P. G. Wodehouse

FIVE COMPLETE NOVELS

About the Author

P. G. (Pelham Grenville) Wodehouse, one of the outstanding humorists of the twentieth century, was born and educated in England. He first came to the United States on a visit in 1909. While here, he sold two short stories to American magazines (*Collier's* and *Cosmopolitan*) for five hundred dollars, then a very impressive sum, which convinced him to unpack his suitcase and settle in for an extended stay. He became an American citizen in 1955.

In his humorous novels, Wodehouse (pronounced "woodhouse") often poked fun at English gentry, especially minor nobility in decline; at America's moneyed classes; and at early Hollywood. He was best known as the creator of Jeeves, the peerless "gentleman's personal gentleman," whose worldly ways, quickness, and unflappability have endeared him to more than one generation of readers.

P. G. Wodehouse, known to his friends as Plum (which is what his first name sounds like when spoken quickly), wrote nearly one hundred books. He also collaborated on more than thirty plays and musical comedies and was the author of a score of film scripts. He died in 1975.

P. G. Wodehouse

FIVE COMPLETE NOVELS

The Return of Jeeves

Bertie Wooster Sees It Through

Spring Fever

The Butler Did It

The Old Reliable

AVENEL BOOKS
New York

This Omnibus edition was previously published in separate volumes
under the titles:
> *Spring Fever* Copyright MCMXLVIII by Pelham Grenville Wodehouse
> *The Old Reliable* Copyright MCML, MCMLI by Pelham Grenville Wodehouse
> *The Return of Jeeves* Copyright MCMLIII, MCMLIV by P. G. Wodehouse
> *Bertie Wooster Sees it Through* Copyright © MCMLV, MCMLVI by P. G. Wodehouse
> *The Butler Did It* Copyright © MCMLVI, MCMLVII by P.G. Wodehouse

> *The Butler Did It* originally appeared in a shorter, substantially different
> form in *Collier's* under the title *Something Fishy*.

This 1983 edition is published by Avenel Books, distributed by Crown Publishers, Inc.,
by arrangement with Scott Meredith Literary Agency, Inc.

Manufactured in the United States of America

Library of Congress Cataloging in Publication Data
Wodehouse, P. G. (Pelham Grenville), 1881–1975.
   P. G. Wodehouse 5 complete novels.

   Contents: Bertie Wooster sees it through—Return of
Jeeves—Spring fever—The butler did it—The old
reliable.
   I. Title.   II. Title: P. G. Wodehouse five complete
novels.
PR6045.053A6   1983   823′.912   82-22633
ISBN: 0-517-405385

h g f e d

CONTENTS

The Return of Jeeves

PART ONE

1

TOWCESTER ABBEY—pronounced Toaster—the seat of William Egerton Ossingham Belfry, ninth Earl of Towcester, is one of those stately homes of England which were a lot statelier in the good old days before the moth got at them. It stands—such portions of it as have not fallen down—in the heart of Southmoltonshire in the midst of smiling country. Though if you had asked Bill Towcester what the dickens the English countryside had to smile about as of even date, he would have been unable to tell you. Its architecture is thirteenth century, fifteenth century and Tudor, its dilapidation twentieth century post-World War Two.

To reach the Abbey you turn off the main road and approach by a mile-long drive thickly incrusted with picturesque weeds and make your way up stone steps, chipped in spots, to a massive front door which badly needs a lick of paint. And this was what Bill's sister Monica and her husband Sir Roderick ('Rory') Carmoyle had done on the summer evening on which this story opens.

Monica, usually addressed as Moke, was small and vivacious, her husband large and stolid. There was something about his aspect and deportment that suggested a more than ordinarily placid buffalo chewing a cud and taking in its surroundings very slowly and methodically, refusing to be hurried. It was thus that, as they stood on the front steps, he took in Towcester Abbey.

"Moke," he said at length, having completed his scrutiny, "I'll tell you something which you may or may not see fit to release to the Press. This bally place looks moldier every time I see it."

Monica was quick to defend her childhood home.

"It might be a lot worse."

Rory considered this, chewing his cud for a while in silence.

"How?" he asked.

"I know it needs doing up, but where's the money to come from? Poor old Bill can't afford to run a castle on a cottage income."

"Why doesn't he get a job like the rest of us? Look at me. Floorwalker at Harrod's."

3

"You needn't stick on side just because you're in trade, you old counterjumper."

"Everybody's doing it, I mean to say. Nowadays the House of Lords is practically empty except on evenings and bank holidays."

"We Towcesters aren't easy to place. The Towcester men have all been lilies of the field. Why, Uncle George didn't even put on his own boots."

"Whose boots did he put on?" asked Rory, interested.

"Ah, that's what we'd all like to know. Of course, Bill's big mistake was letting that American woman get away from him."

"What American woman would that be?"

"It was just after you and I got married. A Mrs. Bessemer. A widow. He met her in Cannes one summer. Fabulously rich and, according to Bill, unimaginably beautiful. It seemed promising for a time, but it didn't come to anything. I suppose someone cut him out. Of course, he was plain Mr. Belfry then, not my lord Towcester, which may have made a difference."

Rory shook his head.

"It wouldn't be that. I was plain Mr. Carmoyle when I met you, and look at the way I snaffled you in the teeth of the pick of the County."

"But then think what you were like in those days. A flick of the finger, a broken heart. And you're not so bad now, either," added Monica fondly. "Something of the old magic remains."

"True," said Rory placidly. "In a dim light I still cast a spell. But the trouble with Bill was, I imagine, that he lacked *drive* . . . the sort of drive you see so much of at Harrod's. The will to win, I suppose you might call it. Napoleon had it. I have it. Bill hasn't. Oh, well, there it is," said Rory philosophically. He resumed his study of Towcester Abbey. "You know what this house wants?" he proceeded. "An atom bomb, dropped carefully on the roof of the main banqueting hall."

"It would help, wouldn't it?"

"It would be the making of the old place. Put it right in no time. Still, atom bombs cost money, so I suppose that's out of the question. What you ought to do is use your influence with Bill to persuade him to buy a lot of paraffin and some shavings and save the morning papers and lay in plenty of matches and wait till some moonless night and give the joint the works. He'd feel a different man, once the old ruin was nicely ablaze."

Monica looked mysterious.

"I can do better than that."

Rory shook his head.

"No. Arson. It's the only way. You can't beat good old arson. Those fellows down in the east end go in for it a lot. They touch a match to the shop, and it's like a week at the seaside to them."

"What would you say if I told you I was hoping to sell the house?"

Rory stared, amazed. He had a high opinion of his wife's resourcefulness, but he felt that she was attempting the impossible.

"Sell it? I don't believe you could give it away. I happen to know Bill offered it for a song to one of these charitable societies as a Home for Reclaimed Juvenile Delinquents, and they simply sneered at him. Probably thought it would give the Delinquents rheumatism. Very damp house, this."

"It is a bit moist."

"Water comes through the walls in heaping handfuls. I suppose because it's so close to the river. I remember saying to Bill once, 'Bill,' I said, 'I'll tell you something about your home surroundings. In the summer the river is at the bottom of your garden, and in the winter your garden is at the bottom of the river.' Amused the old boy quite a bit. He thought it clever."

Monica regarded her husband with that cold, wifely eye which married men learn to dread.

"Very clever," she said frostily. "Extremely droll. And I suppose the first thing you'll do is make a crack like that to Mrs. Spottsworth."

"Eh?" It stole slowly into Rory's mind that a name had been mentioned that was strange to him. "Who's Mrs. Spottsworth?"

"The woman I'm hoping to sell the house to. American. Very rich. I met her when I was passing through New York on my way home. She owns dozens of houses in America, but she's got a craving to have something old and picturesque in England."

"Romantic, eh?"

"Dripping with romance. Well, when she told me that—we were sitting next to each other at a women's lunch—I immediately thought of Bill and the Abbey, of course, and started giving her a sales talk. She seemed interested. After all, the Abbey is chock full of historical associations."

"And mice."

"She was flying to England next day, so I told her when I would be arriving and we arranged that she was to come here and have a look at the place. She should be turning up at any moment."

"Does Bill know she's coming?"

"No. I ought to have sent him a cable, but I forgot. Still, what does it matter? He'll be only too delighted. The important thing is to keep you from putting her off with your mordant witticisms. 'I often say in my amusing way, Mrs. Spottsworth, that whereas in the summer months the river is at the bottom of the garden, in the winter months—ha, ha—the garden—this is going to slay you—is at the bottom of the river, ho, ho, ho.' That would just clinch the sale."

"Now would I be likely to drop a brick of that sort, old egg?"

"Extremely likely, old crumpet. The trouble with you is that, though a king among men, you have no tact."

Rory smiled. The charge tickled him.

"No tact? The boys at Harrod's would laugh if they heard that."

"Do remember that it's vital to put this deal through."

"I'll bear it in mind. I'm all for giving poor old Bill a leg-up. It's a damn

shame," said Rory, who often thought rather deeply on these subjects. "Bill starts at the bottom of the ladder as a mere heir to an Earldom, and by pluck and perseverance works his way up till he becomes the Earl himself. And no sooner has he settled the coronet on his head and said to himself, 'Now to whoop it up!' than they pull a social revolution out of their hats like a rabbit and snitch practically every penny he's got. Ah, well!" said Rory with a sigh. "I say," he went on, changing the subject, "have you noticed, Moke, old girl, that throughout this little chat of ours—which I for one have thoroughly enjoyed—I have been pressing the bell at frequent intervals and not a damn thing has happened? What is this joint, the palace of the sleeping beauty? Or do you think the entire strength of the company has been wiped out by some plague or pestilence?"

"Good heavens," said Monica, "bells at Towcester Abbey don't ring. I don't suppose they've worked since Edward the Seventh's days. If Uncle George wished to summon the domestic staff, he just shoved his head back and howled like a prairie wolf."

"That would have been, I take it, when he wanted somebody else's boots to put on?"

"You just open the door and walk in. Which is what I am about to do now. You bring the bags in from the car."

"Depositing them where?"

"In the hall for the moment," said Monica. "You can take them upstairs later."

She went in, and made her way to that familiar haunt, the living-room off the hall where in her childhood days most of the life of Towcester Abbey had centered. Like other English houses of its size, the Abbey had a number of vast state apartments which were never used, a library which was used occasionally, and this living-room, the popular meeting place. It was here that in earlier days she had sat and read the *Girls' Own Paper* and, until the veto had been placed on her activities by her Uncle George, whose sense of smell was acute, had kept white rabbits. A big, comfortable, shabby room with French windows opening into the garden, at the bottom of which—in the summer months—the river ran.

As she stood looking about her, sniffing the old familiar smell of tobacco and leather and experiencing, as always, a nostalgic thrill and a vague wish that it were possible to put the clock back, there came through the French window a girl in overalls, who, having stared for a moment in astonishment, uttered a delighted squeal.

"Moke . . . *darling!*"

Monica turned.

"Jill, my angel!"

They flung themselves into each other's arms.

2

JILL WYVERN was young, very pretty, slightly freckled and obviously extremely practical and competent. She wore her overalls as if they were a uniform. Like Monica, she was small, and an admirer of hers, from Bloomsbury, had once compared her, in an unpublished poem, to a Tanagra statuette. It was not a very apt comparison, for Tanagra statuettes, whatever their merits, are on the static side, and Jill was intensely alert and alive. She moved with a springy step and in her time had been a flashy outside right on the hockey field.

"My precious Moke," she said. "Is it really you? I thought you were in Jamaica."

"I got back this morning. I picked up Rory in London, and we motored down here. Rory's outside, looking after the bags."

"How brown you are!"

"That's Montego Bay. I worked on this sunburn for three months."

"It suits you. But Bill didn't say anything about expecting you. Aren't you appearing rather suddenly?"

"Yes, I cut my travels short rather suddenly. My allowance met those New York prices and gave up the ghost with a low moan. Ah, here's the merchant prince."

Rory came in, mopping his forehead.

"What have you got in those bags of yours, old girl? Lead?" He saw Jill, and stopped, gazing at her with wrinkled brow. "Oh, hullo," he said uncertainly.

"You remember Jill Wyvern, Rory."

"Of course, yes. Jill Wyvern, to be sure. As you so sensibly observe, Jill Wyvern. Have you been telling her about your sunburn?"

"She noticed it for herself."

"It does catch the eye. She says she's that color all over," said Rory confidentially to Jill. "Might raise a question or two from an old-fashioned husband, what? Still I suppose it all makes for variety. So you're Jill Wyvern, are you? How you've grown!"

"Since when?"

"Since . . . since you started growing."

"You haven't a notion who I am, have you?"

"I wouldn't say *that* . . ."

"I'll help you out. I was at your wedding."

"You don't look old enough."

"I was fifteen. They gave me the job of keeping the dogs from jumping on the guests. It was pouring, you may remember, and they all had muddy paws."

"Good God! Now I have you placed. So *you* were that little squirt. I noticed you bobbing about and thought what a frightful young excrescence you looked."

"My husband is noted for the polish of his manners," said Monica. "He is often called the modern Chesterfield."

7

"What I was about to add," said Rory with dignity, "was that she's come on a lot since those days, showing that we should never despair. But didn't we meet again some time?"

"Yes, a year or two later when you stayed here one summer. I was just coming out then, and I expect I looked more of an excrescence than ever."

Monica sighed.

"Coming out!" The dear old getting-ready-for-market stage! How it takes one back. Off with the glasses and the teeth-braces."

"On with things that push you in or push you out, whichever you needed." This was Rory's contribution, and Monica looked at him austerely.

"What do you know about it?"

"Oh, I get around in our Ladies Foundation department," said Rory.

Jill laughed.

"What I remember best are those agonized family conferences about my hockey-player's hands. I used to walk about for hours holding them in the air."

"And how did you make out? Has it paid off yet?"

"Paid off?"

Monica lowered her voice confidentially.

"A man, dear. Did you catch anything worth while?"

"I think he's worth while. As a matter of fact, you don't know it, but you're moving in rather exalted circles. She whom you see before you is none other than the future Countess of Towcester."

Monica screamed excitedly.

"You don't mean you and Bill are engaged?"

"That's right."

"Since when?"

"Some weeks ago."

"Well, I'm delighted. I wouldn't have thought Bill had so much sense."

"No," agreed Rory in his tactful way. "One raises the eyebrows in astonishment. Bill, as I remember it, was always more of a lad for the buxom, voluptuous type. Many a passionate romance have I seen him through with females who looked like a cross between pantomime Fairy Queens and all-in wrestlers. There was a girl in the Hippodrome chorus—"

He broke off these reminiscences, so fraught with interest to a *fiancée*, in order to say 'Ouch!' Monica had kicked him shrewdly on the ankle.

"Tell me, darling," said Monica. "How did it happen? Suddenly?"

"Quite suddenly. He was helping me give a cow a bolus—"

Rory blinked.

"A—?"

"Bolus. Medicine. You give it to cows. And before I knew what was happening he had grabbed my hand and was saying, 'I say, arising from this, will you marry me?' "

"How frightfully eloquent. When Rory proposed to me, all he said was 'Eh, what?' "

"And it took me three weeks to work up to that," said Rory. His forehead had become wrinkled again. It was plain that he was puzzling over something. "This bolus of which you were speaking. I don't quite follow. You were giving it to a cow, you say?"

"A sick cow."

"Oh, a sick cow? Well, here's the point that's perplexing me. Here's the thing that seems to me to need straightening out. *Why* were you giving boluses to sick cows?"

"It's my job. I'm the local vet."

"What! You don't by any chance mean a veterinary surgeon?"

"That's right. Fully licensed. We're all workers nowadays."

Rory nodded sagely.

"Profoundly true," he said. "I'm a son of toil myself."

"Rory's at Harrod's," said Monica.

"Really?"

"Floorwalker in the Hosepipe, Lawn Mower and Bird Bath department," said Rory. "But that is merely temporary. There's a strong rumor going the rounds that hints at promotion to the Glass, Fancy Goods and Chinaware. And from there to the Ladies Underclothing is but a step."

"My hero!" Monica kissed him lovingly. "I'll bet they'll all be green with jealousy."

Rory was shocked at the suggestion.

"Good God, no. They'll rush to shake me by the hand and slap me on the back. Our esprit de corps is wonderful. It's one for all and all for one in the Brompton Road."

Monica turned back to Jill.

"And doesn't your father mind you running about the country giving boluses to cows? Jill's father," she explained to Rory, "is Chief Constable of the county."

"And very nice, too," said Rory.

"I should have thought he would have objected."

"Oh, no. We're all working at something. Except my brother Eustace. He won a football pool last winter and he's gone frightfully upper class. Very high hat with the rest of the family. Moves on a different plane."

"Damn snob," said Rory warmly. "I hate these class distinctions."

He was about to speak further, for the subject was one on which he held strong opinions, but at this moment the telephone bell rang, and he looked around, startled.

"For heaven's sake! Don't tell me the old boy has paid his telephone bill!" he cried, astounded.

Monica took up the receiver.

"Hullo? . . . Yes, this is Towcester Abbey. . . . No, Lord Towcester is not in at the moment. This is his sister, Lady Carmoyle. The number of his car? It's news to me that he's *got* a car." She turned to Jill. "You don't know the number of Bill's car, do you?"

"No. Why are they asking?"

"Why are you asking?" said Monica into the telephone. She waited a moment, then hung up. "He's rung off."

"Who was it?"

"He didn't say. Just a voice from the void."

"You don't think Bill's had an accident?"

"Good heavens, no," said Rory, "He's much too good a driver. Probably he had to stop somewhere to buy some gas, and they need his number for their books. But it's always disturbing when people don't give their names on the telephone. There was a fellow in Ours . . . chap in the Jams, Sauces and Potted Meats . . . who was rung up one night by a Mystery Voice that wouldn't give its name, and to cut a long story short—"

Monica did so.

"Save it up for after dinner, my king of raconteurs," she said. "If there is any dinner," she added doubtfully.

"Oh, there'll be dinner all right," said Jill, "and you'll probably find it'll melt in the mouth. Bill's got a very good cook."

Monica stared.

"A cook? These days? I don't believe it. You'll be telling me next he's got a housemaid."

"He has. Name of Ellen."

"Pull yourself together, child. You're talking wildly. Nobody has a housemaid."

"Bill has. And a gardener. And a butler. A wonderful butler called Jeeves. And he's thinking of getting a boy to clean the knives and boots."

"Good heavens! It sounds like the home life of the Aga Khan." Monica frowned thoughtfully. "Jeeves?" she said. "Why does that name seem to ring a bell?"

Rory supplied illumination.

"Bertie Wooster. He has a man named Jeeves. This is probably a brother or an aunt or something."

"No," said Jill. "It's the same man. Bill has him on lend lease."

"But how on earth does Bertie get on without him?"

"I believe Mr. Wooster's away somewhere. Anyhow, Jeeves appeared one day and said he was willing to take office, so Bill grabbed him, of course. He's an absolute treasure. Bill says he's an 'old soul,' whatever that means."

Monica was still bewildered.

"But how about the financial end? Does he pay this entourage, or just give them a pleasant smile now and then?"

"Of course he pays them. Lavishly. He flings them purses of gold every Saturday morning."

"Where does the money come from?"

"He earns it."

"Don't be silly. Bill hasn't earned a penny since he was paid twopence a time for taking his castor oil. How could he possibly earn it?"

"He's doing some sort of work for the Farm Board."

"You don't make a fortune out of that."

"Bill seems to. I suppose he's so frightfully good at his job that they pay him more than the others. I don't know what he does, actually. He just goes off in his car. Some kind of inspection, I suppose it is. Checking up on all those questionnaires. He's not very good at figures, so he always takes Jeeves with him."

"Well, that's wonderful," said Monica. "I was afraid he might have started backing horses again. It used to worry me so much in the old days, the way he would dash from race course to race course in a gray topper that he carried sandwiches in."

"Oh, no, it couldn't be anything like that. He promised me faithfully he would never bet on a horse again."

"Very sensible," said Rory. "I don't mind a small flutter from time to time, of course. At Harrod's we always run a Sweep on the big events, five bob chances. The brass hats frown on anything larger."

Jill moved to the French window.

"Well, I mustn't stand here talking," she said. "I've got work to do. I came here to attend to Bill's Irish terrier. It's sick of a fever."

"Give it a bolus."

"I'm giving it some new American ointment. It's got mange. See you later."

Jill went off on her errand of mercy, and Rory turned to Monica. His customary stolidity had vanished. He was keen and alert, like Sherlock Holmes on the trail.

"Moke!"

"Hullo?"

"What do you make of it, old girl?"

"Make of what?"

"This sudden affluence of Bill's. There's something fishy going on here. If it had just been a matter of a simple butler, one could have understood it. A broker's man in disguise, one would have said. But how about the housemaid and the cook and the car and, by Jove, the fact that he's paid his telephone bill."

"I see what you mean. It's odd."

"It's more than odd. Consider the facts. The last time I was at Towcester Abbey, Bill was in the normal state of destitution of the upper-class Englishman of today, stealing the cat's milk and nosing about in the gutters for cigar ends. I come here now, and what do I find? Butlers in every nook and cranny, housemaids as far as the eye can reach, cooks jostling each other in the kitchen, Irish terriers here, there and everywhere, and a lot of sensational talk going on about boys to clean the knives and boots. It's . . . what's the word?"

"I don't know."

"Yes, you do. Begins with 'in.' "

"Influential? Inspirational? Infra red?"

"Inexplicable. That's what it is. The whole thing is utterly inexplicable. One dismisses all that stuff about jobs with the Farm Board as pure eyewash. You don't cut a stupendous dash like this on a salary from the Farm Board." Rory paused, and ruminated for a moment. "I wonder if the old boy's been launching out as a gentleman burglar."

"Don't be an idiot."

"Well, fellows do, you know. Raffles, if you remember. He was one, and made a dashed good thing out of it. Or could it be that he's blackmailing somebody?"

"Oh, Rory."

"Very profitable, I believe. You look around for some wealthy bimbo and nose out his guilty secrets, then you send him a letter saying that you know all and tell him to leave ten thousand quid in small notes under the second milestone on the London road. When you've spent that, you tap him for another ten. It all mounts up over a period of time, and would explain these butlers, housemaids and what not very neatly."

"If you would talk less drivel and take more bags upstairs, the world would be a better place."

Rory thought it over and got her meaning.

"You want me to take the bags upstairs?"

"I do."

"Right ho. The Harrod's motto is Service."

The telephone rang again. Rory went to it.

"Hullo?" He started violently. "The *who?* Good God! All right. He's out now, but I'll tell him when I see him." He hung up. There was a grave look on his face. "Moke," he said, "perhaps you'll believe me another time and not scoff and mock when I advance my theories. That was the police."

"The police?"

"They want to talk to Bill."

"What about?"

"They didn't say. Well, dash it, they wouldn't, would they? Official Secrets Act and all that sort of thing. But they're closing in on him, old girl, closing in on him."

Probably all they want is to get him to present the prizes at the police sports or something."

"I doubt it," said Rory. "Still, hold that thought if it makes you happier. Take the bags upstairs, you were saying? I'll do it instanter. Come along and encourage me with word and gesture."

3

FOR SOME moments after they had gone the peace of the summer evening was broken only by the dull, bumping sound of a husband carrying suitcases upstairs. This died away, and once more a drowsy stillness stole over Towcester Abbey. Then, faintly at first but growing louder, there came from the distance the chugging of a car. It stopped, and there entered through the French window a young man. He tottered in, breathing heavily like a hart that pants for cooling streams when heated in the chase, and having produced his cigarette case lit a cigarette in an overwrought way, as if he had much on his mind.

Or what one may loosely call his mind. William, ninth Earl of Towcester, though intensely amiable and beloved by all who knew him, was far from being a mental giant. From his earliest years his intimates had been aware that, while his heart was unquestionably in the right place, there was a marked shortage of the little gray cells, and it was generally agreed that whoever won the next Nobel prize, it would not be Bill Towcester. At the Drones Club, of which he had been a member since leaving school, it was estimated that in the matter of intellect he ranked somewhere in between Freddie Widgeon and Pongo Twistleton, which is pretty low down on the list. There were some, indeed, who held his I.Q. to be inferior to that of Barmy Fotheringay-Phipps.

Against this must be set the fact that, like all his family, he was extremely good looking, though those who considered him so might have revised their views, had they seen him now. For in addition to wearing a very loud checked coat with bulging, voluminous pockets, and a crimson tie with blue horse-shoes on it, which smote the beholder like a blow, he had a large black patch over his left eye and on his upper lip a ginger mustache of the outsize, or soupstrainer, type. In the clean-shaven world in which we live today it is not often that one sees a mustache of this almost tropical luxuriance, and it is not often, it may be added, that one wants to.

A black patch and a ginger mustache are grave defects, but that the ninth Earl was not wholly dead to a sense of shame was shown by the convulsive start, like the leap of an adagio dancer, which he gave a moment later when, wandering about the room, he suddenly caught sight of himself in an old world mirror that hung on the wall.

"Good Lord!" he exclaimed, recoiling.

With nervous fingers he removed the patch, thrust it into his pocket, tore the fungoid growth from his lip and struggled out of the checked coat. This done, he went to the window, leaned out and called in a low, conspiratorial voice.

"Jeeves!"

There was no answer.

"Hi, Jeeves, where are you?"

Again silence.

Bill gave a whistle, then another. He was still whistling, his body halfway through the French window, when the door behind him opened, revealing a stately form.

The man who entered—or perhaps one should say shimmered into—the room was tall and dark and impressive. He might have been one of the better-class ambassadors or the youngish High Priest of some refined and dignified religion. His eyes gleamed with the light of intelligence, and his finely chiseled face expressed a feudal desire to be of service. His whole air was that of a gentleman's gentleman who, having developed his brain over a course of years by means of a steady fish diet, is respectfully eager to place that brain at the disposal of the young master. He was carrying over one arm a coat of sedate color and a tie of conservative pattern.

"You whistled, m'lord?" he said.

Bill spun around.

"How the dickens did you get over there, Jeeves?"

"I ran the car into the garage, m'lord, and then made my way to the servants' quarters. Your coat, m'lord."

"Oh, thanks. I see you've changed."

"I deemed it advisable, m'lord. The gentleman was not far behind us as we rounded into the straight and may at any moment be calling. Were he to encounter on the threshold a butler in a check suit and a false mustache, it is possible that his suspicions might be aroused. I am glad to see that your lordship has removed that somewhat distinctive tie. Excellent for creating atmosphere on the race course, it is scarcely vogue in private life."

Bill eyed the repellent object with a shudder.

"I've always hated that beastly thing, Jeeves. All those foul horseshoes. Shove it away somewhere. And the coat."

"Very good, m'lord. This coffer should prove adequate as a temporary receptacle." Jeeves took the coat and tie, and crossed the room to where a fine old oak dower chest stood, an heirloom long in the Towcester family. "Yes," he said, " 'Tis not so deep as a well nor so wide as a church door, but 'tis enough, 'twill serve."

He folded the distressing objects carefully, placed them inside and closed the lid. And even this simple act he performed with a quiet dignity which would have impressed any spectator less agitated than Bill Towcester. It was like seeing the plenipotentiary of a great nation lay a wreath on the tomb of a deceased monarch.

But Bill, as we say, was agitated. He was brooding over an earlier remark that had fallen from this great man's lips.

"What do you mean, the gentleman may at any moment be calling?" he asked. The thought of receiving a visit from that red-faced man with the loud voice who had bellowed abuse at him all the way from Epsom Downs to Northamptonshire was not an unmixedly agreeable one.

"It is possible that he observed and memorized the number of our car, m'lord. He was in a position to study our license plate for some considerable time, your lordship will recollect."

Bill sank limply into a chair and brushed a bead of perspiration from his forehead. This contingency, as Jeeves would have called it, had not occurred to him. Placed before him now, it made him feel filleted.

"Oh, golly, I never thought of that. Then he would get the owner's name and come racing along here, wouldn't he?"

"So one would be disposed to imagine, m'lord."

"Hell's bells, Jeeves!"

"Yes, m'lord."

Bill applied the handkerchief to his forehead again.

"What do I do if he does?"

"I would advise your lordship to assume a nonchalant air and disclaim all knowledge of the matter."

"With a light laugh, you mean?"

"Precisely, m'lord."

Bill tried a light laugh.

"How did that sound, Jeeves?"

"Barely adequate, m'lord."

"More like a death rattle?"

"Yes, m'lord."

"I shall need a few rehearsals."

"Several, m'lord. It will be essential to carry conviction."

Bill kicked petulantly at a footstool.

"How do you expect me to carry conviction, feeling the way I do?"

"I can readily appreciate that your lordship is disturbed."

"I'm all of a twitter. Have you ever seen a jelly hit by a cyclone?"

"No, m'lord, I have never been present on such an occasion."

"It quivers. So do I."

"After such an ordeal your lordship would naturally be unstrung."

"Ordeal is the right word, Jeeves. Apart from the frightful peril one is in, it was so dashed ignominious having to leg it like that."

"I should hardly describe our recent activities as legging it, m'lord. 'Strategic retreat' is more the *mot juste*. This is a recognized military maneuver, practiced by all the greatest tacticians when the occasion seemed to call for such a move. I have no doubt that General Eisenhower has had recourse to it from time to time."

"But I don't suppose he had a fermenting punter after him, shouting 'Welsher!' at the top of his voice."

"Possibly not, m'lord."

Bill brooded.

"It was that word 'welsher' that hurt, Jeeves."

"I can readily imagine it, m'lord. Objected to as irrelevant, incompetent and immaterial, as I believe the legal expression is. As your lordship several times asseverated during our precarious homeward journey, you have every intention of paying the gentleman."

"Of course I have. No argument about that. Naturally I intend to brass up to the last penny. It's a case of . . . what, Jeeves?"

"*Noblesse oblige,* m'lord."

"Exactly. The honor of the Towcesters is at stake. But I must have time, dash it, to raise three thousand pounds, two and six."

"Three thousand and five pounds, two and six, m'lord. Your lordship is forgetting the gentleman's original five pound note."

"So I am. You trousered it and came away with it in your pocket."

"Precisely, m'lord. Thus bringing the sum total of your obligations to this Captain Biggar—"

"Was that his name?"

"Yes, m'lord. Captain C. G. Brabazon-Biggar, United Rovers Club, Northumberland Avenue, London W.C. 2. In my capacity as your lordship's clerk I wrote the name and address on the ticket which he now has in his possession. The note which he handed to me and which I duly accepted as your lordship's official representative raises your commitments to three thousand and five pounds, two shillings and sixpence."

"Oh, gosh!"

"Yes, m'lord. It is not an insignificant sum. Many a poor man would be glad of three thousand and five pounds, two shillings and sixpence."

Bill winced.

"I would be grateful, Jeeves, if you could see your way not to keep on intoning those words."

"Very good, m'lord."

"They are splashed on my soul in glorious technicolor."

"Quite so, m'lord."

"Who was it who said that when he or she was dead, the word something would be found carved on his or her heart?"

"Queen Mary, m'lord, the predecessor of the great Queen Elizabeth. The word was 'Calais,' and the observation was intended to convey her chagrin at the loss of that town."

"Well, when I die, which will be very shortly if I go on feeling as I do now, just cut me open, Jeeves—"

"Certainly, m'lord."

"—and I'll bet you a couple of bob you'll find carved on my heart the words, 'Three thousand and five pounds, two and six.' "

Bill rose and paced the room with fevered steps.

"How does one scrape together a sum like that, Jeeves?"

"It will call for thrift, m'lord."

"You bet it will. It'll take years."

"And Captain Biggar struck me as a somewhat impatient gentleman."

"You needn't rub it in, Jeeves."

"Very good, m'lord."

"Let's keep our minds on the present."

"Yes, m'lord. Remember that man's life lies all within this present, as 'twere but a hair's-breadth of time. As for the rest, the past is gone, the future yet unseen."

"Eh?"

"Marcus Aurelius, m'lord."

"Oh? Well, as I was saying, let us glue our minds on what is going to happen if this Biggar suddenly blows in here. Do you think he'll recognize me?"

"I am inclined to fancy not, m'lord. The mustache and the patch formed a very effective disguise. After all, in the past few months we have encountered several gentlemen of your lordship's acquaintance—"

"And not one of them spotted me."

"No, m'lord. Nevertheless, facing the facts, I fear we must regard this afternoon's episode as a setback. It is clearly impossible for us to function at the Derby tomorrow."

"I was looking forward to cleaning up on the Derby."

"I, too, m'lord. But after what has occurred, one's entire turf activities must, I fear, be regarded as suspended indefinitely."

"You don't think we could risk one more pop?"

"No, m'lord."

"I see what you mean, of course. Show up at Epsom tomorrow, and the first person we'd run into would be this Captain Biggar—"

"Straddling, like Apollyon, right across the way. Precisely, m'lord."

Bill passed a hand through his disordered hair.

"If only I had frozen on to the money we made at Newmarket!"

"Yes, m'lord. 'Of all sad words of tongue or pen the saddest are these—It might have been.' Whittier."

"You warned me not to let our capital fall too low."

"I felt that we were not equipped to incur any heavy risk. That was why I urged your lordship so vehemently to lay Captain Biggar's second wager off. I had misgivings. True, the probability of the double bearing fruit at such odds was not great, but when I saw Whistler's Mother pass us on her way to the starting post, I was conscious of a tremor of uneasiness. Those long legs, that powerful rump . . ."

"Don't, Jeeves!"

"Very good, m'lord."

"I'm trying not to think of Whistler's Mother."

"I quite understand, m'lord."

"Who the dickens *was* Whistler, anyway?"

"A figure, landscape and portrait painter of considerable distinction, m'lord, born in Lowell, Massachusetts, in 1834. His 'Portrait of my Mother,' painted in 1872, is particularly esteemed by the cognoscenti and was purchased by the French Government for the Luxembourg Gallery, Paris, in the year 1892. His works are individual in character and notable for subtle color harmony."

Bill breathed a little stertorously.

"It's subtle, is it?"

"Yes, m'lord."

"I see. Thanks for telling me. I was worrying myself sick about his color harmony." Bill became calmer. "Jeeves, if the worst comes to the worst and Biggar does catch me bending, can I gain a bit of time by pleading the Gaming Act?"

"I fear not, m'lord. You took the gentleman's money. A cash transaction."

"It would mean chokey, you feel?"

"I fancy so, m'lord."

"Would you be jugged, too, as my clerk?"

"In all probability, m'lord. I am not quite certain on the point. I should have to consult my solicitor."

"But I would be for it?"

"Yes, m'lord. The sentences, however, are not, I believe, severe."

"But think of the papers. The ninth Earl of Towcester, whose ancestors held the field at Agincourt, skipped from the field at Epsom with a slavering punter after him. It'll be jam for the newspaper boys."

"Unquestionably the circumstance of your lordship having gone into business as a Silver Ring bookmaker would be accorded wide publicity."

Bill, who had been pacing the floor again, stopped in midstride and regarded the speaker with an accusing eye.

"And who was it suggested that I should go into business as a Silver Ring bookie? You, Jeeves. I don't want to be harsh, but you must own that the idea came from you. You were the—"

"*Fons et origo mali,* m'lord? That, I admit, is true. But if your lordship will recall, we were in something of a quandary. We had agreed that your lordship's impending marriage made it essential to augment your lordship's slender income, and we went through the Classified Trades section of the telephone directory in quest of a possible profession which your lordship might adopt. It was merely because nothing of a suitable nature had presented itself by the time we reached the T's that I suggested Turf Accountant *faute de mieux.*"

"*Faute de* what?"

"*Mieux,* m'lord. A French expression. We should say 'for want of anything better.' "

"What asses these Frenchmen are! Why can't they talk English?"

"They are possibly more to be pitied than censured, m'lord. Early upbringing no doubt has a good deal to do with it. As I was saying, it seemed to me a happy solution of your lordship's difficulties. In the United States of

America, I believe, bookmakers are considered persons of a somewhat low order and are, indeed, suppressed by the police, but in England it is very different. Here they are looked up to and courted. There is a school of thought which regards them as the new aristocracy. They make a great deal of money, and have the added gratification of not paying income tax."

Bill sighed wistfully.

"*We* made a lot of money up to Newmarket."

"Yes, m'lord."

"And where is it now?"

"Where, indeed, m'lord?"

"I shouldn't have spent so much doing up the place."

"No, m'lord."

"And it was a mistake to pay my tailor's bill."

"Yes, m'lord. One feels that your lordship did somewhat overdo it there. As the old Roman observed, *ne quid nimis*."

"Yes, that was rash. Still, no good beefing about it now, I suppose."

"No, m'lord. The moving finger writes, and having writ—"

"Hoy!"

"—moves on, nor all your piety and wit can lure it back to cancel half a line nor all your tears wash out one word of it. You were saying, m'lord?"

"I was only going to ask you to cheese it."

"Certainly, m'lord."

"Not in the mood."

"Quite so, m'lord. It was only the appositeness of the quotation—from the works of the Persian poet Omar Khayyam—that led me to speak. I wonder if I might ask a question, m'lord?"

"Yes, Jeeves?"

"Is Miss Wyvern aware of your lordship's professional connection with the turf?"

Bill quivered like an aspen at the mere suggestion.

"I should say not. She would throw fifty-seven fits if she knew. I've rather given her the idea that I'm employed by the Farm Board."

"A most respectable body of men."

"I didn't actually say so in so many words. I just strewed the place with Farm Board report forms and took care she saw them. Did you know that they issue a hundred and seventy-nine different blanks other than the seventeen questionnaires?"

"No, m'lord. I was not aware. It shows zeal."

"Great zeal. They're on their toes, those boys."

"Yes, m'lord."

"But we're wandering from the point, which is that Miss Wyvern must never learn the awful truth. It would be fatal. At the outset of our betrothal she put her foot down firmly on the subject of my tendency to have an occasional flutter, and I promised her faithfully that I would never punt again. Well, you might argue that being a Silver Ring bookie is not the same thing as punting, but I doubt if you would ever sell that idea to Miss Wyvern."

"The distinction is certainly a nice one, m'lord."

"Let her discover the facts, and all would be lost."

"Those wedding bells would not ring out."

"They certainly wouldn't. She would return me to store before I could say 'What ho.' So if she comes asking questions, reveal nothing. Not even if she sticks lighted matches between your toes."

"The contingency is a remote one, m'lord."

"Possibly. I'm merely saying. Whatever happens, Jeeves, secrecy and silence."

"You may rely on me, m'lord. In the inspired words of Pliny the Younger—"

Bill held up a hand.

"Right ho, Jeeves."

"Very good, m'lord."

"I'm not interested in Pliny the Younger."

"No, m'lord."

"As far as I'm concerned, you may take Pliny the Younger and put him where the monkey put the nuts."

"Certainly, m'lord."

"And now leave me, Jeeves. I have a lot of heavy brooding to do. Go and get me a stiffish whisky and soda."

"Very good, m'lord. I will attend to the matter immediately."

Jeeves melted from the room with a look of respectful pity, and Bill sat down and put his head between his hands. A hollow groan escaped him, and he liked the sound of it and gave another.

He was starting in a third, bringing it up from the soles of his feet, when a voice spoke at his side.

"Good heavens, Bill. What on earth's the matter?"

Jill Wyvern was standing there.

4

IN THE interval which had elapsed since her departure from the living room, Jill had rubbed American ointment on Mike the Irish terrier, taken a look at a goldfish belonging to the cook, which had caused anxiety in the kitchen by refusing its ant's eggs, and made a routine tour of the pigs and cows, giving one of the latter a bolus. She had returned to the house agreeably conscious of duty done and looking forward to a chat with her loved one, who, she presumed, would by now be back from his Farm Board rounds and in a mood for pleasant dalliance. For even when the Farm Board know they have got hold of an exceptionally good man and wish (naturally) to get every possible ounce of work out of him, they are humane enough to let the poor peon call it a day around about the hour of the evening cocktail.

To find him groaning with his head in his hands was something of a shock.

"What on earth's the matter?" she repeated.

Bill had sprung from his chair with a convulsive leap. That loved voice, speaking unexpectedly out of the void when he supposed himself to be alone with his grief, had affected him like a buzz-saw applied to the seat of his trousers. If it had been Captain C. G. Brabazon-Biggar, of the United Rovers Club, Northumberland Avenue, he could not have been very much more perturbed. He gaped at her, quivering in every limb. Jeeves, had he been present, would have been reminded of Macbeth seeing the ghost of Banquo.

"Matter?" he said, inserting three *m's* at the beginning of the word.

Jill was looking at him with grave, speculative eyes. She had that direct, honest gaze which many nice girls have, and as a rule Bill liked it. But at the moment he could have done with something that did not pierce quite so like a red-hot gimlet to his inmost soul. A sense of guilt makes a man allergic to direct, honest gazes.

"Matter?" he said, getting the word shorter and crisper this time. "What do you mean, what's the matter? Nothing's the matter. Why do you ask?"

"You were groaning like a foghorn."

"Oh, that. Touch of neuralgia."

"You've got a headache?"

"Yes, it's been coming on some time. I've had rather an exhausting afternoon."

"Why, aren't the crops rotating properly? Or are the pigs going in for smaller families?"

"My chief problem today," said Bill dully, "concerned horses."

A quick look of suspicion came into Jill's gaze. Like all nice girls, she had, where the man she loved was concerned, something of the Private Eye about her.

"Have you been betting again?"

Bill stared.

"*Me?*"

"You gave me your solemn promise you wouldn't. Oh, Bill, you are an idiot. You're more trouble to look after than a troupe of performing seals. Can't you see it's just throwing money away? Can't you get it into your fat head that the punters haven't a hope against the bookmakers? I know people are always talking about bringing off fantastic doubles and winning thousands of pounds with a single fiver, but that sort of thing never really happens. What did you say?"

Bill had not spoken. The sound that had proceeded from his twisted lips had been merely a soft moan like that of an emotional red Indian at the stake.

"It happens sometimes," he said hollowly. "I've heard of cases."

"Well, it couldn't happen to you. Horses just aren't lucky for you."

Bill writhed. The illusion that he was being roasted over a slow fire had become extraordinarily vivid.

"Yes," he said. "I see that now."

Jill's gaze became more direct and penetrating than ever.

"Come clean, Bill. Did you back a loser in the Oaks?"

This was so diametrically opposite to what had actually occurred that Bill perked up a little.

"Of course I didn't."

"You swear?"

"I may begin to at any moment."

"You didn't back anything in the Oaks?"

"Certainly not."

"Then what's the matter?"

"I told you. I've got a headache."

"Poor old thing. Can I get you anything?"

"No, thanks. Jeeves is bringing me a whisky and soda."

"Would a kiss help, while you're waiting?"

"It would save a human life."

Jill kissed him, but absently. She appeared to be thinking.

"Jeeves was with you today, wasn't he?" she said.

"Yes. Yes, Jeeves was along."

"You always take him with you on these expeditions of yours."

"Yes."

"Where do you go?"

"We make the rounds."

"Doing what?"

"Oh, this and that."

"I see. How's the headache?"

"A little better, thanks."

"Good."

There was silence for a moment.

"I used to have headaches a few years ago," said Jill.

"Bad?"

"Quite bad. I suffered agonies."

"They do touch you up, don't they?"

"They do. But," proceeded Jill, her voice rising and a hard note creeping into her voice, "my headaches, painful as they were, never made me look like an escaped convict lurking in a bush listening to the baying of the blood-hounds and wondering every minute when the hand of doom was going to fall on the seat of his pants. And that's how you are looking now. There's guilt written on your every feature. If you were to tell me at this moment that you had done a murder and were worrying because you had suddenly remembered you hadn't hidden the body properly, I would say, 'I thought as much.' Bill, for the last time, what's the matter?"

"Nothing's the matter."

"Don't tell me."

"I am telling you."

"There's nothing on your mind?"

"Not a thing."

"You're as gay and carefree as a lark singing in the summer sky?"

"If anything, rather more so."

There was another silence. Jill was biting her lip, and Bill wished she wouldn't. There is, of course, nothing actually low and degrading in a girl biting her lip, but it is a spectacle that a fiancé with a good deal on his mind can never really enjoy.

"Bill, tell me," said Jill. "How do you feel about marriage?"

Bill brightened. This, he felt, was more the stuff.

"I think it's an extraordinarily good egg. Always provided, of course, that the male half of the sketch is getting someone like you."

"Never mind the pretty speeches. Shall I tell you how I feel about it?"

"Do."

"I feel that unless there is absolute trust between a man and a girl, they're crazy even to think of getting married, because if they're going to hide things from each other and not tell each other their troubles, their marriage is bound to go on the rocks sooner or later. A husband and wife ought to tell each other everything. I wouldn't ever dream of keeping anything from you, and if it interests you to know it, I'm as sick as mud to think that you're keeping this trouble of yours, whatever it is, from me."

"I'm not in any trouble."

"You are. What's happened, I don't know, but a short-sighted mole that's lost its spectacles could see that you're a soul in torment. When I came in here, you were groaning your head off."

Bill's self-control, so sorely tried today, cracked.

"Damn it all," he bellowed. "Why shouldn't I groan? I believe Towcester Abbey is open for being groaned in at about this hour, is it not? I wish to heaven you would leave me alone," he went on, gathering momentum. "Who do you think you are? One of these G-men fellows questioning some rat of the underworld? I suppose you'll be asking next where I was on the night of February the twenty-first. Don't be such an infernal Nosey Parker."

Jill was a girl of spirit, and with girls of spirit this sort of thing soon reaches saturation point.

"I don't know if you know it," she said coldly, "but when you spit on your hands and get down to it, you can be the world's premier louse."

"That's a nice thing to say."

"Well, it's the truth," said Jill. "You're simply a pig in human shape. And if you want to know what I think," she went on, gathering momentum in her turn, "I believe what's happened is that you've gone and got mixed up with some awful female."

"You're crazy. Where the dickens could I have met any awful females?"

"I should imagine you have had endless opportunities. You're always going off in your car, sometimes for a week at a stretch. For all I know, you may have been spending your time festooned with hussies."

"I wouldn't so much as look at a hussy if you brought her to me on a plate with watercress round her."

"I don't believe you."

"And it was you, if memory serves me aright," said Bill, "who some two and a half seconds ago was shooting off your head about the necessity for absolute trust between us. Women!" said Bill bitterly. "Women! My God, what a sex!"

On this difficult situation Jeeves entered, bearing a glass on a salver.

"Your whisky-and-soda, m'lord," he said, much as a President of the United States might have said to a deserving citizen, "Take this Congressional medal."

Bill accepted the restorative gratefully.

"Thank you, Jeeves. Not a moment before it was needed."

"And Sir Roderick and Lady Carmoyle are in the yew alley, asking to see you, m'lord."

"Good heavens! Rory and the Moke? Where did they spring from? I thought she was in Jamaica."

"Her ladyship returned this morning, I understand, and Sir Roderick obtained compassionate leave from Harrod's in order to accompany her here. They desired me to inform your lordship that they would be glad of a word with you at your convenience before the arrival of Mrs. Spottsworth."

"Before the what of who? Who on earth's Mrs. Spottsworth?"

"An American lady whose acquaintance her ladyship made in New York, m'lord. She is expected here this evening. I gathered from what her ladyship and Sir Roderick were saying that there is some prospect of Mrs. Spottsworth buying the house."

Bill gaped.

"Buying the house?"

"Yes, m'lord."

"*This* house?"

'Yes, m'lord."

"Towcester Abbey, you mean?"

"Yes, m'lord."

"You're pulling my leg, Jeeves."

"I would not take such a liberty, m'lord."

"You seriously mean that this refugee from whatever American loony-bin it was where she was under observation until she sneaked out with false whiskers on is actually contemplating paying hard cash for Towcester Abbey?"

"That was the interpretation which I placed on the remarks of her ladyship and Sir Roderick, m'lord."

Bill drew a deep breath.

"Well, I'll be blowed. It just shows you that it takes all sorts to make a world. Is she coming to stay?"

"So I understood, m'lord."

"Then you might remove the two buckets you put to catch the water under the upper hall skylight. They create a bad impression."

"Yes, m'lord. I will also place some more thumb tacks in the wallpaper. Where would your lordship be thinking of depositing Mrs. Spottsworth?"

"She'd better have the Queen Elizabeth room. It's the best we've got."

"Yes, m'lord. I will insert a wire screen in the flue, to discourage intrusion by the bats that nest there."

"We can't give her a bathroom, I'm afraid."

"I fear not, m'lord."

"Still, if she can make do with a shower, she can stand under the upper hall skylight."

Jeeves pursed his lips.

"If I might offer the suggestion, m'lord, it is not judicious to speak in that strain. Your lordship might forget yourself and let fall some such observation in the hearing of Mrs. Spottsworth."

Jill, standing at the French window and looking out with burning eyes, had turned and was listening, electrified. The generous wrath which had caused her to allude to her betrothed as a pig in human shape had vanished completely. It could not compete with this stupendous news. As far as Jill was concerned, the war was over.

She thoroughly concurred with Jeeves's rebuke.

"Yes, you poor fish," she said, "you mustn't even think like that. Oh, Bill, isn't it wonderful! If this comes off, you'll have money enough to buy a farm I'm sure we'd do well running a farm, me as a vet and you with all your expert farming knowledge."

"My what?"

Jeeves coughed.

"I think Miss Wyvern is alluding to the fact that you have had such wide experience working for the Farm Board, m'lord."

"Oh, ah, yes. I see what you mean. Of course, yes, the Farm Board. Thank you, Jeeves."

"Not at all, m'lord."

Jill developed her theme.

"If you could sting this Mrs. Spottsworth for something really big, we could start a prize herd. That pays like anything. I wonder how much you could get for the place."

"Not much, I'm afraid. It's seen better days."

"What are you going to ask?"

"Three thousand and five pounds, two shillings and sixpence."

"What!"

Bill blinked.

"Sorry. I was thinking of something else."

"But what put an odd sum like that into your head?"

"I don't know."

"You must know."

"I don't."

"But you must have had some *reason.*"

"The sum in question arose in the course of his lordship's work in connection with his Farm Board duties this afternoon, miss," said Jeeves smoothly. "Your lordship may recall that I observed at the time that it was a peculiar figure."

"So you did, Jeeves, so you did."

"That was why your lordship said, 'Three thousand and five pounds, two shillings and sixpence.' These momentary mental aberrations are not uncommon, I believe. If I might suggest it, m'lord, I think it would be advisable to proceed to the yew alley without further delay. Time is of the essence."

"Of course, yes. They're waiting for me, aren't they? Are you coming, Jill?"

"I can't, darling. I have patients to attend to. I've got to go all the way over to Stover to see the Mainwarings' Peke, though I don't suppose there's the slightest thing wrong with it. That dog is the worst hypochondriac."

"Well, you're coming to dinner all right?"

"Of course. I'm counting the minutes. My mouth's watering already."

Jill went out through the French window. Bill mopped his forehead. It had been a near thing.

"You saved me there, Jeeves," he said. "But for your quick thinking all would have been discovered."

"I am happy to have been of service, m'lord."

"Another instant, and womanly intuition would have been doing its stuff, with results calculated to stagger humanity. You eat a lot of fish, don't you, Jeeves?"

"A good deal, m'lord."

"So Bertie Wooster has often told me. You sail into the sole and sardines like nobody's business, he says, and he attributes your giant intellect to the effects of the phosphorus. A hundred times, he says, it has enabled you to snatch him from the soup at the eleventh hour. He raves about your great gifts."

"Mr. Wooster has always been gratifyingly appreciative of my humble efforts on his behalf, m'lord."

"What beats me and has always beaten me is why he ever let you go. When you came to me that day and said you were at liberty, you could have bowled me over. The only explanation I could think of was that he was off his rocker ... or more off his rocker than he usually is. Or did you have a row with him and hand in your portfolio?"

Jeeves seemed distressed at the suggestion.

"Oh, no, m'lord. My relations with Mr. Wooster continue uniformly cordial, but circumstances have compelled a temporary separation. Mr. Wooster is attending a school which does not permit its student body to employ gentlemen's personal gentlemen."

"A school?"

"An institution designed to teach the aristocracy to fend for itself, m'lord. Mr. Wooster, though his finances are still quite sound, feels that it is prudent to build for the future, in case the social revolution should set in with even greater severity. Mr. Wooster ... I can hardly mention this without some display of emotion ... is actually learning to darn his own socks. The course he is taking includes boot-cleaning, sock-darning, bed-making and primary-grade cooking."

"Golly! Well, that's certainly a novel experience for Bertie."

"Yes, m'lord. Mr. Wooster doth suffer a sea change into something rich and strange. I quote the Bard of Stratford! Would your lordship care for another quick whisky and soda before joining Lady Carmoyle?"

"No, we mustn't waste a moment. As you were saying not long ago, time is of the ... what, Jeeves?"

"Essence, m'lord."

"Essence? You're sure?"

"Yes, m'lord."

"Well, if you say so, though I always thought an essence was a sort of scent. Right ho, then, let's go."

"Very good, m'lord."

5

SOME TEN miles from Towcester Abbey on the London road there stands the wayside inn called the Goose and Gherkin. Its solitary waiter, who had slipped out to make a quick telephone call, came back into the coffee room of the Goose and Gherkin wearing the starry-eyed look of a man who has just learned that he has backed a long-priced winner. He yearned to share his happiness with someone, and the only possible confidant was the woman at the table near the door, who was having a small gin and tonic and whiling away the time by reading a book of spiritualistic interest. He decided to tell her the good news.

"I don't know if you would care to know, madam," he said, in a voice that throbbed with emotion, "but Whistler's Mother won the Oaks."

The woman looked up, regarding him with large, dark, soulful eyes as if he had been something recently assembled from ectoplasm.

"The what?"

"The Oaks, madam."

"And what are the Oaks?"

It seemed incredible to the waiter that there should be anyone in England who could ask such a question, but he had already gathered that the lady was an American lady, and American ladies, he knew, are often ignorant of the fundamental facts of life. He had once met one who had wanted to know what a football pool was.

"It's an annual horse race, madam, reserved for fillies. By which I mean that it comes off once a year and the male sex isn't allowed to compete. It's run at Epsom Downs the day before the Derby, of which you have no doubt heard."

"Yes, I have heard of the Derby. It is your big race over here, is it not?"

"Yes, madam. What is sometimes termed a Classic. The Oaks is run the day before it, though in previous years the day after. By which I mean," said the waiter, hoping he was not being too abstruse, "it used to be run the day following the Derby, but now they've changed it."

"And Whistler's Mother won this race you call the Oaks?"

"Yes, madam. By a couple of lengths. I was on five bob."

"I see. Well, that's fine, isn't it? Will you bring me another gin and tonic."

"Certainly, madam. Whistler's Mother!" said the waiter, in a sort of ecstasy. "What a beauty!"

He went out. The woman resumed her reading. Quiet descended on the coffee room.

In its general essentials the coffee room at the Goose and Gherkin differed very little from the coffee rooms of all the other inns that nestle by the wayside in England and keep the island race from dying of thirst. It had the usual dim, religious light, the customary pictures of "The Stag at Bay" and "The Huguenot's Farewell" over the mantelpiece, the same cruets and bottles of sauce, and the traditional ozonelike smell of mixed pickles, gravy soup, boiled potatoes, waiters and old cheese.

What distinguished it on this June afternoon and gave it a certain something that the others had not got was the presence in it of the woman the waiter had been addressing. As a general rule, in the coffee rooms of English wayside inns, all the eye is able to feast on is an occasional farmer eating fried eggs or a couple of commercial travelers telling each other improper stories, but the Goose and Gherkin had drawn this strikingly handsome hand across the sea, and she raised the tone of the place unbelievably.

The thing about her that immediately arrested the attention and drew the startled whistle to the lips was the aura of wealth which she exuded. It showed itself in her rings, her hat, her stockings, her shoes, her platinum fur cape and the Jacques Fath sports costume that clung lovingly to her undulating figure. Here, you would have said to yourself, beholding her, was a woman who had got the stuff in sackfuls and probably suffered agonies from coupon-clipper's thumb, a woman at the mention of whose name the bloodsucking leeches of the Internal Revenue Department were accustomed to raise their filthy hats with a reverent intake of the breath.

Nor would have have been in error. She was just as rich as she looked. Twice married and each time to a multimillionaire, she was as nicely fixed financially as any woman could have wished.

Hers had been one of those Horatio Alger careers which are so encouraging to girls who hope to get on in the world, showing as they do that you never know what prizes Fate may be storing up for you around the corner. Born Rosalinda Banks, of the Chillicothe, Ohio, Bankses, with no assets beyond a lovely face, a superb figure and a mild talent for vers libre, she had come to Greenwich Village to seek her fortune and had found it first crack out of the box. At a studio party in McDougal Alley she had met and fascinated Clifton Bessemer, the Pulp Paper Magnate, and in almost no time at all had become his wife.

Widowed owing to Clifton Bessemer trying to drive his car one night through a truck instead of round it, and two years later meeting in Paris and marrying the millionaire sportsman and big-game hunter, A. B. Spottsworth, she was almost immediately widowed again.

It was a confusion of ideas between him and one of the lions he was hunting in Kenya that had caused A. B. Spottsworth to make the obituary column. He thought the lion was dead, and the lion thought it wasn't. The result being that when he placed his foot on the animal's neck preparatory to being photographed by Captain Biggar, the White Hunter accompanying the expedition, a rather unpleasant brawl had ensued, and owing to Captain Biggar having to drop the camera and spend several vital moments looking for his rifle, his bullet, though unerring, had come too late to be of practical assistance. There was nothing to be done but pick up the pieces and transfer the millionaire sportsman's vast fortune to his widow, adding it to the sixteen million or so which she had inherited from Clifton Bessemer.

Such, then, was Mrs. Spottsworth, a woman with a soul and about forty-two million dollars in the old oak chest. And, to clear up such minor points as may require elucidation, she was on her way to Towcester Abbey, where she was to be the guest of the ninth Earl of Towcester, and had stopped off at the Goose and Gherkin because she wanted to stretch her legs and air her Pekinese dog, Pomona. She was reading a book of spiritualistic interest because she had recently become an enthusiastic devotee of psychical research. She was wearing a Jacques Fath sports costume because she liked Jacques Fath sports costumes. And she was drinking gin and tonic because it was one of those warm evenings when a gin and tonic just hits the spot.

The waiter returned with the elixir, and went on where he had left off.

"Thirty-three to one the price was, madam."

Mrs. Spottsworth raised her lustrous eyes.

"I beg your pardon?"

"That's what she started at."

"To whom do you refer?"

"This filly I was speaking of that's won the Oaks."

"Back to her, are we?" said Mrs. Spottsworth with a sigh. She had been reading about some interesting manifestations from the spirit world, and this earthy stuff jarred upon her.

The waiter sensed the lack of enthusiasm. It hurt him a little. On this day of days he would have preferred to have to do only with those in whose veins sporting blood ran.

"You're not fond of racing, madam?"

Mrs. Spottsworth considered.

"Not particularly. My first husband used to be crazy about it, but it always seemed to me so unspiritual: All that stuff about booting them home and goats and beetles and fast tracks and mudders and something he referred to as a boat race. Not at all the sort of thing to develop a person's higher self. I'd bet a grand now and then, just for the fun of it, but that's as far as I would go. It never touched the deeps in me."

"A grand, madam?"

"A thousand dollars."

"Coo!" said the waiter, awed. "That's what I'd call putting your shirt on. Though for me it'd be not only my shirt but my stockings and pantie-girdle as well. Lucky for the bookies you weren't at Epsom today, backing Whistler's Mother."

He moved off, and Mrs. Spottsworth resumed her book.

For perhaps ten minutes after that nothing of major importance happened in the coffee room of the Goose and Gherkin except that the waiter killed a fly with his napkin and Mrs. Spottsworth finished her gin and tonic. Then the door was flung open by a powerful hand, and a tough, square, chunky, weatherbeaten-looking man in the middle forties strode in. He had keen blue eyes, a very red face, a round head inclined to baldness and one of those small, bristly mustaches which abound in such profusion in the outposts of Empire. Indeed, these sprout in so widespread a way on the upper lips of those who bear the white man's burden that it is a tenable theory that the latter hold some sort of patent rights. One recalls the nostalgic words of the poet Kipling, when he sang "Put me somewheres east of Suez, where the best is like the worst, where there ain't no ten commandments and a man can raise a small bristly mustache."

It was probably this mustache that gave the newcomer the exotic look he had. It made him seem out of place in the coffee room of an English inn. You felt, eyeing him, that his natural setting was Black Mike's bar in Pago-Pago, where he would be the life and soul of the party, though of course most of the time he would be out on safari, getting rough with such fauna as happened to come his way. Here, you would have said, was a man who many a time had looked his rhinoceros in the eye and made it wilt.

And again, just as when you were making that penetrating analysis of Mrs. Spottsworth, you would have been perfectly right. This bristly mustached he-man of the wilds was none other than the Captain Biggar whom we mentioned a moment ago in connection with the regrettable fracas which had culminated in A. B. Spottswotrth going to reside with the morning stars, and any of the crowd out along Bubbling Well Road or in the Long Bar at Shanghai could have told you that "Sahib" Biggar had made more rhinoceroses wilt than you could shake a stick at.

At the moment, he was thinking less of our dumb chums than of something cool in a tankard. The evening, as we have said, was warm, and he had driven many miles—from Epsom Downs, where he had started immediately after the conclusion of the race known as the Oaks, to this quiet inn in Southmoltonshire.

"Beer!" he thundered, and at the sound of his voice Mrs. Spottsworth dropped her book with a startled cry, her eyes leaping from the parent sockets.

And in the circumstances it was quite understandable that her eyes should have leaped, for her first impression had been that this was one of those interesting manifestations from the spirit world, of which she had been reading. Enough to make any woman's eyes leap.

The whole point about a hunter like Captain Biggar, if you face it squarely, is that he hunts. And, this being so, you expect him to stay put in and around his chosen hunting grounds. Meet him in Kenya or Malaya or Borneo, and you feel no surprise. "Hullo there, Captain Biggar," you say. "How's the spooring?" And he replies that the spooring is top-hole. Everything perfectly in order.

But when you see him in the coffee room of an English country inn, thousands of miles from his natural habitat, you may be excused for harboring a momentary suspicion that this is not the man in the flesh but rather his wraith or phantasm looking in, as wraiths and phantasms will, to pass the time of day.

"Eek!" Mrs. Spottsworth exclaimed, visibly shaken. Since interesting herself in psychical research, she had often wished to see a ghost, but one likes to pick one's time and place for that sort of thing. One does not want specters muscling in when one is enjoying a refreshing gin and tonic.

To the Captain, owing to the dimness of the light in the Goose and Gherkin's coffee room, Mrs. Spottsworth, until she spoke, had been simply a vague female figure having one for the road. On catching sight of her, he had automatically twirled his mustache, his invariable practice when he observed anything female in the offing, but he had in no sense drunk her in. Bending his gaze upon her now, he quivered all over like a nervous young hippopotamus finding itself face to face with its first White Hunter.

"Well, fry me in butter!" he ejaculated. He stood staring at her. "Mrs. Spottsworth! Well, simmer me in prune juice! Last person in the world I'd have dreamed of seeing. I thought you were in America."

Mrs. Spottsworth had recovered her poise.

"I flew over for a visit a week ago," she said.

"Oh, I see. That explains it. What made it seem odd, finding you here, was that I remember you told me you lived in California or one of those places."

"Yes, I have a home in Pasadena. In Carmel, too, and one in New York and another in Florida and another up in Maine."

"Making five in all?"

"Six. I was forgetting the one in Oregon."

"Six?" The Captain seemed thoughtful. "Oh, well," he said, "it's nice to have a roof over your head, of course."

"Yes. But one gets tired of places after a while. One yearns for something new. I'm thinking of buying this house I'm on my way to now, Towcester Abbey. I met Lord Towcester's sister in New York on her way back from Jamaica, and she said her brother might be willing to sell. But what are you doing in England, Captain? I couldn't believe my eyes at first."

"Oh, I thought I'd take a look at the old country, dear lady. Long time since I had a holiday, and you know the old proverb—all work and no play makes Jack a peh-bah pom bahoo. Amazing the way things have changed since I was here last. No idle rich, if you know what I mean. Everybody working. Everybody got a job of some kind."

"Yes, it's extraordinary, isn't it? Lord Towcester's sister, Lady Carmoyle, tells me her husband, Sir Roderick Carmoyle, is a floor-walker at Harrod's. And he's a tenth Baronet or something."

"Amazing, what? Tubby Frobisher and the Subadar won't believe me when I tell them."

"Who?"

"Couple of pals of mine out in Kuala Lumpur. They'll be astonished. But I like it," said the Captain stoutly. "It's the right spirit. The straight bat."

"I beg your pardon?"

"A cricket term, dear lady. At cricket you've got to play with a straight bat, or ... or, let's face it, you don't play with a straight bat, if you see what I mean."

"I suppose so. But do sit down, won't you?"

"Thanks, if I may, but only for a minute. I'm chasing a foe of the human species."

In Captain Biggar's manner, as he sat down, a shrewd observer would have noted a trace of embarrassment, and might have attributed this to the fact that the last time he and Mrs. Spottsworth had seen each other he had been sorting out what was left of her husband with a view to shipping it to Nairobi. But it was not the memory of that awkward moment that was causing his diffidence. Its roots lay deeper than that.

He loved this woman. He had loved her from the very moment she had come into his life. How well he remembered that moment. The camp among the acacia trees. The boulder-strewn cliff. The boulder-filled stream. Old Simba the lion roaring in the distance, old Tembo the elephant doing this and that in the *bimbo* or tall grass, and A. B. Spottsworth driving up in the car with a vision in jodhpurs at his side. "My wife," A. B. Spottsworth had said, indicating the combination of Cleopatra and Helen of Troy by whom he was accompanied, and as he replied, "Ah, the memsahib,"and greeted her with a civil *"Krai yu ti ny ma pay,"* it was as if a powerful electric shock had passed through Captain Biggar. This, he felt, was It.

Naturally, being a white man, he had not told his love, but it had burned steadily within him ever since, a strong, silent passion of such a caliber that sometimes, as he sat listening to the hyaenas and gazing at the snows of Kilimanjaro, it had brought him within an ace of writing poetry.

And here she was again, looking lovelier than ever. It seemed to Captain Biggar that somebody in the vicinity was beating a bass drum. But it was only the thumping of his heart.

His last words had left Mrs. Spottsworth fogged.

"Chasing a foe of the human species?" she queried.

"A blighter of a bookie. A cad of the lowest order with a soul as black as his finger nails. I've been after him for hours. And I'd have caught him," said the Captain, moodily sipping beer, "if something hadn't gone wrong with my bally car. They're fixing it now at that garage down the road."

"But why were you chasing this bookmaker?" asked Mrs. Spottsworth. It seemed to her a frivolous way for a strong man to be passing his time.

Captain Biggar's face darkened. Her question had touched an exposed nerve.

"The low hound did the dirty on me. Seemed straight enough, too. Chap with a walrus mustache and a patch over his left eye. Honest Patch Perkins, he called himself. 'Back your fancy and fear nothing, my noble sportsman,' he said. 'If you don't speculate, you can't accumulate,' he said. 'Walk up, walk up. Roll, bowl or pitch. Ladies halfway and no bad nuts returned,' he said. So I put my double on with him."

"Your double?"

"A double, dear lady, is when you back a horse in one race and if it wins, put the proceeds on another horse in another race."

. "Oh, what we call a parlay in America."

"Well, you can readily see that if both bounders pull it off, you pouch a princely sum. I've got in with a pretty knowledgeable crowd since I came to London, and they recommended as a good double for today Lucy Glitters and Whistler's Mother."

The name struck a chord.

"The waiter was telling me that Whistler's Mother won."

"So did Lucy Glitters in the previous race. I had a fiver on her at a hundred to six and all to come on Whistler's Mother for the Oaks. She ambled past the winning post at—"

"Thirty-three to one, the waiter was saying. My goodness! You certainly cleaned up, didn't you!"

Captain Biggar finished his beer. If it is possible to drink beer like an overwrought soul, he did so.

"I certainly ought to have cleaned up," he said, with a heavy frown. "There was the colossal sum of three thousand pounds, two shillings and sixpence owing to me, plus my original fiver which I had handed to the fellow's clerk, a chap in a checked suit and another walrus mustache. And what happened? This inky-hearted bookie welshed on me. He legged it in his car with me after him. I've been pursuing him, winding and twisting through the country roads, for what seems an eternity. And just as I was on the point of grappling with him, my car broke down. But I'll have the scoundrel! I'll catch the louse! And when I do, I propose to scoop out his insides with my bare hands and twist his head off and make him swallow it. After which—"

Captain Biggar broke off. It had suddenly come to him that he was monopolizing the conversation. After all, of what interest could these day-dreams of his be to this woman?

"But let's not talk about me any more," he said. "Dull subject. How have you been all these years, dear lady? Pretty fit, I hope? You look right in the pink. And how's your husband? Oh, sorry!"

"Not at all. You mean, have I married again? No, I have not married again, though Clifton and Alexis keep advising me to. They are sweet about it. So broadminded and considerate."

"Clifton? Alexis?"

"Mr. Bessemer and Mr. Spottsworth, my two previous husbands. I get them on the ouija board from time to time. I suppose," said Mrs. Spottsworth, laughing a little self-consciously, "you think it's odd of me to believe in things like the ouija board?"

"Odd?"

"So many of my friends in America call all that sort of thing poppycock."

Captain Biggar snorted militantly.

"I'd like to be there to talk to them! I'd astonish their weak intellects. No, dear lady, I've seen too many strange things in my time, living as I have done in the shadowlands of Mystery, to think anything odd. I have seen barefooted pilgrims treading the path of Ahura-Mazda over burning coals. I've seen ropes tossed in the air and small boys shinning up them in swarms. I've met fakirs who slept on beds of spikes."

"Really?"

"I assure you. And think of it, insomnia practically unknown. So you don't catch me laughing at people because they believe in ouija boards."

Mrs. Spottsworth gazed at him tenderly. She was thinking how sympathetic and understanding he was.

"I am intensely interested in psychical research. I am proud to be one of the little band of devoted seekers who are striving to pierce the veil. I am hoping to be vouchsafed some enthralling spiritual manifestation at this Towcester Abbey where I'm going. It is one of the oldest houses in England, they tell me."

"Then you ought to flush a specter or two," agreed Captain Biggar. "They collect in gangs in these old English country houses. How about another gin and tonic?"

"No, I must be getting along. Pomona's in the car, and she hates being left alone."

"You couldn't stay and have one more quick one?"

"I fear not. I must be on my way. I can't tell you how delightful it has been, meeting you again, Captain."

"Just made my day, meeting you, dear lady," said Captain Biggar, speaking hoarsely, for he was deeply moved. They were out in the open now, and he was able to get a clearer view of her as she stood beside her car bathed in the sunset glow. How lovely she was, he felt, how wonderful, how . . . Come, come, Biggar, he said to himself gruffly, this won't do, old chap. Play the game, Biggar, play the game, old boy!

"Won't you come and see me when I get back to London, Captain? I shall be at the Savoy."

"Charmed, dear lady, charmed," said Captain Biggar. But he did not mean it.

For what would be the use? What would it profit him to renew their acquaintance? Just twisting the knife in the wound, that's what he would be doing. Better, far better, to bite the bullet and wash the whole thing out here and now. A humble hunter with scarcely a bob to his name couldn't go mixing with wealthy widows. It was the kind of thing he had so often heard Tubby Frobisher and the Subadar denouncing in the old Anglo-Malay Club at Kuala Lumpur. "Chap's nothing but a bally fortune-hunter, old boy," they would say, discussing over the gin *pahits* someone who had made a rich marriage. "Simply a blighter gigolo, old boy, nothing more. Can't do that sort of thing, old chap, what? Not cricket, old boy."

And they were right. It couldn't be done. Damn it all, a feller had his code. *"Meh nee pan kong bahn rotfai"* about summed it up.

Stiffening his upper lip, Captain Biggar went down the road to see how his car was getting on, and Mrs. Spottsworth, getting into her car, drove off toward Towcester Abbey.

6

IT WAS with her mind in something of a whirl that she did so. The encounter with Captain C. G. Biggar had stirred her quite a good deal.

Mrs. Spottsworth was a woman who attached considerable importance to what others of less sensitivity would have dismissed carelessly as chance happenings or coincidences. She did not believe in chance. In her lexicon there was no such word as coincidence. These things, she held, were *meant.* This unforeseen return into her life of the White Hunter could be explained, she felt, only on the supposition that some pretty adroit staff work had been going on in the spirit world.

It had happened at such a particularly significant moment. Only two days previously A. B. Spottsworth, chatting with her on the ouija board, had remarked, after mentioning that he was very happy and eating lots of fruit, that it was high time she thought of getting married again. No sense, A. B. Spottsworth had said, in her living a lonely life with all that money in the bank. A woman needs a mate, he had asserted, adding that Cliff Bessemer, with whom he had exchanged a couple of words that morning in the vale of light, felt the same. "And they don't come more level-headed than old Cliff Bessemer," said A. B. Spottsworth.

And when his widow had asked, "But, Alexis, wouldn't you and Clifton *mind* me marrying again?" A. B. Spottsworth had replied in his bluff way, spelling the words out carefully, "Of course we wouldn't, you dumbbell. Go to it, kid."

And right on top of that dramatic conversation who should pop up out of a trap but the man who had loved her with a strong silent passion from the first moment they had met. It was uncanny. One would have said that passing the veil had made the late Messrs. Bessemer and Spottsworth clairvoyant.

Inasmuch as Captain Biggar, as we have seen, had not spoken his love but had let concealment like a worm i' the bud feed on his tomato-colored cheek, it may seem strange that Mrs. Spottsworth should have known anything about the way he felt. But a woman can always tell. When she sees a man choke up and look like an embarrassed beetroot every time he catches her eye over the eland steaks and limejuice, she soon forms an adequate diagnosis of his case.

The recurrence of these phenomena during those moments of farewell outside the Goose and Gherkin showed plainly, moreover, that the passage of time had done nothing to cool off the gallant Captain. She had not failed to observe the popeyed stare in his keen blue eyes, the deepening of the hue of his vermilion face and the way his number eleven feet had shuffled from start to finish of the interview. If he did not still consider her the tree on which the fruit of his life hung, Rosalinda Spottsworth was vastly mistaken. She was a little surprised that nothing had emerged in the way of an impassioned declaration. But how could she know that a feller had his code?

Driving through the pleasant Southmoltonshire country, she found her thoughts dwelling lingeringly on Captain C. G. Biggar.

At their very first meeting in Kenya she had found something about him that attracted her, and two days later this mild liking had become a rather fervent admiration. A woman cannot help but respect a man capable of upping with his big-bored .505 Gibbs and blowing the stuffing out of a charging buffalo. And from respect to love is as short a step as that from Harrod's Glass, Fancy Goods and Chinaware department to the Ladies Underclothing. He seemed to her like someone out of Ernest Hemingway, and she had always had a weakness for those rough, tough, devil-may-care Hemingway characters. Spiritual herself, she was attracted by roughness and toughness in the male. Clifton Bessemer had had those qualities. So had A. B. Spottsworth. What had first impressed her in Clifton Bessemer had been the way he had swatted a charging fly with a rolled-up evening paper at the studio party where they had met, and in the case of A. B. Spottsworth the spark had been lit when she heard him one afternoon in conversation with a Paris taxi-driver who had expressed dissatisfaction with the amount of his fare.

As she passed through the great gates of Towcester Abbey and made her way up the long drive, it was beginning to seem to her that she might do considerably worse than cultivate Captain Biggar. A woman needs a protector, and what better protector can she find than a man who thinks nothing of going into tall grass after a wounded lion? True, wounded lions do not enter largely into the ordinary married life, but it is nice for a wife to know that, if one does happen to come along, she can leave it with every confidence to her husband to handle.

It would not, she felt, be a difficult matter to arrange the necessary preliminaries. A few kind words and a melting look or two ought to be quite sufficient to bring that strong, passionate nature to the boil. These men of the wilds respond readily to melting looks.

She was just trying one out in the mirror of her car when, as she rounded a bend in the drive, Towcester Abbey suddenly burst upon her view, and for the moment Captain Biggar was forgotten. She could think of nothing but that she had found the house of her dreams. Its mellow walls aglow in the rays of the setting sun, its windows glittering like jewels, it seemed to her like some palace of fairyland. The little place in Pasadena, the little place in Carmel, and the little places in New York, Florida, Maine and Oregon were well enough in their way, but this outdid them all. Houses like Towcester Abbey always look their best from outside and at a certain distance.

She stopped the car and sat there, gazing raptly.

Rory and Monica, tired of waiting in the yew alley, had returned to the house and met Bill coming out. All three had gone back into the living room, where they were now discussing the prospects of a quick sale to this female Santa Claus from across the Atlantic. Bill, though feeling a little better after his whisky and soda, was still in a feverish state. His goggling eyes and twitching limbs would have interested a Harley Street physician, had one been present to observe them.

"Is there a hope?" he quavered, speaking rather like an invalid on a sickbed addressing his doctor.

"I think so," said Monica.

"I don't," said Rory.

Monica quelled him with a glance.

"The impression I got at that women's lunch in New York," she said, "was that she was nibbling. I gave her quite a blast of propaganda and definitely softened her up. All that remains now is to administer the final shove. When she arrives, I'll leave you alone together, so that you can exercise that well-known charm of yours. Give her the old personality."

"I will," said Bill fervently. "I'll be like a turtledove cooing to a female turtledove. I'll play on her as on a stringed instrument."

"Well, mind you do, because if the sale comes off, I'm expecting a commission."

"You shall have it, Moke, old thing. You shall be repaid a thousandfold. In due season there will present themselves at your front door elephants laden with gold and camels bearing precious stones and rare spices."

"How about apes, ivory and peacocks?"

"They'll be there."

Rory, the practical, hardheaded businessman, frowned on this visionary stuff.

"Well, will they?" he said. "The point seems to me extremely moot. Even on the assumption that this woman is weak in the head I can't see her paying a fortune for a place like Towcester Abbey. To start with, all the farms are gone."

"That's true," said Bill, damped. "And the park belongs to the local golf club. There's only the house and garden."

"The garden, yes. And we know all about the garden, don't we? I was saying to Moke only a short while ago that whereas in the summer months the river is at the bottom of the garden—"

"Oh, be quiet," said Monica. "I don't see why you shouldn't get fifteen thousand pounds, Bill. Maybe even as much as twenty."

Bill revived like a watered flower.

"Do you really think so?"

"Of course she doesn't," said Rory. "She's just trying to cheer you up, and very sisterly of her, too. I honor her for it. Under that forbidding exterior there lurks a tender heart. But twenty thousand quid for a house from which even Reclaimed Juvenile Delinquents recoil in horror? Absurd. The thing's a relic of the past. A hundred and forty-seven rooms!"

"That's a lot of house," argued Monica.

"It's a lot of junk," said Rory firmly. "It would cost a bally fortune to do it up."

Monica was obliged to concede this.

"I suppose so," she said. "Still, Mrs. Spottsworth's the sort of woman who would be quite prepared to spend a million or so on that. You've been making a few improvements, I notice," she said to Bill.

"A drop in the bucket."

"You've even done something about the smell on the first floor landing."

"Wish I had the money it cost."

"You're hard up?"

"Stony."

"Then where the dickens," said Rory, pouncing like a prosecuting counsel, "do all these butlers and housemaids come from? That girl Jill Stick-in-the-mud—"

"Her name is not Stick-in-the-mud."

"Her name may or may not be Stick-in-the-mud," he said, letting the point go, for after all it was a minor one, "but the fact remains that she was holding us spellbound just now with a description of your domestic amenities which suggested the mad luxury that led to the fall of Babylon. Platoons of butlers, beauty choruses of housemaids, cooks in reckless profusion and stories flying about of boys to clean the knives and boots—I said to Moke after she'd left that I wondered if you had set up as a gentleman bur— . . . That reminds me, old girl. Did you tell Bill about the police?"

Bill leaped a foot, and came down shaking in every limb.

"The police? What about the police?"

"Some blighter rang up from the local gendarmerie. The rozzers want to question you."

"What do you mean, question me?"

"Grill you," explained Rory. "Give you the third degree. And there was another call before that. A mystery man who didn't give his name. He and Moke kidded back and forth for a while."

"Yes, I talked to him," said Monica. "He had a voice that sounded as if he ate spinach with sand in it. He was enquiring about the license number of your car."

"What!"

"You haven't run into somebody's cow, have you? I understand that's a very serious offence nowadays."

Bill was still quivering briskly.

"You mean someone was wanting to know the license number of my car?"

"That's what I said. Why, what's the matter, Bill? You're looking as worried as a prune."

"White and shaken," agreed Rory. "Like a side-car." He laid a kindly hand on his brother-in-law's shoulder. "Bill, tell me. Be frank. Why are you wanted by the police?"

"I'm not wanted by the police."

"Well, it seems to be their dearest wish to get their hands on you. One theory that crossed my mind," said Rory, "was—I mentioned it to you, Moke, if you remember—that you had found some opulent bird with a guilty secret and were going in for a spot of blackmail. This may or may not be the case, but if it is, now is the time to tell us, Bill, old man. You're among friends. Moke's broadminded, and I'm broadminded. I know the police look a bit squiggle-eyed at blackmail, but I can't see any objection to it myself. Quick profits and practically no overhead. If I had a son, I'm not at all sure I wouldn't have him trained for that profession. So if the flatties are after you and you would like a helping hand to get you out of the country before they start watching the ports, say the word, and we'll . . ."

"Mrs. Spottsworth," announced Jeeves from the doorway, and a moment later Bill had done another of those leaps in the air which had become so frequent with him of late.

He stood staring pallidly at the vision that entered.

7

MRS. SPOTTSWORTH had come sailing into the room with the confident air of a woman who knows that her hat is right, her dress is right, her shoes are right and her stockings are right and that she has a matter of forty-two million dollars tucked away in sound securities, and Bill, with a derelict country house for sale, should have found her an encouraging spectacle. For unquestionably she looked just the sort of person who would buy derelict English country houses by the gross without giving the thing a second thought.

But his mind was not on business transactions. It had flitted back a few years and was in the French Riviera, where he and this woman had met and—he could not disguise it from himself—become extremely matey.

It had all been perfectly innocent, of course—just a few moonlight drives, one or two mixed bathings and hobnobbings at Eden Roc and the ordinary exchanges of civilities customary on the French Riviera—but it seemed to him that there was a grave danger of her introducing into their relations now that touch of Auld Lang Syne which is the last thing a young man wants when he has a fiancée around—and a fiancée, moreover, who has already given evidence of entertaining distressing suspicions.

Mrs. Spottsworth had come upon him as a complete and painful surprise. At Cannes he had got the impression that her name was Bessemer, but of course in places like Cannes you don't bother much about surnames. He had, he recalled, always addressed her as Rosie, and she—he shuddered—had addressed him as Billiken. A clear, but unpleasant, picture rose before his eyes of Jill's face when she heard her addressing him as Billiken at dinner tonight. Most unfortunately, through some oversight, he had omitted to mention to Jill his Riviera acquaintance, Mrs. Bessemer, and he could see that she might conceivably take a little explaining away.

"How nice to see you again, Rosalinda," said Monica. "So glad you found your way here all right. It's rather tricky after you leave the main road. My husband, Sir Roderick Carmoyle. And this is—"

"Billiken!" cried Mrs. Spottsworth, with all the enthusiasm of a generous nature. It was plain that if the ecstasy occasioned by this unexpected encounter was a little one-sided, on her side at least it existed in full measure.

"Eh?" said Monica.

"Mr. Belfry and I are old friends. We knew each other in Cannes a few years ago, when I was Mrs. Bessemer."

"Bessemer!"

"It was not long after my husband had passed the veil owing to having a head-on collision with a truck full of beer bottles on the Jericho Turnpike. His name was Clifton Bessemer."

Monica shot a pleased and contgratulatory look at Bill. She knew all about Mrs. Bessemer of Cannes. She was aware that her brother had given this Mrs. Bessemer the rush of a lifetime, and what better foundation could a young man with a house to sell have on which to build.

"Well, that's fine," she said. "You'll have all sorts of things to talk about, won't you? But he isn't Mr. Belfry now, he's Lord Towcester."

"Changed his name," explained Rory. "The police are after him, and an alias was essential."

"Oh, don't be an ass, Rory. He came into the title," said Monica. "You know how it is in England. You start out as something, and then someone dies and you do a switch. Our uncle, Lord Towcester, pegged out not long ago, and Bill was his heir, so he shed the Belfry and took on the Towcester."

"I see. Well, to me he will always be Billiken. How are you, Billiken?"

Bill found speech, though not much of it and what there was rather rasping.

"I'm fine, thanks—er—Rosie."

"Rosie?" said Rory, startled and, like the child of nature he was, making no attempt to conceal his surprise. "Did I hear you say Rosie?"

Bill gave him a cold look.

"Mrs. Spottsworth's name, as you have already learned from a usually well-informed source—*viz*. Moke—is Rosalinda. All her friends—even casual acquaintances like myself—called her Rosie."

"Oh, ah," said Rory. "Quite, quite. Very natural, of course."

"Casual acquaintances?" said Mrs. Spottsworth, pained.

Bill plucked at his tie.

"Well, I mean blokes who just knew you from meeting you at Cannes and so forth."

"Cannes!" cried Mrs. Spottsworth ecstatically. "Dear sunny, gay, delightful Cannes! What times we had there, Billiken! Do you remember—"

"Yes, yes," said Bill. "Very jolly, the whole thing. Won't you have a drink or a sandwich or a cigar or something?"

Fervently he blessed the Mainwarings' Peke for being so confirmed a hypochondriac that it had taken Jill away to the other side of the county. By the time she returned, Mrs. Spottsworth, he trusted, would have simmered down and become less expansive on the subject of the dear old days. He addressed himself to the task of curbing her exuberance.

"Nice to welcome you to Towcester Abbey," he said formally.

"Yes, I hope you'll like it," said Monica.

"It's the most wonderful place I ever saw!"

"Would you say that? Moldering old ruin, I'd call it," said Rory judicially, and was fortunate enough not to catch his wife's eye. "Been decaying for centuries. I'll bet if you shook those curtains, a couple of bats would fly out."

"The patina of Time!" said Mrs. Spottsworth. "I adore it." She closed her eyes. " 'The dead, twelve deep, clutch at you as you go by,' " she murmured.

"What a beastly idea," said Rory. "Even a couple of clutching corpses would be a bit over the odds, in my opinion."

Mrs. Spottsworth opened her eyes. She smiled.

"I'm going to tell you something very strange," she said. "It struck me so strongly when I came in at the front door I had to sit down for a moment. Your butler thought I was ill."

"You aren't, I hope?"

"No, not at all. It was simply that I was . . . overcome. I realized that I had been here before."

Monica looked politely puzzled. It was left to Rory to supply the explanation.

"Oh, as a sightseer?" he said. "One of the crowd that used to come on

Fridays during the summer months to be shown over the place at a bob a head. I remember them well in the days when you and I were walking out, Moke. The Gogglers, we used to call them. They came in charabangs and dropped nut chocolate on the carpets. Not that dropping nut chocolate on them would make these carpets any worse. That's all been discontinued now, hasn't it, Bill? Nothing left to goggle at, I suppose. The late Lord Towcester," he explained to the visitor, "stuck the Americans with all his best stuff, and now there's not a thing in the place worth looking at. I was saying to my wife only a short while ago that by far the best policy in dealing with Towcester Abbey would be to burn it down."

A faint moan escaped Monica. She raised her eyes heavenwards, as if pleading for a thunderbolt to strike this man. If this was her Roderick's idea of selling goods to a customer, it seemed a miracle that he had ever managed to get rid of a single hose pipe, lawn mower or bird bath.

Mrs. Spottsworth shook her head with an indulgent smile.

"No, no, I didn't mean that I had been here in my present corporeal envelope. I meant in a previous incarnation. I'm a Rotationist, you know."

Rory nodded intelligently.

"Ah, yes. Elks, Shriners and all that. I've seen pictures of them, in funny hats."

"No, no, you are thinking of Rotarians. I am a Rotationist, which is quite different. We believe that we are reborn as one of our ancestors every ninth generation."

"Ninth?" said Monica, and began to count on her fingers.

"The mystic ninth house. Of course you've read the Zend Avesta of Zoroaster, Sir Roderick?"

"I'm afraid not. Is it good?"

"Essential, I would say."

"I'll put it on my library list," said Rory. "By Agatha Christie, isn't it?"

Monica had completed her calculations.

"Ninth . . . That seems to make me Lady Barbara, the leading hussy of Charles the Second's reign."

Mrs. Spottsworth was impressed.

"I suppose I ought to be calling you Lady Barbara and asking you about your latest love affair."

"I only wish I could remember it. From what I've heard of her, it would make quite a story."

"Did she get herself sunburned all over?" asked Rory. "Or was she more of an indoor girl?"

Mrs. Spottsworth had closed her eyes again.

"I feel influences," she said. "I even hear faint whisperings. How strange it is, coming into a house that you last visited three hundred years ago. Think of all the lives that have been lived within these ancient walls. And they are all here, all around us, creating an intriguing aura for this delicious old house."

Monica caught Bill's eye.

"It's in the bag, Bill," she whispered.

"Eh?" said Rory in a loud, hearty voice. "What's in the bag?"

"Oh, shut up."

"But what *is* in the . . . Ouch!" He rubbed a well-kicked ankle. "Oh, ah, yes, of course. Yes, I see what you mean."

Mrs. Spottsworth passed a hand across her brow. She appeared to be in a sort of mediumistic trance.

"I seem to remember a chapel. There is a chapel here?"

"Ruined," said Monica.

"You don't need to tell her that, old girl," said Rory.

"I knew it. And there's a Long Gallery."

"That's right," said Monica. "A duel was fought in it in the eighteenth century. You can still see the bullet holes in the walls."

"And dark stains on the floor, no doubt. This place must be full of ghosts."

This, felt Monica, was an idea to be discouraged at the outset.

"Oh, no, don't worry," she said heartily. "Nothing like that in Towcester Abbey," and was surprised to observe that her guest was gazing at her with large, woebegone eyes like a child informed that the evening meal will not be topped off with ice cream.

"But I want ghosts," said Mrs. Spottsworth. "I must have ghosts. Don't tell me there aren't *any?*"

Rory was his usual helpful self.

"There's what we call the haunted lavatory on the ground floor," he said. "Every now and then, when there's nobody near it, the toilet will suddenly flush, and when a death is expected in the family, it just keeps going and going. But we don't know if it's a specter or just a defect in the plumbing."

"Probably a poltergeist," said Mrs. Spottsworth, seeming a little disappointed. "But are there no visual manifestations?"

"I don't think so."

"Don't be silly, Rory," said Monica. "Lady Agatha."

Mrs. Spottsworth was intrigued.

"Who was Lady Agatha?"

"The wife of Sir Caradoc the Crusader. She has been seen several times in the ruined chapel."

"Fascinating, fascinating," said Mrs. Spottsworth. "And now let me take you to the Long Gallery. Don't tell me where it is. Let me see if I can't find it for myself."

She closed her eyes, pressed her fingertips to her temples, paused for a moment, opened her eyes and started off. As she reached the door, Jeeves appeared.

"Pardon me, m'lord."

"Yes, Jeeves?"

"With reference to Mrs. Spottsworth's dog, m'lord, I would appreciate instructions as to meal hours and diet."

"Pomona is very catholic in her tastes," said Mrs. Spottsworth. "She usually dines at five, but she is not at all fussy."

"Thank you, madam."

"And now I must concentrate. This is a test." Mrs. Spottsworth applied her fingertips to her temples once more. "Follow, please, Monica. You, too, Billiken. I am going to take you straight to the Long Gallery."

The procession passed through the door, and Rory, having scrutinized it in his slow, thorough way, turned to Jeeves with a shrug of the shoulders.

"Potty, what?"

"The lady does appear to diverge somewhat from the generally accepted norm, Sir Roderick."

"She's as crazy as a bedbug. I'll tell you something, Jeeves. That sort of thing wouldn't be tolerated at Harrod's."

"No, sir?"

"Not for a moment. If this Mrs. Dogsbody, or whatever her name is, came into—say the Cakes, Biscuits and General Confectionery and started acting that way, the store detectives would have her by the seat of the trousers and be giving her the old heave-ho before the first gibber had proceeded from her lips."

"Indeed, Sir Roderick?"

"I'm telling you, Jeeves. I had an experience of that sort myself shortly after I joined. I was at my post one morning—I was in the Jugs, Bottles and Picnic Supplies at the time—and a woman came in. Well dressed, refined aspect, nothing noticeable about her at all except that she was wearing a fireman's helmet—I started giving her courteous service. 'Good morning, madam,' I said. 'What can I do for you, madam? Something in picnic supplies, madam? A jug? A bottle?' She looked at me keenly. 'Are you interested in bottles, gargoyle?' she asked, addressing me for some reason as 'gargoyle.' 'Why, yes, madam,' I replied. 'Then what do you think of this one,' she said. And with that she whipped out a whacking great decanter and brought it whizzing down on the exact spot where my frontal bone would have been, had I not started back like a nymph surprised while bathing. It shattered itself on the counter. It was enough. I beckoned to the store detectives and they scooped her up."

"Most unpleasant, Sir Roderick."

"Yes, shook me, I confess. Nearly made me send in my papers. It turned out that she had recently been left a fortune by a wealthy uncle in Australia, and it had unseated her reason. This Mrs. Dogsbody's trouble is, I imagine, the same. Inherited millions from a platoon of deceased husbands, my wife informs me, and took advantage of the fact to go right off her onion. Always a mistake, Jeeves, unearned money. There's nothing like having to scratch for a living. I'm twice the man I was since I joined the ranks of the world's workers."

"You see eye to eye with the Bard, Sir Roderick. 'Tis deeds must win the prize.' "

"Exactly. Quite so. And speaking of winning prizes, what about tomorrow?"

"Tomorrow, Sir Roderick?"

"The Derby. Know anything?"

"I fear not, Sir Roderick. It would seem to be an exceptionally open contest. Monsieur Boussac's Voleur is, I understand, the favorite. Fifteen to two at last night's call-over and the price likely to shorten to sixes or even fives for the S.P. But the animal in question is somewhat small and lightly boned for so grueling an ordeal. Though we have, to be sure, seen such a handicap overcome. The name of Manna, the 1925 winner, springs to the mind, and Hyperion, another smallish horse, broke the course record previously held by Flying Fox, accomplishing the distance in two minutes, ninety-four seconds."

Rory regarded him with awe.

"By Jove! You know your stuff, don't you?"

"One likes to keep *au courant* in these matters, sir. It is, one might say, an essential part of one's education."

"Well, I'll certainly have another chat with you tomorrow before I put my bet on."

"I shall be most happy if I can be of service, Sir Roderick," said Jeeves courteously, and oozed softly from the room, leaving Rory with the feeling, so universal among those who encountered this great man, that he had established connection with some wise, kindly spirit in whose hands he might place his affairs without tremor.

A few moments later, Monica came in, looking a little jaded.

"Hullo, old girl," said Rory. "Back from your travels? Did she find the ruddy gallery?"

Monica nodded listlessly.

"Yes, after taking us all over the house. She said she lost the influence for a while. Still, I suppose it wasn't bad after three hundred years."

"I was saying to Jeeves a moment ago that the woman's as crazy as a bedbug. Though, arising from that, how is it that bedbugs have got their reputation for being mentally unbalanced? Now that she's over in this country, I expect she'll soon be receiving all sorts of flattering offers from Colney Hatch and similar establishments. What became of Bill?"

"He didn't stay the course. He disappeared. Went to dress, I suppose."

"What sort of state was he in?"

"Glassy-eyed and starting at sudden noises."

"Ah, still jittery. He's certainly got the jumps all right, our William. But I've had another theory about old Bill," said Rory. "I don't think his nervousness is due to his being one jump ahead of the police. I now attribute it to his having got this job with the Farm Board and, like all these novices, pitching in too strenuously at first. We fellows who aren't used to work have got to learn to husband our strength, to keep something in reserve, if you know what I mean. That's what I'm always preaching to the chaps under me. Most of them listen, but there's one lad—in the Midgets Outfitting—you've never seen such *drive*. That boy's going to burn himself out before he's fifty. Hullo, whom have we here?"

He stared, at a loss, at a tall, good-looking girl who had just entered. A momentary impression that this was the ghost of Lady Agatha, who, wearying of the ruined chapel, had come to join the party, he dismissed. But he could not place her. Monica saw more clearly into the matter. Observing the cap and apron, she deduced that this must be that almost legendary figure, the housemaid.

"Ellen?" she queried.

"Yes, m'lady. I was looking for his lordship."

"I think he's in his room. Anything I can do?"

"It's this gentleman that's just come, asking to see his lordship, m'lady. I saw him driving up in his car and, Mr. Jeeves being busy in the dining-room, I answered the door and showed him into the morning-room."

"Who is he?"

"A Captain Biggar, m'lady."

Rory chuckled amusedly.

"Biggar? Reminds me of that game we used to play when we were kids, Moke—the Bigger Family."

"I remember."

"You do? Then which is bigger, Mr. Bigger or Mrs. Bigger?"

"Rory, really."

"Mr. Bigger, because he's father Bigger. Which is bigger, Mr. Bigger or his old maid aunt?"

"You're not a child, you know."

"Can you tell me, Ellen?"

"No, sir."

"Perhaps Mrs. Dogsbody can," said Rory, as that lady came bustling in. There was a look of modest triumph on Mrs. Spottsworth's handsome face.

"Did you tell Sir Roderick?" she said.

"I told him," said Monica.

"I found the Long Gallery, Sir Roderick."

"Three rousing cheers," said Rory. "Continue along these lines, and you'll soon be finding bass drums in telephone booths. But pigeonholing that for the moment, do you know which is bigger, Mr. Bigger or his old maid aunt?"

Mrs. Spottsworth looked perplexed.

"I beg your pardon?"

Rory repeated his question, and her perplexity deepened.

48 P. G. WODEHOUSE

"But I don't understand."

"Rory's just having one of his spells," said Monica.

"The old maid aunt," said Rory, "because, whatever happens, she's always Bigger."

"Pay no attention to him," said Monica. "He's quite harmless on these occasions. It's just that a Captain Biggar has called. That set him off. He'll be all right in a minute."

Mrs. Spottsworth's fine eyes had widened.

"Captain Biggar?"

"There's another one," said Rory, knitting his brow, "only it eludes me for the moment. I'll get it soon. Something about Mr. Bigger and his son."

"Captain Biggar?" repeated Mrs. Spottsworth. She turned to Ellen. "Is he a gentleman with a rather red face?"

"He's a gentleman with a very red face," said Ellen. She was a girl who liked to get these things right.

Mrs. Spottsworth put a hand to her heart.

"How extraordinary!"

"You know him?" said Monica.

"He is an old, old friend of mine. I knew him when . . . Oh, Monica, could you . . . would you . . . could you possibly invite him to stay?"

Monica started like a war horse at the sound of the bugle.

"Why, of course, Rosalinda. Any friend of yours. What a splendid idea."

"Oh, thank you." Mrs. Spottsworth turned to Ellen. "Where is Captain Biggar?"

"In the morning-room, madam."

"Will you take me there at once. I must see him."

"If you will step this way, madam."

Mrs. Spottsworth hurried out, followed sedately by Ellen. Rory shook his head dubiously.

"Is this wise, Moke, old girl? Probably some frightful outsider in a bowler hat and a made-up tie."

Monica's eyes were sparkling.

"I don't care what he's like. He's a friend of Mrs. Spottsworth's, that's all that matters. Oh, Bill!" she cried, as Bill came in.

Bill was tail-coated, white-tied and white-waistcoated, and his hair gleamed with strange unguents. Rory stared at him in amazement.

"Good God, Bill! You look like Great Lovers through the Ages. If you think I'm going to dress up like that, you're much mistaken. You get the old Carmoyle black tie and soft shirt, and like it. I get the idea, of course. You've dolled yourself up to impress Mrs. Spottsworth and bring back memories of the old days at Cannes. But I'd be careful not to overdo it, old boy. You've got to consider Jill. If she finds out about you and the Spottsworth—"

Bill started.

"What the devil do you mean?"

"Nothing, nothing. I was only making a random remark."

"Don't listen to him, Bill," said Monica. "He's just drooling. Jill's sensible."

"And after all," said Rory, looking on the bright side, "it all happened before you met Jill."

"All what happened?"

"Nothing, old boy, nothing."

"My relations with Mrs. Spottsworth were pure to the last drop."

"Of course, of course."

"Do you sell muzzles at Harrod's, Rory?" asked Monica.

"Muzzles? Oh, rather. In the Cats, Dogs and Domestic Pets."

"I'm going to buy one for you, to keep you quiet. Just treat him as if he weren't there, Bill, and listen while I tell you the news. The most wonderful thing has happened. An old friend of Mrs. Spottsworth's has turned up, and I've invited him to stay."

"An old friend?"

"Another old lover, one presumes."

"Do stop it, Rory. Can't you understand what a marvelous thing this is, Bill! We've put her under an obligation. Think what a melting mood she'll be in after this!"

Her enthusiasm infected Bill. He saw just what she meant.

"You're absolutely right. This is terrific."

"Yes, isn't it a stroke of luck! She'll be clay in your hands now."

"Clay is the word. Moke, you're superb. As fine a bit of quick thinking as I ever struck. Who is the fellow?"

"His name's Biggar. Captain Biggar."

Bill groped for support at a chair. A greenish tinge had spread over his face.

"What!" he cried. "Captain B-b-b—?"

"Ha!" said Rory. "Which is bigger, Mr. Bigger or Master Bigger? Master Bigger, because he's a little Bigger. I knew I'd get it," he said complacently.

PART TWO

8

It was a favorite dictum of the late A. B. Spottsworth, who, though fond of his wife in an absent-minded sort of way, could never have been described as a ladies' man or mistaken for one of those troubadours of the Middle Ages, that the secret of a happy and successful life was to get rid of the women at the earliest possible opportunity. Give the gentler sex the bum's rush, he used to say, removing his coat and reaching for the poker chips, and you could start to go places. He had often observed that for sheer beauty and uplift few sights could compare with that of the female members of a dinner party filing out of the room at the conclusion of the meal, leaving the men to their soothing masculine conversation.

To Bill Towcester at nine o'clock on the night of this disturbing day such an attitude of mind would have seemed incomprehensible. The last thing in the world that he desired was Captain Biggar's soothing masculine conversation. As he stood holding the dining-room door open while Mrs. Spottsworth, Monica and Jill passed through on their way to the living room, he was weighed down by a sense of bereavement and depression, mingled with uneasy speculations as to what was going to happen now. His emotions, in fact, were similar in kind and intensity to those which a garrison beleaguered by savages would have experienced, had the United States Marines, having arrived, turned right around and walked off in the opposite direction.

True, all had gone perfectly well so far. Even he, conscience-stricken though he was, had found nothing to which he could take exception in the Captain's small talk up till now. Throughout dinner, starting with the soup and carrying on to the sardines on toast, the White Hunter had confined himself to such neutral topics as cannibal chiefs he had met and what to do when cornered by African headhunters with poisoned blowpipes. He had told two rather long and extraordinarily dull stories about a couple of friends of his called Tubby Frobisher and the Subadar. And he had recommended to Jill, in case she should ever find herself in need of one, an excellent ointment for use when bitten by alligators. To fraudulent bookmakers, chases across country and automobile licenses he had made no reference whatsoever.

But now that the women had left and two strong men—or three, if you counted Rory—stood face to face, who could say how long this happy state of things would last? Bill could but trust that Rory would not bring the conversation around to the dangerous subject by asking the Captain if he went in for racing at all.

"Do you go in for racing at all, Captain?" said Rory, as the door closed.

A sound rather like the last gasp of a dying zebra shot from Captain Biggar's lips. Bill, who had risen some six inches into the air, diagnosed it correctly as a hollow, mirthless laugh. He had had some idea of uttering something along those lines himself.

"Racing?" Captain Biggar choked. "Do I go in for racing at all? Well, mince me up and smother me in onions!"

Bill would gladly have done so. Such a culinary feat would, it seemed to him, have solved all his perplexities. He regretted that the idea had not occurred to one of the cannibal chiefs of whom his guest had been speaking.

"It's the Derby Dinner tonight," said Rory. "I'll be popping along shortly to watch it on the television set in the library. All the top owners are coming on the screen to say what they think of their chances tomorrow. Not that the blighters know a damn thing about it, of course. Were you at the Oaks this afternoon by any chance?"

Captain Biggar expanded like one of those peculiar fish in Florida which swell when you tickle them.

"Was I at the Oaks? *Chang suark*! Yes, sir, I was. And if ever a man—"

"Rather pretty, this Southmoltonshire country, don't you think, Captain?" said Bill. "Picturesque, as it is sometimes called. The next village to us—Lower Snodsbury—you may have noticed it as you came through—has a—"

"If ever a man got the ruddy sleeve across the bally windpipe," proceeded the Captain, who had now become so bright red that it was fortunate that by a lucky chance there were no bulls present in the dining room, "it was me at Espom this afternoon. I passed through the furnace like Shadrach, Meshach and Nebuchadnezzar or whoever it was. I had my soul tied up in knots and put through the wringer."

Rory tut-tutted sympathetically.

"Had a bad day, did you?"

"Let me tell you what happened."

"—Norman church," continued Bill, faint but persevering, "which I believe is greatly—"

"I must begin by saying that since I came back to the old country, I have got in with a pretty shrewd lot of chaps, fellows who know one end of a horse from the other, as the expression is, and they've been putting me on to some good things. And today—"

"—admired by blokes who are fond of Norman churches," said Bill. "I don't know much about them myself, but according to the nibs there's a nave or something on that order—"

Captain Biggar exploded again.

"Don't talk to me about knaves! *Yogi tulsiram jaginath*! I met the king of them this afternoon, blister his insides. Well, as I was saying, these chaps of mine put me on to good things from time to time, and today they advised a double. Lucy Glitters in the two-thirty and Whistler's Mother for the Oaks."

"Extraordinary, Whistler's Mother winning like that," said Rory. "The consensus of opinion at Harrod's was that she hadn't a hope."

"And what happened? Lucy Glitters rolled in at a hundred to six, and Whistler's Mother, as you may have heard, at thirty-three to one."

Rory was stunned.

"You mean your double came off?"

"Yes, sir."

"At those odds?"

"At those odds."

"How much did you have on?"

"Five pounds on Lucy Glitters and all to come on Whistler's Mother's nose."

Rory's eyes bulged.

"Good God! Are you listening to this, Bill? You must have won a fortune."

"Three thousand pounds."

"Well, I'll be . . . Did you hear that, Jeeves?"

Jeeves had entered, bearing coffee. His deportment was, as ever, serene. Like Bill, he found Captain Biggar's presence in the home disturbing, but where Bill quaked and quivered, he continued to resemble a well-bred statue.

"Sir?"

"Captain Biggar won three thousand quid on the Oaks."

"Indeed, sir? A consummation devoutly to be wished."

"Yes," said the Captain somberly. "Three thousand pounds I won, and the bookie did a bolt."

Rory stared.

"No!"

"I assure you."

"Skipped by the light of the moon?"

"Exactly."

Rory was overcome.

"I never heard anything so monstrous. Did you ever hear anything so monstrous, Jeeves? Wasn't that the frozen limit, Bill?"

Bill seemed to come out of a trance.

"Sorry, Rory, I'm afraid I was thinking of something else. What were you saying?"

"Poor old Biggar brought off a double at Epsom this afternoon, and the swine of a bookie legged it, owing him three thousand pounds."

Bill was naturally aghast. Any good-hearted young man would have been, hearing such a story.

"Good heavens, Captain," he cried, "what a terrible thing to have happened. Legged it, did he, this bookie?"

"Popped off like a jack rabbit, with me after him."

"I don't wonder you're upset. Scoundrels like that ought not to be at large. It makes one's blood boil to think of this . . . this . . . what would Shakespeare have called him, Jeeves?"

"This arrant, rascally, beggarly, lousy knave, m'lord."

"Ah, yes. Shakespeare put these things well."

"A whoreson, beetle-headed, flap-eared knave; a knave, a rascal, an eater of broken meats; a beggarly filthy, worsted-stocking—"

"Yes, yes, Jeeves, quite so. One gets the idea." Bill's manner was a little agitated. "Don't run away, Jeeves. Just give the fire a good stir."

"It is June, m'lord."

"So it is, so it is. I'm all of a doodah, hearing this appalling story. Won't you sit down, Captain? Oh, you are sitting down. The cigars, Jeeves. A cigar for Captain Biggar."

The Captain held up a hand.

"Thank you, no. I never smoke when I'm after big game."

"Big game? Oh, I see what you mean. This bookie fellow. You're a White Hunter, and now you're hunting white bookies," said Bill with a difficult laugh. "Rather good, that, Rory?"

"Dashed good, old boy. I'm convulsed. And now may I get down? I want to go and listen to the Derby Dinner."

"An excellent idea," said Bill heartily. "Let's all go and listen to the Derby Dinner. Come along, Captain."

Captain Biggar made no move to follow Rory from the room. He remained in his seat, looking redder than ever.

"Later, perhaps," he said curtly. "At the moment, I would like to have a word with you, Lord Towcester."

"Certainly, certainly, certainly, certainly, certainly," said Bill, though not blithely. "Stick around, Jeeves. Lots of work to do in here. Polish an ashtray or something. Give Captain Biggar a cigar."

"The gentleman has already declined your lordship's offer of a cigar."

"So he has, so he has. Well, well!" said Bill. "Well, well, well, well, well!" He lit one himself with a hand that trembled like a tuning fork. "Tell us more about this bookie of yours, Captain."

Captain Biggar brooded darkly for a moment. He came out of the silence to express a wistful hope that some day it might be granted to him to see the color of the fellow's insides.

"I only wish," he said, "that I could meet the rat in Kuala Lumpur."

"Kuala Lumpur?"

Jeeves was his customary helpful self.

"A locality in the Straits Settlements, m'lord, a British crown colony in the East Indies including Malacca, Penang and the province of Wellesley, first made a separate dependency of the British Crown in 1853 and placed under the Governor-General of India. In 1887 the Cocos or Keeling Islands were attached to the colony, and in 1889 Christmas Island. Mr. Somerset Maugham has written searchingly of life in those parts."

"Of course, yes. It all comes back to me. Rather a strange lot of birds out there, I gather."

Captain Biggar conceded this.

"A very strange lot of birds. But we generally manage to put salt on their tails. Do you know what happens to a welsher in Kuala Lumpur, Lord Towcester?"

"No, I—er—don't believe I've ever heard. Don't go, Jeeves. Here's an ashtray you've missed. What does happen to a welsher in Kuala Lumpur?"

"We let the blighter have three days to pay up. Then we call on him and give him a revolver."

"That's rather nice of you. Sort of heaping coals of . . . You don't mean a *loaded* revolver?"

"Loaded in all six chambers. We look the louse in the eye, leave the revolver on the table and go off. Without a word. He understands."

Bill gulped. The strain of the conversation was beginning to tell on him.

"You mean he's expected to . . . Isn't that a bit drastic?"

Captain Biggar's eyes were cold and hard, like picnic eggs.

"It's the code, sir. Code! That's a big word with the men who live on the frontiers of empire. Morale can crumble very easily out there. Drink, women and unpaid gambling debts, those are the steps down," he said. "Drink, women and unpaid gambling debts," he repeated, illustrating with jerks of the hand.

"That one's the bottom, is it? You hear that, Jeeves?"

"Yes, m'lord."

"Rather interesting."

"Yes, m'lord."

"Broadens the mind a bit."

"Yes, m'lord."

"One lives and learns, Jeeves."

"One does indeed, m'lord."

Captain Biggar took a Brazil nut, and cracked it with his teeth.

"We've got to set an example, we bearers of the white man's burden. Can't let the Dyaks beat us on code."

"Do they try?"

"A Dyak who defaults on a debt has his head cut off."

"By the other Dyaks?"

"Yes, sir, by the other Dyaks."

"Well, well."

"The head is then given to his principal creditor."

This surprised Bill. Possibly it surprised Jeeves, too, but Jeeves' was a face that did not readily register such emotions as astonishment. Those who knew him well claimed on certain occasions of great stress to have seen a very small muscle at the corner of his mouth give one quick, slight twitch, but as a rule his features preserved a uniform impertubability, like those of a cigar store Indian.

"Good heavens!" said Bill. "You couldn't run a business that way over here. I mean to say, who would decide who was the principal creditor? Imagine the arguments there would be. Eh, Jeeves?"

"Unquestionably, m'lord. The butcher, the baker . . ."

"Not to mention hosts who had entertained the Dyak for week ends, from whose houses he had slipped away on Monday morning, forgetting the Saturday night bridge game."

"In the event of his surviving, it would make such a Dyak considerably more careful in his bidding, m'lord."

"True, Jeeves, true. It would, wouldn't it? He would think twice about trying any of that psychic stuff?"

"Precisely, m'lord! And would undoubtedly hesitate before taking his partner out of a business double."

Captain Biggar cracked another nut. In the silence it sounded like one of those explosions which slay six.

"And now," he said, "with your permission, I would like to cut the *ghazi havildar* and get down to brass tacks, Lord Towcester." He paused a moment, marshalling his thoughts. "About this bookie."

Bill blinked.

"Ah, yes, this bookie. I know the bookie you mean."

"For the moment he has got away, I am sorry to say. But I had the sense to memorize the number of his car."

"You did? Shrewd, Jeeves."

"Very shrewd, m'lord."

"I then made enquiries of the police. And do you know what they told me? They said that that car number, Lord Towcester, was yours."

Bill was amazed.

"Mine?"

"Yours."

"But how could it be mine?"

That is the mystery which we have to solve. This Honest Patch Perkins, as he called himself, must have borrowed your car . . . with or without your permission."

"Incredulous!"

"Incredible, m'lord."

"Thank you, Jeeves. Incredible! How would I know any Honest Patch Perkins?"

"You don't?"

THE RETURN OF JEEVES

"Never heard of him in my life. Never laid eyes on him. What does he look like?"

"He is tall . . . about your height . . . and wears a ginger mustache and a black patch over his left eye."

"No, dash it, that's not possible . . . Oh, I see what you mean. A black patch over his left eye and a ginger mustache on the upper lip. I thought for a moment . . .".

"And a checked coat and a crimson tie with blue horseshoes on it."

"Good heavens! He must look the most ghastly outsider. Eh, Jeeves?"

"Certainly far from *soigné*, m'lord."

"Very far from *soigné*. Oh, by the way, Jeeves, that reminds me. Bertie Wooster told me that you once made some such remark to him, and it gave him the idea for a ballad to be entitled, 'Way down upon the *soigné* river.' Did anything ever come of it, do you know?"

"I fancy not, m'lord."

"Bertie wouldn't have been equal to whacking it out, I suppose. But one can see a song hit there, handled by the right person."

"No doubt, m'lord."

"Cole Porter could probably do it."

"Quite conceivably, m'lord."

"Or Oscar Hammerstein."

"It should be well within the scope of Mr. Hammerstein's talents, m'lord."

It was with a certain impatience that Captain Biggar called the meeting to order.

"To hell with song hits and Cole Porters!" he said, with an abruptness on which Emily Post would have frowned. "I'm not talking about Cole Porter, I'm talking about this bally bookie who was using your car today."

Bill shook his head.

"My dear old pursuer of pumas and what have you, you say you're talking about bally bookies, but what you omit to add is that you're talking through the back of your neck. Neat that, Jeeves."

"Yes, m'lord. Crisply put."

"Obviously what happened was that friend Biggar got the wrong number."

"Yes, m'lord."

The red of Captain Biggar's face deepened to purple. His proud spirit was wounded.

"Are you telling me I don't know the number of a car that I followed all the way from Epsom Downs to Southmoltonshire? That car was used today by this Honest Patch Perkins and his clerk, and I'm asking you if you lent it to him."

"My dear good bird, would I lend my car to a chap in a checked suit and a crimson tie, not to mention a black patch and a ginger mustache? The thing's not . . . what, Jeeves?"

"Feasible, m'lord." Jeeves coughed. "Possibly the gentleman's eyesight needs medical attention."

Captain Biggar swelled portentously.

"My eyesight? *My* eyesight? Do you know who you're talking to? I am Sahib Biggar."

"I regret that the name is strange to me, sir. But I still maintain that you have made the pardonable mistake of failing to read the license number correctly."

Before speaking again, Captain Biggar was obliged to swallow once or twice, to restore his composure. He also took another nut.

"Look," he said, almost mildly. "Perhaps you're not up on these things. You haven't been told who's who and what's what. I am Biggar the White Hunter, the most famous White Hunter in all Africa and Indonesia. I can stand without a tremor in the path of an onrushing rhino . . . and why? Because my eyesight is so superb that I know . . . I *know* I can get him in that one vulnerable spot before he has come within sixty paces. That's the sort of eyesight mine is."

Jeeves maintained his iron front.

"I fear I cannot recede from my position, sir. I grant that you may have trained your vision for such a contingency as you have described, but, poorly informed as I am on the subject of the larger fauna of the East, I do not believe that rhinoceri are equipped with license numbers."

It seemed to Bill that the time had come to pour oil on the troubled waters and dish out a word of comfort.

"This bookie of yours, Captain. I think I can strike a note of hope. We concede that he legged it with what appears to have been the swift abandon of a bat out of hell, but I believe that when the fields are white with daisies he'll pay you. I get the impression that he's simply trying to gain time."

"I'll give him time," said the Captain morosely. "I'll see that he gets plenty. And when he has paid his debt to Society, I shall attend to him personally. A thousand pities we're not out East. They understand these things there. If they know you for a straight shooter and the other chap's a wrong 'un . . . well, there aren't many questions asked."

Bill started like a frightened fawn.

"Questions about what?"

" 'Good riddance' sums up their attitude. The fewer there are of such vermin, the better for Anglo-Saxon prestige."

"I suppose that's one way of looking at it."

"I don't mind telling you that there are a couple of notches on my gun that aren't for buffaloes . . . or lions . . . or elands . . . *or* rhinos."

"Really? What are they for?"

"Cheaters."

"Ah, yes. Those are those leopard things that go as fast as racehorses."

Jeeves had a correction to make.

"Somewhat faster, m'lord. A half mile in forty-five seconds."

"Great Scott! Pretty nippy, what? That's traveling, Jeeves."

"Yes, m'lord."

"That's a cheetah, that was, as one might say."

Captain Biggar snorted impatiently.

"Chea-ters was what I said. I'm not talking about cheetah, the animal . . . though I have shot some of those, too."

"Too?"

"Too."

"I see,"said Bill, gulping a little. "Too."

Jeeves coughed.

"Might I offer a suggestion, m'lord?"

"Certainly, Jeeves. Offer several."

"An idea has just crossed my mind, m'lord. It has occurred to me that it is quite possible that this racecourse character against whom Captain Biggar nurses a justifiable grievance may have substituted for his own license plate a false one—"

"By Jove, Jeeves, you've hit it!"

"—and that by some strange coincidence he selected for this false plate the number of your lordship's car."

"Exactly. That's the solution. Odd we didn't think of that before. It explains the whole thing, doesn't it, Captain?"

Captain Biggar was silent. His thoughtful frown told that he was weighing the idea.

"Of course it does," said Bill buoyantly. "Jeeves, your bulging brain, with its solid foundation of fish, has solved what but for you would have remained one of those historic mysteries you read about. If I had a hat on, I would raise it to you."

"I am happy to have given satisfaction, m'lord."

"You always do, Jeeves, you always do. It's what makes you so generally esteemed."

Captain Biggar nodded.

"Yes, I suppose that might have happened. There seems to be no other explanation."

"Jolly, getting these things cleared up," said Bill. "More port, Captain?"

"No, thank you."

"Then suppose we join the ladies. They're probably wondering what the dickens has happened to us and saying 'He cometh not,' like . . . who, Jeeves?"

"Mariana of the Moated Grange, m'lord. Her tears fell with the dews at even; her tears fell ere the dews were dried. She could not look on the sweet heaven either at morn or eventide."

"Oh, well, I don't suppose our absence has hit them quite as hard as that. Still, it might be as well . . . Coming, Captain?"

"I should first like to make a telephone call."

"You can do it from the living room."

"A private telephone call."

"Oh, right ho. Jeeves, conduct Captain Biggar to your pantry and unleash him on the instrument."

"Very good, m'lord."

Left alone, Bill lingered for some moments, the urge to join the ladies in the living room yielding to a desire to lower just one more glass of port by way of celebration. Honest Patch Perkins had, he felt, rounded a nasty corner.

The only thought that came to mar his contentment had to do with Jill. He was not quite sure of his standing with that lodestar of his life. At dinner, Mrs. Spottsworth, seated on his right, had been chummy beyond his gloomiest apprehensions, and he fancied he had detected in Jill's eye one of those cold, pensive looks which are the last sort of look a young man in love likes to see in the eye of his betrothed.

Fortunately, Mrs. Spottsworth's chumminess had waned as the meal proceeded and Captain Biggar started monopolizing the conversation. She had stopped talking about the old Cannes days and had sat listening in rapt silence as the White Hunter told of antres vast and deserts idle and of the cannibals that each other eat, the anthropophagi, and men whose heads do grow beneath their shoulders.

This to hear had Mrs. Spottsworth seriously inclined, completely switching off the Cannes motif, so it might be that all was well.

Jeeves returned, and he greeted him effusively as one who had fought the good fight.

"That was a brain wave of yours, Jeeves."

"Thank you, m'lord."

"It eased the situation considerably. His suspicions are lulled, don't you think?"

"One would be disposed to fancy so, m'lord."

"You know, Jeeves, even in these disturbed postwar days, with the social revolution turning handsprings on every side and Civilization, as you might say, in the melting pot, it's still quite an advantage to be in big print in Debrett's Peerage."

"Unquestionably so, m'lord. It gives a gentleman a certain standing."

"Exactly. People take it for granted that you're respectable. Take an Earl, for instance. He buzzes about, and people say, 'Ah, an Earl,' and let it go at that. The last thing that occurs to them is that he may in his spare moments be putting on patches and false mustaches and standing on a wooden box in a checked coat and a tie with blue horseshoes, shouting, 'Five to one the field, bar one!' "

"Precisely, m'lord."

"A satisfactory state of things."

"Highly satisfactory, m'lord."

"There have been moments today, Jeeves, I don't mind confessing, when it seemed to me that the only thing to do was to turn up the toes and say, 'This is the end,' but now it would take very little to start me singing like the Cherubim and Seraphim. It was the Cherubim and Seraphim who sang, wasn't it?"

"Yes, m'lord. Hosanna, principally."

"I feel a new man. The odd sensation of having swallowed a quart of butterflies, which I got when there was a burst of red fire and a roll of drums from the orchestra and that White Hunter shot up through a trap at my elbow, has passed away completely."

"I am delighted to hear it, m'lord."

"I knew you would be, Jeeves, I knew you would be. Sympathy and understanding are your middle names. And now," said Bill, "to join the ladies in the living room and put the poor souls out of their suspense."

9

ARRIVING IN the living room, he found that the number of ladies available for being joined there had been reduced to one—reading from left to right, Jill. She was sitting on the settee twiddling an empty coffee cup and staring before her with what are sometimes described as unseeing eyes. Her air was that of a girl who is brooding on something, a girl to whom recent happenings have given much food for thought.

"Hullo there, darling," cried Bill with the animation of a shipwrecked mariner sighting a sail. After that testing session in the dining-room, almost anything that was not Captain Biggar would have looked good to him, and she looked particularly good.

Jill glanced up.

"Oh, hullo," she said.

It seemed to Bill that her manner was reserved, but he proceeded with undiminished exuberance.

"Where's everybody?"

"Rory and Moke are in the library, listening to the Derby Dinner."

"And Mrs. Spottsworth?"

"Rosie," said Jill in a toneless voice, "has gone to the ruined chapel. I believe she is hoping to get a word with the ghost of Lady Agatha."

Bill started. He also gulped a little.

"Rosie?"

"I think that is what you call her, is it not?"

"Why—er—yes."

"And she calls you Billiken. Is she a very old friend?"

"No, no. I knew her slightly at Cannes one summer."

"From what I heard her saying at dinner about moonlight drives and bathing from the Eden Roc, I got the impression that you had been rather intimate."

"Good heavens, no. She was just an'acquaintance, and a pretty mere one, at that."

"I see."

There was a silence.

"I wonder if you remember," said Jill, at length breaking it, "what I was saying this evening before dinner about people not hiding things from each other, if they are going to get married?"

"Er—yes . . . Yes . . . I remember that."

"We agreed that it was the only way."

"Yes . . . Yes, that's right. So we did."

"I told you about Percy, didn't I? And Charles and Squiffy and Tom and Blotto," said Jill, mentioning other figures of Romance from the dead past. "I never dreamed of concealing the fact that I had been engaged before I met you. So why did you hide this Spottsworth from me?"

It seemed to Bill that, for a pretty good sort of chap who meant no harm to anybody and strove always to do the square thing by one and all, he was being handled rather roughly by Fate this summer day. The fellow—Shakespeare, he rather thought, though he would have to check with Jeeves—who had spoken of the slings and arrows of outrageous fortune, had known what he was talking about. Slings and arrows described it to a nicety.

"I didn't hide this Spottsworth from you!" he cried passionately. "She just didn't happen to come up. Lord love a duck, when you're sitting with the girl you love, holding her little hand and whispering words of endearment in her ear, you can't suddenly switch the conversation to an entirely different topic and say, 'Oh, by the way, there was a woman I met in Cannes some years ago, on the subject of whom I would now like to say a few words. Let me tell you all about the time we drove to St. Tropez.' "

"In the moonlight."

"Was it my fault that there was a moon? I wasn't consulted. And as for bathing from the Eden Roc, you talk as if we had the ruddy Eden Roc to ourselves with not another human being in sight. It was not so, but far otherwise. Every time we took a dip, the water was alive with exiled Grand Dukes and stiff with dowagers of the most rigid respectability."

"I still think it odd you never mentioned her."

"I don't."

"I do. And I think it still odder that when Jeeves told you this afternoon that a Mrs. Spottsworth was coming here, you just said, 'Oh, ah?' or something and let it go as if you had never heard the name before. Wouldn't the natural thing have been to say, 'Mrs. Spottsworth? Well, well, bless my soul, I wonder if that can possibly be the woman with whom I was on terms of mere acquaintanceship at Cannes a year or two ago. Did I ever tell you about her, Jill? I used to drive with her a good deal in the moonlight, though of course in quite a distant way.' "

It was Bill's moment.

"No," he thundered, "it would not have been the natural thing to say, 'Mrs. Spottsworth? Well, well,' and so on and so forth, and I'll tell you why. When I knew her . . . slightly, as I say, as one does know people in places like Cannes . . . her name was Bessemer."

"Oh?"

"Precisely. *B* with an *E* with an *S* with an *S* with an *E* with an *M* with an *E* with an *R* Bessemer. I have still to learn how all this Spottsworth stuff arose."

Jeeves came in. Duty called him at about this hour to collect the coffee cups, and duty never called to this great man in vain.

His arrival broke what might be called the spell. Jill, who had more to say on the subject under discussion, withheld it. She got up and made for the French window.

"Well, I must be getting along," she said, still speaking rather tonelessly.

Bill stared.

"You aren't leaving already?"

"Only to go home and get some things. Moke has asked me to stay the night."

"Then Heaven bless Moke! Full marks for the intelligent female."

"You like the idea of my staying the night?"

"It's terrific."

"You're sure I shan't be in the way?"

"What on earth are you talking about? Shall I come with you?"

"Of course not. You're supposed to be a host."

She went out, and Bill, gazing after her fondly, suddenly stiffened. Like a delayed action bomb, those words "You're sure I shan't be in the way?" had just hit him. Had they been mere idle words? Or had they contained a sinister significance?

"Women are odd, Jeeves," he said.

"Yes, m'lord."

"Not to say peculiar. You can't tell what they mean when they say things, can you?"

"Very seldom, m'lord."

Bill brooded for a moment.

"Were you observing Miss Wyvern as she buzzed off?"

"Not closely, m'lord."

"Was her manner strange, do you think?"

"I could not say, m'lord. I was concentrating on coffee cups."

Bill brooded again. This uncertainty was preying on his nerves. "You're sure I shan't be in the way?" Had there been a nasty tinkle in her voice as she uttered the words? Everything turned on that. If no tinkle, fine.But if tinkle, things did not look so good. The question, plus tinkle, could only mean that his reasoned explanation of the Spottsworth-Cannes sequence had failed to get across and that she still harbored suspicions, unworthy of her though such suspicions might be.

The irritability which good men feel on these occasions swept over him. What was the use of being as pure as the driven snow, or possibly purer, if girls were going to come tinkling at you?

"The whole trouble with women, Jeeves," he said, and the philosopher Schopenhauer would have slapped him on the back and told him he knew just how he felt, "is that practically all of them are dotty. Look at Mrs. Spottsworth. Wacky to the eyebrows. Roosting in a ruined chapel in the hope of seeing Lady Agatha."

"Indeed, m'lord? Mrs. Spottsworth is interested in specters?"

"She eats them alive. Is that balanced behavior?"

"Psychical research frequently has an appeal for the other sex, m'lord. My Aunt Emily—"

Bill eyed him dangerously.

"Remember what I said about Pliny the Younger, Jeeves?"

"Yes, m'lord."

"That goes for your Aunt Emily as well."

"Very good, m'lord."

"I'm not interested in your Aunt Emily."

"Precisely, m'lord. During her long lifetime very few people were."

"She is no longer with us?"

"No, m'lord."

"Oh, well, that's something," said Bill.

Jeeves floated out, and he flung himself into a chair. He was thinking once more of that cryptic speech, and now his mood had become wholly pessimistic. It was no longer any question of a tinkle or a non-tinkle. He was virtually certain that the words, "You're sure I shan't be in the way?" had been spoken through clenched teeth and accompanied by a look of infinite meaning. They had been the words of a girl who had intended to make a nasty crack.

He was passing his hands through his hair with a febrile gesture, when Monica entered from the library. She had found the celebrants at the Derby Dinner a little on the long-winded side. Rory was still drinking in every word, but she needed an intermission.

She regarded her hair-twisting brother with astonishment.

"Good heavens, Bill! Why the agony? What's up?"

Bill glared unfraternally.

"Nothing's up, confound it! Nothing, nothing, nothing, nothing, nothing!"

Monica raised her eyebrows.

"Well, there's no need to be stuffy about it. I was only being the sympathetic sister."

With a strong effort Bill recovered the chivalry of the Towcesters.

"I'm sorry, Moke old thing. I've got a headache."

"My poor lamb!"

"It'll pass off in a minute."

"What you need is fresh air."

"Perhaps I do."

"And pleasant society. Ma Spottsworth's in the ruined chapel. Pop along and have a chat with her."

"What!"

Monica became soothing.

"Now don't be difficult, Bill. You know as well as I do how important it is to jolly her along. A flash of speed on your part now may mean selling the house. The whole idea was that on top of my sales talk you were to draw her aside and switch on the charm. Have you forgotten what you said about cooing to her like a turtle dove? Dash off this minute and coo as you have never cooed before."

For a long moment it seemed as though Bill, his frail strength taxed beyond its limit of endurance, was about to suffer something in the nature of spontaneous combustion. His eyes goggled, his face flushed, and burning words trembled on his lips. Then suddenly, as if Reason had intervened with a mild "Tut, tut," he ceased to glare and his cheeks slowly resumed their normal hue. He had seen that Monica's suggestion was good and sensible.

In the rush of recent events, the vitally urgent matter of pushing through the sale of his ancestral home had been thrust into the background of Bill's mind. It now loomed up for what it was, the only existing life preserver bobbing about in the sea of troubles in which he was immersed. Clutch it, and he was saved. When you sold houses, he reminded himself, you got deposits, paid cash down. Such a deposit would be sufficient to dispose of the Biggar menace, and if the only means of securing it was to go to Rosalinda Spottsworth and coo, then go and coo he must.

Simultaneously there came to him the healing thought that if Jill had gone to her cottage to provide herself with things for the night, it would be at least half an hour before she got back, and in half an hour a determined man can do a lot of cooing.

"Moke," he said, "you're right. My place is at her side."

He hurried out, and a moment later Rory appeared at the library door.

"I say, Moke," said Rory, "can you speak Spanish?"

"I don't know. I've never tried. Why?"

"There's a Spaniard or an Argentine or some such bird in there telling us about his horse in his native tongue. Probably a rank outsider, still one would have been glad to hear his views. Where's Bill? Don't tell me he's still in there with the White Man's Burden?"

"No, he came in here just now, and went out to talk to Mrs. Spottsworth."

"I want to confer with you about old Bill," said Rory. "Are we alone and unobserved?"

"Unless there's someone hiding in that dower chest. What about Bill?"

"There's something up, old girl, and it has to do with this chap Biggar. Did you notice Bill at dinner?"

"Not particularly. What was he doing? Eating peas with his knife?"

"No, but every time he caught Biggar's eye, he quivered like an Ouled Nail stomach dancer. For some reason Biggar affects him like an egg whisk. Why? That's what I want to know. Who is this mystery man? Why has he come here? What is there between him and Bill that makes Bill leap and quake and shiver whenever he looks at him? I don't like it, old thing. When you married me, you never said anything about fits in the family, and I consider I have been shabbily treated. I mean to say, it's a bit thick, going to all the trouble and expense of wooing and winning the girl you love, only to discover shortly after the honeymoon that you've become brother-in-law to a fellow with St. Vitus's dance."

Monica reflected.

"Come to think of it," she said, "I do remember, when I told him a Captain Biggar had clocked in, he seemed a bit upset. Yes, I distinctly recall a greenish pallor and a drooping lower jaw. And I came in here just now and found him tearing his hair. I agree with you. It's sinister."

"And I'll tell you something else," said Rory. "When I left the dining-room to go and look at the Derby Dinner, Bill was all for coming too. 'How about it?' he said to Biggar, and Biggar, looking very puff-faced, said, 'Later, perhaps. At the moment, I would like a word with you, Lord Towcester.' In a cold, steely voice, like a magistrate about to fine you a fiver for pinching a policeman's helmet on Boat Race night. And Bill gulped like a stricken bull pup and said, 'Oh, certainly, certainly,' or words to that effect. It sticks out a mile that this Biggar has got something on old Bill."

"But what could he possibly have on him?"

"Just the question I asked myself, my old partner of joys and sorrows, and I think I have the solution. Do you remember those stories one used to read as a kid? The *Strand* Magazine used to be full of them."

"Which stories?"

"Those idol's eye stories. The ones where a gang of blighters pop over to India to pinch the great jewel that's the eye of the idol. They get the jewel all right, but they chisel one of the blighters out of his share of the loot, which naturally makes him as sore as a gumboil, and years later he tracks the other blighters down one by one in their respectable English homes and wipes them out to the last blighter, by way of getting a bit of his own back. You mark my words, old Bill is being chivvied by this chap Biggar because he did him out of his share of the proceeds of the green eye of the little yellow god in the temple of Vishnu, and I shall be much surprised if we don't come down to breakfast tomorrow morning and find him weltering in his blood among the kippers and sausages with a dagger of Oriental design in the small of his back."

"Ass!"

"Are you addressing me?"

"I am, and with knobs on. Bill's never been farther east than Frinton."

"He's been to Cannes."

"Is Cannes east? I never know. But he's certainly never been within smelling distance of Indian idols' eyes."

"I didn't think of that," said Rory. "Yes, that, I admit, does weaken my argument to a certain extent." He brooded tensely. "Ha! I have it now. I see it all. The rift between Bill and Biggar is due to the baby."

"What on earth are you talking about? What baby?"

"Bill's, working in close collaboration with Biggar's daughter, the apple of Biggar's eye, a poor, foolish little thing who loved not wisely but too well. And if you are going to say that girls are all-wise nowadays, I reply, 'Not one brought up in the missionary school at Squalor Lumpit.' In those missionary schools they explain the facts of life by telling the kids about the bees and the flowers till the poor little brutes don't know which is which."

"For heaven's sake, Rory."

"Mark how it all works out with the inevitability of Greek tragedy or whatever it was that was so bally inevitable. Girl comes to England, no mother to guide her, meets a handsome young Englishman, and what happens? The first false step. The remorse . . . too late. The little bundle. The awkward interview with Father. Father all steamed up. Curses a bit in some native dialect and packs his elephant gun and comes along to see old Bill. Caramba! as that Spaniard is probably saying at this moment on the television screen. Still, there's nothing to worry about. I don't suppose he can make him marry her. All Bill will have to do is look after the little thing's education. Send it to school and so on. If a boy, Eton. If a girl, Roedean."

"Cheltenham."

"Oh, yes. I'd forgotten you were an Old Cheltonian. The question now arises, should young Jill be told? It hardly seems fair to allow her to rush unwarned into marriage with a ripsnorting *roué* like William, Earl of Towcester."

"Don't call Bill a ripsnorting *roué*!"

"It is how we should describe him at Harrod's."

"As a matter of fact, you're probably all wrong about Bill and Biggar. I know the poor boy's jumpy, but most likely it hasn't anything to do with Captain Biggar at all. It's because he's all on edge, wondering if Mrs. Spottsworth is going to buy the house. In which connection, Rory, you old fathead, can't you do something to help the thing along instead of bunging a series of spanners into the works?"

"I don't get your drift."

"I will continue snowing. Ever since Mrs. Spottsworth arrived, you've been doing nothing but point out Towcester Abbey's defects. Be constructive."

"In what way, my queen?"

"Well, draw her attention to some of the good things there are in the place."

Rory nodded dutifully, but dubiously.

"I'll do my best," he said. "But I shall have very little raw material to work with. And now, old girl, I imagine that Spaniard will have blown over by this time, so let us rejoin the Derby diners. I've got rather a liking for a beast called Oratory. The Brompton Oratory being just across the road from Harrod's, it's a bit of an omen, what?"

10

MRS. SPOTTSWORTH had left the ruined chapel. After a vigil of some twenty-five minutes she had wearied of waiting for Lady Agatha to manifest herself. Like many very rich women, she tended to be impatient and to demand quick service. When in the mood for specters, she wanted them hot off the griddle. Returning to the garden, she had found a rustic seat and was sitting there smoking a cigarette and enjoying the beauty of the night.

It was one of those lovely nights which occur from time to time in an English June, mitigating the rigors of the island summer and causing manufacturers of raincoats and umbrellas to wonder uneasily if they have been mistaken in supposing England to be an earthly Paradise for men of their profession.

A silver moon was riding in the sky, and a gentle breeze blew from the west, bringing with it the heart-stirring scent of stock and tobacco plant. Shy creatures of the night rustled in the bushes at her side and, to top the whole thing off, somewhere in the woods beyond the river a nightingale had begun to sing with the full-throated zest of a bird conscious of having had a rave notice from the poet Keats and only a couple of nights ago a star spot on the program of the B.B.C.

It was a night made for romance, and Mrs. Spottsworth recognized it as such. Although in her vers libre days in Greenwich Village she had gone in almost exclusively for starkness and squalor, even then she had been at heart a sentimentalist. Left to herself, she would have turned out stuff full of moons, Junes, loves, doves, blisses and kisses. It was simply that the editors of the poetry magazines seemed to prefer rat-ridden tenements, the smell of cooking cabbage, and despair, and a girl had to eat.

Fixed now as solidly financially as any woman in America and freed from the necessity of truckling to the tastes of editors, she was able to take the wraps off her romantic self, and as she sat on the rustic seat, looking at the moon and listening to the nightingale, a stylist like the late Gustave Flaubert, tireless in his quest of the *mot juste*, would have had no hesitation in describing her mood as mushy.

To this mushiness Captain Biggar's conversation at dinner had contributed largely. We have given some indication of its trend, showing it ranging freely from cannibal chiefs to African headhunters, from African headhunters to alligators, and its effect on Mrs. Spottsworth had been very similar to that of Othello's reminiscences on Desdemona. In short, long before the last strawberry had been eaten, the final nut consumed, she was convinced that this was the mate for her and resolved to spare no effort in pushing the thing along. In the matter of marrying again both A. B. Spottsworth and Clifton Bessemer had given her the green light, and there was consequently no obstacle in her path.

There appeared, however, to be one in the path leading to the rustic seat, for at this moment there floated to her through the silent night the sound of a strong man tripping over a flowerpot. It was followed by some pungent remarks in Swahili, and Captain Biggar limped up, rubbing his shin.

Mrs. Spottsworth was all womanly sympathy.

"Oh, dear. Have you hurt yourself, Captain?"

"A mere scratch, dear lady," he assured her.

He spoke bluffly, and only somebody like Sherlock Holmes or Monsieur Poirot could have divined that at the sound of her voice his soul had turned a double somersault, leaving him quivering with an almost Bill-Towcester-like intensity.

His telephone conversation concluded, the White Hunter had prudently decided to avoid the living-room and head straight for the great open spaces, where he could be alone. To join the ladies, he had reasoned, would be to subject himself to the searing torture of having to sit and gaze at the woman he worshipped, a process which would simply rub in the fact of how unattainable she was. He recognized himself as being in the unfortunate position of the moth in Shelley's well-known poem that allowed itself to become attracted by a star, and it seemed to him that the smartest move a level-headed moth could make would be to minimize the anguish by shunning the adored object's society. It was, he felt, what Shelley would have advised.

And here he was, alone with her in the night, a night complete with moonlight, nightingales, gentle breezes and the scent of stock and tobacco plant.

It was a taut, tense Captain Biggar, a Captain Biggar telling himself he must be strong, who accepted his companion's invitation to join her on the rustic seat. The voices of Tubby Frobisher and the Subadar seemed to ring in his ears. "Chin up, old boy," said Tubby in his right ear. "Remember the code," said the Subadar in his left.

He braced himself for the coming tête-à-tête.

Mrs. Spottsworth, a capital conversationalist, began it by saying what a beautiful night it was, to which the Captain replied "Top hole." "The moon," said Mrs. Spottsworth, indicating it and adding that she always thought a night when there was a full moon was so much nicer than a night when there was not a full moon. "Oh, rather," said the Captain. Then, after Mrs.

Spottsworth had speculated as to whether the breeze was murmuring lull-
abies to the sleeping flowers and the Captain had regretted his inability to
inform her on this point, he being a stranger in these parts, there was a
silence.

It was broken by Mrs. Spottsworth, who gave a little cry of concern.

"Oh, dear!"

"What's the matter?"

"I've dropped my pendant. The clasp is so loose."

Captain Biggar appreciated her emotion.

"Bad show," he agreed. "It must be on the ground somewhere. I'll have a
look-see."

"I wish you would. It's not valuable—I don't suppose it cost more than ten
thousand dollars—but it has a sentimental interest. One of my husbands gave
it to me, I never can remember which. Oh, have you found it? Thank you ever
so much. Will you put it on for me?"

As Captain Biggar did so, his fingers, spine and stomach muscles trembled.
It is almost impossible to clasp a pendant round its owner's neck without
touching that neck in spots, and he touched his companion's in several. And
every time he touched it, something seemed to go through him like a knife. It
was as though the moon, the nightingale, the breeze, the stock and the
tobacco plant were calling to him to cover this neck with burning kisses.

Only Tubby Frobisher and the Subadar, forming a solid bloc in opposition, restrained him.

"Straight bat, old boy!" said Tubby Frobisher.

"Remember you're a white man," said the Subadar.

He clenched his fists and was himself again.

"It must be jolly," he said, recovering his bluffness, "to be rich enough to
think ten thousand dollars isn't anything to write home about."

Mrs. Spottsworth felt like an actor receiving a cue.

"Do you think that rich women are happy, Captain Biggar?"

The Captain said that all those he had met—and in his capacity of White
Hunter he had met quite a number—had seemed pretty bobbish.

"They wore the mask."

"Eh?"

"They smiled to hide the ache in their hearts," explained Mrs. Spottsworth.

The Captain said he remembered one of them, a large blonde of the name
of Fish, dancing the can-can one night in her step-ins, and Mrs. Spottsworth
said that no doubt she was just trying to show a brave front to the world.

"Rich women are so lonely, Captain Biggar."

"Are you lonely?"

"Very, very lonely."

"Oh, ah," said the Captain.

It was not what he would have wished to say. He would have preferred to
pour out his soul in a torrent of impassioned words. But what could a fellow
do, with Tubby Frobisher and the Subadar watching his every move?

A woman who has told a man in the moonlight, with nightingales singing their heads off in the background, that she is very, very lonely and received in response the words "Oh, ah" is scarcely to be blamed for feeling a momentary pang of discouragement. Mrs. Spottsworth had once owned a large hound dog of lethargic temperament who could be induced to go out for his nightly airing only by a succession of sharp kicks. She was beginning to feel now as she had felt when her foot thudded against this languorous animal's posterior. The same depressing sense of trying in vain to move an immovable mass. She loved the White Hunter. She admired him. But when you set out to kindle the spark of passion in him, you certainly had a job on your hands. In a moment of bitterness she told herself that she had known oysters on the half shell with more of the divine fire in them.

However, she persevered.

"How strange our meeting again like this," she said softly.

"Very odd."

"We were a whole world apart, and we met in an English inn."

"Quite a coincidence."

"Not a coincidence. It was destined. Shall I tell you what brought you to that inn?"

"I wanted a spot of beer."

"Fate," said Mrs. Spottsworth. "Destiny. I beg your pardon?"

"I was only saying that, come right down to it, there's no beer like English beer."

"The same Fate, the same Destiny," continued Mrs. Spottsworth, who at another moment would have hotly contested this statement, for she thought English beer undrinkable, "that brought us together in Kenya. Do you remember the day we met in Kenya?"

Captain Biggar writhed. It was like asking Joan of Arc if she happened to recall the time she saw that heavenly vision of hers. "How about it, boys?" he enquired silently, looking pleadingly from right to left. "Couldn't you stretch a point?" But Tubby Frobisher and the Subadar shook their heads.

"The code, old man," said Tubby Frobisher.

"Play the game, old boy," said the Subadar.

"Do you?" asked Mrs. Spottsworth.

"Oh, rather," said Captain Biggar.

"I had the strangest feeling, when I saw you that day, that we had met before in some previous existence."

"A bit unlikely, what?"

Mrs. Spottsworth closed her eyes.

"I seemed to see us in some dim, prehistoric age. We were clad in skins. You hit me over the head with your club and dragged me by my hair to your cave."

"Oh, no, dash it, I wouldn't do a thing like that."

Mrs. Spottsworth opened her eyes, and enlarging them to their fullest extent allowed them to play on his like searchlights.

"You did it because you loved me," she said in a low, vibrant whisper. "And I—"

She broke off. Something tall and willowy had loomed up against the skyline, and a voice with perhaps just a quaver of nervousness in it was saying, "Hullo-ullo-ullo-ullo-ullo."

"I've been looking for you everywhere, Rosie," said Bill. "When I found you weren't at the ruined chapel . . . Oh, hullo, Captain."

"Hullo," said Captain Biggar dully, and tottered off. Lost in the shadows a few paces down the path, he halted and brushed away the beads of perspiration which had formed on his forehead.

He was breathing heavily, like a buffalo in the mating season. It has been a near thing, a very near thing. Had this interruption been postponed even for another minute, he knew that he must have sinned against the code and taken the irrevocable step which would have made his name a mockery and a byword in the Anglo-Malay Club at Kuala Lumpur. A pauper with a bank balance of a few meager pounds, he would have been proposing marriage to a woman with millions.

More and more, as the moments went by, he had found himself being swept off his feet, his ears becoming deafer and deafer to the muttered warnings of Tubby Frobisher and the Subadar. Her eyes he might have resisted. Her voice, too, and the skin he had loved to touch. But when it came to eyes, voice, skin, moonlight, gentle breezes from the west and nightingales, the mixture was too rich.

Yes, he felt as he stood there heaving like a stage sea, he had been saved, and it might have been supposed that his prevailing emotion would have been a prayerful gratitude to Fate or Destiny for its prompt action. But, oddly enough, it was not. The first spasm of relief had died quickly away, to be succeeded by a rising sensation of nausea. And what caused this nausea was the fact that, being still within earshot of the rustic seat, he could hear all that Bill was saying. And Bill, having seated himself beside Mrs. Spottsworth, had begun to coo.

Too little has been said in this chronicle of the ninth Earl of Towcester's abilities in this direction. When we heard him promising his sister Monica to contact Mrs. Spottsworth and coo to her like a turtle dove, we probably formed in our minds the picture of one of those run-of-the-mill turtle doves whose cooing, though adequate, does not really amount to anything much. We would have done better to envisage something in the nature of a turtle dove of stellar quality, what might be called the Turtle Dove Supreme. A limited young man in many respects, Bill Towcester could, when in mid-season form, touch heights in the way of cooing which left his audience, if at all impressionable, gasping for air.

These heights he was touching now, for the thought that this woman had it in her power to take England's leading white elephant off his hands, thus stabilizing his financial position and enabling him to liquidate Honest Patch Perkins' honorable obligations, lent him an eloquence which he had not achieved since May Week dances at Cambridge. The golden words came trickling from his lips like syrup.

Captain Biggar was not fond of syrup, and he did not like the thought of the woman he loved being subjected to all this goo. For a moment he toyed with the idea of striding up and breaking Bill's spine in three places, but once more found his aspirations blocked by the code. He had eaten Bill's meat and drunk Bill's drink . . . both excellent, especially the roast duck . . . and that made the feller immune to assault. For when a feller has accepted a feller's hospitality, a feller can't go about breaking the feller's spine, no matter what the feller may have done. The code is rigid on that point.

He is at liberty, however, to docket the feller in his mind as a low-down, fortune-hunting son of a what not, and this was how Captain Biggar was docketing Bill as he lumbered back to the house. And it was—substantially—how he described him to Jill when, passing through the French window, he found her crossing the living room on her way to deposit her things in her sleeping apartment.

"Good gracious!" said Jill, intrigued by his aspect. "You seem very upset, Captain Biggar. What's the matter? Have you been bitten by an alligator?"

Before proceeding, the Captain had to put her straight on this.

"No alligators in England," he said. "Except, of course, in zoos. No, I have been shocked to the very depths of my soul."

"By a wombat?"

Again the Captain was obliged to correct her misapprehensions. An oddly ignorant girl, this, he was thinking.

"No wombats in England, either. What shocked me to the very depths of my soul was listening to a low-down, fortune-hunting English peer doing his stuff." He barked bitterly. "Lord Towcester, he calls himself. Lord Gigolo's what I call him."

Jill started so sharply that she dropped her suitcase.

"Allow me," said the Captain, diving for it.

"I don't understand," said Jill. "Do you mean that Lord Towcester—?"

One of the rules of the code is that a white man must shield women, and especially young, innocent girls, from the seamy side of life, but Captain Biggar was far too stirred to think of that now. He resembled Othello not only in his taste for antres vast and deserts idle but in his tendency, being wrought, to become perplexed in the extreme.

"He was making love to Mrs. Spottsworth in the moonlight," he said curtly.

"What!"

"Heard him with my own ears. He was cooing to her like a turtle dove. After her money, of course. All the same, these effete aristocrats of the old country. Make a noise like a rich widow anywhere in England, and out come all the Dukes and Earls and Viscounts, howling like wolves. Rats, we'd call them in Kuala Lumpur. You should hear Tubby Frobisher talk about them at the club. I remember him saying one day to Doc and Squiffy—the Subadar wasn't there, if I recollect rightly—gone up country, or something—'Doc,' he said . . ."

It was probably going to be a most extraordinarily good story, but Captain Biggar did not continue it any further, for he saw that his audience was walking out on him. Jill had turned abruptly, and was passing through the door. Her head, he noted, was bowed, and very properly, too, after a revelation like that. Any nice girl would have been knocked endways by such a stunning *exposé* of the moral weaknesses of the British aristocracy.

He sat down and picked up the evening paper, throwing it from him with a stifled cry as the words "Whistler's Mother" leaped at him from the printed page. He did not want to be reminded of Whistler's Mother. He was brooding darkly on Honest Patch Perkins and wondering wistfully if Destiny (or Fate) would ever bring their paths together again, when Jeeves came floating in. Simultaneously, Rory entered from the library.

"Oh, Jeeves," said Rory, "will you bring me a flagon of strong drink? I am athirst."

With a respectful movement of his head Jeeves indicated the tray he was carrying, laden with the right stuff, and Rory accompanied him to the table, licking his lips.

"Something for you, Captain?" he said.

"Whisky, if you please," said Captain Biggar. After that ordeal in the moonlit garden, he needed a restorative.

"Whisky? Right. And for you, Mrs. Spottsworth?" said Rory, as that lady came through the French window accompanied by Bill.

"Nothing, thank you, Sir Roderick. On a night like this, moonlight is enough for me. Moonlight and your lovely garden, Billiken."

"I'll tell you something about that garden," said Rory. "In the summer months . . ." He broke off as Monica appeared in the library door. The sight of her not only checked his observations on the garden, but reminded him of her injunction to boost the bally place to this Spottsworth woman. Looking about him for something in the bally place capable of being boosted, his eye fell on the dower chest in the corner and he recalled complimentary things he had heard said in the past about it.

It seemed to him that it would make a good *point d'appui.* "Yes," he proceeded, "the garden's terrific, and furthermore it must never be overlooked that Towcester Abbey, though a bit shopsoiled and falling apart at the seams, contains many an *objet d'art* calculated to make the connoisseur sit up and say 'What ho!' Cast an eye on that dower chest, Mrs. Spottsworth."

"I was admiring it when I first arrived. It's beautiful."

"Yes, it is nice, isn't it?" said Monica, giving her husband a look of wifely approval. One didn't often find Rory showing such signs of almost human intelligence. "Duveen used to plead to be allowed to buy it, but of course it's an heirloom and can't be sold."

"Goes with the house," said Rory.

"It's full of the most wonderful old costumes."

"Which go with the house," said Rory, probably quite incorrectly, but showing zeal.

"Would you like to look at them?" said Monica, reaching for the lid.

Bill uttered an agonized cry.

"They're not in there!"

"Of course they are. They always have been. And I'm sure Rosalinda would enjoy seeing them."

"I would indeed."

"There's quite a romantic story attached to this dower chest, Rosalinda. The Lord Towcester of that time—centuries ago—wouldn't let his daughter marry the man she loved, a famous explorer and discoverer."

"The old boy was against Discoverers," explained Rory. "He was afraid they might discover America. Ha, ha, ha, ha, ha, oh, I beg your pardon."

"The lover sent this chest to the girl, filled with rare embroideries he had brought back from his travels in the East, and her father wouldn't let her have it. He told the lover to come and take it away. And the lover did, and of course inside it was the young man's bride. Knowing what was going to happen, she had hid there."

"And the funny part of the story is that the old blister followed the chap all the way down the drive, shouting 'Get that damn thing out of here!' "

Mrs. Spottsworth was enchanted.

"What a delicious story. Do open it, Monica."

"I will. It isn't locked."

Bill sank bonelessly into a chair.

"Jeeves!"

"M'lord?"

"Brandy!"

"Very good, m'lord."

"Well, for heaven's sake!" said Monica.

She was staring wide-eyed at a check coat of loud pattern and a tie so crimson, so intensely blue horseshoed, that Rory shook his head censoriously.

"Good Lord, Bill, don't tell me you go around in a coat like that? It must make you look like an absconding bookie. And the tie! The cravat! Ye gods! You'd better drop in at Harrod's and see the chap in our haberdashery department. We've got a sale on."

Captain Biggar strode forward. There was a tense, hard expression on his rugged face.

"Let me look at that." He took the coat, felt in the pocket and produced a black patch. "Ha!" he said, and there was a wealth of meaning in his voice.

Rory was listening at the library door.

"Hullo," he said. "Someone talking French. Must be Boussac. Don't want to miss Boussac. Come along, Moke. This girl," said Rory, putting a loving arm round her shoulder, "talks French with both hands. You coming, Mrs. Spottsworth? It's the Derby Dinner on television."

"I will join you later, perhaps," said Mrs. Spottsworth. "I left Pomona out in the garden, and she may be getting lonely."

"You, Captain?"

Captain Biggar shook his head. His face was more rugged than ever.

"I have a word or two to say to Lord Towcester first. If you can spare me a moment, Lord Towcester?"

"Oh, rather," said Bill faintly.

Jeeves returned with the brandy, and he sprang for it like Whistler's Mother leaping at the winning post.

11

BUT BRANDY, when administered in one of those small after-dinner glasses, can never do anything really constructive for a man whose affairs have so shaped themselves as to give him the momentary illusion of having been hit in the small of the back by the Twentieth Century Limited. A tun or a hogshead of the stuff might have enabled Bill fo face the coming interview with a jaunty smile. The mere sip which was all that had been vouchsafed to him left him as pallid and boneless as if it had been sarsaparilla. Gazing through a mist at Captain Biggar, he closely resembled the sort of man for whom the police spread dragnets, preparatory to questioning them in connection with the recent smash and grab robbery at Marks and Schoenstein's Bon Ton Jewelery Store on Eighth Avenue. His face had shaded away to about the color of the under side of a dead fish, and Jeeves, eyeing him with respectful commiseration, wished that it were possible to bring the roses back to his cheeks by telling him one or two good things which had come into his mind from the Collected Works of Marcus Aurelius.

Captain Biggar, even when seen through a mist, presented a spectacle which might well have intimidated the stoutest. His eyes seemed to Bill to be shooting out long, curling flames, and why they called a man with a face as red as that a White Hunter was more than he was able to understand. Strong emotion, as always, had intensified the vermilion of the Captain's complexion, giving him something of the appearance of a survivor from an explosion in a tomato cannery.

Nor was his voice, when he spoke, of a timbre calculated to lull any apprehensions which his aspect might have inspired. It was the voice of a man who needed only a little sympathy and encouragement to make him whip out a revolver and start blazing away with it.

"So!" he said.

There are no good answers to the word "So!" particularly when uttered in the kind of voice just described, and Bill did not attempt to find one.

"So you are Honest Patch Perkins!"

Jeeves intervened, doing his best as usual.

"Well, yes and no, sir."

"What do you mean, yes and no? Isn't this the louse's patch?" demanded the Captain, brandishing Exhibit A. "Isn't that the hellhound's ginger mustache?" he said, giving Exhibit B a twiddle. "And do you think I didn't recognize that coat and tie?"

"What I was endeavoring to convey by the expression 'Yes and no,' sir, was that his lordship has retired from business."

"You bet he has. Pity he didn't do it sooner."

"Yes, sir. Oh, Iago, the pity of it, Iago."

"Eh?"

"I was quoting the Swan of Avon, sir."

"Well, stop quoting the bally Swan of Avon."

"Certainly, sir, if you wish it."

Bill had recovered his faculties to a certain extent. To say that even now he was feeling boomps-a-daisy would be an exaggeration, but he was capable of speech.

"Captain Biggar," he said, "I owe you an explanation."

"You owe me three thousand and five pounds, two and six," said the Captain, coldly corrective.

This silenced Bill again, and the Captain took advantage of the fact to call him eleven derogatory names.

Jeeves assumed the burden of the defense, for Bill was still reeling under the impact of the eleventh name.

"It is impossible to gainsay the fact that in the circumstances your emotion is intelligible, sir, for one readily admits that his lordship's recent activities are of a nature to lend themselves to adverse criticism. But can one fairly blame his lordship for what has occurred?"

This seemed to the Captain an easy one to answer.

"Yes," he said.

"You will observe that I employed the adverb 'fairly,' sir. His lordship arrived on Epsom Downs this afternoon with the best intentions and a capital adequate for any reasonable emergency. He could hardly have been expected to foresee that two such meagerly favored animals as Lucy Glitters and Whistler's Mother would have emerged triumphant from their respective trials of speed. His lordship is not clairvoyant."

"He could have laid the bets off."

"There I am with you, sir. *Rem acu tetigisti.*"

"Eh?"

"A Latin expression, which might be rendered in English by the American colloquialism, 'You said a mouthful.' I urged his lordship to do so."

"You?"

"I was officiating as his lordship's clerk."

The Captain stared.

"You weren't the chap in the pink mustache?"

"Precisely, sir, though I would be inclined to describe it as russet rather than pink."

The Captain brightened.

"So you were his clerk, were you? Then when he goes to prison, you'll go with him."

"Let us hope there will be no such sad ending as that, sir."

"What do you mean, 'sad' ending?" said Captain Biggar.

There was an uncomfortable pause. The Captain broke it.

"Well, let's get down to it," he said. "No sense in wasting time. Properly speaking, I ought to charge this sheepfaced, shambling refugee from hell—"

"The name is Lord Towcester, sir."

"No, it's not, it's Patch Perkins. Properly speaking, Perkins, you slinking reptile, I ought to charge you for petrol consumed on the journey here from Epsom, repairs to my car, which wouldn't have broken down if I hadn't had to push it so hard in the effort to catch you . . . and," he added, struck with an afterthought, "the two beers I had at the Goose and Gherkin while waiting for those repairs to be done. But I'm no hog. I'll settle for three thousand and five pounds, two and six. Write me a check."

Bill passed a fevered hand through his hair.

"How can I write you a check?"

Captain Biggar clicked his tongue, impatient of this shilly-shallying.

"You have a pen, have you not? And there is ink on the premises, I imagine? You are a strong, ablebodied young fellow in full possession of the use of your right hand, aren't you? No paralysis? No rheumatism in the joints? If," he went on, making a concession, "what is bothering you is that you have run out of blotting paper, never mind. I'll blow on it."

Jeeves came to the rescue, helping out the young master, who was still massaging the top of his head.

"What his lordship is striving to express in words, sir, is that while, as you rightly say, he is physically competent to write a check for three thousand and five pounds, two shillings and sixpence, such a check, when presented at your bank, would not be honored."

"Exactly," said Bill, well pleased with this lucid way of putting the thing. "It would bounce like a bounding dervish and come shooting back like a homing pigeon."

"Two very happy images, m'lord."

"I haven't a bean."

"Insufficient funds is the technical expression, m'lord. His lordship, if I may employ the argot, sir, is broke to the wide."

Captain Biggar stared.

"You mean you own a place like this, a bally palace if ever I saw one, and can't write a check for three thousand pounds?"

Jeeves undertook the burden of explanation.

"A house such as Towcester Abbey, in these days is not an asset, sir, it is a liability. I fear that your long residence in the East has rendered you not quite abreast of the changed conditions prevailing in your native land. Socialistic legislation has sadly depleted the resources of England's hereditary aristocracy. We are living now in what is known as the Welfare State, which means—broadly—that everybody is completely destitute."

It would have seemed incredible to any of the native boys, hippopotami, rhinoceri, pumas, zebras, alligators and buffaloes with whom he had come in contact in the course of his long career in the wilds that Captain Biggar's strong jaw was capable of falling like an unsupported stick of asparagus, but it had fallen now in precisely that manner. There was something almost piteous in the way his blue eyes, round and dismayed, searched the faces of the two men before him.

"You mean he can't brass up?"

"You have put it in a nutshell, sir. Who steals his lordship's purse steals trash."

Captain Biggar, his iron self-control gone, became a human semaphore, He might have been a White Hunter doing his daily dozen.

"But I must have the money, and I must have it before noon tomorrow." His voice rose in what in a lesser man would have been a wail. "Listen. I'll have to let you in on something that's vitally secret, and if you breathe a word to a soul I'll rip you both asunder with my bare hands, shred you up into small pieces and jump on the remains with hobnailed boots. Is that understood?"

Bill considered.

"Yes, that seems pretty clear. Eh, Jeeves?"

"Most straightforward, m'lord."

"Carry on, Captain."

Captain Biggar lowered his voice to a rasping whisper.

"You remember that telephone call I made after dinner? It was to those pals of mine, the chaps who gave me my winning double this afternoon. Well, when I say winning double," said Captain Biggar, raising his voice a little, "that's what it would have been but for the degraded chiselling of a dastardly, lop-eared—"

"Quite, quite," said Bill hurriedly. "You telephoned to your friends, you were saying?"

"I was anxious to know if it was all settled."

"If all what was settled?"

Captain Biggar lowered his voice again, this time so far that his words sounded like gas escaping from a pipe.

"There's something cooking—as Shakespeare says, we have an enterprise of great importance."

Jeeves winced.

" 'Enter*prises* of great pith and moment' is the exact quotation, sir."

"These chaps have a big S.P. job on for the Derby tomorrow. It's the biggest cert in the history of the race. The Irish horse, Ballymore."

Jeeves raised his eyebrows.

"Not generally fancied, sir."

"Well, Lucy Glitters and Whistler's Mother weren't generally fancied, were they? That's what makes this job so stupendous. Ballymore's a long-priced outsider. Nobody knows anything about him. He's been kept darker than a black cat on a moonless night. But let me tell you that he has had two secret trial gallops over the Epsom course and broke the record both times."

Despite his agitation, Bill whistled.

"You're sure of that?"

"Beyond all possibility of doubt. I've watched the animal run with my own eyes, and it's like a streak of lightning. All you see is a sort of brown blur. We're putting our money on at the last moment, carefully distributed among a dozen different bookies so as not to upset the price. And now," cried Captain Biggar, his voice rising once more, "you're telling me that I shan't have any money to put on."

His agony touched Bill. He did not think, from what little he had seen of him, that Captain Biggar was a man with whom he could ever form one of those beautiful friendships you read about, the kind that existed between Damon and Pythias, David and Jonathan, or Abercrombie and Fitch, but he could understand and sympathize with his grief.

"Too bad, I agree," he said, giving the fermenting hunter a kindly, brotherly look and almost, but not quite, patting him on the shoulder. "The whole situation is most regrettable, and you wouldn't be far out in saying that the spectacle of your anguish gashes me like a knife. But I'm afraid the best I can manage is a series of monthly payments, starting say about six weeks from now."

"That won't do me any good."

"Nor me," said Bill frankly. "It'll knock the stuffing out of my budget and mean cutting down the necessities of life to the barest minimum. I doubt if I shall be able to afford another square meal till about 1954. Farewell, a long farewell . . . to what, Jeeves?"

"To all your greatness, m'lord. This is the state of man: today he puts forth the tender leaves of hopes; tomorrow blossoms, and bears his blushing honors thick upon him. The third day comes a frost, a killing frost, and when he thinks, good easy man, full surely his greatness is aripening, nips his root."

"Thank you, Jeeves."

"Not at all, m'lord."

Bill looked at him, and sighed.

"You'll have to go, you know, to start with. I can't possibly pay your salary."

"I should be delighted to serve your lordship without emolument."

"That's dashed good of you, Jeeves, and I appreciate it. About as nifty a display of the feudal spirit as I ever struck. But how," asked Bill keenly, "could I keep you in fish?"

Captain Biggar interrupted these courteous exchanges. For some moments he had been chafing, if chafing is the right word to describe a White Hunter who is within an ace of frothing at the mouth. He said something so forceful about Jeeves's fish that speech was wiped from Bill's lips and he stood goggling with the dumb consternation of a man who has been unexpectedly struck by a thunderbolt.

"I've got to have that money!"

"His lordship has already informed you that, owing to the circumstance of his being fiscally crippled, that is impossible."

"Why can't he borrow it?"

Bill recovered the use of his vocal cords.

"Who from?" he demanded peevishly. "You talk as if borrowing money was as simple as falling off a log."

"The point his lordship is endeavoring to establish," explained Jeeves, "is the almost universal tendency of gentlemen to prove un-cooperative when an attempt is made to float a loan at their expense."

"Especially if what you're trying to get into their ribs for is a whacking great sum like three thousand and five pounds, two and six."

"Precisely, m'lord. Confronted by such figures, they become like the deaf adder that hearkens not to the voice of the charmer, charming never so wisely."

"So putting the bite on my social circle is off," said Bill. "It can't be done. I'm sorry."

Captain Biggar seemed to blow flame through his nostrils.

"You'll be sorrier," he said, "and I'll tell you when. When you and this precious clerk of yours are standing in the dock at the Old Bailey, with the Judge looking at you over his bifocals and me in the well of the court making faces at you. Then's the time when you'll be sorry . . . then and shortly afterward, when the Judge pronounces sentence, accompanied by some strong remarks from the bench, and they lead you off to Wormwood Scrubbs to start doing your two years hard or whatever it is."

Bill gaped.

"Oh, dash it!" he protested. "You wouldn't proceed to that . . . what, Jeeves?"

"Awful extreme, m'lord."

"You surely wouldn't proceed to that awful extreme?"

"Wouldn't I!"

"One doesn't want unpleasantness."

"What one wants and what one is going to get are two different things," said Captain Biggar, and went out, grinding his teeth, to cool off in the garden.

He left behind him one of those silences often called pregnant. Bill was the first to speak.

"We're in the soup, Jeeves."

"Certainly a somewhat sharp crisis in our affairs would appear to have been precipitated, m'lord."

"He wants his pound of flesh."

"Yes, m'lord."

"And we haven't any flesh."

"No, m'lord. It is a most disagreeable state of affairs."

"He's a tough egg, that Biggar. He looks like a gorilla with stomach ache."

"There is, perhaps, a resemblance to such an animal, afflicted as your lordship suggests."

"Did you notice him at dinner?"

"To which aspect of his demeanor during the meal does your lordship allude?"

"I was thinking of the sinister way he tucked into the roast duck. He flung himself on it like a tiger on its prey. He gave me the impression of a man without ruth or pity."

"Unquestionably a gentleman lacking in the softer emotions, m'lord."

"There's a word that just describes him. Begins with a *V*. Not vapid. Not vermicelli. Vindictive. The chap's vindictive. I can understand him being sore, about not getting his money, but what good will it do him to ruin me?"

"No doubt he will derive a certain moody satisfaction from it, m'lord."

Bill brooded.

"I suppose there really is nobody one could borrow a bit of cash from?"

"Nobody who springs immediately to the mind, m'lord."

"How about that financier fellow, who lives out Ditchingham way—Sir Somebody Something?"

"Sir Oscar Wopple, m'lord? He shot himself last Friday."

"Oh, then we won't bother him."

Jeeves coughed.

"If I might make a suggestion, m'lord?"

"Yes, Jeeves?"

A faint ray of hope had stolen into Bill's somber eyes. His voice, while still scarcely to be described as animated, no longer resembled that of a corpse speaking from the tomb.

"It occurred to me as a passing thought, m'lord, that were we to possess ourselves of Captain Biggar's ticket, our position would be noticeably stabilized."

Bill shook his head.

"I don't get you, Jeeves. Ticket? What ticket? You speak as if this were a railway station."

"I refer to the ticket which, in my capacity of your lordship's clerk, I handed to the gentleman as a record of his wager on Lucy Glitters and Whistler's Mother, m'lord."

"Oh, you mean his *ticket*?" said Bill, enlightened.

"Precisely, m'lord. As he left the race course so abruptly, it must be still upon his person, and it is the only evidence that exists that the wager was ever made. Once we had deprived him of it, your lordship would be in a position to make payment at your lordship's leisure."

"I see. Yes, that would be nice. So we get the ticket from him, do we?"

"Yes, m'lord."

"May I say one word, Jeeves?"

"Certainly, m'lord."

"How?"

"By what I might describe as direct action, m'lord."

Bill stared. This opened up a new line of thought.

"Set on him, you mean? *Scrag* him? Choke it out of him?"

"Your lordship has interpreted my meaning exactly."

Bill continued to stare.

"But, Jeeves, have you *seen* him? That bulging chest, those rippling muscles?"

"I agree that Captain Biggar is well-nourished, m'lord, but we would have the advantage of surprise. The gentleman went out into the garden. When he returns, one may assume that it will be by way of the French window by which he made his egress. If I draw the curtains, it will be necessary for him to enter through them. We will see him fumbling, and in that moment a sharp tug will cause the curtains to descend upon him, enmeshing him, as it were."

Bill was impressed, as who would not have been.

"By Jove, Jeeves! Now you're talking. You think it would work?"

"Unquestionably, m'lord. The method is that of the Roman retarius, with whose technique your lordship is no doubt familiar."

"That was the bird who fought with net and trident?"

"Precisely, m'lord. So if your lordship approves—"

"You bet I approve."

"Very good, m'lord. Then I will draw the curtains now, and we will take up our stations on either side of them."

It was with deep satisfaction that Bill surveyed the completed preparations. After a rocky start, the sun was coming through the cloud wrack.

"It's in the bag, Jeeves!"

"A very apt image, m'lord."

"If he yells, we will stifle his cries with the ... what do you call this stuff?"

"Velours, m'lord."

"We will stifle his cries with the velours. And while he's groveling on the ground, I shall get a chance to give him a good kick in the tailpiece."

"There *is* that added attraction, m'lord. For blessings ever wait on virtuous deeds, as the playwright Congreve informs us."

Bill breathed heavily.

"Were you in the First World War, Jeeves?"

"I dabbled in it to a certain extent, m'lord."

"I missed that one because I wasn't born, but I was in the Commandos in this last one. This is rather like waiting for the zero hour, isn't it?"

"The sensation is not dissimilar, m'lord."

"He should be coming soon."

"Yes, m'lord."

"On your toes, Jeeves?"

"Yes, m'lord."

"All set?"

"Yes, m'lord."

"Hi!" said Captain Biggar in their immediate rear. "I want to have another word with you two."

A lifetime of braving the snares and perils of the wilds develops in these White Hunters over the years a sort of sixth sense, warning them of lurking danger. Where the ordinary man, happening upon a tiger trap in the jungle, would fall in base over apex, your White Hunter, saved by his sixth sense, walks around it.

With fiendish cunning, Captain Biggar, instead of entering, as expected, through the French window, had circled the house and come in by the front door.

12

ALTHOUGH THE actual time which had elapsed between Captain Biggar's departure and return had been only about five minutes, scarcely long enough for him to take half a dozen turns up and down the lawn, pausing in the course of one of them to kick petulantly at a passing frog, it had been ample for his purposes. If you had said to him as he was going through the French window, "Have you any ideas, Captain?" he would have been forced to reply, "No more than a rabbit." But now his eye was bright and his manner jaunty. He had seen the way.

On occasions of intense spiritual turmoil the brain works quickly. Thwarted passion stimulates the little gray cells, and that painful scene on the rustic seat, when love had collided so disastrously with the code that governs the actions of the men who live on the frontiers of Empire, had stirred up those of Captain Biggar till, if you had X-rayed his skull, you would have seen them leaping and dancing like rice in a saucepan. Not thirty seconds after the frog's rubbing its head, had gone off to warn the other frogs to watch out for atom bombs, he was rewarded with what he recognized immediately as an inspiration.

Here was his position in a nutshell. He loved. Right. He would go further, he loved like the dickens. And unless he had placed a totally wrong construction on her words, her manner and the light in her eyes, the object of his passion loved him. A woman, he meant to say, does not go out of her way to bring the conversation around to the dear old days when a feller used to whack her over the top-knob with clubs and drag her into caves, unless she intends to convey a certain impression. True, a couple of minutes later she had been laughing and giggling with the frightful Towcester excrescence, but that, it seemed to him now that he had had time to simmer down, had been merely a guest's conventional civility to a host. He dismissed the Towcester gumboil. He was convinced that, if one went by the form book, he had but to lay his heart at her feet, and she would pick it up.

So far, so good. But here the thing began to get more complicated. She was rich and he was poor. That was the hitch. That was the snag. That was what was putting the good old sand in the bally machinery.

The thought that seared his soul and lent additional vigor to the kick he had directed at the frog was that, but for the deplorable financial methods of that blackhearted bookmaker, Honest Patch Towcester, it would all have been so simple. Three thousand pounds deposited on the nose of Ballymore at the current odds of fifty to one would have meant a return of a hundred and fifty thousand, just like finding it: and surely even Tubby Frobisher and the Subadar, rigid though their views were, could scarcely accuse a chap of not playing with the straight bat if he married a woman, however wealthy, while himself in possession of a hundred and fifty thousand of the best and brightest.

He groaned in spirit. A sorrow's crown of sorrow is remembering happier things, and he proceeded to torture himself with the recollection of how her neck had felt beneath his fingers as he fastened her pen—

Captain Biggar uttered a short, sharp exclamation. It was in Swahili, a language which always came most readily to his lips in moments of emotion, but its meaning was as clear as if it had been the "Eureka!" of Archimedes.

Her pendant! Yes, now he saw daylight. Now he could start handling the situation as it should be handled.

Two minutes later, he was at the front door. Two minutes and twenty-five seconds later, he was in the living room, eyeing the backs of Honest Patch Towcester and his clerk as they stood—for some silly reason known only to themselves—crouching beside the curtains which they had pulled across the French window.

"Hi!" he cried. "I want to have another word with you two."

The effect of the observation on his audience was immediate and impressive. It is always disconcerting, when you are expecting a man from the northeast, to have him suddenly bark at you from the southwest, especially if he does so in a manner that recalls feeding time in a dog hospital, and Bill went into his quaking and leaping routine with the smoothness that comes from steady practice. Even Jeeves, though his features did not lose their customary impassivity, appeared—if one could judge by the fact that his left eyebrow flickered for a moment as if about to rise—to have been stirred to quite a considerable extent.

"And don't stand there looking like a dying duck," said the Captain, addressing Bill, who, one is compelled to admit, was giving a rather close impersonation of such a bird *in articulo mortis.* "Since I saw you two beauties last," he continued, helping himself to another whisky and soda, "I have been thinking over the situation, and I have now got it all taped out. It suddenly came to me, quick as a flash. I said to myself, 'The pendant!' "

Bill blinked feebly. His heart, which had crashed against the back of his front teeth, was slowly returning to its base, but it seemed to him that the shock which he had just sustained must have left his hearing impaired. It had sounded exactly as if the Captain had said "The pendant!" which, of course, made no sense whatever.

"The pendant?" he echoed, groping.

"Mrs. Spottsworth is wearing a diamond pendant, m'lord," said Jeeves. "It is to this, no doubt, that the gentleman alludes."

It was specious, but Bill found himself still far from convinced.

"You think so?"

"Yes, m'lord."

"He alludes to that, in your opinion?"

"Yes, m'lord."

"But why does he allude to it, Jeeves?"

"That, one is disposed to imagine, m'lord, one will ascertain when the gentleman has resumed his remarks."

"Gone on speaking, you mean?"

"Precisely, m'lord."

"Well, if you say so," said Bill doubtfully. "But it seems a . . . what's that expression you're always using?"

"Remote contingency, m'lord?"

"That's right. It seems a very remote contingency."

Captain Biggar had been fuming silently. He now spoke with not a little asperity.

"If you have quite finished babbling, Patch Towcester—"

"Was I babbling?"

"Certainly you were babbling. You were babbling like a . . . like a . . . well, like whatever the dashed things are that babble."

"Brooks," said Jeeves helpfully, "are sometimes described as doing so, sir. In his widely read poem of that name, the late Lord Tennyson puts the words, 'Oh, brook, oh, babbling brook,' into the mouth of the character Edmund, and later describes the rivulet, speaking in its own person, as observing, 'I chatter over stony ways in little sharps and trebles, I bubble into eddying bays, I babble on the pebbles.' "

Captain Biggar frowned.

"*Ai deng hahp kamoo* for the late Lord Tennyson," he said impatiently. "What I'm interested in is this pendant."

Bill looked at him with a touch of hope.

"Are you going to explain about that pendant? Throw light upon it, as it were?"

"I am. It's worth close on three thousand quid, and," said Captain Biggar, throwing out the observation almost casually, "you're going to pinch it, Patch Towcester."

Bill gaped.

"Pinch it?"

"This very night."

It is always difficult for a man who is feeling as if he has just been struck over the occiput by a blunt instrument to draw himself to his full height and stare at someone censoriously, but Bill contrived to do so.

"What!" he cried, shocked to the core. "Are you, a bulwark of the Empire, a man who goes about setting an example to Dyaks, seriously suggesting that I rob one of my guests?"

"Well, I'm one of your guests, and you robbed me."

"Only temporarily."

"And you'll be robbing Mrs. Spottsworth only temporarily. I shouldn't have used the word 'pinch.' All I want you to do is borrow that pendant till tomorrow afternoon, when it will be returned."

Bill clutched his hair.

"Jeeves!"

"M'lord?"

"Rally round, Jeeves. My brain's tottering. Can you make any sense of what this rhinoceros-biffer is saying?"

"Yes, m'lord."

"You can? Then you're a better man that I am, Gunga Din."

"Captain Biggar's thought-processes seem to me reasonably clear, m'lord. The gentleman is urgently in need of money with which to back the horse Ballymore in tomorrow's Derby, and his proposal, as I take it, is that the pendant shall be abstracted and pawned and the proceeds employed for that purpose. Have I outlined your suggestion correctly, sir?"

"You have."

"At the conclusion of the race, one presumes, the object in question would be redeemed, brought back to the house, discovered, possibly by myself, in some spot where the lady might be supposed to have dropped it, and duly returned to her. Do I err in advancing this theory, sir?"

"You do not."

"Then, could one be certain beyond the peradventure of a doubt that Ballymore will win—"

"He'll win all right. I told you he had twice broken the course record."

"That is official, sir?"

"Straight from the feed box."

"Then I must confess, m'lord, I see little or no objection to the scheme."

Bill shook his head, unconvinced.

"I still call it stealing."

Captain Biggar clicked his tongue.

"It isn't anything of the sort, and I'll tell you why. In a way, you might say that that pendant was really mine."

"Really . . . what was that last word?"

"Mine. Let me," said Captain Biggar, "tell you a little story."

He sat musing for a while, his mind in the past. Coming out of his reverie and discovering with a start that his glass was empty, he refilled it. His attitude was that of a man who, even if nothing came of the business transaction which he had proposed, intended to save something from the wreck by drinking as much as possible of his host's whisky. When the refreshing draught had finished its journey down the hatch, he wiped his lips on the back of his hand, and began.

"Do either of you chaps know the Long Bar at Shanghai? No? Well, it's the Café de la Paix of the East. They always say that if you sit outside the Café de la Paix in Paris long enough, you're sure sooner or later to meet all your pals, and it's the same with the Long Bar. A few years ago, chancing to be in Shanghai, I had dropped in there, never dreaming that Tubby Frobisher and the Subadar were within a thousand miles of the place, and I'm dashed if the first thing I saw wasn't the two old bounders sitting on a couple of stools as large as life. 'Hullo, there, Sahib, old boy,' they said when I rolled up, and I said, 'Hullo, there, Tubby! Hullo there, Subadar, old chap,' and Tubby said, 'What'll you have, old boy?' and I said, 'What are you boys having?' and they said stingahs, so I said that would do me all right, so Tubby ordered a round of stingahs, and we started talking about *chowluangs* and *nai bahn rot fais* and where we had all met last and whatever became of the *poogni* at Lampang, and all that sort of thing. And when the stingahs were finished, I said, 'The next are on me. What for you, Tubby, old boy?' and he said he'd stick to stingahs. 'And for you, Subadar, old boy?' I said, and the Subadar said he'd stick to stingahs, too, so I wigwagged the barman and ordered stingahs all around, and, to cut a long story short, the stingahs came, a stingah for Tubby, a stingah for the Subadar and a stingah for me. 'Luck, old boys!' said Tubby. 'Luck, old boys!' said the Subadar. 'Cheerio, old boys!' I said, and we drank the stingahs."

Jeeves coughed. It was a respectful cough, but firm.

"Excuse me, sir."

"Eh?"

"I am reluctant to interrupt the flow of your narrative, but is this leading somewhere?"

Captain Biggar flushed. A man who is telling a crisp, well-knit story does not like to be asked if it is leading somewhere.

"Leading somewhere? What do you mean, is it leading somewhere? Of course it's leading somewhere. I'm coming to the nub of the thing now. Scarcely had we finished this second round of stingahs, when in through the door, sneaking along like a chap that expects at any moment to be slung out on his fanny, came this fellow in the tattered shirt and dungarees."

The introduction of a new and unexpected character took Bill by surprise.

"Which fellow in the tattered shirt and dungarees?"

"This fellow I'm telling you about."

"Who was he?"

"You may well ask. Didn't know him from Adam, and I could see Tubby Frobisher didn't know him from Adam. Nor did the Subadar. But he came sidling up to us and the first thing he said, addressing me, was, 'Hullo, Bimbo, old boy,' and I stared and said, 'Who on earth are you, old boy?' because I hadn't been called Bimbo since I left school. Everybody called me that there, God knows why, but out East it's been 'Sahib' for as long as I can remember. And he said, 'Don't you know me, old boy? I'm Sycamore; old boy.' And I stared again, and I said, 'What's that, old boy? Sycamore? Sycamore? Not Beau Sycamore that was in the Army Class at Uppingham with me, old boy?' and he said, 'That's right, old boy. Only it's Hobo Sycamore now.' "

The memory of that distressing encounter unmanned Captain Biggar for a moment. He was obliged to refill his glass with Bill's whisky before he could proceed.

"You could have knocked me down with a feather," he said, resuming. "This chap Sycamore had been the smartest, most dapper chap that ever adorned an Army Class, even at Uppingham."

Bill was following the narrative closely now.

"They're dapper in the Army Class at Uppingham, are they?"

"Very dapper, and this chap Sycamore, as I say, the most dapper of the lot. His dapperness was a byword. And here he was in a tattered shirt and dungarees, not even wearing a school tie," Captain Biggar sighed. "I saw at once what must have happened. It was the old, old story. Morale can crumble very easily out East. Drink, women and unpaid gambling debts . . ."

"Yes, yes," said Bill. "He'd gone under, had he?"

"Right under. It was pitiful. The chap was nothing but a bally beachcomber."

"I remember a story of Maugham's about a fellow like that."

"I'll bet your friend Maugham, whoever he may be, never met such a derelict as Sycamore. He had touched bottom, and the problem was what was to be done about it. Tubby Frobisher and the Subadar, of course, not having been introduced, were looking the other way and taking no part in the conversation, so it was up to me. Well, there isn't much you can do for these chaps who have let the East crumble their morale except give them something to buy a couple of drinks with, and I was just starting to feel in my pocket for a *baht* or a *tical*, when from under that tattered shirt of his this chap Sycamore produced something that brought a gasp to my lips. Even Tubby Frobisher and the Subadar, though they hadn't been introduced, had to stop trying to pretend there wasn't anybody there and sit up and take notice '*Sabaiga*!' said Tubby. '*Pom behoo*!' said the Subadar. And I don't wonder they were surprised. It was this pendant which you have seen tonight on the neck . . ." Captain Biggar faltered for a moment. He was remembering how that neck had felt beneath his fingers. ". . . on the neck," he proceeded, calling all his manhood to his aid, "of Mrs. Spottsworth."

"Golly!" said Bill, and even Jeeves, from the fact that the muscle at the side of his mouth twitched briefly, seemed to be feeling that after a slow start the story had begun to move. One saw now that all that stingah stuff had been merely the artful establishing of atmosphere, the setting of the stage for the big scene.

" 'I suppose you wouldn't care to buy this, Bimbo, old boy?' this chap Sycamore said, waggling the thing to make it glitter. And I said, 'Fry me in olive oil, Beau, old boy, where did you get that?' "

"That's just what I was going to ask," said Bill, all agog. "Where did he?"

"God knows. I ought not to have enquired. It was dashed bad form. That's one thing you learn very early out East of Suez—never ask questions. No doubt there was some dark history behind the thing . . . robbery . . . possibly murder. I didn't ask. All I said was, 'How much?' and he named a price far beyond the resources of my purse, and it looked as though the thing was going to be a washout. But fortunately Tubby Frobisher and the Subadar—I'd introduced them by this time—offered to chip in, and between us we met his figure and he went off, back into the murk and shadows from which he had emerged. Sad thing, very sad. I remember seeing this chap Sycamore make a hundred and forty-six in a house cricket match at school before being caught low down in the gully off a googly that dipped and swung away late. On a sticky wicket, too," said Captain Biggar, and was silent for a while, his thoughts in the past.

He came back into the present.

"So there you are," he said, with the air of one who has told a well-rounded tale.

"But how did you get it?" said Bill.

"Eh?"

"The pendant. You said it was yours, and the way I see it is that it passed into the possession of a syndicate."

"Oh, ah, yes, I didn't tell you that, did I? We shook dice for it, and I won. Tubby was never lucky with the bones. Nor was the Subadar."

"And how did Mrs. Spottsworth get it?"

"I gave it to her."

"You *gave* it to her."

It was impossible for Captain Biggar to become redder than he already was, so not even an eye as keen as Jeeves's could detect whether or not he was blushing, but an embarrassed look came into his eyes.

"Why not?" he said bluffly. "The dashed thing was no use to me, and I had received many kindnesses from Mrs. Spottsworth and her husband. Poor chap was killed by a lion and what was left of him shipped off to Nairobi, and when Mrs. Spottsworth was leaving the camp on the following day, I thought it would be a civil thing to give her something as a memento and all that, so I lugged out the pendant and asked her if she'd care to have it. She said she would, so I slipped it to her, and she went off with it. That's what I meant when I said you might say that the bally thing was really mine," said Captain Biggar, and helped himself to another whisky.

Bill was impressed.

"This puts a different complexion on things, Jeeves."

"Distinctly, m'lord."

"After all, as Pop Biggar says, the pendant practically belongs to him, and he merely wants to borrow it for an hour or two."

"Precisely, m'lord."

Bill turned to the Captain. His mind was made up.

"It's a deal," he said.

"You'll do it?"

"I'll have a shot."

"Stout fellow!"

"Let's hope it comes off."

"It'll come off all right. The clasp is loose."

"I meant I hoped nothing would go wrong."

Captain Biggar scouted the idea. He was all buoyancy and optimism.

"Go wrong? What can go wrong? You'll be able to think of a hundred ways of getting the dashed thing, two brainy fellers like you. Well," said the Captain, finishing his whisky, "I'll be going out and doing my exercises."

"At this time of night?"

"Breathing exercises," explained Captain Biggar. "Yoga. And with it, of course, communion with the Jivatma, or soul. Toodle-oo, chaps."

He pushed the curtains aside, and passed through the French window.

13

A LONG and thoughtful silence followed his departure. The room seemed very still, as rooms always did when Captain Biggar went out of them. Bill was sitting with his chin supported by his hand, like Rodin's "Penseur." Then he looked at Jeeves and, having looked, shook his head.

"No, Jeeves," he said.

"M'lord?"

"I can see that feudal gleam in your eye, Jeeves. You are straining at the leash, all eagerness to lend the young master a helping hand. Am I right?"

"I was certainly feeling, m'lord, that in view of our relationship of thane and vassal it was my duty to afford your lordship all the assistance that lay within my power."

Bill shook his head again.

"No, Jeeves, that's out. Nothing will induce me to allow you to go getting yourself mixed up in an enterprise which, should things not pan out as planned, may quite possibly culminate in a five-year stretch at one of our popular prisons. I shall handle this binge alone, and I want no back chat about it."

"But, m'lord—"

"No back chat, I said, Jeeves."

"Very good, m'lord."

"All I require from you is advice and counsel. Let us review the position of affairs. We have here a diamond pendant which at moment of going to press is on the person of Mrs. Spottsworth. The task confronting me—I said me, Jeeves—is somehow to detach this pendant from this person and nip away with it unobserved. Any suggestions?"

"The problem is undoubtedly one that presents certain points of interest, m'lord."

"Yes, I'd got as far as that myself."

"One rules out anything in the nature of violence, I presume, placing reliance wholly on stealth and finesse."

"One certainly does. Dismiss any idea that I propose to swat Mrs. Spottsworth on the napper with a blackjack."

"Then I would be inclined to say, m'lord, that the best results would probably be obtained from what I might term the spider sequence."

"I don't get you, Jeeves."

"If I might explain, m'lord. Your lordship will be joining the lady in the garden?"

"Probably on a rustic seat."

"Then, as I see it, m'lord, conditions will be admirably adapted to the plan I advocate. If shortly after entering into conversation with Mrs. Spottsworth, your lordship were to affect to observe a spider on her hair, the spider sequence would follow as doth the night the day. It would be natural for your lordship to offer to brush the insect off. This would enable your lordship to operate with your lordship's fingers in the neighborhood of the lady's neck. And if the clasp, as Captain Biggar assures us, is loose, it will be a simple matter to unfasten the pendant and cause it to fall to the ground. Do I make myself clear, m'lord?"

"All straight so far. But wouldn't she pick it up?"

"No, m'lord, because in actual fact it would be in your lordship's pocket. Your lordship would institute a search in the surrounding grass, but without avail, and eventually the search would be abandoned until the following day. The object would finally be discovered late tomorrow evening."

"After Biggar gets back?"

"Precisely, m'lord."

"Nestling under a bush?"

"Or on the turf some little distance away. It had rolled."

"Do pendants roll?"

"This pendant would have done so, m'lord."

Bill chewed his lower lip thoughtfully.

"So that's the spider sequence?"

"That is the spider sequence, m'lord."

"Not a bad scheme at all."

"It has the merit of simplicity, m'lord. And if your lordship is experiencing any uneasiness at the thought of opening cold, as the theatrical expression is, I would suggest our having what in stage parlance is called a quick run-through."

"A rehearsal, you mean?"

"Precisely, m'lord. It would enable your lordship to perfect yourself in lines and business. In the Broadway section of New York, where the theater industry of the United States of America is centered, I am told that this is known as ironing out the bugs."

Bill laughed hollowly.

"Ironing out the spiders."

"Ha, ha, m'lord. But, if I may venture to say so, it is unwise to waste the precious moments in verbal pleasantries."

"Time is of the essence?"

"Precisely, m'lord. Would your lordship like to walk the scene?"

"Yes, I think I would, if you say it's going to steady the nervous system. I feel as if a troupe of performing fleas were practicing buck-and-wing steps up and down my spine."

"I have heard Mr. Wooster complain of a similar malaise in moments of stress and trial, m'lord. It will pass."

"When?"

"As soon as your lordship has got the feel of the part. A rustic seat, your lordship said?"

"That's where she was last time."

"Scene, A rustic seat," murmured Jeeves. "Time, A night in summer. Discovered at rise, Mrs. Spottsworth. Enter Lord Towcester. I will portray Mrs. Spottsworth, m'lord. We open with a few lines of dialogue to establish atmosphere, then bridge into the spider sequence. Your lordship speaks."

Bill marshalled his thoughts.

"Er—Tell me, Rosie—"

"Rosie, m'lord?"

"Yes, Rosie, blast it. Any objection?"

"None whatever, m'lord."

"I used to know her at Cannes."

"Indeed, m'lord? I was not aware. You were saying, m'lord?"

"Tell me, Rosie, are you afraid of spiders?"

"Why does your lordship ask?"

"There's rather an outsize specimen crawling on the back of your hair." Bill sprang about six inches in the direction of the ceiling. "What on earth did you do that for?" he demanded irritably.

Jeeves preserved his calm.

"My reason for screaming, m'lord, was merely to add verisimilitude. I supposed that that was how a delicately nurtured lady would be inclined to react on receipt of such a piece of information."

"Well, I wish you hadn't. The top of my head nearly came off."

"I am sorry, m'lord. But it was how I saw the scene. I felt it, felt it *here*," said Jeeves, tapping the left side of his waist-coat. "If your lordship would be good enough to throw me the line once more."

"There's rather an outize specimen crawling on the back of your hair."

"I would be grateful if your lordship would be so kind as to knock it off."

"I can't see it now. Ah, there it goes. On your neck."

"And that," said Jeeves, rising from the settee on which in his role of Mrs. Spottsworth he had seated himself, "is cue for business, m'lord. Your lordship will admit that it is really quite simple."

"I suppose it is."

"I am sure that after this try-out the performing fleas to which your lordship alluded a moment ago will have substantially modified their activities."

"They've slowed up a bit, yes. But I'm still nervous."

"Inevitable on the eve of an opening performance, m'lord. I think your lordship should be starting as soon as possible. If 'twere done, then 'twere well 'twere done quickly. Our arrangements have been made with a view to a garden set, and it would be disconcerting were Mrs. Spottsworth to return to the house, compelling your lordship to adapt your technique to an interior."

Bill nodded.

"I see what you mean. Right ho, Jeeves. Good-bye."

"Good-bye, m'lord."

"If anything goes wrong—"

"Nothing will go wrong, m'lord."

"But if it does . . . You'll write me in Dartmoor occasionally, Jeeves? Just a chatty letter from time to time, giving me the latest news from the outer world?"

"Certainly, m'lord."

"It'll cheer me up as I crack my daily rock. They tell me conditions are much better in these modern prisons than they used to be in the old days."

"So I understand, m'lord."

"I might find Dartmoor a regular home from home. Solid comfort, I mean to say."

"Quite conceivably, m'lord."

"Still, we'll hope it won't come to that."

"Yes, m'lord."

"Yes . . . Well, good-bye once again, Jeeves."

"Good-bye, m'lord."

Bill squared his shoulders and strode out, a gallant figure. He had summoned the pride of the Towcesters to his aid, and it buoyed him up. With just this quiet courage had a Towcester of the seventeenth century mounted the scaffold at Tower Hill, nodding affably to the headsman and waving to friends and relations in the audience. When the test comes, blood will tell.

He had gone a few moments, when Jill came in.

It seemed to Jeeves that in the course of the past few hours the young master's betrothed had lost a good deal of the animation which rendered her as a rule so attractive, and he was right. Her recent interview with Captain Biggar had left Jill pensive and inclined to lower the corners of the mouth and stare mournfully. She was staring mournfully now.

"Have you seen Lord Towcester, Jeeves?"

"His lordship has just stepped into the garden, miss."

"Where are the others?"

"Sir Roderick and her ladyship are still in the library, miss."

"And Mrs. Spottsworth?"

"She stepped into the garden shortly before his lordship."

Jill stiffened.

"Oh?" she said, and went into the library to join Monica and Rory. The corners of her mouth were drooping more than ever, and her stare had increased in mournfulness some twenty per cent. She looked like a girl who is thinking the worst, and that was precisely the sort of girl she was.

Two minutes later, Captain Biggar came bustling in with a song on his lips. Yoga and communion with the Jivatma, or soul, seemed to have done him good. His eyes were bright and his manner alert. It is when the time for action has come that you always catch these White Hunters at their best.

"Pale hands I loved beside the Shalimar, where are you now, where are you now?" sang Captain Biggar. "I . . . how does the dashed thing go . . . I sink beneath your spell. La, la, la, . . . La, la, la, la. Where are you now? Where *are* you now? For they're hanging Danny Deever in the morning," he caroled, changing the subject.

He saw Jeeves, and suspended the painful performance.

"Hullo," he said. "*Quai hai,* my man. How are things?"

"Things are in a reasonably satisfactory state, sir."

"Where's Patch Towcester?"

"His lordship is in the garden, sir."

"With Mrs. Spottsworth?"

"Yes, sir. Putting his fate to the test, to win or lose it all."

"You thought of something, then?"

"Yes, sir. The spider sequence."

"The how much?"

Captain Biggar listened attentively as Jeeves outlined the spider sequence, and when he had finished paid him a stately compliment.

"You'd do well out East, my boy."

"It is extremely kind of you to say so, sir."

"That is to say if that scheme was your own."

"It was, sir."

"Then you'd be just the sort of fellow we want in Kuala Lumpur. We need chaps like you, chaps who can use their brains. Can't leave brains all to the Dyaks. Makes the blighters get above themselves."

"The Dyaks are exceptionally intelligent, sir?"

"Are they! Let me tell you of something that happened to Tubby Frobisher and me one day when we . . ." He broke off, and the world was deprived of another excellent story. Bill was coming through the French window.

A striking change had taken place in the ninth Earl in the few minutes since he had gone out through that window, a young man of spirit setting forth on a high adventure. His shoulders, as we have indicated, had then been square. Now they sagged like those of one who bears a heavy weight. His eyes were dull, his brow furrowed. The pride of the Towcesters appeared to have packed up and withdrawn its support. No longer was there in his bearing any suggestion of that seventeenth century ancestor who had infused so much of the party spirit into his decapitation on Tower Hill. The ancestor he most closely resembled now was the one who was caught cheating at cards by Charles James Fox at Wattier's in 1782.

"Well?" cried Captain Biggar.

Bill gave him a long, silent mournful look, and turned to Jeeves.

"Jeeves!"

"M'lord?"

"That spider sequence."

"Yes, m'lord?"

"I tried it."

"Yes, m'lord?"

"And things looked good for a moment. I detached the pendant."

"Yes, m'lord?"

"Captain Biggar was right. The clasp was loose. It came off."

Captain Biggar uttered a pleased exclamation in Swahili.

"Gimme," he said.

"I haven't got it. It slipped out of my hand."

"And fell?"

"And fell."

"You mean it's lying in the grass?"

"No," said Bill, with a somber shake of the head. "It isn't lying in any ruddy grass. It went down the front of Mrs. Spottsworth's dress, and is now somewhere in the recesses of her costume."

14

It is not often that one sees three good men struck all of a heap simultaneously, but anybody who chanced to stroll into the living room of Towcester Abbey at this moment would have been able to observe that spectacle. To say that Bill's bulletin had had a shattering effect on his companions would be, if anything, to understate it. Captain Biggar was expressing his concern by pacing the room with whirling arms, while the fact that two of the hairs of his right eyebrow distinctly quivered showed how deeply Jeeves had been moved. Bill himself, crushed at last by the blows of Fate, appeared formally to have given up the struggle. He had slumped into a chair, and was sitting there looking boneless and despairing. All he needed was a long white beard, and the resemblance to King Lear on one of his bad mornings would have been complete.

Jeeves was the first to speak.

"Most disturbing, m'lord."

"Yes," said Bill dully. "Quite a nuisance, isn't it? You don't happen to have any little-known Asiatic poison on you, do you, Jeeves?"

"No, m'lord."

"A pity," said Bill. "I could use it."

His young employer's distress pained Jeeves, and as it had always been his view that there was no anodyne for the human spirit, when bruised, like a spot of Marcus Aurelius, he searched in his mind for some suitable quotation from the Emperor's works. And he was just hesitating between 'Whatever may befall thee, it was preordained for thee from everlasting' and 'Nothing happens to any man which he is not fitted by nature to bear,' both excellent, when Captain Biggar, who had been pouring out a rapid fire of ejaculations in some native dialect, suddenly reverted to English.

"*Doi wieng lek!*" he cried. "I've got it! Fricassee me with stewed mushrooms on the side, I see what you must do."

Bill looked up. His eyes were glazed, his manner listless.

"Do?" he said. "Me?"

"Yes, you."

"I'm sorry," said Bill. "I'm in no condition to do anything except possibly expire, regretted by all."

Captain Biggar snorted, and having snorted uttered a tchah, a pah and a bah.

"*Mun py nawn lap lao!*" he said impatiently. "You can dance, can't you?"

"Dance?"

"Preferably the Charleston. That's all I'm asking of you, a few simple steps of the Charleston."

Bill stirred slightly, like a corpse moving in its winding sheet. It was an acute spasm of generous indignation that caused him to do so. He was filled with what, in his opinion, was a justifiable resentment. Here he was, in the soup and going down for the third time, and this man came inviting him to dance before him as David danced before Saul. Assuming this to be merely the thin end of the wedge, one received the impression that in next to no time the White Hunter, if encouraged, would be calling for comic songs and conjuring tricks and imitations of footlight favorites who are familiar to you all. What, he asked himself bitterly, did the fellow think this was? The revival of vaudeville? A village concert in aid of the church organ restoration fund?

Groping for words with which to express these thoughts, he found that the Captain was beginning to tell another of his stories. Like Marcus Aurelius, Kuala Lumpur's favorite son always seemed to have up his sleeve something apposite to the matter in hand, whatever that matter might be. But where the Roman Emperor, a sort of primitive Bob Hope or Milton Berle, had contented himself with throwing off wisecracks, Captain Biggar preferred the narrative form.

"Yes, the Charleston," said Captain Biggar, "and I'll tell you why. I am thinking of the episode of Tubby Frobisher and the wife of the Greek consul. The recollection of it suddenly flashed upon me like a gleam of light from above."

He paused. A sense of something omitted, something left undone, was nagging at him. Then he saw why this was so. The whisky. He moved to the table and filled his glass.

"Whether it was Smyrna or Joppa or Stamboul where Tubby was stationed at the time of which I speak," he said, draining half the contents of his glass and coming back with the rest, "I'm afraid I can't tell you. As one grows older, one tends to forget these details. It may even have been Baghdad or half a dozen other places. I admit frankly that I have forgotten. But the point is that he was at some place somewhere and one night he attended a reception or a *soirée* or whatever they call these binges at one of the embassies. You know the sort of thing I mean. Fair women and brave men, all dolled up and dancing their ruddy heads off. And in due season it came to pass that Tubby found himself doing the Charleston with the wife of the Greek consul as his partner. I don't know if either of you have ever seen Tubby Frobisher dance the Charleston?"

"Neither his lordship nor myself have had the privilege of meeting Mr. Frobisher, sir," Jeeves reminded him courteously.

Captain Biggar stiffened.

"Major Frobisher, damn it."

"I beg your pardon, sir. Major Frobisher. Owing to our never having met him, the Major's technique when performing the Charleston is a sealed book to us."

"Oh?" Captain Biggar refilled his glass. "Well, his technique, as you call it, is vigorous. He does not spare himself. He is what in the old days would have been described as a three-collar man. By the time Tubby Frobisher has finished dancing the Charleston, his partner knows she has been in a fight, all right. And it was so on this occasion. He hooked on to the wife of the Greek consul and he jumped her up and he jumped her down, he whirled her about and he spun her round, he swung her here and he swung here there, and all of a sudden what do you think happened?"

"The lady had heart failure, sir?"

"No, the lady didn't have heart failure, but what occurred was enough to give it to all present at that gay affair. For, believe me or believe me not, there was a tinkling sound, and from inside her dress there began to descend to the floor silver forks, silver spoons and, Tubby assures me, a complete toilet set in tortoiseshell. It turned out that the female was a confirmed kleptomaniac and had been using the space between her dress and whatever she was wearing under her dress—I'm not a married man myself, so can't go into particulars—as a safe deposit."

"Embarrassing for Major Frobisher, sir."

Captain Biggar stared.

"For Tubby? Why? He hadn't been pinching the things, he was merely the instrument for their recovery. But don't tell me you've missed the whole point of my story, which is that I am convinced that if Patch Towcester here were to dance the Charleston with Mrs. Spottsworth with one tithe of Tubby Frobisher's determination and will to win, we'd soon rout that pendant out of its retreat. Tubby would have had it in the open before the band had played a dozen bars. And talking of that, we shall need music. Ah, I see a gramophone over there in the corner. Excellent. Well? Do you grasp the scheme?"

"Perfectly, sir. His lordship dances with Mrs. Spottsworth, and in due course the pendant droppeth as the gentle rain from heaven upon the place beneath."

"Exactly. What do you think of the idea?"

Jeeves referred the question to a higher court.

"What does your lordship think of it?" he asked deferentially.

"Eh?" said Bill. "What?"

Captain Biggar barked sharply.

"You mean you haven't been listening? Well, of all the—"

Jeeves intervened.

"In the circumstances, sir, his lordship may, I think, be excused for being distrait," he said reprovingly. "You can see from his lordship's lackluster eye that the native hue of his resolution is sicklied o'er with the pale cast of thought. Captain Biggar's suggestion is, m'lord, that your lordship shall invite Mrs. Spottsworth to join you in performing the dance known as the Charleston. This, if your lordship infuses sufficient vigor into the steps, will result in the pendant becoming dislodged and falling to the ground, whence it can readily be recovered and placed in your lordship's pocket."

It was perhaps a quarter of a minute before the gist of these remarks penetrated to Bill's numbed mind, but when it did, the effect was electric. His eyes brightened, his spine stiffened. It was plain that hope had dawned, and was working away once more at the old stand. As he rose from his chair, jauntily and with the aid of a man who is ready for anything, he might have

been that debonair ancestor of his who in the days of the Restoration had by
his dash and gallantry won from the ladies of King Charles the Second's
court the affectionate sobriquet of Tabasco Towcester.

"Lead me to her!" he said, and his voice rang out clear and resonant.
"Lead me to her, that is all I ask, and leave the rest to me."

But it was not necessary, as it turned out, to lead him to Mrs. Spottsworth,
for at this moment she came in through the French window with her Peking-
ese dog Pomona in her arms.

Pomona, on seeing the assembled company, gave vent to a series of
piercing shrieks. It sounded as if she were being torn asunder by red-hot
pincers, but actually this was her method of expressing joy. In moments of
ecstasy she always screamed partly like a lost soul and partly like a scalded
cat.

Jill came running out of the library, and Mrs. Spottsworth calmed her
fears.

"It's nothing, dear," she said. "She's just excited. But I wish you would put
her in my room, if you are going upstairs. Would it be troubling you too
much?"

"Not at all," said Jill aloofly.

She went out, carrying Pomona, and Bill advanced on Mrs. Spottsworth.
"Shall we dance?" he said.

Mrs. Spottsworth was surprised. On the rustic seat just now, especially in
the moments following the disappearance of her pendant, she had found her
host's mood markedly on the Byronic side. She could not readily adjust
herself to this new spirit of gaiety.

"You want to *dance*?"

"Yes, with *you,*" said Bill, infusing into his manner a wealth of Restoration
gallantry. "It'll be like the old days at Cannes."

Mrs. Spottsworth was a shrewd woman. She had not failed to observe
Captain Biggar lurking in the background, and it seemed to her that an
admirable opportunity had presented itself of rousing the fiend that slept in
him . . . far too soundly, in her opinion. What it was that was slowing up the
White Hunter in his capacity of wooer, she did not know: but what she did
know was that there is nothing that so lights a fire under a laggard lover as the
spectacle of the woman he loves treading the measure in the arms of another
man, particularly another man as good-looking as William, Earl of
Towcester.

"Yes, won't it!" she said, all sparkle and enthusiasm. "How well I
remember those days! Lord Towcester dances so wonderfully," she added,
addressing Captain Biggar and imparting to him a piece of first-hand infor-
maton which, of course, he would have been sorry to have missed. "I love
dancing. The one unpunished rapture left on earth."

"What ho!" said Bill, concurring. "The old Charleston . . . do you
remember it?"

"You bet I do."

"Put a Charleston record on the gramophone, Jeeves."

"Very good, m'lord."

When Jill returned from depositing Pomona in Mrs. Spottsworth's sleeping quarters, only Jeeves, Bill and Mrs. Spottsworth were present in the living room, for at the very outset of the proceedings Captain Biggar, unable to bear the sight before him, had plunged through the French window into the silent night.

The fact that it was he himself who had suggested this distressing exhibition, recalling, as it did in his opinion, the worst excesses of the Carmagnole of the French Revolution combined with some of the more risqué features of native dances he had seen in Equatorial Africa, did nothing to assuage the darkness of his mood. The frogs on the lawn, which he was now pacing with a black scowl on his face, were beginning to get the illusion that it was raining number eleven boots.

His opinion of the Charleston, as rendered by his host and the woman he loved, was one which Jill found herself sharing. As she stood watching from the doorway, she was conscious of much the same rising feeling of nausea which had afflicted the White Hunter when listening to the exchanges on the rustic seat. Possibly there was nothing in the way in which Bill was comporting himself that rendered him actually liable to arrest, but she felt very strongly that some form of action should have been taken by the police. It was her view that there ought to have been a law.

Nothing is more difficult than to describe in words a Charleston danced by, on the one hand, a woman who loves dancing Charlestons and throws herself right into the spirit of them, and, on the other hand, by a man desirous of leaving no stone unturned in order to dislodge from some part of his associate's anatomy a diamond pendant which has lodged there. It will be enough, perhaps, to say that if Major Frobisher had happened to walk into the room at this moment, he would instantly have been reminded of old days in Smyrna or Joppa or Stamboul or possibly Baghdad. Mrs. Spottsworth he would have compared favorably with the wife of the Greek consul, while Bill he would have patted on the back, recognizing his work as fully equal, if not superior, to his own.

Rory and Monica, coming out of the library, were frankly amazed.

"Good heavens!" said Monica.

"The old boy cuts quite a rug, does he not?" said Rory. "Come, girl, let us join the revels."

He put his arm about Monica's waist, and the action became general. Jill, unable to bear the degrading spectacle any longer, turned and went out. As she made her way to her room, she was thinking unpleasant thoughts of her betrothed. It is never agreeable for an idealistic girl to discover that she has linked her lot with a libertine, and it was plain to her now that William, Earl of Towcester, was a debauchee whose correspondence course might have been taken with advantage by Casanova, Don Juan and the rowdier Roman Emperors.

"When I dance," said Mrs. Spottsworth, cutting, like her partner, quite a rug, "I don't know I've got feet."

Monica winced.

"If you danced with Rory, you'd know you've got feet. It's the way he jumps on and off that gets you down."

"Ouch!" said Mrs. Spottsworth suddenly. Bill had just lifted her and brought her down with a bump which would have excited Tubby Frobisher's generous admiration, and she was now standing rubbing her leg. "I've twisted something," she said, hobbling to a chair.

"I'm not surprised," said Monica, "the way Bill was dancing."

"Oh, gee, I hope it is just a twist and not my sciatica come back. I suffer so terribly from sciatica, especially if I'm in a place that's at all damp."

Incredible as it may seem, Rory did not say, 'Like Towcester Abbey, what?' and go on to speak of the garden which, in the winter months, was at the bottom of the river. He was peering down at an object lying on the floor.

"Hullo," he said. "What's this? Isn't this pendant yours, Mrs. Spottsworth?"

"Oh, thank you," said Mrs. Spottsworth. 'Yes, it's mine. It must have ... Ouch!" she said, breaking off, and writhed in agony once more.

Monica was all concern.

"You must get straight to bed, Rosalinda."

"I guess I should."

With a nice hot-water bottle."

"Yes."

"Rory will help you upstairs."

"Charmed," said Rory. "But why do people always speak of a 'nice' hot-water bottle? We at Harrod's say 'nasty' hot-water bottle. Our electric pads have rendered the hot-water bottle obsolete. Three speeds ... Autumn Glow, Spring Warmth and Mae West."

They moved to the door, Mrs. Spottsworth leaning heavily on his arm. They passed out, and Bill, who had followed them with a bulging eye, threw up his hands in a wide gesture of despair.

"Jeeves!"

"M'lord?"

"This is the end!"

"Yes, m'lord."

"She's gone to ground."

"Yes, m'lord."

"Accompanied by the pendant."

"Yes, m'lord."

"So unless you have any suggestions for getting her out of that room, we're sunk. Have you any suggestions?"

"Not at the moment, m'lord."

"I didn't think you would have. After all, you're human, and the problem is one which is not within . . . what, Jeeves?"

"The scope of human power, m'lord."

"Exactly. Do you know what I am going to do?"

"No, m'lord."

"Go to bed, Jeeves. Go to bed and try to sleep and forget. Not that I have the remotest chance of getting to sleep, with every nerve in my body sticking out a couple of inches and curling at the ends."

"Possibly if your lordship were to count sheep—"

"You think that would work?"

"It is a widely recognized specific, m'lord."

"H'm." Bill considered. "Well, no harm in trying it. Good night, Jeeves."

"Good night, m'lord."

15

EXCEPT FOR the squeaking of mice behind the wainscoting and an occasional rustling sound as one of the bats in the chimney stirred uneasily in its sleep, Towcester Abbey lay hushed and still. 'Twas now the very witching time of night, and in the Blue Room Rory and Monica, pleasantly fatigued after the activities of the day, slumbered peacefully. In the Queen Elizabeth Room Mrs. Spottsworth, Pomona in her basket at her side, had also dropped off. In the Anne Boleyn Room Captain Biggar, the good man taking his rest, was dreaming of old days on the Me Wang River, which, we need scarcely inform our public, is a tributary of the larger and more crocodile-infested Wang Me.

Jill, in the Clock Room, was still awake, staring at the ceiling with hot eyes, and Bill, counting sheep in the Henry the Eighth room, had also failed to find oblivion. The specific recommended by Jeeves might be widely recognized, but so far it had done nothing toward enabling him to knit up the raveled sleave of care.

"Eight hundred and twenty-two," murmured Bill. "Eight hundred and twenty-three. Eight hundred and . . . "

He broke off, leaving the eight hundred and twenty-fourth sheep, an animal with a more than usually vacuous expression on its face, suspended in the air into which it had been conjured up. Someone had knocked on the door, a knock so soft and deferential that it could have proceeded from the knuckle of only one man. It was consequently without surprise that a moment later he perceived Jeeves entering.

"Your lordship will excuse me," said Jeeves courteously. "I would not have disturbed your lordship, had I not, listening at the door, gathered from your lordship's remarks that the strategem which I proposed had proved unsuccessful."

"No, it hasn't worked yet," said Bill, "but come in, Jeeves, come in." He would have been glad to see anything that was not a sheep. "Don't tell me," he said, starting as he noted the gleam of intelligence in his visitor's eye, "that you've thought of something?"

"Yes, m'lord, I am happy to say that I fancy I have found a solution to the problem which confronted us."

"Jeeves, you're a marvel!"

"Thank you very much, m'lord."

"I remember Bertie Wooster saying to me once that there was no crisis which you were unable to handle."

"Mr. Wooster has always been far too flattering, m'lord."

"Nonsense. Not nearly flattering enough. If you have really put your finger on a way of overcoming the superhuman difficulties in our path—"

"I feel convinced that I have, m'lord."

Bill quivered inside his mauve pajama jacket.

"Think well, Jeeves," he urged. "Somehow or other we have got to get Mrs. Spottsworth out of her room for a lapse of time sufficient to enable me to bound in, find that pendant, scoop it up and bound out again, all this without a human eye resting upon me. Unless I have completely misinterpreted your words owing to having suffered a nervous breakdown from counting sheep, you seem to be suggesting that you can do this. How? That is the question that springs to the lips. With mirrors?"

Jeeves did not speak for a moment. A pained look had come into his finely chiselled face. It was as though he had suddenly seen some sight which was occasioning him distress.

"Excuse me, m'lord. I am reluctant to take what is possibly a liberty on my part—"

"Carry on Jeeves. You have our ear. What is biting you?"

"It is your pajamas, m'lord. Had I been aware that your lordship was in the habit of sleeping in mauve pajamas, I would have advised against it. Mauve does not become your lordship. I was once compelled, in his best interests, to speak in a similar vein to Mr. Wooster, who at that time was also a mauve-pajama addict."

Bill found himself at a loss.

"How have we got on to the subject of pajamas?" he asked, wonderingly.

"They thrust themselves on the notice, m'lord. That very aggressive purple. If your lordship would be guided by me and substitute a quiet blue or possibly a light pistachio green—"

"Jeeves!"

"M'lord?"

"This is no time to be prattling of pajamas."

"Very good, m'lord."

"As a matter of fact, I rather fancy myself in mauve. But that, as I say, is neither here nor there. Let us postpone the discussion to a more suitable moment. I will, however, tell you this. If you really have something to suggest with reference to that pendant and that something brings home the bacon, you may take these mauve pajamas and raze them to the ground and sow salt on the foundations."

"Thank you very much, m'lord."

"It will be a small price to pay for your services. Well, now that you've got me all worked up, tell me more. What's the good news? What is this scheme of yours?"

"A quite simple one, m'lord. It is based on—"

Bill uttered a cry.

"Don't tell me. Let me guess. The psychology of the individual?"

"Precisely, m'lord."

Bill drew in his breath sharply.

"I thought as much. Something told me that was it. Many a time and oft, exchanging dry Martinis with Bertie Wooster in the bar of the Drones Club, I have listened to him, rapt, as he spoke of you and the psychology of the individual. He said that, once you get your teeth into the psychology of the individual, it's all over except chucking one's hat in the air and doing spring dances. Proceed, Jeeves. You interest me strangely. The individual whose psychology you have been brooding on at the present juncture is, I take it, Mrs. Spottsworth? Am I right or wrong, Jeeves?"

"Perfectly correct, m'lord. Has it occurred to your lordship what is Mrs. Spottsworth's principal interest, the thing uppermost in the lady's mind?"

Bill gaped.

"You haven't come here at one in the morning to suggest that I dance the Charleston with her again?"

"Oh, no, m'lord."

"Well, when you spoke of her principal interest—"

"There is another facet of Mrs. Spottsworth's character which you have overlooked, m'lord. I concede that she is an enthusiastic Charleston performer, but what principally occupies her thoughts is psychical research. Since her arrival at the Abbey, she has not ceased to express a hope that she may be granted the experience of seeing the specter of Lady Agatha. It was that that I had in mind when I informed your lordship that I had formulated a scheme for obtaining the pendant, based on the psychology of the individual."

Bill sank back on the pillows, a disappointed man.

"No, Jeeves," he said. "I won't do it."

"M'lord?"

"I see where you're heading. You want me to dress up in a farthingale and wimple and sneak into Mrs. Spottsworth's room, your contention being that if she wakes and sees me, she will simply say, 'Ah, the ghost of Lady Agatha,' and go to sleep again. It can't be done, Jeeves. Nothing will induce me to dress up in women's clothes, not even in such a deserving cause as this one. I might stretch a point and put on the old mustache and black patch."

"I would not advocate it, m'lord. Even on the race-course I have observed clients, on seeing your lordship, start back with visible concern. A lady, discovering such an apparition in her room, might quite conceivably utter a piercing scream."

Bill threw his hands up with a despondent groan.

"Well, there you are, then. The thing's off. Your scheme falls to the ground and becomes null and void."

"No, m'lord. Your lordship has not, if I may say so, grasped the substance of the plan I am putting forward. The essential at which one aims is the inducing of Mrs. Spottsworth to leave her room, thus rendering it possible for your lordship to enter and secure the pendant. I propose now, with your lordship's approval, to knock on Mrs. Spottsworth's door and request the loan of a bottle of smelling salts."

Bill clutched at his hair.

"You said, Jeeves?"

"Smelling salts, m'lord."

Bill shook his head.

"Counting those sheep has done something to me," he said. "My hearing has become affected. It sounded to me just as if you had said, 'Smelling salts.'"

"I did, m'lord. I would explain that I required them in order to restore your lordship to consciousness."

"There again. I could have sworn that I heard you say, 'Restore your lordship to consciousness.'"

"Precisely, m'lord. Your lordship has sustained a severe shock. Happening to be in the vicinity of the ruined chapel at about the hour of midnight, your lordship observed the wraith of Lady Agatha and was much overcome. How your lordship contrived to totter back to your room, your lordship will never know, but I found your lordship there in a highly emotional state and immediately applied to Mrs. Spottsworth for the loan of her smelling salts."

Bill was still at a loss.

"I don't get the gist, Jeeves."

"If I might elucidate my meaning still further, m'lord. The thought I had in mind was that, learning that Lady Agatha was, if I may so term it, on the wing, Mrs. Spottsworth's immediate reaction would be an intense desire to hasten to the ruined chapel in order to observe the manifestation for herself. I would offer to escort her thither, and during her absence—"

It is never immediately that the ordinary man, stunned by some revelation of genius, is able to find words with which to express his emotion. When Alexander Graham Bell, meeting a friend one morning in the year 1878, said, 'Oh, hullo, George, heard the latest? I invented the telephone yesterday,' it is probable that the friend merely shuffled his feet in silence. It was the same with Bill now. He could not speak. He lay there dumbly, while remorse flooded over him that he could ever have doubted this man. It was just as Bertie Wooster had so often said. Let this fish-fed mastermind get his teeth into the psychology of the individual, and it was all over except chucking your hat in the air and doing spring dances.

"Jeeves," he began, at length finding speech, but Jeeves was shimmering through the door.

"Your smelling salts, m'lord," he said, turning his head on the threshold. "If your lordship will excuse me."

It was perhaps two minutes, though to Bill it seemed longer, before he returned, bearing a small bottle.

"Well?" said Bill eagerly.

"Everything has gone according to plan, m'lord. The lady's reactions were substantially as I had anticipated. Mrs. Spottsworth, on receiving my communication, displayed immediate interest. Is your lordship familiar with the expression 'Jiminy Christmas!'?"

"No, I don't think I ever heard it. You don't mean 'Merry Christmas'?"

"No, m'lord. 'Jiminy Christmas!' It was what Mrs. Spottsworth observed on receiving the information that the phantasm of Lady Agatha was to be seen in the ruined chapel. The words, I gathered, were intended to convey surprise and elation. She assured me that it would take her but a brief time to hop into a dressing gown and that at the conclusion of that period she would be with me with, I understood her to say, her hair in a braid. I am to return in a moment and accompany her to the scene of the manifestation. I will leave the door open a few inches, so that your lordship, by applying your lordship's eye to the crack, may be able to see us depart. As soon as we have descended the staircase, I would advocate instant action, for I need scarcely remind your lordship that speed is—"

"Of the essence? No, you certainly don't have to tell me that. You remember what you were saying about cheetahs?"

"With reference to their speed of foot, m'lord?"

"That's right. Half a mile in forty-five seconds, I think you said?"

"Yes, m'lord."

"Well, the way I shall move would leave the nippiest cheetah standing at the post."

"That will be highly satisfactory, m'lord. I, on my side, may mention that on the dressing table in Mrs. Spottsworth's room I observed a small jewel case, which I have no doubt contains the pendant. The dressing table is immediately beneath the window. Your lordship will have no difficulty in locating it."

He was right, as always. It was the first thing that Bill saw when, having watched the little procession of two out of sight down the stairs, he hastened along the corridor to the Queen Elizabeth room. There, as Jeeves had stated, was the dressing table. On it was the small jewel case of which he had spoken. And in that jewel case, as he opened it with shaking hands, Bill saw the pendant. Hastily he slipped it into the pocket of his pajamas, and was turning to leave, when the silence, which had been complete but for his heavy breathing, was shattered by a series of dreadful screams.

Reference has been made earlier to the practice of the dog Pomona of shrieking loudly to express the ecstasy she always felt on beholding a friend or even what looked to her like a congenial stranger. It was ecstasy that was animating her now. In the course of that session on the rustic seat, when Bill had done his cooing, she had taken an immediate fancy to her host, as all dogs did. Meeting him now in this informal fashion, just at a moment when she had been trying to reconcile herself to the solitude which she so disliked, she make no attempt to place any bounds on her self-expression.

Screams sufficient in number and volume to have equipped a dozen Baronets stabbed in the back in libraries burst from her lips, and their effect on Bill was devastating. The author of "The Hunting of the Snark" says of one of his protagonists in a powerful passage:

> 'So great was his fright
> That his waistcoat turned white'

and the experience through which he was passing nearly caused Bill's mauve pajamas to do the same.

Though fond of Pomona, he did not linger to fraternize. He shot out of the door at a speed which would have had the most athletic cheetah shrugging its shoulders helplessly, and arrived in the corridor just as Jill, roused from sleep by those awful cries, came out of the Clock Room. She watched him steal softly into the Henry the Eighth room, and thought in bitter mood that a more suitable spot for him could scarcely have been found.

It was some quarter of an hour later, as Bill, lying in bed, was murmuring, "Nine hundred and ninety-eight . . . Nine hundred and ninety-nine . . . One thousand . . ." that Jeeves entered.

He was carrying a salver.

On that salver was a ring.

"I encountered Miss Wyvern in the corridor a few moments ago, m'lord," he said. "She desired me to give this to your lordship."

PART THREE

16

WYVERN HALL, the residence of Colonel Aubrey Wyvern, father of Jill and Chief Constable of the county of Southmoltonshire, lay across the river from Towcester Abbey, and on the following afternoon Colonel Wyvern, having worked his way scowlingly through a most inferior lunch, stumped out of the dining-room and went to his study and rang for his butler. And in due course the butler entered, tripping over the rug with a muffled "Whoops!" his invariable practice when crossing any threshold.

Colonel Wyvern was short and stout, and this annoyed him, for he would have preferred to be tall and slender. But if his personal appearance gave him pangs of discomfort from time to time, they were as nothing compared to the pangs the personal appearance of his butler gave him. In England today the householder in the country has to take what he can get in the way of domestic help, and all Colonel Wyvern had been able to get was the scrapings and scourings of the local parish school. Bulstrode, the major-domo of Wyvern Hall, was a skinny stripling of some sixteen summers, on whom Nature in her bounty had bestowed so many pimples that there was scarcely room on his face for the vacant grin which habitually adorned it.

He was grinning now, and once again, as always happened at these staff conferences, his overlord was struck by the closeness of the lad's resemblance to a halfwitted goldfish peering out of a bowl.

"Bulstrode," he said, with a parade-ground rasp in his voice.

"Yus?" replied the butler affably.

At another moment, Colonel Wyvern would have had something to say on the subject of this unconventional verbal approach, but today he was after bigger game. His stomach was still sending up complaints to the front office about that lunch, and he wanted to see the cook.

"Bulstrode," he said, "Bring the cook to me."

The cook, conducted into the presence, proved also to be one of the younger set. Her age was fifteen. She bustled in, her pigtails swinging behind her, and Colonel Wyvern gave her an unpleasant look.

"Trelawny!" he said.

"Yus?" said the cook.

This time there was no reticence on the part of the Chief Constable. The Wyverns did not as a rule war upon women, but there are times when chivalry is impossible.

"Don't say 'Yus?' you piefaced little excrescence," he thundered. "Say 'Yes, sir?' and say it in a respectful and soldierly manner, coming smartly to attention with the thumbs on the seam of the trousers. Trelawny, that lunch you had the temerity to serve up today was an insult to me and a disgrace to anyone daring to call herself a cook, and I have sent for you to inform you that if there is any more of this spirit of slackness and *laissez faire* on your part . . ." Colonel Wyvern paused. The "I'll tell your mother," with which he had been about to conclude his sentence, seemed to him to lack a certain something. "You'll hear of it," he said and, feeling that even this was not as good as he could have wished, infused such vigor and venom into his description of underdone chicken, watery Brussels sprouts and potatoes you couldn't get a fork into that a weaker girl might well have wilted.

But the Trelawnys were made of tough stuff. They did not quail in the hour of peril. The child met his eye with iron resolution, and came back strongly.

"Hitler!" she said, putting out her tongue.

The Chief Constable started.

"Did you call me Hitler?"

"Yus, I did."

"Well, don't do it again," said Colonel Wyvern sternly. "You may go, Trelawny."

Trelawny went, with her nose in the air, and Colonel Wyvern addressed himself to Bulstrode.

A proud man is never left unruffled when worsted in a verbal duel with a cook, especially a cook aged fifteen with pigtails, and in the Chief Constable's manner as he turned on his butler there was more than a suggestion of a rogue elephant at the height of its fever. For some minutes he spoke well and forcefully, with particular reference to the other's habit of chewing his candy ration while waiting at table, and when at length he was permitted to follow Evangeline Trelawny to the lower regions in which they had their being, Bulstrode, if not actually shaking in every limb, was at any rate subdued enough to omit to utter his customary "Whoops!" when tripping over the rug.

He left the Chief Constable, though feeling a little better after having cleansed his bosom of the perilous stuff that weighs upon the soul, still definitely despondent. "Ichabod," he was saying to himself, and he meant it. In the golden age before the social revolution, he was thinking, a gaping, pimpled tripper over rugs like this Bulstrode would have been a lowly hall-boy, if that. It revolted a Tory of the old school's finer feelings to have to regard such a blot on the Southmoltonshire scene in the sacred light of a butler.

He thought nostalgically of his young manhood in London at the turn of the century and of the vintage butlers he had been wont to encounter in those brave days . . . butlers who weighed two hundred and fifty pounds on the hoof, butlers with three chins and bulging abdomens, butlers with large, goose-berry eyes and that austere, supercilious, butlerine manner which has passed away so completely from the degenerate world of the nineteen-fifties. Butlers had been butlers then in the deepest and holiest sense of the word. Now they were mere chinless boys who sucked toffee and said "Yus?" when you spoke to them.

It was almost inevitable that a man living so near to Towcester Abbey and starting to brood on butlers should find his thoughts turning in the direction of the Abbey's principal ornament, and it was with a warm glow that Colonel Wyvern now began to think of Jeeves. Jeeves had made a profound impression on him. Jeeves, in his opinion, was the goods. Young Towcester himself was a fellow the Colonel, never very fond of his juniors, could take or leave alone, but this man of his, this Jeeves, he had recognized from their first meeting as something special. Out of the night that covered the Chief Constable, black as the pit—after that disturbing scene with Evangeline Trelawny—from pole to pole, there shone a sudden gleam of light. He himself might have his Bulstrode, but at least he could console himself with the thought that his daughter was marrying a man with a butler in the fine old tradition on his payroll. It put heart into him. It made him feel that this was not such a bad little old world, after all.

He mentioned this to Jill when she came in a moment later, looking cold and proud, and Jill tilted her chin and looked colder and prouder. She might have been a Snow Queen or something of that sort.

"I am not going to marry Lord Towcester," she said curtly.

It seemed to Colonel Wyvern that his child must be suffering from some form of amnesia, and he set himself to jog her memory.

"Yes, you are," he reminded her. "It was in the *Times*. I saw it with my own eyes. The engagement is announced between—."

"I have broken off the engagement."

That little gleam of light of which we were speaking a moment ago, the one we showed illuminating colonel Wyvern's darkness, went out with a pop, like a stage moon that has blown a fuse. He stared incredulously.

"Broken off the engagement?"

"I am never going to speak to Lord Towcester again."

"Don't be an ass," said Colonel Wyvern. "Of course you are. Not going to speak to him again? I never heard such nonsense. I suppose what's happened is that you've had one of these lovers' tiffs."

Jill did not intend to allow without protest what was probably the world's greatest tragedy since the days of Romeo and Juliet to be described in this inadequate fashion. One really must take a little trouble to find the *mot juste*.

"It was not a lovers' tiff," she said, all the woman in her flashing from her eyes. "If you want to know why I broke off the engagement, it was because of the abominable way he has been behaving with Mrs. Spottsworth."

Colonel Wyvern put a finger to his brow.

"Spottsworth? Spottsworth? Ah, yes. That's the American woman you were telling me about."

"The American trollop," corrected Jill coldly.

"Trollop?" said Colonel Wyvern, intrigued.

"That was what I said."

"Why do you call her that? Did you catch them—er—trolloping?"

"Yes, I did."

"Good gracious!"

Jill swallowed once or twice, as if something jagged in her throat were troubling her.

"It all seems to have started," she said, speaking in that toneless voice which had made such a painful impression on Bill, "in Cannes some years ago. Apparently she and Lord Towcester used to swim together at Eden Roc and go for long drives in the moonlight. And you know what that sort of thing leads to."

"I do indeed," said Colonel Wyvern with animation, and was about to embark on an anecdote of his interesting past, when Jill went on, still speaking in that same strange, toneless voice.

"She arrived at the Abbey yesterday. The story that has been put out is that Monica Carmoyle met her in New York and invited her to stay, but I have no doubt that the whole thing was arranged between her and Lord Towcester, because it was obvious how matters stood between them. No sooner had she appeared than he was all over her . . . making love to her in the garden, dancing with her like a cat on hot bricks, and," said Jill nonchalantly, wearing the mask like the Mrs. Fish who had so diverted Captain Biggar by doing the can-can in her step-ins in Kenya, "coming out of her room at two o'clock in the morning in mauve pajamas."

Colonel Wyvern choked. He had been about to try to heal the rift by saying that it was quite possible for a man to exchange a few civil remarks with a woman in a garden and while away the long evening by partnering her in the dance and still not be in any way culpable, but this statement wiped the words from his lips.

"Coming out of her room in mauve pajamas?"

"Yes."

"*Mauve* pajamas?"

"Bright mauve."

"God bless my soul!"

A club acquaintance, annoyed by the eccentricity of the other's bridge game, had once told Colonel Wyvern that he looked like a retired member of Singer's troupe of midgets who for years had been doing himself too well on the starchy foods, and this was in a measure true. He was, as we have said, short and stout. But when the call to action came, he could triumph over his brevity of stature and rotundity of waistcoat and became a figure of dignity and menace. It was an impressive Chief Constable who strode across the room and rang the bell for Bulstrode.

"Yus?" said Bulstrode.

Colonel Wyvern choked down the burning words he would have liked to utter. He told himself that he must conserve his energies.

"Bulstrode," he said, "bring me my horsewhip."

Down in the forest of pimples on the butler's face something stirred. It was a look of guilt.

"It's gorn," he mumbled.

Colonel Wyvern stared.

"Gone? What do you mean, gone? Gone where?"

Bulstrode choked. He had been hoping that this investigation might have been avoided. Something had told him that it would prove embarrassing.

"To the mender's. To be mended. It got cracked."

"Cracked?"

"Yus," said Bulstrode, in his emotion adding the unusual word 'sir'. "I was cracking it in the stable yard, and it cracked. So I took it to the mender's."

Colonel Wyvern pointed an awful finger at the door.

"Get out, you foul blot," he said. "I'll talk to you later." Seating himself at his desk, as he always did when he wished to think, he drummed his fingers on the arm of the chair. "I'll have to borrow young Towcester's," he said at length, clicking his tongue in evident annoyance. "Infernally awkward, calling on a fellow you're going to horsewhip and having to ask him for the loan of his horsewhip to do it with. Still, there it is," said Colonel Wyvern philosophically. "That's how it goes."

He was a man who could always adjust himself to circumstances.

17

LUNCH AT Towcester Abbey had been a much more agreeable function than lunch at Wyvern Hall, on a different plane altogether. Where Colonel Wyvern had been compelled to cope with the distressing efforts of a pigtailed incompetent apparently under the impression that she was catering for a covey of buzzards in the Gobi Desert, the revelers at the Abbey had been ministered to by an expert. Earlier in this chronicle passing reference was made to the virtuosity of Bill's O.C. Kitchen, the richly gifted Mrs. Piggott, and in dishing up the midday meal today she had in no way fallen short of her high ideals. Three of the four celebrants at the table had found the food melting in their mouths and had downed it with cries of appreciation.

The exception was the host himself, in whose mouth it had turned to ashes. What with one thing and another . . . the instability of his financial affairs, last night's burglarious interlude and its devastating sequel, the shattering of his romance . . . Bill was far from being the gayest of all that gay company. In happier days he had sometimes read novels in which characters were described as pushing their food away untasted, and had often wondered, being a man who enjoyed getting his calories, how they could have brought themselves to do it. But at the meal which was now coming to an end he had been doing it himself, and, as we say, what little nourishment he had contrived to take had turned to ashes in his mouth. He had filled in the time mostly by crumbling bread, staring wildly and jumping like a galvanized frog when spoken to. A cat in a strange alley would have been more at its ease.

Nor had the conversation at the table done anything to restore his equanimity. Mrs. Spottsworth would keep bringing it round to the subject of Captain Biggar, regretting his absence from the feast, and each mention of the White Hunter's name had had a seismic effect on his sensitive conscience. She did it again now.

"Captain Biggar was telling me—," she began, and Rory uttered one of his jolly laughs.

"He was, was he?" he said in his tactful way. "Well, I hope you didn't believe him."

Mrs. Spottsworth stiffened. She sensed a slur on the man she loved.

"I beg your pardon?"

"Awful liar, that chap."

"Why do you say that, Sir Roderick?"

"I was thinking of those yarns of his at dinner last night."

"They were perfectly true."

"Not a bit of it," said Rory buoyantly. "Don't you let him pull your leg, my dear Mrs. Dogsbody. All these fellows from out East are the most frightful liars. It's due, I believe, to the ultra-violet rays of the sun in those parts. They go out without their solar topees, and it does something to them. I have this from an authoritative source. One of them used to come to headquarters a lot when I was in the Guns, Pistols and Ammunition, and we became matey. And one night, when in his cups, he warned me not to swallow a single word any of them said. 'Look at me,' he reasoned. 'Did you ever hear a chap tell the ghastly lies I do? Why, I haven't spoken the truth since I was so high. And so low are the standards east of Suez that my nickname out there is George Washington.' "

"Coffee is served in the living room, m'lord," said Jeeves, intervening in his polished way and averting what promised, judging from the manner in which Mrs. Spottsworth's fine eyes had begun to glitter, to develop into an ugly brawl.

Following his guests into the living room, Bill was conscious of a growing sense of uneasiness and alarm. He had not supposed that anything could have increased his mental discomfort, but Rory's words had done so a hundredfold. As he lowered himself into a chair, accepted a cup of coffee and spilled it over his trousers, one more vulture had added itself to the little group already gnawing at his bosom. For the first time he had begun to question the veracity of Captain Biggar's story of the pendant, and at the thought of what he had let himself in for if that story had not been true his imagination boggled.

Dimly he was aware that Rory and Monica had collected all the morning papers and were sitting surrounded by them, their faces grave and tense. The sands were running out. Less than an hour from now the Derby would be run, and soon, if ever, they must decide how their wagers were to be placed.

"*Racing News,*" said Monica, calling the meeting to order. "What does the *Racing News* say, Rory?"

Rory studied that sheet in his slow, thorough way.

"Lot of stuff about the Guineas form. Perfect rot, all of it. You can't go by the Guineas. Too many unknowns. If you want my considered opinion, there's nothing in sight to beat Taj Mahal. The Aga has the mares, and that's what counts. The sires don't begin to matter compared with the mares."

"I'm glad to hear you pay this belated tribute to my sex."

"Yes, I think for my two quid it's Taj Mahal on the nose."

"That settles Taj Mahal for me. Whenever you bet on them, they start running backwards. Remember that dog race."

Rory was obliged to yield this point.

"I admit my nominee let the side down on that occasion," he said. "But when a real rabbit gets loose on a dog track, it's bound to cause a bit of confusion. Taj Mahal gets my two o'goblins."

"I thought your money was going on Oratory."

"Oratory is my outsider bet, ten bob each way."

"Well, here's another hunch for you. Escalator."

"Escalator?"

"Wasn't H's the first store to have escalators?"

"By Jove, yes. We've got the cup, you know. Our safety landing device has enabled us to clip three seconds off Selfridge's record. The Selfridge boys are livid. I must look into this Escalator matter."

"Lester Piggott is riding it."

"That settles it. L. Piggott is the name of the chap stationed in the Trunks, Bags and Suitcases, as fine a man as ever punched a time clock. I admit his L. stands for Lancelot, but that's a good enough omen for me."

Monica looked across at Mrs. Spottsworth.

"I suppose you think we're crazy, Rosalinda?"

Mrs. Spottsworth smiled indulgently.

"Of course not, dear. This brings back the old days with Mr. Bessemer. Racing was all he ever thought of. We spent our honeymoon at Sheepshead Bay. It's the Derby, is it, you're so interested in?"

"Just our silly little annual flutter. We don't bet high. Can't afford to. We of Harrod's have to watch the pennies."

"Rigidly," said Rory. He chuckled amusedly, struck by a whimsical idea. "I was just thinking," he went on in explanation of his mirth, "that the smart thing for me to have done would have been to stick to that pendant of yours I picked up last night and go off to London with it and pawn it, thus raising a bit of . . . Yes, old man?"

Bill swallowed.

"I didn't speak."

"I thought you did."

"No, just a hiccup."

"To which," Rory conceded, "you were fully entitled. If a man can't hiccup in his own house, in whose house can he hiccup? Well, summing up, Taj Mahal two quid. Escalator ten bob each way. I'll go and send off my wire." He paused. "But wait. Is it not rash to commit oneself without consulting Jeeves?"

"Why Jeeves?"

"My dear Moke, what that man doesn't know about form isn't worth knowing. You should have heard him yesterday when I asked him if had any views on the respective contestants in England's premier classic race. He just stood there rattling off horses and times and records as if he were the Archbishop of Canterbury."

Monica was impressed.

"I didn't konw he was as hot as that. Are there no limits to the powers of this wonder man? We'll go and confer with him at once."

They hurried out, and Bill, having cleared his throat, said, "Er."

Mrs. Spottsworth looked up enquiringly.

"Er, Rosie. That pendant of yours. The one Rory was speaking of."

"Yes?"

"I was admiring it last night."

"It's nice, isn't it?"

"Beautiful. You didn't have it at Cannes, did you?"

"No. I hadn't met Mr. Spottsworth then. It was a present from him."

Bill leaped. His worst suspicions had been confirmed.

"A present from Mr. Sp——?" he gasped.

Mrs. Spottsworth laughed.

"It's too funny," she said. "I was talking to Captain Biggar about it last night, and I told him one of my husbands gave it to me, but I couldn't remember which. It was Mr. Spottsworth, of course. So silly of me to have forgotten."

Bill gulped.

"Are you sure?"

"Oh, quite."

"It . . . It wasn't given to you by some fellow on one of those hunting expeditions . . . as a . . . as a sort of memento?"

Mrs. Spottsworth stared.

"What *do* you mean?"

"Well, I thought . . . fellow grateful for kindness . . . saying good-bye . . . might have said Won't you accept this as a little memento . . . and all that sort of thing."

The suggestion plainly offended Mrs. Spottsworth.

"Do you imagine that I accept diamond pendants from 'fellows,' as you call them?"

"Well, I—"

"I wouldn't dream of such a thing. Mr. Spottsworth bought that pendant when we were in Bombay. I can remember it as if it were yesterday. A funny little shop with a very fat Chinese behind the counter, and Mr. Spottsworth would insist on trying to speak Chinese. And just as he was bargaining, there was an earthquake. Not a bad one, but everything was all red dust for about ten minutes, and when it cleared, Mr. Spottsworth said, 'Let's get out of here!' and paid what the man was asking and grabbed the pendant and we raced out and never stopped running till we had got back to the hotel."

A dull despair had Bill in its grip. He heaved himself painfully to his feet.

"I wonder if you would excuse me," he said. "I have to see Jeeves about something."

"Well, ring for Jeeves."

Bill shook his head.

"No, I think, if you don't mind, I'll go and see him in his pantry."

It had occurred to him that in Jeeves's pantry there would be a drop of port, and a drop of port or some similar restorative was what his stricken soul craved.

18

WHEN RORY and Monica entered Jeeves's pantry, they found its proprietor reading a letter. His fine face, always grave, seemed a little graver than usual, as if the letter's contents had disturbed him.

"Sorry to interrupt you, Jeeves," said Monica.

"Not at all, m'lady."

"Finish your reading."

"I had already done so, m'lady. A communication from Mr. Wooster."

"Oh?" said Rory. "Bertie Wooster, eh? How is the old bounder? Robust?"

"Mr. Wooster says nothing to indicate the contrary, sir."

"Good. Rosy cheeks, eh? Eating his spinach, no doubt? Capital. Couldn't be better. Still, be that as it may," said Rory, "what do you think of Taj Mahal for this afternoon's beano at Epsom Downs? I thought of slapping my two quid on its nose, with your approval."

"And Moke the Second," said Monica. "That's my fancy."

Jeeves considered.

"I see no objection to a small wager on the animal you have named, sir, nor on yours, m'lady. One must bear in mind, however, that the Derby is always an extremely open race."

Don't I know it!"

"It would be advisable, therefore, if the funds are sufficient, to endeavor to save your stake by means of a bet each way on some other horse."

"Rory thought of Escalator. I'm hesitating."

Jeeves coughed.

"Has your ladyship considered the Irish horse, Ballymore?"

"Oh, Jeeves, for heaven's sake. None of the nibs even mention it. No, not Ballymore, Jeeves. I'll have to think of something."

"Very good, m'lady. Would there be anything further?"

"Yes," said Rory. "Now that we're all here together, cheek by jowl as it were, a word from our sponsor on a personal matter, Jeeves. What was all that that Mrs. Dogsbody was saying at lunch about you and her being out on the tiles last night?"

"Sir?"

"Weren't you in the room when she was talking about it?"

"No, m'lady."

"She said you bowled off together in the small hours to the ruined chapel."

"Ah, yes, m'lady. I apprehend Sir Roderick's meaning now. Mrs. Spottsworth did desire me to escort her to the ruined chapel last night. She was hoping to see the wraith of Lady Agatha, she informed me."

"Any luck?"

"No, m'lady."

"She says Bill saw the old girl."

"Yes, m'lady."

Rory uttered the gratified exclamation of one who has solved a mystery.

"So that's why Bill's looking like a piece of cheese today. It must have scared him stiff."

"I believe Lord Towcester was somewhat moved by the experience, Sir Roderick. But I fancy that if, as you say, there is a resemblance between his lordship and a portion of cheese, it is occasioned more by the circumstance of his lordship's matrimonial plans having been cancelled than by any manifestation from the spirit world."

Monica squeaked excitedly.

"You don't mean Bill's engagement is off?"

"That is what I was endeavoring to convey, m'lady. Miss Wyvern handed me the ring in person, to return to his lordship. 'Am I to infer, miss,' I ventured to enquire, 'that there is a symbolical significance attached to this gesture?' and Miss Wyvern replied in the affirmative."

"Well, I'll be blowed. Poor old Bill!"

"Yes, m'lady."

"The heart bleeds."

"Yes, Sir Roderick."

It was at this moment that Bill came charging in. Seeing his sister and her husband, he stopped.

"Oh, hullo, Rory," he said. "Hullo, Moke. I'd forgotten you were here."

Rory advanced with outstretched hand. The dullest eye could have seen that he was registering compassion. He clasped Bill's right hand in his own, and with his left hand kneaded Bill's shoulder. A man, he knew, wants sympathy at a time like this. It is in such a crisis in his affairs that he thanks heaven that he has an understanding brother-in-law, a brother-in-law who knows how to give a pep talk.

"We are not only here, old man," he said, "but we have just heard from Jeeves a bit of news that has frozen our blood. He says the girl Jill has returned you to store. Correct? I see it is. Too bad, too bad. But don't let it get you down, boy. You must . . . how would you put it, Jeeves?"

"Stiffen the sinews, summon up the blood, Sir Roderick."

"Precisely. You want to take the big, broad, spacious view, Bill. You are a fiancée short, let's face it, and your immediate reaction is, no doubt, a disposition to rend the garments and scatter ashes on the head. But you've got to look at these things from every angle, Bill, old man. Remember what Shakespeare said . . . 'A woman is only a woman, but a good cigar is a smoke.' "

Jeeves winced.

"Kipling, Sir Roderick."

"And here's another profound truth. I don't know who said this one. All cats are gray in the dark."

Monica spoke. Her lips, as she listened, had been compressed. There was a strange light in her eyes.

"Splendid. Go on."

Rory stopped kneading Bill's shoulder and patted it.

"At the moment," he resumed, "you are reeling from the shock, and very naturally, too. You feel you've lost something valuable, and of course I suppose one might say you have, for Jill's a nice enough kid, no disputing that. But don't be too depressed about it. Look for the silver lining, whenever clouds appear in the blue, as I have frequently sung in my bath and you, I imagine, in yours. Don't forget you're back in circulation again. Personally, I think it's an extremely nice slice of luck for you that this has happened. A bachelor's life is the only happy one, old man. When it comes to love, there's a lot to be said for the 'à la carte' as opposed to the 'table d'hôte.' "

"Jeeves," said Monica.

"M'lady?"

"What was the name of the woman who drove a spike into her husband's head? It's in the Bible somewhere."

"I fancy your ladyship is thinking of the story of Jael. But she and the gentleman into whose head she drove the spike were not married, merely good friends."

"Still, her ideas were basically sound."

"It was generally considered so in her circle of acquaintance, m'lady."

"Have you a medium-sized spike, Jeeves? No? I must look in at the ironmonger's," said Monica. "Good-bye, Table d'hôte."

She walked out, and Rory watched her go, concerned. His was not a very quick mind, but he seemed to sense something wrong.

"I say! She's miffed. Eh, Jeeves?"

"I received that impression, Sir Roderick."

"Dash it all, I was only saying that stuff about marriage to cheer you up, Bill. Jeeves, where can I get some flowers? And don't say, 'At the flower shop,' because I simply can't sweat all the way to the town. Would there be flowers in the garden?"

"In some profusion, Sir Roderick."

"I'll go and pluck her a bouquet. That's a thing you'll find it useful to remember, Bill, if you ever get married, not that you're likely to, of course, the way things are shaping. Always remember that when the gentler sex get miffed, flowers will bring them around every time."

The door closed. Jeeves turned to Bill.

"Your lordship wished to see me about something?" he said courteously.

Bill passed a hand over his throbbing brow.

"Jeeves," he said, "I hardly know how to begin. Have you an aspirin about you?"

"Certainly, m'lord. I have just been taking one myself."

He produced a small tin box, and held it out.

"Thank you, Jeeves. Don't slam the lid."

"No, m'lord."

"And now," said Bill, "to tell you all."

Jeeves listened with gratifyingly close attention while he poured out his tale. There was no need for Bill at its conclusion to ask him if he had got the gist. It was plain from the gravity of his, "Most disturbing, m'lord," that he had got it nicely. Jeeves always got gists.

"If ever a man was in the soup," said Bill, summing up, "I am. I have been played up and made a sucker of. What are those things people get used as, Jeeves?"

"Catspaws, m'lord?"

"That's right. Catspaws. This blighted Biggar has used me as a catspaw. He told me the tale. Like an ass, I believed him. I pinched the pendant, swallowing that whole story of his about it practically belonging to him and he only wanted to borrow it for a few hours, and off he went to London with it, and I don't suppose we shall ever see him again. Do you?"

"It would appear improbable, m'lord."

"One of those remote contingencies, what?"

"Extremely remote, I fear, m'lord."

"You wouldn't care to kick me, Jeeves?"

"No, m'lord."

"I've been trying to kick myself, but it's so dashed difficult if you aren't a contortionist. All that stuff about stingahs and long bars and the chap Sycamore! We ought to have seen through it in an instant."

"We ought, indeed, m'lord."

"I suppose that when a man has a face as red as that, one tends to feel that he must be telling the truth."

"Very possibly, m'lord."

"And his eyes were so bright and blue. Well, there it is," said Bill. "Whether it was the red face or the blue eyes that did it, one cannot say, but the fact remains that as a result of the general color scheme I allowed myself to be used as a catspaw and pinched an expensive pendant which the hellhound Biggar has gone off to London with, thus rendering myself liable to an extended sojourn in the cooler . . . unless—"

"M'lord?"

"I was going to say, 'Unless you have something to suggest.' Silly of me," said Bill, with a hollow laugh. "How could you possibly have anything to suggest?"

"I have, m'lord."

Bill stared.

"You wouldn't try to be funny at a time like this, Jeeves?"

"Certainly not, m'lord."

"You really have a life belt to throw me before the gumbo closes over my head?"

"Yes, m'lord. In the first place, I would point out to your lordship that there is little or no likelihood of your lordship becoming suspect of the theft of Mrs. Spottsworth's ornament. It has disappeared. Captain Biggar has disappeared. The authorities will put two and two together, m'lord, and automatically credit him with the crime."

"Something in that."

"It would seem impossible, m'lord, for them to fall into any other train of thought."

Bill brightened a little, but only a little.

"Well, that's all to the good, I agree, but it doesn't let me out. You've overlooked something, Jeeves."

"M'lord?"

"The honor of the Towcesters. That is the snag we come up against. I can't go through life feeling that under my own roof—leaky, but still a roof—I have swiped a valuable pendant from a guest filled to the eyebrows with my salt.

How am I to reimburse La Spottsworth? That is the problem to which we have to bend our brains."

"I was about to touch on that point, m'lord. Your lordship will recall that in speaking of suspicion falling upon Captain Biggar I said, 'In the first place.' In the second place, I was about to add, restitution can readily be made to Mrs. Spottsworth, possibly in the form of notes to the correct amount dispatched anonymously to her address, if the lady can be persuaded to purchase Towcester Abbey."

"Great Scott, Jeeves!"

"M'lord?"

"The reason I used the expression 'Great Scott!' "said Bill, his emotion still causing him to quiver from head to foot, "was that in the rush and swirl of recent events I had absolutely forgotten all about selling the house. Of course! That would fix up everything, wouldn't it?"

"Unquestionably, m'lord. Even a sale at a sacrifice price would enable your lordship to do—"

"The square thing?"

"Precisely, m'lord. I may add that while on our way to the ruined chapel last night, Mrs. Spottsworth spoke in high terms of the charms of Towcester Abbey and was equally cordial in her remarks as we were returning. All in all, m'lord, I would say that the prospects were distinctly favorable, and if I might offer the suggestion, I think that your lordship should now withdraw to the library and obtain material for what is termed a sales talk by skimming through the advertisements in *Country Life,* in which, as your lordship is possibly aware, virtually every large house which has been refused as a gift by the National Trust is offered for sale, The language is extremely persuasive."

"Yes, I know the sort of thing. 'This lordly demesne, with its avenues of historic oaks, its tumbling streams alive with trout and tench, its breath-taking vistas lined with flowering shrubs . . .' Yes, I'll bone up."

"It might possibly assist your lordship if I were to bring a small bottle of champagne to the library."

"You think of everything, Jeeves."

"Your lordship is too kind."

"Half a bot should do the trick."

"I think so, m'lord, if adequately iced."

It was some minutes later, as Jeeves was passing through the living-room with the brain-restorer on a small tray, that Jill came in through the French window.

19

IT IS a characteristic of women as a sex, and one that does credit to their gentle hearts, that—unless they are gangster's molls or something of that kind—they shrink from the thought of violence. Even when love is dead, they dislike the idea of the man to whom they were once betrothed receiving a series of juicy ones from a horsewhip in the competent hands of an elderly, but still muscular, Chief Constable of a county. When they hear such a Chief Constable sketching out plans for an operation of this nature, their instinct is to hurry to the prospective victim's residence and warn him of his peril by outlining the shape of things to come.

It was to apprise Bill of her father's hopes and dreams that Jill had come to Towcester Abbey, and not being on speaking terms with her former fiancé, she had been wondering a little how the information she was bringing could be conveyed to him. The sight of Jeeves cleared up this point. A few words of explanation to Jeeves, coupled with the suggestion that he should advise Bill to lie low till the old gentleman had blown over, would accomplish what she had in mind, and she could then go home again, her duty done and the whole unpleasant affair disposed of.

"Oh, Jeeves," she said.

Jeeves had turned, and was regarding her with respectful benevolence.

"Good afternoon, miss. You will find his lordship in the library."

Jill stiffened haughtily. There was not much of her, but what there was she drew to its full height.

"No, I won't," she replied in a voice straight from the frigidaire. "because I'm jolly well not going there. I haven't the slightest wish to speak to Lord Towcester. I want you to give him a message."

"Very good, miss."

"Tell him my father is coming here to borrow his horsewhip to horsewhip him with."

"Miss?"

"It's quite simple, isn't it? You know my father?"

"Yes, miss."

"And you know what a horsewhip is?"

"Yes, miss."

"Well, tell Lord Towcester the combination is on its way over."

"And if his lordship should express curiosity as to the reason for Colonel Wyvern's annoyance?"

"You may say it's because I told him about what happened last night. Or this morning, to be absolutely accurate. At two o'clock this morning. He'll understand."

"At two o'clock this morning, miss? That would have been at about the hour when I was escorting Mrs. Spottsworth to the ruined chapel. The lady had expressed a wish to establish contact with the apparition of Lady Agatha. The wife of Sir Caradoc the Crusader, miss, who did well, I believe, at the Battle of Joppa. She is reputed to haunt the ruined chapel."

Jill collapsed into a chair. A sudden wild hope, surging through the cracks in her broken heart, had shaken her from stem to stern, making her feel boneless.

"What . . . what did you say?"

Jeeves was a kindly man, and not only a kindly man but a man who could open a bottle of champagne as quick as a flash. It was in something of the spirit of the Sir Philip Sidney who gave the water to the stretcher case that he now whisked the cork from the bottle he was carrying. Jill's need, he felt, was greater than Bill's.

"Permit me, miss."

Jill drank gratefully. Her eyes had widened, and the color was returning to her face.

"Jeeves, this is a matter of life and death," she said. "At two o'clock this morning I saw Lord Towcester coming out of Mrs. Spottsworth's room looking perfectly frightful in mauve pajamas. Are you telling me that Mrs. Spottsworth was not there?"

"Precisely, miss. She was with me in the ruined chapel, holding me spellbound with her account of recent investigations of the Society of Psychical Research."

"Then what was Lord Towcester doing in her room?"

"Purloining the lady's pendant, miss."

It was unfortunate that as he said these words Jill should have been taking a sip of champagne, for she choked. And as her companion would have considered it a liberty to slap her on the back, it was some moments before she was able to speak.

"Purloining Mrs. Spottsworths's pendant?"

"Yes, miss. It is a long and somewhat intricate story, but if you would care for me to run through the salient points, I should be delighted to do so. Would it interest you to hear the inside history of his lordship's recent activities, culminating, as I have indicated, in the abstracting of Mrs. Spottsworth's ornament?"

Jill drew in her breath with a hiss.

"Yes, Jeeves, it would."

"Very good, miss. Then must I speak of one who loved not wisely but too well, of one whose subdued eyes, albeit unused to the melting mood, drop tears as fast as the Arabian trees their medicinal gum."

"Jeeves!"

"Miss?"

"What on earth are you talking about?"

Jeeves looked a little hurt.

"I was endeavoring to explain that it was for love of you, miss, that his lordship became a Silver Ring bookmaker."

"A what?"

"Having plighted his troth to you, miss, his lordship felt—rightly, in my opinion—that in order to support a wife he would require a considerably larger income than he had been enjoying up to that moment. After weighing and rejecting the claims of other professions, he decided to embark on the career of a bookmaker in the Silver Ring, trading under the name of Honest Patch Perkins. I officiated as his lordship's clerk. We wore false mustaches."

Jill opened her mouth, then, as if feeling that any form of speech would be inadequate, closed it again.

"For a time the venture paid very handsomely. In three days at Doncaster we were so fortunate as to amass no less a sum than four hundred and twenty pounds, and it was in optimistic mood that we proceeded to Epsom for the Oaks. But disaster was lurking in wait for his lordship. To use the metaphor that the tide turned would be inaccurate. What smote his lordship was not so much the tide as a single tidal wave. Captain Biggar, miss. He won a double at his lordship's expense—five pounds on Lucy Glitters at a hundred to six, all to come on Whistler's Mother, S.P."

Jill spoke faintly.

"What was the S.P.?"

"I deeply regret to say, miss, thirty-three to one. And as he had rashly refused to lay the wager off, this cataclysm left his lordship in the unfortunate position of owing Captain Biggar in excess of three thousand pounds, with no assets with which to meet his obligations."

"Golly!"

"Yes, miss. His lordship was compelled to make a somewhat hurried departure from the course, followed by Captain Biggar, shouting 'Welsher!' but when we were able to shake off our pursuer's challenge some ten miles from the Abbey, we were hoping that the episode was concluded and that to Captain Biggar his lordship would remain merely a vague, unidentified figure in a false mustache. But it was not to be, miss. The Captain tracked his lordship here, penetrated his incognito and demanded an immediate settlement."

"But Bill had no money."

"Precisely, miss. His lordship did not omit to stress that point. And it was then that Captain Biggar proposed that his lordship should secure possession of Mrs. Spottsworth's pendant, asserting, when met with a *nolle prosequi* on his lordship's part, that the object in question had been given by him to the lady some years ago, so that he was morally entitled to borrow it. The story, on reflection, seems somewhat thin, but it was told with so great a wealth of corroborative detail that it convinced us at the time, and his lordship, who had been vowing that he would ne'er consent, consented. Do I make myself clear, miss?"

"Quite clear. You don't mind my head swimming?"

"Not at all, miss. The question then arose of how the operation was to be carried through, and eventually it was arranged that I should lure Mrs. Spottsworth from her room on the pretext that Lady Agatha had been seen in the ruined chapel, and during her absence his lordship should enter and obtain the trinket. This ruse proved successful. The pendant was duly handed to Captain Biggar, who has taken it to London with the purpose of pawning it and investing the proceeds on the Irish horse, Ballymore, concerning whose chances he is extremely sanguine. As regards his lordship's mauve pajamas, to which you made a derogatory allusion a short while back, I am hoping to convince his lordship that a quiet blue or a pistachio green—"

But Jill was not interested in the Towcester pajamas and the steps which were being taken to correct their mauveness. She was hammering on the library door.

"Bill! Bill!" she cried, like a woman wailing for her demon lover, and Bill, hearing that voice, came out with the promptitude of a cork extracted by Jeeves from a bottle.

"Oh, Bill!" said Jill, flinging herself into his arms. "Jeeves has told me everything!"

Over the head that rested on his chest Bill shot an anxious glance at Jeeves.

"When you say everything, do you mean *everything*?"

"Yes, m'lord. I deemed it advisable."

"I know all about Honest Patch Perkins and your mustache and Captain Biggar and Whistler's Mother and Mrs. Spottsworth and the pendant," said Jill, nestling closely.

It seemed so odd to Bill that a girl who knew all this should be nestling closely that he was obliged to release her for a moment and step across and take a sip of champagne.

"And you really mean," he said, returning and folding her in his embrace once more, "that you don't recoil from me in horror?"

"Of course I don't recoil from you in horror. Do I look as if I were recoiling from you in horror?"

"Well, no," said Bill, having considered this. He kissed her lips, her forehead, her ears and the top of her head. "But the trouble is that you might just as well recoil from me in horror, because I don't see how the dickens we're ever going to get married. I haven't a bean, and I've somehow got to raise a small fortune to pay Mrs. Spottsworth for her pendant. *Noblesse oblige,* if you follow my drift. So if I don't sell her the house—"

"Of course you'll sell her the house."

"Shall I? I wonder—I'll certainly try. Where on earth she's disappeared to? She was in here when I came through into the library just now. I wish she'd show up. I'm all full of that *Country Life* stuff, and if she doesn't come soon, it will evaporate."

"Excuse me, m'lord," said Jeeves, who during the recent exchanges had withdrawn discreetly to the French window. "Mrs. Spottsworth and her ladyship are at this moment crossing the lawn."

With a courteous gesture he stepped to one side, and Mrs. Spottsworth entered, followed by Monica.

"Jill!" cried Monica, halting, amazed. "Good heavens!"

"Oh, it's all right," said Jill. "There's been a change in the situation. Sweethearts still."

"Well, that's fine. I've been showing Rosalinda round the place—"

"—with its avenues of historic oaks, its tumbling streams alive with trout and tench, and its breath-taking vistas lined with flowering shrubs . . . How did you like it?" said Bill.

Mrs. Spottsworth clasped her hands and closed her eyes in an ecstasy.

"It's wonderful, wonderful!" she said. "I can't understand how you can bring yourself to part with it, Billiken."

Bill gulped.

"Am I going to part with it?"

"You certainly are," said Mrs. Spottsworth emphatically, "if I have anything to say about it. This is the house of my dreams. How much do you want for it—lock, stock and barrel?"

"You've taken my breath away."

"Well, that's me. I never could endure beating about the bush. If I want a thing, I say so and write a note. I'll tell you what let's do. Suppose I pay you a deposit of two thousand, and we can decide on the purchase price later?"

"You couldn't make it three thousand?"

"Sure." Mrs. Spottsworth unscrewed the top of her fountain pen and having unscrewed it, paused. "There's just one thing, though, before I sign on the dotted line. This place isn't damp, is it?"

"*Damp*?" said Monica. "Why, of course not."

"You're sure?"

"Dry as a bone."

"Well, that's swell. Damp is death to me. Fibrositis *and* sciatica."

Rory came in through the French window, laden with roses.

"A nosegay for you, Moke, old girl, with comps. of R. Carmoyle," he said, pressing the blooms into Monica's hands. "I say, Bill, it's starting to rain."

"What of it?"

"What *of* it?" echoed Rory, surprised. "My dear old boy, you know what happens in this house when it rains. Water through the roof, water through the walls, water, water everywhere. I was merely about to suggest in a kindly, Boy Scout sort of spirit that you had better put buckets under the upstairs skylight. Very damp house, this," he said, addressing Mrs. Spottsworth in his genial, confidential way. "So near the river, you know. I often say that whereas in the summer months the river is at the bottom of the garden, in the winter months the garden is at the bottom of the—"

"Excuse me, m'lady," said the housemaid Ellen, appearing in the doorway. "Could I speak to Mrs. Spottsworth, m'lady?"

Mrs. Spottsworth, who had been staring, aghast, at Rory, turned, pen in hand. "Yes?"

"Moddom," said Ellen, "your pendant's been pinched."

She had never been a girl for breaking things gently.

With considerable gratification Ellen found herself the center of attraction. All eyes were focussed upon her, and most of them were bulging. Bill's, in particular, struck her as being on the point of leaving their sockets.

"Yes," she proceeded, far too refined to employ the Bulstrode-Trelawny 'Yus,' "I was laying out your clothes for the evening, moddom, and I said to myself that you'd probably be wishing to wear the pendant again tonight, so I ventured to look in the little box, and it wasn't there, moddom. It's been stolen."

Mrs. Spottsworth drew a quick breath. The trinket in question was of little intrinsic worth—it could not, as she had said to Captain Biggar, have cost more than ten thousand dollars—but, as she had also said to Captain Biggar, it had a sentimental value for her. She was about to express her concern in words, but Bill broke in.

"What do you mean, it's been stolen?" he demanded hotly. You could see that the suggestion outraged him. "You probably didn't look properly."

Ellen was respectful, but firm.

"It's gone, m'lord."

"You may have dropped it somewhere, Mrs. Spottsworth," said Jill. "Was the clasp loose?"

"Why, yes," said Mrs. Spottsworth. "The clasp was loose. But I distinctly remember putting it in its case last night."

"Not there now, moddom," said Ellen, rubbing it in.

"Let's go up and have a thorough search," said Monica.

"We will," said Mrs. Spottsworth. "But I'm afraid . . . very much afraid—"

She followed Ellen out of the room. Monica, pausing at the door, eyed Rory balefully for an instant.

"Well, Bill," she said, "so you don't sell the house, after all. And if Big Mouth there hadn't come barging in prattling about water and buckets, that check would have been signed."

She swept out, and Rory looked at Bill, surprised.

"I say, did I drop a brick?"

Bill laughed hackingly.

"If one followed you about for a month, one would have enough bricks to build a house."

"In re this pendant. Anything I can do?"

"Yes, keep out of it."

"I could nip off in the car and fetch some of the local constabulary."

"Keep right out of it." Bill looked at his watch. "The Derby will be starting in a few minutes. Go in there and get the television working."

"Right," said Rory. "But if I'm needed, give me a shout."

He disappeared into the library, and Bill turned to Jeeves, who had once again effaced himself. In times of domestic crisis, Jeeves had the gift, possessed by all good butlers, of creating the illusion that he was not there. He was standing now at the extreme end of the room, looking stuffed.

"Jeeves!"

"M'lord?" said Jeeves, coming to life like a male Galatea.

"Any suggestions?"

"None of practical value, m'lord. But a thought has just occurred which enables me to take a somewhat brighter view of the situation. We were speaking not long since of Captain Biggar as a gentleman who had removed himself permanently from our midst. Does it not seem likely to your lordship that in the event of Ballymore emerging victorious the Captain, finding himself in possession of ample funds, will carry out his original plan of redeeming the pendant, bringing it back and affecting to discover it on the premises?"

Bill chewed his lip.

"You think so?"

"It would be the prudent course for him to pursue, m'lord. Suspicion, as I say, must inevitably rest upon him, and failure to return the ornament would place him in the disagreeable position of becoming a hunted man in hourly danger of being apprehended by the authorities. I am convinced that if Ballymore wins, we shall see Captain Biggar again."

"*If* Ballymore wins."

"Precisely, m'lord."

"Then one's whole future hangs on whether it does."

"That is how matters stand, m'lord."

Jill uttered a passionate cry.

"I'm going to start praying!"

"Yes, do," said Bill. "Pray that Ballymore will run as he has never run before. Pray like billy-o. Pray all over the house. Pray—"

Monica and Mrs. Spottsworth came back.

"Well," said Monica, "it's gone. There's no doubt about that. I've just phoned for the police."

Bill reeled.

"What!"

"Yes, Rosalinda didn't want me to, but I insisted. I told her you wouldn't dream of not doing everything you could to catch the thief."

"You . . . You think the thing's been stolen?"

"It's the only possible explanation."

Mrs. Spottsworth sighed.

"Oh, dear! I really am sorry to have started all this trouble."

"Nonsense, Rosalinda. Bill doesn't mind. All Bill wants is to see the crook caught and bunged into the cooler. Isn't it, Bill?"

"Yes, *sir*!" said Bill.

"For a good long stretch, too, let's hope."

"We musn't be vindictive."

"No," said Mrs. Spottsworth. "You're quite right. Justice, but not vengeance."

"Well, one thing's certain," said Monica. "It's an inside job."

Bill stirred uneasily.

"Oh, do you think so?"

"Yes, and I've got a pretty shrewd idea who the guilty party is."

"Who?"

"Someone who was in a terrible state of nerves this morning."

"Oh?"

"His cup and saucer were rattling like castanets."

"When was this?"

"At breakfast. Do you want me to name names?"

"Go ahead."

"Captain Biggar!"

Mrs. Spottsworth started.

"What!"

"You weren't down, Rosalinda, or I'm sure you would have noticed it, too. He was as nervous as a treeful of elephants."

"Oh, no, no! Captain Biggar? That I can't and won't believe. If Captain Biggar were guilty, I should lose my faith in human nature. And that would be a far worse blow than losing the pendant."

"The pendant is gone, and he's gone. It adds up, don't you think? Oh, well," said Monica, "we shall soon know."

"What makes you so sure of that?"

"Why, the jewel case, of course. The police will take it away and test it for fingerprints. What on earth's the matter, Bill?"

"Nothing's the matter," said Bill, who had leaped some eighteen inches into the air but saw no reason for revealing the sudden agonized thought which had motivated this adagio exhibiton. "Er, Jeeves."

"M'lord?"

"Lady Carmoyle is speaking of Mrs. Spottsworth's jewel case."

"Yes, m'lord?"

"She threw out the interesting suggestion that the miscreant might have forgotten to wear gloves, in which event the bally thing would be covered with his fingerprints. That would be lucky, wouldn't it?"

"Extremely fortunate, m'lord."

"I'll bet he's wishing he hadn't been such an ass."

"Yes, m'lord."

"And that he could wipe them off."

"Yes, m'lord."

"You might go and get the thing, so as to have it ready for the police when they arrive."

"Very good, m'lord."

"Hold it by the edges, Jeeves. You don't want to disturb those fingerprints."

"I will exercise the greatest care, m'lord," said Jeeves, and went out, and almost simultaneously Colonel Wyvern came in through the French window.

At the moment of his entry Jill, knowing that when a man is in a state of extreme agitation there is nothing he needs more than a woman's gentle sympathy, had put her arms round Bill's neck and was kissing him tenderly. The spectacle brought the Colonel to a halt. It confused him. With this sort of thing going on, it was difficult to lead up to the subject of horsewhips.

"Ha, hrr'mph!" he said, and Monica spun round, astounded.

"My goodness!" she said. "You have been quick. It's only five minutes since I phoned."

"Eh?"

"Hullo, father," said Jill. "We were just waiting for you to show up. Have you brought your bloodhounds and magnifying glass?"

"What the dickens are you talking about?"

Monica was perplexed.

"Didn't you come in answer to my phone call, Colonel?"

"You keep talking about a phone call. What phone call? I came to see Lord Towcester on a personal matter. What's all this about a phone call?"

"Mrs. Spottsworth's diamond pendant has been stolen, father."

"What? What? What?"

"This is Mrs. Spottsworth," said Monica. "Colonel Wyvern, Rosalinda, our Chief Constable."

"Charmed," said Colonel Wyvern, bowing gallantly, but an instant later he was the keen, remorseless police officer again. "Had your pendant stolen, eh? Bad show, bad show." He took out a notebook and a pencil. "An inside job, was it?"

"That's what we think."

"Then I'll have to have a list of everybody in the house."

Jill stepped forward, her hands extended.

"Wyvern, Jill," she said. "Slip on the bracelets, officer. I'll come quietly."

"Oh, don't be an ass," said Colonel Wyvern.

Something struck the door gently. It might have been a foot. Bill opened the door, revealing Jeeves. He was carrying the jewel case, a handkerchief at its extreme edges.

"Thank you, m'lord," he said.

He advanced to the table and lowered the case on to it very carefully.

"Here is the case the pendant was in," said Mrs. Spottsworth.

"Good." Colonel Wyvern eyed Jeeves with approval. "Glad to see you were careful about handling it, my man."

"Oh, trust Jeeves for that," said Bill.

"And now," said Colonel Wyvern, "for the names."

As he spoke, the library door burst open, and Rory came dashing out, horror written on his every feature.

21

"I SAY, chaps," said Rory, "the most appalling thing has happened!"

Monica moaned.

"Not something *more*?"

"This is the absolute frozen limit. The Derby is just starting—"

"Rory, the Chief Constable is here."

"—and the television set has gone on the blink. Oh, it's my fault, I suppose. I was trying to get a perfect adjustment, and I must have twiddled the wrong thingummy."

"Rory, this is Colonel Wyvern, the Chief Constable."

"How are you, Chief C.? Do you know anything about television?"

The Colonel drew himself up.

"I do not!"

"You couldn't fix a set?" said Rory wistfully. "Not that there's time, of course. The race will be over. What about the radio?"

"In the corner, Sir Roderick," said Jeeves.

"Oh, thank heaven!" cried Rory, galloping to it. "Come on and give me a hand, Jeeves!"

The Chief Constable spoke coldly.

"Who is this gentleman?"

"Such as he is," said Monica apologetically, "my husband, Sir Roderick Carmoyle."

Colonel Wyvern advanced on Rory as majestically as his lack of inches permitted, and addressed the seat of his trousers, the only portion of him visible as he bent over the radio.

"Sir Roderick, I am conducting an investigation."

"But you'll hold it up to listen to the Derby?"

"When on duty, Sir Roderick, I allow nothing to interfere. I want a list—"

The radio suddenly blaring forth, gave him one.

"... Taj Mahal, Sweet William, Garniture, Moke the Second, Voleur ... Quite an impressive list, isn't it?" said the refined B.B.C. voice of one whose name, one felt instinctively, was Lionel. One could picture him easing the sleeves of his canary-colored pullover. "Oh, and there's Bellwether, he's turning round now and walking back to the gate. . . . They should be off in just a moment. . . . Oo noo, two mo-ah have turned round. One of them is being *very* temperamental. It looks like Simple Simon. No, it's the Irish outsider, Ballymore."

The Chief Constable frowned.

"Really, I must ask—"

"Okay. I'll turn it down," said Rory, and immediately, being Rory, turned it up.

"They're in line now," yelled the radio, like a costermonger calling attention to his blood oranges, "all twenty-six of them. . . . They're OFF. . . . Ballymore is left at the post."

Jill screamed shrilly.

"Oh, *no*!"

"Vaurien," proceeded the radio, now, owing to Rory's ministrations, speaking in an almost inaudible whisper, like an invalid uttering a few last words from a sick bed, "is in front, the Boussac pacemaker." Its voice strengthened a little. "Taj Mahal is just behind. I see Escalator. Escalator's going very strong. I see Sweet William. I see Moke the Second. I see . . ." Here the wasting sickness set in again, and the rest was lost in a sort of mouselike squeak.

The Chief Constable drew a relieved breath.

"Ha! At last! Now then, Lord Towcester. What servants have you here?"

Bill did not answer. Like a mechanical figure he was moving toward the radio, as if drawn by some invisible force.

"There's a cook," said Monica.

"A widow, sir," said Jeeves. "Mary Jane Piggott."

Rory looked round.

"Piggott? Who said Piggott?"

"A housemaid," said Monica, as Jill, like Bill, was drawn toward the radio as if in a trance. "Her name's Ellen. Ellen what, Jeeves?"

"French, m'lady. Ellen Tallulah French."

"The French horse," bellowed the radio, suddenly acquiring a new access of strength, "is still in front, then Moke the Second, Escalator, Taj Mahal . . ."

"What about the gardener?"

"No, not Gardener," said Rory. "You mean Garniture."

". . . Sweet William, Oratory . . . Vaurien's falling back, and Garniture—"

"You see?" said Rory.

"—and Moke the Second moving up."

"That's mine," said Monica, and with a strange, set look on her face began to move toward the radio.

"Looks quite as though Gordon Richards might be going to win the Derby at last. They're down the hill and turning Tattenham Corner, Moke the Second in front, with Gordon up. Only three and a half furlongs to go . . ."

"Yes, sir," said Jeeves, completely unmoved, "there is a gardener, an old man named Percy Wellbeloved."

The radio suddenly broke into a frenzy of excitement.

"Oo! . . . Oo!! . . . There's a horse coming up on the outside. It's coming like an express train. I can't identify . . ."

"Gee, this is exciting, isn't it!" said Mrs. Spottsworth.

She went to the radio. Jeeves alone remained at the Chief Constable's side. Colonel Wyvern was writing laboriously in his notebook.

"It's Ballymore! The horse on the outside is Ballymore. He's challenging the Moke. Hear that crowd roaring 'Come on, Gordon!' "

"Moke . . . The Moke . . . Gordon," wrote Colonel Wyvern.

"Come on, Gordon!" shouted Monica.

The radio was now becoming incoherent.

"It's Ballymore . . . No, it's the Moke . . . No, Ballymore . . . No, the Moke . . . No . . ."

"Make up your mind," advised Rory.

For some moments Colonel Wyvern had been standing motionless, his notebook frozen in his hand. Now a sort of shudder passed through him, and his eyes grew wide and wild. Brandishing his pencil, he leaped toward the radio.

"Come on, Gordon!" he roared, "COME ON, GORDON!!!"

"Come on, Ballymore," said Jeeves with quiet dignity.

Lionel at the B.B.C. had now given up all thoughts of gentlemanly restraint. It was as though a dozen Percys and Ronalds had been puncturing his pullover with pins.

"Photo finish!" he shrieked. "Photo finish! Photo finish! First time in the history of the Derby. Photo finish. Escalator in third place."

Rather sheepishly the Chief Constable turned away and came back to Jeeves.

"The gardener's name you said was what?"

"Percy Wellbeloved, sir."

"Odd name."

"Shropshire, I believe, sir."

"Ah? Percy Wellbeloved. Does that complete the roster of the staff?"

"Yes, sir, except for myself."

Rory came away from the radio, mopping his forehead.

"Well, that Taj Mahal let me down with a bang," he said bitterly. "Why is it one can never pick a winner in this bally race?"

" 'The Moke' didn't suggest a winner to you?" said Monica.

"Eh? No. Why? Why should it?"

"God bless you, Roderick Carmoyle."

Colonel Wyvern was himself again now.

"I would like," he said, in a curt, official voice, "to inspect the scene of the robbery."

"I will take you there," said Mrs. Spottsworth. "Will you come, too, Monica?"

"Yes, yes, of course," said Monica. "Listen in, some of you, will you, and see what that photo shows."

"And I'll send this down to the station," said Colonel Wyvern, picking up the jewel case by one corner, "and find out what it shows."

They went out, and Rory moved to the door of the library.

"I'll go and see if I really have damaged that T.V. set," he said. "All I did was twiddle a thingummy." He stretched himself with a yawn. "Dam dull Derby," he said. "Even if Moke the Second wins, the old girl's only got ten bob on it at eights."

The library door closed behind him.

"Jeeves," said Bill, "I've got to have a drink."

"I will bring it immediately, m'lord."

"No, don't bring it. I'll come to your pantry."

"And I'll come with you," said Jill. "But we must wait to hear that result. Let's hope Ballymore had sense enough to stick out his tongue."

"Ha!" cried Bill.

The radio had begun to speak.

"Hundreds of thousands of pounds hang on what that photograph decides," Lionel was saying in the rather subdued voice of a man recovering from a hangover. He seemed to be a little ashamed of his recent emotion. "The numbers should be going up at any moment. Yes, here it is . . ."

"Come on, Ballymore!" cried Jill.

"Come on, Ballymore!" shouted Bill.

"Come on, Ballymore," said Jeeves reservedly.

"Moke the Second wins," said Lionel. "Hard luck on Ballymore. He ran a wonderful race. If it hadn't been for that bad start, he would have won in a canter. His defeat saves the bookies a tremendous loss. A huge sum was bet on the Irish horse ten minutes before starting time, obviously one of those S.P. jobs which are so . . ."

Dully, with something of the air of a man laying a wreath on the tomb of an old friend, Bill turned the radio off.

"Come on," he said. "After all, there's still champagne."

22

MRS. SPOTTSWORTH came slowly down the stairs. Monica and the Chief Constable were still conducting their examination of the scene of the crime, but she had been unable to endure their society any longer. Both had been speaking freely of Captain Biggar, and the trend of their remarks had been such as to make her feel that knives were being driven through her heart. When a woman loves a man with every fiber of a generous nature, it can never be pleasant for her to hear this man alluded to as a redfaced thug (Monica) and as a scoundrel who can't possibly get away but must inevitably ere long be caught and slapped into the jug (Colonel Wyvern). It was her intention to make for that rustic seat and there sit and think of what might have been.

The rustic seat stood at a junction of two moss-grown paths facing the river which lay—though only, as we have seen, during the summer months—at the bottom of the garden. Flowering bushes masked it from the eye of one approaching, and it was not till she had turned the last corner that Mrs. Spottsworth was able to perceive that it already had an occupant. At the sight of that occupant she stood for a moment transfixed. Then there burst from her lips a cry so like that of a zebu calling to its mate that Captain Biggar, who had been sitting in a deep reverie, staring at a snail, had the momentary illusion that he was back in Africa. He sprang to his feet, and for a long instant they stood there motionless, gazing at each other wide-eyed while the various birds, bees, wasps, gnats and other insects operating in the vicinity went about their business as if nothing at all sensational had happened. The snail, in particular, seemed completely unmoved.

Mrs. Spottsworth did not share its detached aloofness. She was stirred to her depths.

"You!" she cried. "Oh, I knew you would come. They said you wouldn't, but I knew."

Captain Biggar was hanging his head. The man seemed crushed, incapable of movement. A rhinoceros, seeing him now, would have plucked up heart and charged on him without a tremor, feeling that this was going to be easy.

"I couldn't do it," he muttered. "I got to thinking of you and of the chaps at the club, and I couldn't do it."

"The club?"

"The old Anglo-Malay Club in Kuala Lumpur, where men are white and honesty goes for granted. Yes, I thought of the chaps. I thought of Tubby Frobisher. Would I ever be able to look him again in that one good eye of his? And then I thought that you had trusted me because . . . because I was an Englishman. And I said to myself, it isn't only the old Anglo-Malay and Tubby and the Subadar and Doc and Squiffy, Cuthbert Biggar—you're letting down the whole British Empire."

Mrs. Spottsworth choked.

"Did . . . did you take it?"

Captain Biggar threw up his chin and squared his shoulders. He was so nearly himself again, now that he had spoken those brave words, that the rhinoceros, taking a look at him, would have changed its mind and decided to remember an appointment elsewhere.

"I took it, and I brought it back," he said in a firm, resonant voice, producing the pendant from his hip pocket. "The idea was merely to borrow it for the day, as security for a gamble. But I couldn't do it. It might have meant a fortune, but I couldn't do it."

Mrs. Spottsworth bent her head.

"Put it around my neck, Cuthbert," she whispered.

Captain Biggar stared incredulously at her back hair.

"You want me to? You don't mind if I touch you?"

"Put it round my neck," repeated Mrs. Spottsworth.

Reverently the Captain did so, and there was a pause.

"Yes," said the Captain, "I might have made a fortune, and shall I tell you why I wanted a fortune? Don't run away with the idea that I'm a man who values money. Ask any of the chaps out East, and they'll say, 'Give Sahib

Biggar his .505 Gibbs, his eland steak of a night, let him breathe God's clean air and turn his face up to God's good sun and he asks nothing more.' But it was imperative that I should lay my hands on a bit of the stuff so that I might feel myself in a position to speak my love. Rosie . . . I heard them calling you that, and I must use that name . . . Rosie, I love you. I loved you from that first moment in Kenya when you stepped out of the car and I said, 'Ah, the memsahib.' All these years I have dreamed of you, and on this very seat last night it was all I could do to keep myself from pouring out my heart. It doesn't matter now. I can speak now because we are parting forever. Soon I shall be wandering out into the sunset . . . alone."

He paused, and Mrs. Spottsworth spoke. There was a certain sharpness in her voice.

"You won't too be wandering out into any old sunset alone," she said. "Jiminy Christmas! What do you want to wander out into sunsets alone for?"

Captain Biggar smiled a faint, sad smile.

"I don't *want* to wander out into sunsets alone, dear lady. It's the code. The code that says a poor man must not propose marriage to a rich woman, for if he does, he loses his self-respect and ceases to play with a straight bat."

"I never heard such nonsense in my life. Who started all the applesauce?"

Captain Biggar stiffened a little.

"I cannot say who started it, but it is the rule that guides the lives of men like Squiffy and Doc and the Subadar and Augustus Frobisher."

Mrs. Spottsworth uttered an exclamation.

"*Augustus* Frobisher? For Pete's sake! I've been thinking all along that there was something familiar about that name Frobisher, and now you say Augustus . . . This friend of yours, this Frobisher. Is he a fellow with a red face?"

"We all have red faces east of Suez."

"And a small, bristly mustache?"

"Small, bristly mustaches, too."

"Does he stammer slightly? Has he a small mole on the left cheek? Is one of his eyes green and the other glass?"

Captain Biggar was amazed.

"Good God! That's Tubby. You've met him?"

"Met him? You bet I've met him. It was only a week before I left the States that I was singing, 'Oh, Perfect Love' at his wedding."

Captain Biggar's eyes widened.

"*Howki wa hoo!*" he exclaimed. "Tubby is married?"

"He certainly is. And do you know who he's married to? Cora Rita Rockmetteller, widow of the late Sigsbee Rockmetteller, the Sardine King, a woman with a darned sight more money than I've got myself. Now you see how much your old code amounts to. When Augustus Frobisher met Cora and heard that she had fifty million smackers hidden away behind the brick in the fireplace, did he wander out into any sunset alone? No, sir! He bought a clean collar and a gardenia for his buttonhole and snapped into it."

Captain Biggar had lowered himself on to the rustic seat and was breathing heavily through the nostrils.

"You have shaken me, Rosie!"

"And you needed shaking, talking all that malarkey. You and your old code!"

"I can't take it in."

"You will, if you sit and think it over for awhile. You stay here and get used to the idea of walking down the aisle with me, and I'll go in and phone the papers that a marriage has been arranged and will shortly take place between Cuthbert . . . have you any other names, my precious lamb?"

"Gervase," said the Captain in a low voice. "And it's Brabazon-Biggar. With a hyphen."

". . . between Cuthbert Gervase Brabazon-Biggar and Rosalinda Bessemer Spottsworth. It's a pity it isn't Sir Cuthbert. Say!" said Mrs. Spottsworth, struck with an idea. "What's wrong with buying you a knighthood? I wonder how much they cost these days. I'll have to ask Sir Roderick. I might be able to get it at Harrod's. Well, good-bye for the moment, my wonder man. Don't go wandering off into any sunsets."

Humming gaily, for her heart was light, Mrs. Spottsworth tripped down the moss-grown path, tripped across the lawn and tripped through the French window into the living room. Jeeves was there. He had left Bill and Jill trying mournfully to console each other in his pantry, and had returned to the living room to collect the coffee cups. At the sight of the pendant encircling Mrs. Spottsworth's neck, no fewer than three hairs of his left eyebrow quivered for an instant, showing how deeply he had been moved by the spectacle.

"You're looking at the pendant, I see," said Mrs. Spottsworth, beaming happily. "I don't wonder you're surprised. Captain Biggar found it just now in the grass by that rustic seat where we were sitting last night."

It would be too much to say that Jeeves stared, but his eyes enlarged the merest fraction, a thing they did only on special occasions.

"Has Captain Biggar returned, madam?"

"He got back a few mintues ago. Oh, Jeeves, do you know the telephone number of the *Times*?"

"No, madam, but I could ascertain."

"I want to announce my engagement to Captain Biggar."

Four hairs of Jeeves's right eyebrow stirred slightly as if a passing breeze had disturbed them.

"Indeed, madam? May I wish you every happiness?"

"Thank you, Jeeves."

"Shall I telephone the *Times*, madam?"

"If you will, and the *Telegraph* and *Mail* and *Express* and . . . the *Daily Express,* do you think?"

"I doubt whether more than a scattered handful of the *Daily Express* public are able to read, madam."

"Perhaps you're right. Just those, then."

"Very good, madam. Might I venture to ask, madam, if you and Captain Biggar will be taking up your residence at the Abbey?"

Mrs. Spottsworth sighed.

"No, Jeeves, I wish I could buy it . . . I love the place . . . but it's damp. This English climate!"

"Our English summers *are* severe."

"And the winters worse."

Jeeves coughed.

"I wonder if I might make a suggestion, madam, which I think should be satisfactory to all parties."

"What's that?"

"Buy the house, madam, take it down stone by stone and ship it to California."

"And put it up there?" Mrs. Spottsworth beamed. "Why, what a brilliant idea!"

"Thank you, madam."

"William Randolph Hearst used to do it, didn't he? I remember visiting at San Simeon once, and there was a whole French Abbey lying on the grass near the gates. I'll do it, Jeeves. You've solved everything. Oh, Lord Towcester," said Mrs. Spottsworth. "Just the man I wanted to see."

Bill had come in with Jill, walking with slow, despondent steps. As he saw the pendant, despondency fell from him like a garment. Unable to speak, he stood pointing a trembling finger.

"It was discovered in the grass adjoining a rustic seat in the garden, m'lord, by Mrs. Spottsworth's *fiancé,* Captain Biggar," said Jeeves.

Bill found speech, though with difficulty.

"Biggar's back?"

"Yes, m'lord."

"And he found the pendant?"

"Yes, m'lord."

"And he's engaged to Mrs. Spottsworth?"

"Yes, m'lord. And Mrs. Spottsworth has decided to purchase the Abbey."

"What!"

"Yes, m'lord."

"I do believe in fairies!" said Bill, and Jill said she did, too.

"Yes, Lord Towcester," said Mrs. Spottsworth, "I'm going to buy the Abbey. I don't care what you're asking for it. I want it, and I'll write you a check the moment I come back from apologizing to that nice Chief Constable. I left him very abruptly just now, and I'm afraid he may be feeling offended. Is he still up in my room, Jeeves?"

"I believe so, madam. He rang for me not long ago to ask if I could provide him with a magnifying glass."

"I'll go and see him," said Mrs. Spottsworth. "I'm taking the Abbey with me to America, Lord Towcester. It was Jeeves's idea."

She went out, and Jill hurled herself into Bill's arms.

"Oh, Bill! Oh, Bill! Oh, Bill!" she cried. "Though I don't know why I'm kissing you," she said. "I ought to be kissing Jeeves. Shall I kiss you, Jeeves?"

"No, miss."

"Just think, Jeeves. You'll have to buy that fish slice after all."

"It will be a pleasure and a privilege, miss."

"Of course, Jeeves," said Bill, "you must never leave us, wherever we go, whatever we do."

Jeeves sighed apologetically.

"I am very sorry, m'lord, but I fear I cannot avail myself of your kindness. Indeed, I fear I am compelled to hand in my notice."

"Oh, Jeeves!"

"With the deepest regret, miss, I need scarcely say. But Mr. Wooster needs me. I received a letter from him this morning."

"Has he left that school of his, then?"

Jeeves sighed again.

"Expelled, m'lord."

"Good heavens!"

"It is all most unfortunate, m'lord. Mr. Wooster was awarded the prize for sock-darning. Two pairs of his socks were actually exhibited on Speech Day. It was then discovered that he had used a crib . . . an old woman whom he smuggled into his study at night."

"Poor old Bertie!"

"Yes, m'lord. I gather from the tone of his communication that the scandal has affected him deeply. I feel that my place is at his side."

Rory came in from the library, looking moody.

"I can't fix it," he said.

"Rory," said Bill, "do you know what's happened?"

"Yes, old boy, I've busted the television set."

"Mrs. Spottsworth is going to marry Captain Biggar, and she's buying the Abbey."

"Oh?" said Rory. His manner was listless. "Well, as I was saying, I can't fix the bally thing, and I don't believe any of the local yokels can, either, so the only thing to do is to go to the fountain head." He went to the telephone. "Give me Sloane one two three four," he said.

Captain Biggar came bustling through the French window, humming a Swahili wedding march.

"Where's my Rosie?" he asked.

"Upstairs," said Bill. "She'll be down in a minute. She's just been telling us the news—congratulations, Captain."

"Thank you, thank you."

"I say," said Rory, the receiver at his ear, "I've just remembered another one. Which is bigger, Captain Biggar or Mrs. Biggar? Mrs. Biggar, because she became Biggar. Ha, ha. Ha, ha, ha! Meanwhile, I'm trying to get—"

His number came through.

"Oh, hullo," he said. "Harrod's?"

Bertie Wooster Sees It Through

Dedication

TO

PETER SCHWED
(Of the firm of Simon and Schuster)

DEAR PETE,

I have rather gone off dedications these last forty years or so. To hell with them about sums up my attitude. Today, when I write a book, it's just a book, with no trimmings.

It was not always so. Back at the turn of the century I and the rest of the boys would as soon have gone out without our spats as allowed a novel of ours to go out practically naked, as you might say. The dedication was the thing on which we spread ourselves. I once planned a book which was to consist entirely of dedications, but abandoned the idea because I could not think of a dedication for it.

We went in for variety in those days. When you opened a novel, you never knew what you were going to get. It might be the curt take-it-or-leave-it dedication:

TO J. SMITH

the somewhat warmer

To My Friend

PERCY BROWN

or one of those cryptic dedications with a bit of poetry shoved in underneath in italics, like

TO F.B.O.

*Stark winds
And sunset over the moors.*

> *Why?*
> *Whither?*
> *Whence?*
> *And the sound of distant drums . . .*

> J. FRED MUGGS
> *Lower-Smattering-on-the-Wissel,*
> *1912*

or possibly, if we were feeling a bit livery, the nasty dedication:

TO THE CRITICS
THESE PEARLS

It was all great fun and kept our pores open and brought the roses to our cheeks, but most authors have given it up. Inevitably a time came when there crept into their minds the question "What is there in this for me?" I know it was so in my case. "What is Wodehouse getting out of this?" I asked myself, and the answer, as far as I could see, was, "Not a ruddy thing."

When the eighteenth-century writer inserted on Page One something like

To

THE MOST NOBLE AND PUISSANT
LORD KNUBBLE OF KNOPP

From

HIS VERY HUMBLE SERVANT
THE AUTHOR

My Lord.
It is with inexpressible admiration for your lordship's transcendent gifts that the poor slob who now addresses your lordship presents to your lordship this trifling work, so unworthy of your lordship's distinguished consideration

he expected to clean up. Lord Knubble was his patron and could be relied on, if given the old oil in liberal doses, to come through with at least a couple of guineas. But where does the modern author get off? He plucks—let us say—P. B. Biffen from the unsung millions and makes him immortal, and what does Biffen do in return? He does nothing. He just stands there. If he is like all the Biffens I know, the author won't get so much as a lunch out of it.

Nevertheless, partly because I know I shall get a very good lunch out of you but principally because you told Jack Goodman that you thought *Bertie Wooster Sees It Through* was better than *War and Peace* I inscribe this book

TO PETER SCHWED
TO MY FRIEND PETER SCHWED

TO P.S.

Half a league
Half a league
Half a league
Onward
With a hey-nonny-nonny
And a hot cha-cha

P. G. WODEHOUSE
Colney Hatch, 1954

1

As I sat in the bath tub, soaping a meditative foot and singing, if I remember correctly, "Pale Hands I Loved Beside The Shalimar," it would be deceiving my public to say that I was feeling boomps-a-daisy. The evening that lay before me promised to be one of those sticky evenings, no good to man or beast. My Aunt Dahlia, writing from her country residence, Brinkley Court down in Worcestershire, had asked me as a personal favor to take some acquaintances of hers out to dinner, a couple of the name of Trotter.

They were, she said, creeps of the first water and would bore the pants off me, but it was imperative that they be given the old oil, because she was in the middle of a very tricky business deal with the male half of the sketch and at such times every little helps. "Don't fail me, my beautiful bountiful Bertie," her letter had concluded, on a note of poignant appeal.

Well, this Dahlia is my good and deserving aunt, not to be confused with Aunt Agatha, the one who kills rats with her teeth and devours her young, so when she says Don't fail me, I don't fail her. But, as I say, I was in no sense looking forward to the binge. The view I took of it was that the curse had come upon me.

It had done so, moreover, at a moment when I was already lowered spiritually by the fact that for the last couple of weeks or so Jeeves had been away on his summer holiday. Round about the beginning of July each year he downs tools, the slacker, and goes off to Bognor Regis for the shrimping, leaving me in much the same position as those poets one used to have to read at school who were always beefing about losing gazelles. For without this righthand man at his side Bertram Wooster becomes a mere shadow of his former self and in no condition to cope with any ruddy Trotters.

Brooding darkly on these Trotters, whoever they might be, I was starting to scour the left elbow and had switched to "Ah, Sweet Mystery of Life," when my reverie was interrupted by the sound of a soft footstep in the bedroom, and I sat up, alert and, as you might say, agog, the soap frozen in my grasp. If feet were stepping softly in my sleeping quarters, it could only mean, I felt, unless of course a burglar had happened to drop in, that the prop of the establishment had returned from his vacation, no doubt looking bronzed and fit.

A quiet cough told me that I had reasoned astutely, and I gave tongue.

"Is that you, Jeeves?"

"Yes, sir."

"Home again, what?"

"Yes, sir."

"Welcome to 3 A Berkeley Mansions, London W.1," I said, feeling like a shepherd when a strayed sheep comes trickling back to the fold. "Did you have a good time?"

"Most agreeable, thank you, sir."

"You must tell me all about it."

"Certainly, sir, at your convenience."

"I'll bet you hold me spellbound. What are you doing in there?"

"A letter has just arrived for you, sir. I was placing it on the dressing table. Will you be dining in, sir?"

"No, out, blast it. A blind date with some slabs of gorgonzola sponsored by Aunt Dahlia. So if you want to go to the club, carry on."

As I have mentioned elsewhere in these memoirs of mine, Jeeves belongs to a rather posh club for butlers and valets called the Junior Ganymede, situated somewhere in Curzon Street, and I knew that after his absence from the metropolis he would be all eagerness to buzz round there and hobnob with the boys, picking up the threads and all that sort of thing. When I've been away for a week or two, my first move is always to make a beeline for the Drones.

"I'll bet you get a rousing welcome from the members, with a hey-nonny-nonny and a hot-cha-cha," I said. "Did I hear you say something about there being a letter for me?"

"Yes, sir. It was delivered a moment ago by special messenger."

"Important, do you think?"

"One can only conjecture, sir."

"Better open it and read contents."

"Very good, sir."

There was a stage wait of about a minute and a half, during which, my moodiness now much lightened, I rendered "Roll Out The Barrel," "I Love a Lassie," and "Every Day I Bring Thee Violets," in the order named. In due season his voice filtered through the woodwork.

"The letter is of considerable length, sir. Perhaps if I were to give you its substance?"

"Do so, Jeeves. All ready at this end."

"It is from a Mr. Percy Gorringe, sir. Omitting extraneous matter and concentrating on essentials, Mr. Gorringe wishes to borrow a thousand pounds from you."

I started sharply, causing the soap to shoot from my hand and fall with a dull thud on the bath mat. With no preliminary warning to soften the shock, his words had momentarily unmanned me. It is not often that one is confronted with ear-biting on so majestic a scale, a fiver till next Wednesday being about the normal tariff.

"You said . . . *what,* Jeeves? A thousand pounds? But who is this hound of hell? I don't know any Gorringes."

"I gather from his communication that you and the gentleman have not met, sir. But he mentions that he is the stepson of a Mr. L. G. Trotter, with whom Mrs. Travers appears to be acquainted."

I nodded. Not much use, of course, as he couldn't see me.

"Yes, he's on solid ground there," I admitted. "Aunt Dahlia does know Trotter. He's the bloke she has asked me to put the nosebag on with tonight. So far, so good. But I don't see that being Trotter's stepson entitles this Gorringe to think he can sit on my lap and help himself to the contents of my wallet. I mean, it isn't a case of 'Any stepson of yours, L. G. Trotter, is a stepson of mine.' Dash it, Jeeves, once start letting yourself be touched by stepsons, and where are you? The word flies round the family circle that you're a good provider, and up roll all the sisters and cousins and aunts and nephews and uncles to stake out their claims, several being injured in the crush. The place becomes a shambles."

"There is much in what you say, sir, but it appears to be not so much a loan as an investment that the gentleman is seeking. He wishes to give you the opportunity of contributing the money to the production of his dramatization of Lady Florence Craye's novel *Spindrift.* "

"Oh, that's it, is it? I see. Yes, one begins to follow the trend of thought."

This Florence Craye is . . . well, I suppose you would call her a sort of step-cousin of mine or cousin once removed or something of that nature. She is Lord Worplesdon's daughter, and old W. in a moment of temporary insanity recently married my Aunt Agatha *en secondes noces,* as I believe the expression is. She is one of those intellectual girls, her bean crammed to bursting point with the little gray cells, and about a year ago, possibly because she was full of the divine fire but more probably because she wanted something to take her mind off Aunt Agatha, she wrote this novel and it was well received by the intelligentsia, who notoriously enjoy the most frightful bilge.

"Did you ever read *Spindrift?* " I asked, retrieving the soap.

"I skimmed through it, sir."

"What did you think of it? Go on, Jeeves, don't be coy. The word begins with an l."

"Well, sir, I would not go so far as to apply to it the adjective which I fancy you have in mind, but it seemed to me a somewhat immature production, lacking in significant form. My personal tastes lie more in the direction of

Dostoyevsky and the great Russians. Nevertheless, the story was not wholly devoid of interest and might quite possibly have its appeal for the theater-going public."

I mused awhile. I was trying to remember something, but couldn't think what. Then I got it.

"But I don't understand this," I said. "I distinctly recall Aunt Dahlia telling me that Florence had told her that some manager had taken the play and was going to put it on. Poor misguided sap, I recollect saying. Well, if that is so, why is Percy dashing about trying to get into people's ribs like this? What does he want a thousand quid for? These are deep waters, Jeeves."

"That is explained in the gentleman's letter, sir. It appears that one of the syndicate financing the venture, who had promsied the sum in question, finds himself unable to fullfill his obligations. This, I believe, frequently happens in the world of the theater."

I mused again, letting the moisture from the sponge slide over the torso. Another point presented itself.

"But why didn't Florence tell Percy to go and have a pop at Stilton Cheesewright? She being engaged to him, I mean. One would have thought that Stilton, linked to her by bonds of love, would have been the people's choice."

"Possibly Mr. Cheesewright has not a thousand pounds at his disposal, sir."

"That's true. I see what you're driving at. Whereas I have, you mean?"

"Precisely, sir."

The situation had clarified somewhat. Now that I had the facts, I could discern that Percy's move had been based on sound principles. When you are trying to raise a thousand quid, the first essential, of course, is to go to someone who has got a thousand quid, and no doubt he had learned from Florence that I was stagnant with the stuff. But where he had made his error was in supposing that I was the king of the mugs and in the habit of scattering vast sums like birdseed to all and sundry.

"Would you back a play, Jeeves?"

"No, sir."

"Nor would I. I meet him with a firm nolle prosequi, I think, don't you, and keep the money in the old oak chest?"

"I would certainly advocate such a move, sir."

"Right. Percy gets the bird. Let him eat cake. And now to a more urgent matter. While I'm dressing, will you be mixing me a strengthening cocktail?"

"Certainly, sir. A martini or one of my specials?"

"The latter."

I spoke in no uncertain voice. It was not merely the fact that I was up against an evening with a couple whom Aunt Dahlia, always a good judge, had described as creeps that influenced this decision on my part. I needed fortifying for another reason.

These last few days, with Jeeves apt to return at any moment, it had been borne in upon me quite a good deal that when the time came for us to stand face to face I should require something pretty authoritative in the way of bracers to nerve me for what would inevitably be a testing encounter, calling for all that I had of determination and the will to win. If I was to emerge from it triumphant, no stone must be left unturned and no avenue unexplored.

You know how it is when two strong men live in close juxtaposition, if juxtaposition is the word I want. Differences arise. Wills clash. Bones of contention pop up and start turning handsprings. No one was more keenly alive than I to the fact that one such bone was scheduled to make its debut the instant I swam into his ken, and mere martinis, I felt, despite their numerous merits, would not be enough to see me through the ordeal that confronted me.

It was in quite fairly tense mood that I dried and clothed the person, and while it would perhaps be too much to say that as I entered the sitting-room some quarter of an hour later I was a-twitter, I was unquestionably conscious of a certain jumpiness. When Jeeves came in with the shaker, I dived at it like a seal going after a slice of fish and drained a quick one, scarcely pausing to say "Skin off your nose."

The effect was magical. That apprehensive feeling left me, to be succeeded by a quiet sense of power. I cannot put it better than by saying that as the fire coursed through my veins, Wooster the timid fawn became in a flash Wooster the man of iron will, ready for anything. What Jeeves inserts in these specials of his I have never ascertained, but their morale-building force is extraordinary. They wake the sleeping tiger in a chap. Well, to give you some idea, I remember once after a single one of them striking the table with clenched fist and telling my Aunt Agatha to stop talking rot. And I'm not sure it wasn't "bally rot."

"One of your best and brightest, Jeeves," I said, refilling the glass. "The weeks among the shrimps have not robbed your hand of its cunning."

He did not reply. Speech seemed to have been wiped from his lips, and I saw, as I had foreseen would happen, that his gaze was riveted on the upper slopes of my mouth. It was a cold, disapproving gaze, such as a fastidious luncher who was not fond of caterpillars might have directed at one which he had discovered in his portion of salad, and I knew that the clash of wills for which I had been bracing myself was about to raise its ugly head.

I spoke suavely but firmly. You can't beat suave firmness on these occasions, and thanks to that life-giving special I was able to be as firmly suave as billy-o. There was no mirror in the sitting-room, but had there been and had I caught a glimpse of myself in it, I have no doubt I should have seen something closely resembling a haughty seigneur of the old regime about to tell the domestic staff just where it got off.

"Something appears to be arresting your attention, Jeeves. Is there a smut on my nose?"

His manner continued frosty. There are moments when he looks just like a governess, one of which was this one.

"No, sir. It is on the upper lip. A dark stain like mulligatawny soup."

I gave a careless nod.

"Ah, yes," I said. "The moustache. That is what you are alluding to, is it not? I grew it while you were away. Rather natty, don't you think?"

"No, sir, I do not."

I moistened my lips with the special, still suave to the gills. I felt strong and masterful.

"You dislike the little thing?"

"Yes, sir."

"You don't feel it gives me a sort of air? A . . . how shall I put it? . . . a kind of diablerie?"

"No, sir."

"You hurt and disappoint me, Jeeves," I said, sipping a couple of sips and getting suaver all the time. "I could understand your attitude if the object under advisement were something bushy and waxed at the ends like a sergeant major's, but it is merely the delicate wisp of vegetation with which David Niven has for years been winning the applause of millions. When you see David Niven on the screen, you don't recoil in horror, do you?"

"No, sir. His moustache is very becoming to Mr. Niven."

"But mine isn't to me?"

"No, sir."

It is at moments like this that a man realizes that the only course for him to pursue, if he is to retain his self-respect, is to unship the velvet hand in the iron glove, or, rather, the other way about. Weakness at such a time is fatal.

There are limits, I mean to say, and sharply defined limits at that, and these limits I felt that he had passed by about a mile and a quarter. I yield to nobody in my respect for Jeeves's judgment in the matter of socks, shoes, shirts, hats and cravats, but I was dashed if I was going to have him muscling in and trying to edit the Wooster face. I finished my special and spoke in a quiet, level voice.

"I am sorry, Jeeves. I had hoped for your sympathy and cooperation, but if you are unable to see your way to sympathizing and cooperating, so be it. Come what may, however, I shall maintain the status quo. It is status quos that people maintain, isn't it? I have been put to considerable trouble and anxiety growing this moustache, and I do not propose to hew it off just because certain prejudiced parties, whom I will not specify, don't know a good thing when they see one. *J'y suis, j'y reste,* Jeeves," I said, becoming a bit Parisian.

Well, after this splendid exhibition of resolution on my part I suppose there was nothing much the chap could have said except "Very good, sir" or something of that sort, but, as it happened, he hadn't time to say even that, for the final word had scarcely left my lips when the front door bell tootled. He shimmered out, and a moment later shimmered in again.

"Mr. Cheesewright," he announced.

And in clumped the massive form of the bird to whom he alluded. The last person I had expected to see, and, for the matter of that, about the last one I wanted to.

2

I DON'T know if you have had the same experience, but I have always found that there are certain blokes whose mere presence tends to make me ill at ease, inducing the nervous laugh, the fiddling with the tie and the embarrassed shuffling of the feet. Sir Roderick Glossop, the eminent looney doctor, until circumstances so arranged themselves that I was enabled to pierce the forbidding exterior and see his better, softer side, was one of these. J. Washburn Stoker, with his habit of kidnaping people on his yacht and generally throwing his weight about like a pirate of the Spanish Main, was another. And a third is this G. D'Arcy (Stilton) Cheesewright. Catch Bertram Wooster *vis-à-vis* with him, and you do not catch him at his best.

Considering that he and I have known each other since, as you might say, we were so high, having been at private school, Eton and Oxford together, we ought, I suppose, to be like Damon and what's-his-name, but we aren't by any means. I generally refer to him in conversation as "that blighter Stilton," while he, I have been informed by usually reliable sources, makes no secret of his surprise and concern that I am still on the right side of the walls of Colney Hatch or some similar institution. When we meet, there is always a certain stiffness and what Jeeves would call an imperfect fusion of soul.

One of the reasons for this is, I think, that Stilton used to be a policeman. He joined the Force on coming down from Oxford with the idea of rising to a position of eminence at Scotland Yard, a thing you find a lot of the fellows you know doing these days. True, he turned in his truncheon and whistle shortly afterwards because his uncle wanted him to take up another walk in life, but these rozzers, even when retired, never quite shake off that "Where were you on the night of June the fifteenth?" manner, and he seldom fails, when we run into another, to make me feel like a rat of the underworld detained for questioning in connection with some recent smash-and-grab raid.

Add the fact that this uncle of his wins his bread as a magistrate at one of the London police courts, and you will understand why I avoid him as much as possible and greatly prefer him elsewhere. The man of sensibility shrinks from being closeted with an ex-bluebottle with magistrate blood in him.

In my demeanor, accordingly, as I rose to greet him, a close observer would have noted more than a touch of that To-what-am-I-indebted-for-the-honor-of-this-visit stuff. I was at a loss to imagine what he was doing invading my privacy like this, and another thing that had me fogged was why, having invaded it, he was standing staring at me in a stern, censorious sort of way, as if the sight of me had got right in amongst him, revolting his finest feelings. I might have been some dreg of society whom he had caught in the act of slipping a couple of ounces of cocaine to some other dreg.

"Ho!" he said, and this alone would have been enough to tell an intelligent bystander, had there been one, that he had spent some time in the ranks of the Force. One of the first things the Big Four teach the young recruit is to say "Ho!" "I thought as much," he went on, knitting the brow. "Swilling cocktails, eh?"

This was the moment when, had conditions been normal, I would no doubt have laughed nervously, fingered the tie and shuffled the feet, but with two of Jeeves's specials under my belt, still exercising their powerful spell, I not only remained intrepid but retorted with considerable spirit, putting him right in his place.

"I fail to understand you, officer," I said coldly. "Correct me if I am wrong, but I believe this is the hour when it is customary for an English gentleman to partake of a short snifter. Will you join me?"

His lip curled. Most unpleasant. These coppers are bad enough when they leave their lips in statu quo.

"No, I won't," he replied, curtly and offensively. "*I* don't want to ruin my constitution. What do you suppose those things are going to do to your eye and your power of control? How can you expect to throw doubles if you persist in stupefying yourself with strong drink? It's heartbreaking."

I saw all. He was thinking of the Darts sweep.

The annual Darts sweep is one of the high spots of life at the Drones Club. It never fails to stir the sporting instincts of the members, causing them to roll up in dense crowds and purchase tickets at ten bob a go, with the result that the sum in the kitty is always colossal. This time my name had been drawn by Stilton, and as Horace Pendlebury-Davenport, last year's winner, had gone and got married and at his wife's suggestion resigned his membership, the thing was pretty generally recognized as a sitter for me, last year's runner-up. "Wooster," the word flew to and fro, "is the deadest of snips. He throws a beautiful dart."

So I suppose it was only natural in a way that, standing, if all went well, to scoop in a matter of fifty-six pounds ten shillings, Stilton should feel that it was his mission in life to see that I kept at the peak of my form. But that didn't make this incessant surveillance of his easier to endure. Ever since he had glanced at his ticket, seen that it bore the name Wooster, and learned that I was a red-hot favorite for the tourney, his attitude towards me had been that of an official at Borstal told off to keep an eye on a more than ordinarily up-and-coming juvenile delinquent. He had a way of looming up beside me at the club, sniffing quickly at my glass and giving me an accusing look, coupled with a sharp whistling intake of the breath, and here he was now doing the same thing in my very home. It was worse than being back in a Little Lord Fauntleroy suit and ringlets and having a keen-eyed nurse always at one's elbow, watching one's every move like a bally hawk.

I was about to say how deeply I resented being tailed up in this manner, when he resumed.

"I have come here tonight to talk seriously to you, Wooster," he said, frowning in a most unpleasant manner. "I am shocked at the casual, frivolous way in which you are treating this Darts tournament. You seem not to be taking the most elementary precautions to ensure victory on the big day. It's the old, old story. Overconfidence. All these fatheads keep telling you you're sure to win, and you suck it down like one of your beastly cocktails. Well, let me tell you you're living in a fool's Paradise. I happened to look in at the Drones this afternoon, and Freddie Widgeon was at the Darts board, stunning all beholders with a performance that took the breath away. His accuracy was sensational."

I waved a hand and tossed the head. In fact, I suppose you might say I bridled. He had wounded my *amour propre*.

"Tchah!" I said, registering scorn.

"Eh?"

"I said 'Tchah!' With ref. to F. Widgeon. I know his form backwards. Flashy, but no staying power. The man will be less than the dust beneath my chariot wheels."

"That's what you think. As I said before, overconfidence. You can take it from me that Freddie is a very dangerous competitor. I happen to know that he has been in strict training for weeks. He's knocked off smoking and has a cold bath every morning. Did you have a cold bath this morning?"

"Certainly not. What do you suppose the hot tap's for?"

"Do you do Swedish exercises before breakfast?"

"I wouldn't dream of such a thing. Leave these excesses to the Swedes, I say."

"No," said Stilton bitterly. "All you do is riot and revel and carouse. I am told that you were at that party of Catsmeat Potter-Pirbright's last night. You probably reeled home at three in the morning, rousing the neighborhood with drunken shouts."

I raised a haughty eyebrow. This police persecution was intolerable. Was I in Russia?

"You would scarcely expect me, constable," I said coldly, "to absent myself from the farewell supper of a boyhood friend who is leaving for Hollywood in a day or two and may be away from civilization for years. Catsmeat would have been pained in his foundations if I had oiled out. And it wasn't three in the morning, it was two-thirty."

"Did you drink anything?"

"The merest sip."

"And smoke?"

"The merest cigar."

"I don't believe you. I'll bet, if the truth was known," said Stilton morosely, intensifying the darkness of his frown, "you lowered yourself to the level of the beasts of the field. I'll bet you whooped it up like a sailor in a Marseilles *bistro*. And from the fact that there is a white tie round your neck and a white waistcoat attached to your foul stomach at this moment I gather that you are planning to be off shortly to some other nameless orgy."

I laughed one of my quiet laughs. The words amused me.

"Orgy, eh? I'm giving dinner to some friends of my Aunt Dahlia's, and she strictly warned me to lay off the old Falernian because my guests are tee-totalers. When the landlord fills the flowing bowl, it will be with lemonade, barley water, or possibly lime juices. So much for your nameless orgies."

This, as I had expected, had a mollifying effect on his acerbity, if acerbity is the word I want. He did not become genial, because he couldn't, but he became as nearly genial as it was in his power to be. He practically smiled.

"Capital," he said. "Capital. Most satisfactory."

"I'm glad you're pleased. Well, good night."

"Teetotalers, eh? Yes, that's excellent. But avoid all rich foods and sauces and be sure to get to bed early. What was that you said?"

"I said good night. You'll be wanting to run along, no doubt."

"I'm not running along." He looked at his watch. "Why the devil are women always late?" he asked peevishly. "She ought to have been here long ago. I've told her over and over again that if there's one thing that makes Uncle Joe furious, it's being kept waiting for his soup."

This introduction of the sex motif puzzled me.

"She?"

"Florence. She is meeting me here. We're dining with my uncle."

"Oh, I see. Well, well. So Florence will be with us ere long, will she? Splendid, splendid, splendid."

I spoke with quite a bit of warmth and animation, trying to infuse a cheery note into the proceedings, and immediately wished I hadn't, because he quivered like a palsy patient and gave me a keen glance, and I saw that we had got on to dangerous ground. A situation of considerable delicacy had been precipitated.

One of the things which make it difficult to bring about a beautiful friendship between G. D'Arcy Cheesewright and self is the fact that not long ago I unfortunately got tangled up in his love life. Incensed by some crack he had made about modern enlightened thought, modern enlightened thought being practically a personal buddy of hers, Florence gave him the swift heave-ho and—much against my will, but she seemed to wish it—became betrothed to me. And this had led Stilton, a man of volcanic passions, to express a desire to tear me limb from limb and dance buck-and-wing dances on my remains. He also spoke of stirring up my face like an omelette and buttering me over the West End of London.

Fortunately before matters could proceed to this awful extreme love resumed work at the old stand, with the result that my nomination was canceled and the peril passed, but he has never really got over the distressing episode. Ever since then the green-eyed monster has always been more or less round and about, ready to snap into action at the drop of the hat, and he has tended to docket me as a snake in the grass that can do with a lot of watching.

So, though disturbed, I was not surprised that he now gave me that keen glance and spoke in a throaty growl, like a Bengal tiger snarling over its breakfast coolie.

"What do you mean, splendid? Are you so anxious to see her?"

I saw that tact would be required.

"Not anxious, exactly," I said smoothly. "The word is too strong. It's just that I would like to have her opinion of this moustache of mine. She is a girl of taste, and I would be prepared to accept the verdict. Shortly before you arrived, Jeeves was subjecting the growth to some destructive criticism, and it shook me a little. What do you think of it, by the way?"

"I think it's ghastly."

"Ghastly?"

"Revolting. You look like something in the chorus line of a touring revue. But you say Jeeves doesn't like it?"

"He didn't seem to."

"Ah, so you'll have to shave it. Thank God for that."

I stiffened. I resent the view, so widely held in my circle of acquaintance, that I am a mere Hey-you in the home, bowing to Jeeves's behests like a Hollywood yes-man.

"Over my dead body I'll shave it. It stays just where it is, rooted to the spot. A fig for Jeeves, if I may use the expression."

He shrugged his shoulders.

"Well, it's up to you, I suppose. If you don't mind making yourself an eyesore—"

I stiffened a bit further.

"Did you say eyesore?"

"Eyesore was what I said."

"Oh, it was, was it?" I riposted, and it is possible that, had we not been interrupted, the exchanges would have become heated, for I was still under the stimulating influence of those specials and in no mood to brook backchat. But before I could tell him that he was a fatheaded ass, incapable of recognizing the rare and the beautiful if handed to him on a skewer, the doorbell rang again and Jeeves announced Florence.

3

IT's JUST occurred to me, thinking back, that in that passage where I gave a brief pen portrait of her—fairly near the start of this narrative, if you remember,—I may have made a bloomer and left you with a wrong impression of Florence Craye. Informed that she was an intellectual girl who wrote novels and was like ham and eggs with the boys with the bulging foreheads out Bloomsbury way, it is possible that you conjured up in your mind's eye the picture of something short and dumpy with ink spots on the chin, as worn by so many of the female intelligentsia.

Such is far from being the truth. She is tall and willowy and handsome, with a terrific profile and luxuriant platinum blonde hair, and might, so far as looks are concerned, be the star unit of the harem of one of the better class sultans. I have known strong men to be bowled over by her at first sight, and it is seldom that she takes her walks abroad without being whistled at by visiting Americans.

She came breezing in, dressed up to the nines, and Stilton received her with a cold eye on his wrist watch.

"So there you are at last," he said churlishly. "About time, dash it. I suppose you had forgotten that Uncle Joe has a nervous breakdown if he's kept waiting for his soup."

I was expecting some haughty response to this crack for I knew her to be a girl of spirit, but she ignored the rebuke, and I saw that her eyes, which are bright and hazel in color, were resting on me with a strange light in them. I don't know if you have ever seen a female of what they call teen-age gazing raptly at Humphrey Bogart in a cinema, but her deportment was much along those lines. More than a touch of the Soul's Awakening, if I make my meaning clear.

"Bertie!" she yipped, shaking from stem to stern. "The moustache! It's *lovely!* Why have you kept this from us all these years? It's wonderful. It gives you such a dashing look. It alters your whole appearance."

Well, after the bad press the old fungus had been getting of late, you might have thought that a rave notice like this would have been right up my street. I mean, while one lives for one's Art, so to speak, and cares little for the public's praise or blame and all that sort of thing, one can always do with something to paste into one's scrapbook, can one not? But it left me cold, particularly in the vicinity of the feet. I found my eye swiveling round to Stilton, to see how he was taking it, and was concerned to note that he was taking it extremely big.

Pique. That's the word I was trying to think of. He was looking definitely piqued, like a diner in a restaurant who has bitten into a bad oyster, and I wasn't sure I altogether blamed him, for his loved one had not only patted my cheek with an affectionate hand but was drinking me in with such wide-eyed admiration that any fiancé, witnessing the spectacle, might well have been excused for growing a bit hot under the collar. And Stilton, of course, as I have already indicated, was a chap who could give Othello a couple of bisques and be dormy one at the eighteenth.

It seemed to me that unless prompt steps were taken through the proper channels, raw passions might be unchained, so I hastened to change the subject.

"Tell me all about your uncle, Stilton," I said. "Fond of soup, is he? Quite a boy for the bouillon, yes?"

He merely gave a grunt like a pig dissatisfied with its ration for the day, so I changed the subject again.

"How is *Spindrift* going?" I asked Florence. "Still selling pretty copiously?"

I had said the right thing. She beamed.

"Yes, it's doing splendidly. It has just gone into another edition."

"That's good."

"You knew it had been made into a play?"

"Eh? Oh, yes. Yes, I heard about that."

"Do you know Percy Gorringe?"

I winced a trifle. Proposing, as I did, to expunge the joy from Percy's life by giving him the uncompromising miss-in-baulk before tomorrow's sun had set, I would have preferred to keep him out of the conversation. I said the name seemed somehow familiar, as if I had heard it somewhere in some connection.

"He did the dramatization. He has made a splendid job of it."

Here Stilton, who appeared to be allergic to Gorringes, snorted in his uncouth way. There are two things I particulary dislike about G. D'Arcy Cheesewright—one, his habit of saying "Ho!" the other his tendency, when moved, to make a sound like a buffalo pulling its foot out of a swamp.

"We have a manager who is going to put it on and he's got the cast and all that, but there has been an unfortunate hitch."

"You don't say?"

"Yes. One of the backers has failed us, and we need another thousand pounds. Still, it's going to be all right. Percy assures me he can raise the money."

Again I winced, and once more Stilton snorted. It is always difficult to weigh snorts in the balance, but I think this second one had it over the first in offensiveness by a small margin.

"That louse?" he said. "He couldn't raise tuppence."

These, of course, were fighting words. Florence's eyes flashed.

"I won't have you calling Percy a louse. He is very attractive and very clever."

"Who says so?"

"I say so."

"Ho!" said Stilton. "Attractive, eh? Who does he attract?"

"Never mind whom he attracts."

"Name three people he ever attracted. And clever? He may have just about enough intelligence to open his mouth when he wants to eat, but no more. He's a halfwitted gargoyle."

"He is not a gargoyle."

"Of course he's a gargoyle. Are you going to look me in the face and deny that he wears short side-whiskers?"

"Why shouldn't he wear short side-whiskers?"

"I suppose he has to, being a louse."

"Let me tell you—"

"Oh, come on," said Stilton brusquely, and hustled her out. As they wended their way, he was reminding her once more of his Uncle Joseph's reluctance to be kept waiting for his soup.

It was a pensive Bertram Wooster, with more than a few furrows in his forehead, who returned to his chair and put match to cigarette. And I'll tell you why I was pensive and furrowed. The recent slab of dialogue between the young couple had left me extremely uneasy.

Love is a delicate plant that needs constant tending and nurturing, and this cannot be done by snorting at the adored object like a gas explosion and calling her friends lice. I had the disquieting impression that it wouldn't take too much to make the Stilton-Florence axis go p'fft again, and who could say that in this event, the latter, back in circulation, would not decide to hitch on to me once more? I remembered what had happened that other time and, as the fellow said, the burned child fears the spilled milk.

You see, the trouble with Florence was that though, as I have stated, indubitably comely and well equipped to take office as a pinup girl, she was, as I have also stressed, intellectual to the core, and the ordinary sort of bloke like myself does well to give this type of female as wide a miss as he can manage.

You know how it is with these earnest, brainy beazels of what is called strong character. They can't let the male soul alone. They want to get behind it and start shoving. Scarcely have they shaken the rice from their hair in the car driving off for the honeymoon than they pull up their socks and begin molding the partner of joys and sorrows, and if there is one thing that gives me the pip, it is being molded. Despite adverse criticism from many quarters—the name of my Aunt Agatha is one that springs to the lips—I like B. Wooster the way he is. Lay off him, I say. Don't try to change him, or you may lose the flavor.

Even when we were merely affianced, I recalled, this woman had dashed the mystery thriller from my hand, instructing me to read instead a perfectly frightful thing by a bird called Tolstoi. At the thought of what horrors might ensue after the clergyman had done his stuff and she had a legal right to bring my gray hairs in sorrow to the grave, the imagination boggled. It was a subdued and apprehensive Bertram Wooster who some moments later reached for the hat and light overcoat and went off to the Savoy to shove food into the Trotters.

The binge, as I had anticipated, did little or nothing to raise the spirits. Aunt Dahlia had not erred in stating that my guests would prove to be creeps of no common order. L. G. Trotter was a little man with a face like a weasel, who scarcely uttered during the meal because, whenever he tried to, the moon of his delight shut him up, and Mrs. Trotter was a burly heavyweight with a beaked nose who talked all the time, principally about some woman she disliked named Blenkinsop. And nothing to help me through the grim proceedings except the faint, far-off echo of those specials of Jeeves's. It was a profound relief when they finally called it a day and I was at liberty to totter off to the Drones for the restorative I so sorely needed.

The almost universal practice of the inmates being to attend some form of musical entertainment after dinner, the smoking room was empty when I arrived, and it would not be too much to say that five minutes later, a cigarette between my lips and a brimming flagon at my side, I was enveloped in a deep peace. The strained nerves had relaxed. The snootered soul was at rest.

It couldn't last, of course. These lulls in life's battle never do. Came a moment when I had that eerie feeling that I was not alone and, looking round, found myself gazing at G. D'Arcy Cheesewright.

4

THIS CHEESEWRIGHT, I should perhaps have mentioned earlier, is a bimbo who from the cradle up has devoted himself sedulously to aquatic exercise. He was Captain of Boats at Eton. He rowed four years for Oxford. He sneaks off each summer at the time of Henley Regatta and sweats lustily with his shipmates on behalf of the Leander Club. And if he ever goes to New York, I have no doubt he will squander a fortune sculling about the lake in Central Park at twenty-five cents a throw. It is only rarely that the oar is out of his hand.

Well, you can't do that sort of thing without developing the thews and sinews, and all this galley-slave stuff has left him extraordinarily robust. His chest is broad and barrel-like and the muscles of his brawny arms strong as iron bands. I remember Jeeves once speaking of someone of his acquaintance whose strength was as the strength of ten, and the description would have fitted Stilton nicely. He looks like an all-in wrestler.

Being a pretty broadminded chap and realizing that it takes all sorts to make a world, I had always till now regarded this beefiness of his with kindly toleration. The way I look at it is, if blighters want to be beefy, let them be beefy. Good luck to them, say I. What I did not like at moment of going to press was the fact that in addition to bulging in all directions with muscle he was glaring at me in a sinister manner, his air that of one of those Fiends with Hatchet who are always going about the place Slaying Six. He was plainly much stirred about something, and it would not be going too far to say that as I caught his eye, I wilted where I sat.

Thinking that it must be the circumstance of his having found me restoring the tissues with a spot of the right stuff that was causing his chagrin, I was about to say that the elixir in my hand was purely medicinal and had been recommended by a prominent Harley Street physician when he spoke.

"If only I could make up my mind!"

"About what, Stilton?"

"About whether to break your foul neck or not."

I did a bit more wilting. It seemed to me that I was alone in a deserted smoking-room with a homicidal looney. It is a type of looney I particularly bar, and the homicidal looney I like least is one with a forty-four chest and biceps in proportion. His fingers, I noticed, were twitching, always a bad sign. Oh, for the wings of a dove about summed up my feelings as I tried not to look at them.

"Break my foul neck?" I said, hoping for further information. "Why?"

"You don't know?"

"I haven't the foggiest."

"Ho!"

He paused at this point to dislodge a fly which had sauntered in through the open window and become mixed up with his vocal cords. Having achieved his object, he resumed.

"Wooster!"

"Still here, old man."

"Wooster," said Stilton, and if he wasn't grinding his teeth, I don't know a ground tooth when I see one, "what was the thought behind that moustache of yours? Why did you grow it?"

Well, rather difficult to say, of course. One gets these whims. I scratched the chin a moment.

"I suppose I felt it might brighten things up," I hazarded.

"Or had you an ulterior motive? Was it part of a subtle plot for stealing Florence from me?"

"My dear Stilton!"

"It all looks very fishy to me. Do you know what happened just now, when we left my uncle's?"

"I'm sorry, no. I'm a stranger in these parts myself."

He ground a few more teeth.

"I will tell you. I saw Florence home in a cab, and all the way there she was raving about that foul moustache of yours. It made me sick to listen to her."

I weighed the idea of saying something to the effect that girls would be girls and must be expected to have their simple enthusiasms, but decided better not.

"When we got off at her door and I turned after paying the driver, I found she was looking at me intently, examining me from every angle, her eyes fixed on my face."

"You enjoyed that, of course?"

"Shut up. Don't interrupt me."

"Right ho. I only meant it must have been pretty gratifying."

He brooded for a space. Whatever had happened at that lovers' get-together, one could see that the memory of it was stirring him like a dose of salts.

"A moment later," he said, and paused, wrestling with his feelings, "a moment later," he went on, finding speech again, "she announced that she wished me to grow a moustache, too. She said—I quote her words—that when a man has a large pink face and a head like a pumpkin, a little something around the upper lip often does wonders in the way of easing the strain. Would you say my head was like a pumpkin, Wooster?"

"Not a bit, old man."

"Not like a pumpkin?"

"No, not like a pumpkin. A touch of the dome of St. Paul's, perhaps."

"Well, that is what she compared it to, and she said that if I split it in the middle with a spot of hair, the relief to pedestrians and traffic would be enormous. She's crazy. I wore a moustache my last year at Oxford, and it looked frightful. Nearly as loathsome as yours. Moustache, forsooth!" said Stilton, which surprised me, for I hadn't supposed he knew words like "Forsooth." " 'I wouldn't grow a moustache to please a dying grandfather,' I told her. 'A nice fool I'd look with a moustache,' I said. 'It's how you look without one,' she said. 'Is that so?' I said. 'Yes, it is,' she said. 'Oh?' I said. 'Yes,' she said. 'Ho!' I said, and she said 'Ho to you!' "

If she had added "With knobs on," it would, of course, have made it stronger, but I must say I was rather impressed by Florence's work as described in this slice of dialogue. It seemed to me snappy and forceful. I suppose girls learn this sort of cut-and-thrust stuff at their finishing schools. And Florence, one must remember, had been moving a good deal of late in bohemian circles—Chelsea sudios and the rooms of the intelligentsia in Bloomsbury and places like that—where the repartee is always of a high order.

"So that was that," proceeded Stilton, having brooded for a space. "One thing led to another, hot words passed to and fro, and it was not long before she was returning the ring and saying she would be glad to have her letters back at my earliest convenience."

I tut-tutted. He asked me rather abruptly not to tut-tut, so I stopped tut-tutting, explaining that my reason for having done so was that his tragic tale had moved me deeply.

"My heart aches for you," I said.

"It does, does it?"

"Profusely."

"Ho!"

"You doubt my sympathy?"

"You bet I doubt your ruddy sympathy. I told you just now that I was trying to make up my mind, and what I'm trying to make it up about is this. Had you foreseen that that would happen? Did your cunning fiend's brain spot what was bound to occur if you grew a moustache and flashed it on Florence?"

I tried to laugh lightly, but you know how it is with these light laughs, they don't always come out just the way you would wish. Even to me it sounded more like a gargle.

"Am I right? Was that the thought that came into your cunning fiend's brain?"

"Certainly not. As a matter of fact, I haven't got a cunning fiend's brain."

"Jeeves has. The plot could have been his. Was it Jeeves who wove this snare for my feet?"

"My dear chap! Jeeves doesn't weave snares for feet. He would consider it a liberty. Besides, I told you he is the spearhead of the movement which disapproves of my moustache."

"I see what you mean. Yes, on second thought I am inclined to acquit Jeeves of complicity. The evidence points to your having thought up the scheme yourself."

"Evidence? How do you mean, evidence?"

"When we were at your flat and I said I was expecting Florence, I noticed a very significant thing—your face lit up."

"It didn't."

"Pardon me. I know when a face lights up and when it doesn't. I could read you like a book. You were saying to yourself, 'This is the moment! This is where I spring it on her!' "

"Nothing of the sort. If my face lit up—which I gravely doubt—it was merely because I reasoned that as soon as she arrived you would be leaving."

"You wanted me to leave?"

"I did. You were taking up space which I required for other purposes."

It was plausible, of course, and I could see it shook him. He passed a hamlike hand, gnarled with toiling at the oar, across his brow.

"Well, I shall have to think it over. Yes, yes, I shall have to think it over."

"Go away and start now, is what I would suggest."

"I will. I shall be scrupulously fair. I shall weigh this and that. But if I find my suspicions are correct, I shall know what to do about it."

And with these ominous words he withdrew, leaving me not a little bowed down with weight of woe. For apart from the fact that when a bird of Stilton's impulsive temperament gets it into his nut that you have woven snares for his feet, practically anything can happen in the way of violence and mayhem, it gave me goose pimples to think of Florence being at large once more. It was with heavy heart that I finished my whisky and splash and tottered home. "Wooster," a voice seemed to be whispering in my ear, "things are getting hot, old sport."

Jeeves was at the telephone when I reached the sitting-room.

"I am sorry," he was saying, and I noticed that he was just as suave and firm as I had been at our recent get-together. "No, please, further discussion is useless. I am afraid you must accept my decision as final. Good night."

From the fact that he had not chucked in a lot of "Sirs" I presumed that he had been talking to some pal of his, though from the curtness of his tone probably not the one whose strength was as the strength of ten.

"What was that, Jeeves?" I asked. "A little tiff with one of the boys at the club?"

"No, sir. I was speaking to Mr. Percy Gorringe, who rang up shortly before you entered. Affecting to be yourself, I informed him that his request for a thousand pounds could not be entertained. I thought that this might spare you discomfort and embarrassment."

I must say I was touched. After being worsted in that clash of wills of ours, one might have expected him to show dudgeon and be loath to do the feudal thing by the young master. But Jeeves and I, though we may have our differences—as it might be on the subject of lip-joy—do not allow them to rankle.

"Thank you, Jeeves."

"Not at all, sir."

"Lucky you came back in time to do the needful. Did you enjoy yourself at the club?"

"Very much, sir."

"More than I did at mine."

"Sir?"

I ran into Stilton Cheesewright there and found him in difficult mood. Tell me, Jeeves, what do you do at this Junior Ganymede of yours?"

"Well, sir, many of the members play a sound game of bridge. The conversation, too, is always of a high order. And should one desire more frivolous entertainment, there is the club book."

"The . . . oh, yes, I remember."

Perhaps you do, too, if you happened to be around when I was relating the doings at Totleigh Towers, the country seat of Sir Watkyn Bassett, when this club book had enabled me to put it so crushingly across the powers of darkness in the shape of Roderick Spode. Under Rule Eleven at the Junior Ganymede, you may recall, members are required to supply intimate details concerning their employers for inclusion in the volume, and its pages revealed that Spode, who was an amateur Dictator of sorts, running a gang called the Black Shorts, who went about in black footer bags shouting, "Heil, Spode!," also secretly designed ladies' underclothing under the trade name of Eulalie Soeurs. Armed with this knowledge, I had had, of course, little difficulty in reducing him to the level of a third-class power. These Dictators don't want a thing like that to get spread about.

But though the club book had served me well on that occasion, I was far from approving of it. Mine has been in many ways a checkered career, and it was not pleasant to think that full details of episodes I would prefer to be buried in oblivion were giving a big laugh daily to a bunch of valets and butlers.

"You couldn't tear the Wooster material out of that club book, could you, Jeeves?"

"I fear not, sir."

"It contains matter that can fairly be described as dynamite."

"Very true, sir."

"Suppose the contents were bruited about and reached the ears of my Aunt Agatha?"

"You need have no concern on that point, sir. Each member fully understands that perfect discretion is a *sine qua non.*"

"All the same I'd feel happier if that page—"

"Those eleven pages, sir."

"—if those eleven pages were consigned to the flames." A sudden thought struck me. "Is there anything about Stilton Cheesewright in the book?"

"A certain amount, sir."

"Damaging?"

"Not in any real sense of the word, sir. His personal attendant merely reports that he has a habit, when moved, of saying 'Ho' and does Swedish exercises in the nude each morning before breakfast."

I sighed. I hadn't really hoped, and yet it had been a disappointment. I have always held—rightly, I think—that nothing eases the tension of a difficult situation like a well-spotted bit of blackmail, and it would have been agreeable to have been in a position to go to Stilton and say "Cheesewright, I know your secret!" and watch him wilt. But you can't fulfill yourself to any real extent in that direction if all the party of the second part does is say "Ho!" and tie himself into knots before sailing into the eggs and b. It was plain that with Stilton there could be no such moral triumph as I had achieved in the case of Roderick Spode.

"Ah, well," I said resignedly, "if that's that, that's that, what?"

"So it would appear, sir."

"Nothing to do but keep the chin up and the upper lip as stiff as can be managed. I think I'll go to bed with an improving book. Have you read *The Mystery of the Pink Crayfish* by Rex West?"

"No, sir, I have not enjoyed that experience. Oh, pardon me, sir, I was forgetting. Lady Florence Craye spoke to me on the telephone shortly before you came in. Her ladyship would be glad if you would ring her up. I will get the number, sir."

I was puzzled. I could make nothing of this. No reason, of course, why she shouldn't want me to give her a buzz, but on the other hand no reason that I could see why she should.

"She didn't say what she wanted?"

"No, sir."

"Odd, Jeeves."

"Yes, sir. . . . One moment, m'lady. Here is Mr. Wooster."

I took the instrument from him and hullo-ed.

"Bertie?"

"On the spot."

"I hope you weren't in bed?"

"No, no."

"I thought you wouldn't be. Bertie, will you do something for me? I want you to take me to a night club tonight."

"Eh?"

"A night club. Rather a low one. I mean garish and all that sort of thing. It's for the book I'm writing. Atmosphere."

"Oh, ah," I said, enlightened. I knew all about this atmosphere thing. Bingo Little's wife, the well-known novelist Rosie M. Banks, is as hot as a pistol on it, Bingo has often told me. She frequently sends him off to take notes of this and that so that she shall have plenty of ammo for her next chapter. If you're a novelist, apparently, you have to get your atmosphere correct, or your public starts writing you stinkers beginning "Dear Madam, are you aware . . .?" "You're doing something about a night club?"

"Yes, I'm just coming to the part where my hero goes to one, and I've never been to any except the respectable ones where everybody goes, which aren't the sort of thing I want. What I need is something more—"

"Garish?"

"Yes, garish."

"You want to go tonight?"

"It must be tonight, because I'm off tomorrow afternoon to Brinkley."

"Oh, you're going to stay with Aunt Dahlia?"

"Yes. Well, can you manage it?"

"Oh, rather. Delighted."

"Good. D'Arcy Cheesewright," said Florence, and I noted the steely what-d'you-call-it in her voice, "was to have taken me, but he finds himself unable to. So I've had to fall back on you."

This might, I thought, have been more tactfully put, but I let it go.

"Right ho," I said. "I'll call for you at about half-past eleven."

You are surprised? You are saying to yourself "Come, come, Wooster, what's all this?" wondering why I was letting myself in for a beano from which I might well have shrunk? The matter is susceptible of a ready explanation.

My quick mind, you see, had spotted instantly that this was where I might quite conceivably do myself a bit of good. Having mellowed this girl with food and drink, who knew but that I might succeed in effecting a reconciliation between her and the piece of cheese with whom until tonight she had been headed for the altar rails, thus averting the peril which must always loom on the Wooster horizon while she remained unattached and at a loose end? It needed, I was convinced, only a few kindly words from a sympathetic man of the world, and these I was prepared to supply in full measure.

"Jeeves," I said, "I shall be going out again. This will mean having to postpone finishing the mystery of the pink crayfish to a later date, but that can't be helped. As a matter of fact, I rather fancy I have already wrested its secret from it. Unless I am very much mistaken, the man who bumped off Sir Eustace Willoughby, Bart., was the butler."

"Indeed, sir?"

"That is what I think, having sifted the clues. All that stuff throwing suspicion on the vicar doesn't fool me for an instant. Will you ring up The Mottled Oyster and book a table in my name."

"Not too near the band, sir?"

"How right you are, Jeeves. Not too near the band."

5

I DON'T know why it is, but I'm not much of a lad for night clubs these days. Age creeping on me, I suppose. But I still retain my membership in about half a dozen, including this Mottled Oyster at which I had directed Jeeves to book me a table.

The old spot has passed a somewhat restless existence since I first joined, and from time to time I get a civil note from its proprietors saying that it has changed its name and address once more. When it was raided as The Feverish Cheese, it became The Frozen Limit, and when it was raided as The Frozen Limit, it bore for a while mid snow and ice the banner with the strange device The Startled Shrimp. From that to The Mottled Oyster was, of course, but a step. In my hot youth I had passed not a few quite pleasant evenings beneath its roof in its various incarnations, and I thought that if it preserved anything approaching the old form, it ought to be garish enough to suit Florence. As I remembered, it rather prided itself on its garishness. That was why the rozzers were always raiding it.

I picked her up at her flat at eleven-thirty, and found her in somber mood, the lips compressed, the eyes inclined to gaze into space with a sort of hard glow in them. No doubt something along these lines is always the aftermath of a brisk dust-up with the heart-throb. During the taxi drive she remained *sotto voce* and the silent tomb, and from the way her foot kept tapping on the floor of the vehicle I knew that she was thinking of Stilton, whether or not in agony of spirit I was, of course, unable to say, but I thought it probable. Following her into the joint, I was on the whole optimistic. It seemed to me that with any luck I ought to be successful in the task that lay before me—viz. softening her with well-chosen words and jerking her better self back to the surface.

When we took our seats and I looked about me, I must confess that, having this object in mind, I could have done with dimmer lights and a more romantic *tout ensemble*, if *tout ensemble* is the expression I want. I could also have dispensed with the rather strong smell of kippered herrings which hung over the establishment like a fog. But against these drawbacks could be set the fact that up on the platform where the band was, a man with adenoids was singing through a megaphone and, like all men who sing through megaphones nowadays, ladling out stuff well calculated to melt the hardest heart.

It's an odd thing. I know one or two song writers and have found them among the most cheery of my acquaintances, ready of smile and full of merry quips and so forth. But directly they put pen to paper they never fail to take the dark view. All that We're-drifting-apart-you're-breaking-my-heart stuff, I mean to say. The thing this bird was putting across per megaphone at the moment was about a chap crying into his pillow because the girl he loved was getting married next day, but—and this was the point or nub—not to him. He didn't like it. He viewed the situation with concern. And the megaphonist was extracting every ounce of juice from the setup.

Some fellows, no doubt, would have taken advantage of this outstanding goo to plunge without delay into what Jeeves calls *medias res,* but I, being shrewd, knew that you have to give these things time to work. So, having ordered kippers and a bottle of what would probably turn out to be rat poison, I opened the conversation on a more restrained note, asking her how the new novel was coming along. Authors, especially when female, like to keep you posted about this.

She said it was coming along very well but not quickly, because she was a slow, careful worker who mused a good bit in between paragraphs and spared no pains to find the exact word with which to express what she wished to say. Like Flaubert, she said, and I said I thought she was on the right lines.

"Those," I said, "were more or less my methods when I wrote that thing of mine for the *Boudoir*."

I was alluding to the weekly paper for the delicately nurtured, *Milady's Boudoir,* of which Aunt Dahlia is the courteous and popular proprietor or proprietress. She has been running it now for about three years, a good deal to the annoyance of Uncle Tom, her husband, who has to foot the bills. At her request I had once contributed an article—or "piece," as we journalists call it—on What the Well-Dressed Man Is Wearing.

"So you're off to Brinkley tomorrow," I went on. "You'll like that. Fresh air, gravel soil, company's own water, Anatole's cooking and so forth."

"Yes. And of course it will be wonderful meeting Daphne Dolores Morehead."

The name was new to me.

"Daphne Dolores Morehead?"

"The novelist. She is going to be there. I admire her work so much. I see, by the way, she is doing a serial for the *Boudoir*."

"Oh, yes?" I said, intrigued. One always likes to hear about the activities of one's fellow-writers.

"It must have cost your aunt a fortune. Daphne Dolores Morehead is frightfully expensive. I can't remember what it is she gets a thousand words, but it's something enormous."

"The old sheet must be doing well."

"I suppose so."

She spoke listlessly, seeming to have lost interest in *Milady's Boudoir*. Her thoughts, no doubt, had returned to Stilton. She cast a dull eye hither and thither about the room. It had begun to fill up now, and the dance floor was congested with frightful bounders of both sexes.

"What horrible people," she said. "I must say I am surprised that you should be familiar with such places, Bertie. Are they all like this?"

I weighed the question.

"Well, some are better and some are worse. I would call this one about average. Garish, of course, but then you said you wanted something garish."

"Oh, I'm not complaining. I shall make some useful notes. It is just the sort of place to which I pictured Rollo going that night."

"Rollo?"

"The hero of my novel. Rollo Beaminster."

"Oh, I see. Yes, of course. Out on the tiles, was he?"

"He was in wild mood. Reckless. Desperate. He had lost the girl he loved."

"What ho!" I said. "Tell me more."

I spoke with animation and vim, for whatever you may say of Bertram Wooster, you cannot say that he does not know a cue when he hears one. Throw him the line, and he will do the rest. I hitched up the larynx. The kippers and the bot had arrived by now, and I took a mouthful of the former and a sip of the latter. It tasted like hair-oil.

"You interest me strangely," I said. "Lost the girl he loved, had he?"

"She had told him she never wished to see or speak to him again."

"Well, well. Always a nasty knock for a chap, that."

"So he comes to this low night club. He is trying to forget."

"But I'll bet he doesn't."

"No, it is useless. He looks about him at the glitter and garishness and feels how hollow it all is. I think I can use that waiter over there in the night club scene, the one with the watery eyes and the pimple on his nose," she said, jotting down a note on the back of the bill of fare. She was plainly collecting some useful material.

I fortified myself with a swig of whatever the stuff was in the bottle and prepared to give her the works.

"Always a mistake," I said, starting to do the sympathetic man of the world, "fellows losing girls and—conversely—girls losing fellows. I don't know how you feel about it, but the way it seems to me is that it's a silly idea giving the dream man the raspberry just because of some trifling tiff. Kiss and make up, I always say. I saw Stilton at the Drones tonight," I said, getting down to it.

She stiffened and took a reserved mouthful of kipper. Her voice, when consignment had passed down the hatch and she was able to speak, was cold and metallic.

"Oh, yes?"

"He was in wild mood."

"Oh, yes?"

"Reckless. Desperate. He looked about him at the Drones smoking-room, and I could see he was feeling what a hollow smoking-room it was."

"Oh, yes?"

Well, I suppose if someone had come along at this moment and said to me "Hullo there, Wooster, how's it going? Are you making headway?" I should have had to reply in the negative. "Not perceptibly, Wilkinson,"—or Banks or Smith or Knatchbull-Huguessen or whatever the name might have been, I would have said. I had the uncomfortable feeling of having been laid a stymie. However, I persevered.

"Yes, he was in quite a state of mind. He gave me the impression that it wouldn't take much to make him go off to the Rocky Mountains and shoot grizzly bears. Not a pleasant thought."

"You mean if one is fond of grizzly bears?"

"I was thinking more if one was fond of Stiltons."

"I'm not."

"Oh? Well, suppose he joined the Foreign Legion?"

"It would have my sympathy."

"You wouldn't like to think of him tramping through the hot sand without a pub in sight, with Riffs or whatever they're called potting at him from all directions."

"Yes, I would. If I saw a Riff trying to shoot D'Arcy Cheesewright, I would hold his hat for him and egg him on."

Once more I had that sense of not making progress. Her face, I observed, was cold and hard, like my kipper, which of course during these exchanges I had been neglecting, and I began to understand how those birds in Holy Writ must have felt after their session with the deaf adder. I can't recall all the details, though at my private school I once won a prize for Scripture Knowledge, but I remember that they had the dickens of an uphill job trying to charm it, and after they had sweated themselves to a frazzle no business resulted. It is often this way, I believe, with deaf adders.

"Do you know Horace Pendlebury-Davenport?" I said, after a longish pause during which we worked away at our respective kippers.

"The man who married Valerie Twistleton?"

"That's the chap. Formerly the Drones Club Darts champion."

"I've met him. But why bring him up?"

"Because he points the moral and adorns the tale. During the period of their betrothal he and Valerie had a row similar in caliber to that which has occurred between you and Stilton and pretty nearly parted for ever."

She gave me the frosty eye.

"Must we talk about Mr. Cheesewright?"

"I see him as tonight's big topic."

"I don't, and I think I'll go home."

"Oh, not yet. I want to tell you about Horace and Valerie. They had this row of which I speak and might, as I say, have parted forever, had they not been reconciled by a woman who, so Horace says, looked as if she bred cocker spaniels. She told them a touching story, which melted their hearts. She said she had once loved a bloke and quarreled with him about some trifle, and he turned on his heel and went off to the Federated Malay States and married the widow of a rubber planter. And each year from then on there arrived at her address a simple posy of white violets, together with a slip of paper bearing the words 'It might have been.' You wouldn't like that to happen with you and Stilton, would you?"

"I'd love it."

"It doesn't give you a pang to think that at this very moment he may be going the rounds of the shipping offices, inquiring about sailings to the Malay States?"

"They'd be shut at this time of night."

"Well, first thing tomorrow morning, then."

She laid down her knife and fork and gave me an odd look.

"Bertie, you're extraordinary," she said.

"Eh? How do you mean, extraordinary?"

"All this nonsense you have been talking, trying to reconcile me and D'Arcy. Not that I don't admire you for it. I think it's rather wonderful of you. But then everybody says that though you have a brain like a peahen, you're the soul of kindness and generosity."

Well, I was handicapped here by the fact that, never having met a peahen, I was unable to estimate the quality of these fowls' intelligence, but she had spoken as if they were a bit short of the gray matter, and I was about to ask her who the hell she meant by "everybody," when she resumed.

"You want to marry me yourself, don't you?"

I had to take another mouthful of the hell-brew before I could speak. One of those difficult questions to answer.

"Oh, rather," I said, for I was anxious to make the evening a success. "Of course. Who wouldn't?"

"And yet you—"

She did not proceed further than the word "you," for at this juncture, with the abruptness with which these things always happen, the joint was pinched. The band stopped in the middle of a bar. A sudden hush fell upon the room. Square-jawed men shot up through the flooring, and one, who seemed to be skippering the team, stood out in the middle and in a voice like a foghorn told everybody to keep their seats. I remember thinking how nicely timed the whole thing was—breaking loose, I mean, at a moment when the conversation had taken a distasteful turn and threatened to become fraught with embarrassment. I have heard hard things said about the London police force—notably by Catsmeat Potter-Pirbright and others on the morning after the annual Oxford and Cambridge boat race—but a fairminded man had to admit that there were occasions when they showed tact of no slight order.

I wasn't alarmed, of course. I had been through this sort of thing many a time and oft, as the expression is, and I knew what happened. So, noting that my guest was giving a rather close imitation of a cat on hot bricks, I hastened to dispel her alarm.

"No need to get the breeze up," I said. "Nothing is here for tears, nothing to wail or knock the breast," I added, using one of Jeeves's gags which I chanced to remember. "Everything is quite in order."

"But won't they arrest us?"

I laughed lightly. These novices!

"Absurd. No danger of that whatsoever."

"How do you know?"

"All this is old stuff to me. Here in a nutshell is the procedure. They round us up, and we push off in an orderly manner to the police station in plain vans. There we assemble in the waiting-room and give our names and addresses, exercising a certain latitude as regards the details. I, for example, generally call myself Ephraim Gadsby of The Nasturtiums, Jubilee Road, Streatham Common. I don't know why. Just a whim. You, if you will be guided by me, will be Matilda Bott of 365 Churchill Avenue, East Dulwich. These formalities concluded, we shall be free to depart, leaving the proprietor to face the awful majesty of Justice."

She refused to be consoled. The resemblance to a cat on hot bricks became more marked. Though instructed by the foghorn chap to keep her seat, she shot up as if a spike had come through it.

"I'm sure that's not what happens."

"It is, unless they've changed the rules."

"You have to appear in court."

"No, no."

"Well, I'm not going to risk it. Good night."

And getting smoothly off the mark she made a dash for the service door, which was not far from where we sat. And an adjacent constable, baying like a bloodhound, started off in hot pursuit.

Whether I acted judiciously at this point is a question which I have never been able to decide. Sometimes I think yes, reflecting that the Chevalier Bayard in my place would have done the same, sometimes no. Briefly what occurred was that as the gendarme came galloping by, I shoved out a foot, causing him to take the toss of a lifetime. Florence withdrew, and the guardian of the peace, having removed his left boot from his right ear, with which it had become temporarily entangled, rose and informed me that I was in custody.

As at the moment he was grasping the scruff of my neck with one hand and the seat of my trousers with the other, I saw no reason to doubt the honest fellow.

6

I SPENT the night in what is called durance vile, and bright and early next day was haled before the beak at Vinton Street police court, charged with assaulting an officer of the law and impeding him in the execution of his duties, which I suppose was a fairly neat way of putting it. I was extremely hungry and needed a shave.

It was the first time I had met the Vinton Street chap, always hitherto having patronized his trade rival at Bosher Street, but Barmy Fotheringay-Phipps, who was introduced to him on the morning of January the first one year, had told me he was a man to avoid, and the truth of this was now borne in upon me in no uncertain manner. It seemed to me, as I stood listening to the cop running through the story sequence, that Barmy, in describing this Solon as a twenty-minute egg with many of the less lovable qualities of some high-up official of the Spanish Inquisition, had understated rather than exaggerated the facts.

I didn't like the look of the old blister at all. His manner was austere, and as the tale proceeded his face, such as it was, grew hard and dark with menace. He kept shooting quick glances at me through his pince-nez, and the dullest eye could see that the constable was getting all the sympathy of the audience and that the citizen cast for the role of Heavy in this treatment was the prisoner Gadsby. More and more the feeling stole over me that the prisoner Gadsby was about to get it in the gizzard and would be lucky if he didn't fetch up on Devil's Island.

However, when the *J'accuse* stuff was over and I was asked if I had anything to say, I did my best. I admitted that on the occasion about which we had been chatting I had extended a foot, causing the officer to go base over apex, but protested that it had been a pure accident without any *arrière pensée* on my part. I said I had been feeling cramped after a longish sojourn at the table and had merely desired to unlimber the leg muscles.

"You know how sometimes you want a stretch," I said.

"I am strongly inclined," responded the beak, "to give you one. A good long stretch."

Rightly recognizing this as comedy, I uttered a cordial guffaw to show that my heart was in the right place, and an officious blighter in the well of the court shouted "Silence!" I tried to explain that I was convulsed by His Worship's ready wit, but he shushed me again, and His Worship came to the surface once more.

"However," he went on, adjusting his pince-nez, "in consideration of your youth I will exercise clemency."

"Oh, fine," I said.

"Fine," replied the other half of the cross-talk act, who seemed to know all the answers, "is right. Ten pounds. Next case."

I paid my debt to Society, and pushed off.

Jeeves was earning the weekly envelope by busying himself at some domestic task when I reached the old home. He cocked an inquiring eye at me, and I felt that an explanation was due him. It would have surprised him, of course, to discover that my room was empty and my bed not been slept in.

"A little trouble last night with the minions of the law, Jeeves," I said. "Quite a bit of that Eugene-Aram-Walked-between-with-gyves-upon-his wrists stuff."

"Indeed, sir? Most vexing."

"Yes, I didn't like it much, but the magistrate—with whom I have just been threshing the thing out—had a wonderful time. I brought a ray of sunshine into his drab life, all right. Did you know that these magistrates were expert comedians?"

"No, sir. The fact had not been drawn to my attention."

"Think of Groucho Marx and you will get the idea. One gag after another, and all at my expense. I was just the straight man, and I found the experience most unpleasant, particularly as I had had no breakfast that any conscientious gourmet could call breakfast. Have you ever passed the night in chokey, Jeeves?"

"No, sir. I have been fortunate in that respect."

"It renders the appetite unusually keen. So rally round, if you don't mind, and busy yourself with the skillet. We have eggs on the premises, I presume?"

"Yes, sir."

"I shall need about fifty, fried, with perhaps the same number of pounds of bacon. Toast, also. Four loaves will probably be sufficient, but stand by to weigh in with more if necessary. And don't forget the coffee—say sixteen pots."

"Very good, sir."

"And after that," I said with a touch of bitterness, "I suppose you will go racing round to the Junior Ganymede to enter this spot of bother of mine in the club book."

"I fear I have no alternative, sir. Rule Eleven is very strict."

"Well, if you must, you must, I suppose. I wouldn't want you to be hauled up in a hollow square of butlers and have your buttons snipped off. That club book, Jeeves. You're absolutely sure there's nothing in it in the C's under 'Cheesewright'?"

"Nothing but what I outlined last night, sir."

"And a lot of help that is," I said moodily. "I don't mind telling you, Jeeves, that this Cheesewright has become a menace."

"Indeed, sir?"

"And I had hoped that you might have found something in the club book which would have enabled me to spike his guns. Still, if you can't, you can't, of course. All right, rush along and dish up that breakfast."

I had slept but fitfully on the plank bed which was all that the Vinton Street Gestapo had seen their way to provide for the use of clients, so after partaking of a hearty meal I turned in between the sheets. Like Rollo Beaminster, I wanted to forget. It must have been well after the luncheon hour when the sound of the telephone jerked me out of the dreamless. Feeling a good deal refreshed, I shoved on a dressing gown and went to the instrument.

It was Florence.

"Bertie?" she yipped.

"Hullo? I thought you said you were going to Brinkley today."

"I'm just starting. I rang up to ask how you got on after I left last night."

I laughed a mirthless laugh.

"Not so frightfully well," I replied. "I was scooped in by the constabulary."

"What! You told me they didn't arrest you."

"They don't. But they did."

"Are you all right now?"

"Well, I have a pinched look."

"But I don't understand. Why did they arrest you?"

"It's a long story. Cutting it down to the gist, I noticed that you were anxious to leave, so, observing that a rozzer was after you hell-for-leather, I put a foot out, tripping him up and causing him to lose interest in the chase."

"Good gracious!"

"It seemed to me the prudent policy to pursue. Another moment and he would have had you by the seat of the pants, and of course we can't have that sort of thing going on. The upshot of the affair was that I spent the night in a prison cell and had rather a testing morning with the magistrate at Vinton Street police court. However, I'm pulling round all right."

"Oh, Bertie!" Seeming deeply moved, she thanked me brokenly, and I said Don't mention it. Then she gasped a sudden gasp, as if she had received a punch on the third waistcoat button. "Did you say Vinton Street?"

"That's right."

"Oh, my goodness. Do you know who that magistrate was?"

"I couldn't tell you. No cards were exchanged. We boys in court called him Your Worship."

"He's D'Arcy's uncle!"

I goshed. It had startled me not a little.

"You don't mean that?"

"Yes."

"What, the one who likes soup?"

"Yes. Just imagine if after having dinner with him last night I had appeared before him in the dock this morning!"

"Embarrassing. Difficult to know what to say."

"D'Arcy would never have forgiven me."

"Eh?"

"He would have broken the engagement."

I didn't get this.

"How do you mean?"

"How do I mean what?"

"How do you mean he would have broken the engagement? I thought it was off already."

She gave what I believe is usually called a rippling laugh.

"Oh, no. He rang me up this morning and climbed down. And I forgave him. He's starting to grow a moustache today."

I was profoundly relieved.

"Well, that's splendid," I said, and when she O-Bertie-ed and I asked her what she was Oh-Bertie-ing about, she explained that what she had had in mind was the fact that I was so chivalrous and generous.

"Not many men in your place, feeling as you do about me, would behave like this."

"Quite all right."

"I'm very touched."

"Don't give it another thought. It's really all on again, is it?"

"Yes. So mind you don't breathe a word to him about my being at that place with you."

"Of course not."

"D'Arcy is so jealous."

"Exactly. He must never know."

"Never, Why, if he even found out I was telephoning to you now, he would have a fit."

I was about to laugh indulgently and say that this was what Jeeves calls a remote contingency, because how the dickens could he ever learn that we had been chewing the fat, when my eye was attracted by a large object just within my range of vision. Slewing the old bean round a couple of inches, I was enabled to perceive that this large o. was the bulging form of G. D'Arcy Cheesewright. I hadn't heard the door bell ring, and I hadn't seen him come in, but there unquestionably he was, haunting the place once more like a resident specter.

7

IT WAS a moment for quick thinking. One doesn't want fellows having fits all over one's sitting-room. I was extremely dubious, moreover, as to whether, should he ascertain who was at the other end of the wire, he would confine himself to fits.

"Certainly, Catsmeat," I said. "Of course, Catsmeat. I quite understand, Catsmeat. But I'll have to ring off now, Catsmeat, as our mutual friend Cheesewright has just come in. Goodbye, Castmeat." I hung up the receiver and turned to Stilton. "That was Catsmeat," I said.

He made no comment on this information, but stood glowering darkly. Now that I had been apprised of the ties of blood linking him with mine host of Vinton Street, I could see the family resemblance. Both uncle and nephew had the same way of narrowing their gaze and letting you have it from beneath the overhanging eyebrow. The only difference was that whereas the former pierced you to the roots of the soul through rimless pince-nez, with the latter you got the eye nude.

For a moment I was under the impression that my visitor's emotion was due to his having found me at this advanced hour in pyjamas and a dressing gown, a costume which, if worn at three o'clock in the afternoon, is always liable to start a train of thought. But it seemed that this was not so. More serious matters were on the agenda paper.

"Wooster," he said, in a rumpling voice like the Cornish express going through a tunnel, "where were you last night?"

I own the question rattled me. For an instant, indeed, I rocked on my base. Then I reminded myself that nothing could be proved against me, and was strong again.

"Ah, Stilton," I said cheerily, "come in, come in. Oh, you are in, aren't you? Well, take a seat and tell me all your news. A lovely day, is it not? You'll find a lot of people who don't like July in London, but I am all for it myself. It always seems to me there's a certain sort of something about it."

He appeared to be one of those fellows who are not interested in July in London, for he showed no disposition to pursue the subject, merely giving one of those snorts of his.

"Where were you last night, you blighted louse?" he said, and I noticed that the face was suffused, the cheek muscles twitching and the eyes, like stars, starting from their spheres.

I had a pop at being cool and nonchalant.

"Last night?" I said, musing. "Let me see, that would be the night of July the twenty-second, would it not? H'm. Ha. The night of—"

He swallowed a couple of times.

"I see you have forgotten. Let me assist your memory. You were in a low night club with Florence Craye, my fiancée."

"Who, me?"

"Yes, you. And this morning you were in the dock at Vinton Street police court."

"You're sure you mean me?"

"Quite sure. I had the information from my uncle, who is the magistrate there. He came to lunch at my flat today, and as he was leaving he caught sight of your photograph on the wall."

"I didn't know you kept my photograph on your wall, Stilton. I'm touched."

He continued to ferment.

"It was a group photograph," he said curtly, "and you happened to be in it. He looked at it, sniffed sharply and said 'Do you know this young man?' I explained that we belonged to the same club, so it was not always possible to avoid you, but that that was the extent of our association. I was going on to say that, left to myself, I wouldn't touch you with a ten-foot pole, when he proceeded. Still sniffing, he said he was glad I was not a close friend of yours, because you weren't at all the sort of fellow he liked to think of any nephew of his being matey with. He said you had been up before him this morning, charged with assaulting a policeman, who stated that he had arrested you for tripping him up while he was chasing a girl with platinum hair in a night club."

I pursed the lips. Or, rather I tried to, but something seemed to have gone wrong with the machinery. Still, I spoke boldly and with spirit.

"Indeed?" I said. "Personally I would be inclined to attach little credence to the word of the sort of policeman who spends his time chasing platinum-haired girls in night clubs. And as for this uncle of yours, with his wild stories of me having been up before him—well, you know what magistrates are. The lowest form of pond life. When a fellow hasn't the brains and initiative to sell jellied eels, they make him a magistrate."

"You mean that when he said that about your photograph he was deceived by some slight resemblance?"

I waved a hand.

"Not necessarily a slight resemblance. London's full of chaps who look like me. I'm a very common type. People have told me that there is a fellow called Ephraim Gadsby—one of the Streatham Common Gadsbys—who is positively my double. I shall, of course, take this into consideration when weighing the question of bringing an action for slander and defamation of character against this uncle of yours, and shall probably decide to let justice be tempered with mercy. But it would be a kindly act to warn the old son of a bachelor to be more careful in future how he allows his tongue to run away with him. There are limits to one's forbearance."

He brooded darkly for about forty-five seconds.

"Platinum hair, the policeman said," he observed at the end of this lull. "This girl had platinum hair."

"No doubt very becoming."

"I find it extremely significant that Florence has platinum hair."

"I don't see why. Hundreds of girls have. My dear Stilton, ask yourself if it is likely that Florence would have been at a night club like the . . . what did you say the name was?"

"I didn't. But I believe it was called The Mottled Oyster."

"Ah, yes, I have heard of it. Not a very nice place, I understand. Quite incredible that she would have gone to a joint like that. A fastidious, intellectual girl like Florence? No, no."

He pondered. It seemed to me that I had him going.

"She wanted me to take her to a night club last night," he said. "Something to do with getting material for her new book."

"But you very properly refused?"

"No, as a matter of fact, I said I would. Then we had that bit of trouble, so of course it was off."

"And she, of course, went home to bed. What else would any pure, sweet English girl have done? It amazes me that you can suppose even for a moment that she would have gone to one of these dubious establishments without you. Especially a place where, as I understand your story, squads of policemen are incessantly chasing platinum-haired girls hither and thither, and probably even worse things happening as the long night wears on. No, Stilton, dismiss these thoughts—which, if you will allow me to say so, are unworthy of you—and . . . Ah, here is Jeeves," I said, noting with relief that the sterling fellow, who had just oozed in, was carrying the old familiar shaker. "What have you there, Jeeves? Some of your specials?"

"Yes, sir. I fancied that Mr. Cheesewright might possibly be glad of refreshment."

"He's just in the vein for it. I won't join you, Stilton, because, as you know, with this Darts tournament coming on, I am in more or less strict training these days, but I must insist on your trying one of these superb mixtures of Jeeves's. You have been anxious . . . worried . . . disturbed . . . and it will pull you together. Oh, by the way, Jeeves."

"Sir?"

"I wonder if you remember, when I came home last night after chatting with Mr. Cheesewright at the Drones, my saying to you that I was going straight to bed with an improving book?"

"Certainly, sir."

"*The Mystery of the Pink Crayfish,* was it not?"

"Precisely, sir."

"I think I said something to the effect that I could hardly wait till I could get at it?"

"As I recollect, those were your exact words, sir. You were, you said, counting the minutes until you could curl up with it."

"Thank you, Jeeves."

"Not at all, sir."

He oozed off, and I turned to Stilton, throwing the arms out in a sort of wide gesture. I don't suppose I have ever come closer in my life to saying *"Voilà!"*

"You heard?" I said. "If that doesn't leave me without a stain on my character, it is difficult to see what it does leave me without. But let me help you to your special. You will find it rare and refreshing."

It's a curious thing about those specials of Jeeves's, and one on which many revelers have commented, that while, as I mentioned earlier, they wake the sleeping tiger in you, they also work the other way round. I mean, if the tiger in you isn't sleeping but on the contrary up and doing with a heart for any fate, they lull it. You come in like a lion, you take your snootful, and you go out like a lamb. Impossible to explain it, of course. One can merely state the facts.

It was so now with Stilton. In his pre-special phase he had been all steamed up and fit for treasons, stratagems and spoils, as the fellow said, and he became a better, kindlier man beneath my very gaze. Halfway through the initial snifter he was admitting in the friendliest way that he had wronged me. I might be the most consummate ass that ever eluded the vigilance of the talent scouts of Colney Hatch, he said, but it was obvious that I had not taken Florence to The Mottled Oyster. And dashed lucky for me I hadn't, he added, for had such been the case, he would have broken my spine in three places. In short, all very chummy and cordial.

"Harking back to the earlier portion of our conversation, Stilton," I said, changing the subject after we had agreed that his Uncle Joseph was a cockeyed fathead who would do well to consult some good oculist, "I noticed that when you spoke of Florence, you used the expression 'My fiancée.' Am I to infer from this that the dove of peace has pulled a quick one since I saw you last? That broken engagement, has it been soldered?"

He nodded.

"Yes," he said. "I made certain concessions and yielded certain points." Here his hand strayed to his upper lip and a look of pain passed over his face. "A reconciliation took place this morning."

"Splendid!"

"You're pleased?"

"Of course."

"Ho!"

"Eh?"

He eyed me fixedly.

"Wooster, come off it. You know you're in love with her yourself."

"Absurd."

"Absurd, my foot. You needn't think you can fool me. You worship that girl, and I am still inclined to believe that the whole of this moustache sequence was a vile plot on your part to steal her from me. Well, all I have to say is that if I ever catch you oiling round her and trying to alienate her affections, I shall break your spine in four places."

"Three, I thought you said."

"No, four. However, she will be out of your reach for some little time, I am glad to say. She goes today to visit your aunt, Mrs. Travers, in Worcestershire."

Amazing how with a careless word you can land yourself in the soup. I was within the merest toucher of saying Yes, so she had told me, which would, of course, have been fatal. In the nick of time I contrived to substitute an "Oh, really?"

"She's going to Brinkley, is she? You also?"

"I shall be following in a few days."

"You aren't going with her?"

"Talk sense. You don't suppose I intend to appear in public during the early stages of growing that damned moustache she insists on. I shall remain confined to my room till the foul thing has started to sprout a bit.

Goodbye, Wooster. You will remember what I was saying about your spine?"

I assured him that I would bear it in mind, and he finished his special and withdrew.

8

THE DAYS that followed saw me at the peak of my form, fizzy to an almost unbelievable extent and enchanting one and all with my bright smile and merry sallies. During this halcyon period, if halcyon is the word I want, it would not be too much to say that I revived like a watered flower.

It was as if a great weight had been rolled off the soul. Only those who have had to endure the ordeal of having G. D'Arcy Cheesewright constantly materialize from thin air and steal up behind them, breathing down the back of their necks as they took their ease in their smoking-room, can fully understand the relief of being able to sink into a chair and order a restorative, knowing that the place would be wholly free from this pre-eminent scourge. My feelings, I suppose, were roughly what those of Mary would have been, had she looked over her shoulder one morning and found the lamb no longer among those present.

And then—*bing*—just as I was saying to myself that this was the life, along came all those telegrams.

The first to arrive reached me at my residence just as I was lighting the after-breakfast cigarette, and I eyed it with something of the nervous discomfort of one confronted with a ticking bomb. Telegrams have so often been the heralds or harbingers or whatever they're called of sharp crises in my affairs that I have come to look on them askance, wondering if something is going to pop out of the envelope and bite me in the leg. It was with a telegram, it may be recalled, that Fate teed off in the sinister episode of Sir Watkyn Bassett, Roderick Spode and the silver cow-creamer which I was instructed by Aunt Dahlia to pinch from the first-named's collection at Totleigh Towers.

Little wonder, then, that as I brooded over this one—eyeing it, as I say, askance—I was asking myself if Hell's foundations were about to quiver again.

Still, there the thing was, and it seemed to me, weighing the pros and cons, that only one course lay before me—viz. to open it.

I did so. Handed in at Brinkley-cum-Snodsfield-in-the-Marsh, it was signed "Travers," this revealing it as the handiwork either of Aunt Dahlia or Thomas P. Travers, her husband, a pleasant old bird whom she had married at her second pop some years earlier. From the fact that it started with the words "Bertie, you worm," I deduced that it was the former who had taken post-office pen in hand. Uncle Tom is more guarded in his speech than the female of the species. He generally calls me "Me boy."

This was the substance of the communication:

> BERTIE, YOU WORM, YOUR EARLY PRESENCE DESIRED. DROP EVERYTHING AND COME DOWN HERE PRONTO, PREPARED FOR LENGTHY VISIT. URGENTLY NEED YOU TO BUCK UP A BLIGHTER WITH WHISKERS. LOVE. TRAVERS.

I brooded over this for the rest of the morning, and on my way to lunch at the Drones shot off my answer, a brief request for more light:

> DID YOU SAY WHISKERS OR WHISKY? LOVE. WOOSTER.

I found another from her on returning:

> WHISKERS, ASS. THE SON OF A WHAT-NOT HAS SHORT BUT DISTINCT SIDE-WHISKERS. LOVE. TRAVERS.

It's an odd thing about memory, it so often just fails to spear the desired object. At the back of my mind there was dodging about a hazy impression that somewhere at some time I heard someone mention short side-whiskers in some connection, but I couldn't pin it down. It eluded me. So, pursuing the sound old policy of going to the fountainhead for information, I stepped out and dispatched the following:

> WHAT SHORT-SIDE-WHISKERED SON OF A WHAT-NOT WOULD THIS BE, AND WHY DOES HE NEED BUCKING UP? WIRE FULL DETAILS, AS AT PRESENT FOGGED, BEWILDERED AND MYSTIFIED. LOVE. WOOSTER.

She replied with the generous warmth which causes so many of her circle to hold on to their hats when she lets herself go:

> LISTEN, YOU FOUL BLOT. WHAT'S THE IDEA OF MAKING ME SPEND A FORTUNE ON TELEGRAMS LIKE THIS? DO YOU THINK I AM MADE OF MONEY? NEVER YOU MIND WHAT SHORT-SIDE-WHISKERED SON OF A WHAT-NOT IT IS OR WHY HE NEEDS BUCKING UP. YOU JUST COME AS I TELL YOU AND LOOK SLIPPY ABOUT IT. OH, AND BY THE WAY, GO TO ASPINALL'S IN BOND STREET AND GET PEARL NECKLACE OF MINE THEY HAVE THERE AND BRING IT DOWN

WITH YOU. HAVE YOU GOT THAT? ASPINALL'S. BOND STREET.
PEARL NECKLACE. SHALL EXPECT YOU TOMORROW. LOVE.
TRAVERS.

A little shaken but still keeping the flag flying, I responded with the ensuing:

FULLY GRASP ALL THAT ASPINALL'S-BOND-STREET-PEARL-
NECKLACE STUFF, BUT WHAT YOU ARE OVERLOOKING IS THAT
COMING TO BRINKLEY AT PRESENT JUNCTURE NOT SO JOLLY
SIMPLE AS YOU SEEM TO THINK. THERE ARE COMPLICATIONS AND
WHAT NOT. WHEELS WITHIN WHEELS, IF YOU GET WHAT I
MEAN. WHOLE THING CALLS FOR DEEP THOUGHT. WILL WEIGH
MATTERS CAREFULLY AND LET YOU KNOW DECISION. LOVE.
WOOSTER.

You see, though Brinkley Court is a home from home and gets five stars in Baedeker as the headquarters of Monsieur Anatole, Aunt Dahlia's French cook—a place, in short, to which in ordinary circ. I race, when invited, with a whoop and a holler, it had taken me but an instant to spot that under existing conditions there were grave objections to going there. I need scarcely say that I allude to the fact that Florence was on the premises and Stilton expected shortly.

It was this that was giving me pause. Who could say that the latter, finding me in residence on his arrival, would not leap to the conclusion that I had rolled up in pursuit of the former like young Lochinvar coming out of the west? And should this thought flit into his mind, what, I asked myself, would the harvest be? His parting words about my spine were still green in my memory. I knew him to be a man rather careful in his speech, on whose promises one could generally rely, and if he said he was going to break spines in four places, you could be quite sure that four places was precisely what he would break them in.

I passed a restless and uneasy evening. In no mood for revelry at the Drones, I returned home early and was brushing up on my *Mystery of the Pink Crayfish* when the telephone rang, and so disordered was the nervous system that I shot ceilingwards at the sound. It was as much as I could do to totter across the room and unhook the receiver.

The voice that floated over the wire was that of Aunt Dahlia.

Well, when I say floated, possibly thundered would be more the *mot juste*. A girlhood and early womanhood spent in chivvying the British fox in all weathers under the auspices of the Quorn and Pytchley have left this aunt brick-red in color and lent amazing power to her vocal cords. I've never pursued foxes myself, but apparently, when you do, you put in a good bit of your time shouting across ploughed fields in a high wind, and this becomes a habit. If Aunt Dahlia has a fault, it is that she is inclined to talk to you when face to face in a small drawing-room as if she were addressing some crony a quarter of a mile away whom she had observed riding over hounds. For the rest, she is a large, jovial soul, built rather on the lines of Mae West, and is beloved by all including the undersigned. Our relations have always been chummy to the last drop.

"Hullo, hullo, hullo!" she boomed. The old hunting stuff coming to the surface, you notice. "Is that you, Bertie, darling?"

I said it was none other.

"Then what's the idea, you halfwitted Gadarene swine, of all this playing hard-to-get? You and your matter-weighing! I never heard such nonsense in my life. You've got to come here, and immediately, if you don't want an aunt's curse delivered on your doorstep by return of post. If I have to cope unaided with that ruddy Percy any longer, I shall crack beneath the strain."

She paused to take in breath, and I put a question.

"Is Percy the whiskered bloke?"

"That's the one. He's casting a thick pall of gloom over the place. It's like living in a fog. Tom says if something isn't done soon, he will take steps."

"But what's the matter with the chap?"

"He's madly in love with Florence Craye."

"Oh, I see. And it depresses him to think that she's engaged to Stilton Cheesewright?"

"Exactly. He's as sick as mud about it. He moons broodingly to and fro, looking like Hamlet. I want you to come and divert him. Take him for walks, dance before him, tell him funny stories. Anything to bring a smile to that whiskered, tortoiseshell-rimmed face."

I saw her point, of course. No hostess wants a Hamlet on the premises. But what I couldn't understand was how a chap like that came to be polluting the pure air of Brinkley. I knew the old relative to be quite choosey in the matter of guests. Cabinet ministers have sometimes failed to crash the gate. I put this to her, and she said the explanation was perfectly simple.

"I told you I was in the middle of a spot of business with Trotter. I've got the whole family here—Percy's stepfather, L. G. Trotter, Percy's mother, Mrs. Trotter, and Percy in person. I only wanted Trotter, but Mrs. T. and Percy rang themselves in."

"I see. What they call a package deal." I broke off, aghast. Memory had returned to its throne, and I knew now why that stuff about short side-whiskers had seemed to have a familiar ring. "Trotter?" I cried.

She whooped censoriously.

"Don't yell like that. You nearly broke my eardrum."

"But did you say Trotter?"

"Of course I said Trotter."

"This Percy's name isn't Gorringe?"

"That's what it unquestionably is. He admits it."

"Then I'm frightfully sorry, old thing, but I can't possibly come. It was only the other day that the above Gorringe was trying to nick me for a thousand quid to put into this play he's made of Florence's book, and I turned him down like a bedspread. You can readily see, then, how fraught with embarrassment a meeting in the flesh would be. I shouldn't know which way to look."

"If that's all that's worrying you, forget it. Florence tells me he has raised that thousand elsewhere."

"Well, I'm dashed. Where did he get it?"

"She doesn't know. He's secretive about it. He just said it was all right, he had got the stuff and they could go ahead. So you needn't be shy about meeting him. What if he does think you the world's premier louse? Don't we all?"

"Something in that."

"Then you'll come?"

I chewed the lower lip dubiously. I was thinking of Stilton.

"Well, speak, dumbbell," said the relative with asperity. "What's all the silence about?"

"I was musing."

"Then stop musing and give me the good word. If it will help to influence your decision, I may mention that Anatole is at the top of his form just now."

I started. If this was so, it would clearly be madness not to be one of the company ranged around the festive board.

I have touched so far only lightly on this Anatole, and I take the opportunity now of saying that his was an output which had to be tasted to be believed, mere words being inadequate to convey the full facts with regard to his amazing virtuosity. After one of Anatole's lunches has melted in the mouth, you unbutton the waistcoat and loll back, breathing heavily and feeling that life has no more to offer, and then, before you know where you are, along comes one of his dinners, with even more on the ball, the whole layout constituting something about as near Heaven as any reasonable man could wish.

I felt, accordingly, that no matter how vehemently Stilton might express and fulfill himself on discovering me ... well, not perhaps exactly cheek by jowl with the woman he loved but certainly hovering in her vicinity, the risk of rousing the fiend within him was one that must be taken. It cannot ever, of course, be agreeable to find yourself torn into a thousand pieces with a fourteen-stone Othello doing a Shuffle off to Buffalo on the scattered fragments, but if you are full at the time of Anatole's *Timbale de ris de veau Toulousiane,* the discomfort unquestionably becomes modified.

"I'll come," I said.

"Good boy. With you taking Percy off my neck, I shall be free to concentrate on Trotter. And every ounce of concentration will be needed, if I'm to put this deal through."

"What is the deal? You never told me. Who is this Trotter, if any?"

"I met him at Agatha's. He's a friend of hers. He owns a lot of papers up in Liverpool and wants to establish a beachhead in London. So I'm trying to get him to buy a *Boudoir.*"

I was amazed. Absolutely the last thing I would have expected. I had always supposed *Milady's Boudoir* to be her ewe lamb. To learn that she contemplated selling it stunned me. It was like hearing that Rodgers had decided to sell Hammerstein.

"But why on earth? I thought you loved it like a son."

"I do, but the strain of having to keep going to Tom and trying to get money out of him for its support has got me down. Every time I start pleading with him for another check, he says 'But isn't it paying its way yet?' and he says 'H'm!' adding that if this sort of thing goes on, we shall all be on the dole by next Chrismas. It's become too much for me. It makes me feel like one of those women who lug babies around in the streets and want you to buy white heather. So when I met Trotter at Agatha's, I decided that he was the man who was going to take over, if human ingenuity could work it. What did you say?"

"I said 'Oh, ah.' I was about to add that it was a pity."

"Yes, quite a pity, but unavoidable. Tom gets more difficult to touch daily. He says he loves me dearly, but enough is sufficient. Well, I'll expect you tomorrow, then. Don't forget the necklace."

"I'll send Jeeves over for it in the morning."

"Right."

I think she would have spoken further, but at this moment a female voice off stage said "Three-ee-ee minutes," and she hung up with the sharp cry of a woman who fears she is going to be soaked for another couple of bob or whatever it is.

Jeeves came trickling in.

"Oh, Jeeves," I said, "we shall be heading for Brinkley tomorrow."

"Very good, sir."

"Aunt Dahlia wants me there to infuse a bit of the party spirit into our old pal Percy Gorringe, who is at the moment infesting the joint."

"Indeed, sir? I wonder, sir, if it would be possible for you to allow me to return to London next week for the afternoon?"

"Certainly Jeeves, certainly. You have some beano in prospect?"

"It is the monthly luncheon of the Junior Ganymede Club, sir. I have been asked to take the chair."

"Take it by all means, Jeeves. A well-deserved honor."

"Thank you, sir. I shall of course return the same day."

"You'll make a speech, no doubt?"

"Yes, sir. A speech from the chair is of the essence."

"I'll bet you have them rolling in the aisles. Oh, Jeeves, I was nearly forgetting. Aunt Dahlia wants me to bring her necklace. It's at Aspinall's in Bond Street. Will you toddle over and get it in the morning?"

"Certainly, sir."

"And another thing I almost forgot to mention. Percy has raised that thousand quid."

"Indeed, sir?"

"He must have approached someone with a more biteable ear than mine. One wonders who the mug was."

"Yes, sir."

"Some halfwit, one presumes."

"No doubt, sir."

"Still, there it is. It just bears out what the late Barnum used to say about there being one born every minute."

"Precisely, sir. Would that be all, sir?"

"'Yes, that's all. Good night, Jeeves."

"Good night, sir. I will attend to the packing in the morning."

9

IT WAS getting on for the quiet evenfall on the morrow when after a pleasant drive through the smiling countryside I steered the two-seater in at the gates of Brinkley Court and ankled along to inform my hostess that I had come aboard. I found her in her snuggery or den, taking it easy with a cup of tea and an Agatha Christie. As I presented myself, she gave the moustache a swift glance, but apart from starting like a nymph surprised while bathing and muttering something about "Was this the face that stopped a thousand clocks?" made no comment. One received the impression that she was saving it up.

"Hullo, reptile," she said. "You're here, are you?"

"Here I am," I responded, "with my hair in a braid and ready to the last button. A very merry Pip-pip to you, aged relative."

"The same to you, fathead. I suppose you forgot to bring that necklace?"

"Far from it. Here it is. It's the one Uncle Tom gave you at Christmas, isn't it?"

"That's right. He likes to see me wearing it at dinner."

"As who wouldn't?" I said courteously. I handed it over and helped myself to a slice of buttered toast. "Well, nice to be in the old home once more. I'm in my usual room, I take it? And how is everything in and around Brinkley Court? Anatole all right?"

"Never better."

"You look pretty roguish."

"Oh, I'm fine."

"And Uncle Tom?"

A cloud passed over her shining evening face.

"Tom's still a bit low, poor old buster."

"Owing to Percy, you mean?"

"That's right."

"There has been no change then in this Gorringe's gloom?"

"Naturally not. He's been worse than ever since Florence got here. Tom winces every time he sees him, especially at meals. He says that having to watch Percy push away untasted food cooked by Anatole gives him a rush of blood to the head, and that gives him indigestion. You know how sensitive his stomach is."

I patted her hand.

"Be of good cheer," I said. "I'll buck Perce up. Freddie Widgeon was showing me a trick with two corks and a bit of string the other night which cannot fail to bring a smile to the most tortured face. It had the lads at the Drones in stitches. You will doubtless be able to provide a couple of corks?"

"Twenty, if you wish."

"Good." I took a cake with pink icing on it. "So much for Percy. What of the rest of the personnel? Anybody here besides the Trotter gang and Florence?"

"Not yet. Tom said something about somebody named Lord Sidcup looking in for dinner tomorrow on his way to the brine baths at Droitwich. Do you know him?"

"Never heard of him. He's a sealed book to me."

"He's some man Tom met in London. Apparently he's a bit of nib on old silver, and Tom wants to show him his collection."

I nodded. I knew this uncle to be greatly addicted to the collecting of old silver. His apartments both at Brinkley Court and at his house in Charles Street are full of things I wouldn't be seen dead in a ditch with.

"What they call a virtuoso this Lord Sidcup would be, I presume?"

"Something on those lines."

"Ah well, it takes all sorts to make a world, does it not?"

"We shall also have with us tomorrow the boy friend Cheesewright, and the day after that Daphne Dolores Morehead. She's the novelist."

"I know. Florence was telling me about her. You've bought a serial from her, I understand."

"Yes. I thought it would be a shrewd move to salt the mine."

I didn't get this. She seemed to me an aunt who was talking in riddles.

"How do you mean, salt the mine? What mine? This is the first I've heard of any mines."

I think that if her mouth had not been full of buttered toast, she would have clicked her tongue, for as soon as she had cleared the gangway with a quick swallow she spoke impatiently, as if my slowness in the uptake had exasperated her.

"You really are an abysmal ass, young Bertie. Haven't you ever heard of salting mines? It's a recognized business precaution. When you've got a dud mine you want to sell to a mug, you sprinkle an ounce or two of gold over it and summon the mug to come along and inspect the property. He rolls up, sees the gold, feels that this is what the doctor ordered and reaches for his check book. I worked on the same principle."

I was still at a loss, and said so, and this time she did click her tongue.

"Can't you grasp it, chump? I bought the serial to make the paper look good to Trotter. He sees the announcement that a Daphne Morehead opus is coming along and is terrifically impressed. 'Gosh!' he says to himself. 'Daphne Dolores Morehead and everything! *Milady's Boudoir* must be hot stuff.' "

"But don't these blokes want to see books and figures and things before they brass up?"

"Not if they've been having Anatole's cooking for a week or more. That's why I asked him down here."

I saw what she meant, and her reasoning struck me as sound. There is something about those lunches and dinners of Anatole's that mellows you and saps your cool judgment. After tucking into them all this time I presumed that L. G. Trotter was going about in a sort of rosy mist, wanting to do kind acts right and left like a Boy Scout. Continue the treatment a few more days, and he would probably beg her as a personal favor to accept twice what she was asking.

"Very shrewd," I said. "Yes, I think you're on the right lines. Has Anatole been giving you his *Rognons aux Montagnes?*"

"*And* his *Selle d'Agneau au laitues à la Grecque.*"

"Then I would say the thing was in the bag. All over but the cheering. But here's a point that has been puzzling me," I said. "Florence tells me that La Morehead is one of the more costly of our female pen-pushers and has to have purses of gold flung to her in great profusion before she will consent to sign on the dotted line. Correct?"

"Quite correct."

"Then how the dickens," I said, getting down to it in my keen way, "did you contrive to extract the necessary ore from Uncle Tom? Didn't he pay his income tax this year?"

"You bet he did. I should have thought you would have heard his screams in London. Poor old boy, how he does suffer on these occasions."

She spoke sooth. Uncle Tom, though abundantly provided with the chips, having been until his retirement one of those merchant princes who scoop it up in sackfuls out East, has a rooted objection to letting the hellbounds of the Inland Revenue dip in and get theirs. For weeks after they have separated him from his hard-earned he is inclined to go off into corners and sit with his head between his hands, muttering about ruin and the sinister trend of socialistic legislation and what is to become of us all if this continues.

"He certainly does," I assented. "Quite the soul in torment, what? And yet, despite this, you succeeded in nicking him for what must have been a small fortune. How did you do it? From what you were saying on the phone last night I got the impression that he was in more than usually non-parting mood these days. You conjured up in my mind's eye the picture of a man who was sticking his ears back and refusing to play ball, like Balaam's ass."

"What do you know about Balaam's ass?"

"Me? I know Balaam's ass from soup to nuts. Have you forgotten that when a pupil at the Rev. Aubrey Upjohn's educational establishment at Bramley-on-Sea I once won a prize for Scripture Knowledge?"

"I'll bet you cribbed."

"Not at all. My triumph was due to sheer merit. But, getting back to it, how did you induce Uncle Tom to scare the moths from his pocketbook? It must have required quite a scuttleful of wifely wiles on your part?"

I wouldn't like to say of a loved aunt that she giggled, but unquestionably the sound that proceeded from her lips closely resembled a giggle.

"Oh, I managed."

"But how?"

"Never mind how, you pestilential young Nosey Parker. I managed."

"I see," I said, letting it go. Something told me she did not wish to spill the data. "And how is the Trotter deal coming along?"

I seemed to have touched an exposed nerve. The giggle died on her lips, and her face—always, as I have said, on the reddish side—deepened in color to a rich mauve.

"Blister his blighted insides!" she said, speaking with the explosive heat which had once made fellow-members of the Quorn and Pytchley leap convulsively in their saddles. "I don't know what's the matter with the son of Belial. Here he is, with nine of Anatole's lunches and eight of Anatole's dinners tucked away among the gastric juices, and he refuses to get down to brass tacks. He hums—"

"What on earth does he do that for?"

"—and haws. He evades the issue. I strain every nerve to make him talk turkey, but I can't pin him down. He doesn't say Yes and he doesn't say No."

"There's a song called that . . . or, rather, 'She Didn't Say Yes and She Didn't Say No.' I sing it a good deal in my bath. It goes like this."

I started to render the refrain in a pleasant light baritone, but desisted on receiving Agatha Christie abaft the frontal bone. The old relative seemed to have fired from the hip like somebody in a Western B picture.

"Don't try me too high, Bertie dear," she said gently, and fell into what looked like a reverie. "Do you know what I think is the trouble?" she went on, coming out of it. "I believe Ma Trotter is responsible for this non-cooperation of his. For some reason she doesn't want him to put the deal through, and has told him he mustn't. It's the only explanation I can think of. When I met him at Agatha's, he spoke as if it were just a matter of arranging terms, but these last few days he has come over all coy, as if acting under orders from up top. When you stood them dinner that night, did he strike you as being crushed beneath her heel?"

"Very much so. He wept with delight when she gave him a smile and trembled with fear at her frown. But why would she object to him buying the *Boudoir?*"

"Don't ask me. It's a complete mystery."

"You haven't put her back up somehow since she got here?"

"Certainly not. I've been fascinating."

"And yet there it is, what?"

"Exactly. There it blasted well is, curse it."

I heaved a sympathetic sigh. Mine is a tender heart, easily wrung, and the spectacle of this good old egg mourning over what might have been had wrung it like a ton of bricks.

"Too bad," I said. "One had hoped for better things."

"One had," she assented. "I was so sure that Morehead serial would have brought home the bacon."

"Of course, he may be just thinking it over."

"That's true."

"A fellow thinking it over would naturally hum."

"And haw?"

"And, possibly, also haw. You could scarcely expect him to do less."

We would no doubt have proceeded to go more deeply into the matter, subjecting this humming and hawing of L. G. Trotter's to a close analysis, but at this moment the door opened and a careworn face peered in, a face disfigured on either side by short whiskers and in the middle by tortoise-shell-rimmed spectacles.

"I say," said the face, contorted with anguish, "have you seen Florence?"

Aunt Dahlia replied that she had not been privileged to do so since lunch.

"I thought she might be with you."

"She isn't."

"Oh," said the face, still running the gamut of the emotions, and began to recede.

"Hey!" cried Aunt Dahlia, arresting it as it was about to disappear. She went to the desk and picked up a buff envelope. "This telegram came for her just now. Will you give it to her if you see her. And while you're here, meet my nephew Bertie Wooster, the pride of Piccadilly."

Well, I hadn't expected him on learning of my identity to dance about the room on the tips of his toes, and he didn't. He gave me a long, reproachful look, similar in its essentials to that which a black beetle gives a cook when the latter is sprinkling insect powder on it.

"I have corresponded with Mr. Wooster," he said coldly. "We have also spoken on the telephone."

He turned and was gone, gazing at me reproachfully to the last. It was plain that the Gorringes did not lightly forget.

"That was Percy," said Aunt Dahlia.

I replied that I had divined as much.

"Did you notice how he looked when he said 'Florence' ? Like a dying duck in a thunderstorm."

"And did you notice," I inquired in my turn, "how he looked when you said 'Bertie Wooster' ? Like someone finding a dead mouse in his pint of beer. Not a bonhommous bird. Not my type."

"No. You would scarcely suppose that even a mother could view him without nausea, would you? And yet he is the apple of Ma Trotter's eye. She loves him as much as she hates Mrs. Alderman Blenkinsop. Did she touch on Mrs. Alderman Blenkinsop at that dinner of yours?"

"At several points during the meal. Who is she?"

"Her bitterest social rival up in Liverpool."

"Do they have social rivals up in Liverpool?"

"You bet they do, in droves. I gather that it is nip and tuck between the Trotter and the Blenkinsop as to who shall be the uncrowned queen of Liverpudlian society. Sometimes one gets her nose in front, sometimes the other. It's like what one used to read about the death struggles for supremacy in New York's Four Hundred in the old days. But why am I telling you all this? You ought to be out there in the sunset, racing after Percy and bucking him up with your off-color stories. You have a fund of off-color stories, I presume?"

"Oh, rather."

"Then get going, laddie. Once more unto the breach, dear friends, once more, or close the wall up with our English dead. Yoicks! Tally-ho! Hark for'ard!" she added, reverting to the argot of the hunting field.

Well, when Aunt Dahlia tells you to get going, you get going, if you know what's good for you. But I was in no cheery mood as I made my way into the great open spaces. That look of Percy's had told me he was going to be a hard audience. It had had in it much of the austerity which I had noticed in Stilton Cheesewright's Uncle Joseph during our get-together at Vinton Street police court.

It was with not a little satisfaction, accordingly, that I found on arriving in the open no signs of him. Relieved, I abandoned the chase and started to stroll hither and thither, taking the air. And I hadn't taken much of it, when there he was, rounding a rhododendron bush in my very path.

10

I<small>F IT</small> hadn't been for the whiskers, I don't believe I would have recognized him. It was only about ten minutes since he had shoved his face in at the door of Aunt Dahlia's lair, but in that brief interval his whole aspect had changed. No longer the downcast duck in a thunderstorm from whom I had so recently parted, he had become gay and bobbish. His air was jaunty, his smile bright, and there was in his demeanor more than a suggestion of a man who might at any moment break into a tap dance. It was as if he had spent a considerable time watching that trick of Freddie Widgeon's with the two corks and the bit of string.

"Hullo there, Wooster," he cried buoyantly, and you would have supposed that finding Bertram in his midst had just about made his day. "Taking a stroll, eh?"

I said Yes, I was taking a stroll, and he beamed as though feeling that I could have pursued no wiser and more admirable course. *Sensible chap, Wooster,* he seemed to be saying. *He takes strolls.*

There was a short intermission here, during which he looked at me lovingly and slid his feet about a bit in the manner of one trying out dance steps. Then he said it was a beautiful evening, and I endorsed this.

"The sunset," he said, indicating it.

"Very fruity," I agreed, for the whole horizon was aflame with glorious technicolor.

"Seeing it," he said, "I am reminded of a poem I wrote the other day for *Parnassus*. Just a little thing I dashed off. You might care to hear it."

"Oh, rather."

"It's called 'Caliban at Sunset.' "

"What at sunset?"

"Caliban."

He cleared his throat, and began:

> *I stood with a man*
> *Watching the sun go down.*
> *The air was full of murmurous summer scents*
> *And a brave breeze sang like a bugle*
> *From a sky that smoldered in the west,*
> *A sky of crimson, amethyst and gold and sepia*
> *And blue as blue as were the eyes of Helen*
> *When she sat*
> *Gazing from some high tower in Ilium*
> *Upon the Grecian tents darkling below.*
> *And he,*
> *This man who stood beside me,*
> *Gaped like some dull, halfwitted animal*
> *And said,*
> *"I say,*

> *Doesn't that sunset remind you*
> *Of a slice*
> *Of underdone roast beef?"*

He opened his eyes, which he had closed in order to render the *morceau* more effectively.

"Bitter, of course."

"Oh, frightfully bitter."

"I was feeling bitter when I wrote it. I think you know a man named Cheesewright. It was he I had in mind. Actually, we had never stood watching a sunset together, but I felt it was just the sort of thing he would have said if he had been watching a sunset, if you see what I mean. Am I right?"

"Quite right."

"A soulless clod, don't you think?"

"Soulless to the core."

"No finer feelings?"

"None."

"Would I be correct in describing him as a pumpkin-headed oaf?"

"Quite correct."

"Yes," he said, "she is well out of it."

"She?"

"Florence."

"Oh, ah. Well out of what?"

He eyed me speculatively, heaving gently like a saucepan of porridge about to reach the height of its fever. I am a man who can observe and deduce, and it was plain to me, watching him sizzle, that something had happened pretty recently in his affairs which had churned him up like a seidlitz powder, leaving him with but two alternatives—(a) to burst where he stood and (b) to decant his pent-up emotions on the first human being who came along. No doubt he would have preferred this human being to have been of a non-Wooster nature, but one imagines that he was saying to himself that you can't have everything and that he was in no position to pick and choose.

He decided on Alternative B.

"Wooster," he said, placing a hand on my shoulder, "may I ask you a question? Has your aunt told you that I love Florence Craye?"

"She did mention it, yes."

"I thought she might have done. She is not what I would call a reticent woman, though of course with many excellent qualities. I was forced to take her into my confidence soon after my arrival here, because she asked me why the devil I was going about looking like a dead codfish."

"Or like Hamlet?"

"Hamlet or a dead codfish. The point is immaterial. I confessed to her that it was because I loved Florence with a consuming passion and had discovered

that she was engaged to the oaf Cheesewright. It had been, I explained, as if I
had received a crushing blow on the head."

"Like Sir Eustace Willoughby."

"I beg your pardon?"

"In *The Mystery of the Pink Crayfish*. He was conked on the bean in his
library one night, and if you ask me it was the butler who did it. But I
interrupted you."

"You did."

"I'm sorry. You were saying it was as if you had received a crushing blow
on the head."

"Exactly. I reeled beneath the shock."

"Must have been a nasty jar."

"It was. I was stunned. But now . . . You remember that telegram your aunt
gave me to give to Florence?"

"Ah, yes, the telegram."

"It was from Cheesewright, breaking the engagement."

I had no means of knowing, of course, what his form was when reeling
beneath shocks, but I doubted whether he could have put up a performance
topping mine as I heard these words. The sunset swayed before my eyes as if
it were doing the shimmy, and a bird close by which was getting outside its
evening worm looked for an instant like two birds, both flickering.

"What!" I gurgled, rocking on my base.

"Yes."

"He's broken the engagement?"

"Precisely."

"Oh, golly! Why?"

He shook his head.

"Ah, that I couldn't tell you. All I know is that I found Florence in the
stable yard tickling a cat behind the ear, and I came up and said 'Here's a
telegram for you,' and she said 'Really? I suppose it's from D'Arcy.' I
shuddered at the name, and while I was shuddering, she opened the envelope. It was a long telegram, but she had not read more the first words when
she uttered a sharp cry. 'Bad news?' I queried. Her eyes flashed, and a cold,
proud look came into her face. 'Not at all,' she replied. 'Splendid news.
D'Arcy Cheesewright has broken the engagement.' "

"Gosh!"

"You may well say 'Gosh'!"

"She didn't tell you any more than that?"

"No. She said one or two incisive things about Cheesewright with which I
thoroughly concurred and strode off in the direction of the kitchen garden.
And I came away, walking, as you may well imagine, on air. I deprecate the
modern tendency to use slang, but I am not ashamed to confess that what I
was saying to myself was the word 'Whoopee!' Excuse me, Wooster, I must
now leave you. I can't keep still."

And with these words he pranced off like a mustang, leaving me to face the changed conditions alone.

It was with a brooding sense of peril that I did so. And if you are saying "But why, Wooster? Surely everything is pretty smooth? What matter if the girl's nuptials with Cheesewright have been canceled, when here is Percy Gorringe all ready and eager to take up the white man's burden?" I reply "Ah, but you've not seen Percy Gorringe." I mean to say, I couldn't picture Florence, however much on the rebound, accepting the addresses of a man who voluntarily wore side-whiskers and wrote poems about sunsets. Far more likely, it seemed to me, that having a vacant date on her hands she would once again reach out for the old and tried—viz. poor old Bertram. It was what she had done before, and these things tend to become a habit.

I was completely at a loss to imagine what could have caused this in-and-out running on Stilton's part. The thing didn't make sense. When last seen, it will be remembered, he had had all the earmarks of one about whom Love had twined its silken fetters. His every word at that parting chat of ours had indicated this beyond peradventure and doubt. Dash it, I mean, you don't go telling people you will break their spines in four places if they come oiling round the adored object unless you have more than a passing fancy for the bally girl.

So what had occurred to dim the lamp of love and all that sort of thing?

Could it be, I asked myself, that the strain of growing that moustache had proved too much for him? Had he caught sight of himself in the mirror about the third day—the third day is always the danger spot—and felt that nothing in the way of wedded bliss could make the venture worth while? Called upon to choose between the woman he loved and a hairless upper lip, had he cracked, with the result that the lip had had it by a landslide?

With a view to getting the inside stuff straight from the horse's mouth, I hurried to the kitchen garden, where, if Percy was to be relied on, Florence would now be, probably pacing up and down with lowered head.

She was there with lowered head, though not actually pacing up and down. She was bending over a gooseberry bush, eating gooseberries in an over-wrought sort of way. Seeing me, she straightened up, and I snapped into the *res* without preamble.

"What's all this I hear from Percy Gorringe?" I said.

She swallowed a gooseberry with a passionate gulp that spoke eloquently of the churned-up soul, and I saw, as Percy's words had led me to expect, that she was madder than a wet hen. Her whole aspect was that of a girl who would have given her year's dress allowance for the privilege of beating G. D'Arcy Cheesewright over the head with a parasol.

I continued.

"He says there has been a rift within the lute."

"I beg your pardon?"

"You and Stilton. According to Percy, the lute is not the lute it was. Stilton has broken the engagement, he tells me."

"He has. I'm delighted, of course."

"Delighted? You like the setup?"

"Of course I do. What girl would not be delighted who finds herself unexpectedly free from a man with a pink face and a head that looks as if it had been blown up with a bicycle pump?"

I clutched the brow. I am a pretty astute chap, and I could see that this was not the language of love. I mean, if you had heard Juliet saying a thing like that about Romeo, you would have raised the eyebrows in quick concern, wondering if all was well with the young couple.

"But when I saw him last, everything seemed perfectly okey-doke. I could have sworn that, however reluctantly, he had reconciled himself to growing that moustache."

She stooped and took another gooseberry.

"It has nothing to do with moustaches," she said, reappearing on the surface. "The whole thing is due to the fact that D'Arcy Cheesewright is a low, mean, creeping, crawling, slinking, spying, despicable worm," she proceeded, dishing out the words from between clenched teeth. "Do you know what he did?"

"I haven't a notion."

She refreshed herself with a further gooseberry and returned to the upper air, breathing a few puffs of flame through the nostrils.

"He sneaked round to that night club yesterday and made inquiries."

"Oh, my gosh!"

"Yes. You wouldn't think a man could stoop so low, but he bribed people and was allowed to look at the head waiter's book and found that a table had been reserved that night in your name. This confirmed his degraded suspicions. He knew that I had been there with you. I suppose," said Florence, diving at the gooseberry bush once more and starting to strip it of its contents, "a man gets a rotten, spying mind like that from being a policeman."

To say that I was appalled would not be putting it any too strongly. I was, moreover, astounded. It was a revelation to me that a puff-faced poop like Stilton could have been capable of detective work on this uncanny scale. I had always respected his physique, of course, but had supposed that the ability to fell an ox with a single blow more or less let him out. Not for an instant had I credited him with reasoning powers which might well have made Hercule Poirot himself draw the breath in with a startled "What ho." It just showed how one ought never to underestimate a man simply because he devotes his life to shoving oars into rivers and pulling them out again, this being about as silly a way of passing the time as could be hit upon.

No doubt, as Florence had said, this totally unforeseen snakiness was the result of his having been, if only briefly, a member of the police force. One presumes that when the neophyte has been issued his uniform and regulation boots, the men up top take him aside and teach him a few things likely to be of use to him in his chosen profession. Stilton, it was plain, had learned his lesson well and, if one did but know, was probably capable of measuring blood stains and collecting cigar ash.

However, it was only fleeting attention that I gave to this facet of the situation. My thoughts were concentrated on something of far greater pith and moment, as Jeeves would say. I allude to the position—now that the man knew all—of B. Wooster, which seemed to me sticky to a degree. Florence, having sated herself with gooseberries, was starting to move off, and I arrested her with a sharp "Hoy!"

"That telegram," I said.

"I don't want to talk about it."

"I do. Was there anything about me in it?"

"Oh, yes, quite a lot."

I swallowed a couple of times and passed a finger round the inside of my collar. I had thought there might be.

"Did he hint at any plans he had with regard to me?"

"He said he was going to break your spine in five places."

"*Five* places?"

"I think he said five. Don't you let him," said Florence warmly, and it was nice, of course, to know that she disapproved. "Breaking spines! I never heard of such a thing. He ought to be ashamed of himself."

And she moved off in the direction of the house, walking like a tragedy queen on one of her bad mornings.

What I have heard Jeeves call the glimmering landscape was now fading on the sight, and it was getting on for the hour when dressing-gongs are beaten. But though I knew how rash it is ever to be late for one of Anatole's dinners, I could not bring myself to go in and don the soup-and-fish. I had so much to occupy the mind that I lingered on in a sort of stupor. Winged creatures of the night kept rolling up and taking a look at me and rolling off again, but I remained motionless, plunged in thought. A man pursued by a thug like D'Arcy Cheesewright has need of all the thought he can get hold of.

And then, quite suddenly, out of the night that covered me, black as the pit from pole to pole, there shone a gleam of light. It spread, illuminating the entire horizon, and I realized that, taken by and large, I was sitting pretty.

You see, what I had failed till now to spot was the fact that Stilton hadn't a notion that I was at Brinkley. Thinking me to be in the metropolis, it was there that he would be spreading his dragnet. He would call at the flat, ring bells, get no answer and withdraw, baffled. He would haunt the Drones, expecting me to drop in, and eventually, when I didn't so drop, would slink away, baffled again. "He cometh not" he would say, no doubt grinding his teeth, and a fat lot of good that would do him.

And of course, after what had occurred, there was no chance of him visiting Brinkley. A man who has broken off his engagement doesn't go to the country house where he knows the girl to be. Well, I mean, I ask you. Naturally he doesn't. If there was one spot on earth which could be counted on as of even date to be wholly free from Cheesewrights, it was Brinkley Court, Brinkley-cum-Snodsfield-in-the-Marsh, Worcestershire.

Profoundly relieved, I picked up the feet and hastened to my room with a song on my lips. Jeeves was there, not actually holding a stop watch but obviously shaking his head a bit over the young master's tardiness. His left eyebrow quivered perceptibly as I entered.

"Yes, I know I'm late, Jeeves," I said, starting to shed the upholstery. "I went for a stroll."

He accepted the explanation indulgently.

"I quite understand, sir. It had occurred to me that, the evening being so fine, you were probably enjoying a saunter in the grounds. I told Mr. Cheesewright that this was no doubt the reason for your absence."

11

HALF IN and half out of the shirt, I froze like one of those fellows in the old fairy stories who used to talk out of turn to magicians and have spells cast upon them. My ears were sticking up like a wirehaired terrier's, and I could scarcely believe that they had heard aright.

"Mr. Chuch?" I quavered. "What's that, Jeeves?"

"Sir?"

"I don't understand you. Are you saying . . . are you telling me . . . are you actually asserting that Stilton Cheesewright is on the premises?"

"Yes, sir. He arrived not long ago in his car. I found him waiting here. He expressed a desire to see you and appeared chagrined at your continued absence. Eventually, the dinner hour becoming imminent, he took his departure. He is hoping, I gathered from his remarks, to establish contact with you at the conclusion of the meal."

I slid dumbly into the shirt and started to tie the tie. I was quivering, partly with apprehension but even more with justifiable indignation. To say that I felt that this was a bit thick would not be straining the facts unduly. I mean, I knew D'Arcy Cheesewright to be of coarse fiber, the sort of bozo who, as Percy had said, would look at a sunset and see in it only a resemblance to a slice of underdone roast beef, but surely one is entitled to expect even bozos of coarse fiber to have a certain amount of delicacy and decent feeling and what not. This breaking off his engagement to Florence with one hand and coming thrusting his society on her with the other struck me, as it would have struck any fineminded man, as about as near the outside rim as it was possible to go.

"It's monstrous, Jeeves!" I cried. "Has this pumpkin-headed oaf no sense of what is fitting? Has he no tact, no discretion? Are you aware that this very evening, through the medium of a telegram which I have every reason to believe was a stinker, he severed his relations with Lady Florence?"

"No, sir, I had not been apprised. Mr. Cheesewright did not confide in me."

"He must have stopped off en route to compose the communication for it arrived not so very long before he did. Fancy doing the thing by telegram, thus giving some post-office clerk the laugh of a lifetime. And then actually having the crust to come barging in here! That, Jeeves, is serving it up with cream sauce. I don't want to be harsh, but there is only one word for D'Arcy Cheesewright—the word 'uncouth.' What are you goggling at?" I asked, noticing that his gaze was fixed upon me in a meaning manner.

He spoke with quiet severity.

"Your tie, sir. It will not, I fear, pass muster."

"Is this a time to talk of ties?"

"Yes, sir. One aims at the perfect butterfly shape, and this you have not achieved. With your permission, I will adjust it."

He did so, and I must say made a very fine job of it, but I continued to chafe.

"Do you realize, Jeeves, that my life is in peril?"

"Indeed, sir?"

"I assure you. That hunk of boloney . . . I allude to G. D'Arcy Cheesewright . . . has formally stated his intention of breaking my spine in five places."

"Indeed, sir? Why is that?"

I gave him the facts, and he expressed his opinion that the position of affairs was disturbing.

I shot one of my looks at him.

"You would go so far as that, Jeeves?"

"Yes, sir. Most disturbing."

"Ho!" I said, borrowing a bit of Stilton's stuff, and was about to tell him that if he couldn't think of a better word than that to describe what was probably the ghastliest imbroglio that had ever broken loose in the history of the human race, I would be glad to provide him with a Roget's *Thesaurus* at my personal expense, when the gong went and I had to leg it for the trough.

I do not look back to that first dinner at Brinkley Court as among the pleasantest functions which I have attended. Ironically, considering the circumstances, Anatole, that wizard of the pots and pans, had come through with one of his supremest efforts. He had provided the company with, if memory serves me correctly,

Le Caviar Frais
Le Consommé aux Pommes d'Amour
Les Sylphides à la crème d'Ecrevisses
Les Fried Smelts
Le Bird of some kind with chipped potatoes
Le Ice Cream

and, of course, *les fruits* and *le café,* but for all its effect on the Wooster soul it might have been corned beef hash. I don't say I pushed it away untasted, as Aunt Dahlia had described Percy doing with his daily ration, but the successive courses turned to ashes in my mouth. The sight of Stilton across the table blunted appetite.

I suppose it was just imagination, but he seemed to have grown quite a good deal both upwards and sideways since I had last seen him, and the play of expression on his salmon-colored face showed only too clearly the thoughts that were occupying his mind, if you could call it that. He gave me from eight to ten dirty looks in the course of the meal, but except for a remark at the outset to the effect that he was hoping to have a word with me later, did not address me.

Nor, for the matter of that, did he address anyone. His demeanor throughout was that of a homicidal deaf mute. The Trotter female, who sat on his right, endeavored to entertain him with a saga about Mrs. Alderman Blenkinsop's questionable behavior at a recent church bazaar, but he confined his response to gaping at her like some dull, halfwitted animal, as Percy would have said, and digging silently into the foodstuffs.

Sitting next to Florence, who spoke little, merely looking cold and proud and making bread pills, I had ample leisure for thought during the festivities, and by the time the coffee came round I had formed my plans and perfected my strategy. When eventually Aunt Dahlia blew the whistle for the gentler sex to buzz off and leave the men to their port, I took advantage of their departure to execute a quiet sneak through the French windows into the garden, being well in the open before the first of the procession had crossed the threshold. Whether or not this clever move brought a hoarse cry to Stilton's lips, I cannot say for certain, but I fancied I heard something that sounded like the howl of a timber wolf that has stubbed its toe on a passing rock. Not bothering to go back and ask if he had spoken, I made my way into the spacious grounds.

Had circumstances been different from what they were—not, of course, that they ever are—I might have derived no little enjoyment from this after-dinner saunter, for the air was full of murmurous summer scents and a brave breeze sang like a bugle from a sky liberally studded with stars. But to appreciate a starlit garden one has to have a fairly tranquil mind, and mine was about as far from being tranquil as it could jolly well stick.

What to do? I was asking myself. It seemed to me that the prudent course, if I wished to preserve a valued spine intact, would be to climb aboard the two-seater first thing in the morning and ho for the open spaces. To remain in statu quo would, it was clear, involve a distasteful nippiness on my part, for only by the most unremitting activity could I hope to elude Stilton and foil his sinister aims. I would be compelled, I saw, to spend a substantial portion of my time flying like a youthful hart or roe over the hills where spices grow, as I remembered having heard Jeeves once put it, and the Woosters resent having to sink to the level of harts and roes, whether juvenile or getting on in years. We have our pride.

I had just reached the decision that on the morrow I would melt away like snow on the mountain tops and go to America or Australia or the Fiji Islands or somewhere for awhile, when the murmurous summer scents were augmented by the aroma of a powerful cigar and I observed a dim figure approaching. After a tense moment when I supposed it to be Stilton and braced myself for a spot of that youthful-hart-or-roe stuff, I got it placed. It was only Uncle Tom, taking his nightly prowl.

Uncle Tom is a great lad for prowling in the garden. A man with grayish hair and a face like a walnut–not that that has anything to do with it, of course–I just mention it in passing–he likes to be among the shrubs and flowers early and late, particularly late, for he suffers a bit from insomnia and the tribal medicine man told him that a breath of fresh air before hitting the hay would bring relief.

Seeing me, he paused for station identification.

"Is that you, Bertie, me boy?"

I conceded this, and he hove alongside, puffing smoke.

"Why did you leave us?" he asked, alluding to that quick duck of mine from the dining-room.

"Oh, I thought I would."

"Well, you didn't miss much. What a set! That man Trotter makes me sick."

"Oh, yes?"

"His stepson Percy makes me sick."

"Oh, yes?"

"And that fellow Cheesewright makes me sick. They all make me sick," said Uncle Tom. He is not one of your jolly-innkeeper-with-entrance-number-in-act-one hosts. He looks with ill-concealed aversion on at least ninety-four per cent of the guests within his gates and spends most of his time dodging them. "Who invited Cheesewright here? Dahlia, I suppose, though why we shall never know. A deleterious young slab of damnation, if ever I saw one. But she will do these things. I've even known her to invite her sister Agatha. Talking of Dahlia, Bertie, me boy, I'm worried about her."

"Worried?"

"Exceedingly worried. I believe she's sickening for something. Has her manner struck you as strange since you got here?"

I mused.

"No, I don't think so," I said. "She seemed to be about the same as usual. How do you mean, strange?"

He waved a concerned cigar. He and the old relative are a fond and united couple.

"It was just now, when I looked in on her in her room to ask if she would care to come for a stroll. She said No, she didn't think she would, because if she went out at night she always swallowed moths and midges and things and she didn't believe it was good for her on top of a heavy dinner. And we were talking idly of this and that, when she suddenly seemed to come all over faint."

"Swooned, do you mean?"

"No, I wouldn't say she actually swooned. She continued perpendicular. But she tottered, pressing her hand to the top of her head. Pale as a ghost she looked."

"Odd."

"Very. It worried me. I'm not at all easy in my mind about her."

I pondered.

"It couldn't have been something you said that upset her?"

"Impossible. I was talking about this fellow Sidcup who's coming tomorrow to look at my silver collection. You've never met him, have you?"

"No."

"Rather a fatheaded ass," said Uncle Tom, who thinks most of his circle fatheaded asses, "but apparently knows quite a bit about old silver and jewelry and all that sort of thing and anyway he'll only be here for dinner, thank God," he added in his hospitable way. "But I was telling you about your aunt. As I was saying, she tottered and looked as pale as a ghost. The fact of the matter is, she's been overdoing it. This paper of hers, this *Madame's Nightshirt* or whatever it's called. It's wearing her to a shadow. Silly nonsense. What does she want with a weekly paper? I'll be thankful if she sells it to this man Trotter and gets rid of the damned thing, because apart from wearing her to a shadow it's costing me a fortune. Money, money, money, there's no end to it."

He then spoke with considerable fervor for a while of income tax and surtax, and after making a tentative appointment to meet me in the breadline at an early date popped off and was lost in the night. And I, feeling that, the hour being now advanced, it might be safe to retire to my room, made my way thither.

As I started to get into something loose, I continued to brood on what he had told me about Aunt Dahlia. I found myself mystified. At dinner I had, of course, been distrait and preoccupied, but even so I would, I thought, have noticed if she had shown any signs of being in the grip of a wasting sickness or anything of that kind. As far as I could recollect, she had appeared to be tucking into the various items on the menu with her customary zip and *brio*.

Yet Uncle Tom had spoken of her as looking as pale as a ghost, a thing which took some doing with a face as red as hers.

Odd, not to say mysterious.

I was still musing on this and wondering what Osborne Cross, the sleuth in *The Mystery of the Pink Crayfish,* would have made of it, when I was jerked out of my meditations by the turning of the door handle. This was followed by a forceful bang on the panel, and I realized how prudent I had been in locking up before settling in for the night. For the voice that now spoke was that of Stilton Cheesewright.

"Wooster!"

I rose, laying down my *Crayfish,* into which I had been about to dip, and put my lips to the keyhole.

"Wooster!"

"All right, my good fellow," I said coldly. "I heard you the first time. What do you want?"

"A word with you."

"Well, you jolly well aren't going to have it. Leave me, Cheesewright. I would be alone. I have a slight headache."

"It won't be slight, if I get at you."

"Ah, but you can't get at me," I riposted cleverly, and returning to my chair resumed my literary studies, pleasantly conscious of having worsted him in debate. He called me a few derogatory names through the woodwork, banged and handle-rattled a bit more, and finally shoved off, no doubt muttering horrid imprecations.

It was about five minutes later that there was another knock on the door, this time so soft and discreet that I had no difficulty in identifying it.

"Is that you, Jeeves?"

"Yes, sir."

"Just a moment."

As I crossed the room to admit him, I was surprised to find that the lower limbs were feeling a bit filleted. That verbal duel with my recent guest had shaken me more than I had suspected.

"I have just had a visit from Stilton Cheesewright, Jeeves," I said.

"Indeed, sir? I trust the outcome was satisfactory."

"Yes, I rather nonplused the simple soul. He had imagined that he could penetrate into my sanctum without let or hindrance, and was struck all of a heap when he found the door locked. But the episode has left me a little weak, and I would be glad if you could dig me out a whisky-and-soda."

"Certainly, sir."

"It wants to be prepared in just the right way. Who was that pal of yours you were speaking about the other day whose strength was as the strength of ten?"

"A gentleman of the name of Galahad, sir. You err, however, in supposing him to have been a personal friend. He was the subject of a poem by the late Alfred, Lord Tennyson."

"Immaterial, Jeeves. All I was going to say was that I would like the strength of this whisky-and-soda to be as that of ten. Don't flinch when pouring."

"Very good, sir."

He departed on his errand of mercy, and I buckled down to the *Crayfish* once more. But scarcely had I started to collect clues and interview suspects when I was interrupted again. A clenched fist had sloshed against the portal with a disturbing booming sound. Assuming that my visitor was Stilton, I was about to rise and rebuke him through the keyhole as before, when there penetrated from the outer spaces an ejaculation so fruity and full of vigor that it could have proceeded only from the lips of one who had learned her stuff among the hounds and foxes.

"Aunt Dahlia?"

"Open this door!"

I did so, and she came charging in.

"Where's Jeeves?" she asked, so plainly all of a twitter that I eyed her in considerable alarm. After what Uncle Tom had been saying about her tottering I didn't like this febrile agitation.

"Is something the matter?" I asked.

"You bet something's the matter. Bertie," said the old relative, sinking on to the chaise longue and looking as if at any moment she might start blowing bubbles, "I'm up against it, and only Jeeves can save my name in the home from becoming mud. Produce the blighter, and let him exercise that brain of his as never before."

12

I ENDEAVORED to soothe her with a kindly pat on the topknot.

"Jeeves will be back in a moment," I said, "and will doubtless put everything right with one wave of his magic wand. Tell me, my fluttering old aspen, what seems to be the trouble?"

She gulped like a stricken bull pup. I had rarely seen a more jittery aunt.

"It's Tom!"

"The uncle of that name?"

"How many Toms do you think there are in this joint, for goodness' sake?" she said, with a return of her normal forcefulness. "Yes, Thomas Portarlington Travers, my husband."

"Portarlington?" I said, a little shocked.

"He came pottering into my room just now."

I nodded intelligently. I remembered that he had spoken of having done so. It was on that occasion, you recall, that he had observed her pressing her hand to the top of her head.

"I see. Yes, so far I follow you. Scene, your room. Discovered sitting, you. Enter Uncle Tom, pottering. What then?"

She was silent for a space. Then she spoke in what was for her a hushed voice. That is to say, while rattling the vases on the mantelpiece, it did not bring plaster down from the ceiling.

"I'd better tell you the whole thing."

"Do, old ancestor. Nothing like getting it off the chest, whatever it is."

She gulped like another stricken bull pup.

"It's not a long story."

"Good," I said, for the hour was late and I had had a busy day.

"You remember when we were talking after you got here this evening . . . Bertie, you revolting object," she said, deviating momentarily from the main thread, "that moustache of yours is the most obscene thing I ever saw outside of a nightmare. It seems to take one straight into another and a dreadful world. What made you commit this rash act?"

I tut-tutted a bit austerely.

"Never mind my moustache, old flesh and blood. You leave it alone, and it'll leave you alone. When we were talking this evening, you were saying?"

She accepted the rebuke with a moody nod.

"Yes, I mustn't get side-tracked. I must stick to the point."

"Like glue."

"When we were talking this evening, you said you wondered how I had managed to get Tom to cough up the price of that Daphne Dolores Morehead serial. You remember?"

"I do. I'm still wondering."

"Well, it's quite simple. I didn't."

"Eh?"

"Tom didn't contribute a penny."

"Then how—?"

"I'll tell you how. I pawned my pearl necklace."

I gazed at her . . . well, I suppose "awestruck" would be the word. Acquaintance with this woman dating from the days when I was an infant mewling and puking in my nurse's arms, if you will excuse the expression, had left me with the feeling that her guiding motto in life was "Anything goes," but this seemed pretty advanced stuff even for one to whom the sky had always been the limit.

"Pawned it?" I said.

"Pawned it."

"Hocked it, you mean? Popped it? Put it up the spout?"

"That's right. It was the only thing to do. I had to have that serial in order to salt the mine, and Tom absolutely refused to give me so much as a fiver to slake the thirst for gold of this blood-sucking Morehead. 'Nonsense, non-sense,' he kept saying. 'Quite out of the question, quite out of the question.' So I slipped up to London, took the necklace to Aspinall's, told them to make a replica, and then went along to the pawnbroker's. Well, when I say pawnbroker's, that's a figure of speech. My fellow was much higher class. More of a moneylender, you would call him."

"I whistled a bar or two.

"Then that thing I picked up for you this morning was a dud?"

"Cultured stuff."

"Golly!" I said. "You aunts do live!" I hesitated. I was loath to bruise that gentle spirit, especially at a moment when she was worried about something, but it seemed to me a nephew's duty to point out the snag. "And when . . . I'm afraid this is going to spoil your day, but what happens when Uncle Tom finds out?"

"That's exactly the trouble."

"I thought it might be."

She gulped like a third stricken bull pup.

"If it hadn't been for a foul bit of bad luck, he wouldn't have found out in a million years. I don't suppose Tom, bless him, would know the difference between the Kohinoor and something from Woolworth's."

I saw her point. Uncle Tom, as I have indicated, is a red-hot collector of old silver and there is nothing you can teach him about sconces, foliation, scrolls and ribbon wreaths, but jewelry is to him, as to most of the male sex, a sealed book.

"But he's going to find out tomorrow evening, and I'll tell you why. I told you he came to my room just now. Well, we had been kidding back and forth for a few moments, all very pleasant and matey, when he suddenly . . . Oh, my God!"

I administered another sympathetic pat on the bean.

"Pull yourself together, old relative. What did he suddenly do?"

"He suddenly told me that this Lord Sidcup who is coming tomorrow is not only an old-silver hound but an expert on jewelry, and he was going to ask him, while here, to take a look at my necklace."

"Gosh!"

"He said he had often had a suspicion that the bandits who sold it to him had taken advantage of his innocence and charged him a lot too much. Sidcup, he said, would be able to put him straight about it."

"Golly!"

" 'Gosh!' is right, and so is 'Golly!' "

"Then that's why you clutched the top of your head and tottered?"

"That's why. How long do you suppose it will take this fiend in human shape to see through that dud string of pearls and spill the beans? Just about ten seconds, if not less. And then what? Can you blame me for tottering?"

I certainly couldn't. In her place, I would have tottered myself and tottered like nobody's business. A far duller man than Bertram Wooster would have been able to appreciate that this aunt who sat before me clutching feverishly at her perm was an aunt who was in the dickens of a spot. A crisis had been precipitated in her affairs which threatened, unless some pretty adroit staffwork was pulled by her friends and well-wishers, to put the home right plumb spang in the melting pot.

I have made a rather close study of the married state, and I know what happens when one turtle dove gets the goods on the other turtle dove. Bingo Little has often told me that if Mrs. Bingo had managed to get on him some of the things it seemed likely she was going to get, the moon would have been turned to blood and Civilization shaken to its foundations. I have heard much the same thing from other husbands of my acquaintance, and of course similar upheavals occur when it is the little woman who is caught bending.

Always up to now Aunt Dahlia had been the boss of Brinkley Court, maintaining a strong centralized government, but let Uncle Tom discover that she had pawned her pearl necklace in order to buy a serial story for what for some reason he always alluded to as *Madame's Nightshirt,* a periodical which from the very start he had never liked, and she would be in much the same position as one of those monarchs or dictators who wake up one morning to find that the populace had risen against them and is saying it with bombs. Uncle Tom is a kindly old bimbo, but even kindly old bimbos can make themselves dashed unpleasant when the conditions are right.

"Egad!" I said, fingering the chin. "This is not so good."

"It's the end of all things."

"You say this Sidcup bird will be here tomorrow? It doesn't give you much time to put your affairs in order. No wonder you're sending out S.O.S.'s for Jeeves."

"Only he can save me from the fate that is worse than death."

"But can even Jeeves adjust matters?"

"I'm banking on him. After all, he's a hell of an adjuster."

"True."

"He's got you out of some deepish holes in his time."

"Quite. I often say there is none like him, none. He should be with us at any moment now. He stepped out to get me a tankard of the old familiar juice."

Her eyes gleamed with a strange light.

"Bags I first go at it!"

I patted her hand.

"Of course," I said, "of course. You may take that as read. You don't find Bertram Wooster hogging the drink supply when a suffering aunt is at his side with her tongue hanging out. Your need is greater than mine, as whoever-it-was said to the stretcher case. Ah!"

Jeeves had come in bearing the elixir, not a split second before we were ready for it. I took the beaker from him and offered it to the aged relative with a courteous gesture. With a brief "Mud in your eye" she drank deeply. I then finished what was left at a gulp.

"Oh, Jeeves," I said.

"Sir?"

"Lend me your ear."

"Very good, sir."

It had needed but a glance at my late father's sister to tell me that if there was going to be any lucid exposition of the *res,* I was the one who would have to attend to it. After moistening her clay she had relapsed into a sort of frozen coma, staring before her with unseeing eyes and showing a disposition to pant like a hart when heated in the chase. Nor was this to be wondered at. Few women would have been in vivacious mood, had Fate touched off beneath them a similar stick of trinitrotoluol. I imagine her emotions after Uncle Tom had said his say must have been of much the same nature as those which she had no doubt frequently experienced in her hunting days when her steed, having bucked her from the saddle, had proceeded to roll on her. And while the blushful Hippocrene of which she had just imbibed her share had been robust and full of inner meaning, it had obviously merely scratched the surface.

"A rather tight place has popped up out of a trap, Jeeves, and we should be glad of your counsel and advice. This is the posish. Aunt Dahlia has a pearl necklace, the Christmas gift of Uncle Tom, whose second name, I'll bet you didn't know, is Portarlington. The one you picked up at Aspinall's this morning. Are you with me?"

"Yes, sir."

"Well, this is where the plot thickens. It isn't a pearl necklace, if I make my meaning clear. For reasons into which we need not go, she put the Uncle-Tom-Merry-Christmas one up the spout. What is now in her possession is an imitation of little or no intrinsic value."

"Yes, sir."

"You don't seem amazed."

"No, sir. I became aware of the fact when I saw the necklace this morning. I perceived at once that what had been given to me was a cultured replica."

"Good Lord! Was it as easy to spot as that?"

"Oh, no, sir. I have no doubt that it would deceive the untutored eye. But I spent some months at one time studying jewelry under the auspices of a cousin of mine who is in the trade. The genuine pearl has no core."

"No what?"

"Core, sir. In its interior. The cultured pearl has. A cultured pearl differs from a real one in this respect, that it is the result of introducing into the oyster a foreign substance designed to irritate it and induce it to coat the substance with layer upon layer of nacre. Nature's own irritant is invariably so small as to be invisible, but the core in the cultured imitation can be discerned, as a rule merely by holding the cultured pearl up before a strong light. This was what I did in the matter of Mrs. Travers' necklace. I had no need of the endoscope."

"The what?"

"Endoscope, sir. An instrument which enables one to peer into the culured pearl's interior and discern the core."

I was conscious of a passing pang for the oyster world, feeling—and I think correctly—that life for these unfortunate bivalves must be one damn thing after another, but my principal emotion was one of astonishment.

"Great Scott, Jeeves! Do you know everything?"

"Oh, no, sir. It just happens that jewelry is something of a hobby of mine. With diamonds, of course, the test would be different. One might ascertain the genuineness of a diamond, for example, by taking a sapphire-point phonograph needle—which is, as you are no doubt aware, corundum having a hardness of 9—and trying to make a small test scratch on the underside of the suspect stone. A genuine diamond, I need scarcely remind you, is the only substance with a hardness of 10—Moh's scale of hardness. Most of the hard objects we see about us are approximately 7 in the hardness scale. But you were saying, sir?"

I was still blinking a bit. When Jeeves gets going nicely, he often has this effect on me. With a strong effort I pulled myself together and was able to continue.

"Well, that's the nub of the story," I said. "Aunt Dahlia's necklace, the one now in her possesion, is, as your trained senses told you, a seething mass of cores and not worth the paper it's written on. Right. Well, here's the point. If no complications had been introduced into the scenario, all would be well, because Uncle Tom couldn't tell the difference betwen a real necklace and an imitation one if he tried for months. But a whale of a complication has been introduced. A pal of his is coming tomorrow to look at the thing, and this pal, like you, is an expert on jewelry. You see what will happen the moment he cocks an eye at the worthless substitute. Exposure, ruin, desolation and despair. Uncle Tom, learning the truth, will blow his top, and Aunt Dahlia's prestige will be down among the wines and spirits. You get me, Jeeves?"

"Yes, sir."

"Then let us have your views."

"It is disturbing, sir."

I wouldn't have thought that anything would have been able to rouse that crushed aunt from her trance, but this did the trick. She came up like a rocketing pheasant from the chair into which she had slumped.

"Disturbing! What a word to use!"

I sympathized with her distress, but checked her with an upraised hand.
"Please, old relative! Yes, Jeeves, it is, as you say, a bit on the disturbing
side, but one feels that you will probably have something constructive to
place before the board. We shall be glad to hear your solution."

He allowed a muscle at the side of his mouth to twitch regretfully.

"With a problem of such magnitude, sir, I fear I am not able to provide a
solution offhand, if I may use the expression. I should require to give the
matter thought. Perhaps if I might be permitted to pace the corridor for
awhile?"

"Certainly, Jeeves. Pace all the corridors you wish."

"Thank you, sir. I shall hope to return shortly with some suggestion which
will give satisfaction."

I closed the door behind him and turned to the aged r., who, her face bright
purple, was still muttering "Disturbing."

"I know just how you feel, old flesh and blood," I said. "I ought to have
warned you that Jeeves never leaps about and rolls the eyes when you spring
something sensational on him, preferring to preserve the calm impassivity of
a stuffed frog."

"Disturbing!"

"I have grown not to mind this much myself, though occasionally, as I was
about to do tonight, administering a rather stern rebuke, for experience has
taught me—"

"Disturbing, for God's sake! *Disturbing!*"

"I know, I know. That manner of his does afflict the nerve centers quite a
bit, does it not? But, as I was saying, experience has taught me that there
always follows some ripe solution of whatever the problem may be. As the
fellow said, if stuffed frogs come, can ripe solutions be far behind?"

She sat up. I could see the light of hope dawning in her eyes.

"You really think he will find the way?"

"I am convinced of it. He always finds the way. I wish I had a quid for every
way he has found since first he started to serve under the Wooster banner.
Remember how he enabled me to put it across Roderick Spode at Totleigh
Towers."

"He did, didn't he?"

"He certainly did. One moment, Spode was a dark menace, the next a mere
blob of jelly with all his fangs removed, groveling at my feet. You can rely
implicitly on Jeeves. Ah," I said, as the door opened. "Here he comes, his
head sticking out at the back and his eyes shining with intelligence and what
not. You have thought of something, Jeeves?"

"Yes, sir."

"I knew it. I was saying a moment ago that you always find the way. Well,
let us have it."

"There is a method by means of which Mrs. Travers can be extricated from
her sea of troubles. Shakespeare."

I didn't know why he was addressing me as Shakespeare, but I motioned him to continue.

"Proceed, Jeeves."

He did so, turning now to Aunt Dahlia, who was gazing at him like a bear about to receive a bun.

"If, as Mr. Wooster has told me, madam, this jewelry expert is to be with us shortly, it would seem that your best plan is to cause the necklace to disappear before he arrives. If I may make my meaning clearer, madam," he went on in response to a query from the sizzling woman as to whether he supposed her to be a bally conjurer. "What I had in mind was something in the nature of a burglarious entry, as the result of which the piece of jewelry would be abstracted. You will readily see, madam, that if the gentleman, coming to examine the necklace, finds that there is no necklace for him to examine—"

"He won't be able to examine it?"

"Precisely, madam. *Rem acu tetigisti.*"

I shook the lemon. I had expected something better than this. It seemed to me that that great brain had at last come unglued, and this saddened me.

"But, Jeeves," I said gently, "where do you get your burglar? From the Army and Navy Stores?"

"I was thinking that you might consent to undertake the task, sir."

"Me?"

"Gosh, yes," said Aunt Dahlia, her dial lighting up like a stage moon. "How right you are, Jeeves. You wouldn't mind doing a little thing like that for me, would you, Bertie? Of course you wouldn't. You've grasped the idea? You get a ladder, prop it up against my window, pop in, pinch the necklace and streak off with it. And tomorrow I go to Tom in floods of tears and say 'Tom! My pearls! They've gone! Some low bounder sneaked in last night and snitched them as I slept!' That's the idea, isn't it, Jeeves?"

"Precisely, madam. It would be a simple task for Mr. Wooster. I notice that since my last visit to Brinkley Court the bars which protected the windows have been removed."

"Yes, I had that done after that time when we were all locked out. You remember?"

"Very vividly, madam."

"So there's nothing to stop you, Bertie."

"Nothing but—"

I paused. I had been about to say "Nothing but my total and absolute refusal to take on the assignment in any shape or form," but I checked the words before they could pass the lips. I saw that I was exaggerating what I had supposed to be the dangers and difficulties of the enterprise.

After all, I felt, there was nothing so very hazardous about it. All I had to do was to procure a ladder and climb up it, a ludicrously simple feat for one of my agility and lissomness. A nuisance, of course, having to turn out at this time of night, but I was quite prepared to do so in order to bring the roses back to the cheeks of a woman who in my bib and cradle days had frequently dandled me on her knee, not to mention saving my life on one occasion when I had half swallowed a rubber comforter.

"Nothing at all," I replied cordially. "Nothing whatever. You provide the necklace, and I will do the rest. Which is your room?"

"The last one on the left."

"Right."

"Left, fool. I'll be going there now, so as to be in readiness. Golly, Jeeves, you've taken a weight off my mind. I feel a new woman. You won't mind if you hear me singing about the house?"

"Not at all, madam."

"I shall probably start first thing tomorrow."

"Any time that suits you, madam."

He closed the door behind her with an indulgent smile, or something as nearly resembling a smile as he ever allows to appear on his map.

"One is glad to see Mrs. Travers so happy, sir."

"Yes, you certainly bucked her up like a tonic. No difficulty about finding a ladder, I take it?"

"Oh, no, sir. I chanced to observe one outside the tool shed by the kitchen garden."

"So did I, now you mention it. No doubt it's still there, so let's go. If it were . . . what's that expression of yours?"

"If it were done when 'tis done, then 'twere well it were done quickly, sir."

"That's right. No sense in standing humming and hawing."

"No, sir. There is a tide in the affairs of men which, taken at the flood, leads on to fortune."

"Exactly," I said.

I couldn't have put it better myself.

The venture went with gratifying smoothness. I found the ladder, by the tool shed as foreshadowed, and lugged it across country to the desired spot. I propped it up. I climbed it. In next to no time I was through the window and moving silently across the floor.

Well, not so dashed silently, as a matter of fact, because I collided with a table which happened to be in the fairway and upset it with quite a bit of noise.

"Who's there?" asked a voice from the darkness in a startled sort of way.

This tickled me. Ah, I said to myself amusedly, Aunt Dahlia throwing herself into her part and giving the thing just the touch it needed to make it box-office. What an artist, I felt.

Then it said "Who's there?" again, and it was as though a well-iced hand had been laid upon my heart.

Because the voice was not the voice of any ruddy aunt, it was the voice of

Florence Craye. The next moment light flooded the apartment and there she
was, sitting up in bed in a pink boudoir cap.

13

I DON'T know if you happen to be familiar with a poem called "The Charge of
the Light Brigade" by the bird Tennyson whom Jeeves had mentioned when
speaking of the fellow whose strength was as the strength of ten. It is, I
believe, fairly well known, and I used to have to recite it at the age of seven or
thereabouts when summoned to the drawing-room to give visitors a glimpse
of the young Wooster. "Bertie recites so nicely," my mother used to
say—getting her facts twisted, I may mention, because I practically always
fluffed my lines—and after trying to duck for safety and being hauled back I
would snap into it. And very unpleasant the whole thing was, so people have
told me.

Well, what I was about to say, when I rambled off a bit on the subject of the
dear old days, was that though in the course of the years most of the poem of
which I speak has slid from the memory, I still recall its punch line. The thing
goes, as you probably know,

Tum tiddle umpty-pum
Tum tiddle umpty-pum
Tum tiddle umpty-pum

and this brought you to the napperoo or payoff, which was

Someone had blundered

I always remember that bit, and the reason I bring it up now is that, as I
stood blinking at this pink-boudoir-capped girl, I was feeling just as those
Light Brigade fellows must have felt. Obviously someone had blundered
here, and that someone was Aunt Dahlia. Why she should have told me that
her window was the last one on the left, when the last one on the left was what
it was anything but, was more than I could imagine. One sought in vain for
what Stilton Cheesewright would have called the ulterior motive.

However, it is hopeless to try to fathom the mental processes of aunts, and
anyway this was no time for idle speculation. The first thing the man of
sensibility has to do on arriving like a sack of coals in a girl's bedroom in the
small hours is to get the conversation going, and it was to this that I now

addressed myself. Nothing is worse on these occasions than the awkward pause and the embarrassed silence.

"Oh, hullo," I said, as brightly and cheerily as I could manage. "I say, I'm most frightfully sorry to pop in like this at a moment when you were doubtless knitting up the ravelled sleave of care, but I went for a breather in the garden and found I was locked out, so I thought my best plan was not to rouse the house but to nip in through the first open window. You know how it is when you rouse houses. They don't like it."

I would have spoken further, developing the theme, for it seemed to me that I was on the right lines . . . so much better, I mean to say, than affecting to be walking in my sleep. All that *Where am I?* stuff, I mean. Too damn silly . . . but she suddenly gave one of those rippling laughs of hers.

"Oh, Bertie!" she said, and not, mark you, with that sort of weary fed-upness with which girls generally say "Oh, Bertie!" to me. "What a romantic you are!"

"Eh!"

She rippled again. It was a relief, of course, to find that she did not propose to yell for help and all that sort of thing, but I must say I found this mirth a bit difficult to cope with. You've probably had the same experience yourself—listening to people guffawing like hyenas and not having the foggiest what the joke is. It makes you feel at a disadvantage.

She was looking at me in an odd kind of way, as if at some child for whom, while conceding that it had water on the brain, she felt a fondness.

"Isn't this just the sort of thing you would do!" she said. "I told you I was no longer engaged to D'Arcy Cheesewright, and you had to fly to me. You couldn't wait till the morning, could you? I suppose you had some sort of idea of kissing me softly while I slept?"

I leaped perhaps six inches in the direction of the ceiling. I was appalled, and I think not unjustifiably so. I mean, dash it, a fellow who has always prided himself on the scrupulous delicacy of his relations with the other sex doesn't like to have it supposed that he deliberately shins up ladders at one in the morning in order to kiss girls while they sleep.

"Good Lord, no," I said, replacing the chair which had knocked over in my agitation. "Nothing further from my thoughts. I take it your attention happened to wander for a moment when I was outlining the facts just now. What I was saying, only you weren't listening, was that I went for a breather in the garden and found I was locked out—"

She rippled once more. That looking-fondly-at-idiot-child expression on her face had become intensified.

"You don't think I'm angry, do you? Of course I'm not. I'm very touched. Kiss me, Bertie."

Well, one has to be civil. I did as directed, but with an uneasy feeling that this was a bit above the odds. I didn't at all like the general trend of affairs, the whole thing seeming to me to be becoming far too French. When I broke out of the clinch and stepped back, I found the expression on her face had changed. She was now regarding me in a sort of speculative way, if you know what I mean, rather like a governess taking a gander at the new pupil.

"Mother's quite wrong," she said.

"Mother?"

"Your Aunt Agatha."

This surprised me.

"You call her Mother? Oh, well, okay, if you like it. Up to you, of course. What was she wrong about?"

"You. She keeps insisting that you are a vapid and irreflective nitwit who ought years ago to have been put in some good mental home."

I drew myself up haughtily, cut more or less to the quick. So this was how the woman was accustomed to shoot off her bally head about me in my absence, was it! A pretty state of affairs. The woman, I'll trouble you, whose repulsive son Thos I had for years practically nursed in my bosom. That is to say, when he passed through London on his way back to school, I put him up at my residence and not only fed him luxuriously but with no thought of self took him to the Old Vic and Madame Tussaud's. Was there no gratitude in the world?

"She does, does she?"

"She's awfully amusing about you."

"Amusing, eh?"

"It was she who said that you had a brain like a peahen."

Here, of course, if I had wished to take it, was an admirable opportunity to go into this matter of peahens and ascertain just where they stood in the roster of our feathered friends as regarded the I.Q., but I let it go.

She adjusted the boudoir cap, which the recent embrace had tilted a bit to one side. She was still looking at me in that speculative way.

"She says you are a guffin."

"A what?"

"A guffin."

"I don't understand you."

"It's one of those old-fashioned expressions. What she meant, I think, was that she considered you a wet smack and a total loss. But I told her she was quite mistaken and that there is a lot more in you than people suspect. I realized that when I found you in that bookshop that day buying *Spindrift*. Do you remember?"

I had not forgotten the incident. The whole thing had been one of those unfortunate misunderstandings. I had promised Jeeves to buy him the works of a cove of the name of Spinoza—some kind of philosopher or something, I gathered—and the chap at the bookshop, expressing the opinion that there was no such person as Spinoza, had handed me *Spindrift* as being more probably what I was after, and scarcely had I grasped it when Florence came in. To assume that I had purchased the thing and to autograph it for me in green ink with her fountain pen had been with her the work of an instant.

"I knew then that you were groping dimly for the light and trying to educate yourself by reading good literature, that there was something lying hidden deep down in you that only needed bringing out. It would be a fascinating task, I told myself, fostering the latent potentialities of your budding mind. Like watching over some timid, backward flower."

I bridled pretty considerably. Timid, backward flower, my left eyeball, I was thinking. I was on the point of saying something stinging like "Oh, yes?" when she proceeded.

"I know I can mold you, Bertie. You want to improve yourself, and that is half the battle. What have you been reading lately?"

"Well, what with one thing and another, my reading has been a bit cut into these last days, but I am in the process of plugging away at a thing called *The Mystery of the Pink Crayfish.*"

Her slender frame was more or less hidden beneath the bedclothes, but I got the impression that a shudder had run through it.

"Oh, Bertie!" she said, this time with something more nearly approaching the normal intonation.

"Well, it's dashed good," I insisted stoutly. "This baronet, this Sir Eustace Willoughby, is discovered in his library with his head bashed in—"

A look of pain came into her face.

"Please!" She sighed. "Oh, dear," she said, "I'm afraid it's going to be uphill work fostering the latent potentialities of your budding mind."

"I wouldn't try, if I were you. Give it a miss, is my advice."

"But I hate to think of leaving you in the darkness, doing nothing but smoke and drink at the Drones Club."

I put her straight about his. She had her facts wrong.

"I also play Darts."

"Darts!"

"As a matter of fact, I shall very soon be this year's club champion. The event is a snip for me. Ask anybody."

"How can you fritter away your time like that, when you might be reading T. S. Eliot? I would like to see you—"

What it was she would have liked to see me doing she did not say, though I presumed it was something foul and educational, for at this juncture someone knocked on the door.

It was the last contingency I had been anticipating, and it caused my heart to leap like a salmon in the spawning season and become entangled with my front teeth. I looked at the door with what I have heard Jeeves call a wild surmise, and persp. breaking out on my brow.

Florence, I noticed, seemed a bit startled, too. One gathered that she hadn't expected, when setting out for Brinkley Court, that her bedroom was going to be such a social center. There's a song I used to sing a good deal at one time, the refrain or burthen of which began with the words "Let's all go round to Maud's." Much the same sentiment appeared to be animating the guests beneath Aunt Dahlia's roof, and it was, of course, upsetting for the poor child. At one in the morning girls like a bit of privacy, and she couldn't have had much less privacy if she had been running a snack bar on a racecourse.

"Who's that?" she cried.

"Me," responded a deep, resonant voice, and Florence clapped a hand to her throat, a thing I didn't know anybody ever did off the stage.

For the d.r.v. was that of G. D'Arcy Cheesewright. To cut a long story short, the man was in again.

It was with a distinctly fevered hand that Florence reached out for a dressing gown, and in her deportment, as she hopped from between the sheets, I noted a marked suggestion of a pea on a hot shovel. She is one of those cool, calm, well-poised modern girls from whom as a rule you can seldom get more than a raised eyebrow, but I could see that this thing of having Stilton a pleasant visitor at a moment when her room was all cluttered up with Woosters had rattled her more than slightly.

"What do you want?"

"I have brought your letters."

"Leave them on the mat."

"I will not leave them on the mat. I wish to confront you in person."

"At this time of night! You aren't coming in here!"

"That," said Stilton crisply, "is where you make your ruddy error. I *am* coming in there."

I remember Jeeves saying something once about the poet's eye in a fine frenzy rolling and glancing from Heaven to earth, from earth to Heaven. It was in much the same manner that Florence's eye now rolled and glanced. I could see what was disturbing her, of course. It was that old problem which always bothers chaps in mystery thrillers—viz. how to get rid of the body—in this case, that of Bertram. If Stilton proposed to enter, it was essential that Bertram be placed in storage somewhere for the time being, but the question that arose was where.

There was a cupboard on the other side of the room, and she nipped across and flung open the door.

"Quick!" she hissed, and it's all rot to say you can't hiss a word that hasn't an 's' in it. She did it on her head. "In here!"

The suggestion struck me as a good one. I popped in and she closed the door behind me.

Well, actually, the fingers being, I suppose, nerveless, she didn't, but left it ajar. I was able, consequently, to follow the ensuing conversation as clearly as if it had been coming over the wireless.

Stilton began it.

"Here are your letters," he said stiffly.

"Thank you," she said stiffly.

"Don't mention it," he said stiffly.

"Put them on the dressing table," she said stiffly.

"Right ho," he said stiffly.

I don't know when I've known a bigger night for stiff speakers.

After a brief interval, during which I presumed that he was depositing the correspondence as directed, Stilton resumed.

"You got my telegram?"

"Of course I got your telegram."

"You notice I have shaved my moustache?"

"I do."

"It was my first move on finding out about your underhanded skulduggery."

"What do you mean, my underhanded skulduggery?"

"If you don't call it underhanded skulduggery, sneaking off to night clubs with the louse Wooster, it would be extremely entertaining to be informed how you would describe it."

"You know perfectly well that I wanted atmosphere for my book."

"Ho!"

"And don't say 'Ho.' "

"I will say 'Ho!' " retorted Stilton with spirit. "Your book, my foot. I don't believe there is any book. I don't believe you've ever written a book."

"Indeed? How about *Spindrift,* now in its fifth edition and soon to be translated into the Scandinavian?"

"Probably the work of the louse Gorringe."

I imagine that at this coarse insult Florence's eyes flashed fire. The voice in which she spoke certainly suggested it.

"Mr. Cheesewright, you have had a couple!"

"Nothing of the kind."

"Then you must be insane, and I wish you would have the courtesy to take that pumpkin head of yours out of here."

I rather think, though I can't be sure, that at these words Stilton ground his teeth. Certainly there was a peculiar sound, as if a coffee mill had sprung into action. The voice that filtered through to my cozy retreat quivered hoarsely.

"My head is not like a pumpkin!"

"It is, too, like a pumpkin."

"It is not like a pumpkin at all. I have this on the authority of Bertie Wooster, who says it is more like the dome of St. Paul's." He broke off, and there was a smacking sound. He had apparently smitten his brow. "Wooster!" he cried, emitting an animal snarl. "I didn't come here to talk about my head, I came to talk about Wooster, the slithery serpent who slinks behind chaps' backs, stealing fellows' girls from them. Wooster the home-wrecker! Wooster the snake in the grass from whom no woman is safe! Wooster the modern Don what's-his-name! You've been conducting a clandestine intrigue with him right along. You thought you were fooling me, didn't you? You thought I didn't see through your pitiful . . . your pitiful . . . Dammit, what's the word? . . . your pitiful . . . No, it's gone."

"I wish you would follow its excellent example."

"Subterfuges! I knew I'd get it. Do you think I didn't see through your pitiful subterfuges? All that bilge about wanting me to grow a moustache. Do you think I'm not on to it that the whole of that moustache sequence was just a ruse to enable you to break it off with me and switch over to the grass snake Wooster. 'How can I get rid of this Cheesewright?' you said to yourself. 'Ha, I have it!' you said to yourself. 'I'll tell him he's got to grow a moustache. He'll say like hell he'll grow any bally moustache. And then I'll say Ho! You won't, won't you? All right, then all is over between us. That'll fix it.' It must have been a nasty shock to you when I yielded to your request. Upset your plans quite a bit, I imagine? You hadn't bargained for that, had you?"

Florence spoke in a voice that would have frozen an Eskimo.

"The door is just behind you, Mr. Cheesewright. It opens if you turn the handle."

He came right back at her.

"Never mind the door. I'm talking about you and the leper Wooster. I suppose you will now hitch on to him, or what's left of him after I've finished stepping on his face. Am I right?"

"You are."

"It is your intention to marry this human gumboil?"

"It is."

"Ho!"

Well, I don't know how you would have behaved in my place, hearing these words and realizing for the first time that the evil had spread as far as this. You would probably have started violently, as I did. No doubt I ought to have spotted the impending doom, but for some reason or other, possibly because I had been devoting so much thought to Stilton, I hadn't. This abrupt announcement of my betrothal to a girl of whom I took the gravest view shook me to my depths, with the result, as I say, that I started violently.

And, of course, the one place where it is unwise to start violently, if you wish to remain unobserved and incognito, is a cupboard in a female bedroom. What exactly it was that now rained down on me, dislodged by my sudden movement, I cannot say, but I think it was hat boxes. Whatever it was, it sounded in the stilly night like coal being lowered down a chute into a cellar, and I heard a sharp exclamation. A moment later a hand wrenched open the door and a suffused face glared in on me as I brushed the hat boxes, if they were hat boxes, from my hair.

"Ho!" said Stilton, speaking with difficulty like a cat with a fishbone in its throat. "Come on out of there, serpent," he added, attaching himself to my left ear and pulling vigorously.

I emerged like a cork out of a bottle.

14

I⊤ ɪs always a bit difficult to know just what to say on occasions like this. I said "Oh, there you are, Stilton. Nice evening," but it seemed to be the wrong thing, for he merely quivered as if he had got a beetle down his back and increased the incandescence of his gaze. I saw that it was going to require quite a good deal of suavity and tact on my part to put us all at our ease.

"You are doubtless surprised—" I began, but he held up a hand as if he had been back in the Force directing the traffic. He then spoke in a quiet, if rumbling, voice.

"You will find me waiting in the corridor, Wooster," he said, and strode out.

I understood the spirit which had prompted the words. It was the *preux chevalier* in him coming to the surface. You can stir up a Cheesewright till he froths at the mouth, but you cannot make him forget that he is an Old Etonian and a pukka Sahib. Old Etonians do not brawl in the presence of the other sex. Nor do pukka Sahibs. They wait till they are alone with the party of the second part in some secluded nook.

I thoroughly approved of this fineness of feeling, for it had left me sitting on top of the world. It would now, I saw, be possible for me to avoid anything in the nature of unpleasantness by executing one of those subtle rearward movements which great Generals keep up their sleeves for moments when things are beginning to get too hot. You think you have got one of these Generals cornered and are all ready to swoop on him, and it is with surprise and chagrin that, just as you are pulling up your socks and putting a final polish on your weapons, you observe that he isn't there. He has withdrawn on his strategic railway, taking his troops with him.

With that ladder waiting in readiness for me, I was in a similarly agreeable position. Corridors meant nothing to me. I didn't need to go into any corridors. All I had to do was slide through the window, place my foot on the top rung and carry on with a light heart to terra firma.

But there is one circumstance which can dish the greatest of Generals—viz. if, toddling along to the station to buy his ticket, he finds that since he last saw it the strategic railway has been blown up. That is the time when you will find him scratching his head and chewing the lower lip. And it was a disaster of this nature that now dished me. Approaching the window and glancing out, I saw that the ladder was no longer there. At some point in the course of the recent conversations it had vanished, leaving not a wrack behind.

What had become of it was a mystery I found myself unable to solve, but that was a thing that could be gone into later. At the moment it was plain that the cream of the Wooster brain must be given to a more urgent matter—to wit, the question of how I was to get out of the room without passing through the door and finding myself alone in a confined space with Stilton, the last person in his present frame of mind with whom a man of slender physique would wish to be alone in confined spaces. I put this to Florence, and she agreed, like Sherlock Holmes, that the problem was one which undoubtedly presented certain points of interest.

"You can't stay here all night," she said.

I admitted the justice of this, but added that I didn't at the moment see what the dickens else I could do.

"You wouldn't care to knot your sheets and lower me to the ground with them?"

"No, I wouldn't. Why don't you jump?"

"And smash myself to hash?"

"You might not."

"On the other hand, I might."

"Well, you can't make an omelette without breaking eggs."

I gave her a look. It seemed to me the silliest thing I had ever heard a girl say, and I have heard girls say some pretty silly things in my time. I was on the point of saying "You and your bally omelettes!" when something seemed to go off with a pop in my brain and it was as though I had swallowed a brimming dose of some invigorating tonic, the sort of pick-me-up that makes a bedridden invalid rise from his couch and dance the Carioca. Bertram was himself again. With a steady hand I opened the door. And when Stilton advanced on me like a mass murderer about to do his stuff, I quelled him with the power of the human eye.

"Just a moment, Stilton," I said suavely. "Before you give rein, if that's the expression I want, to your angry passions, don't forget you've drawn me in the Drones Club Darts sweep."

It was enough. Halting abruptly, as if he had walked into a lamp post, he stood goggling like a cat in an adage. Cats in adages, Jeeves tells me, let "I dare not" wait upon "I would," and I could see with the naked eye that this was what Stilton was doing.

Flicking a speck of dust from my sleeve and smiling a quiet smile, I proceeded to rub it in.

"You appreciate the position of affairs?" I said. "By drawing my name, you have set yourself apart from ordinary men. To make it clear to the meanest intelligence . . . I allude to yours, my dear Cheesewright . . . where the ordinary man, seeing me strolling along Piccadilly, merely says 'Ah, there goes Bertie Wooster,' you, having drawn me in the sweep, say 'There goes my fifty-six pounds ten shillings,' and you probably run after me to tell me to be very careful when crossing the street because the traffic nowadays is so dangerous."

He raised a hand and fingered his chin. I could see that my words were not being wasted. Shooting my cuffs, I resumed.

"In what sort of condition shall I be to win that Darts tourney and put nearly sixty quid in your pocket, if you pull the strong arm stuff you are contemplating? Try that one on your bazooka, my dear Cheesewright."

It was a tense struggle, of course, but it didn't last long. Reason prevailed. With a low grunt which spoke eloquently of the overwrought soul, he stepped back, and with a cheery "Well, good night, old man" and a benevolent wave of the hand I left him and made my way to my room.

As I entered it, Aunt Dahlia in a maroon dressing gown rose from the chair in which she had been sitting and fixed me with a blazing eye, struggling for utterance.

"Well!" she said, choking on the word like a Pekinese on a chump chop too large for its frail strength. After which, speech failing her, she merely stood and gargled.

I must say that this struck me in the circs as a bit thick. I mean, if anyone was entitled to have blazing eyes and trouble with the vocal cords, it was, as I saw it, me. I mean, consider the facts. Owing to this woman's clothheaded blundering when issuing divisional orders, I was slated to walk down the aisle with Florence Craye and had been subjected to an ordeal which might well have done permanent damage to the delicate nerve centers. I was strongly of the opinion that so far from being glared and gargled at I was in a position to demand a categorical explanation and to see that I got it.

As I cleared my throat in order to put this to her, she mastered her emotion sufficiently to be able to speak.

"Well?" she said, looking like a female minor prophet about to curse the sins of the people. "May I trespass on your valuable time long enough to ask you what in the name of everything bloodsome you think you're playing at, young piefaced Bertie? It is now some twenty minutes past one o'clock in the morning, and not a spot of action on your part. Do you expect me to sit up all night waiting for you to get around to a simple, easy task which a crippled child of six could have had all done and washed up in a quarter of an hour? I suppose this is just the shank of the evening to you dissipated Londoners, but we rustics like to get our sleep. What's the idea? Why the delay? What on earth have you been doing all this while, you revolting young piece of cheese?"

I laughed a hollow, mirthless laugh. Getting quite the wrong angle on it, she begged me to postpone my farmyard imitations to a more suitable moment. I told myself that I must be calm . . . calm.

"Before replying to your questions, aged relative," I said, holding myself in with a strong effort, "let me put one to you. Would you mind informing me in a few simple words why you told me that your window was the end one on the left?"

"It is the end one on the left."

"Pardon me."

"Looking from the house."

"Oh, looking *from* the house?" A great light dawned on me. "I thought you meant looking *at* the house."

"Looking at the house it would of course be . . ." She broke off with a startled yowl, staring at me with quite a good deal of that wild surmise stuff. "Don't tell me you got into the wrong room?"

"It could scarcely have been wronger."

"Whose was it?"

"Florence Craye's."

She whistled. It was plain that the drama of the situation had not escaped her.

"Was she in bed?"

"With a pink boudoir cap on."

"And she woke up and found you there?"

"Almost immediately. I knocked over a table or something."

She whistled again.

"You'll have to marry the girl."

"Quite."

"Though I doubt if she would have you."

"I have positive inside information to the contrary."

"You fixed it up?"

"She fixed it up. We are affianced."

"In spite of the moustache?"

"She likes the moustache."

"She does? Morbid. But what about Cheesewright? I thought he and she were affianced, as you call it?"

"No longer. It's off."

"They've bust up?"

"Completely."

"And now she's taken you on?"

"That's right."

A look of concern came into her face. Despite the occasional brusqueness of her manner and the fruity names she sees fit to call me from time to time, she loves me dearly and my well-being is very near her heart.

"She's pretty highbrow for you, isn't she? If I know her, she'll have you reading W.H. Auden before you can say 'What ho.' "

"She rather hinted at some such contingency, though, if I recollect, T.S. Eliot was the name that was mentioned."

"She proposes to mold you?"

"I gathered so."

"You won't like that."

"No."

She nodded understandingly.

"Men don't. I attribute my own happy marriage to the fact that I have never so much as laid a finger on old Tom. Agatha is trying to mold Worplesdon, and I believe his agonies are frightful. She made him knock off smoking the other day, and he behaved like a cinnamon bear with its foot in a trap. Has Florence told you to knock off smoking?"

"Not yet."

"She will. And after that it'll be cocktails." She gazed at me with a good deal of what-do-you-call-it. You could see that remorse had her in its grip. "I'm afraid I've got you into a bit of a jam, my poppet."

"Don't give it a thought, old blood relation," I said. "These things happen. It is your predicament, not mine, that is exercising me. We've got to get you out of your sea of troubles, as Jeeves calls it. Everything else is relatively unimportant. My thoughts of self are merely in about the proportion of the vermouth to the gin in a strongish dry martini."

She was plainly touched. Unless I am very much mistaken, her eyes were wet with unshed tears.

"That's very altruistic of you, Bertie dear."

"Not at all, not at all."

"One wouldn't think it, to look at you, but you have a noble soul."

"*Who* wouldn't think it, to look at me?"

"And if that's the way you feel, all I can say is that it does you credit and let's get going. You'd better go and shift that ladder to the right window."

"You mean the left window."

"Well, let's call it the correct window."

I braced myself to break the bad news.

"Ah," I said, "but what you're overlooking—possibly because I forgot to tell you—is that a snag has arisen which threatens to do our aims and objects a bit of no good. The ladder isn't there."

"Where?"

"Under the right window, or perhaps I should say the wrong window. When I looked out, it was gone."

"Nonsense. Ladders don't melt into thin air."

"They do, I assure you, at Brinkley Court, Brinkley-cum-Snodsfield-in-the-Marsh. I don't know what conditions prevail elsewhere, but at Brinkley Court they vanish if you take your eye off them for so much as an instant."

"You mean the ladder's disappeared?"

"That is precisely the point I was endeavoring to establish. It has folded its tents like the Arabs and silently stolen away."

She turned bright mauve, and I think was about to rap out something in the nature of a Quorn-and-Pytchley expletive, for she is a woman who seldom minces her words when stirred, but at this juncture the door opened and Uncle Tom came in. I was too distrait to be able to discern whether or not he was pottering, but a glance was enough to show me that he was definitely all of a doddah.

"Dahlia!" he exclaimed. "I thought I heard your voice. What are you doing up at this hour?"

"Bertie had a headache," replied the old relative, a quick thinker. "I have been giving him an aspirin. The head a little better now, Bertie?"

"One notes a slight improvement," I assured her, being a quick thinker myself. "You're out and about a bit late, aren't you, Uncle Tom?"

"Yes," said Aunt Dahlia. "What are *you* doing up at this hour, my old for-better-and-for-worser? You ought to have been asleep ages ago."

Uncle Tom shook his head. His air was grave.

"Asleep, old girl? I shan't get any sleep tonight. Far too worried. The place is alive with burglars."

"Burglars? What gives you that idea? I haven't seen any burglars. Have you, Bertie?"

"Not one. I remember thinking how odd it was."

"You probably saw an owl or something, Tom."

"I saw a ladder. When I was taking my stroll in the garden before going to bed. Propped up against one of the windows. I took it away in the nick of time. A minute later, and burglars would have been streaming up it in their thousands."

Aunt Dahlia and I exchanged a glance. I think we were both feeling happier now that the mystery of the vanishing l. had been solved. It's an odd thing, but however much of an aficionado one may be of mysteries in book form, when they pop up in real life they seldom fail to give one the pip.

She endeavored to soothe his agitation.

"Probably just a ladder one of the gardeners was using and forgot to put back where it belonged. Though, of course," she went on thoughtfully, feeling no doubt that a spot of paving the way would do harm, "I suppose there is always a chance of a cracksman having a try for that valuable pearl necklace of mine. I had forgotten that."

"I hadn't," said Uncle Tom. "It was the first thing I thought of. I went straight to your room and got it and locked it up in the safe in the hall. A burglar will have to be pretty smart to get it out of there," he added with modest pride, and pushed off, leaving behind him what I have sometimes heard called a pregnant silence.

Aunt looked at nephew, nephew looked at aunt.

"Hell's whiskers!" said the former, starting the conversation going again. "Now what do we do?"

I agreed that the situation was sticky. Indeed, offhand it was difficult to see how it could have been more glutinous.

"What are the chances of finding out the combination?"

"Not a hope."

"I wonder if Jeeves can crack a safe."

She brightened.

"I'll bet he can. There's nothing Jeeves can't do. Go and fetch him."

I Lord-love-a-duck-ed impatiently.

"How the dickens can I fetch him? I don't know which his room is. Do you?"

"No."

"Well, I can't go from door to door, rousing the whole domestic staff. Who do you think I am? Paul Revere?"

I paused for a reply, and as I did so who should come in but Jeeves in person. Late though it was, the hour had produced the man.

"Excuse me, sir," he said. "I am happy to find that I have not interrupted your slumbers. I ventured to come to inquire whether matters had developed satisfactorily. Were you successful in your enterprise, sir?"

I shook the cocoanut.

"No, Jeeves. I moved in a mysterious way my wonders to perform, but was impeded by a number of Acts of God," I said, and in a few crisp words put him abreast. "So the necklace is now in the safe," I concluded, "and the problem as I see it, and as Aunt Dahlia sees it, is how the dickens to get it out. You grasp the position?"

"Yes, sir. It is disturbing."

Aunt Dahlia uttered a passionate cry.

"Don't *do* it!" she boomed with extraordinary vehemence. "If I hear that word 'disturbing' once more . . . Can you bust a safe, Jeeves?"

"No, madam."

"Don't say 'No, madam' in that casual way. How do you know you can't?"

"It requires a specialized education and upbringing, madam."

"Then I'm for it," said Aunt Dahlia, making for the door. Her face was grim and set. She might have been a marquise about to hop into the tumbril at the time when there was all that unpleasantness over in France. "You weren't through the San Francisco earthquake, were you, Jeeves?"

"No, madam. I have never visited the western coastal towns of the United States."

"I was only thinking that if you had been, what's going to happen tomorrow when this Lord Sidcup arrives and tells Tom the awful truth would have reminded you of old times. Well, good night, all. I'll be running along and getting my beauty sleep."

She buzzed off, a gallant figure. The Quorn trains its daughters well. No weakness there. In the fell clutch of circumstance, as I remember Jeeves putting it once, they do not wince or cry aloud. I mentioned this to him as the door closed, and he agreed that it was substantially so.

"Under the tiddly-poms of whatever-it-is . . . How does the rest of it go?"

"Under the bludgeonings of chance their heads are . . . pardon me . . . bloody but unbowed, sir."

"That's right. Your own?"

"No, sir. The late William Ernest Henley, 1849-1903."

"Ah?"

"The title of the poem is 'Invictus.' But did I understand Mrs. Travers to say that Lord Sidcup was expected, sir?"

"He arrives tomorrow."

"Would he be the gentleman of whom you were speaking, who is to examine Mrs. Travers' necklace?"

"That's the chap."

"Then I fancy that all is well, sir."

I started. It seemed to me that I must have misunderstood him. Either that, or he was talking through his hat.

"All is *well,* did you say, Jeeves?"

"Yes, sir. You are not aware who Lord Sidcup is, sir?"

"I never heard of him in my life."

"You will possibly remember him, sir, as Mr. Roderick Spode."

I stared at him. You could have knocked me down with a toothpick.

"Roderick Spode?"

"Yes, sir."

"You mean the Roderick Spode of Totleigh Towers?"

"Precisely, sir. He recently succeeded to the title on the demise of the late Lord Sidcup, his uncle."

"Great Scott, Jeeves!"

"Yes, sir. I think you will agree with me, sir, that in these circumstances the problem confronting Mrs. Travers is susceptible of a ready solution. A word to his lordship, reminding him of the fact that he sells ladies' underclothing under the trade name of Eulalie Soeurs, should go far towards inducing him to preserve a tactful silence with regard to the spurious nature of the necklace. At the time of our visit to Totleigh Towers you will recollect that Mr. Spode, as he then was, showed unmistakably his reluctance to let the matter become generally known."

"Egad, Jeeves!"

"Yes, sir. I thought I would mention it, sir. Good night, sir."

He oozed off.

15

WE WOOSTERS are never very early risers, and the sun was highish in the heavens next morning when I woke to greet a new day. And I had just finished tucking away a refreshing scrambled eggs and coffee, when the door opened as if a hurricane had hit it and Aunt Dahlia came pirouetting in.

I use the word "pirouetting" advisedly, for there was an elasticity in her bearing which impressed itself immediately upon the eye. Of the drooping mourner of last night there remained no trace. The woman was plainly right above herself.

"Bertie," she said, after a brief opening speech in the course of which she described me as a lazy young hound who ought to be ashamed to be wallowing in bed on what, if you asked her, was the maddest merriest day of all the glad new year, "I've just been talking to Jeeves, and if ever a lifesaving friend in need drew breath, it is he. Hats off to Jeeves is the way I look at it."

Pausing for a moment to voice the view that my moustache was an offense against God and man but that she saw in it nothing that a good weed-killer couldn't cure, she resumed.

"He tells me this Lord Sidcup who's coming here today is none other than our old pal Roderick Spode."

I nodded. I had divined from her exuberance that he must have been spilling the big news.

"Correct," I said. "Apparently, all unknown to us, Spode was right from the start the secret nephew of the holder of the title, and since that sojourn of ours at Totleigh Towers the latter has gone to reside with the morning stars, giving him a stepup. Jeeves has also, I take it, told you about Eulalie Soeurs?"

"The whole thing. Why didn't you ever let me in on that? You know how I enjoy a good laugh."

I spread the hands in a dignified gesture, upsetting the coffee pot, which was fortunately empty.

"My lips were sealed."

"You and your lips!"

"All right, me and my lips. But I repeat. The information was imparted to me in confidence."

"You could have told Auntie."

I shook my head. Women do not understand these things. *Noblesse oblige* means nothing to the gentler sex.

"One does not impart confidential confidences even to Auntie, not if one is a confidant of the right sort."

"Well, anyway, I now have the facts, and I hold Spode, alias Sidcup, in the hollow of my hand. Bless my soul," she went on, a far-off ecstatic look on her face, "how well I remember that day at Totleigh Towers. There he was, advancing on you with glittering eyes and foam-flecked lips, and you drew yourself up as cool as some cucumbers, as Anatole would say, and said 'One minute, Spode, just one minute. It may interest you to learn that I know all about Eulalie.' Gosh, how I admired you!"

"I don't wonder."

"You were like one of those lion tamers in circuses who defy murderous man-eating monarchs of the jungle."

"There was a resemblance, no doubt."

"And how he wilted! I've never seen anything like it. Before my eyes he wilted like a wet sock. And he's going to do it again when he gets here this evening."

"You propose to draw him aside and tell him you know his guilty secret?"

"Exactly. Strongly recommending him, when Tom shows him the necklace, to say it's a lovely bit of work and worth every penny he paid for it. It can't fail. Fancy him owning Eulalie Soeurs! He must make a packet out of it. I was in there last month, buying some cami-knickers, and the place was doing a roaring trade. Money pouring in like a tidal wave. By the way, laddie, talking of cami-knickers, Florence was showing me hers just now. Not the ones she had on, I don't mean, her reserve supply. She wanted my opinion of them. And I'm sorry to tell you, my poor lamb," she said, eyeing me with auntly pity, "that things look pretty serious in that quarter."

"They do?"

"Extremely serious. She's all set to start those wedding bells ringing out. Somewhere around next November she seems to think, at St. George's, Hanover Square. Already she is speaking freely of bridesmaids and caterers." She paused, and looked at me in a surprised sort of way. "You don't seem very upset," she said. "Are you one of these men of chilled steel one reads about?"

I spread the hands again, this time without disaster to the breakfast tray.

"Well, I'll tell you, old ancestor. When a fellow has been engaged as often as I have and each time saved from the scaffold at the eleventh hour, he comes to have faith in his star. He feels that all is not lost till they have actually got him at the altar rails with the organ playing 'Oh, Perfect Love' and the clergyman saying 'Wilt thou?' At the moment, admittedly, I am in the soup, but it may well be that in God's good time it will be granted to me to emerge unscathed from the tureen."

"You don't despair?"

"Not at all. I have high hopes that, after they have thought things over, these two proud spirits who have parted brass rags will come together and be reconciled, thus letting me out. The rift was due—"

"I know. She told me."

"—to the fact that Stilton learned that I had taken Florence to The Mottled Oyster one night about a week ago, and he refused to believe that I had done so merely in order to enable her to accumulate atmosphere for her new book. When he has cooled off and reason has returned to its throne, he may realize how mistaken he was and beg her to forgive him for his low suspicions. I think so. I hope so."

She agreed that there was something in this and commended me for my spirit, which in her opinion was the right one. My intrepidity reminded her, she said, of the Spartans at Thermopylae, wherever that may be.

"But he's a long way from being in that frame of mind at the moment, according to Florence. She says he is convinced that you two were on an unbridled toot together. And, of course, his finding you in the cupboard in her bedroom at one in the morning was unfortunate."

"Most. One would gladly have avoided the occurrence."

"Must have given the man quite a start. What beats me is why he didn't hammer the stuffing out of you. I should have thought that would have been his first move."

I smiled quietly.

"He has drawn me in the Drones Club Darts sweep."

"What's that got to do with it?"

"My dear old soul, does a fellow hammer the stuffing out of a chap on whose virtuosity at the Darts board he stands to win fity-six pounds, ten shillings?"

"Oh, I see."

"So did Stilton. I made the position thoroughly clear to him, and he has ceased to be a menace. However much his thoughts may drift in the direction of stuffing-hammering, he will have to continue to maintain the non-belligerent status of a mild cat in an adage. I have bottled him up good and proper. There was nothing further you wished to discuss?"

"Not that I know of."

"Then if you will withdraw, I will be getting up and dressing."

I rose from the hay as the door closed, and having bathed, shaved and clad the outer man, took my cigarette out for a stroll in the grounds and messuages.

The sun was now a good bit higher in the heavens than when last observed, and its genial warmth increased the optimism of my mood. Thinking of Stilton and the dead stymie I had laid him, I found myself feeling that it was not such a bad little old world, after all. I don't know anything that braces you more thoroughly than outgeneraling one of the baser sort who has been chucking his weight about and planning to start something. It was with much the same quiet satisfaction which I had experienced when bending Roderick Spode to my will at Totleigh Towers that I contemplated Stilton in his bottled-up state. As Aunt Dahlia had said, quite the lion tamer.

True, as against this, there was Florence—already, it appeared, speaking freely of bridesmaids, caterers and St. George's, Hanover Square—and a lesser man might have allowed her dark shadow to cloud his feeling of *bien être*. But it is always the policy of the Woosters to count their blessings one by one, and I concentrated my attention exclusively on the bright side of the picture, telling myself that even if an eleventh hour reprieve failed to materialize and I was compelled to drain the bitter cup, I wouldn't have to do it with two black eyes and a fractured spine, wedding presents from G. D'Arcy Cheesewright. Come what might, I was that much ahead of the game.

I was, in short, in buoyant mood and practically saying "Tra la," when I observed Jeeves shimmering up in the manner of one desiring audience.

"Ah, Jeeves," I said. "Nice morning."

"Extremely agreeable, sir."

"Did you want to see me about something?"

"If you could spare me a moment, sir. I was anxious to ascertain if it would be possible for you to dispense with my services today in order that I may go to London. The Junior Ganymede luncheon, sir."

"I thought that was next week."

"The date has been put forward to accommodate Sir Everard Everett's butler, who leaves with his employer tomorrow for the United States of America. Sir Everard is assuming his duties as Britannic ambassador at Washington."

"Is that so? Good luck to the old blister."

"Yes, sir."

"One likes to see these public servants bustling about and earning their salaries."

"Yes, sir."

"If one is a taxpayer, I mean, contributing one's whack to those salaries."

"Precisely, sir. I should be glad if you could see your way to allowing me to attend the function, sir. As I informed you, I am taking the chair."

Well, of course, when he puts it like that, I had no option but to right-ho.

"Certainly, Jeeves. Push along and revel till your ribs squeak. It may be your last chance," I added significantly.

"Sir?"

"Well, you've often stressed how fussy the brass hats are about members not revealing the secrets of the club book, and Aunt Dahlia tells me you've just been spilling the whole inner history of Spode and Eulalie Soeurs to her. Won't they drum you out if this becomes known?"

"The contingency is a remote one, sir, and I gladly took the risk, knowing that Mrs. Travers' happiness was at stake."

"Pretty white, Jeeves."

"Thank you, sir. I endeavor to give satisfaction. And now I think perhaps, if you will excuse me, sir, I should be starting for the station. The train for London leaves very shortly."

"Why not drive up in the two-seater?"

"If you could spare it, sir?"

"Of course."

"Thank you very much, sir. It will be a great convenience."

He pushed off in the direction of the house, no doubt to go and get the bowler hat which is his inseparable companion when in the metropolis, and scarcely had he left me when I heard my name called in a bleating voice and turned to perceive Percy Gorringe approaching, his tortoise-shell-rimmed spectacles glistening in the sunshine.

My first emotion on beholding him was one of surprise, a feeling that of all the in and out performers I had ever met he was the most unpredictable. I mean, you couldn't tell from one minute to another what aspect he was going to present to the world, for he switched from Stormy to Set Fair and from Set Fair to Stormy like a barometer with something wrong with its works. At dinner on the previous night he had been all gaiety and effervescence, and here he was now, only a few hours later, once more giving that impersonation of a dead codfish which had caused Aunt Dahlia to take so strong a line with him. Fixing me with lack-luster eyes, if lack-luster is the word I want, and wasting no time on preliminary pip-pippings and *pourparlers,* he started straight off cleansing his bosom of the perilous stuff that weighs upon the heart.

"Wooster," he said, "Florence has just told me a story that shocked me!"

Well, difficult to know what to say to that, of course. One's impulse was to ask what story, adding that if it was the one about the bishop and the lady snake charmer, one had heard it. And one could, no doubt, have shoved in a thoughtful word or two deploring the growing laxity of speech of the modern girl. I merely said "Oh, ah?" and waited for further details.

His eye, as Florence's had done on the previous night, rolled in a fine frenzy and glanced from heaven to earth, from earth to heaven. You could see the thing had upset him.

"Shortly after breakfast," he continued, retrieving the eye and fixing it on me once more, "finding her alone in the herbaceous border, cutting flowers, I hastened up and asked if I might be allowed to hold the basket."

"Very civil."

"She thanked me and said she would be glad if I would do so, and for awhile we talked of neutral subjects. One topic led to another, and eventually I asked her to be my wife."

" 'At-a-boy!"

"I beg your pardon?"

"I only said ' 'At-a-boy!' "

"Why did you say ' 'At-a-boy!'?"

"Sort of cheering you on, as it were."

"I see. Cheering me on. The expression is a corruption, one assumes, of the phrase 'That is the boy' and signifies friendly encouragement?"

"That's right."

"Then I am surprised in the circumstances—and may I say more than a little disgusted—to hear it from your lips, Wooster. It would have been in better taste to have refrained from cheap taunts and jeers."

"Eh?"

"If you have triumphed, that is no reason why you should mock those who have been less fortunate."

"I'm sorry. If you could give me a few footnotes . . . "

He tchah-ed impatiently.

"I told you that I asked Florence to be my wife, and I also told you that she said something which shocked me profoundly. It was that she was engaged to you."

I got it now. I saw what he was driving at.

"Oh, ah, yes, of course. Quite. Yes, we would appear to be betrothed."

"When did this happen, Wooster?"

"Fairly recently."

He snorted.

"Very recently, I should imagine, seeing that it was only yesterday that she was engaged to Cheesewright. It's all most confusing," said Percy peevishly. "It makes one's head swim. One doesn't know where one is."

I could see his point.

"Bit of a mixup," I agreed.

"It's bewildering. I cannot think what she can possibly see in you."

"No. Very odd, the whole thing."

He brooded darkly awhile.

"Her recent infatuation for Cheesewright," he said, teeing off again, "one could dimly understand. Whatever his mental defects, he is a vigorous young animal, and it is not uncommon to find girls of intellect attracted by vigorous young animals. Bernard Shaw made this the basis of his early novel, *Cashel Byron's Profession*. But *you!* It's inexplicable. A mere weedy butterfly."

"Would you call me a weedy butterfly?"

"If you can think of a better description, I shall be happy to hear it. I am unable to discern in you the slightest vestige of charm, the smallest trace of any quality that could reasonably be expected to appeal to a girl like Florence. It amazes one that she should wish to have you permanently about the house."

I don't know if you would call me a touchy man. As a rule, I should say not. But it is not pleasant to find yourself chalked upon the slate as a weedy butterfly, and I confess that I spoke a little shortly.

"Well, there it is," I said, and went into the silence. And as he, too, seemed disinclined for chit-chat, we stood for some moments like a couple of Trappist monks who have run into each other by chance at the dog races. And I think I would pretty soon have nodded curtly and removed myself, had he not arrested me with an exclamation similar in tone and volume to the one which Stilton had uttered on finding me festooned with hat boxes in Florence's cupboard. He was looking at me through the windshields with what appeared to be concern, if not horror. It puzzled me. It couldn't have taken him all this time, I felt, to notice the moustache.

"Wooster! Good gracious! You are not wearing a hat!"

"I don't much in the country."

"But in this hot sun! You might get sunstroke. You ought not to take such risks."

I must say I was touched by this solicitude. Much of the pique I had been feeling left me. It isn't many fellows, I mean to say, who get all worked up about the well-being of birds who are virtually strangers. It just showed, I thought, that a man may talk a lot of rot about weedy butterflies and still have a tender heart beneath what I should imagine was pretty generally recognized as a fairly repulsive exterior.

"Don't worry," I said, soothing his alarm.

"But I do worry," he responded sharply. "I feel very strongly that you ought either to get a hat or else stay in the shade. I don't want to appear fussy, but your health is naturally a matter of greatest concern to me. You see, I have drawn you in the Drones Club Darts sweep."

This got right past me. I could make nothing of it. It sounded to me like straight delirium.

"You've what? How do you mean you've drawn me in the Drones Club Darts sweep?"

"I put it badly. I was agitated. What I should have said was that I have bought you from Cheesewright. He has sold me the ticket bearing your name. So can you wonder that it makes me nervous when I see you going about in this hot sun without a hat?"

In a career liberally spotted with nasty shocks I have had occasion to do quite a bit of reeling and tottering from time to time, but I have seldom reeled and tottered more heartily than I did on hearing these frightful words. I had addressed Aunt Dahlia earlier in the morning, if you remember, as a fluttering aspen. The description would have fitted me at this moment like the paper on the wall.

This surge of emotion will, I think, be readily understood. My whole foreign policy, as I have made clear, had been built on the fact that I had bottled Stilton up good and proper, and it now appeared, dash it, that I hadn't bottled him up at all. He was once more in the position of an Assyrian fully licensed to come down like a wolf on the fold with his cohorts all gleaming with purple and gold, and the realization that his thirst for vengeance was so pronounced that, rather than forgo his war aims, he was prepared to sacrifice fifty-six quid and a bender was one that froze the marrow.

"There must be a lot of hidden good in Cheesewright," proceeded Percy. "I confess frankly that I misjudged him, and if I had not alredy returned the galley proofs, I would withdraw that 'Caliban at Sunset' thing of mine from *Parnassus*. He tells me that you are a certain winner of this Darts contest, and yet he voluntarily offered to sell me for quite a trivial sum the ticket bearing your name, because, he said, he had taken a great fancy to me and would like to do me a good turn. A big, generous, warmhearted gesture, and one that restores one's faith in human nature. By the way, Cheesewright is looking for you. He wants to see you about something."

He repeated his advice with ref. to the hat and moved off, and for quite a while I stood where I was, rigid to the last limb, my numbed bean trying to grapple with this hideous problem which had arisen. It was plain that some diabolically clever counter move would have to be made and made slippily, but what diabolically clever counter move? There was what is called the rub.

You see, it wasn't as if I could just leg it from the danger zone, which was what I would have liked to do. It was imperative that I be among those present at Brinkley Court when Spode arrived this evening. Airily though Aunt Dahlia had spoken of making the man play ball, it was quite conceivable that the program might blow a fuse, in which event the presence on the spot of a quick-thinking nephew would be of the essence. The Woosters do not desert aunts in the time of need.

Eliminating, therefore, the wings of the dove, for which I would gladly have been in the market, what other course presented itself? I freely own that for five minutes or so the thing had me snookered.

But it has often been said of Bertram Wooster that in moments of intense peril he has an uncanny knack of getting inspiration, and this happened now. Suddenly a thought came like a full-blown rose, flushing the brow, and I picked up the feet and lit out for the stables, where my two-seater was housed. It might be that Jeeves had not yet started on the long trail that led to the Junior Ganymede Club, and if he hadn't, I saw the way out.

16

IF YOU are one of the better element who are never happier than when curled up with the works of B. Wooster, you possibly came across a previous slab of these reminiscences of mine in which I dealt with a visit Jeeves and I paid to Deverill Hall, the rural seat of Esmond Haddock, J.P., and will recall that while under the Haddock roof Jeeves found my Aunt Agatha's son Thos in possession of what is known as a cosh and very prudently impounded it, feeling—as who wouldn't—that it was the last thing that ought to be at the disposal of that homicidal young thug. The thought which had flushed my brow in the manner described was . . . Had Jeeves still got it? Everything turned on that.

I found him, richly appareled and wearing the bowler hat, at the wheel of the car, on the point of putting foot to self-starter. Another moment, and I should have been too late. Racing up, I inaugurated the quiz without delay.

"Jeeves," I said, "throw your mind back to that time we stayed at Deverill Hall. Are you throwing?"

"Yes, sir."

"Then continue to follow me closely. My Aunt Agatha's son, young Thos, was there."

"Precisely, sir."

"With the idea of employing it on a schoolmate of his called Stinker, who had incurred his displeasure for some reason, he had purchased before leaving London a cosh."

"Or blackjack, to use the American term."

"Never mind American terms, Jeeves. You took the weapon from him."

"I deemed it wisest, sir."

"It was wisest. No argument about that. Let a plug-ugly like young Thos loose in the community with a cosh, and you are inviting disasters and . . . what's the word? Something about cats."

"Cataclysms, sir?"

"That's it. Cataclysms. Unquestionably you did the right thing. But all that is beside the point. What I am leading up to is this. That cosh, where is it?"

"Among my effects at the apartment, sir."

"I'll drive with you to London and pick it up."

"I could bring it with me on my return, sir."

I did a brief dance step. On his return, forsooth! When would that be? Late at night, probably, because the gang at a hot spot like the Junior Ganymede don't break up a party at the end of lunch. I know what happens when these wild butlers let themselves go. They sit around till all hours, drinking deep and singing close harmony and generally whooping it up like a bunch of the boys at the Malemute saloon. It would mean that for the whole of the long summer day I should be defenseless, an easy prey for a Stilton who, as I had just been informed, was prowling about, seeking whom he might devour.

"That's no good, Jeeves. I require it immediately. Not tonight, not a week from Wednesday, but at the earliest possible moment. I am being hotly pursued by Cheesewright, Jeeves."

"Indeed, sir?"

"And if I am to stave off the Cheesewright challenge, I shall have need of a weapon. His strength is as the strength of ten, and unarmed I should be corn before his sickle."

"Extremely well put, sir, if I may say so, and your diagnosis of the situation is perfectly accurate. Mr. Cheesewright's robustness would enable him to crush you like a fly."

"Exactly."

"He would obliterate you with a single blow. He would break you in two with his bare hands. He would tear you limb from limb."

I frowned slightly. I was glad to see that he appreciated the gravity of the situation, but these crude physical details seemed to me uncalled for.

"No need to make a production number of it, Jeeves," I said with a touch of coldness. "What I am driving at is that, armed with the cosh, I can face the blighter without a tremor. You agree?"

"Most decidedly, sir."

"Then shift-ho," I said, and hurled myself into the vacant seat.

This cosh of which I have been speaking was a small rubber bludgeon which at first sight you might have supposed unequal to the task of coping with an adversary of Stilton Cheesewright's tonnage. In repose, I mean to say, it didn't look like anything so frightfully hot. But I had seen it in action and was hep to what Florence would have called its latent potentialities. At Deverill Hall one night, for the soundest of reasons but too long to go into here, Jeeves had had occasion to bean a policeman with it—Constable Dobbs, a zealous officer—and the smitten slop had dropped as the gentle rain from heaven upon the place beneath.

There is a song, frequently sung by curates at village concerts, which runs:

> *I fear no foe in shining armor,*
> *Though his lance be bright and keen.*

Or is it "swift and keen"? I can't remember. Not that it matters. The point is that those words summed up my attitude to a nicety. They put what I was feeling in a nutshell. With that cosh on my person, I should feel debonair and confident, no matter how many Cheesewrights came bounding at me with slavering jaws.

Everything went according to plan. After an agreeable drive we dropped anchor at the door of Berkeley Mansions and made our way to the flat. There, as foreshadowed, was the cosh. Jeeves handed it over, I thanked him in a few well-chosen words, he went off to his orgy, and I, after a bite of lunch at the Drones, settled myself in the two-seater and turned its nose Worcestershirewards.

The first person I met as I passed thorugh the portals of Brinkley Court some hours later was Aunt Dahlia. She was in the hall, pacing up and down like a distraught tigress. Her exuberance of the morning had vanished completely, leaving her once more the haggard aunt of yesterday, and I was conscious of a quick pang of concern.

"Golly!" I said. "What's up, old relative? Don't tell me that scheme of yours didn't work?"

She kicked morosely at a handy chair, sending it flying into the unknown.

"It hasn't had a chance to work."

"Why not? Didn't Spode turn up?"

She gazed about her with somber eyes, apparently in the hope of finding another chair to kick. There not being one in her immediate sphere of influence, she kicked the sofa.

"He turned up all right, and what happened? Before I could draw him aside and get so much as a word in, Tom swooped on him and took him off to the collection room to look at his foul silver. They've been in there for more than an hour, and how much longer they're going to be, Heaven knows."

I pursed the lips. One ought, I felt, to have anticipated something of this sort.

"Can't you detach him?"

"No human power can detach a man to whom Tom is talking about his silver collection. He holds him with a glittering eye. All I can hope is that he will be so wrapped up in the silver end of the thing that he'll forget all about the necklace."

The last thing a nephew of the right sort wants to do is to shove a wallowing aunt still more deeply beneath the surface of the slough of despond than she is already, but I had to shake my head at this.

"I doubt it."

She gave the sofa another juicy one.

"So do I doubt it. That's why I'm going steadily cuckoo and may at any moment start howling like a banshee. Sooner or later he'll remember to take Spode to the safe, and what I am saying to myself is When? When? I feel like . . . who was the man who sat with a sword dangling over him, suspended by a hair, wondering how long it was going to be before it dropped and gave him a nasty flesh wound?"

She had me there. Nobody I had met. Certainly not one of the fellows at the Drones, or I should have heard about it.

"I couldn't tell you, I'm afraid. Jeeves might know."

At the mention of that honored name her eyes lit up.

"Jeeves! Of course! He's the man I want. Where is he?"

"In London. He asked me if he could take the day off. It was the Junior Ganymede monthly luncheon today."

She uttered a cry which might have been the howl of the banshee to which she had alluded, and gave me the sort of look which in the old tally-ho days she would have given a mentally deficient hound which she had observed suspending its professional activities in order to chase a rabbit.

"You let Jeeves go away at a time like this, when one has never needed him more?"

"I hadn't the heart to refuse. He was taking the chair. He'll be back soon."

"By which time . . ."

She would have spoken further . . . a good deal further, if I read aright the message in her eyes . . . but before she could even get going something whiskered came down the stairs and Percy was with us.

Seeing me, he halted abruptly.

"Wooster!" His agitation was very marked. "Where have you been all day, Wooster?"

I told him I had driven to London, and he drew his breath in with a hiss.

"In this hot weather? It can't be good for you. You must not overtax yourself, Wooster. You must husband your strength."

He had chosen the wrong moment for horning in. The old relative turned on him as if he had been someone she had observed heading off the fox, if not shooting it.

"Gorringe, you ghastly sheepfaced fugitive from hell," she thundered, forgetting, or so I imagine, that she was a hostess, "get out of here, blast you. We're in conference."

I suppose mixing with editors of poetry magazines toughens a fellow, rendering him impervious to verbal assault, for Percy, who might well have been expected to wilt, didn't wilt by a damn sight but drew himself up to his full height, which was about six feet two, and came back at her strongly.

"I am sorry to have intruded at an unseasonable moment, Mrs. Travers," he said, with a simple dignity that became him well, "but I have a message for you from Moth-aw, Moth-aw would like to speak to you. She desired me to ask if it would be convenient if she came to your room."

Aunt Dahlia flung her hands up emotionally. I could understand how she felt. The last thing a woman wants, when distraught, is a chat with someone like Ma Trotter.

"Not now!"

"Later, perhaps?"

"Is it important?"

"I received the impression that it was most important."

Aunt Dahlia heaved a deep sigh, the sigh of a woman who feels that they are coming over the plate too fast for her.

"Oh, all right. Tell her I'll see her in half an hour. I'm going back to the collection room, Bertie. It's just possible that Tom may have run down by now. But one last word," she added, as she moved away. "The next sub-human gargoyle that comes butting in and distracting my thoughts when I am trying to wrestle with vital problems takes his life in his hands. Let him make his will and put in his order for lilies!"

She disappeared at some forty m.p.h., and Percy followed her retreating form with an indulgent eye.

"A quaint character," he said.

I agreed that the old relative was quaint in spots.

"She reminds me a little of the editress of *Parnassus*. The same tendency to wave her hands and shout, when stirred. But about this drive of yours to London, Wooster. What made you go there?"

"Oh, just one or two things I had to attend to."

"Well, I am thankful that you got back safely. The toll of the roads is so high these days. I trust you always drive carefully, Wooster? No speeding? No passing on blind corners? Capital, capital. But we were all quite anxious about you. We couldn't think where you could have got to. Cheesewright was particularly concerned. He appeared to think that you had vanished permanently and he said there were all sorts of things he had been hoping to discuss with you. I must let him know you are back. It will relieve his mind."

He trotted off, and I lit a nonchalant cigarette, calm and collected to the eyebrows. I was perhaps halfway through it and had just blown quite a goodish smoke ring, when clumping footsteps made themselves heard and Stilton loomed up on the skyline.

I reached a hand into my pocket and got a firm grasp on the old Equalizer.

17

I DON'T know if you have ever seen a tiger of the jungle drawing a deep breath preparatory to doing a swan dive and landing with both feet on the backbone of one of the minor fauna. Probably not, nor, as a matter of fact, have I. But I should imagine that a t. of the j. at such a moment would look . . . allowing, of course, for the fact that it would not have a pink face and a head like a pumpkin . . . exactly as G. D'Arcy Cheesewright looked as his eyes rested on the Wooster frame. For perhaps a couple of ticks he stood there inflating and deflating his chest. Then he said, as I had rather supposed he would:

"Ho!"

His signature tune, as you might say.

My nonchalance continued undiminished. It would have been idle to pretend that the blister's attitude was not menacing. It was about as menacing as it could jolly well stick. But with my hand on the cosh I faced him without a tremor. Like Caesar's wife, I was ready for anything.

I gave him a careless nod.

"Ah, Stilton," I said. "How are tricks?"

The question appeard to set the seal on his hotted-up-ness. He gnashed a tooth or two.

"I'll show you how tricks are! I've been looking for you all day."

"You wished to see me about something?"

"I wished to pull your head off at the roots and make you swallow it."

I nodded again, carelessly as before.

"Ah, yes. You rather hinted at some such desire last night, did you not? It all comes back to me. Well, I'm sorry, Stilton, but I'm afraid it's off. I have made other plans. Percy Gorringe will no doubt have told you that I ran up to London this morning. I went to get this," I said, and producing the man of slender physique's best friend, gave it a suggestive waggle.

There is one drawback to not wearing a moustache, and that is that if you don't have one, you've got nothing to twirl when baffled. All you can do is stand with your lower jaw drooping like a tired lily, looking a priceless ass, and that is what Stilton was doing now. His whole demeanor was that of an Assyrian who, having come down like a wolf on the fold, finds in residence not lambs but wildcats, than which, of course, nothing makes an Assyrian feel sillier.

"Amazingly effective little contrivances, these," I proceeded, rubbing it in. "You read about them a good deal in mystery thrillers. Coshes they are called, though blackjack is, I believe, the American term."

He breathed stertorously, his eyes bulging. I suppose he had never come up against anything like this before. One gets new experiences.

"You put that thing down!" he said hoarsely.

"I propose to put it down," I replied, quick as a flash. "I propose to put it down jolly dashed hard, the moment you make a move, and though I am the merest novice in the use of the cosh, I don't see how I can help hitting a head the size of yours somewhere. And then where will you be, Cheesewright? On the floor, dear old soul, that's where you will be, with me carelessly dusting my hands and putting the instrument back in my pocket. With one of these things in his possession the veriest weakling can lay out the toughest egg colder than a halibut on ice. To put it in a word, Cheesewright, I am armed, and the setup, as I see it, is this. I take a comfortable stance with the weight balanced on both feet, you make a spring, and I, cool as some cucumbers . . ."

It was a silly thing to say, that about making springs, because it put ideas into his head. He made one on the word "cucumbers" with such abruptness that I was caught completely unawares. That's the trouble with beefy fellows like Stilton. They are so massive that you don't credit them with the ability to get off the mark like jack rabbits and fly through the air with the greatest of ease. Before I knew what had happend, the cosh, wrenched from my grasp, was sailing across the hall, to come to rest on the floor near Uncle Tom's safe.

I stood there defenseless.

Well, "stood" is putting it loosely. In crises like this we Woosters do not stand. It was soon made abundantly clear that Stilton was not the only one of our little circle who could get off marks like jack rabbits. I doubt if in the whole of Australia, where this species of animal abounds, you could have found a jack rabbit capable of a tithe of the swift smoothness with which I removed myself from the pulsating center of things. To do a backward jump of some eleven feet and install myself behind the sofa was with me the work of an instant, and there for awhile the matter rested, because every time he came charging round to my side like a greyhound I went whizzing round to his side like an electric hare, rendering his every effort null and void. Those great Generals, of whom I was speaking earlier, go in for this maneuver quite a bit. Strategic redeployment is the technical term.

How long this round-and-round-the-mulberry-bush sequence would have continued, it is not easy to say, but probably not any great length of time, for already my partner in the rhythmic doings was beginning to show signs of feeling the pace. Stilton, like so many of these beefy birds, is apt, when not in training for some aquatic contest, to yield to the lure of the fleshpots. This takes its toll. By the end of the first dozen laps, while I remained as fresh as a daisy, prepared to fight it out on this line if it took all summer, he was puffing quite considerably and his brow had become wet with honest sweat.

But as so often happens on these occasions, the fixture was not played to a finish. Pausing for a moment before starting on lap thirteen, we were interrupted by the entry of Seppings, Aunt Dahlia's butler, who came toddling in, looking rather official.

I was glad to see him myself, for some sort of interruption was just what I had been hoping for, but this turning of the thing into a threesome plainly displeased Stilton, and I could understand why. The man's presence hampered him and prevented him from giving of his best. I have already explained that the Cheesewright code prohibits brawling if there are females around. The same rule holds good when members of the domestic staff appear at the ringside. If butlers butt in while they are in the process of trying to ascertain the color of some acquaintance's insides, the Cheesewrights cheese it.

But, mark you, they don't like cheesing it, and it is not to be wondered at that, compelled by this major-domo's presence to suspend hostilities, Stilton should have eyed him with ill-concealed animosity. His manner, when he spoke, was brusque.

"What do you want?"

"The door, sir."

Stilton's ill-concealed animosity became rather worse concealed. So packed indeed, with deleterious animal magnetism was the glance he directed at Seppings that one felt that there was a considerable danger of Aunt Dahlia at no distant date finding herself a butler short.

"What do you mean, you want the door? Which door? What door? What on earth do you want a door for?"

I saw that it was almost impossible that he would ever get the thing straight in his mind without a word of explanation, so I supplied it. I always like, if I can, to do the square thing by one and all on these occasions. Scratch Bertram Wooster, I sometimes say, and you find a Boy Scout.

"The front door, Stilton, old dance partner, is what one presumes Pop Seppings has in mind," I said. "I would hazard the guess that the bell rang. Correct, Seppings?"

"Yes, sir," he replied with quiet dignity. "The front door bell rang, and in pursuance of my duties I came to answer it."

And, his manner suggesting that that in his opinion would hold Stilton for awhile, he carried on as planned.

"What I'll bet has happened, Stilton, old scone," I said, clarifying the whole situation, "is that some visitor waits without."

I was right. Seppings flung wide the gates, there was a flash of blonde hair and a whiff of Chanel Number Five, and a girl came sailing in, a girl whom I was able to classify at a single glance as a pipterino of the first water.

Those who know Bertram Wooster best are aware that he is not a man who readily slops over when speaking of the opposite sex. He is cool and critical. He weighs his words. So when I describe this girl as a pipterino, you will gather that she was something pretty special. She could have walked into any assembly of international beauty contestants, and the committee of judges would have laid down the red carpet for her. One could imagine fashionable photographers fighting to the death for her custom.

Like the heroine of *The Mystery of the Pink Crayfish* and, indeed, the heroines of all the thrillers I have ever come across, she had hair the color of ripe wheat and eyes of cornflower blue. Add a tiptilted nose and a figure as full of curves as a scenic railway, and it will not strike you as strange that Stilton, sheathing the sword, should have stood gaping at her dumbly, his aspect that of a man who has been unexpectedly struck by a thunderbolt.

"Is Mrs. Travers around?" inquired this vision, addressing herself to Seppings. "Will you tell her Miss Morehead has arrived."

I was astounded. For some reason, possibly because she had three names, the picture I had formed in my mind of Daphne Dolores Morehead was that of an elderly female with a face like a horse and gold-rimmed pince-nez attached to her top button with a black string. Seeing her steadily and seeing her whole, I found myself commending Aunt Dahlia's sagacity in inviting her to Brinkley Court, presumably to help promote the sale of the *Boudoir*. A word from her, advising its purchase, would, I felt, go a long way with L.G. Trotter. He was doubtless a devoted and excellent husband, true as steel to the wife of his b., but even devoted and excellent husbands are apt to react powerfully when girls of the D. D. Morehead type start giving them Treatment A.

Stilton was still goggling at her like a bulldog confronted with a pound of steak, and now, her eyes of cornflower blue becoming accustomed to the dim light of the hall, she took a dekko at him and uttered an exclamation that seemed—oddly, considering what Stilton was like—one of pleasure.

"Mr. Cheesewright!" she said. "Well, fancy! I thought your face was familiar." She took another dekko. "You *are* D'Arcy Cheesewright, who used to row for Oxford?"

Stilton inclined the bean dumbly. He seemed incapable of speech.

"I thought so. Somebody pointed you out to me at the Eights Week ball one year. But I almost didn't recognize you. You had a moustache then. I'm so glad you haven't any longer. You look so much handsomer without it. I do think moustaches are simply awful. I always say that a man who can lower himself to wearing a moustache might just as well grow a beard."

I could not let this pass.

"There are moustaches and moustaches," I said, twirling mine. Then, seeing that she was asking herself who this slim, distinguished-looking stranger might be, I tapped myself on the wishbone. "Wooster, Bertram," I said. "I'm Mrs. Travers' nephew, she being my aunt. Should I lead you into her presence? She is probably counting the minutes."

She pursed the lips dubiously, as if the program I had suggested deviated in many respects from the ideal.

"Yes, I suppose I ought to be going and saying Hello, but what I would really like would be to explore the grounds. It's such a lovely place."

Stilton, who was now a pretty vermilion, came partially out of the ether, uttering odd, strangled noises like a man with no roof to his mouth trying to recite "Gunga Din." Finally something coherent emerged.

"May I show you round?" he said hoarsely.

"I'd love it."

"Ho!" said Stilton. He spoke quickly, as if feeling he had been remiss in not saying that earlier, and a moment later they were up and doing. And I, with something of the emotions of Daniel passing out of the stage door of the lions' den, went to my room.

It was cool and restful there. Aunt Dahlia is a woman who believes in doing her guests well in the matter of arm chairs and chaise longues, and the chaise longue allotted to me yielded gratefully to the form. It was not long before a pleasant drowsiness stole over me. The weary eyelids closed. I slept.

When I woke up half an hour later, my first act was to start with some violence. The brain cleared by slumber, I had remembered the cosh.

I rose to my feet, appalled, and shot from the room. It was imperative that I should recover possession of that beneficent instrument with all possible speed, for though in our recent encounter I had outgeneraled Stilton in round one, foiling him with my superior footwork and ring science, there was no knowing when he might not be feeling ready for round two. A setback may discourage a Cheesewright for the moment, but does not dispose of him as a logical contender.

The cosh, you will recall, had flashed through the air like a shooting star, to wind up its trip somewhere near Uncle Tom's safe, and I proceeded to the spot on winged feet. And picture my concern on finding on arrival that it wasn't there. The way things disappeared at Brinkley Court . . . ladders, coshes and what not . . . was enough to make a man throw in his hand and turn his face to the wall.

At this moment I actually did turn my face to the wall, the one the safe was wedged into, and having done so gave another of those violent starts of mine.

And what I saw was enough to make a fellow start with all the violence at his disposal. For two or three ticks I simply couldn't believe it. "Bertram," I said to myself, "the strain has been too much for you. You are cockeyed." But no. I blinked once or twice to clear the vision, and when I had finished blinking there it was, just as I had seen it the first time.

The safe door was open.

18

IT IS at moments like this that you catch Bertram Wooster at his superb best, his ice-cold brain working like a machine. Many fellows, I mean to say, seeing that safe door open, would have wasted precious time standing goggling at it, wondering why it was open, who had opened it and why whoever had opened it hadn't shut it again, but not Bertram. Hand him something on a plate with watercress round it, and he does not loiter and linger. He acts. A quick dip inside and a rapid rummaging, and I had the thing all sewed up.

There were half a dozen jewel cases stowed away on the shelves, and it took a minute or two to open them and examine contents, but investigation revealed only one pearl necklace, so I was spared anything in the nature of a perplexing choice. Swiftly trouser-pocketing the *bijouterie*, I shot off to Aunt Dahlia's den like the jack rabbit I had so closely resembled at my recent conference with Stilton. She should, I thought, be there by now, and it was a source of considerable satisfaction to me to feel that I was about to bring the sunshine back into the life of this deserving old geezer. When last seen, she had so plainly been in need of a bit of sunshine.

I found her in statu quo, as foreseen, smoking a gasper and spelling her way through her Agatha Christie, but I didn't bring the sunshine into her life, because it was there already. I was amazed at the change in her demeanor since she had gone off droopingly to see if Uncle Tom had finished talking to Spode about old silver. Then, you will recall, her air had been that of one caught in the machinery. Now, she conveyed the impression of having found the bluebird. As she looked up on discovering me in her midst, her face was shining like the seat of a busdriver's trousers, and it wouldn't have surprised me much if she had started yodeling. Her whole aspect was that of an aunt who on honeydew had fed and drunk the milk of Paradise, and the thought crossed my mind that if she was feeling as yeasty as this before hearing the good news, she might quite easily, when I spilled same, explode with a loud report.

I was not able, however, to reveal the chunk of secret history which I had up my sleeve, for, as so often happens when I am closeted with this woman, she made it impossible for me to get a syllable in edgeways. Even as I crossed the threshold, words began to flutter from her like bats out of a barn.

"Bertie!" she boomed. "Just the boy I wanted to see. Bertie, my pet, I have fought the good fight. Do you remember the hymn about 'See the troops of Midian prowl and prowl around'? It goes on 'Christian, up and smite them,' and that is what I have done in no uncertain manner. Let me tell you what happened. It will make your eyes pop."

"I say," I said, but was able to get no further. She rolled over me like a steam roller.

"When we parted in the hall not long ago, you will remember, I was bewitched, bothered and bewildered because I couldn't get hold of Spode to put the bite on him about Eulalie Soeurs, and was going to the collection room on the off chance of there having been a lull. But when I arrived, I found Tom still gassing away, so I took a seat and sat there hoping that Spode would eventually make a break for the open and give me a chance of having a word with him. But he continued to take it without a murmur, and Tom went rambling on. And then suddenly my bones were turned to water and the collection room swam before my eyes. Without any warning Tom suddenly switched to the subject of the necklace. 'You might like to look at it now,' he said. 'Certainly,' said Spode. 'It's in the safe in the hall,' said Tom. 'Let's go,' said Spode, and off they went."

She paused for breath, as even she has to do sometimes.

"I say—" I said.

The lungs refilled, she carried on again.

"I wouldn't have thought my limbs would have been able to support me to the door, much less down a long passage into the hall, but they did. I followed in the wake of the procession, giving at the knees but somehow managing to navigate. What I thought I was doing, joining the party, I don't know, but I suppose I had some vague idea of being present when Tom got the bad news and pleading brokenly for forgiveness. Anyway, I went. Tom opened the safe, and I stood there as if I had been turned into a pillar of salt, like Lot's wife."

I recalled the incident to which she referred, it having happened to come up in the examination paper that time I won that prize for Scripture Knowledge at my private school, but it's probably new to you, so I will give a brief synopsis. For some reason which has escaped my memory they told this Mrs. Lot, while out walking one day, not to look round or she would be turned into a pillar of salt, so of course she immediately did look round and by what I have always thought an odd coincidence she *was* turned into a pillar of salt. It just shows you, what? I mean to say, you never know where you are these days.

"Time marched on. Tom took out the jewel case and passed it over to Spode, who said 'Ah, this is it, is it?' or some damn silly remark like that, and at that moment, with the hand of doom within a toucher of descending, Seppings. Woof!" she said, and paused for breath again.

was wanted on the phone. 'Eh? What? What?' said Tom, his invariable practice when told he is wanted on the phone, and legged it, followed by Seppings. Woof!" she said, and paused for breath again.

"I say—" I said.

"You can imagine how I felt. That stupendous bit of luck had changed the whole aspect of affairs. For hours I had been wondering how on earth I could get Spode alone, and now I had got him alone. You can bet I didn't waste a second. 'Just think, Lord Sidcup,' I said winningly, 'I haven't had a moment yet to talk to you about all our mutual friends and those happy days at Totleigh Towers. How is dear Sir Watkyn Bassett!' I asked, still winningly. I fairly cooed to the man."

"I say—" I said.

She squelched me with an imperious gesture.

"Don't interrupt, curse you. I never saw such a chap for wanting to collar the conversation. Gabble, gabble, gabble. Listen, can't you, when I'm telling you the biggest story that has broken around these parts for years. Where was I? Oh, yes. 'How is dear Sir Watkyn?' I said, and he said dear Sir Watkyn was pretty oojah-cum-spiff. 'And dear Madeline?' I said, and he said dear

Madeline was ticking over all right. And then I drew a deep breath and let him have it. 'And how is that ladies' underclothing place of yours getting along?' I said. 'Eulalie Soeurs, isn't it called? still coining money, I trust?' And next moment you could have knocked me down with a feather. For with a jolly laugh he replied, 'Eulalie Soeurs? Oh, I haven't anything to do with that any longer. I sold out ages ago. It's a company now.' And as I stood gaping at him, my whole plan of campaign in ruins, he said 'Well, I may as well have a look at this necklace. Mr. Travers says he is anxious to have my opinion of it.' And he pressed his thumb to the catch and the jewel case flew open. And I was just commending my soul to God and saying to myself that this was the end, when I stubbed my foot against something and looked down and there, lying on the floor . . . you'll scarcely believe this . . . was a cosh."

She paused again, took on a cargo of breath quickly, and resumed.

"Yessir, a cosh! You wouldn't know what a cosh is, of course, so I'll explain. It's a small rubber instrument, much used by the criminal classes for socking their friends and relations. They wait till their mother-in-law's back is turned and then let her have it. It's all the rage in underworld circles, and there it was, as I say, lying at my feet."

"I say—" I said.

I got the imperious gesture between the eyes once more.

"Well, for a moment, it rang no bell. I picked it up automatically, the good housewife who doesn't like to see things lying around on floors, but it held no message for me. It simply didn't occur to me that my guardian angel had been directing my footsteps and was showing me the way out of my troubles and perplexities. And then suddenly, in a blinding flash, I got it. I realized what that good old guardian angel was driving at. He had at last succeeded in penetrating the bone and getting it into my fat head. There was Spode, with his back turned, starting to take the necklace out of the case . . ."

I gasped gurglingly.

"You didn't cosh him?"

"Certainly I coshed him. What would you have had me do? What would Napoleon have done? I took a nice easy half-swing and let go with lots of follow-through, and he fell to earth he knew not where."

I could readily believe it. Just so had Constable Dobbs fallen at Deverill Hall.

"He's in bed now, convinced that he had a touch of vertigo and hit his head on the floor. Don't worry about Spode. A good night's rest and a bland diet, and he'll be as right as rain tomorrow. And I've got the necklace, I've got the necklace, I've got the bally necklace, and I feel as if I could pick up a couple of tigers and knock their heads together!"

I gaped at her. The bean was swimming. Through the mist that had risen before the eyes she appeared to be swaying like an aunt caught in a high wind.

"You say you've got the necklace?" I quavered.

"I certainly have."

"Then what," I said, in about as hollow a voice as ever proceeded from human lips, "is the one I've got?"

And I produced my exhibit.

For quite a while it was plain that she had failed to follow the story sequence. She looked at the necklace, then at me, then at the necklace again. It was not until I had explained fully that she got the strength of it.

"Of course, yes," she said, her brow clearing. "I see it all now. What with yelling for Tom and telling him Spode had had some sort of seizure and listening to him saying 'Oh, my God! Now we'll have to put the frightful fellow up for the night!' and trying to comfort him and helping Seppings tote the remains to bed and all that, I forgot to suggest shutting the safe door. And Tom, of course, never thought of it. He was much too busy tearing his hair and saying this was certainly the last time he would invite a club acquaintance to his house, by golly, it being notorious that the first thing club acquaintances do on finding themselves in somebody's home is to have fits and take advantage of them to stay dug into the woodwork for weeks. And then you came along—"

"—and rummaged in the safe and found a pearl necklace and naturally thought it was yours—"

"—and swiped it. Very decent of you, Bertie, dear, and I appreciate the kind thought. If you had been here this morning, I would have told you that Tom insisted on everybody putting their valuables in the safe, but you had dashed up to London. What took you there, by the way?"

"I went to get the cosh, formerly the property of Aunt Agatha's son, Thos. I have been having a little trouble of late with Menaces."

She gazed at me with worshiping eyes, deeply moved.

"Was it you, my heart of gold," she said brokenly, "who provided that cosh? I had been putting it down as straight guardian angel stuff. Oh, Bertie, if ever I called you a brainless poop who ought to be given a scholarship at some good lunatic asylum, I take back the words."

I thanked her briefly.

"But what happens now?"

"I give three rousing cheers and start strewing roses from my hat."

I frowned with a touch of impatience.

"I am not talking about you, my dear old ancestor, but about your nephew Bertram, the latter being waist-high in the mulligatawny and liable at any moment to sink without trace. Here I am in possession of somebody's pearl necklace—"

"Ma Trotter's. I recognize it now. She wears it in the evenings."

"Right. So far, so good. The choker belongs, we find, to Ma Trotter. That point established, what do I do for the best?"

"You put it back."

"In the safe?"

"That's it. You put it back in the safe."

It struck me as a most admirable idea, and I wondered why I hadn't thought of it myself.

"You've hit it!" I said. "Yes, I'll put it back in the safe."

"I'd run along now, if I were you. No time like the present."

"I will. Oh, by the way, Daphne Dolores Morehead has arrived. She's out in the grounds with Stilton."

"What did you think of her?"

"A sight for sore eyes, if I may use the expression. I had no idea they were making female novelists like that these days."

I would have gone on to amplify the favorable impression the young visitor's outer crust had made on me, but at this moment Mrs. Trotter loomed up in the doorway. She looked at me as if feeling that I was on the whole pretty superfluous.

"Oh, good evening, Mr. Wooster," she said in a distant sort of way. "I was hoping to find you alone, Mrs. Travers," she added with the easy tact which had made her the toast of Liverpool.

"I'm just off," I assured her. "Nice evening."

"Very nice."

"Well, toodle-oo," I said, and set a course for the hall, feeling pretty bobbish, for at least a portion of my troubles would soon be over. If, of course, the safe was still open.

It was. And I had reached it and was on the point of whipping out the jewel case and depositing it, when a voice spoke behind me, and turning like a startled fawn, I perceived L. G. Trotter.

Since my arrival at Brinkley Court I had not fraternized to any great extent with this weasel-faced old buster. He gave me the impression, as he had done at that dinner of mine, of not being too frightfully keen on the society of his juniors. I was surprised that he should be wanting to chat with me now, and wished that he could have selected some more suitable moment. With that necklace on my person, solitude was what I desired.

"Hey," he said. "Where's your aunt?"

"She's in her room," I replied, "talking to Mrs. Trotter."

"Oh? Well, when you see her, tell her I've gone to bed."

This surprised me.

"To bed? Surely the night is yet young?"

"I've got one of my dyspeptic attacks. You haven't a digestive pill on you?"

"I'm sorry. I came out without any."

"Hell!" he said, rubbing the abdomen. "I'm in agony. I feel as if I'd swallowed a couple of wildcats. Hullo," he proceeded, changing the subject, "What's that safe door doing open?"

I threw out the suggestion that somebody must have opened it, and he nodded as if thinking well of the theory.

"Damned carelessness," he said. "That's the way things get stolen."

And before my bulging eyes he stepped across and gave the door a shove. It closed with a clang.

"Oof !" he said, massaging the abdomen once more, and with a curt "Good night" passed up the stairs, leaving me frozen to the spot. Lot's wife couldn't have been stiffer.

Any chance I had of putting things back in the safe had gone with the wind.

19

I DON'T know that I have a particularly vivid imagination—possibly not, perhaps—but in circs like those which I have just outlined you don't need a very vivid imagination to enable you to spot the shape of things to come. As plainly as if it had been the top line on an oculist's chart, I could see what the future held for Bertram.

As I stood there gaping at that closed door, a vision rose before my eyes, featuring me and an inspector of police, the latter having in his supporting cast an unusually nasty-looking sergeant.

"Are you coming quietly, Wooster?" the inspector was saying.

"Who, me?" I said, quaking in every limb. "I don't know what you mean."

"Ha, ha," laughed the imspector. "That's good. Eh, Fotheringay?"

"Very rich, sir," said the sergeant. "Makes me chuckle, that does."

"Too late to try anything of that sort, my man," went on the inspector, becoming grave again. "The game is up. We have evidence to prove that you went to this safe and from it abstracted a valuable pearl necklace, the property of Mrs. L. G. Trotter. If that doesn't mean five years in the jug for you, I miss my bet."

"But, honestly, I thought it was Aunt Dahlia's."

"Ha, ha," laughed the inspector.

"Ha, ha," chirped the sergeant.

"A pretty story," said the inspector. "Tell that to the jury and see what they think of it. Fotheringay, the handcuffs!"

Such was the v. that rose before my e. as I gaped at that c.d., and I wilted like a salted snail. Outside in the garden birds were singing their evensong, and it seemed to me that each individual bird was saying "Well, boys, Wooster is for it. We shan't see much of Wooster for the next few years. Too bad, too bad. A nice chap till he took to crime."

A hollow groan escaped my lips, but before another could follow it I was racing for Aunt Dahlia's room. As I reached it, Ma Trotter came out, gave me an austere look and passed on her way, and I went on into the presence. I found the old relative sitting bolt upright in her chair, staring before her with unseeing eyes, and it was plain that once more something had happened to inject a black frost into her sunny mood. The Agatha Christie had fallen unheeded to the floor, displaced from her lap, no doubt, by a shudder of horror.

Normally, I need scarcely say, my policy on finding this sterling old soul looking licked to a splinter would have been to slap her between the shoulder blades and urge her to keep her tail up, but my personal troubles left me with little leisure for bracing aunts. Whatever the disaster or cataclysm that had come upon her, I felt, it could scarcely claim to rank in the same class as the one that had come upon me.

"I say," I said. "The most frightful thing has happened!"

She nodded somberly. A martyr at the stake would have been cheerier.

"You bet your heliotrope socks it has," she responded. "Ma Trotter has thrown off the mask, curse her. She wants Anatole."

"Who wouldn't?"

It seemed for a moment as if she were about to haul off and let a loved nephew have it on the side of the head, but with a strong effort she calmed herself. Well, when I say "calmed herself," she didn't cease to boil briskly, but she confined her activities to the spoken word.

"Don't you understand, ass? She has come out into the open and stated her terms. She says she won't let Trotter buy the *Boudoir* unless I give her Anatole."

It just shows how deeply my predicament had stirred me that my reaction to this frightful speech was practically nil. Informed at any other time that there was even a remote prospect of that superb disher-up handing in his portfolio and going off to waste his sweetness on the desert air of the Trotter home, I should unquestionably have blenched and gasped and tottered but now, as I say, I heard those words virtually unmoved.

"No, really?" I said. "I say, listen, old flesh and blood. Just as I got to the safe and was about to restore the Trotter pearls, that chump L. G. Trotter most officiously shut the door, foiling my aims and objects and leaving me in the dickens of a jam. I'm trembling like a leaf."

"So am I."

"I don't know what to do."

"I don't, either."

"I search in vain for some way out of this what the French call *impasse*."

"Me, too," she said, picking up the Agatha Christie and hurling it at a passing vase. When deeply stirred, she is always inclined to kick things and throw things. At Totleigh Towers, during one of our more agitated conferences, she had cleared the mantelpiece in my bedroom of its entire contents, including a terra cotta elephant and a porcelain statuette of the Infant Samuel in Prayer. "I don't suppose any woman ever had such a problem to decide. On the one hand, life without Anatole is a thing almost impossible—"

"Here I am, stuck with this valuable pearl necklace, the property of Mrs. L. G. Trotter, and when its loss—"

"—to contemplate. On the other—"

"—is discovered, hues and cries will be raised, inspectors and sergeants sent for—"

"—hand, I must sell the *Boudoir*, or I can't take that necklace of mine out of hock. So—"

"—and I shall be found with what is known as hot ice on my person."

"Ice!"

"And you know as well as I do what happens to people who are caught in possession of hot ice."

"Ice!" she repeated, and sighed dreamily. "I think of those prawns in iced aspic of his, and I say to myself that I should be mad to face a lifetime without Anatole's cooking. That *Selle d'Agneau à la Grecque!* That *Mignonette de Poulet Roti Petit Duc!* Those *Nonats de la Méditerranée au Fenouil!* And then I feel I must be practical. I've got to get that necklace back, and if the only way of getting it back is to . . . Sweet suffering soupspoons!" she vociferated, if that's the word, anguish written on her every feature. "I wonder what Tom will say when he hears Anatole is leaving!"

"And I wonder what he'll say when he hears his nephew is doing a stretch in Dartmoor."

"Eh?"

"Stretch in Dartmoor."

"Who's going to do a stretch in Dartmoor?"

"I am."

"You?"

"Me."

"Why?"

I gave her a look which I suppose, strictly speaking, no nephew should have given an aunt. But I was sorely exasperated.

"Haven't you been listening?" I demanded.

She came back at me with equal heat.

"Of course I haven't been listening. Do you think that when I am faced with the prospect of losing the finest cook in the midland counties I have time to pay attention to your vapid conversation? What were you babbling about?"

I drew myself up. The word "babbling" had wounded me.

"I was merely mentioning that, owing to that ass L. G. Trotter having shut the door of the safe before I could deposit the fatal necklace, I am landed with the thing. I described it as hot ice."

"Oh, that was what you were saying about ice?"

"That was what. I also hazarded the prediction that in about two shakes of a duck's tail inspectors and sergeants would come scooping me up and taking me off to chokey."

"What nonsense. Why should anyone think you had anything to do with it?"

I laughed. One of those short, bitter ones.

"You don't think it may arouse their suspicions when they find the ruddy thing in my trouser pocket? At any moment I may be caught with the goods on me, and you don't have to read many thrillers to know what happens to unfortunate slobs who are caught with the goods on them. They get it in the neck."

I could see she was profoundly moved. In my hours of ease this aunt is sometimes uncertain, coy and hard to please and, when I was younger, not infrequently sloshed me on the earhole if my behavior seemed to her to call for the gesture, but let real peril threaten Bertram and she is in there swinging every time.

"This isn't good," she said, picking up a small foot-stool and throwing it at a china shepherdess on the mantelpiece.

I endorsed this view, expressing the opinion that it was dashed awful.

"You'll have to—"

"Hist!"

"Eh?"

"Hist!"

"What do you mean, Hist?"

What I had meant by the monosollyable was that I had heard footsteps approaching the door. Before I could explain this, the handle turned sharply and Uncle Tom came in.

My ear told me at once that all was not well with this relative by marriage. When Uncle Tom has anything on his mind, he rattles his keys. He was jingling now like a xylophone. His face had the haggard, careworn look which it wears when he hears that week-end guests are expected.

"It's a judgment!" he said, bursting into speech with a whoosh.

Aunt Dahlia masked her agitation with what I imagine she thought to be a genial smile.

"Hullo, Tom, come and join the party. What's a judgment?"

"This is. On me. For weakly allowing you to invite those infernal Trotters here. I knew something awful would happen. I felt it in my bones. You can't fill the house up with people like that without courting disaster. Stands to reason. He's got a face like a weasel, she's twenty pounds overweight, and that son of hers wears whiskers. It was madness ever to let them cross the threshold. Do you know what's happened?"

"No, what?"

"Somebody's pinched her necklace!"

"Good heavens!"

"I thought that would make you sit up," said Uncle Tom, with gloomy triumph. "She collared me in the hall just now and said she wanted the thing to wear at dinner tonight, and I took her to the safe and opened it and it wasn't there."

I told myself that I must keep very cool.

"You mean," I said, "that it had gone?"

He gave me rather an unpleasant look.

"You've got a lightning brain!" he said.

Well, I have, of course.

"But how could it have gone?" I asked. "Was the safe open?"

"No, shut. But I must have left it open. All that fuss of putting that frightful fellow Sidcup to bed distracted my attention."

I think he was about to say that it just showed what happened when you let people like that into the house, but checked himself on remembering that he was the one who had invited him.

"Well, there it is," he said. "Somebody seems to have come along while we were upstairs, seen the safe door open and helped himself. The Trotter woman is raising cain, and it was only my urgent entreaties that kept her from sending for the police there and then. I told her we could get much better results by making secret inquiries. Didn't want a scandal, I said. But I doubt if I could have persuaded her if it hadn't been that young Gorringe came along and backed me up. Quite an intelligent young fellow, that; though he does wear whiskers."

I cleared my throat nonchalantly. At least, I tried to do it nonchalantly.

"Then what steps are you taking, Uncle Tom?"

"I'm going to excuse myself during dinner on the plea of a headache—which I've got, I don't mind telling you—and go and search the rooms. Just possible I might dig up something. Meanwhile, I'm off to get a drink. The whole thing has upset me considerably. Will you join me in a quick one, Bertie, me boy?"

"I think I'll stick on here, if you don't mind," I said. "Aunt Dahlia and I are talking of this and that."

He produced a final obligato on the keys.

"Well, suit yourself. But it seems odd to me in my present frame of mind that anyone can refuse a drink. I wouldn't have thought it possible."

As the door closed behind him, Aunt Dahlia expelled her breath like a death rattle.

"Golly!" she said.

It seemed to me the *mot juste*.

"What should we do now, do you think?" I queried.

"I know what I'd like to do. I'd like to put the whole thing up to Jeeves, if certain fatheads hadn't let him go off on toots in London just when we need him most."

"He may be back by now."

"Ring for Seppings, and ask."

I pressed the bell.

"Oh, Seppings," I said, as he entered and You-rang-madam-ed. "Has Jeeves got back yet?"

"Yes, sir."

"Then send him here with all speed," I said.

And a few moments later the man was with us, looking so brainy and intelligent that my heart leaped up as if I had beheld a rainbow in the sky.

"Oh, Jeeves," I yipped.

"Oh, Jeeves," yipped Aunt Dahlia, dead heating with me.

"After you," I said.

"No, go ahead," she replied, courteously yielding the floor. "Your predicament is worse than my predicament. Mine can wait."

I was touched.

"Very handsome of you, old egg," I said. "Much appreciated. Jeeves, your close attention, if you please. Certain problems have arisen."

"Yes, sir?"

"Two in all."

"Yes, sir?"

"Shall we call them Problem A. and Problem B.?"

"Certainly, sir, if you wish."

"Then here is Problem A., the one affecting me."

I ran through the scenario, putting the facts clearly and well.

"So there you are, Jeeves. Bend the brain to it. If you wish to pace the corridor, by all means do so."

"It will not be necessary, sir. One sees what must be done."

I said I would be glad if he could arrange it so that two could.

"You must restore the necklace to Mrs. Trotter, sir."

"Give it back to her, you mean?"

"Precisely, sir."

"But, Jeeves," I said, my voice shaking a little, "isn't she going to wonder how I come to have my hooks on the thing? Will she not probe and question, and having probed and questioned rush to the telephone and put in her order for inspectors and sergeants?"

A muscle at the side of his mouth twitched indulgently.

"The restoration would, of course, have to be accomplished with secrecy, sir. I would advocate placing the piece of jewelry in the lady's bedchamber at a moment when it was unoccupied. Possibly while she was at the dinner table."

"But I should be at the dinner table, too. I can't say 'Oh, excuse me' and dash upstairs in the middle of the fish course."

"I was about to suggest that you allow me to attend to the matter, sir. My movements will be less circumscribed."

"You mean you'll handle the whole binge?"

"If you will give me the piece of jewelry, sir, I shall be most happy to do so."

I was overcome. I burned with remorse and shame. I saw how mistaken I had been in supposing that he had been talking through the back of his neck.

"Golly, Jeeves! This is a pretty feudal."

"Not at all, sir."

"You've solved the whole thing. Rem . . . what's that expression of yours?"

"*Rem acu tetigisti,* sir?"

"That's it. It does mean 'You have put your finger on the nub,' doesn't it?"

"That would be a rough translation of the Latin, sir. I am happy to have given satisfaction. But did I understand you to say that there was a further matter that was troubling you, sir?"

"Problem B. is mine, Jeeves," said Aunt Dahlia, who during this slice of dialogue had been waiting in the wings, chafing a bit at being withheld from taking the stage. "It's about Anatole."

"Yes, madam?"

"Mrs. Trotter wants him."

"Indeed, madam?"

"And she says she won't let Trotter buy the *Boudoir* unless she gets him. And you know how vital it is that I sell the *Boudoir.* Sweet spirits of niter!" cried the old relative passionately. "If only there was some way of inserting a bit of backbone into L. G. Trotter and making him stand up to the woman and defy her!"

"There is, madam."

Aunt Dahlia leaped about a foot and a quarter. It was as though that calm response had been a dagger of Oriental design thrust into the fleshy part of her leg.

"What did you say, Jeeves? Did you say there was?"

"Yes, madam. I think it will be a reasonably simple matter to induce Mr. Trotter to override the lady's wishes."

I didn't want to cast a damper over the proceedings, but I had to put in a word here.

"Frightfully sorry to have to dash the cup of joy from your lips, old tortured spirit," I said, "but I fear that all this comes under the head of wishful thinking. Pull yourself together, Jeeves. You speak . . . is it airily?"

"Airily or glibly, sir."

"Thank you, Jeeves. You speak airily or glibly of inducing L. G. Trotter to throw off the yoke and defy his considerably better half, but are you not too . . . dash it, I've forgotten the word."

"Sanguine, sir?"

"That's it. Sanguine. Brief though my acquaintance with these twain has been, I have got L. G. Trotter's number, all right. His attitude towards Ma Trotter is that of an exceptionally diffident worm towards a sinewy Plymouth

Rock or Orpington. A word from her, and he curls up into a ball. So where do you get off with that simple-matter-to-override-wishes stuff?"

I thought I had him there, but no.

"If I might explain. I gather from Mr. Seppings, who has had opportunities of overhearing the lady's conversation, that Mrs. Trotter, being socially ambitious, is extremely anxious to see Mr. Trotter knighted, madam."

Aunt Dahlia nodded.

"Yes, that's right. She's always talking about it. She thinks it would be one in the eyes for Mrs. Alderman Blenkinsop."

"Precisely, madam."

I was rather surprised.

"Do they knight birds like him?"

"Oh, yes, sir. A gentleman of Mr. Trotter's prominence in the world of publishing is always in imminent danger of receiving the accolade."

"Danger? Don't these bozos like being knighted?"

"Not when they are of Mr. Trotter's retiring disposition, sir. He would find it a very testing ordeal. It involves wearing satin knee-breeches and walking backwards with a sword between the legs, not at all the sort of thing a sensitive gentleman of regular habits would enjoy. And he shrinks, no doubt, from the prospect of being addressed for the remainder of his life as Sir Lemuel."

"His name's not Lemuel?"

"I fear so, sir."

"Couldn't he use his second name?"

"His second name is Gengulphus."

"Golly, Jeeves," I said, thinking of old Uncle Tom Portarlington, "there's some raw work pulled at the font from time to time, is there not?"

"There is, indeed, sir."

Aunt Dahlia seemed perplexed, like one who strives in vain to put her finger on the nub.

"Is this all leading up to something, Jeeves?"

"Yes, madam. I was about to hazard the suggestion that were Mr. Trotter to become aware that the alternative to buying *Milady's Boudoir* was the discovery by Mrs. Trotter that he had been offered a knighthood and had declined it, you might find the gentleman more easily molded than in the past, madam."

It took Aunt Dahlia right between the eyes like a sock full of wet sand. She tottered, and grabbed for support at the upper part of my right arm, giving it the dickens of a pinch. The anguish caused her next remark to escape me, though as it was no doubt merely "Gosh!" or "Lord love a duck!" or something of that sort, I suppose I didn't miss much. When the mists had cleared from my eyes and I was myself again, Jeeves was speaking.

"It appears that Mrs. Trotter some months ago insisted on Mr. Trotter engaging the services of a gentleman's personal gentleman, a young fellow named Worple, and Worple contrived to secure the rough draft of Mr. Trotter's letter of refusal from the wastepaper basket. He had recently become a member of the Junior Ganymede, and in accordance with Rule Eleven he forwarded the document to the secretary for inclusion in the club archives. Through the courtesy of the secretary I was enabled to peruse it after luncheon, and a photostatic copy is to be dispatched to me through the medium of the post. I think that if you were to mention this to Mr. Trotter, madam—"

Aunt Dahlia uttered a whoop similar in timbre to those which she had been accustomed to emit in the old Quorn and Pytchley days when encouraging a bevy of hounds to get on the scent and give it both nostrils.

"We've got him cold!"

"So one is disposed to imagine, madam."

"I'll tackle him right away."

"You can't," I pointed out. "He's gone to bed. Touch of dyspepsia."

"Then tomorrow directly after breakfast," said Aunt Dahlia. "Oh, Jeeves!"

Emotion overcame her, and she grabbed at my arm again. It was like being bitten by an alligator.

20

AT ABOUT the hour of nine next morning a singular spectacle might have been observed on the main staircase of Brinkley Court. It was Bertram Wooster coming down to breakfast.

It is a fact well known to my circle that only on very rare occasions do I squash in at the communal morning meal, preferring to chew the kipper or whatever it may be in the seclusion of my bedchamber. But a determined man can nerve himself to almost anything, if necessary, and I was resolved at all cost not to miss the dramatic moment when Aunt Dahlia tore off her whiskers and told a cowering L. G. Trotter that she knew all. It would, I felt, be value for money.

Though slightly on the somnambulistic side, I don't know when I have felt more strongly that the lark was on the wing and the snail on the thorn and God in His Heaven and all right with the world. Thanks to Jeeves's outstanding acumen, Aunt Dahlia's problems were solved, and I was in a position—if I cared to be rude enough—to laugh in the faces of any inspectors and sergeants who might blow in. Furthermore, before retiring to rest on the previous night I had taken the precaution to recover the cosh from the old relative, and it was securely on my person once more. Little wonder that, as I entered the dining-room, I was within an ace of bursting into song and piping as the linnets do, as I have heard Jeeves put it.

The first thing I saw on crossing the threshold was Stilton wolfing ham, the next Daphne Dolores Morehead finishing off her repast with toast and marmalade.

"Ah, Bertie, old man," cried the former, waving a fork in the friendliest manner. "So there you are, Bertie, old fellow. Come in, Bertie, old chap, come in. Splendid to see you looking so rosy."

His cordiality would have surprised me more, if I hadn't seen in it a ruse or stratagem designed to put me off my guard and lull me into a false sense of security. Keenly alert, I went to the sideboard and helped myself with my left hand to sausages and bacon, keeping the right hand on the cosh in my side pocket. This jungle warfare teaches a man to take no chances.

"Nice morning," I said, having taken my seat and dipped the lips into a cup of coffee.

"Lovely," agreed the Morehead, who was looking more than ever like a dewy flower at daybreak. "D'Arcy is going to take me for a row on the river."

"Yes," said Stilton, giving her a burning glance. "One feels that Daphne ought to see the river. You might tell your aunt we shall not be back for lunch. Sandwiches and hardboiled eggs are being provided."

"By that nice butler."

"By, as you say, that nice butler, who also thought it might run to a bottle of the best from the oldest bin. We shall be starting almost immediately."

"I'll be going and getting ready," said the Morehead.

She rose with a bright smile, and Stilton, full though he was of ham, bounded gallantly to open the door for her. When he returned to the table, he found me rather ostentatiously brandishing the cosh. It seemed to surprise him.

"Hullo!" he said. "What are you doing with that thing?"

"Oh, nothing," I replied nonchalantly, resting it by my plate. "I just thought I would like to have it handy."

He swallowed a chunk of ham in a puzzled way. Then his face cleared.

"Good Lord! You didn't think I was going to set about you?"

I said that some such idea had crossed my mind, and he uttered an amused laugh.

"Good heavens, no. Why, I look on you as my dearest pal, old man."

It seemed to me that if yesterday's session was a specimen of the way he comported himself towards his dearest pals, the ones who weren't quite so dear must have a pretty thin time of it. I said as much, and he laughed again as heartily as if he had been standing in the dock at Vinton Street police court with His Worship getting off those nifties of his which convulsed all and sundry.

"Oh, that?" he said, dismissing the incident with an airy wave of the hand. "Forget all that, dear old chap. Put it right out of your mind. Perhaps I was a little cross on the occasion to which you refer, but no longer."

"No?" I said guardedly.

"Definitely not. I see now that I owe you a deep debt of gratitude. But for you, I might still be engaged to that pill Florence. Thank you, Bertie, old man."

Well, I said "Not at all" or "Don't mention it" or something of that sort, but my head was swimming. What with getting up for breakfast and hearing this Cheesewright allude to Florence as a pill, I felt in a sort of dream.

"I thought you loved her," I said, digging a bewildered fork into my sausage.

He laughed again. Only a beefy mass of heartiness like G. D'Arcy Cheesewright could have been capable of so much merriment at such an hour.

"Who, me? Good heavens, no. I may have imagined I did once . . . one of those boyish fancies . . . but when she said I had a head like a pumpkin, the scales fell from my eyes and I came out of the ether. Pumpkin, forsooth! I don't mind telling you, Bertie, old chap, that there are others—I mention no names—who have described my head as majestic. Yes, I have it from a reliable source that it makes me look a king among men. That will give you a rough idea of what a silly young geezer that blighted Florence Craye is. It is a profound relief to me that you have enabled me to get her out of my hair."

He thanked me again, and I said "Don't mention it," or it may have been "Not at all." I was feeling dizzier than ever.

"Then you don't think," I said with a quaver in the v., "that later on, when the hot blood has cooled, there might be a reconciliation?"

"Not a hope."

"It happened before."

"It won't happen again. I know now what love really is, Bertie. I tell you, when somebody—who shall be nameless—gazes into my eyes and says that the first time she saw me—in spite of the fact that I was wearing a moustache fully as foul as that one of yours—something went over her like an electric shock, I feel as if I had just won the Diamond Sculls at Henley. It's all washed up between Florence and me. She's yours, old man. Take her, old chap, take her."

Well, I said something civil like "Oh, thanks," but he wasn't listening. A silvery voice had called his name, and pausing but an instant to swallow the last of his ham he shot from the room, his face aglow and his eyes a-sparkle.

He left me with the heart like lead within the bosom and the sausage and bacon turning to ashes in my mouth. This, I could see, was the end. It was plain to the least observant eye that G. D'Arcy Cheesewright had got it properly up his nose. Morehead Preferred was booming, and Craye Ordinaries down in the cellar with no takers.

And I had been so certain that in due season wiser counsels would prevail, causing these two sundered hearts to regret the rift in the lute and decide to have another pop at it, thus saving me from the scaffold once more. But it was not to be. Bertram was for it. He would have to drain the bitter cup, after all.

I was starting on a second installment of coffee—it tasted like the bitter cup—when L. G. Trotter came in.

The one thing I didn't want in my enfeebled state was to have to chew the fat with Trotters, but when you're alone in a dining-room with a fellow, something in the nature of conversation is inevitable, so, as he poured himself out a cup of tea, I said it was a beautiful morning and recommended the sausages and bacon.

He reacted strongly, shuddering from head to foot.

"Sausages?" he said. "Bacon?" he said. "Don't talk to me about sausages and bacon," he said. "My dyspepsia's worse than ever."

Well, if he wanted to thresh out the subject of his aching tum, I was prepared to lend a ready ear, but he skipped on to another topic.

"You married?" he asked.

I winced a trifle and said I wasn't actually married yet.

"And you won't ever be, if you've got a morsel of sense," he proceeded, and brooded darkly over his tea for a moment. "You know what happens when you get married? You're bossed. You can't call your soul your own. You become just a cipher in the home."

I must say I was a bit surprised to find him so confidential to one who was, after all, a fairly mere stranger, but I put it down to the dyspepsia. No doubt the shooting pains had robbed him of his cool judgment.

"Have an egg," I said, by way of showing him that my heart was in the right place.

He turned green and tied himself into a lovers' knot.

"I won't have an egg! Don't keep telling me to have things. Do you think I could look at eggs, feeling the way I do? It's all this infernal French cooking. No digestion can stand up against it. Marriage!" he said, getting back to the old subject. "Don't talk to me about marriage. You get married, and first thing you know, you have stepsons rung in on you who grow whiskers and don't do a stroke of honest work. All they do is write poems about sunsets. Pah!"

I'm pretty shrewd, and it flashed upon me at this point that it might quite possibly be his stepson Percy to whom he was guardedly alluding. But before I could verify this suspicion the room had begun to fill up. Round about nine-twenty, which it was now, you generally find the personnel of a country house lining up for the eats. Aunt Dahlia came in and took a fried egg. Mrs. Trotter came in and took a sausage. Percy and Florence came in and took respectively a slice of ham and a portion of haddock. As there were no signs of Uncle Tom, I presumed that he was breakfasting in bed. He generally does, rarely feeling equal to facing his guests till he has fortified himself a bit for the stern ordeal.

Those present had got their heads down and their elbows squared and were busily employed getting theirs, when Seppings appeared with the morning papers, and conversation, not that there had ever been much of it, flagged. It was to a silent gathering that there now entered a newcomer, a man about seven feet in height with a square, powerful face, slightly moustached toward the center. It was some time since I had set eyes on Roderick

Spode, but I had no difficulty in recognizing him. He was one of those distinctive-looking blisters who, once seen, are never forgotten.

He was looking a little paler, I thought, as if he had recently had an attack of vertigo and hit his head on the floor. He said "Good morning" in what for him was rather a weak voice, and Aunt Dahlia glanced up from her *Daily Mirror.*

"Why, Lord Sidcup!" she said. "I never expected that you would be able to come to breakfast. Are you sure it's wise? Do you feel better this morning?"

"Considerably better, thank you," he responded bravely. "The swelling has to some extent subsided."

"I'm so glad. That's those cold compresses. I was hoping they would bring home the bacon. Lord Sidcup," said Aunt Dahlia, "had a nasty fall yesterday evening. We think it must have been a sudden giddiness. Everything went black, didn't it, Lord Sidcup?"

He nodded, and was plainly sorry next moment that he had done so, for he winced as I have sometimes winced when rashly oscillating the bean after some outstanding night of revelry at the Drones.

"Yes," he said. "It was all most extraordinary. I was standing there feeling perfectly well—never better, in fact—when it was as though something hard had hit me on the head, and I remembered no more till I came to in my room, with you smoothing my pillow and your butler mixing me a cooling drink."

"That's life," said Aunt Dahlia gravely. "Yessir, that's life all right. Here today and gone tomorrow, I often say. Bertie, you hellhound, take that beastly cigarette of yours outside. It smells like guano."

I rose, always willing to oblige, and had sauntered about halfway to the french window, when from the lips of Mrs. L. G. Trotter there suddenly proceeded what I can only describe as a screech. I don't know if you have ever inadvertently trodden on an unseen cat. Much the same sort of thing. Taking a quick look at her, I saw that her face had become almost as red as Aunt Dahlia's.

"Well!" she ejaculated.

She was staring at the *Times,* which was what she had drawn in the distribution of the morning journals, in much the same manner as a resident of India would have stared at a cobra, had he found it nestling in his bathtub.

"Of all the—!" she said, and then words failed her.

L. G. Trotter gave her the sort of look the cobra might have given the resident of India who had barged in on its morning bath. I could understand how he felt. A man with dyspepsia, already out of harmony with his wife, does not like to hear that wife screaming her head off in the middle of breakfast.

"What on earth's the matter?" he said testily.

Her bosom heaved like a stage sea.

"I'll tell you what's the matter. They've gone and knighted Robert Blenkinsop!"

"They have?" said L. G. Trotter. "Gosh!"

The stricken woman seemed to think "Gosh!" inadequate.

It wasn't. He now said "Ba goom!" She continued to erupt like one of those volcanoes which spill over from time to time and make the neighboring householders think a bit.

"Robert Blenkinsop! Robert Blenkinsop! Of all the iniquitous pieces of idiocy! I don't know what things are coming to nowadays. I never heard of such a . . . May I ask why you are laughing?"

L. G. Trotter curled up beneath her eye like a sheet of carbon paper.

"Not laughing," he said meekly. "Just smiling. I was thinking of Bobby Blenkinsop walking backwards with satin knee-breeches on."

"Oh?" said Ma Trotter, and her voice rang through the room like that of a costermonger indicating to his public that he has Brussels sprouts and blood oranges for sale. "Well, let me tell you that that is never going to happen to you. If ever you are offered a knighthood, Lemuel, you will refuse it. Do you understand? I won't have you cheapening yourself."

There was a crash. It was Aunt Dahlia dropping her coffee cup, and I could appreciate her emotion. She was feeling precisely as I had felt on learning from Percy that the Wooster Darts sweep ticket had changed hands, leaving Stilton free to attack me with tooth and claw. There is nothing that makes a woman sicker than the sudden realization that somebody she thought she was holding in the hollow of her hand isn't in the hollow of her hand by a jugful. So far from being in the hollow of her hand, L. G. Trotter was stepping high, wide and handsome with his hat on the side of his head, and I wasn't surprised that the thing had shaken her to her foundation garments.

In the silence which followed L. G. Trotter's response to this wifely ultimatum—it was, if I remember correctly, "Okay"—Seppings appeared in the doorway.

He was carrying a silver salver, and on this salver lay a pearl necklace.

21

It is pretty generally recognized in the circles in which he moves that Bertram Wooster is not a man who lightly throws in the towel and admits defeat. Beneath the thingummies of what-d'you-call-it his head, wind and weather permitting, is as a rule bloody but unbowed, and if the slings and arrows of outrageous fortune want to crush his proud spirit, they have to pull their socks up and make a special effort.

Nevertheless, I must confess that when, already weakened by having come down to breakfast, I beheld the spectacle which I have described, I definitely quailed. The heart sank, beads of persp. sprang out upon the brow and, as had happened in the case of Spode, everything went black. Through a murky mist I seemed to be watching a Negro butler presenting an inky salver to a Ma Trotter who looked like the end man in a minstrel show.

The floor heaved beneath my feet as if an earthquake had set in with unusual severity. My eye, in a fine frenzy rolling, met Aunt Dahlia's, and I saw that hers was rolling, too.

Still, she did her best, as always.

" 'At-a-boy, Seppings!" she said heartily. "We were all wondering where that necklace could have got to. It is yours, isn't it, Mrs. Trotter?"

Ma Trotter was scrutinizing the salver though a lorgnette.

"It's mine, all right," she said. "But what I'd like to know is how it came into this man's possession."

Aunt Dahlia continued to do her best.

"You found it on the floor of the hall, I suppose, Seppings, where Lord Sidcup dropped it when he had his seizure?"

A dashed good suggestion, I thought, and it might quite easily have clicked, had not Spode, the silly ass, shoved his oar in.

"I fail to see how that could be so, Mrs. Travers," he said in that supercilious way of his which has got him so disliked on all sides. "The necklace I was holding when my senses left me was yours. Mrs. Trotter's was presumably in the safe."

"Yes," said Ma Trotter, "and pearl necklaces don't jump out of safes. I think I'll step to the telephone and have a word with the police."

Aunt Dahlia raised her eyebrows. It must have taken a bit of doing, but she did it.

"I don't understand you, Mrs. Trotter," she said, very much the *grande dame*. "Do you suppose that my butler would break into the safe and steal your necklace?"

Spode horned in again. He was one of those unpleasant men who never know when to keep their big mouths shut.

"Why break?" he said. "It would not have been necessary to *break* into the safe. The door was already open."

"Ho!" cried Ma Trotter, reckless of the fact that the copyright of the word was Stilton's. "So that's how it was. All he had to do was reach in and help himself. The telephone is in the hall, I think?"

Seppings made his first contribution to the feast of reason and flow of soul.

"If I might explain, madam."

He spoke austerely. The rules of their guild do not permit butlers to give employers' guests dirty looks, but while stopping short of the dirty look he was not affectionate. Her loose talk about police and telephones had caused him to take umbrage, and it was pretty clear that whoever he might select as a companion on his next long walking tour, it would not be Ma Trotter.

"It was not I who found the necklace, madam. Acting upon instructions from Mr. Travers, I instituted a search through the rooms of the staff and

discovered the object in the bedchamber of Mr. Wooster's personal attendant, Mr. Jeeves. Upon my drawing this to Mr. Jeeves's attention, he informed me that he had picked it up in the hall."

"Is that so? Well, tell this man Jeeves to come here at once."

"Very good, madam."

Seppings withdrew, and I would have given a good deal to have been able
to withdraw myself, for in about another two ticks, I saw, it would be
necessary for Bertram Wooster to come clean and reveal all, blazoning forth
to the world Aunt Dahlia's recent activities, if blazoning forth to the world is
the expression I want, and bathing the unfortunate old egg in shame and
confusion. Feudal fidelity would no doubt make Jeeves seal his lips, but you
can't let fellows go sealing their lips if it means rendering themselves liable to
an exemplary sentence, coupled with some strong remarks from the Bench.
Come what might, the dirt would have to be dished. The code of the Woosters
is rigid on points like this.

Looking at Aunt Dahlia, I could see that her mind was working along the
same lines, and she wasn't liking it by any means. With a face as red as hers
she couldn't turn pale, but her lips were tightly set and her hand, as it lathered
a slice of toast with marmalade, plainly shook. The look on her dial was the
look of a woman who didn't need a fortune teller and a crystal ball to apprise
her of the fact that it would not be long before the balloon went up.

I was gazing at her so intently that it was only when a soft cough broke the
silence that I realized that Jeeves had joined the gang. He was standing on the
outskirts looking quietly respectful.

"Madam?" he said.

"Hey, you!" said Ma Trotter.

He continued to look quietly respectful. If he resented having the words
"Hey, you!" addressed to him, there was nothing in his manner to show it.

"This necklace," said Ma Trotter, giving him a double whammy through
the lorgnette. "The butler says he found it in your room."

"Yes, madam. I was planning after breakfast to make inquiries as to its
ownership."

"You were, were you?"

"I presumed that it was some trinket belonging to one of the housemaids."

"It was . . . what?"

He coughed again, that deferential cough of his which sounds like a
well-bred sheep clearing its throat on a distant mountain top.

"I perceived at once that it was merely an inexpensive imitation made from
cultured pearls, madam," he said.

I don't know if you happen to know the expression "a stunned silence."
I've come across it in books when one of the characters has unloaded a hot
one on the assembled company, and I have always thought it a neat way of
describing that sort of stilly hush that pops up on these occasions. The silence
that fell on the Brinkley Court breakfast table as Jeeves uttered these words
was as stunned as the dickens.

L. G. Trotter was the first to break it.

"What's that? Inexpensive imitation? I paid five thousand pounds for that necklace."

"Of course you did," said Ma Trotter with a petulant waggle of the bean. "The man's intoxicated."

I felt compelled to intervene in the debate and dispel the miasma of suspicion which had arisen, or whatever it is that miasmas do.

"Intoxicated?" I said. "At ten in the morning? A laughable theory. But the matter can readily be put to the test. Jeeves, say 'Theodore Oswaldtwistle, the thistle sifter, in sifting a sack of thistles thrust three thorns through the thick of his thumb.' "

He did so with an intonation as clear as a bell, if not clearer.

"You see," I said, and rested my case.

Aunt Dahlia, who had blossomed like a flower revived with a couple of fluid ounces of the right stuff from a watering can, chipped in with a helpful word.

"You can bank on Jeeves," she said. "If he thinks it's a dud, it is a dud. He knows all about jewelry."

"Precisely," I added. "He has the full facts. He studied under an aunt of his in the profession."

"Cousin, sir."

"Of course, yes, cousin. Sorry, Jeeves."

"Not at all, sir."

Spode came butting in again.

"Let me see that necklace," he said authoritatively.

Jeeves drew the salver to his attention.

"You will, I think, support my view, my lord."

Spode took contents, glanced at them, sniffed and delivered judgment.

"Perfectly correct. An imitation, and not a very good one."

"You can't be sure," said Percy, and got withered by a look.

"Can't be sure?" Spode bristled like a hornet whose feelings have been wounded by a tactless remark. "Can't be *sure?*"

"Of course he's sure," I said, not actually slapping him on the back but giving him a back-slapping look designed to show him he had got Bertram Wooster in his corner. "He knows, as everybody knows, that cultured pearls have a core. You spotted the core in a second, didn't you, Spode, old man, or rather Lord Sidcup, old man?"

I was going on to speak of the practice of introducing a foreign substance into the oyster in order to kid it along and induce it to cover this f.s. with layers of nacre—which I still think is a dirty trick to play on a shellfish which simply wants to be left alone with its thoughts—but Spode had risen. There was dudgeon in his manner.

"All this sort of thing at breakfast!" he said, and I saw what he meant. At home, no doubt, he wrapped himself around the morning egg in cozy seclusion, his daily paper propped up against the coffee pot and none of this business of naked passions buzzing all over the place. He wiped his mouth, and left via the french window, wincing with a hand to his head as L. G. Trotter spoke in a voice that nearly cracked his tea cup.

"Emily! Explain this!"

Ma Trotter got the lorgnette working on him, but for all the good it did she might as well have used a monocle. He stared right back at her, and I imagine—couldn't be certain, of course, because his back was to me—that there was in his gaze a steely hardness that turned her bones to water. At any rate, when she spoke, it was like what I have heard Jeeves describe as the earliest pipe of half-awakened birds.

"I can't explain it," she . . . yes, quavered. I was going to say "murmured," but quavered hits it off better.

L. G. Trotter barked like a seal.

"I can," he said. "You've been giving money on the sly again to that brother of yours."

This was the first I had heard of any brother of Ma Trotter's, but I wasn't surprised. My experience is that all wives of prosperous businessmen have shady brothers in the background to whom they slip a bit from time to time.

"I haven't!"

"Don't lie to me!"

"Oh!" cried the shrinking woman, shrinking a bit more, and the spectacle was too much for Percy. All this while he had been sitting tensely where he sat, giving the impression of something stuffed by a good taxidermist, but now, moved by a mother's distress, he rose rather in the manner of one about to reply to the toast of The Ladies. He was looking a little like a cat in a strange alley which is momentarily expecting a half brick in the short ribs, but his voice, though low, was firm.

"I can explain everything. Moth-aw is innocent. She wanted her necklace cleaned. She entrusted it to me to take to the jeweler's, and I pawned it and had an imitation made. I needed money urgently."

Aunt Dahlia well-I'll-be-blowed.

"What an extraordinary thing to do!" she said. "Did you ever hear of anybody doing anything like that, Bertie?"

"New to me, I must confess."

"Amazing, eh?"

"Bizarre, you might call it."

"Still, that's how it goes."

"Yes, that's how it goes."

"I needed a thousand pounds to put into the play," said Percy.

L. G. Trotter, who was in good voice this morning, uttered a howl that set the silverware rattling. It was fortunate for Spode that he had removed himself from earshot, for it would certainly have done that head of his no good. Even I, though a strong man, leaped about six inches.

"You put a thousand pounds into a *play?*"

"Into *the* play," said Percy. "Florence's and mine. My dramatization of her novel, *Spindrift*. One of our backers had failed us, and rather than disappoint the woman I loved—"

Florence was staring at him, wide-eyed. If you remember, I described her aspect on first glimpsing my moustache as having had in it a touch of the Soul's Awakening. The S.A. was now even more pronounced. It stuck out a mile.

"Percy! You did that for me?"

"And I'd do it again," said Percy.

L. G. Trotter began to speak. As to whether he opened his remarks with the words "Ba goom!" I cannot be positive, but there was a "Ba goom!" implicit in every syllable. The man had got it right up his nose, and one felt a gentle pity for Ma Trotter, little as one liked her. Her reign was over. She had had it. From now on it was plain who was going to be the Führer of the Trotter home. The worm of yesterday—or you might say the worm of ten minutes ago—had become a worm in tiger's clothing.

"This settles it!" he vociferated, if vociferated is the word. "There won't be any more loafing about London for you, young man. We leave this house this morning—"

"What!" yipped Aunt Dahlia.

"—and the moment we get back to Liverpool you start in at the bottom of the business, as you ought to have done two years ago if I hadn't let myself be persuaded against my better judgment. Five thousand pounds I paid for that necklace, and you . . ."

Emotion overcame him, and he paused.

"But, Mr. Trotter!" There was anguish in Aunt Dahlia's voice. "You aren't leaving this morning!"

"Yes, I am. Think I'm going to go through another of that French cook's lunches?"

"But I was hoping you would not be going away before we had settled this matter of buying the *Boudoir*. If you could give me a few moments in the library?"

"No time for that. I'm going to drive in to Market Snodsbury and see a doctor. Just a chance he may be able to do something to relieve the pain. It's about there that it seems to catch me," said L. G. Trotter, indicating the fourth button of his waistcoat.

"Tut-tut," said Aunt Dahlia, and I tut-tutted, too, but nobody else expressed the sympathy the writhing man had a right to expect. Florence was still drinking in Percy with every eye at her disposal, and Percy was bending solicitously over Ma Trotter, who was sitting looking like a toad beneath the harrow.

"Come, Moth-aw," said Percy, hoiking her up from where she roosted. "I will bathe your temples with eau-de-Cologne."

With a reproachful look at L. G. Trotter he led her gently from the room. A mother's best friend is her boy.

Aunt Dahlia was still looking aghast, and I knew what was in her mind.

Once let this Trotter get away to Liverpool and she would be dished. Delicate negotiations like selling a weekly paper for the gentler sex to a customer full of sales resistance can't be conducted successfully by mail. You have to have men like L. G. Trotter on the spot, kneading their arms and generally giving them the old personality.

"Jeeves!" I cried. I don't know why, because I couldn't see what he could do to help.

He sprang respectfully to life. During the late give-and-take he had been standing in the background with that detached, stuffed-frog look on his face which it always wears when he is present at a free-for-all in which his sense of what is fitting does not allow him to take part. And the spirits rose as I saw from his eye that he was going to rally round.

"If I might make a suggestion, sir."

"Yes, Jeeves?"

"It occurs to me that one of those morning mixtures of mine would bring relief to Mr. Trotter."

I gargled. I got his meaning.

"You mean those pick-me-ups you occasionally prepare for me when the state of the old head seems to call for it?"

"Precisely, sir."

"Would they hit the trot with Mr. Spotter, or rather the other way round?"

"Oh, yes, sir. They act directly on the internal organs."

It was enough. I saw that, as always, he had *tetigisti*-ed the *rem*. I turned to L. G. Trotter.

"You heard?"

"No, I didn't. How do you expect me to hear things—?"

I checked him with one of my gestures.

"Well, listen now," I said. "Be of good cheer, L. G. Trotter, for the United States Marines have arrived. No need for any doctors. Go along with Jeeves, and he will mix you a mixture which will put the old tum in midseason form before you can say 'Lemuel Gengulphus.' "

He looked at Jeeves with a wild surmise. I heard Aunt Dahlia gasp a gasp.

"Is that right?"

"Yes, sir. I can guarantee the efficacy of the preparation."

L. G. Trotter emitted a loud "Woof!"

"Let's go," he said briefly.

"I'll come with you and hold your hand," said Aunt Dahlia.

"Just one word," I said, as the procession started to file out. "On swallowing the stuff you will have the momentary illusion that you have been struck by lightning. Pay no attention. It's all part of the treatment. But watch the eyeballs, as they are liable, unless checked, to start from the parent sockets and rebound from the opposite wall."

They passed from the room, and I was alone with Florence.

22

IT'S AN odd thing, but it hadn't occurred to me in the rush and swirl of recent events that, with people drifting off in twos and threes and—in the case of Spode—in ones, the time must inevitably come when this beasel and I would be left face to face in what is called a *solitude à deux*. And now that this unpleasant state of affairs had come about, it was difficult to know how to start the conversation. However, I had a pop at it, the same pop I had had when finding myself closeted with L. G. Trotter.

"Can I get you a sausage?" I said.

She waved it away. It was plain that the unrest in her soul could not be lulled with sausages.

"Oh, Bertie," she said, and paused.

"Or a slice of ham?"

She shook her head. Ham appeared to be just as much a drug in the market as sausages.

"Oh, Bertie," she said again.

"Right opposite you," I said encouragingly.

"Bertie, I don't know what to do."

She signed off once more, and I stood there waiting for something to emerge. A half-formed idea of offering her a kipper I dismissed. Too silly, I mean, keeping on suggesting items on the menu like a waiter trying to help a customer make up his mind.

"I feel awful!" she said.

"You look fine," I assured her, but she dismissed the pretty compliment with another wave of the hand.

She was silent again for a moment, and then it came out with a rush.

"It's about Percy."

I was nibbling a slice of toast as she spoke, but lowered it courteously.

"Percy?" I said.

"Oh, Bertie," she proceeded, and from the way her nose wiggled I could see that she was in quite a state. "All that that happened just now . . . when he said that about not disappointing the woman he loved . . . when I realized what he had done . . . just for me . . ."

"I know what you mean," I said. "Very white."

"Something happened to me. It was as though for the first time I was seeing the real Percy. I had always admired his intellect, of course, but now it was different. I seemed to be gazing into his naked soul, and what I saw there . . ."

"Pretty good, was it?" I queried, helping the thing along.

She drew a deep breath.

"I was overcome. I was stunned. I realized that he was just like Rollo Beaminster."

For a moment I was not abreast. Then I remembered.

"Oh, ah, yes. You didn't get around to telling me much about Rollo, except that he was in wild mood."

"Oh, that was quite early in the story, before he and Sylvia came together again."

"They came together, did they?"

"Yes. She gazed into his naked soul and knew that there would be no other man for her."

I have already stressed the fact that I was mentally at my brightest this morning, and hearing these words I got the distinct idea that she was feeling pretty pro-Percy as of even date. I might be wrong, of course, I didn't think so, and it seemed to me that this was a good thing that wanted pushing along. There is, as Jeeves had so neatly put it, a tide in the affairs of men which, taken at the flood, leads on to fortune.

"I say," I said, "here's a thought. Why don't you marry Percy?"

She started. I saw that she was trembling. She moved, she stirred, she seemed to feel the rush of life along her keel. In her eyes, as she gazed at me, it wasn't difficult to spot the light of hope.

"But I'm engaged to you," she faltered, rather giving the impression that she could have kicked herself for being such a chump.

"Oh, that can be readily adjusted," I said heartily. "Call it off, is my advice. You don't want a weedy butterfly like me about the home, you want something more in the nature of a soulmate, a chap with a number nine hat you can sit and hold hands and talk about T. S. Eliot with. And Percy fills the bill."

She choked a bit. The light of hope was now very pronounced.

"Bertie! You will release me?"

"Certainly, certainly. Frightful wrench, of course, and all that sort of thing, but consider it done."

"Oh, Bertie!"

She flung herself upon me and kissed me. Unpleasant, of course, but these things have to be faced. As I once heard Anatole remark, one must learn to take a few roughs with a smooth.

We were still linked together in a close embrace, when the silence—we were embracing fairly silently—was broken by what sounded like the heart-cry of one of the local dogs which had bumped its nose against the leg of the table.

It wasn't a dog. It was Percy. He was standing there looking overwrought, and I didn't blame him. Agony, of course, if you love a girl, to come into a room and find her all tangled up with another fellow.

He pulled himself together with a powerful effort.

"Go on," he said, "go on. I'm sorry I interrupted you."

He broke off with a choking gulp, and I could see it was quite a surprise to him when Florence, abruptly detaching herself from me, did a jack rabbit leap that was almost in the Cheesewright-Wooster class and hurled herself into his arms.

"Eh, what?" he said, plainly missing the gist.

"I love you, Percy!"

"You do?" His face lit up for an instant. Then there was a blackout. "But you're engaged to Wooster," he said moodily, eyeing me in a manner that seemed to suggest that in his opinion it was fellows like me who caused half the trouble in the world.

I moved over to the table and took another slice of toast. Cold, of course, but I rather like cold toast, provided there's plenty of butter.

"No, that's off," I said. "Carry on, old sport. You have the green light."

Florence's voice shook.

"Bertie has released me, Percy. I was kissing him because I was so grateful. When I told him I loved you, he released me."

You could see that Percy was impressed.

"I say! That was very decent of him."

"He's like that. Bertie is the soul of chivalry."

"He certainly is. I'm amazed. Nobody would think it, to look at him."

I was getting about fed up with people saying nobody would think it, to look at me, and it is quite possible that I might at this point have said something a bit biting . . . I don't know what, but something. But before I could assemble the makings Florence suddenly uttered something that was virtually tantamount to a wail of anguish.

"But, Percy, what are we to do? I've only a small dress allowance."

I didn't follow the trend of her thought. Nor did Percy. Cryptic, I considered it, and I could see he thought so, too.

"What's that got to do with it?" he said.

Florence wrung her hands, a thing I've often heard about but never seen done. It's a sort of circular movement, starting from the wrists.

"I mean, I haven't any money and you haven't any money, except what your stepfather is going to pay you when you join the business. We should have to live in Liverpool. I can't live in Liverpool!"

Well, of course, lots of people do, or so I have been given to understand, but I saw what she meant. Her heart was in London's Bohemia, Bloomsbury, Chelsea, sandwiches and absinthe in the old studio, all that sort of thing, and she hated to give it up. I don't suppose they have studios up Liverpool way.

"M-m-yes," said Percy.

"You see what I mean?"

"Oh, quite," said Percy.

He was plainly ill at ease. A strange light had come into his tortoise-shell-rimmed spectacles, and his whiskers quivered gently. For a moment he stood there letting "I dare not" wait upon "I would." Then he spoke.

"Florence, I have a confession to make. I hardly know how to tell you. The truth is that my financial position is reasonably sound. I am not a rich man, but I have a satisfactory income, quite large enough to support the home. I have no intention of going to Liverpool."

Florence goggled. I have an idea that she was thinking, early though it was, that he had had one over the eight. Her air was that of a girl on the point of asking him to say "Theodore Oswaldtwistle, the thistle sifter, in sifting a sack of thistles thrust three thorns through the thick of his thumb." However, all she said was:

"But, Percy darling, you surely can't make much out of your poetry?"

He twiddled his fingers for a moment. You could see he was trying to nerve himself to reveal something he would much have preferred to keep under his hat. I have had the same experience when had up on the carpet by my Aunt Agatha.

"I don't," he said. "I only got fifteen shillings for that 'Caliban at Sunset' thing of mine in *Parnassus,* and I had to fight like a tiger to get that. The editress wanted to beat me down to twelve-and-six. But I have a . . . an alternative source of revenue."

"I don't understand."

He bowed his head.

"You will. My receipts from this—er—alternative source of revenue amounted last year to nearly eight hundred pounds, and this year it should be double that, for my agent has succeeded in establishing me in the American market. Florence, you will shrink from me, but I have to tell you. I write detective stories under the pseudonym of Rex West."

I wasn't looking at Florence, so I don't know if she shrank from him, but I certainly didn't. I stared at him, agog.

"Rex West? Lord-love-a-duck! Did you write *The Mystery of the Pink Crayfish?* " I gasped.

He bowed his head again.

"I did. And *Murder in Mauve, The Case of the Poisoned Doughnut* and *Inspector Biffen Views the Body.*"

I hadn't happened to get hold of those, but I assured him that I would lose no time in putting them on my library list, and went on to ask a question which had been occupying my mind for quite a while.

"Then who was it who bumped off Sir Eustace Willoughby, Bart., with the blunt instrument?"

In a low, toneless voice he said:

"Burwash, the butler."

I uttered a cry.

"As I suspected! As I suspected from the first!"

I would have probed further into this Art of his, asking him how he thought up these things and did he work regular hours or wait for inspiration, but Florence had taken the floor again. So far from shrinking from him, she was nestling in his arms and covering his face with burning kisses.

"Percy!" She was all over the blighter. "I think it's wonderful! How frightfully clever of you!"

He tottered.

"You aren't revolted?"

"Of course I'm not. I'm tremendously pleased. Are you working on something now?"

"A novelette. I think of calling it *Blood Will Tell*. It will run to about thirty thousand words. My agent says these American magazines like what they call one-shotters—a colloquial expression, I imagine, for material of a length suitable for publication in a single issue."

"You must tell me all about it," said Florence, taking his arm and heading for the French window.

"Hey, just a moment," I said.

"Yes?" said Percy, turning. "What is it, Wooster? Talk quickly. I am busy."

"May I have your autograph?"

He beamed.

"You really want it?"

"I am a great admirer of your work."

"That is the boy!" said Percy.

He wrote it on the back of an envelope, and they went out hand in hand, those two young folks starting on the long journey together. And I, feeling a bit peckish after this emotional scene, sat down and had another go at the sausages and bacon.

I was still thus engaged when the door opened and Aunt Dahlia came in. A glance was enough to tell me that all was well with the aged relative. On a previous occasion I have described her face as shining like the seat of a bus-driver's trousers. It was doing so now. If she had been going to be Queen of the May, she could not have looked chirpier.

"Has L. G. Trotter signed the papers?" I asked.

"He's going to, the moment he gets his eyeballs back. How right you were about his eyeballs. When last seen, they were ricocheting from wall to wall, with him in hot pursuit. Bertie," said the old ancestor, speaking in an awed voice, "what does Jeeves put into those mixtures of his?"

I shook my head.

"Only he and his God know that," I said gravely.

"They seem powerful stuff. I remember reading somewhere once about a dog that swallowed a bottle of tabasco sauce. It was described as putting up quite a performance. Trotter reacted in a somewhat similar manner. I should imagine dynamite was one of the ingredients."

"Very possibly," I said. "But let us not talk of dogs and tabasco sauce. Let us rather discuss these happy endings of ours."

"Endings? In the plural? I've had a happy ending, all right, but you—"

"Me, too. Florence—"

"You don't mean it's off?"

"She's going to marry Percy."

"Bertie, my beamish boy!"

"Didn't I tell you I had faith in my star? The moral of the whole thing, as I see it, is that you can't keep a good man down, or . . ." I bowed slightly in her direction . . . "a good woman. What a lesson this should be to us, old flesh and blood, never to give up, never to despair. However dark the outlook . . ."

I was about to add "and however black the clouds" and go on to speak of
the sun sooner or later smiling through, but at this moment Jeeves shimmered in.

"Excuse me, madam. Would it be convenient for you to join Mr. Trotter in
the library, madam? He is waiting for you there."

Aunt Dahlia really needs a horse to help her get up speed, but though afoot
she made excellent time to the door.

"How is he?" she asked, turning on the threshold.

"Completely restored to health, madam, I am happy to say. He speaks of
venturing on a sandwich and a glass of milk at the conclusion of your
conference."

She gave him a long, reverent look.

"Jeeves," she said, "you stand alone. I knew you would save the day."

"Thank you very much, madam."

"Have you ever tried those mixtures of yours on a corpse?"

"Not yet, madam."

"You should," said the old relative, and curvetted out like one of those
mettlesome steeds which, though I have never heard one do it myself, say
"Ha!" among the trumpets.

A silence followed her departure, for I was plunged in thought. I was
debating within myself whether to take a step of major importance or
whether, on the other hand, not to, and at such times one does not talk, one
weighs the pros and cons. I was, in short, standing at a man's crossroads.

That moustache of mine . . .

Pro: I loved the little thing. I fancied myself in it. I had hoped to nursed it
through the years with top dressing till it became the talk of the town.

Con: But was it, I asked myself, *safe?* Recalling the effect of its impact on
Florence Craye, I saw clearly that it had made me too fascinating. There peril
lurked. When you become too fascinating, all sorts of things are liable to
occur which you don't want to occur, if you follow me.

A strange calm descended on me. I had made my decision.

"Jeeves," I said, and if I felt the passing pang, why not? One is but human.
"Jeeves," I said, "I'm going to shave my moustache."

His left eyebrow flickered, showing how deeply the words had moved him.

"Indeed, sir?"

"Yes, you have earned this sacrifice. When I have eaten my fill . . . Good
sausages, these."

"Yes, sir."

"Made, no doubt, from contented pigs. Did you have some for your
breakfast?"

"Yes, sir."

"Well, as I was saying, when I have eaten my fill, I shall proceed upstairs to
my room, I shall lather the upper lip, I shall take razor in hand . . . and
voilà."

"Thank you very much, sir," he said.

Spring Fever

BOOK ONE

1

SPRING HAD come to New York, the eight-fifteen train from Great Neck had come to the Pennsylvania terminus, and G. Ellery Cobbold, that stout economic royalist, had come to his downtown office, all set to prise another wad of currency out of the common people.

It was a lovely morning, breathing of bock beer and the birth of a new baseball season, and the sap was running strongly in Mr. Cobbold's veins. He looked like a cartoon of Capital in a labor paper, but he felt fine. It would not have taken much to make him break into a buck-and-wing dance, and if he had had roses in his possession it is more than probable that he would have strewn them from his hat.

Borne aloft in the elevator, he counted his blessings one by one and found them totting up to a highly satisfactory total. The boil on the back of his neck had yielded to treatment. His golf handicap was down to twenty-four. His son Stanwood was in London, safely removed from the wiles of Miss Eileen Stoker of Beverly Hills, Cal. He was on the point of concluding remunerative deals with the Messrs. Simms and Weinstein of Detroit and the Consolidated Nail File and Eyebrow Tweezer Corporation of Scranton, Pa. And a fortunate glance at Debrett's Peerage that morning had reminded him that tomorrow was Lord Shortlands' birthday.

He floated lightly into the office and found Miss Sharples, his efficient secretary, there, right on the job as always, and a mass of torn envelopes in the wastepaper basket told him that she had attended to his correspondence and was all ready to give him the headline news. But though that correspondence almost certainly included vital communications from both Simms and Weinstein and the Nail File and Eyebrow Tweezer boys, it was the matter of Lord Shortlands' natal day that claimed his immediate attention.

"Morning, Miss Sharples," he said, and you could see that what he really meant was 'Good morning, good morning, Miss Sharples, what a beautiful morning it is, is it not? With a Hey and a Ho and a Hey nonny no, Miss Sharples.' "Take a memo."

"Yes, Mr. Cobbold."

"Western Union."

"Western Union," echoed Miss Sharples, inscribing on her tablet something that resembled an impressionistic sketch of a pneumonia germ.

"Tell them to put in a personal call at . . . Say, what time do you reckon an English peer would be waking up in the morning?"

He had come to the woman who knew.

"Eleven, Mr. Cobbold."

"*Eleven?*"

"That's the time young Lord Peebles wakes up in the novel I'm reading. He props his eyes open with his fingers and presses the bell, and Meadowes, his man, brings him a bromo-seltzer and an anchovy on hot toast."

Mr. Cobbold uttered a revolted "Pshaw."

"This fellow isn't one of those dissolute society playboys. He lives in the country, and he's fifty-two. At least, he will be tomorrow. Seems to me seven would be more like it. Have Western Union put in a personal call at seven, English time, tomorrow to the Earl of Shortlands, Beevor Castle, Kent, and sing 'Happy birthday,' to him."

" 'Happy birthday,' " murmured Miss Sharples, pencilling in two squiggles and a streptococcus.

"Tell them to pick out a fellow with a nice tenor voice."

"Yes, Mr. Cobbold."

"Or maybe they tear it off in a bunch, like a barbershop quartette?"

"I don't think so, Mr. Cobbold. Just one vocalist, I believe."

"Ah? Well, see that they do it, anyway. It's important. I wouldn't like Lord Shortlands to think I'd forgotten his birthday. He's the head of my family."

"You don't say!"

"Sure. Cobbold's the family name. There's a son, Lord Beevor, who's out in Kenya, but all the others are Cobbolds. Three daughters. The eldest married a fellow named Topping I was in college with. I'll tell you how I first came to hear of them. I was in the club one day, and I happened to pick up one of those English illustrated weeklies, and there was a photograph of a darned pretty girl with the caption under it 'Lady Teresa Cobbold, youngest daughter of the Earl of Shortlands.' 'Hello,' I said to myself. 'Cobbold? Well, what do you know about that?', and I had the College of Arms in London get busy and look into the thing."

"And it turned out that you were a relation?"

"That's right. Just what kind I couldn't exactly tell you. Sort of cousin is the way I figure it out. I've written Lord Shortlands a letter or two about it and sent him a few cables, but he hasn't got around to answering yet. Busy, maybe. Still, there it is. Seems that in 1700 or thereabouts one of the younger sons sailed for America——"

Mr. Cobbold broke off the gossip from the old home and gave a rather formal cough. He perceived that the spirit of Spring had lured him on to jeopardize office discipline by chewing the fat with one who, however efficient and however capital a listener, was after all an underling.

"Well, that's that," he said. "And now," becoming his business self after this frivolous interlude, "what's new?"

Miss Sharples would have been glad to hear more of the younger son who had sailed for America and all the rest of the Hands-Across-the-Sea stuff, for hers was a romantic nature, but she, too, recognized that this was not the time and place. She consulted her notes.

"Simms and Weinstein will meet your terms, Mr. Cobbold," she said, translating the one that looked like part of Grover Whalen's moustache.

"They better."

"But the Nail File and Eyebrow Tweezer people don't seem any too well pleased."

"They don't, don't they?"

"They say they are at a loss to comprehend."

"Is that so? I'll fix 'em. Anything else?"

"No letters of importance, Mr. Cobbold. There is a cable from Mr. Stanwood."

"Asking for money?"

"Yes, Mr. Cobbold."

"He would be. Seems to me he spends more in London than he did over here."

A frown came into Ellery Cobbold's bulbous face. He was a man of enviable financial standing, for despite the notorious hardness of the times, he always managed to get his, but this did not make it any the more agreeable to him to be tapped by his son. A great many prosperous fathers have this adhesive attitude towards their wealth when the issue show a disposition to declare themselves in on the gross.

A song of his youth flitted through Mr. Cobbold's mind:

> My son Joshu-ay
> Went to Philadelphi-ay;
> Writes home sayin' he's doin' mighty well:
> But seems kind of funny
> That he's always short of money,
> And Ma says the boy's up to some kind of hell.

Then he brightened. Whatever kind of hell Stanwood might be up to, his father's heart had this consolation, that he was not up to it in the society of Miss Eileen Stoker. With restored equanimity he dismissed him from his thoughts and settled down to dictate a letter to the Consolidated Nail File and Eyebrow Tweezer Corporation of Scranton, Pa., which would make them realize that life is stern and earnest and that Nail File and Eyebrow Tweezer Corporations are not put into this world for pleasure alone.

The morning wore on, filled with its little tasks and duties. Lunch time came. The afternoon followed. In due season everything needed to keep Mr.

Cobbold's affairs in apple-pie order for another day had been done, and he took the six-ten train back to his Great Neck home. At eight he dined, and by nine he was in his favorite armchair, a cigar between his lips and a highball at his side, preparing to read the evening paper which the intrusion of a garrulous neighbor had prevented him perusing on the train.

But even when settled in his chair he did not begin to read immediately. Dreamily watching the smoke curl up from his perfecto, he found his thoughts turning to his son Stanwood and the adroitness with which he had flung the necessary spanner into that young man's incipient romance with Miss Eileen Stoker of Hollywood.

The discovery that his offspring was contemplating marrying into celluloid circles had come as an unpleasant shock to Mr. Cobbold, filling him with alarm and, until he rallied and took action, despondency. During the first anxious days he had twice refused a second helping of spaghetti Caruso at lunch, and his golf handicap, always a sensitive plant, had gone up into the thirties.

He mistrusted Stanwood's ability to choose wisely in this vital matter of selecting a life partner, for though he loved his child he did not think highly of his intelligence. Stanwood, a doughty performer on the football field during his college career, was a mass of muscle and bone, and it was Mr. Cobbold's opinion that the bone extended to his head. And he had a good deal of support for this view. Even those who had applauded the young man when he made the All-American in his last season had never claimed for him that he was bright. Excellent at blocking a punt or giving a playmate the quick sleeve across the windpipe, but not bright. It seemed to Mr. Cobbold that he must be saved from himself.

If the bride-to-be had been the Lady Teresa Cobbold whose photograph he had seen in the English illustrated weekly, that would have been a vastly different matter. A union between his son and the daughter of the head of the family he would have welcomed with fervour. But a film star, no. He knew all about film stars. Scarcely had they settled down in the love nest before they were bringing actions for divorce on the ground of ingrowing incompatibility or whatever it might be and stinging the bridegroom for slathers of alimony. And the thought that at the conclusion of the romance under advisement it would be he, the groom's father, who would be called upon to foot the bills had acted on him as a powerful spur, causing him to think on his feet and do it now.

He had shipped Stanwood off to England on the next boat in the custody of an admirable fellow named Augustus Robb, whom he had engaged, principally on the strength of the horn-rimmed spectacles he wore, at an agency which supplied gentlemen's personal gentlemen, with instructions to remain in England till further notice. It is one of the great advantages of being a tycoon that your life trains you to take decisions at the drop of the hat. Where lesser men scratch their heads and twiddle their fingers, the tycoon acts.

To Mr. Cobbold, as he sat there drawing at his cigar, it was a very soothing reflection that three thousand miles of land and another three thousand miles of water separated his son and Miss Stoker, and for some moments he savoured it like some rare and refreshing fruit. Then with a contented sigh he opened his paper.

It was to the financial section that he turned first; then to the funnies, in which he surprisingly retained a boyish interest. After that he allowed his eye to wander at random through the remainder of the sheet. And it was while it was doing so, flitting idly from spot to spot like a hovering butterfly, that it found itself arrested by a photograph on one of the inner pages of a personable young woman with large eyes, curving lips and apparently lemon-coloured hair.

He had been on the verge of sleep at the moment, for he generally sank into a light doze at about this time in the evening, but there was something about those wistful eyes gazing into his, with their suggestion of having at last found a strong man on whom they could rely, which imparted sufficient wakefulness to lead him to glance at the name under the photograph. And having done so, he sat up with a jerk.

MISS EILEEN STOKER

A snort broke from Mr. Cobbold's lips. He frowned, as if he had found a snake on his lap.

So this was Eileen by golly Stoker, was it? No devotee of the silver screen, he had never seen her before, and now that he was seeing her he did not like her looks. A siren, he thought. Designing, he felt. Not to be trusted as far as you could throw an elephant, he considered, and just the sort who would spring with joy to the task of nicking a good man's bank roll. He eyed the lady askance, as he eyed all things askance that seemed potential threats to his current account.

MISS EILEEN STOKER

Universally Beloved Hollywood Star

The phrase "universally beloved" is, of course, a loose one. It cannot ever really include everybody. In this instance it did not include Mr. Cobbold. All over the United States, and in other countries, too, for Art knows no frontiers, there were clubs in existence whose aim it was to boost for Eileen Stoker, to do homage to Eileen Stoker and to get the public thinking the Eileen Stoker way, but the possibility of Ellery Cobbold joining one of them was remote. A society for dipping Eileen Stoker in tar and sprinkling feathers on her he would have supported with pleasure.

There were a few lines in smaller print below this absurd statement that Miss Stoker was universally beloved, and Mr. Cobbold's eye, having nothing better to do at the moment, gave them a casual glance. And scarcely had it done so when its proprietor leaped in his chair with a wordless cry like that of a sleeping cat on whose tail some careless number-eleven shoe has descended.

Once at the country club, coming out of the showers in the nude and sitting down on the nearest bench to dry himself, Mr. Cobbold's attention had been drawn to the fact that a fellow member had left a lighted cigar there, and until tonight he had always regarded this as the high spot of his emotional life. He was now inclined to relegate it to second place.

For this was what he had read:

MISS EILEEN STOKER

Universally Beloved Hollywood Star

Has arrived in England to take up her contract for two pictures
with the Beaumont Co. of London.

The words seemed to print themselves in letters of fire on his soul. So devastating was their effect that for quite an appreciable time he sat paralysed, blowing little air bubbles and incapable of movement. Then, once more his alert, executive self, he rose and bounded to the telephone.

"Gimme Western Union!"

It occurred to him as a passing thought that he seemed to be putting a lot of business in the way of Western Union these days.

"Western Union?"

He was suffering much the same mental anguish as that experienced by generals who have allowed themselves to become outflanked. But how, he asked himself, could he have anticipated this? How could he have foreseen this mobility on the part of the foe? He had always supposed that Hollywood stars were a permanency in Hollywood, like swimming pools and the relations by marriage of a studio chief.

"Western Union?" said Mr. Cobbold, still finding a difficulty in controlling his voice. "I want to send a couple of cables."

2

ON THE following morning, at about the time when the Lord Peebles of whose habits Miss Sharples had spoken was accustomed to begin his day, a young man lay sleeping in the bedroom of a service flat at Bloxham House, Park Lane, London. A silk hat, dress trousers, a pair of evening shoes, two coloured ballons and a squeaker were distributed about the floor beside the bed. From time to time the young man moaned softly, as if in pain. He was dreaming that he was being bitten in half by a shark, which is always trying.

We really do not know why we keep saying "young man" in this guarded way. There is no need for secrecy and concealment. It was Stanwood Cobbold, and he was sleeping at this advanced hour because he had got home at four in the morning from the party which he had given to welcome Miss Eileen Stoker to England.

Except for the bulge under the bedclothes which covered his enormous frame, very little of Stanwood Cobbold was visible, and that little scarcely worth a second look, for Nature, doubtless with the best motives, had given him, together with a heart of gold, a face like that of an amiable hippopotamus. And everybody knows that unless you are particularly fond of hippopotami, a single cursory glance at them is enough. Many blasé explorers do not even take that.

Augustus Robb came softly in, bearing a tray. Augustus Robb always came into rooms softly. Before getting saved at a revival meeting and taking up valeting as a career, he had been a burglar in a fair way of practice, and coming into rooms softly had grown to be a habit.

Once in, his movements became less stealthy. He deposited the tray on the table with a bang and a rattle and raised the blind noisily.

"Hoy!" he cried in a voice like someone calling the cattle home across the Sands of Dee. He had rather a bad bedside manner.

Stanwood parted company with his shark and returned to the world of living things. Having done so, he clasped his forehead with both hands and said "Oh, God!" He had the illusion that everything, including his personal attendant, had turned yellow.

"Brekfuss," roared Augustus Robb, still apparently under the impression that he was addressing a deaf friend a quarter of a mile away. "Eat it while it's hot, cocky. I've done you a poached egg."

There are certain words which at certain times seem to go straight to the foundations of the soul. "Egg" is one of these, especially when preceded by the participle "poached." A strong shudder passed through Stanwood's sensitive person.

"Take it away," he said in a low, tense voice. "And quit making such a darned noise. I've got a headache."

Augustus Robb adjusted the horn-rimmed spectacles which had made so powerful an appeal to Mr. Cobbold senior, and gazed down at the fishy-eyed ruin before him with something of the air of a shepherd about to chide an unruly lamb. He was a large, spreading man with a bald forehead, small eyes, extensive ears and a pasty face. He sucked a front tooth censoriously, his unpleasant habit when in reproachful mood.

"Got a headache, have you? Well, don't forget you asked for it, chum. I heard you come in this morning. Stumbling all over the place you was and knocking down the furniture. 'Ah,' I says to myself. 'You wait,' I says. 'The day of retribution is at hand,' I says, 'when there will be wailing and gnashing of teeth.' And so there is, cocky, so there is. Well, now you're awake, better eat your brekfuss and get up and go out and 'ave a good brisk walk around the park."

The suggestion seemed to strike Stanwood Cobbold like a blow. He drew the bedclothes higher, partly to exclude the light, but principally so that he might avoid seeing his personal attendant. Even when at his most robust he found the sight of the latter disagreeable, for there seemed to him something all wrong about a valet in horn-rimmed spectacles, and at a time like this it was insupportable.

"It's a lovely day, the sun's shining a treat and the little dicky birds are singing fit to bust," said his personal attendant, by way of added inducement. "Upsy-daisy, and I'll have your clobber all ready for you by the time you're out of your tub."

The effort was almost too much for his frail strength, but Stanwood managed to open an eye.

"Get me a highball."

"I won't get you no such thing."

"You're fired!"

"No, I'm not. Don't talk so silly. Fired, indeed! No, cocky, you can't have no highball, but I'll tell you what you can have. I stepped out to the chemist's just now and asked him to recommend something suitable for your condition, and he give me this."

Stanwood, examining the bottle, brightened a little, as if he had met an old friend.

"This is good stuff," he said, shaking up its dark contents. "I've tried it before, and it's always saved my life."

Removing the cork, he took a hearty draft, and after a brief interval, during which his eyeballs revolved in their sockets and his whole aspect became that of one struck by a thunderbolt, seemed to obtain a certain relief. His drawn features relaxed, and he was able to remove the hand which he had placed on top of his head to prevent it coming off.

"Wow!" he said in a self-congratulatory manner.

Augustus Robb was still amused at the idea of his employer dispensing with his services.

"Fired?" he said, chuckling at the quaint conceit. "How can you fire me, when I was specially engaged by your pop to look after you and be your good angel? 'Robb,' he says to me. I can see him now, standing in his office with his weskit unbuttoned and that appealing look in his eyes. 'Robb, my faithful feller,' he says, 'I put my son in your charge. Take the young barstard over to England, cocky, and keep an eye on him and try to make him like what you are,' he says. Meaning by that a bloke of religious principles and a strict teetotaller."

"And a burglar?" said Stanwood with a flicker of spirit.

"Ex-burglar," corrected Augustus Robb coldly. It was a point on which he was touchy. "Seen the light this many a year past, hallelujah, and put all that behind me. And listen," he went on, stirred by a grievance. "Why did you go and tell Mr. Cardinal I'd been a burglar once?"

"I didn't."

"Yes, you did, and you know it. How else could he have found out? I wish I'd never mentioned it now. That's the trouble with you, chum. You're a babbler. You can't keep from spilling the beans. 'So you used to be a burglar used you?' says Mr. Cardinal, day before yesterday it was, when you'd asked me to step over to his apartment and borrow his new *Esquire*. 'And your name's Robb.' 'What about it?' I says. 'Ha, ha,' he says, laughing a sort of silvery laugh. 'Very suitable name for a burglar,' he says. 'You're the fifty-seventh feller that's told me that,' I says. 'Then you have known fifty-seven brilliantly witty people,' he says. 'I congratulate you.' And he takes a couple of little whatnots off the mantelpiece and locks 'em in a cupboard, as it were ostentatiously. Wounding, that was. I wish you'd be more careful."

"Mike won't tell anyone."

"That's not the point. It's the principle of the thing. A feller that's been saved don't want his sinful past jumping out at him all the time like a ruddy jack-in-the-box. Was he at that do of yours last night?"

"Yes, Mike was along," said Stanwood.

He spoke with a trace of flatness in his voice, for the question had awakened unpleasant memories. It might have been his imagination, but it had seemed to him that during the course of the festivities alluded to his friend Mike Cardinal had paid rather too marked attentions to Miss Stoker and that the latter had not been insensible to his approaches. Of course, the whole thing might have been just a manifestation of the party spirit, but Mike was such an exceptionally good-looking bird that a lover, especially a lover who had no illusions about his own appearance, was inclined to be uneasy.

"And was strictly moderate in his potations, I've no doubt," proceeded Augustus Robb. "Always is. I've seen Mr. Cardinal dine here with you and be perfectly satisfied with his simple half-bot. And him with his spirit on the rack, as you might say, and so with every excuse for getting stinko. Fine feller. You ought to take example by him."

Stanwood found himself mystified.

"How do you mean?"

"How do I mean what?"

"Why is Mike's spirit on the rack?"

"Because he's suffering the torments of frustrated love because he can't get the little bit of fluff to say Yus. That's why his ruddy spirit's on the rack."

"What little bit of fluff?"

"This Lady Teresa Cobbold."

Stanwood was intrigued. Terry Cobbold was an old friend of his.

"You don't say!"

"Yus, I do."

"This is the first I've heard of this."

"The story's only just broke."

"Mike never said a word to me."

"Why would he? Fellers don't go around singing of their love like tenors in a comic opera. Specially if the girl's giving 'em the raspberry and they can't seem to make no 'eadway."

"Well, he told you."

"No, he didn't any such thing. So 'appened that when I was in his apartment day before yesterday there was an envelope lying on the desk addressed to Lady Teresa Cobbold, Beevor Castle, Kent, and beside it a 'alf-finished letter, beginning 'Terry, my wingless angel.' I chanced to glance at it, and it told the 'ole story."

"You've got a hell of a nerve, reading people's letters."

"Language. There's a habit you want to break yourself of. Let your Yea be Yea and your Nay be Nay, as the Good Book says. I've a tract in my room that bears on that. I'll fetch it along. Yus, pleading with her to be his, this letter was. Very well expressed, I thought, as far as he'd got, and so I told him."

A sudden spasm of pain contorted Stanwood's homely features, and the comment he had been about to make died on his lips. The telephone at his side had rung with a shattering abruptness.

"Gimme," said Augustus Robb. "I'll answer it. 'Ullo? Yus? Oh, 'ullo, Mr. Cardinal, we was just talking about you. Yus, cocky, I'll tell him. It's Mr. Cardinal. Says not to forget you're giving him lunch at Barribault's Hotel today."

"Lunch?" Stanwood quivered. "Tell him it's off. Tell him I'm dead."

"I won't do no such thing. You can't evade your social obligations. Yus, that's all right, chum. One-fifteen pip emma in the small bar. Right. Goo'bye. What I'd advise," said Augustus Robb, replacing the receiver, "is a nice Turkish bath. That'll bring the roses back to your cheeks, and Gawd knows they need 'em. You look more like a blinkin' corpse than anything 'uman. Well, I can't stand here all day chinning with you, cocky. Got my work to do. 'Ullo, the front doorbell. Wonder who that is."

"If it's anyone for me, don't let them in."

"Unless it's the undertaker, eh? Haw, haw, haw," laughed Augustus Robb, and exited trilling.

Left alone, Stanwood gave himself up to his thoughts, and very pleasant thoughts they were, too, though interrupted at intervals by the activities of some unseen person who appeared to be driving white-hot rivets into his skull. The news about Mike Cardinal and Terry Cobbold had taken a great weight off his mind and, his being a mind not constructed to bear heavy weights, the relief was enormous.

For obviously, he reasoned, if Mike Cardinal was that way about young Terry, he could scarcely be making surreptitious passes at Eileen Stoker.

Or could he?

Surely not?

No, definitely not, Stanwood decided. What he had witnessed at last night's supper party must have been merely the routine civilities of a conscientious guest making himself agreeable to his host's future bride. Odd, of course, that Mike had said nothing to him about Terry. But then, if things were not going too well, no doubt, as Augustus Robb had pointed out, he wouldn't.

Too bad, felt Stanwood, that the course of true love was not batting .400. Inexplicable, moreover. To him, Mike Cardinal seemed to have everything: looks, personality and, seeing that he was a partner in one of Hollywood's most prosperous firms of motion-picture agents, money, of course, to burn. Difficult to see why Terry should be giving him the run-around.

He grieved for Mike Cardinal. Mike was his best friend, and he wished him well. He had, besides, during the month or two which she had spent in London as a member of the chorus of a popular musical comedy, conceived a solid affection for Terry. They had lunched together a good deal, and he had told her about his love for Eileen Stoker and she had told him about her life at home and the motives which had led her to run away from that home and try to earn her living.

A peach of a girl, was Stanwood's view, pretty and cheerful and abounding in pep. Just, in short, the sort for Mike. Nothing would have given Stanwood more pleasure than to have seen the young couple fading out on the clinch.

Still, that was the way things went, he supposed, and he turned his thoughts to the more agreeable subject of Eileen Stoker and the big times they were going to have together, now that she had hit London. So soothing was the effect of these meditations that he fell asleep.

His slumber was not long-lived. "Hoy!" roared a voice almost before he had closed his eyes, and he saw that Augustus Robb was with him once more.

"Now what?" he said wearily.

Augustus Robb was brandishing a document.

"Cable from your pop," he announced. "I'll read it and give you the gist."

He removed his spectacles, fished in his pocket, produced a case, opened it, took out another pair of spectacles, placed these on his nose, put the first pair in the case and the case in his pocket and cleared his throat with a sound like the backfiring of a motor truck, causing Stanwood, who had sat up, to sag down again as if he had been hit over the head with a blunt instrument.

"Here's the substance, chum. He says——"

"Is it money?"

"Yus, he's cabled a thousand dollars to your account, if you must know, but you think too much of money, cocky. Money is but dross, and the sooner you get that clearly into your nut, the 'appier you'll be. But that's only the start. There's a lot more. He says . . . 'Ullo, what's this?"

"What?"

"Well, well, well!"

"What is it?"

"Well, well, well, *well!* Quite a coincidence, I'd call that. Your pop," said Augustus Robb, becoming less cryptic, "says you're to proceed immediately to Beevor Castle——"

It was foreign to Stanwood's policy to keep sitting up, for the process accentuated the unpleasant illusion that somebody was driving white-hot rivets into his skull, but in his emotion he did so now.

"What's that?"

"You 'eard. You're to proceed immediately to Beevor Castle and stay there till he blows the All Clear. You can guess what's happened, of course. He's been apprised that this Stoker jane of yours has come to London, and he's took steps. But you see what I meant about it being a coincidence. Beevor Castle's where this little number of Mr. Cardinal's lives that we was talking about."

Stanwood was still endeavouring to grasp the appalling news.

"Leave London and go to some darned castle?"

"I shall enjoy a breath of country air. Do you good, too. It's what you need, cocky. Fresh air, milk and new-laid eggs."

Stanwood struggled for utterance.

"I'm not going anywhere near any darned castle."

"That's what *you* say. Cloth-headed remark to make, if you ask me. You've got to do what your pop tells you, or he'll cut off supplies, and then where'll you be? It's like in the Good Book, where the feller said 'Go' and they goeth and 'Come' and they cometh. Or, putting it another way, when Father says 'Turn,' we all turn. It's an am-parce."

Even to Stanwood, clouded though his mind was at the moment, the truth of this was evident. With a hollow groan he buried his face in the pillow.

"Oh, gosh!"

Fruitless now those dreams of sitting beside Eileen Stoker with her little hand in his and pouring into her little ear all the good stuff he had been storing up for so many weeks. Goodbye to all that. She would be in London, pursuing her art, and he would be at this blasted castle. As so often occurred in the pictures in which she appeared, two young hearts in springtime had been torn asunder.

"Beevor Castle," said Augustus Robb, seeming to roll the words round his tongue like some priceless wine. No more fervent worshipper of the aristocracy than he existed among London's millions. He read all the society columns, and the only episode of his burglarious past to which in his present saved condition he could look back with real pleasure was the occasion when he had got in through a scullery window belonging to a countess in her own right and had been bitten in the seat of his trousers by what virtually amounted to a titled wirehaired terrier. "Come to think of it, I've seen Beevor Castle. Cycled there once when I was a lad. Took sandwiches. Nice place. Romantic. One of those stately homes of England they talk about. Who'd have thought I'd of ever got inside of it? It just shows, don't it? What I mean is, you never know. And now, cocky, you'd better hop out of that bed and go and have your Turkish bath. I'll be putting out your things. The blue suit with a heliotrope shirt and similarly coloured socks will be about the ticket, I think," said Augustus Robb, who had an eye for the rare and the beautiful.

Nothing, in his opinion, could actually convert his employer into an oil painting, but the blue suit and the heliotrope shirt might help to some small extent.

3

SOME FOUR and a quarter hours after a silver-voiced Western Union songster, even more of a human nightingale than usual owing to sucking throat pastilles, had chanted into the receiver of his telephone that beautiful lyric which begins:

> Happy birthday to you,
> Happy birthday to you,

and goes on (in case the reader has forgotten):

> Happy birthday to you,
> Happy birthday to you.

Claude Percival John Delamere Cobbold, the fifth Earl of Shortlands, was standing at the window of his study on the ground floor of Beevor Castle in the county of Kent, rattling in his trousers pocket the two shillings and eightpence which was all that remained of his month's pocket money and feeling how different everything would be if only it were two hundred pounds.

The sun which had evoked the enthusiasm of Augustus Robb in London at eleven o'clock was shining with equal, or even superior, radiance on Beevor Castle at eleven-fifteen. It glittered on the moat. It also glittered on the battlements and played about the ivied walls, from the disused wing which had been built in 1259 to the modernized section where the family lived and had their being. But when a couple of rays of adventurous disposition started to muscle into the study, they backed out hastily at the sight of this stout, smooth-faced man who looked like a discontented butler, finding his aspect forbidding and discouraging.

For the morning of May the twelfth, the fifty-second anniversary of his birth, had caught Lord Shortlands in poor shape. A dark despondency had him in its grip, and he could see no future for the human race. He glowered at the moat, thinking, as he had so often thought before, what a beastly moat it was.

As a matter of fact, except for smelling a little of mud and dead eels, it was, as moats go, rather a good moat. But you would have been wasting your time if you had tried to sell that idea to Lord Shortlands. A sullen dislike for the home of his ancestors and everything connected with it had been part of his spiritual make-up for some years now, and today, as has been indicated, he was in the acute stage of that malady which, for want of a better name, scientists call the heebie-jeebies.

It generally takes a man who likes to sleep till nine much more than four and a quarter hours to recover from the shock of having "Happy birthday" sung to him over the transatlantic telephone at seven, and in addition to this shattering experience there had been other slings and arrows of outrageous Fortune whistling about the fifth earl's ears this morning.

His dog Whiskers was sick of a fever. His favourite hat, the one with the broken rim and the grease stains, had disappeared, stolen, he strongly suspected, by his daughter Clare, who was collecting odds and ends for the vicar's jumble sale. Breakfast, in the absence of Mrs. Punter, the cook, away visiting relatives in Walham Green, had been prepared by the kitchenmaid, an indifferent performer who had used the scorched-earth policy on the bacon again. Cosmo Blair, the playwright, who had been staying at the castle for the past week, much against his lordship's wishes, was extending his visit indefinitely, in spite of the fact that there had been a clean-cut gentleman's agreement that he would leave this afternoon.

And, shrewdest buffet of all, his daughter Adela, a woman who, being the wife of Desborough Topping, one of those Americans at the mention of whose name Bradstreet raises his hat with a deferential flourish, could have fed such sums to the birds, had refused to lend him two hundred pounds.

Wanted to know why he wanted two hundred pounds, of all silly questions. As if he could possibly tell her that he wanted it in order to buy a public house and marry Mrs. Punter, the cook.

What the average rate or norm of misfortune for earls on their birthdays might be Lord Shortlands did not know, but he would have been greatly surprised to discover that he had not been given an unusually liberal helping; and he was about to sink for the third time in a sea of self-pity when he became aware of a presence and, turning, saw that his daughter Clare had entered the room.

Self-pity gave way to righteous wrath. There are men from whom old hats can be snitched with impunity, and men from whom they cannot. Lord Shortlands was a charter member of the second and sturdier class. His prominent eyes glowed dangerously, and he spoke in a voice the tones of which King Lear, had he been present, would have memorized for personal use.

"Clare," he boomed, "did you take that hat of mine?"

She paid no attention to the question. She was a girl who had an annoying habit of paying no attention to questions, being brisk and masterful and concentrated on her own affairs; the sort of girl, so familiar a feature of the English countryside, who goes about in brogue shoes and tweeds and meddles vigorously in the lives of the villagers, sprucing up their manners and morals till you wonder that something in the nature of a popular uprising does not take place. The thought sometimes crossed Lord Shortlands' mind that if he had been a villager compelled to cope with Lady Clare Cobbold and her sister Lady Adela Topping, he would have turned his face to the wall and given up the struggle.

"Whose is this, Father?" she asked, and he saw that she was extending towards him a battered volume of some kind. It might have been, as indeed it was, an album for the reception of postage stamps.

It is interesting to reflect that this stamp album, which was to play so considerable a part in Lord Shortlands' affairs, made upon him at its first introduction but a slight impression. It was to be instrumental before the week was out in leading him to break Commandments and court nervous prostration, but now he merely looked at it in distaste, like a butler inspecting a bottle of wine of an inferior vintage. Coming events do not always cast their shadows before them.

"Don't point that beastly thing at me," he said. "It's all over dust. What is it?"

"A stamp album."

"Well, it's caked with grime. Put it on the table. Where did you get it?"

"I found it in a cupboard," said Clare, deviating from her practice of not answering questions. "Whose is it, do you know? Because if it doesn't belong to anyone, I want it for my jumble sale."

This would have been an excellent cue for the restating of the hat motif, but Lord Shortlands had now begun to be interested in this album. Like most people, he had once collected stamps, and strange nostalgic emotions were stirring within him. He approached the table and gave the book a tentative prod with the tip of his finger, like a puppy pawing at a tortoise.

"Why, this is mine."

"Why should it be yours?"

"I used to collect stamps."

"I should imagine it's Tony's."

"Why should it be Tony's any more than mine?"

"I've told Desborough, and he's coming here to look through it. He knows all about stamps."

This was true. A confirmed philatelist from his early years, Desborough Topping was as much looked up to by Stanley Gibbons as by Bradstreet. Stamps and the reading of detective stories were his two great passions.

"There may be something valuable in it. If there is," said Clare, who, while she believed in supporting jumble sales in aid of indigent villagers, did not believe in overdoing it, "we can take it out."

She moved towards the door, and Lord Shortlands remembered that the vital issue was still unsettled.

"Just a minute. How about that hat? Somebody has taken my hat. I left it last night hanging on a peg in the coatroom. I go there this morning, and no hat. Hats don't run away. Hats don't leap lightly off pegs and take to the great open spaces. Have you seen my hat?"

"Have you seen Terry?" asked Clare. Unquestionably she was a difficult girl to talk to about hats.

The eccentricity of her conversational methods bewildered Lord Shortlands, who had never been nimble-minded.

"Terry?"

"Have you seen her?"

"No."

"Well, if you do, tell her that Cosmo Blair wants to read her his second act."

The name seemed to grate upon Lord Shortlands' sensibilities.

"Cosmo Blair!"

"Why do you say 'Cosmo Blair' like that?"

"Like what?"

"Like you did."

"I didn't."

"Yes, you did."

"Well, why shouldn't I?" demanded Lord Shortlands, driven out into the open. "He's a potbellied perisher."

Clare quivered from head to foot.

"Don't call him a potbellied perisher!"

"Well, what else can you call him?" asked Lord Shortlands, like Roget trying to collect material for his Thesaurus. "I've studied him closely, and I say he's a potbellied perisher."

"He's a very brilliant man," said Clare, and swept from the room, banging the door behind her.

"His last play ran nine months in London," she added, reopening and rebanging the door.

"And a year in New York," she said, opening the door again and closing it with perhaps the loudest bang of the series.

Lord Shortlands was not a patient man. He resented the spectacle of a daughter behaving like a cuckoo in a cuckoo clock. When the door opened once more a moment later, he was all ready with a blistering reproof, and was on the point of delivering it when he perceived that this was not his child playing a return date, but a godlike figure with short side whiskers that carried a glass of malted milk on a salver. One of Lord Shortlands' numerous grievances against his daughter Adela was the fact that she made him drink a glass of malted milk every morning, and this was Spink, the butler, bringing it.

Nature is a haphazard caster, and no better example of her sloppy methods could have been afforded than by the outer husks of the fifth Earl of Short-lands and Spink, his butler. Called upon to provide an earl and a butler, she had produced an earl who looked like a butler and a butler who looked like an earl. Mervyn Spink was tall and aristocratic and elegant, Lord Shortlands square and stout and plebeian. No judge in a beauty contest would have hesitated between them for an instant, and no one was more keenly aware of this than Lord Shortlands. He would willingly have given half his fortune—amounting at the moment, as we have seen, to two shillings and eightpence—to have possessed a tithe of this malted milk carrier's lissomeness and grace. For something even remotely resembling his profile he would probably have gone still higher.

The butler advanced into the room with the air of an ambassador about to deliver important dispatches to a reigning monarch, and Lord Shortlands turned to the window, to avoid looking at him. He did not like Mervyn Spink.

It is to be doubted if he would have liked him even in the most favourable circumstances; say, just after the other had saved him from drowning or death by fire, for some people are made incompatible by nature, like film stars and their husbands. And the circumstances were very far from favour-able. Lord Shortlands wanted to marry Mrs. Alice Punter, the cook, and so did Spink. And it not agreeable for the last of a proud line to have his butler as a rival in love.

Not that you have to be the last of a proud line to chafe at such a state of affairs. No householder would like it. In a race for which the hand of a cook is the prize a butler starts with the enormous advantage of being constantly at her side. While the seigneur has to snatch what surreptitious interviews he can, quivering all the while at the thought that his daughter Adela may pop in at any moment and catch him, the butler can hobnob with her by the hour, freely exerting the full force of his fascination.

And you simply could not afford to be handicapped like that in a struggle against such an adversary as Mervyn Spink, facially a feast for the eye and in addition a travelled sophisticate who had seen men and cities. Spink had been for a time in service in the United States, and so was able to bring to his wooing a breath of the great world outside. He also had a nephew on the stage. And while it was true that this nephew had so far played only minor character parts, and those only intermittently, a nephew on the stage is always a nephew on the stage.

Add the fact that he could imitate Spencer Tracy and do tricks with bits of string, and it was only too easy to picture the impact of such a personality on a woman of Mrs. Punter's cloistered outlook. Lord Shortlands, who was doing it now, shuddered and gave vent to a little sighing sound like the last gurgle of an expiring soda-water syphon.

Had happier conditions prevailed, there might have taken place at this juncture a word or two of that genial conversation which does so much to smooth relations between employer and employed. Such snatches as "Nice day, Spink," "Yes indeed, m'lord," or "Your malted milk, m'lord," "Eh? Oh? Ah. Right. Thanks!" suggest themselves. But now the silence was strained and unbroken. Spink put the salver on the table without comment, and Lord Shortlands continued to present a chilly back. The shadow of Alice Punter lay between these men.

Spink withdrew, gracefully and sinuously, with a touch of the smugness of the ambassador who is pluming himself on having delivered the important despatches without dropping them, and Lord Shortlands pursued the train of thought which the man's entry had started. He was musing dejectedly on Mervyn Spink's profile, and trying to make himself believe that it was not really so perfectly chiselled as he knew in his heart it was, when the telephone rang.

He approached it warily, as any man would have done whose most recent unhooking of the receiver had resulted in the impact on his eardrum of a Western Union tenor's "Happy birthday." The burned child fears the fire.

"Hullo?" he said.

"Hello," replied a pleasant male voice. "Can I speak to Lady Teresa?"

"Terry? I haven't seen her this morning."

"Who is that speaking?"

"Lord Shortlands."

"Oh, how do you do, Lord Shortlands? You've probably forgotten me. Mike Cardinal."

Lord Shortlands was obliged to confess that the name did not seem familiar.

"I was afraid it wouldn't. Well, would you mind telling Terry I called up. Good-bye."

"Good-bye," said Lord Shortlands, and returned to his meditations. He was sinking steadily again into the slough of despond in which he had spent most of the morning, when the door opened again, this time to admit the Lady Teresa of whom the pleasant voice had spoken.

"Ha!" said Lord Shortlands, brightening.

To say that he beamed at the girl would be too much. A man who has lost his favourite hat and is contending in the lists of love against a butler who might have stepped out of a collar advertisement in a magazine does not readily beam. But his gloom perceptibly lightened. A moment before, you would have taken him for a corpse that had been some days in the water. Now, he might have passed for such a corpse at a fairly early stage of its immersion. After his trying morning the sight of Terry had come to him like that of a sail on the horizon to a shipwrecked mariner.

Even at the nadir of his depression Lord Shortlands, contemplating the inky clouds that loomed about him as far as the eye could reach, had always recognized that there was among them a speck of silver lining; the fact that his youngest daughter, who some time previously had run off to London to seek a venturous freedom in the chorus of a musical comedy, had now run back again and was once more at his side to comfort and advise.

His eldest daughter Adela might be hard to bear, his second daughter Clare difficult to endure. A man might well come near to cracking under the strain of Mervyn Spink and Cosmo Blair. But Terry, God bless her, was all right.

4

LADY TERESA Cobbold was considerably better worth looking at than the Lady Clare, her sister. The latter took after her father in appearance, which was an unfortunate thing for any girl to do, for it has already been stressed that the fifth Earl of Shortlands, though a worthy soul and no thicker in the head than the average member of the House of Peers, presented to the eye the façade of an Eric Blore rather than that of a Robert Taylor. Terry had had the good sense to resemble her late mother, who had been in her day one of the prettiest debutantes in London. Slim, blue-eyed, fair-haired and bearing Youth like a banner, she was the sort of girl at the sight of whom strong men quiver and straighten their ties.

"Good morning, Shorty," she said. "Many happy returns, darling."

"Thank you, my dear."

"Here's my little gift. Only a pipe, I'm afraid."

"It's a jolly good pipe," said Lord Shortlands stoutly. "Just what I wanted. There was a fellow on the phone for you just now."

"Name of Cardinal?"

"Yes. Seemed to know me, but I couldn't place him."

"You wouldn't. It's years since you saw him. Well, never mind young Mike Cardinal," said Terry, perching herself on the end of the battered sofa. "How have you come out on the takings? Did the others do their bit?"

Lord Shortlands' face clouded. He had had a lean birthday.

"Adela gave me a couple of ties. Desborough gave me a book called *Murder at* some dashed placed or other. Clare——"

"No cash?"

"Not a penny."

"What a shame. I was hoping we could have slunk up to London and had lunch somewhere. How much have you got?"

"Two and eightpence. How much have you?"

"Three bob."

"You see. That's how it goes."

"That's how it goes, Shorty."

"Yes, that's how it goes," said Lord Shortlands, and fell into a moody silence.

These times in which we live are not good times for earls. Theirs was a great racket while it lasted, but the boom days are over. A scattered few may still have a pittance, but the majority, after they have paid their income tax and their land tax and all their other taxes and invested in one or two of the get-rich-quick schemes thrown together for their benefit by bright-eyed gentlemen in the City, are generally pretty close to the bread line. Lord Shortlands, with two and eightpence in his pocket, was more happily situated than most.

But even he cannot be considered affluent. There had been a time, for he had seen better days, when he had thought nothing of walking into his club and ordering a bottle of the best. We find him now reduced to malted milk and dependent for the necessities of life on the bounty of his daughter Adela, that levelheaded girl who had had the intelligence to marry into Bradstreet.

Dependence in itself was not a state of being which would have grated on the fifth earl. He had always preferred not to have to pay for things. But it was another matter to be dependent on a daughter who checked his expenditure so closely; who so consistently refused to loosen up—as it might be when a fellow wanted two hundred pounds in order to marry the cook; and, above all, who was so devoted to the ancestral home that she insisted on staying in it all the year round.

Why anyone with the money to live elsewhere should elect to live at Beevor Castle, which was stuffy in summer and cold in winter, was one of the mysteries which Lord Shortlands knew that he would never solve.

"Do you realize, Terry," he said, his thoughts during the lull in the conversation having turned to his perennial grievance, "that the last time I was away from this place for even a couple of hours was when those Americans took it last summer? And then Adela made me go with her to Harrogate, of all loathsome holes. Some nonsense about Desborough's lumbago. I offered to rough it at my club, but she said she couldn't trust me alone in London."

"I suppose you aren't the sort of man who can be trusted alone in London."

"I suppose not," said Lord Shortlands with modest pride.

"You used to paint it red in the old days, didn't you?"

"Reddish," admitted Lord Shortlands. "And since then I've not been out of the damned place. I'm just a bird in a gilded cage."

"Would you call it a gilded cage?"

"Well, a bird in a bally mausoleum."

"Poor old Shorty. You don't like Ye Olde much, do you?"

"And this infernal feeling of dependence. 'Adela, could I have a shilling?' 'What do you want a shilling for?' 'For tobacco.' 'I thought you had tobacco.' 'I've smoked it.' 'Oh? Well, here you are. But you smoke a great deal too much.' It offends one's manly pride. I can't tell you how much I admired your spirited behavior, Terry, in breaking away as you did. It thrilled me to the core. A bold bid for freedom. I wish I had the nerve to do it, too."

"Perhaps the mistake we made was in not going away together and working as a team. We might have got bookings in vaudeville as a cross-talk act."

"What on earth made you come back?"

"Hunger, my angel. The show I was in collapsed, and I couldn't get another job. Have you ever tried not eating, Shorty?"

"Do you mean you didn't get enough to eat?"

"If it hadn't been for one faithful friend, who was a perfect lamb, I should have starved. He used to take me out to lunch and tell me about the girl he was in love with. His father had sent him to England to get him out of her way. He was an American, and, oddly enough, his name was the same as mine."

"What, Cobbold?"

"Well, you didn't think I meant Teresa?"

Lord Shortlands was interested. Since seven that morning the name Cobbold had been graven on his heart.

"I wonder if he was any relation of that lunatic of mine. There's a border-line case in New York named Ellery Cobbold who keeps writing me letters and sending me cables. And this morning he incited some blasted friend of his to ring me up on the telephone and howl into my ear a lot of dashed rot about 'Happy birthday.' At seven! Seven sharp. The stable clock was just striking when the beastly outrage occurred."

"I should imagine Stanwood is his son. He told me his father lived in New York, or somewhere just outside. Well, he kept me alive, though growing thinner every day, but I found I couldn't take it, Shorty, so I came back."

"Why couldn't you get another job? I should have thought a girl as pretty as you could have walked into something."

"I couldn't even crawl. And I couldn't afford to wait."

"No cash?"

"No cash."

Lord Shortlands nodded.

"Yes, that's it. The problem of cash. One comes up against it at every turn. Look at me. If I had two hundred pounds, I could strike off the shackles. Mrs. Punter still sticks rigidly to her terms."

"I know. She told me."

"She will only marry a man who can set her up in a pub in London. Wants to chuck service and settle down. Enjoy the evening of her life, and all that. One can understand it, of course. Women must have the little home with their own sticks of furniture about them. But it makes it dashed awkward. I don't see how I can raise the money, and there's Spink piling it up hand over fist. I saw that chap Blair slip him a quid the other day. It nearly made me sick. And who knows what those Rossiters may not have tipped him last summer? Spink must be getting very near the goal by now."

"But he bets."

"Yes, and suppose one of these days he strikes a long-priced winner."

"According to Mrs. Punter, he loses all the time, and it prejudices her against him. She wants a steady husband."

"Did she tell you that?"

"Yes, that comes straight from the horse's mouth. I went to her just before she left for her holiday, and pleaded your cause. It seems that she once had a sad experience in her life. She didn't tell me what it was, but I gathered that some man had let her down pretty badly, and now she's looking for someone she can rely on."

"The sturdy oak, not the sapling."

"Exactly. I plugged your reliable qualities, and she quite agreed. 'Your pa hasn't got Mr. Spink's fascination and polish,' she said. 'He isn't so much the gentleman as Mr. Spink. But he's steady.' "

"Ha!"

"So carry on and fear nothing, is my advice. Don't give a thought to Spink's fascination and polish. It's the soul that counts, and that's where you have the bulge on him. I think you're Our Five Horse Special and Captain Coe's Final Selection. You'll romp home, darling."

Lord Shortlands, though not insensible to this pep talk, was unable to bring himself to rejoice wholeheartedly. The sort of life he had been living for the last few years makes a man a realist.

"Not if I can't get that two hundred."

"Yes, we shall have to look into that."

The telephone rang, and Lord Shortlands went to it more confidently this time, like one who feels that the danger is past.

"It's for you."

"Mike Cardinal?"

"Yes. He says did you get his letter."

"Yes, I did. Tell him I won't."

"Won't?"

"Won't."

"Won't what?"

"Just won't. He'll understand."

"Yes," said Lord Shortlands into the instrument, mystified but dutifully obeying instructions, "she says she did, but she won't. Eh? I'll ask her. He wants to know if you're still doing your hair the same way."

"Yes."

"She says yes. Eh? Yes, I'll tell her. Good-bye. He says very sensible of you, because it makes you look like a Botticelli angel. What won't you do?" asked Lord Shortlands, who still found the phrase perplexing.

Terry laughed.

"Marry him."

"Does he want to marry you?"

"He keeps saying so."

Lord Shortlands looked as like a conscientious father with his child's welfare at heart as it was possible for him to do.

"You ought to marry."

"I suppose so."

"Think what it would mean. Liberty. Freedom. You would never have to see that moat again."

"Adela wants me to marry Cosmo Blair."

"Don't do it."

"I won't."

"That's the spirit. I mean to say, dash it, it's all very well wanting to get away from the moat, but you can pay too high a price."

"I feel like that, too. Besides, he's going to marry Clare."

"Good God! Does he know it?"

"Not yet. But he will."

Lord Shortlands reflected.

"By George, I believe you're right. She bit my head off just now because I called him a potbellied perisher. Even at the time it struck me as significant. Well, I'm glad there's no danger as far as you're concerned."

"None whatever. I can't stand that superior manner of his. He talks to me as if I were a child."

"He talks to me as if I were a bally fathead," said Lord Shortlands, who, being one, was sensitive about it. "Well, tell me about this fellow Cardinal. When did you meet him?"

"Do you remember Tony bringing a school friend of his here for the summer holidays about eight years ago?"

"How can I possibly remember all Tony's repulsive friends?"

"This one wasn't repulsive. Dazzlingly good-looking. I met him again when I was lunching with Stanwood Cobbold one day. They knew each other in America."

"He's American, is he?"

"Yes. He was at school with Tony, but he comes from California. He came up and asked me if I remembered him."

"And did you?"

"Vividly. So he sat down and joined us, and after lunch Stanwood went off to write to his girl and Mike immediately proposed to me over the coffee cups."

"Quick work."

"So I pointed out to him. He then said he had loved me from the first moment we met, but had been too shy to speak."

"He doesn't sound shy."

"I suppose he's got over it."

"What is he?"

"A Greek god, Shorty. No less."

"I mean, what does he do?"

"He's a motion-picture agent in Hollywood. Motion-picture agents are the people who fix up the stars with engagements at the studios. They get ten per cent of the salaries."

Lord Shortlands' eyes widened. He had read all about motion-picture stars' salaries.

"Good heavens. He must make a fortune."

"Well, he's only a junior partner, but I suppose he does pretty well."

Lord Shortlands gulped emotionally.

"I'd have grabbed him."

"Well, I didn't."

"Don't you like him?"

"Yes, I do. Very much. But I'm not going to marry him."

"Why not?"

"There's a reason."

"What reason?"

"Oh, just a reason. But don't let's talk about me any more. Let's talk about you—you and your two hundred pounds."

Lord Shortlands would have preferred to continue the probe into his daughter's reasons for being unwilling to marry a rich and good-looking young man, whom she admitted to liking, but it was plain that she considered the subject closed. And he was always ready to talk about his two hundred pounds.

"That still remains the insuperable obstacle. I don't see how I can raise it."

"Have you tried Desborough?"

"I keep starting to pave the way, but he always vanishes like a homing rabbit. The impression he gives me is that he sees it coming."

"Well, he'll be here at any moment to look at that stamp album Clare found. And he can't vanish like a rabbit this time, because he's got lumbago again."

"That's true."

"Tackle him firmly. Don't pave the way. Use shock tactics. Oh, hullo, Desborough."

A small, slight, pince-nezed man in the middle forties, who looked like the second vice-president of something, had entered. He came in slowly, for he was supporting himself with a walking stick, but his manner was eager. When there were stamps about, Desborough Topping always resembled a second vice-president on the verge of discovering some leakage in the monthly accounts.

"Hello, Terry. Say, where's this . . . Ah," he said, sighting the album and becoming lost to all external things.

The eyes of Lord Shortlands and his daughter met in a significant glance. "Do it now," said Terry's. "Quite. Certainly. Oh, rather," said Lord Shortlands'. He advanced to the table and laid a gentle hand on his son-in-law's shoulder.

"Some interesting stamps here, eh?" he said affectionately. "Desborough, old chap, can you lend me two hundred pounds?"

The invalid started, as any man might on finding so substantial a touch coming out of a blue sky.

"Two hundred pounds?"

"It would be a great convenience."

"Why don't you ask Adela?"

"I did. But she wouldn't."

Desborough Topping was looking like a stag at bay.

"Well, you know me. I'd give you the shirt off my back."

Lord Shortlands disclaimed any desire for the shirt off his son-in-law's back. What he wanted, he stressed once more, was not haberdashery but two hundred pounds.

"Well, look. Here's the trouble. Adela and I have a joint account."

It was the end. A man cannot go on struggling against Fate beyond a certain point. Lord Shortlands turned and walked to the window, where he gave the moat a look compared with which all previous looks had been loving and appreciative.

"This whole matter of joint accounts for married couples—" he was beginning, speaking warmly, for the subject was one on which he held strong views, when his observations were interrupted. The door had opened again, and his eldest daughter was coming in.

Lady Adela Topping, some fifteen years younger than her husband, was tall and handsome and built rather on the lines of Catherine of Russia, whom she resembled also in force of character and that imperiousness of outlook which makes a woman disinclined to stand any nonsense. And that she had recently been confronted with nonsense of some nature was plainly shown in her demeanour now. She was visibly annoyed; so visibly that if Desborough Topping had not become immersed in the stamp album once more and so missed the tilt of her chin and the flash of her eye, he would have curled up in a ball and rolled under the sofa.

"Do you know a man named Cobbold, Father?" she said. She consulted the buff sheet of paper in her hand. "Ellery Cobbold he signs himself."

Like a bull which, suddenly annoyed by a picador, turns from the matador who had previously engrossed its attention, Lord Shortlands shelved the thought of joint accounts for the time being and puffed belligerently.

"Ellery Cobbold? That fellow in New York? I should say I do. He sours my life."

"But how do you come to be connected with him?"

"He's connected with me. Or says he is. Claims he's a sort of cousin."

"Well, I cannot see that that entitles him to expect us to put his son Stanwood up for an indeterminate visit."

"Does he?"

"That's what he says in his cable. I never heard such impertinence."

"Bally crust," agreed Lord Shortlands, indignant but not surprised. After what had occurred that morning when the stable clock was striking seven, he could scarcely be astonished at any excesses on Mr. Cobbold's part.

Only Terry seemed pleased.

"Is Stanwood Cobbold coming here?" she said. "Splendid."

"Do you know him?"

"We're like ham and eggs."

"Like what?"

"I mean that's how well we get along together. Stanwood's an angel. He saved my life in London."

Down at the table something stirred. It was Desborough Topping coming to the surface.

"Ellery Cobbold?" he said, the name having just penetrated to his stamp-drugged consciousness. "I was in college with Ellery Cobbold. Fat fellow."

"Indeed?"

"Very rich now, I believe."

Lady Adela started.

"Rich?"

"Worth millions, I guess," said Desborough, and dived back into the album.

A change had come over Lady Adela's iron front. Her eyes seemed softer. They had lost their stern anti-Cobbold glare.

"Oh, is he? And you say he's some connection of ours, Father? And his son is friend of yours, Terry? Then of course we must ask him here," said Lady Adela heartily. "Desborough, go and send him a telegram—here's the address—saying that we shall be delighted to put him up. Sign it 'Shortlands.' The cable was addressed to you, Father."

"Was that why you opened it?" asked Lord Shortlands, who had begun to feel ruffled again about that joint account.

"Say that Father will be coming in this afternoon in the car——"

A sigh escaped Lord Shortlands. Permission to go to London, and only two-and-eightpence to spend when he got there. This, he supposed, was the sort of thing Cosmo Blair had been alluding to at dinner last night, when he had spoken of tragic irony.

"—and will bring him back with him. Have you got that clear? Then run along. Oh, and you had better cable Mr. Cobbold, saying how delighted we are. Pistachio, New York. New York is one word."

"Yes, dear. I'll take this album with me. It's quite interesting. I've already found a stamp that's worth several pounds."

"Then Clare must certainly not give the thing to her jumble sale until you have thoroughly examined it," said Lady Adela with decision. She shared her sister's views about not overdoing it when you are aiding indigent villagers.

It seemed to Lord Shortlands that the time had come to get his property rights firmly established. The mention of stamps worth several pounds had stirred him profoundly, and all this loose talk about jumble sales, he felt, must be checked without delay.

"Just a minute, just a minute," he said. "Clare isn't going to have that album. Ridiculous. Absurd."

"What do you mean?"

"Perfect rot. Never heard of such a thing."

"But what has it to do with you?"

"It's my album."

"Nonsense."

"It is, I tell you. I used to collect stamps."

"Years ago."

"Well, the thing's probably been in that cupboard for years. Look at the dust on it. What more likely than that I should have put my album in a cupboard and forgotten all about it?"

"Well, I haven't time to discuss it now. Run along, Desborough."

"Yes, dear."

As the door closed, Lady Adela had another idea.

"It might be a good thing, Father, if you were to start at once. Then you could give Mr. Cobbold lunch."

"What!"

Lady Adela repeated her remark, and Lord Shortlands closed his eyes for a moment, as if he were praying.

"An excellent idea," he said in a hushed voice. "At the Ritz."

"You're behind the times, Shorty," said Terry. "Barribault's is the posh place now."

"Then make it Barribault's," said Lord Shortlands agreeably.

"And you can take Terry with you."

Terry blinked.

"Did you hear what I heard, Shorty?"

" 'Take Terry with you' was the way I got it."

"That's what it sounded like to me, too. Do you really mean this, Adela?"

"Make yourself look nice."

"A vision," said Terry, and started off to do so.

She left Lord Shortlands uplifted but bewildered. He was at a loss to account for this sudden spasm of openhandedness in a daughter generally prudent to a fault. He found himself reminded of the Christmas Day activities of the late Scrooge.

"This may be a most fortunate thing that has happened, Father," said Adela. "Terry is a very attractive girl, and apparently she and this Mr. Cobbold are good friends already. And he saved her life, she says. Odd she should not have mentioned that before. I wonder how it happened. It seems to me that, being here together, they might quite easily——"

"Good Lord!" said Lord Shortlands, enlightened. He was also a little shocked. "Don't you women ever think of anything but trying to fix up weddings?"

"Well, it's quite time that Terry got married. It would steady her."

"Terry doesn't need steadying."

"How can you talk like that, Father, after the way she ran off and——"

"Oh, all right, all right. And now," said Lord Shortlands, for he felt that too much time was being wasted on these trivialities, "in the matter of expenses. I shall need quite a bit of working capital."

"Nonsense. Two pounds will be ample."

It is not often that anyone sees an earl in the act of not believing his ears. Lady Adela was privileged to do so now. Lord Shortlands' prominent eyes, so well adapted for staring incredulously, seemed in danger of leaping from their sockets.

"Two pounds?" he cried. "Great heavens! How about cocktails? How about cigars? How about wines, liqueurs and spirits?"

"I'm not going to have you stuffing yourself with wines and liqueurs. You know how weak your head is."

"My head is not weak. It's as strong as an ox. And it is not a question of stuffing myself, as you call it, with wines and liqueurs. I shall have to do this boy well, shan't I? You don't want him thinking he's accepting the hospitality of Gaspard the miser, do you? It's a little hard," said Lord Shortlands, quivering with the self-pity which came so easily to him. "You bundle me off to London at a moment's notice, upsetting my day and causing me all sorts of inconvenience, to entertain a young man of whom I know nothing except that his father is off his bally onion, and you expect me to keep the expenses down to an absurd sum like two pounds."

"Oh, very well."

"It's going to be a nice thing for me at the end of lunch, when the coffee is served and this young fellow gazes at me with a wistful look in his eyes, to have to say 'No liqueurs, Cobbold. It won't run to them. Chew a toothpick.' I should blush to my very bones."

"Oh, very well, very well. Here is five pounds."

"Couldn't you make it ten?"

"No, I could not make it ten," said Lady Adela with the testiness of a conjurer asked to do too difficult a trick.

"Well, all right. Though it's running it fine. I foresee a painful moment at the table, when the chap is swilling down his wine and I am compelled to say 'Not quite so rapidly, young Cobbold. Eke it out, my boy, eke it out. There isn't going to be a second bottle.' How about seven pounds ten? Splitting the difference, if you see what I mean. Well, I merely asked," said Lord Shortlands, addressing the closing door.

For some moments after the founder of the feast had left him, he stood gazing—in a kindlier spirit now—at the moat. In spite of the misgivings which he had expressed, he was not really ill pleased. For a proper slap-up binge, of course, on the lines of Belshazzar's Feast, five pounds is an inadequate capital, but you can unquestionably do something with it. Many a poor earl, he knew, would have screamed with joy at the sight of a fiver. It was only that he did wish that some angel could have descended from on high and increased his holdings to ten, in his opinion the minimum sum for true self-expression.

So softly did the door open that it was not until he heard his emotional breathing that he became aware of his son-in-law's presence. Desborough Topping had stolen into the room furtively, like a nervous member of the Black Hand attending his first general meeting.

"Psst!" he said.

He glanced over his shoulder. The door was well and truly closed. Nevertheless, he continued to speak in a hushed, conspiratorial whisper.

"Say, look, about that two hundred. I can't manage two hundred, but—"

Something crisp and crackling slid into Lord Shortlands' hand. Staring, he saw his son-in-law receding towards the door. His pince-nezed eyes were shining with an appealing light, and Lord Shortlands had no difficulty in reading their message. It was that fine old family slogan "Not a word to the wife!" The next moment his benefactor had gone.

Terry, returning some minutes later, was stunned by a father's tale of manna in the wilderness.

"Ten quid, Terry! Desborough's come across with ten quid! I cannot speak in too high terms of the fellow's courage—no, dash it, heroism. Men have got the V.C. for less. Fifteen quid in my kick that makes. Fifteen solid jimmy-o'-goblins. Not counting my two-and-eightpence."

"Golly, Shorty, what a birthday you've had."

"Nothing to the birthday I'm going to have. Today, my child, a luncheon will be served in Barribault's Hotel which will ring through the ages. It will go down in story and song."

"That will be nice for Stanwood."

"Stanwood?" Lord Shortlands snorted. "Stanwood isn't going to get a smell of it. Just you and I, my dear. A pretty thing, wasting my hard-earned money on a fellow whose father eggs his confederates on to getting people out of bed at seven in the morning and bellowing 'Happy birthday' at them," said Lord Shortlands severely.

In the drawing room Lady Adela had rung the bell.

"Oh, Spink," she said as the butler slid gracefully over the threshold.

"M'lady?"

"A Mr. Cobbold who is over here from America will be coming to stay this afternoon. Will you put him in the Blue Room."

"Very good, m'lady." A touch of human interest showed itself in Mervyn Spink's frigid eye. "Pardon me, m'lady, but would that be Mr. Ellery Cobbold of Great Neck, Long Island?"

"His son. You know Mr. Cobbold?"

"I was for some time in his employment, m'lady, during my sojourn in the United States of America."

"Then you have met Mr. Stanwood Cobbold?"

"Oh yes, m'lady. A very agreeable young gentleman."

"Ah," said Lady Adela.

She had invited this guest of hers to the castle in the spirit of the man who bites into a luncheon-counter sausage, hoping for the best but not quite knowing what he is going to get, and this statement from an authoritative source relieved her.

5

IT IS pleasant to be able to record that Stanwood Cobbold's Turkish bath did him a world of good, proving itself well worth the price of admission. They took him and stripped him and stewed him till he bubbled at every seam and rubbed him and kneaded him and put him under a cold shower and dumped him into a cold plunge and sent him out into the world a pinker and stronger young man. It was with almost the old oomph and elasticity that shortly after one o'clock he strode into Barribault's Hotel and made purposefully for the smaller of its two bars. This was not because he had anything against the large bar—he yielded to none in his appreciation of its catering and service—but it was in the small bar, it will be remembered, that he had arranged to meet Mike Cardinal.

His friend was not yet at the tryst, the only occupant of the room, except for the white-jacketed ministering angel behind the counter, being a stout, smooth-faced man in the early fifties of butlerine aspect. He was seated at one of the tables, sipping what Stanwood's experienced eye told him was a McGuffy's Special, a happy invention on the part of the ministering angel, whose name—not that it matters, for except for this one appearance he does not come into the story—was Aloysius St. X. McGuffy. He had the air of a man in whose edifice of revelry this McGuffy's Special was not the foundation stone but one of the bricks somewhat higher up. Unless Stanwood's eye deceived him, and it seldom did in these matters, this comfortable stranger had made an early start.

And such was indeed the case. A lunch of really majestic proportions, a lunch that is to ring down the ages, a lunch, in short, of the kind to which Lord Shortlands had been looking forward ever since his daughter Adela with that wave of her magic wand had transformed the world for him, demands a certain ritual of preparation. The fifth earl's first move, on arriving in the centre of things and giving Terry three pounds and sending her off to buy a hat, after arranging to meet her in the lobby of Barribault's Hotel at one-thirty, had been to proceed to his club and knock back a bottle of his favorite champagne, following this with a stiff whiskey and soda. Then, and only then, was he ready for Aloysius McGuffy and his Specials.

Stanwood took a seat at an adjoining table, and after he in his turn had called on the talented Aloysius to start pouring, a restful silence reigned in the bar. From time to time Stanwood shot a sidelong glance at Lord Shortlands, and from time to time Lord Shortlands shot a sidelong glance at Stanwood. Neither spoke, not even to comment on the beauty of the weather, which was still considerable, yet each found in the other's personality much that was attractive.

There is probably something about men crossed in love which tends to draw them together, some subtle aura or emanation which tells them that they have found a kindred soul. At any rate, every time Lord Shortlands looked at Stanwood, he felt that, while Stanwood unquestionably resembled a hippopotamus in appearance, it would be a genuine pleasure to fraternize with him. And every time Stanwood looked at Lord Shortlands, it was to say to himself: "Granted that this bimbo looks like a butler out on the loose, nevertheless something whispers to me that we could be friends." But for a while they remained mute and aloof. It was only when London's first wasp thrust itself into the picture that the barriers fell.

One is inclined to describe this wasp as the Wasp of Fate. Only by supposing it an instrument of destiny can one account for its presence that morning in the small bar of Barribault's Hotel. Even in the country its arrival on the twelfth of May would have been unusual, the official wasping season not beginning till well on in July, and how it came to be in the heart of London's steel and brick at such a time is a problem from which speculation recoils.

Still there it was, and for a space it volplaned and looped the loop about Lord Shortlands' nose, occasioning him no little concern. It then settled down for a brief breather on the back of Stanwood's coat, and Lord Shortlands, feeling that this was an opportunity which might not occur again, remembered his swashing blow, like Gregory in *Romeo and Juliet*, and downed it in its tracks with a large, flat hand.

A buffet between the shoulder blades does something to a man who is drinking a cocktail at the moment. Stanwood choked and turned purple.

Recovering his breath, he said (with some justice) "Hey!", and Lord Short-lands hastened to explain. He said:

"Wasp."

"Wasp?"

"Wasp," repeated Lord Shortlands, and with a pointing finger directed the other's attention to the remains. "Wasp," he added, driving the thing home.

Stanwood viewed the body, and all doubt concerning the purity of his preserver's motives left him.

"Wasp," he said, fully concurring.

"Wasp," said Lord Shortlands, summing the thing up rather neatly. "Messing about on your back. I squashed it."

"Darned good of you."

"Not at all."

"Courageous, too."

"No, no. Perhaps a certain presence of mind. Nothing more. Offer you a cocktail?"

"Or me you?"

"No, me you."

"Well, you me this time," said Stanwood, yielding the point with a pleasant grace. "But next time me you."

The ice was broken.

When two men get together who are not only crossed in love but are both reasonably full of McGuffy's Specials, it is inevitable that before long confidences will be exchanged. The bruised heart demands utterance. Gradually, as he sat there drawing closer and closer spiritually to this new friend, there came upon Stanwood an irresistible urge to tell his troubles to Lord Shortlands.

The orthodox thing, of course, would have been to tell them to Aloysius McGuffy, who may be said to have been there more or less for the purpose, but this would have involved getting up and walking to the bar and putting his foot on the rail and leaning forward and pawing at Aloysius McGuffy's shoulder. Far simpler to dish it out to this sympathetic stranger.

Very soon, accordingly, he was explaining his whole unhappy position to Lord Shortlands in minute detail. He told him of his great love for Eileen Stoker, of his father's short way with sons who loved Eileen Stoker, of his ecstasy on learning of Eileen Stoker's impending arrival in London, of his welcome to her when she did arrive and finally of the crushing blow which had befallen him, knocking his new-found happiness base over apex; this wholly unforeseen cable from his father, ordering him to leave the metropolis immediately and go to some ghastly castle, the name of which had escaped him for the moment.

Throughout the long and at times rambling expositon Lord Shortlands had listened with the owlish intentness of a man who has already started lunch-ing, uttering now a kindly "Ah?" and anon a commiserating "Good gad!" At this mention of going to castles a grave look came into his face. He had grown fond of this young man, and did not like to see him heading for misery and disaster.

"Keep away from castles," he advised.

"But I can't, darn it."

"Castles," said Lord Shortlands, speaking the word with a bitter intonation. "I could tell you something about castles. They have moats."

"Yay, but——"

"Nasty smelly moats. Stinking away there since the Middle Ages. Be guided by me, my dear boy, and steer jolly clear of all castles."

Stanwood was beginning to wonder if it would not have been wiser to stick to the sound old conservative policy of telling his troubles to the barman. This stranger, though sympathetic, seemed slow in the uptake.

"But don't you understand? I've got to go to this castle."

"Why?"

"My father says so."

Lord Shortlands considered this. Until now, though Stanwood had been at some pains to elaborate it, the point had escaped him. It was not long before a happy solution presented itself.

"Kick him in the eye."

"How can I? He's in America."

"Your father is?"

"Yay."

"I could tell you something about fathers in America, too," said Lord Shortlands. "This very morning, as the stable clock was striking seven——"

"If I don't do what he tells me to, he'll slice off my allowance. It's like in the Bible," said Stanwood, searching for an illustration and recalling Augustus Robb's observations on the subject. "You remember? Where the bozo said 'Come' and they goeth."

Lord Shortlands had now a complete, if muzzy, grip of the position of affairs.

"Ah, now I see. Now I understand. You are financially dependent on your father?"

"That's right."

"As I am on my daughter Adela. Most unpleasant, being dependent on people."

"You betcher."

"Especially one's daughter. Adela—I wouldn't tell this to everyone, but I like your face—Adela oppresses me. You have heard of men being henpecked. I am chickpecked. She makes me live all the time at my castle."

"Have you a castle?"

"I have indeed. One of the worst. And she makes me live there. I feel like a caged skylark."

"I feel like a piece of cheese. Run out of London just at the very moment when I want to be sticking to Eileen like a poultice, and chased off to this damned castle. A hell of a setup, don't you think?"

Lord Shortlands, who had a feeling heart, admitted that his young friend's predicament was such as to extort the tear of pity.

"Though it is scarcely," he went on to say, "to be compared with the one in which I find myself. I'm just a toad beneath the harrow."

"You said you were a skylark."

"A toad, too."

"Have you got to go to a castle?"

"I'm at a castle already. I told you that before."

"Gee, that's tough."

"You . . . What was that expression you used just now? Ah yes, You betcher."

"Must grind you a good deal, being at a castle already."

"You betcher. But that, serious though it is, is not my principal trouble."

"What's your principal trouble?"

Lord Shortlands hesitated for a moment. So far his British reserve had triumphed over a pint of champagne, a double whiskey and splash and three McGuffy Specials; but now he felt it weakening. A brief spiritual conflict, and he, too, had decided to tell all.

"It is this. At my castle there is a cook."

"Look, look, lookie, here comes cookie!"

"I beg your pardon?"

"Just a song I happened to remember."

"I see. Well, as I was saying, at my castle there is a cook."

"Another cook?"

"No, the same cook. And the fact is, well, I—er—I want to marry her."

"Good for you."

"You approve?"

"You betcher."

"I am delighted to hear you say so, my dear boy. You know how much your sympathy means to me. Marry her, you suggest?"

"You betcher."

"But here is the difficulty. My butler wants to marry her, too."

"The butler at your castle?"

"You betcher. It is a grave problem."

Stanwood knitted his brows. He was thinking the thing out.

"You can't both marry her."

"Exactly." This clear-sightedness delighted Lord Shortlands. An old head on young shoulders, he felt. "You have put your finger on the very core of the dilemma. What do you advise?"

"Seems to me the cagey move would be to fire the butler."

"Impossible. When I spoke of him as 'my' butler, I used the word loosely. His salary is paid by my daughter Adela. Firing butlers is her prerogative, and she guards it jealously."

"Gee, that's like it is with me and Augustus Robb. Well, then, you'll have to cut him out."

"Easier said than done. He is a man of terrific personal attractions. His profile alone . . . The only thing that gives me hope is that he bets."

"Would he know anything good for Kempton Park next Friday?"

"Most unlikely. He seems to pick nothing but losers. That is why the fact that he is a betting man causes me to hope. He squanders his money, and Alice disapproves."

"Who's Alice?"

"The cook."

"The cook at your castle? The cook we've been talking about?"

"That very cook. She wants a steady husband. And she thinks me steady."

"She does?"

"I have it from a reliable source."

"Then you're set. It's in the bag. All you've got to do is keep plugging away and giving her the old personality. I think you'll nose him out."

"Do you, my dear boy? You are certainly most comforting. But unfortunately there is one very formidable obstacle in my path. She won't marry anyone who cannot put up two hundred pounds to buy a public house."

"Ah? So the real trouble is dough?"

"You betcher. In this world," said Lord Shortlands weightily, "the real trouble is always dough. All through my life I have found that out. And mine has been a long life. I'm fifty-two today."

Stanwood started as if a chord in his soul had been touched. He threw back his head and began to sing in a booming bass:

> "I'm fifty-two today,
> Fifty-two today.
> I've got the key of the door,
> Never been fifty-two before.
> And Father says I can do as I like,
> So shout Hip-hip-hooray,
> He's a jolly good fellow,
> Fifty-two——"

He broke off abruptly and pressed both hands to his temples. Too late he realized that the whole enterprise of throwing his head back and singing old music-hall ballads, however apposite, was one against which his best friends would have warned him.

"If you'll excuse me," he said, rising, "I think I'll just go to the washroom and put my head under the cold tap. Have you ever had that feeling that someone is driving white-hot rivets into your bean?"

"Not in recent years," said Lord Shortlands with a touch of wistfulness. "As a young man——"

"Ice, of course, would be better," said Stanwood, "but you look so silly ordering a bucket of ice and sticking your head in it. But maybe cold water will do something."

He tottered out, hoping for the best, and Lord Shortlands, allowing his lower jaw to droop restfully, gave himself up to meditation.

He thought of Mrs. Punter, and wondered how she was enjoying herself with her relatives at Walham Green. He thought of Terry, and hoped she would buy a nice hat. He thought of ordering another McGuffy Special, but decided that it was not worth the effort. And then suddenly he found himself thinking of something else, something that sent an icy chill trickling down his spine and restored him to a sobriety which could not have been more complete if he had been spending the morning drinking malted milk.

Had he been wise, he asked himself, had he been entirely prudent in confiding to that charming young fellow who had just gone out to put his head under the tap the secret of his love? Suppose the thing were to come to Adela's ears?

A look of glassy horror came into Lord Shortlands' eyes. Perspiration bedewed his forehead, and the word "Crikey!" trembled on his lips. From the very inception of his wooing he had been troubled by the thought of what the deuce would happen if Adela ever got to hear of it.

Then Reason reassured him. The young fellow and he were just ships that pass in the night. They had met and spoken, and now they would part, never to meet again. There could be no possibility of the other ever coming into Adela's orbit. He had been alarming himself unnecessarily.

Comforted and relieved, but feeling an imperative need for an immediate restorative, he turned, with the purpose of establishing communication with Aloysius McGuffy, and found that he was being scrutinized by a pair of extraordinarily good-looking twins, who on closer inspection coalesced into one extraordinarily good-looking young man in a grey suit, who had come in unperceived and taken a seat at the adjoining table. And to his surprise this young man now rose and approached him with outstretched hand.

"How do you do?" he said.

6

Lord Shortlands blinked.

"How do you do," he replied cautiously. Sixteen years ago he had once been stung for five by an agreeable stranger who had scraped acquaintance with him in a bar, and he could not forget that he had at this moment nearly twelve pounds on his person. "Be on the alert, Claude Percival John Delamere," he was saying to himself.

"I have not got my facts twisted?" the other proceeded. "You are Lord Shortlands?"

Though still wary, the fifth earl saw no harm in conceding this. He said he was, and the young man said he had been convinced of it; he, the fifth earl, having changed very little since the old days; looking, in fact, or so it seemed to him, younger than ever.

Lord Shortlands, though continuing to keep a hand on the money in his pocket, began to like this young man.

"You don't remember me. You wouldn't, of course. It's a long time since we met. Your son Tony brought me to Beevor for the summer holidays once, when we were boys together. Cardinal is the name."

"Cardinal?"

"I mentioned that on the phone this morning, if you remember, but nothing seemed to stir. Nice running into one another like this. How is Tony?"

"He's all right. Cardinal? Out in Kenya, growing coffee and all that. Cardinal?" said Lord Shortlands, his McGuffy-Specialized brain at last answering the call. "Why, you're the chap who's in love with my daughter Terry."

The young man bowed.

"I could wish no neater description of myself," he said. "It cuts out all superfluities and gets right down to essentials. One of these days I shall be President of the United States, but I am quite content to live in history as the chap who was in love with your daughter Terry. It must be a very wonderful thing to have such a daughter."

"Oh, decidedly."

"Makes you chuck the chest out more than somewhat, I should imagine?"

"You betcher."

"I'm surprised you don't go around singing all the time. It was a great relief to me when you told me she was still doing her hair the same way. It would be madness to go fooling about with that superb superstructure. And yet I don't know. I doubt whether any rearrangement of the tresses could destroy their charm. The first time I saw her, she had them down her back in pigtails, and I remember thinking the effect perfect."

"Yes, Terry has pretty hair."

"I would have said gorgeous. I love her eyes too, don't you?"

Lord Shortlands said that he thought his daughter had nice eyes, and the young man frowned.

"Not 'nice.' If we are going to talk about Terry, we must take a little trouble to get the right word. Her eyes are heavenly. I don't suppose there's another pair of eyes like that in existence. How do you check up on her nose? That way it turns up slightly at the tip."

"Ah," said Lord Shortlands, wisely refraining from a more definite expression of opinion in the presence of this evidently meticulous critic, and the young man paused to light a cigarette.

Lord Shortlands goggled at him with a solemn intentness. He could see what Terry had meant about the fellow being good-looking. The word understated it. He was sort of super-Spink. Sitting where he did, he presented his profile to Lord Shortlands, and the latter was able to study its clean-cut lines. There was no getting away from it. The chap began where Spink left off.

Mike Cardinal had finished lighting his cigarette and was ready to talk once more.

"Yes, she's got everything, hasn't she? I don't suppose you've the slightest conception of how I love that girl. What a great day that was when she came back into my life; on the hoof, as it were, and not merely as a golden, insubstantial memory. It happened quite by chance, and at a moment, oddly enough, when I was not thinking of her but of chump chops, Brussels sprouts and French-fried potatoes. I was sauntering through the grillroom here, looking for a table, and I saw a friend of mine sitting with a girl and went over to exchange a word, and——"

"Yes, she told me."

"Ah, she has been talking about me, has she? A promising sign. By the way, have I your permission to pay my addresses to your daughter? One likes to get these things settled."

"Well, dash it, you have been paying your addresses to her."

"Unofficially, yes. But unsuccessfully. And why unsuccessfully? Because unofficially."

"Say that again," said Lord Shortlands, whose mental powers were not at their keenest.

"What I mean is that I have not been going at this thing in the right way. I need official backing. If I had your approval of my suit, I feel sure I could swing the deal. A father's influence means so much. You could put in an occasional good word for me, guiding her mind in the right direction. Above all, you could invite me to Beevor for an indefinite stay, and in those romantic surroundings——"

"No, I couldn't. I can't invite people to Beevor."

"Nonsense. A child could do it."

Well, I can't. My daughter Adela won't let me."

"Ah? A nuisance, that. It's a pity I have never met Lady Adela."

"Wasn't she at Beevor when you were there?"

"No."

"Those were the days," sighed Lord Shortlands.

Mike rose to a point of order. His voice, when he spoke, was a little stern.

"Then how about Stanwood Cobbold?"

"Eh?"

"It seems to me that your whole story about not being able to invite people to Beevor falls to the ground. I was round at his place just now, and his man told me a telegram had arrived for him from you, freely extending your hospitality. I shall be glad to hear what you have to say to that."

"I never sent that telegram. It was Adela. Why should I want the chap messing around? He's probably a perisher."

"Not at all."

"Well, his father is."

"Ah, there I cannot speak with firsthand knowledge. I have never met his father. But you'll like Stanwood. Everybody does. He's the best fellow that ever stepped, and I love him like a brother. When you get Stanwood, you've got something. However, to return to myself, I should have thought that, considering that I have already visited the castle and apparently gave satisfaction, seeing that nobody slung me out, Lady Adela would have stretched a point."

"Not a hope. She never asks anyone down who doesn't write or paint or something. They have to be these bally artistic blighters."

"Stanwood isn't an artistic blighter."

"He's an exception."

"I don't get in, then?"

"No, you don't."

"Well, it's all very exasperating. You see how I'm handicapped. No wooer can possibly give of his best if he's in London and the divine object is in Kent and won't answer the telephone. Have you a vacancy for a butler?"

Lord Shortlands sighed wistfully.

"I wish I had. But it wouldn't be any use you coming to Beevor. Terry won't marry you."

"She thinks she won't. But once let me get there——"

"There's some reason. She didn't tell me what."

Mike frowned.

"The reason is that she's a little fathead and doesn't know what's good for her," he said. "It is that fatheaded streak that I am straining every nerve to correct. I keep pointing out to her that it's no use looking like an angel if you can't spot a good man when you see one. And that she does look like an angel no one in his senses would deny. For the last five years I've been living in Hollywood, positively festooned with beautiful women, and I've never set eyes on one fit to be mentioned in the same breath with Terry. She stands alone."

"Yes, Terry told me you worked in Hollywood. Motion-picture agent or something, aren't you?"

"That's right."

"Must make a good thing out of it, what?"

"Quite satisfactory. Have no fear that I shall not be able, when the moment comes, to support your daughter in the style to which she has become accustomed. But it is absolutely essential, as I say, that I come to Beevor, for this business of pressing my suit by mail and having her tell someone to say 'She says she won't' on the telephone is getting me nowhere. Try to think of some method whereby I can be eased into the dear old place."

Lord Shortlands thought hard. An obviously amiable and well-disposed son-in-law with a lucrative connection in Hollywood was just what he had been scouring the country for for years. He was still thinking when Stanwood Cobbold returned, looking brighter and fitter. The cold-water cure had proved effective.

"Hiya, Mike," he cried, in quite a buoyant tone.

"Hello, there," said Mike, "You look extraordinarily roguish. How come? I stopped in at your place on my way here, and Augustus Robb told me you were a sort of living corpse."

"I had a Turkish bath, and I've just been putting my head under the cold tap."

"I see. Do you know Lord Shortlands?"

"Never heard of the guy."

"This is Lord Shortlands."

"Oh, sure, I know him. We've just been chatting. He was telling me about his cook."

"And this, Lord Shortlands, is the Stanwood Cobbold of whom you have heard so much; your forthcoming guest, who . . . Why, what's the trouble?" asked Mike, concerned. Some powerful upheaval appeared to be taking place in the older man's system, manifesting itself outwardly in a sagging jaw and a popeyed stare of horror.

"Is your name Stanwood Cobbold?" cried Lord Shortlands, seeming to experience some difficulty in finding utterance.

"Sure. Why not? What's biting him, Mike?"

Mike was wondering the same thing himself. He hazarded a possible conjecture.

"I think it's joy. Augustus Robb tells me you are leaving today for Beevor Castle in the county of Kent. Lord Shortlands, who owns Beevor Castle, will consequently be your host. Apprised of this, he registers ecstasy. As who would not?"

Lord Shortlands was still finding it hard to speak.

"But this is terrible!"

"Oh, come. There's nothing wrong with Stanwood."

"You see, I want to marry my cook——"

"Well, that's all right by me. How about you, Stanwood?"

"—and I told him. Suppose, when he gets to Beevor, he lets it out to my daughter Adela?"

"She would not be pleased?"

"She would make my life a hell on earth. Is he the sort of chap who's likely to go babbling?" asked Lord Shortlands, fastening his protruding eyes on Stanwood as if seeking to read his very soul.

"I fear he is."

"Good Lord!"

"There is no vice in Stanwood Cobbold. His heart is the heart of a little child. But like the little child whom in heart he so resembles, he has a tendency to lisp artlessly whatever comes into his head. His reputation is that of a man who, if there are beans to be spilled, will spill them with a firm and steady hand. He has never kept a secret, and never will. His mother was frightened by a B.B.C. announcer."

"Oh, my God!"

"Inevitably there will come a time at Beevor Castle when, closeted with Lady Adela and hunting around for some theme to interest, elevate and amuse, he will turn the conversation to the subject of you and the cook. He will mean no harm, of course. His only thought will be to make the party go."

"Great heavens!"

"Most probably the disaster will occur at the dinner table this very night. One can picture the scene. The fish and chips have been dished out, and Stanwood starts digging in. 'Egad, Lady Adela,' he says, speaking with his mouth full. 'You have a darned good cook.' 'Glad you think so, Mr. Cobbold. Eat hearty.' 'Is that the cook Lord Shortlands wants to marry?' says Stanwood. 'I'm not surprised. I'd like to marry her myself.' That's a thing you want to be prepared for."

"This is frightful!"

"Yes, one can picture your embarrassment. That'll be the time to keep cool. But fortunately I have a suggestion to make which, if adopted, will, I think, ease the situation quite a good deal. How do you react to the idea of his staying in London and not going to Beevor at all?"

Stanwood frowned. He had been feeling so much better, and now all this.

"But I've got to go to Beevor, you poor fish. Father says so."

Lord Shortlands, too, seemed displeased.

"Exactly. It is not kind, my dear fellow, to talk drivel at such a moment. Adela sent me in to fetch him. What's she going to say if I return alone?"

"You won't return alone. I shall be at your side. I ought to have mentioned that earlier."

"You?"

"It seems the logical solution. I want to go to Beevor, Stanwood wants to remain in London, you want a guest who can be relied on not to introduce the cook motif into the conversation. The simple ruse which I have suggested would appear to make things all right for everybody."

Lord Shortlands was a slow thinker.

"But Adela doesn't want you. She wants him."

"Naturally, in embarking on such an enterprise, I should assume an incognito. The name Stanwood Cobbold suggests itself."

Stanwood uttered a piercing cry of ecstasy. It made his head start aching again, but one cannot always be thinking of heads.

"Gosh, Mike, could we swing it?"

"It's in the bag."

"This is genius."

"You must expect that when you string along with me."

"Gee, and it's only about half an hour since I was calling Eileen up and telling her I'd got to leave her. I must rush around and see her at once."

"How about our lunch?"

"To hell with lunch."

"And how about Augustus Robb?"

"To hell with Augustus Robb."

"His heart was set on this visit."

"To hell with Augustus Robb's heart and his lungs and his liver, too. If he starts acting up, I'll poke him in the eye," said Stanwood, and departed like one walking on air.

Lord Shortlands, who could work things out if you gave him time, was beginning to get it now.

"You mean you'll come to Beevor instead of him?"

"Exactly."

"Pretending to be him, and so forth?"

"That's right. It's a treat to see the way you're taking hold."

"But, dash it."

"Something on your mind?"

"How can you? Terry knows you. And, by Jove, now I remember, she knows him, too. Used to lunch with him and all that."

"I had not overlooked the point you raise. I am taking it for granted that a daughter's love will ensure her silence."

"That's true. Yes, I suppose it will."

"It might, however, be as well to call her up and prepare her."

"But she's here. Is it half-past one?"

"Just on."

"Then she'll be out in the lobby. I told her to be there at half-past one."

"This is glorious news. A chat with Terry is just what I wanted, to make my day. I have a bone to pick with that young half-wit. She and her 'She says she won't's. Hello, what's this?"

A small boy in buttons had entered the bar. All the employees of Barribault's Hotel have sweet, refined voices. This lad's sweet, refined voice was chanting "Lord Shortlands. Lord Shortlands."

Lord Shortlands cocked an enquiring eye at Mike.

"He wants me."

"Who wouldn't?"

"Here, boy."

"Lord Shortlands, m'lord? Wanted on the telephone, m'lord."

"Now, who the deuce can that be?" mused Lord Shortlands.

"Go and see," suggested Mike. "I, meanwhile, will be having the necessary word with Terry. Do you mind if I rub her turned-up little nose in the carpet?"

"Eh?"

" 'She says she won't,' indeed!" said Mike austerely.

7

BARRIBAULT'S HOTEL being a favourite haunt of the wealthy, and the wealthy being almost uniformly repulsive, its lobby around the hour of one-thirty is always full of human eyesores. Terry in her new hat raised the tone quite a good deal. Or so it seemed to Mike Cardinal. She was sitting at a table near two financiers with four chins, and he made his way there and announced his presence with a genial "Boo!" in her left ear. Having risen some six inches in a vertical direction, she stared at him incredulously.

"You!"

"You should have put your hand to your throat and rolled your eyeballs," said Mike. "It is the only way when you're saying 'You!' Still, I know what you mean. I do keep bobbing up, don't I? One realizes dimly how Mary must have felt."

"Yes, I think you must have lamb blood in you. Delighted to see you, of course."

"Naturally."

"But how did you know I was here?"

"Your father told me."

"You've met him?"

"Just now."

"It's a small world, isn't it?"

"Not in the least. Why do you speak of it in that patronizing way? Because I met your father? We could hardly have helped meeting. He was in the bar, and I came in, and there we were, face to face."

"Was he enjoying himself? Till then, I mean."

"He seemed happy."

"Not too happy?"

"Oh no."

"You see, today is his birthday, and he rather hinted that he intended to celebrate. I don't quite like this lounging in bars."

"He has ceased to lounge. He was called to the telephone."

"Called to the telephone?"

"Called to the telephone, Mister Bones. Why not?"

"But who could have been calling him?"

"I'm afraid I couldn't tell you. I'm a stranger in these parts myself."

"Nobody knows he's here, I mean. Except the family at home, of course."

"Then perhaps it was the family at home. Look, do you mind if we change the subject? I think we've about exhausted it. Let us speak of that letter I wrote you. Well-expressed, didn't you think? Full of good stuff? The phrases neatly turned?"

"Very."

"So a friend of mine named Augustus Robb considered. I came in and found him reading it. A winner, he said cordially, and Augustus Robb is not a man who praises lightly. Personally, I thought it a composition calculated to melt a heart of stone. 'That's going to drag home the gravy,' I said to myself as

325

I licked the stamp. But I was wrong, it seems. Or did your father report you incorrectly when he said 'She says she won't'?"

"No. That was what I told him to say."

"Your idea being to break it gently?"

"You wouldn't have had me be abrupt?"

"Of course not. So you won't marry me?"

"No."

"Somebody's got to."

"Not me."

"That's what you say now, but I don't despair."

"Don't you?"

"Not by a jugful. Much may be done by persistence and perseverance. I shall follow you around a good deal and keep gazing at you with the lovelight in my eyes, and one of these days my hypnotic stare will do the trick. It's like a dog at mealtime. You say to yourself 'I will not feed this dog. It is not good for him,' but he keeps his pleading eye glued on you, and you weaken. Talking of marrying, your father tells me he wants to marry the cook. I said he might."

"Oh, Shorty! I knew something would happen if I let him run around loose in London with all that money in his pocket. Did he really get as confidential as that? You won't go spreading it about, will you?"

"My lips are sealed."

"If my sister Adela ever heard about it, his life would not be worth a moment's purchase."

"She shall never learn his secret from me. Clams take my correspondence course."

"That's good. And now tell me how you come to be here. Lunching with some girl, I suppose?"

"Not at all. Stanwood Cobbold."

"Really? Dear old Stanwood. Bless his heart."

"Amen. He brought us together. Do you remember that day? You were sitting there in the grillroom, listening to him telling you about La Stoker, and I came along. 'Good Lord,' I said to myself. 'I believe it's Terry!' "

"And was it?"

"Yes."

"I don't call that much of a story."

"It's a peach of a story. I don't know what more you want."

"Has Stanwood told you that he's coming to Beevor?"

"He isn't."

"Yes, he is. We're taking him back with us this afternoon. His father cabled Shorty, asking him to put Stanwood up."

"I know all that. The old man wants to get him out of the orbit of the Stoker, who has just arrived in London. But you haven't got the scenario absolutely correct. To give you a complete grasp of it I shall have to go back to the beginning. I came here to meet Stanwood, and ran into your father. All straight so far?"

"Quite."

"Good. Well, for a while, as I told you, he appeared quietly happy. I introduced myself, and we chatted at our ease. About you, and how lovely your hair was and how your nose turned up at the tip and how I was going to marry you, and so on and so forth. All very pleasant and cosy. And then Stanwood blew in, and his happiness waned."

"Didn't he like Stanwood?"

"That's just the trouble. He loved him not wisely but too well. Apparently they had met earlier in the proceedings and formed a beautiful friendship. You know those friendships where Friend A can conceal nothing from Friend B, and vice versa."

"You don't mean he——"

"Exactly."

"Oh, Shorty, Shorty, Shorty!"

"No doubt Stanwood began by telling your father all about the Stoker, and your father, not to be outdone in the courtesies, told Stanwood all about the cook. Not being aware who he was, of course. In these casual encounters in bars names are rarely exchanged. Until I introduced them, Stanwood had been to your father merely a pleasant stranger who looked like a hippopotamus."

"He does look like a hippopotamus, doesn't he?"

"Much more than most hippopotamuses do."

"Not that it matters."

"Not in the least."

"The important thing is, can he keep a secret? Because if he's coming to Beevor——"

"——He will meet your sister Adela. And if he mentions this little matter to your sister Adela, hell's foundations are going to quiver. Precisely. That was the reflection which cast a shadow on your father's sunny mood. He sought for reassurance, but I was not able to give him any. In the lexicon of Stanwood Cobbold, I was compelled to tell him, there is no such word as reticence. He is a beans-spiller of the first order. Over in America we seldom advertise in the papers now. If there is anything we want known, we just tell Stanwood. It's cheaper."

"But this is frightful."

"Exactly what your father said."

"Oh, my goodness."

"I'm not sure if he said that, too, but I think so. The drama gets you, does it? I thought it would. But it's all right. I've only been working up the agony in order to make the happy ending more of a punch."

"Is there a happy ending?"

"There always is when I take things in hand. I found the solution first crack out of the box."

"Are there no limits to the powers of this wonder man?"

"None have yet been discovered. My solution was a very simple one. I suggested that Stanwood should remain in London and that I should go to Beevor in his place."

"As him, do you mean?"

"As him," said Mike.

He beamed at her in the manner of one expecting the approving smile and the word of praise, but Terry was looking thoughtful.

"I see."

"Ingenious?"

"Very."

"It's the only way out of what Augustus Robb would call the am-parce. I am taking it for granted, of course, that you will not gum the game by denouncing me."

"Well, naturally. I can't let Shorty down."

"Of course not. Stoutly spoken, young pip-squeak. Well, that's the scheme, and it seems to me ideal. Your sister wants to entertain Stanwood Cobbold, and she will get a far better Stanwood Cobbold than the original blueprints called for. Stanwood wants to stay in London, because of the Stoker. Your father wants him to stay in London, so that his fatal secret may be preserved. And I want to be at Beevor in order to buckle down to my wooing at close range. It is difficult to see how the setup could be improved. We seem to have a full hand. As one passes through this world, one strives always to scatter light and sweetness and to promote the happiness of the greatest number, and here everybody will be pleased."

"Except me."

"Come, come. Is this the tone?"

"I repeat, except me."

"Don't you want me at Beevor, Lady Teresa?"

"I do not, Mr. Cardinal."

"You say that now, but wait till I start growing on you. Wait till my beautiful nature begins to expand before your eyes like some lovely flower unfolding its petals. Don't you see what a wonderful opportunity this will be for you to become hep to my hidden depths?"

"You haven't any."

"I have, too. Dozens."

"I still stick to it that I don't want you at Beevor."

"Well, it's a mercy I'm coming there. How vividly I remember dear old Beevor, with all its romantic nooks and corners. A lovers' paradise. Sauntering in the shrubberies, seated on the rustic benches, pacing the velvet lawns in the scented dusk and fishing for eels together in the moat, we shall soon get all this nonsense about not marrying me out of your head. 'Golly,' you'll say to yourself, 'what a little mutt I must have been not to have recognized at the very outset that this bimbo was my destined mate!' And you will probably shed a tear or two at the thougtht of all the time you've wasted. Do you realize that we might have been an old married couple by now if you had let yourself think along the right lines?"

"Aren't you keeping Stanwood waiting?"

"He's left. Our lunch is off. I shall take potluck with you and your father."

"You haven't been invited."

"I don't need to be. I'm from Hollywood. Look, he approaches."

Lord Shortlands was crossing the lobby towards them from the direction of the telephone booths, and so arresting was his aspect that Terry gave a little squeak of surprise.

"What on earth is the matter with him?"

The impression Mike Cardinal received was that someone had been feeding his future father-in-law meat, and he said so.

And certainly in Lord Shortlands' demeanour there was a quite unusual effervescence. Though solidly built, he seemed to skip and amble. His whole appearance closely resembled that of Stanwood Cobbold immediately after taking the healing medicine which Augustus Robb had bought at the drugstore. Stanwood's eyes had revolved in their sockets. His did the same. Stanwood had had the air of a man struck behind the ear by an unexpected thunderbolt. So had Lord Shortlands.

"Terry," he cried, "you know that album?"

He had to swallow once or twice before he could proceed.

"I've just been talking to Desborough on the telephone. He says he's found a stamp in it worth well over a thousand pounds!"

BOOK TWO

8

FROM DOWN Westminster way there floated over London the sound of Big Ben striking half-past two, and Augustus Robb came softly into the living room of Number 7 Bloxham House, Park Lane. He had just finished a late lunch, and was now planning to top it off with a good cigar from his employer's box. He was surprised and disconcerted, having made his selection, to observe Stanwood lying on the sofa.

"Why, 'ullo, cocky," he said, hastily thrusting the corona into the recesses of his costume. "I didn't 'ear you come in."

Stanwood did not speak. His face was turned to the wall, and Augustus Robb, eyeing him, came to a not unnatural conclusion.

"Coo!" he exclaimed. "What, *again?* You do live, chum. Only a few hours since you 'ad one of the biggest loads on I ever beheld in my mortal puff, and here you are once more, equally stinko. Beats me how you do it. Well, it's lucky for you you ain't in my old line of business, because there intemperance hampers you. Yus. I knew a feller once, Harry Corker his name was, Old Suction Pump we used to call him, got into a house while under the influence, caught hold of the safe as it come round for the second time, started twiddling the knobs, and first thing you know he'd got dance music from a continental station. If he hadn't retained the presence of mind to dive through the window, taking the glass with him, he'd have been for it. Steadied him a good deal, that experience. Well, I suppose I'll have to step out and fetch along another bottle of that stuff. I'll tell the young fellow behind the counter to make it a bit stronger this time."

Stanwood sat up. His features were drawn, but his voice was clear and his speech articulate.

"I'm not plastered."

"Ain't you?" said Augustus Robb, surprised. "Well, you look it. Country air's what you need. I've packed."

"Then unpack."

"What? Aren't we going to this Beevor Castle?"

"No," said Stanwood, and proceeded to explain.

One points at Augustus Robb with pride. A snob from the crown of his

331

thinly covered head to the soles of his substantial feet, his heart had been set on going to stay at Beevor Castle. He had looked forward to writing letters to his circle of friends on crested stationery and swanking to them later about his pleasant intimacy with the titled and blue-blooded, and, as he listened to Stanwood's story, he felt like a horn-rimmed spectacled peri excluded from paradise.

But his sterling nature triumphed over the blow. A few muttered "Coo's," and he was himself again. Of all the learned professions none is so character-building as that of the burglar. The man who has been trained in the hard school of porch climbing, where you often work half the night on a safe only to discover that all it contains is a close smell and a dead spider, learns to take the rough with the smooth and to bear with fortitude the disappointments from which no terrestrial existence can be wholly free.

But, though philosophic, he could not approve.

"No good's going to come of this," he said.

"Why not?"

"Never does, cocky, from lies and deceptions. Sooner or later you'll find you've gone and got yourself into a nasty mess with these what I might call subterfuges. 'Oh, what a tangled web we weave, when first we practise to deceive!' I used to recite that as a nipper. Many a time I remember my old uncle Fred giving me a bag of peppermints to stop. Said it 'ampered 'im in the digesting of his dinner. Used to keep the peppermints handy, in case I started. Well, if you're not stinko, what are you looking like that for?"

"Like what?"

"Like the way you are. You look like three penn'orth of last week's cat's meat," said Augustus Robb, who was nothing if not frank.

In ordinary circumstances Stanwood might have hesitated to confide his more intimate secrets to the flapping ears of one whose manner he sometimes found a little familiar and who, he suspected, needed but very slight encouragement to become more familiar still. But a great sorrow had just come into his life, earthquakes and black frosts had been playing havoc with his garden of dreams, and at such moments the urge to tell all to anyone who happens to be handy cannot be resisted.

"If you really want to know," he said hollowly, "my heart's broken."

"Coo! Is it?" Augustus Robb was surprised and intrigued. "Lumme, no that this Stoker jane of yours is in London and you 'aven't got to leave her, I'd have thought you'd have been as happy as a lark. What's gone wrong? Been playing you up, has she? Always the way with these spoiled public favorites. You young fellows will keep giving them flattery and adulation, when what they really need is a good clump over the ear'ole, and that makes 'em get above themselves. Found somebody else, has she, and gone and handed you your hat? I thought something like that would happen."

Stanwood groaned. He was finding his companion's attitude trying, but the urge to confide still persisted.

"No, it's not that. But I went to see her just now——"

"Shouldn't have done that, cocky. Rash step to take. Girls often wake up cross after a binge."

"She wasn't cross. But she told me she had been thinking it over and had made up her mind she wasn't going to get married again unless the fellow had money."

"Mercenary, eh? You're well out of it, chum."

"She's not mercenary, blast you."

"Language!"

"It's just that she says she's tried it a couple of times and it doesn't work. She says you can't stop marriage being a bust if the wife has all the dough."

Augustus Robb seated himself on the sofa and, having shifted his employer's knees to one side, for they were interfering with his comfort, put the tips of his fingers together like Counsel preparing to give an opinion in chambers.

"Well, she's quite right," he said. "You can't get away from that. I wouldn't have thought a Hollywood star would have had so much sense. Never does for the old man to have to keep running to the missus every time he wants a bob for a packet of gaspers or half a dollar to put on some 'orse he's heard good reports of. Prevents him being master in the 'ome, if you follow my meaning. It's 'appened in me own family. My uncle Reginald——"

"Damn your uncle Reginald!"

"Language again." Augustus Robb rose, offended. "Very well, I was going to tell you about him, and now I won't. But the fact remains she's perfectly correct. I'd have thought you'd have seen that for yourself. You don't want to be supported by your old woman, do you? Where's your self-respect?"

"To hell with self-respect!"

"Language once more. I wonder if you've ever considered the risk you're running of everlasting fire? Well what are you going to do about it?"

"I don't know."

"Nor me. Well, I'll tell you what I'll do, seeing that things has arrived at such a pass that it's only 'umane to relax the rules a bit. I'll fetch you a brandy and soda."

"Make it brandy straight."

"All right, chum, if you prefer it. No use spoiling the ship for a ha'p'orth of tar."

It was some little time before Augustus Robb returned, for a ring at the front doorbell had delayed him. When he did so, he found his employer sitting up and taking nourishment in the shape of a cigarette.

"I'll tell you what I'm going to do," said Stanwood, accepting the brandy gratefully. He had the air of one who has been thinking things over. "I'm going to talk her out of it."

Augustus Robb shook his head.

"Can't see how that's to be done," he said. "You aren't in the posish. It would mean pursuing 'er with your addresses; going to 'er and pleading with 'er, if you see what I mean, using all the eloquence at your disposal."

"That's what I'm going to do."

"No, you're not, chum. Talk sense. How can you pursue her with your addresses if she's in London and you're in the country? It's the identical am-parce Mr. Cardinal found himself up against, only there the little parcel of goods was in the country and 'im in London. Still, the principle's the same."

Stanwood, though feeling better after the brandy, was still ill disposed to listen to the gibberings of a valet who appeared to have become mentally deranged. He stared bleakly at Augusuts Robb.

"What are you talking about? I told you I wasn't going to the country."

"But you'll have to, chum, now this cable's arrived."

"What cable?"

Augustus Robb slapped his forehead self-reproachfully.

"Forgot you 'adn't seen it. Be forgettin' me own 'ead next. It come while I was fetching you that brandy, and I was reading it in the hall and left it on the hall table. It's from your pop. There's been a new development."

"Oh, my God! What's happened now?"

"It's about these photografts."

"What photographs?"

"All right, all right, don't bustle me. I'm coming to that. It's a long cable, and I can't remember it all, but here's the nub. Your pop, taking it for granted, as you might say, that you're going to this Beevor Castle, says he wants you to send along a lot of photografts of its interior, with you in 'em."

"What!"

"Yus. Seems funny," said Augustus Robb with an indulgent smile, "anyone wanting photografts of a dial like yours, don't it? But there's a reason. He don't say so in so many words, but, reading between the lines, as the expression is, it's obvious that why he wants 'em is so's he can show 'em around among his cronies in New York and stick on dog. See what I mean? He meets one of his gentlemen friends at the club or wherever it may be, and the gentleman friend says, 'Tell me, cocky, what's become of that son of yours? Don't seem to have seen 'im around in quite a while.' 'Ho,' says your pop. 'Ain't you 'eard? He's residing with this aristocratic English earl at his old-world castle.' 'Coo!' says his pal. 'An earl?' 'Yus,' says your pop. 'One of the best of 'em, and the castle has to be seen to be believed. My boy's just sent me some photografts of the place. Look, this is 'im lounging in the amber droring room, and 'ere's another where he's sauntering around the portrait gallery. Nice little place, ain't it, and they treat him like one of the family, he tells me.' And then he puffs out his blinkin' chest and goes off to tell the tale to someone else. Sinful pride, of course, like Jeshurun who waxed fat and kicked, but there you are."

A greenish pallor had manifested itself on Stanwood's face.

"Oh, gosh!"

"You may well say 'Gosh!', though I'm not sure as I'd pass the expression, coming as it does under the 'ead of Language, or something very like it."

"But how can I get photographs of the inside of this foul castle?"

"R. That's what we'd all like to know, isn't it? Properly up against it, you are, ain't you? The Wages of Sin you might call it. Seems to me the only thing you can do is 'urry and catch Mr. Cardinal before he starts and tell him you're going to this Beevor Castle, after all. Look slippy, I should."

Stanwood looked slippy. He was out of the flat in five seconds. A swift taxi took him to Barribault's Hotel. He shot from its interior and grasped the arm of the ornate attendant at the door, a man who knew both Mike and himself well.

"Say, listen," he gasped. "Have you seen Mr. Cardinal?"

"Why, yes, sir," said the attendant. "He's just this minute left, Mr. Cobbold. Went off in a car with an elderly gent and a young lady."

It seemed to Stanwood that there was but one thing to do. He tottered to the small bar, and feebly asked Aloysius McGuffy for one of his Specials. As he consumed it, staring with haggard eyes into the murky future, he looked like something cast up by the tide, the sort of flotsam and jetsam that is passed over with a disdainful jerk of the beak by the discriminating sea gull.

9

THE CAR rolled in through the great gates of Beevor Castle, rolled up the winding drive, crossed the moat and drew up at the front door; and Mike, looking out, heaved a sentimental sigh.

"How all this takes me back," he said. "It was here that I saw you for the first time."

"Was it?" said Terry. "I don't remember."

"I do. A big moment, that. You were leaning out of that window up there."

"The schoolroom."

"So I deduced from the fact that there was jam on your face. It hinted at schoolroom tea."

"I never had jam on my face."

"Yes, you did. Raspberry jam. I loved every pip of it. It seemed to set off to perfection the exquisite fairness of your skin."

Lord Shortlands heaved like an ocean billow, preparatory to alighting. For the last twenty miles he had been siting in a sort of stupor, engrossed in thought, but before that, and during the luncheon which had preceded the drive, he had been very communicative. There was nothing now that Mike did not know concerning the Shortlands-Punter romance and the rivalry, happily no longer dangerous, of Spink, the butler. He could also have passed an examination with regard to the stamp.

The stamp, Lord Shortlands had told him, not once but many times, was a Spanish 1851 *dos reales* blue unused. Desborough, whose industry and acumen could not in his opinion be overpraised, had happened upon it just as the luncheon gong was sounding, with such stirring effects on his morale that for the first time in his association with his wife Lady Adela he had become the dominant male, stoutly refusing to go to the table until he had telephoned the great news to his father-in-law. According to Desborough, a thousand pounds for such a stamp might be looked upon as a conservative figure. A similar one had sold only the other day for fifteen hundred.

"As far as I could follow him, there's an error in colour or something," said Lord Shortlands, returning to the theme as the car stopped. He had mentioned this before, during lunch at least six times and in the earlier stages of the drive another four, but it seemed to him worth saying again. "An error in colour. Those were the words he used. Why that should make it so valuable I'm blessed if I know."

"From what I recall of my stamp-collecting days," said Mike, "an error in colour was always something to start torchlight processions about."

"Used you to collect stamps?" asked Terry.

"As a boy. Why, don't you remember——"

"What?"

"I forget what I was going to say."

"This is disappointing."

"It was probably nothing of importance."

"But one hangs on your lightest word."

"I know. Still, it can't be helped. It may come back. It'll be something to look forward to."

What he was looking forward to, Lord Shortlands said with a grim smile, was the meeting with the viper Spink. By this time, he explained, the news of his sudden accession to wealth must have seeped through to the Servants Hall, and he made no attempt to conceal the fact that he was anticipating considerable entertainment from the sight of his rival's face, the play of expression on which would, no doubt, in the circumstances be well worth watching. He could hardly wait, he said. A mild and kindly man as a rule, Lord Shortlands could be a tough nut in his dealings with vipers.

It was consequently with keen disappointment that he stared at the small maid who had opened the door. To a man who has been expecting to see a butler with heart bowed down, small maids are a poor substitute.

"Hullo! Where's Spink?"

"Mr. Spink's gone off on his motorcycle, m'lord."

"Gone off on his motorcycle?" said Lord Shortlands, obviously disapproving of this athleticism. "What's he gone off on his motorcycle for?"

But the butler, it appeared, was one of those strong, silent butlers. He had not revealed to the maid the motive behind the excursion.

"Oh? Well, all right. Just wanted to see him about something. It'll have to wait. Lady Adela in the drawing room?"

"Yes, m'lord."

"Then come along, Cobbold, my boy. I'll take you to her."

The maid passed out of earshot, and Lord Shortlands seemed to preen himself.

"Notice how I called you Cobbold?"

"Very adroit."

"Can't start too early."

"The start is everything."

"Don't go forgetting."

"Trust me."

"And you, Terry, don't you go forgetting."

"I won't."

"One false step, and ruin stares us in the face."

"Right in the face. But isn't there something you're forgetting, Shorty?"

"Eh? What's that?"

"The possibility of Adela sticking to this stamp."

Lord Shortlands gaped.

"Sticking to it? You mean keeping it?"

"That's what I mean. I feel I can speak freely before this synthetic Cobbold——"

"Do," said Mike. "Go right ahead. I like this spirit of wholesome confidence."

"—because there isn't much about your private affairs that you haven't already told him. He could write your biography by this time. Suppose she decides to set the stamp against services rendered?"

Lord Shortlands' jaw fell limply.

"She wouldn't do that?"

"She will. I can feel it in my bones."

"And what bones they are!" said Mike cordially. "Small and delicate. When I was a boy, I promised my mother I would never marry a girl who hadn't small, delicate bones."

"You must go and look for one. You and I and Clare between us, Shorty, must owe Desborough well over a thousand pounds by this time for board and lodging, and it isn't a thing Adela is likely to have overlooked."

"Then what the devil are we to do?"

"Would you care to hear my plan?" asked Mike, ever helpful.

"Have you a plan?"

"Cut and dried."

"He always has," said Terry. "They call him the One-Man Brains Trust."

"And not without reason," said Mike. "I'm good. Here is the procedure, as I see it. When we arrive in Lady Adela's presence, you introduce me to her. 'Shake hands with Mr. Cobbold' is a formula that suggests itself."

" 'Mitt Mr. Cobbold' would be friendlier."

"She mitts you."

"Exactly. And I hold her hand as in a vise. While she is thus rendered powerless, your father snatches up the album and rushes out and hides it somewhere. This is what is called teamwork."

Lord Shortlands' eyes did not readily sparkle, but they were sparkling now. As far as he was concerned, Mike had got one vote.

"What an admirable idea!"

"I told you I was good. With my other hand I could be choking her."

"I don't think I'd do that."

"It's how I see the scene. Still, just as you please. Tell me," said Mike, the trend of the conversation and certain previous observations on the part of both his host and his host's youngest daughter having suggested a thought to him. "If I am not intruding on delicate family secrets, is your sister Adela what is technically known as a tough baby?"

"None tougher. Her bite spells death."

"I thought as much. Yet here I am, about to stroll calmly into her presence, impersonating an honoured guest, a thing which, if discovered, must infallibly bring her right to the boil. You must be admiring me a good deal."

"Oh, I am."

" 'My hero!' you are possibly saying to yourself."

"Those very words."

"So I supposed. Women always admire courage. And how quickly admiration turns to love. Like a flash. It won't be long before you are weeping salt tears and asking me if I can ever forgive you for having tortured me with your coldness. A week at the outside. What is this door before which we have paused?"

"The drawing room. You seem to have forgotten the geography of the house."

"They didn't allow me in the drawing room much, when I was here before. Rightly or wrongly, they considered that my proper place was in the tool shed, playing ha'penny nap with Tony and the second footman. All right, Lord Shortlands, lead on."

Lord Shortlands led on.

There was a moment, when Mike caught his first glimpse of Lady Adela Topping, when even his iron courage faltered a trifle. He had been warned, of course. They had told him that the chatelaine of Beevor Castle was a tough baby. But he had not been prepared for anything quite so formidable as this. Lady Adela had just returned from the garden and was still holding a stout pair of shears, and the thought of what a nasty flesh wound could be inflicted with these had a daunting effect.

And apart from the shears he found her appearance intimidating. She was looking even more like Catherine of Russia than usual, and it is pretty generally agreed that Catherine of Russia, despite many excellent qualities, was not everybody's girl.

However, he rallied quickly and played his part well in the scene of introduction, helped not a little by the fact that his hostess was showing her most affable and agreeable side. His spectacular good looks had made a powerful impression on the woman behind the shears, who noted with approval that Terry also was looking her best. It seemed to Lady Adela that it would be a very young man who could fail to be attracted by so alluring a girl, and that Terry, for her part, unaccountable though she was in many ways, could scarcely remain indifferent for long to such outstanding physical qualities in a man whose father was a millionaire. She was cordiality itself to Mike.

"So delighted that you were able to come, Mr. Cobbold."

"So kind of you to have me, Lady Adela."

"I hope you will like it here. Terry must show you round after tea."

"She was just suggesting it."

"The rose garden——"

"She particularly mentioned the rose garden. She was telling me how romantic and secluded it was. 'We shall be quite alone there,' she said."

"Your window looks out on it. You might show Mr. Cobbold his room, Terry. There is just time before tea. He is in the Blue Room."

The door closed behind Terry and Mike, and Lord Shortlands, who during these polished exchanges had been shuffling his feet with some impatience, opened the subject nearest his heart.

"Where's that stamp?" he demanded.

"Stamp?" Lady Adela seemed to come out of a trance. In moving to the door Mike had shown his profile to her and she had been musing on it in a sort of ecstasy. Surely, she was feeling, a profile like that, taken in conjunction with a father's bank balance . . . "Oh, the stamp? You mean the one Desborough found."

"Yes. I want it in my possession."

"But it's not yours."

"Yes, it is. Certainly it's mine."

"Oh, of course. I had forgotten. You don't know. That wasn't your album. After lunch Clare started hunting around for things for her jumble sale, and she found yours at the back of one of the drawers of the desk in your study. It had your name on it, so there can't be any mistake. So the other one must belong to Spink."

A nightmare feeling that the solid floor was slipping from under him gripped Lord Shortlands.

"Spink!"

The name Spink has qualities—that "s" at the begining, which you can hiss, and that strong, culminating "k"—which render it almost perfect for shouting at the top of his voice. It was at the top of his voice that Lord Shortlands had shouted it, and his daughter quivered as if he had hit her.

"Father! You nearly deafened me."

"Spink?" repeated Lord Shortlands, a little more on the piano side, but still loudly.

"Yes. Desborough was talking about the stamp at lunch, and Clare was telling Mr. Blair how she had found the album in a cupboard, and after lunch Spink came to me and explained that it was one which had been given him by Mr. Rossiter, the son of those Americans who took the castle last summer. He said he had been looking for it everywhere."

Lord Shortlands clutched for support at a chair. He was conscious of a feeling that it was very hard that a man with a high blood pressure should be subjected to this kind of thing. He could not forget that it was the death by apoplectic stroke of his uncle Gervase that had enabled him to succeed to the title.

"Spink said that?"

"Yes."

Lord Shortlands suddenly came to life.

"It's a ramp!" he cried passionately.

Every instinct told him that Mervyn Spink's story was a tissue or, putting it another way, a farrago of falsehood. Do Americans who take castles for summers give butlers stamp albums? Of course they don't. They haven't any, to start with, and if they have they don't give them away. What on earth would they give them away for? And who ever heard of a philatelist butler? Preposterous, felt Lord Shortlands.

"It's a bally try-on!" he thundered.

"I don't know what you mean. Spink tells me he has collected stamps since he was a boy, and I see nothing improbable in his story. Anyhow, he claims the thing."

"I don't care if he claims it till he's blue in the face."

Lady Adela's eyebrows rose.

"Well, really, Father, I can't see why you are making such a fuss."

"Fuss!"

"I mean, it isn't as if there were any chance of it being yours. And it must belong to somebody, so why not Spink? No doubt Mr. Rossiter did give it to him. It's just the sort of thing an American would do."

"Well, I strongly protest against your handing this stamp over to Spink till he produces Rossiter. His statement is that Rossiter gave it to him. All right, then, let him produce Rossiter."

"He's going to."

A faint gleam of hope illumined Lord Shortlands' darkness.

"Then you haven't given it to him?"

"Naturally not on his unsupported word. He says he thinks Mr. Rossiter is in London, and he has gone up to try to find him. In the meantime the stamp will be quite safe. I have got it locked away. Ah, tea," said Lady Adela welcomingly.

Lord Shortlands, though generally fond of his cup at this hour, exhibited no corresponding elation. He was staring before him with unseeing eyes and wishing that the kindly Aloysius McGuffy could have been at his side, to start shaking up six or seven of his justly famous Specials.

10

A SONG on his lips and the sparkle of triumph in his eye, opening his throttle gaily and tooting his horn with a carefree exuberance, Mervyn Spink sped home from London on his motorcycle, his air that of a man who sits on top of the world. Only the necessity of keeping both hands on the handle bars prevented him patting himself on the back.

The world was looking very beautiful to Mervyn Spink. He gazed at the blue skies, the fleecy clouds, the fluttering butterflies, the hedgerows bright with wild flowers and the spreading fields of wheat that took on the appearance of velvet rubbed the wrong way as the light breeze played over them, and approved of them all, in the order named. He did not actually sing "tra-la," but it was a very close thing. In the whole of Kent at that moment you could not have found a more cheerio butler.

The sight of Lord Shortlands standing in the road outside the castle gates increased his feeling of *bien-être*. He had been looking forward to meeting Lord Shortlands. A nasty knock, he felt correctly, this stamp sequence would be for his rival, and he wished to gloat on his despair. Mervyn Spink was a man who believed in treating rivals rough.

He braked his motorcycle, removed trousers seat from saddle and alighted. "Ah, Shortlands," he said.

Lord Shortlands started. His face, already mauve, took on a deeper shade, and his eyes seemed to be suspended at the end of stalks, like those of a snail or prawn.

"How dare you address me like that?"

A frown marred the alabaster smoothness of Mervyn Spink's brow.

"We'd better get this settled once and for all, Shortlands," he said coldly. "Want me to call you 'm'lord,' do you? Well, if we were the other side of those gates, I'd call you 'm'lord' till my eyes bubbled. But when I'm off duty and we meet in the public highway, I am no longer your employee."

It was a nice piece of reasoning, well expressed, but Lord Shortlands continued dissatisfied.

"Yes, you are."

"No, I'm not. We're man and man. If you think otherwise, you can complain to her ladyship. It'll mean telling her the whole story and explaining just how matters stand between us, but I don't mind that, if you don't."

The purple flush died out of Lord Shortlands' face. A man with his consistently high blood pressure could not actually blench, but he came reasonably near to doing so. The picture those words had conjured up had made him feel as if his spine had been suddenly removed and the vacancy filled with gelatine. His manner, which had had perhaps almost too much in it of the mediaeval earl dealing with a scurvy knave or varlet, changed, taking on the suggestion of a cushat dove calling to its mate.

"Well, never mind, Spink. Quite all right. The point is—er—immaterial."

"Okey-doke, Shortlands."

"Just a technicality. And now what's all this about that stamp?"

"What about it?"

"My daughter tells me you've claimed it."

"I have."

"Says you say you were given it by this fellow Rossiter. I don't believe it," cried Lord Shortlands, recapturing something of the first fine careless rapture of his original manner. The spirit of his fighting ancestors was once more strong within him, and if he had been Lady Adela Topping herself he could not have been more resolutely determined to stand no nonsense. "It's a bally swindle!"

It seemed for an instant as though Mervyn Spink, in defiance of the first rule laid down by the Butlers Guild for the guidance of its members, was about to laugh. But he managed to check the impulse and to substitute for the guffaw a quiet smile.

"Listen," he said. "I'll tell you something."

Until now we have seen this butler only at his best, a skilful carrier of malted milk and a man whose appearance would have shed lustre on a ducal home; his only fault, as far as we have been able to ascertain, the venial one of liking to have an occasional ten bob on the two-thirty. He now strips the mask from his face and stands revealed as the modern Machiavelli he was. The typewriter falters as it records his words, and even Lord Shortlands, though he had known all along that dirty work was in progress in some form or other, found himself stunned and amazed.

"You're quite right, Shortlands. It *is* a bally swindle, and what are you going to do about it? Nothing. Because you can't."

He was right, and Lord Shortlands realized it. However bally the swindle, he could make no move to cope with it. His fear of his daughter Adela held him gagged and bound. Tortured by the humiliating sense of impotence, he uttered a wordless sound at the back of his throat. Augustus Robb, in a similar situation, would have said "Coo!" Both would have meant the same thing.

"Young Rossiter didn't give me that album. I've never seen the thing in my life. But I've a nephew on the stage who plays character parts and doesn't stick at much, so long as he knows there's something in it for him. Well, he's going to play another character part tomorrow. I've just been to see him, and we've fixed everything up."

He paused for an instant, his face darkening a little. The only flaw in his contentment was the lurking feeling that a shade more energy on his part during the initial bargaining might have resulted in his nephew closing for fifty quid, instead of sticking out, as he had done, for ten down and a further ninety on the completion of the deal. But a man about to collect fifteen hundred can afford to be spacious, and he had brightened again when he resumed his remarks.

"I'm telling her ladyship that I had the good luck to catch Mr. Rossiter on the eve of his departure for France, and that he'll be delighted to stop off at the castle tomorrow on his way to Dover and substantiate my claim. You'll be seeing him about lunch time. So there you are. All nice and smooth, I call it."

Lord Shortlands did not reply. He turned and started to totter home. Mervyn Spink wheeled his motorcycle beside him.

"Beautiful evening, m'lord," he said deferentially. They had passed through the gates. "Weather keeps up nicely, m'lord."

He contemplated his companion's face with all the pleasure he had known he was going to feel at the sight of it. Lord Shortlands was looking like Stanwood Cobbold on the morning after. Transferring his gaze to the local flora and fauna, Mervyn Spink felt more uplifted than ever. He drew satisfaction from the lilac bush that blossomed to the left and from the bird with the red beak which had settled on a tree to the right. And perhaps the best proof of his exalted frame of mind is that he found something exhilarating even in the appearance of Cosmo Blair, the playwright, who came towards them at the moment, smoking a cigarette. For this gifted man, though the author of half a dozen dramas which had brought him pots of money both in England and in the United States, was in no sense an eyeful. The normal eye, resting upon Cosmo Blair, was apt to blink and turn away.

Successful playwrights as a class are slender. Vertically there may be quite a lot, though not more than their admirers desire, of George S. Kaufman and, in a greater degree, of Robert E. Sherwood, but you can hardly see them sideways. Cosmo Blair struck a new note by being short and tubby. Lord Shortlands had called him a potbellied perisher; and though the fifth earl was prejudiced, his young guest having an annoying habit of addressing him as "My dear Shortlands" and contradicting every second thing he said, it must be admitted that there was something in the charge.

He scanned the pair through a glistening eyeglass.

"Ah, my dear Shortlands."

Lord Shortlands uttered a sound like a cinnamon bear with a bone in its throat.

"Ah, Spink."

"Good evening, sir."

"Been out for a ride?"

"Yes, sir."

"Nice evening."

"Extremely, sir."

"Oh, by the way, Spink," said Cosmo Blair.

He, too, was feeling serene and contented. There had been crumpets for tea, dripping with butter, as he liked them, and after tea he had read his second act again to Clare. Her outspoken admiration had been very pleasant to him, inducing a sensation of benevolence towards his fellows, and this benevolence had been increased by the beauty of the spring evening. He looked at Mervyn Spink and was glad that it was within his power to do him a kindness.

"By the way, Spink, you remember asking me the other day to do something for that nephew of yours, the actor? Roland Winter, didn't you say his name was?"

"Roland Winter, yes, sir."

"Is he fixed up just now?"

"No, sir. He is at present at liberty."

"Well, I've got something for him in this thing I'm writing. It's an odd thing, my dear Shortlands," said Cosmo Blair, drawing at his cigarette, "how one forgets people. This nephew of our good friend Spink. I've been trying ever since he spoke to me to think why the name Roland Winter was familiar, and I only remembered this afternoon. I had him in a show of mine last year, and he was quite——"

He had been about to say "good," but the word changed on his lips to a startled exclamation. The motorcycle had fallen from Mervyn Spink's nerveless fingers with a crash.

"You know my nephew, sir?"

"Oh, rather. Tall, thin chap with a slight squint and a funny-shaped mouth. Red hair hasn't he got? Yes, now I recall it, red hair. Well, tell him to go and see Charlie Cockburn at the St. George's. I'll drop Charlie a line."

Cosmo Blair went on his way, conscious of a good deed done, and Lord Shortlands uttered an explosive "Ha!"

"Now how about it, you Spink?" he cried exultantly.

Mervyn Spink did not speak. His face was very sad.

"If this blighter Blair knows your blighted nephew so well," proceeded Lord Shortlands, elaborating his point and making it clear to the meanest intelligence, "how the dickens do you propose to introduce him into the place as this blighted Rossiter? You're pipped, Spink. Your whole vile scheme strikes a snag."

Mervyn Spink did not deign to reply. Sombrely he picked up the motorcycle, sombrely mounted it, sombrely opened the throttle and rode off in the direction of the village.

His heart, so light before, was heavy now. He looked at the blue skies and fleecy clouds and took an instant dislike to them. He resented the presence of the fluttering butterflies. The fields of wheat jarred upon his eye. There are few things which more speedily modify the Pippa Passes outlook on life of a butler who has been congratulating himself on having formulated a cast-iron scheme for putting large sums of money in his pocket than the discovery that that scheme, through the most capricious and unforeseeable of chances, has come unstuck.

"Hell!" mused Mervyn Spink, brooding darkly.

At the post office he alighted and dispatched a telegram to his nephew, briefly cancelling all arrangements; then rode sombrely back to the castle and sought refuge in the seclusion of his pantry.

He had been sitting there for some little time, feeling with the poet that of all sad words of tongue or pen the saddest are these—It might have been, when the bell of Lady Adela's room rang.

Bells must be answered, though the heart is aching.

"M'lady?"

"Oh, Spink, Mr. Cobbold has arrived. Will you go and see that he has everything he wants."

"Very good, m'lady."

"Did you find Mr. Rossiter?"

"No, m'lady. I regret to say that the gentleman is not at the moment in London."

"But you will be able to get in touch with him?"

"No doubt, m'lady."

Mervyn Spink departed on his errand. He experienced no soaring of the spirits at the prospect of renewing his acquaintance with one with whom his relations had once been cordial. During their association in Mr. Ellery Cobbold's palatial home at Great Neck he had found Stanwood a pleasant and congenial companion, practically a buddy; for Stanwood, a gregarious soul, had often dropped in on him for a drink and a chat and on several occasions they had attended prize fights together.

But as he approached the Blue Room his heart was still heavy.

11

IN THE Blue Room, Mike, dressed and ready for dinner, was thoroughly approving of his quarters. To Lord Shortlands, that modern Prisoner of Chillon, everything connected with Beevor Castle might be the abomination of desolation, but to Mike, coming to it with a fresh eye, the Blue Room seemed about as satisfactory a Blue Room as a man could wish for.

Its windows, as his hostess had stated, looked out upon the rose garden and beyond it on a pleasing panorama of woods and fields, rooks cawing in the former, rabbits moving briskly to and fro in the latter, and its interior was comfortable, even luxurious. He particularly like the easy chair. Too often in

English country-house bedrooms the guest finds himself fobbed off with something hard and upright constructed to the order of some remote ancestor by the upholsterer of the Spanish Inquisition, but this one invited repose.

He was reclining in it with his feet on the table, thinking long, lingering thoughts of Terry, when his reverie was interrupted. The door had opened, to reveal a handsome stranger, from his dress and deportment apparently the castle butler. He eyed him with interest. This, then, was the Spink whose rivalry had caused Lord Shortlands so much concern, the cork-drawing Adonis who had threatened at one time to play the Serpent in his lordship's Garden of Eden. He could understand how any earl might have feared such a man.

"Good evening, sir."

"Good evening."

On Spink's mobile lips, in spite of his heaviness of heart, there had appeared a faint, respectful smile; the smile of a butler who sees that an amusing blunder has been made by those higher up. G.H.Q. had told him that he would find Stanwood Cobbold in the Blue Room. This was unquestionably the Blue Room, but the man before him was not his old buddy.

"Excuse me, sir, I must have misunderstood her ladyship. I supposed her to say that Mr. Cobbold was occupying this apartment."

"I'm Mr. Cobbold."

Butlers do not start. Spink merely rippled a little.

"Mr. Stanwood Cobbold?"

"That's right."

There was a short pause. Then Spink said, "Indeed, sir?"

It is a very unintelligent butler who, expecting to see in a Blue Room a Stanwood Cobbold with a face like a hippopotamus and finding himself confronted by one with a face like a Greek god, does not suspect that there is funny business afoot. To Spink, who was highly intelligent, the very air seemed thick with funny business, and his eye grew stern and bleak.

And simultaneously there came to him, for his was a mind that worked like a steel spring where his financial interests were concerned, the thought that here was where he might be able to do something towards repairing the ruin of his fortunes. Young men who come to castles calling themselves Stanwood Cobbold when they are not Stanwood Cobbold not do so without an important reason, and a butler who knows their secret may reasonably expect to exact the price of his silence. It seemed to Mervyn Spink that things were looking up.

"I wonder if I might make an observation, sir?"

"Go ahead."

"I would merely wish to remark that I know Mr. Stanwood Cobbold extremely well."

Mike saw that he had made a mistake about that easy chair. He had supposed it comfortable, and in reality it was red hot. He left it quickly.

"You do?"

"Yes, sir. I was for nearly a year in the employment of Mr. Cobbold senior at his home in Great Neck, Long Island, and saw Mr. Stanwood daily."

Mike ran a finger around the inside of his collar. It had seemed, when he put it on, a well-fitting collar, but now it felt unpleasantly tight.

"This opens a new line of thought," he said.

"I fancied it might, sir."

"A new and very interesting line of thought."

"Yes, sir."

The fact that he was still calling him "sir" suggested to Mike that the other had not, as a lesser butler would have done, leaped immediately to the conclusion that he was visiting Beevor Castle in the hope of making away with the spoons. No doubt some subtle something in his appearance, some touch of natural dignity in his bearing, had caused the man to reject what on the face of it would have been the obvious explanation of his presence.

This encouraged him. He would have been the last person to dispute that the situation still presented certain embarrassing features, but the thought came to him, remembering that all men have their price, that it might be possible by exploring every avenue to find some formula that would be acceptable to both parties. There were, in short, in the Blue Room at that moment two minds with but a single thought.

He proceeded to try to pave the way to an understanding.

"Your name is Spink, I believe?"

"Yes, sir."

"Then sit down at this table, Spink. It is, you will notice, a round table, always essential on these occasions. Now, first and foremost, Spink, we must keep quite cool."

"Yes, sir."

"We must not lose our heads. We must get together over the round table and thresh this thing out quietly and calmly in a spirit of mutual co-operation."

"Yes, sir."

"I will begin by conceding a point. I am not Stanwood Cobbold."

"No, sir."

"Very good. We make progress. The question now arises, Who *am* I? Any suggestions?"

"I am not aware of your surname, sir, but I would hazard the conjecture that your first name is Michael."

"This is uncanny."

"I would also hazard the conjecture that you are a friend of Mr. Stanwood, and that you obtained his permission to impersonate him here because you desired to be in the society of Lady Teresa."

"How do you do it? With mirrors?"

Mervyn Spink smiled gently.

"A letter recently arrived for Lady Teresa, couched in impassioned terms and signed 'Mike.'"

"Good God! She didn't show it around?"

"No, sir. A member of the domestic staff came upon it while accidentally glancing through the contents of her ladyship's dressing table and, having perused it, reported its substance to the Servants Hall."

A pretty blush suffused Mike's cheeks. He ground his teeth a little.

"He did, did he?"

"She, sir. It was one of the maids. I rebuked her."

"You didn't wring her neck?"

"That did not occur to me, sir."

"You missed a bet. Did she enjoy it?"

"No, sir. I chided her severely."

"I mean the letter. It entertained her?"

"Yes, sir."

"Fine. One likes to feel that one's letters have given pleasure. Augustus Robb thought it good, too. He looked it over before it left."

"Sir?"

"A London critic. You haven't met him. If you ever do, introduce him to the maid. They will want to swap views on my literary style. Well, seeing that you are so well informed, I will admit that I did come here for the reason you suggest. So where do we go from here? My name, by the way, is Cardinal."

"I have often heard Mr. Stanwood speak of you, sir."

"Very likely. We're old friends. And you're right in supposing that I have his full sympathy and approval in the venture which I have undertaken. He was all for it."

"It is the attitude which one would have expected in Mr. Stanwood. He has a big heart and would, of course, do all that lay in his power to further a friend's romance. But you were saying, sir——"

"Yes, let's get back to it. Where do we go from here?"

"Sir?"

"Come, come, Spink, use the bean. The first essential, as you must see for yourself, is the ensuring of your silence. One word from you to the lady up top, and I am undone."

"Yes, sir."

"How is this silence to be contrived?"

"Well, sir, if I might make the suggestion——"

"You have the floor."

"—I would propose that we came to some amicable arrangement."

"Of a financial nature?"

"Precisely, sir."

Mike drew a breath of relief. It was as he had hoped. They had explored every avenue, and here came the formula, hot from the griddle. He beamed upon Mervyn Spink, as the inhabitants of Ghent no doubt beamed upon the men who brought the good news to that city from Aix.

"Now you're tooting. Now the fog of misundertanding is dissipated and we can talk turkey. How do you react to the idea of a tenner?"

"Unenthusiastically, sir."

"Ten pounds is nice sugar, Spink."

"Inferior to two hundred, sir."

There was a pause. Mike laughed.

"Funny how one's ears play one tricks. It sounded to me for a moment as though you had said two hundred. Something to do with the acoustics, no doubt."

"That was the sum I mentioned, sir."

Mike clicked his tongue.

"Now listen, Spink. Your comedy is good, and we all enjoy a little wholesome fun, but we mustn't waste time. Twenty was what you meant, wasn't it?"

"No, sir. Two hundred. Mr. Stanwood has frequently spoken of the large income which you make in the exercise of your profession in Hollywood, and I am sure you will feel that two hundred pounds is a small price to pay for the privilege of making an extended stay at the castle. Judging by the tone of your letter."

"I wouldn't harp too much on that letter. I might plug you in the eye."

"Very good, sir."

"Already I feel a strong urge in that direction."

"I am sorry to hear that, sir."

"Two hundred pounds!"

"I require the sum for a particular purpose, sir."

"I know."

"His lordship has confided in you, sir?"

"From soup to nuts. And that's another thing that gives me pause. Apart from the disagreeableness of having to cough up two hundred pounds, there is the Lord Shortlands angle. This is going to be tough on him. It will dish his hopes and dreams."

"Into each life some rain must fall."

"Eh?"

"I was merey wishing to indicate, sir, that you cannot make an omelette without breaking eggs."

"Is this time to talk of omelettes, Spink? You realize, of course, that you are a lop-eared blackmailer?"

"Yes, sir."

"And you don't shudder?"

"No, sir."

"Then there is no more to be said."

"You will find pen and ink on the writing table, sir."

Mike made his way slowly to the writing table, and took pen in hand.

"Well, it's a comfort to think that this sort of thing is bound to grow on you and that eventually you will get it in the neck," he said. "I can read your future like a book. Before long another opportunity of stinging some member of the general public will present itself, and you will be unable to resist it. And after that you will go on and on, sinking deeper and deeper into the mire of crime. The appetite grows by what it feeds on, Spink."

"Yes, sir."

"You don't feel like pulling up while there is yet time?"

"No, sir."

"Just as you say. Let us hurry on, then, to the melancholy end. You will, as I say, go on and on, blackmailing the populace like nobody's business, until one day you make that false step which they all make and—bingo!—into the dock for yours, with the judge saying 'Well, prisoner at the bar, it's been nice knowing you——' And then off to the cooler for an exemplary sentence. I shall come on visiting days and make faces at you through the bars."

"I shall be delighted to receive you, sir."

"You won't be when you see the faces. What's the date?"

"The twelfth of May, sir."

"And your first name?"

"Mervyn, sir."

"A sweet name."

"So my mother felt, sir."

"Can you think of your mother at a moment when you are gouging a stranger, scarcely an acquaintance, for two hundred of the best and brightest?"

"Yes, sir."

"Ponder well, Spink. She is looking down on you from heaven——"

"She lives in East Dulwich, sir."

"Well, from East Dulwich, then. It makes no difference to my argument. She is looking down on you from East Dulwich——"

"If you would kindly make the check open——"

"All right. Here you are."

"Thank you, sir."

"Yes, she is ——"

Mike paused. Somebody had knocked on the door.

"Come in."

Lady Adela entered.

"I thought I would come and see if you were all right, Mr. Cobbold," said Lady Adela brightly. "Are you quite comfortable?"

"Very, thank you."

"I suppose you and Spink have been having a talk about old times? He tells me he used to be your father's butler. Did you find Mr. Cobbold just the same, Spink?"

There were things about Mervyn Spink which many people did not like, but he always gave value for money.

"Just the same, m'lady. The sight of him brought back many happy memories. Mr. Stanwood was always very kind to me during the period of my sojourn in the United States of America, m'lady."

From down the corridor came the plaintive note of a husband in distress.

Desborough Topping, hampered by lumbago, was experiencing a difficulty in tying his tie. Like a tigress hearing the cry of her cub, Lady Adela hurried from the room.

"Thank you, Spink," said Mike.

"Not all, sir."

"That handsome testimonial should fix me nicely."

"Yes, sir."

"I wish there was something I could do for you in return."

Mervyn Spink smiled benevolently.

"You have done something, sir."

"The check? You feel satisfied?"

"Entirely, sir."

"Well, that's fine. but you're easily pleased. That check's no good. You will have noted that it is signed 'Michael Cardinal,' which will cause the bank to sling it back at you like a bouncer ejecting a cash customer. For you were mistaken in supposing Michael to be my Christian name. It is Mycroft, like Sherlock Holmes's brother, and that is my official signature. You see what I mean?"

Mervyn Spink reeled. His clean-cut face twisted. If he had had a moustache, he would have looked like a baffled baronet.

"I'll go straight to her ladyship——"

"And tell her that you were mistaken in stating that I was the Stanwood Cobbold who was so kind to you during the period of your sojourn in the United States of America? I wouldn't. It would mean a good deal of tedious explaining. No, no, I think we may look on the incident as closed. This is a glad day for your mother, Spink. The son she loves has been saved from the perpetration of a crime at which her gentle spirit would have shuddered. If you ask me," said Mike, "my bet is that she'll go singing about East Dulwich."

12

LORD SHORTLANDS was beginning to perk up.

For a father whose daughter treats him as a problem child, and is inclined at the slightest offense to stand him in the corner and stop his pocket money, it must always be a matter of extreme delicacy and danger to introduce into that daughter's home a changeling in place of the guest she is expecting to entertain, and during the early stages of Mike's stay at Beevor Castle the fifth earl, fully appreciating this, had run the gamut of the emotions.

At first fear had reigned supreme, causing him to start at sudden noises and to understand with a ghastly clarity what must have been the feelings of that

Damocles of whom he had read in his school days. Then gradually hope had come stealing in, stiffening the jellied backbone. But it was only on the evening of the third day, as he sat in his study before dinner prodding the ribs of his dog Whiskers, happily cured of his recent indisposition, that he was able to view the position of affairs with any real confidence. It seemed to him that, as far as the great imposture was concerned, things had settled down nicely.

With regard to the activities of the viper Spink, he continued to feel apprehensive. So far, that snakelike man had been foiled, but he feared for the future. Butlers, he knew, though crushed to earth, will rise again, and he shuddered to think how nearly Mervyn Spink had triumphed already. If it had not been for the quick brainwork of his young friend Cardinal, he realized, this would have been a big week end for vipers.

Mike's description of his duel with Mervyn Spink had thrilled Lord Shortlands to the core. He had no words to express his admiration for the splendid qualities which this beardless youth had displayed in circumstances which might well have proved too much for a veteran strategist, and more and more did it seem to him inexplicable that his daughter Terry, wooed by such a suiter, should not scoop him in with a cry of joy and grapple him to her soul with hoops of steel.

He looked at Terry meditatively, planning the word in season. She had come in a few moments before and was assisting him in his kindly attentions to the dog Whiskers by tickling the latter's stomach.

"Terry," he said.

But before he could proceed further the door had opened and Mike was standing on the threshold.

A gentle glow permeated Mike's system as he surveyed the charming domestic scene. His future wife, his future father-in-law and his future dog by marriage all on the spot and doing their stuff before him. What could be sweeter? It pained him to have to break up the pretty picture, but he had come to impart news, and it must be imparted.

"Good evening, good evening, Lord Shortlands," he said. "Though I'm not sure I like that 'Lord Shortlands.' If you're going to be my father-in-law, I really ought to begin calling you something not quite so formal. 'Pop' or 'Dad' or something. In this connection, I find Desborough Topping a disappointing guide. I had hoped to pick up some hints from him, but he doesn't seem to call you anything, except occasionally 'Er.' I don't like 'Er.'"

"Adela wanted Desborough to call Shorty 'Pater,'" said Terry.

"I don't like 'Pater,' either."

"Nor did Desborough. It was too much for him. So now he just coughs."

"Coughing should be well within my scope."

Lord Shortlands had a better idea.

"Call me 'Shorty,' as Terry does."

"You solve the whole difficulty," said Mike gratefully. "I doubt if coughing would have been really satisfactory. In constant association with a roupy son-in-law, a father-in-law's love falters and dies. Too tedious, always having to be passing the lozenges. Well, Shorty, you are doubtless wondering what brings me here, intruding on your privacy."

"My dear fellow!"

"Intruding, I repeat. No need to tell me I am butting in. But the fact is, I bring news. And not too good news, I'm afraid. Hang on to your chair."

In spite of the fact that his mind, such as it was, was a good deal easier than it had been, it took very little to alarm Lord Shortlands nowadays. At these ominous words he quivered like a blancmange and, as Mike had advised, clutched the arms of his chair in a fevered grip.

"Has Adela found out?" he gasped.

"No, no, no. Not quite so bad as that. It has to do with Stanwood Cobbold. I regret to have to inform you that dear old Stanwood is in our midst."

As far as a man can reel who is seated in an armchair, Lord Shortlands reeled.

"You don't mean that?"

"I do. Stanwood is here. Himself. Not a picture."

Terry squeaked.

"Here in the house?"

"Not actually in the house, no. He is at present infesting the local inn. He sent me a note from there this afternoon, asking me to go and confer with him. But he speaks of paying us a visit."

The dog Whiskers indicated with a gesture that there was still an area of his person which had not been attended to, but Lord Shortlands was in no mood now for massaging dogs.

"My God! He'll meet Adela!"

Mike said that that was precisely the thought which he, too, found disturbing.

"And if he does, and she asks him who he is, you can bet that his instant reply will be 'Stanwood Cobbold, ma'am.' He would never let slip such a gorgeous opportunity of spilling the beans. So I did my best to make him see how essential it was that he should remain at the inn and not move a step in this direction. I assured him that the finest brains at the castle would be strained to their utmost capacity to find a solution for his problem. You see, what has happened is that his father has cabled telling him to send along a number of photographs of the interior of the house with himself prominently displayed in the foreground."

"Good God!"

"The cable apparently arrived the day we left London, and Stanwood has been pondering ever since on what was to be done about it. Last night he got the bright idea that if he came down here, I would be able to sneak him into the place in the early morning and act as his photographer. He has brought a camera."

Lord Shortlands writhed like a wounded snake, and Terry squeaked again.

"The early morning?" moaned Lord Shortlands. "Fatal!"

"The very worst time," agreed Terry. "The place will be seething with housemaids——"

"Who'll take him for a burglar——"

"And scream——"

"Thus bringing Lady Adela to the spot with her foot in her hand and putting us right in the soup," said Mike. "That was the very picture that rose before my eyes when he outlined the scheme. But cheer up. There's nothing to be worried about."

It was a well-intentioned remark, but Terry appeared to take exception to it. Her squeak this time was one of justifiable indignation, and provoked a thoughtful comment from Mike.

"Tell me," he said. "How do you manage to produce that extraordinary sound? It's like a basketful of puppies. I wouldn't have thought the human voice could have done it."

Terry was not to be lured into a discussion on voice production.

"What do you mean by scaring us stiff like that, and then saying there's nothing to be worried about?"

"There isn't. Have I ever let you down?"

"You've never had the chance."

"No, that's true. But I should have thought you would have realized by this time that there is no am-parce so sticky that the Cardinal brain cannot make it play ball. I have the situation well in hand."

"You haven't thought of something?"

"Of course I've thought of something."

"Then I think you might have told us before, instead of giving us heart failure. Shorty has high blood pressure."

"Very high," said Lord Shortlands. "Runs in the family."

Mike saw their point.

"Yes. I suppose you're right. I was to blame. I don't know if you've noticed that I have a rather unpleasant habit of painting a setup in the darkest colours in order to make the joy bells, when they ring, sound louder. It has got me a good deal disliked."

"I don't wonder."

"It's the artist in me. I have to play for Suspense. But you are waiting for the low-down. Here it comes. Is it not a fact that on Saturday afternoons throughout the spring and summer months this historic joint is thrown open to the general public on payment of an entrance fee of a bob a nob?"

"Why, of course!"

"Don't say 'of course' in that light way. You wouldn't have thought of it in a million years."

"Stanwood can come with the crowd——"

"Complete with camera."

"He can get all the photographs he wants."

"Without incurring the least suspicion."

"But how about Spink? He shows them round."

"Disregard Spink. He can't do a thing. We have the Indian sign on him. Spink is as the dust beneath our chariot wheels."

Terry drew a deep breath.

"You know, you're rather wonderful."

"Why 'rather'?"

"Have you told Stanwood?"

"Not yet. The brain wave came after I had left him. I propose to look in on him tomorrow morning and set his mind at rest. He seemed a little feverish when we parted. That's the trouble with Stanwood. He worries. He lets things prey on his mind. And now ought we not to be making our way to the drawing room? I should imagine that your sister Adela is a woman who throws her weight about a good deal if people are late for dinner."

Lord Shortlands started.

"Has the gong gone?"

"Not yet. But it's past eight."

"Come on, come on, come on!" cried Lord Shortlands, stirred to his depths, and was out of the room in two impressive leaps.

Mike and Terry followed more slowly.

"Did you know," said Mike, "that a flea one twelfth of an inch long, weighing one eighty thousandth of an ounce, can broad-jump thirteen inches?"

"No," said Terry.

"A fact, I believe. Watching your father brought it to my mind. He's very agile."

"Well, you scared him. He's frightened to death of Adela."

"I don't blame him. If the Cardinals knew what fear is, I should be frightened of her myself. As hard an egg as ever stepped out of the saucepan."

"You ought to see her doing her imitation of an angry headmistress."

"Well worth watching, I imagine. Odd how different sisters can be. I can't imagine you scaring anyone. Yours is a beautiful nature: kind, sweet, gentle, dovelike, the very type of nature that one wants to have around the house. Will you marry me?"

"No."

"I think you're wrong. One of these days, when we are walking down the aisle together, with the choir singing 'The Voice That Breathed o'er Eden,' I shall remind you of this. 'Aha!' I shall say. 'Who said she wouldn't marry me?' That'll make you look silly."

They caught Lord Shortlands up at the drawing-room door, and soothed him into something resembling calm. The gong, they pointed out, is the acid test as to whether you are in time for or late for dinner, and the gong had not yet sounded.

So firmly based on reason was their argument that the fifth earl was able to enter the room with almost a swagger. It subsided a little as he saw that they were the last arrivals, but he still maintained a fairly firm front.

"Hullo, hullo," he said. "Dinner's a bit late, isn't it?"

There was no frown on Lady Adela's face. She appeared quite amiable.

"Yes," she said. "I told Spink to put it back ten minutes. We're waiting for Mr. Rossiter."

At the moment of his entry Lord Shortlands had paused at an occasional table and picked up a china ornament, in order to fortify his courage by fiddling with it. At these words, it slipped from his grasp, crashing to ruin on the parquet floor.

"Rossiter!"

"Yes. I wish you wouldn't break things, Father."

At another moment Lord Shortlands would have wilted at the displeasure in his daughter's voice, and would probably have thrown together some hasty story about somebody having joggled his arm. But now he had no thought for such minor matters.

"Rossiter?" he cried. "How do you mean Rossiter?"

"Apparently Mr. Rossiter has been staying at the inn in the village for the fishing. Quite a coincidence that he should have been there just when Spink was trying to find him. Spink happened to go to the inn this evening, and met him. Of course I asked him to come to the castle."

The door opened, and Mervyn Spink appeared. His eye, as it rested upon Lord Shortlands, had in it a lurking gleam.

"Mr. Rossiter," he announced.

Stanwood Cobbold walked into the room, tripping over a rug, as was his habit when he entered rooms.

13

"IT's NO good looking to me for guidance, my dear Shorty," said Mike. "I'm sunk."

He spoke in response to a certain wild appeal in the other's eye, which he had just caught. Dinner was over, and a council of three had met in Lord Shortlands' study to discuss the latest development. Its president was pacing the floor with his hands behind his back, occasionally removing them in order to gesticulate in a rather frenzied manner. Mike and Terry, the remaining delegates to the conference, were seated. The dog Whiskers was present, but took no part in the proceedings. He was trying to locate a flea which had been causing him some annoyance.

"Sunk," Mike repeated. "I am stunned, bewildered and at a loss. *Bouleversé*, if you would like a little French."

Lord Shortlands groaned and flung his arms up like a despairing semaphore. He was thinking of Mervyn Spink's face as he had seen it during the recent meal. For the most part, as befitted a butler performing his official duties, it had been impassive; but once, on Lady Adela asking Mr. Rossiter if he remembered having given her head of staff his stamp album and Mr. Rossiter who seemed a nervous young man, inclined to start violently and try to swallow his uvula when spoken to, upsetting his glass and replying "Oh, sure," it had softened into a quick smile. And in the gesture with which the fellow had offered him the potatoes there had been something virtually tantamount to a dig in the ribs. It had gone through Lord Shortlands like a knife through butter.

"No," said Mike, proceeding, "it's no use my trying to pretend that I am hep. I am not hep. What is all this Rossiter stuff?"

Terry clicked her tongue impatiently, like a worried schoolmistress with a child of slow intelligence.

"Weren't you listening when Adela said that to Stanwood at dinner?"

"Said what?"

"About the album."

"I'm sorry. I missed it."

"Well, Spink is pretending that the album was given him by the son of some Americans named Rossiter who took the castle last summer——"

"The viper!" interpolated Lord Shortlands.

"—and somehow, I can't imagine how, he has got Stanwood to say he is Mr. Rossiter. And when Adela asked him if had given Spink the album, he said he had. Now do you see?"

Mike whistled. Lord Shortlands, whose nervous system had been greatly impaired by the night's happenings, asked him not to whistle, and Mike said that he would endeavour not to do so in future but that this particular whistle had been forced from him by the intense stickiness of the situation.

"I should say I do see," he said. "Has Spink got the stamp, then?"

"No, not yet. He came to the drawing room after dinner and asked for it, but Adela said that it would be much better for her to keep it till Desborough was well enough to go to London. She said he would be able to get a better price than Spink could, because he knows the right people to go to."

"Very shrewd."

"Spink argued a bit, but Adela squashed him."

"Good for her. Well, this is fine. This gives us a respite."

Lord Shortlands was not to be comforted.

"What's the good of a respite? What the dickens does it matter if the fellow gets the thing tonight or the day after tomorrow?"

"The delay, my dear Shorty, is of the utmost importance. It means everything. I have a plan."

"He has a plan," said Terry.

"I have a plan," said Mike. "No need to be surprised. You know my lightning brain. In the interval which elapses before Desborough Topping's lumbago slackens its grip and he is able to travel, we will act. Boys and girls, we are going to pinch this stamp."

"What!"

"Pinch it," said Mike firmly. "Swipe it. Obtain possession of it by strong-arm tactics. Up against this dark and subtle butler, we cannot afford to be too nice in our methods. He has raised the banner with the strange device 'Anything goes.' Let that slogan be ours."

Terry was a girl who believed in giving praise where praise was due, even though there was the risk that such praise might increase the tendency of its recipient to get above himself.

"What a splendid idea. How nice it is to come across someone with a really criminal mind. I suppose this is one of those hidden depths of yours that you were speaking of?"

"That's right. I'm full of them."

Lord Shortlands' conscience appeared to be less elastic than his daughter's. Where she had applauded, he fingered the chin dubiously.

"But I can't go about pinching things."

"Why not?"

"Well, dash it."

"Oh, Shorty."

"No, he's quite right," said Mike. "I see what he means. He shrinks from smirching the old escutcheon, and I honor him for his scruples. But have no qualms, my dear Shorty. In pinching this stamp you will simply be restoring it to its rightful owner. That album belongs to Terry."

Terry shook her head.

"Well meant, but no good. Shorty knows I haven't collected stamps since I was in the schoolroom."

"It was in the schoolroom that you collected this one. I was on the point of mentioning it when we were getting out of the car the day I arrived, only Shorty was so sure the thing was his that I had hadn't the heart to. Throw your mind back. A rainy afternoon eight years ago. You were sitting at the schoolroom table, covered with glue, poring over your childish collection. I entered and said 'Hello, looking at your stamps?' You came clean. Yes, you said, you were looking at your stamps. 'You don't seem to have many,' I said. 'Would you like mine?', adding that I had recently been given an album full of the dam' things as a birthday present by an uncle who wasn't abreast of affairs and didn't know that it was considered bad form at the dear old school to collect stamps. A pastime only fit for kids."

"Oh, golly. Yes, I remember now."

"I thought you would. So I wrote for it and presented it to you."

"Little knowing that it was a gold mine."

"It would have made no difference if I had known. We Cardinals are like that. Lavish to those we love. You can imagine what excellent husbands we make."

"Well, we Cobbolds have scruples about accepting gifts worth hundreds of pounds from young men who look like Caesar Romero."

"I don't look in the least like Caesar Romero. And I don't see what you can do about it. You took it."

"I can give it back."

"A happy way out of the difficulty would be to turn it over to Shorty."

"That's a wonderful idea. Yes, I'll do that. So you see the stamp does belong to you, Shorty," said Terry. "Thank the gentleman, dear."

"Thanks," said Lord Shortlands dazedly. Things were happening a little too rapidly tonight for his orderly mind, and he had the sense of having been caught up in a cyclone. He was also conscious of a lurking feeling that there was a catch somewhere, if only he could pin it down.

"You are now able," said Mike, pointing out the happy ending, "to tie a can to your spiritual struggles. Your conscience, satisfied that it is being asked to do nothing raw, can spit on its hands and charge ahead without a tremor. Or don't you agree with me?"

"Oh, quite. Oh, certainly. But——"

"Now what?"

"Well, dash it, this stamp's worth fifteen hundred pounds, Desborough says. I can't take fifteen hundred pounds from you, Terry." This was not actually the catch which Lord Shortlands was trying to pin down—that still eluded him—but it was a point that needed to be touched on. "If you could let me have two hundred as a loan——"

"Nonsense, darling. What's mine is yours."

"Well, it's extremely kind of you, my dear. I hardly know what to say."

"Mike's the one you ought to be grateful to."

"I am. His generosity is princely."

"Yes," said Mike. "What an extraordinarily fine fellow this chap Cardinal is turning out to be. But let's stick to business. The proposal before the meeting is that we pinch this stamp before Spink can get his hooks on it. Carried, unanimously, I fancy? Yes, carried unanimously. It only remains, therefore, to decide on the best means to that end. It should not be difficult. A little cunning questioning of Desborough Topping will inform us where Lady Adela is keeping the things. No doubt in the drawer of her escritoire or somewhere. Having ascertained this, we procure a stout chisel and go to it."

"But——"

"Now, don't *make* difficulties, Shorty darling," said Terry maternally. "You must see that this is the only way. I'll go and question Desborough cunningly."

She went out, and Lord Shortlands continued to exhibit evidence of the cold foot and the sagging spine. Mike looked at him solicitously.

"I still note a faint shadow on your brow, Shorty," he said. "What seems to be the trouble? Not the conscience again?"

Lord Shortlands had found the catch.

"But, my dear fellow, if Adela finds the drawer of her escritoire broken open and the stamp gone, she'll suspect me."

"Well, what do you care? You'll simply laugh at her. 'What are you going to do about it?' you will say, adding or not adding 'Huh?' according to taste. And she will bite her lip in silence."

"Silence?" said Lord Shortlands dubiously.

"She won't have a thing to say. What can she say?"

"H'm," said Lord Shortlands, and so joyless was his manner that Mike felt constrained to pat him on the back.

"Tails up," he urged.

Lord Shortlands' manner continued joyless.

"It's all very well to say 'Tails up.' I don't like it. Apart from anything else, I don't believe I could ever bring myself to break open an escritoire drawer with a chisel. *Anybody's* escritoire drawer."

"My dear Shorty, is that what's worrying you? I shall attend to that, of course."

"You will?"

"Naturally. It's young man's work."

"Well, I'm very much obliged to you."

"Not at all."

"I wish to goodness Terry would marry you. She'll never get a better husband."

"Keep telling her that. It's exactly what I've always felt. Has she given you any inkling as to what seems to be the difficulty?"

"Not the slightest."

The door opened. Terry had returned. She sat down, and Mike noticed that her manner, which had been one of radiant confidence, was now subdued. Lord Shortlands would have noticed it, too, had he been in better condition tonight for noticing things.

"Well?" said Mike.

"Well?" said Lord Shortlands.

"Well," said Terry, "I saw Desborough."

"Did you find out what you wanted?"

"I found out something I didn't want."

"Less of the mysterious stuff."

Terry sighed.

"I was only trying to break it gently. If you must have it, Desborough suspects Stanwood."

"Suspects him?" cried Lord Shortlands.

"What of?" said Mike.

"Of not being Rossiter."

"But Spink has given him the okay."

"Yes, and that has made Desborough suspect Spink, too. He thinks it's a plot. 'After all,' he said, 'what do we really know of Spink?', and he quoted authorities to show that in nine cases out of ten the butler at a country house turns out to be one of the Black Onion gang or something. I wish he hadn't read so many detective stories."

"But what on earth has made him suspect Stanwood?"

"He took him off after dinner to talk stamps, and of course Stanwood knew nothing about stamps and gave it away in the first minute. The way Desborough has figured it out is that Stanwood and Spink are working together to loot the house. What a pity it is that Stanwood looks so like something out of a crook play. I never saw anything so obviously criminal as his face during dinner."

"So what steps is he planning to take?"

"I don't know. But a step he has taken is to put the stamp in an envelope and lock it up in the safe."

There was a silence.

"In the safe?" said Mike at length.

"Yes."

"Is there a safe?"

"Yes. In the library."

"Of all silly things to have in a house! Well, this, I admit, is a development which I had not foreseen. I shall have to leave you for a while and ponder apart. You will find me in my room, if you want me. Safes, forsooth!" said Mike bitterly, and went out with knitted brow.

It was clear to him that he had here one of those brain-teasers which Sherlock Holmes used to call three-pipe problems, and he made his way to the Blue Room to get his smoking materials.

As he entered, the vast form of Stanwood Cobbold rose from the easy chair.

14

STANWOOD WAS not looking his best. Dinner, with its enforced propinquity to a hostess who had scared the daylights out of him at first sight, and the subsequent tête-à-tête with Desborough Topping had taken their toll. There had been moments in his life when, with representatives of Notre Dame and Minnesota walking about on his face or pressing the more jagged parts of their persons into his stomach, Stanwood Cobbold had experienced a certain discomfort, but nothing in his career to date had ever reduced him to such a ruin of a fine young man as the ordeal which had been thrust upon him tonight. Gazing at him, you would have said that his soul had passed through the furnace, and you would have been perfectly correct. Mike's first act, before asking any questions, was to hurry to the chest of drawers, take out a flask and press it upon his friend.

"Thanks," said Stanwood, handing it back empty. "Gosh, I needed that. I've had one hell of a time, Mike."

Mike, having satisfied the humane side of his nature, was now prepared to be stern.

"Well, you asked for it."

"Who's the little guy with the nose glasses?"

"Desborough Topping, your hostess's husband."

"He's been talking stamps to me," said Stanwood with a reminiscent shudder.

"Well, what did you think he would do? If you horn into a house pretending to be a stamp collector and that house contains another stamp collector, you must expect to be talked stamps at."

"It's the darnedest thing. I don't believe I ever met anyone before who collected stamps. I thought only sissies did. And now I don't seem to meet anyone who doesn't. Kind of a loony setup, don't you think?"

Mike was not to be diverted into an academic discussion of the looniness of the conditions prevailing at Beevor Castle.

"What the devil did you come here for? I told you to stay at the inn till you heard from me."

"Sure, I know. But I had a feeling that you weren't going to deliver. Seemed to me you had lost your grip. So when Spink came along with his proposition, I was ready to do business."

"How did you meet Spink?"

"He blew in just after you had left, and we got together. We had known each other before. We used to be buddies over on the other side. He was Father's butler."

"So he told me."

"Well, I gave him the low-down about the cable and the photographs and asked him if he had anything to suggest, and he said it was a pipe. All I had to do was to say I was this bozo Rossiter, and I was set. I would have the run of the joint, and we could fix up the photographs any time that suited me. Naturally I said Check, and he went to the phone and called Her Nibs up, and she told him to tell me to come along and join the gang."

"What did he say about the album?"

"Nothing much. Just that he wanted it."

"You bet he wanted it. There's a stamp in it worth fifteen hundred pounds."

"Gosh! Really?"

"Which belongs to Terry. Of course she can't prove it, and of course Spink,

now that you've gone and butted in, can. What you've done, you poor mutt, is
to chisel that unhappy child out of fifteen hundred smackers. A girl who has
eaten your salt."

"I don't get this."

"I'll explain it in words of one syllable," said Mike, and proceeded to do so.
When he had finished, it was plain that Stanwood was feeling the bitter
twinges of remorse. You could see the iron twisting about in his soul.

"Why the hell didn't you wise me up about this before?" he said,
aggrieved.

"How was I to know you were going to go haywire and come to the castle?"

"Let's get this straight. If Spink has this stamp old Shortlands won't be able
to marry that cook of his."

"No."

"Spink will buy her with his gold."

"Yes."

Stanwood wagged his head disapprovingly.

"No nice cook ought to marry a man like Spink. Funny I never got on to
him. I always thought him a swell guy. I used to go to his pantry, dying of
thirst, and he would dish out the lifesaver. How was I to know he was a fiend
in human shape? If a fellow's a fiend in human shape," said Stanwood, with a
good deal of justice, "he ought to act like one. Well, it's pretty clear what your
next move is, Mike, old man. Only rough stuff will meet the situation. You
want to chuck all the lessons you learned at mother's knee into the ash can
and get tough. You'll have to swipe that stamp."

"Yes, I thought of that. But it's locked up in a safe."

"Then bust the safe."

"How?"

"Why, get Augustus Robb to do it, of course."

Mike started. An awed look had come into his face; the sort of look which
members of garrisons beleaguered by savages give one another when
somebody says "Here come the United States Marines."

"Good Lord! I'd clean forgotten that Augustus used to be a burglar."

"It'll be pie to him."

"Did you bring him with you?"

"Sure."

"Stanwood, old man," said Mike in a quivering voice, "I take back all the
things I said about you. Forget that I called you a dish-faced moron."

"You didn't."

"Well, I meant to. You may have started badly, but you've certainly come
through nicely at the finish. Augustus Robb! Of course. The hour has
produced the man. It always does. Excuse me a moment. I must go and tell
the boys in the back room about this."

But as he reached the door it opened, and Terry came in, followed by Lord
Shortlands.

"We couldn't wait any longer. We had to come and see if you had ... Oh, hullo, Stanwood."

"Hello, Terry. Hiya, Lord Shortlands."

Terry's eye was cold and reproachful.

"You've made a nice mess of things, Stanwood."

"Yay. Mike's been telling me. I'm sorry."

"Too late to be sorry now," said Lord Shortlands sepulchrally.

His despondency was so marked that Mike thought it only kind to do something to raise his spirits. The method he chose was to utter a piercing "Whoopee!" It caused Lord Shortlands to leap like a gaffed salmon and Terry to quiver all over.

"Good news," he said. "Tidings of great joy. The problem is solved."

"What!"

"I have everything taped out. It turns out, after all, to be extraordinarily simple. We bust the safe."

Terry closed her eyes. She seemed in pain.

"You see, Shorty. He always finds the way. We bust the safe."

Lord Shortlands was feeling unequal to the intellectual pressure of the conversation.

"Can you—er—bust safes?"

"Myself, no. But I have influential friends. We send for Augustus Robb."

"Augustus Robb?"

"Who is this mysterious Augustus Robb you're always talking about?" asked Terry.

"My man," said Stanwood. "He's downstairs with the rest of the help."

"And before he got converted at a revival meeting," said Mike, "he used to be a burglar."

Terry's face had lost its drawn look. It had become bright and animated.

"How absolutely marvellous! Was he a good burglar?"

"One of the very best. There was a time, he gave me to understand, when the name of Robb was one to conjure with in the underworld."

"Rather a good name for a burglar, Robb."

"I told him that myself, and I thought it very quick and clever of me. Very quick and clever of you, too. If you're as good as that, we shall have many a lively duel of wit over the fireside. According to Augustus, the same crack has been made by fifty-six other people, but I don't see that that matters. You and I can't expect to be the only ones in the world with minds like rapiers."

"But if he's got religion, he'll probably have a conscience."

"We shall be able to overcome it. He will see the justice of our cause, which, of course, sticks out like a sore thumb, and, apart from that, he's a snob. He will be quite incapable of resisting an earl's appeal. Have you a coronet, Shorty?"

"Eh? Coronet? Oh yes, somewhere about."

"Then stick it on when you're negotiating with him, with a rakish tilt over one eye, and I don't think we shall have any trouble."

But there was no time to secure this adventitious aid. He had scarcely finished speaking when a hearty fist banged on the door, a hearty voice cried "Hoy!", and the man whom the hour had produced appeared in person.

"Well, cocky. I just came to see how you were getting al— Why, 'ullo," said Augustus Robb, pausing on the threshold and surveying the mob scene before him. "I didn't know you had company, chum. Excuse me."

He made as if to withdaw, but Mike, leaping forward, seized his coat in a firm grip.

"Don't be coy, Augustus. Come right in. You're just the fellow we want. Your name was on our lips at that very moment, and we were on the point of sending the bloodhounds out in search of you. So you've got to Beevor Castle, after all?"

"Yus, though it went against my conscience." Augustus Robb drew Mike aside and spoke in a hoarse whisper. "Do they know about it?"

"Oh yes. All pals here."

"That's all right, then. Wouldn't have wanted to make a bloomer of any description. Nice little place you've got here," said Augustus Robb, speaking less guardedly. "Done you proud, ain't they? Where does that window look out on? The rose garden? Coo! Got a rose garden, 'ave they? Every luxury, as you might say. Well, enjoy it while you can, chum. It won't be long before you're bunged out on your blinkin' ear."

"Why do you strike this morbid note?"

"Just a feeling I 'ave. The wicked may flourish like a ruddy bay tree, as the Good Book says, but they always cop it in the end."

"You rank me among the wicked?"

"Well, you're practisin' deceit, ain't you? Living a lie, I call it. There's a tract I'd like you to read, bearing on that, only coming away in a hurry, I left me tracts behind." Augustus Robb cocked an appreciative eye at Terry and, placing a tactful hand before his mouth, spoke out of the corner of the latter in his original hoarse whisper. "Who's the little bit of fluff?" he asked.

"You recall me to my duties as a host, Augustus," said Mike. "Come and get acquainted. Stanwood, of course, you know. But I don't think you have met Lord Shortlands."

"How do you do, Mr. Robb?"

"Pip-pip, m'lord," said Augustus Robb, visibly moved.

"Welcome—ah—to Beevor Castle."

"Thanks, m'lord. Seems funny bein' inside here, m'lord. Only seen the place from the outside before, m'lord. Cycled here one Bank Holiday, when I was a lad. Took sandwiches."

"It must have seemed strange, too," said Mike, "coming in by the door. Your natural impulse, I imagine, would have been to climb through the scullery window."

Augustus Robb, displeased, pleaded for a little tact, and Mike apologized.

"Sorry. But it's a subject we shall be leading up to before long. And this is Lord Shortlands' daughter, Lady Teresa Cobbold, whose name will be familiar to you from my correspondence. Thank you, Augustus," said Mike, acknowledging the other's wink and upward jerk of the thumbs. "I'm glad you approve. Do sit down. You will find this chair comfortable."

"Have a cushion, Mr. Robb," said Terry.

"A cigar?"said Lord Shortlands.

"I'd offer you a drink," said Mike, "but Stanwood has cleaned me out."

Too late, he saw that he had said the wrong thing. Augustus Robb, the ecstasy of finding himself in such distinguished company having induced in him a state of mind comparable to the nirvana of the Buddhists, had been leaning back in his chair with a soft, contented smile on his lips. This statement brought him up with a jerk, his face hard.

"Ho! So you've been drinking again, have you?" he observed austerely, giving Stanwood a stern look. "After all I said. All right, I wash me 'ands of you. If you want a 'obnailed liver, carry on, cocky. And if eventually you kick the bucket, what of it? I don't care. It's a matter of complete in-bleedin'- difference to me."

This generous outburst brought about one of those awkward pauses. Mike looked at Lord Shortlands. Terry looked at Stanwood. She also frowned significantly, and Stanwood took the hint. His was not a very high I.Q., but even he had realized the vital necessity of conciliating this man.

"Gee, Augustus, I'm sorry."

Augustus Robb sucked his front tooth.

"I'm sure he won't do it again, Mr. Robb."

Augustus Robb preserved an icy silence.

"Augustus," said Mike gently, "Lady Teresa Cobbold is speaking to you. She is, of course, the daughter of the fifth Earl of Shortlands, connected on her mother's side with the Byng-Brown-Byngs and the Foster-Frenches. The Sussex Foster-Frenches, not the Devonshire lot."

It was as if Augustus Robb had come out of a swoon and was saying "Where am I?" He blinked at Terry through his horn-rimmed spectacles, seeming to drink in her Byng-Brown-Byngness, and looked for a moment as if he were about to rise and bow. The cold sternness died out of his eyes, and he inclined his head forgivingly.

"Right ho. Say no more about it."

"That's the way to talk. Everything hotsy-totsy once more? Fine. Sure you're quite comfortable, Augustus?"

"Another cushion, Mr.Robb?" said Terry.

"How's the cigar?" said Lord Shortlands.

And Stanwood, showing an almost human intelligence, muttered something about how he had long thought of taking the pledge and would start looking into the matter tomorrow.

"Well, Augustus," said Mike, satisfied with the success of the preliminary operations and feeling that brass tacks could now be got down to, "as I was saying, you couldn't have come at a more fortunate moment. I did mention that his name was on our lips, didn't I?"

"You betcher," said Stanwood.
"You betcher," said Lord Shortlands.
"We were saying such nice things about you, Mr. Robb," said Terry. She knew she was being kittenish, but there are moments when a girl must not spare the kitten.
Augustus Robb choked on his cigar. His head was swimming a little.
"The fact is, Augustus, we are in a spot, and only you can get us out of it. When I say 'us,' I allude primarily to the fifth Earl of Shortlands, whose family, as you probably know, came over with the Conqueror. You have it in your power to do the fifth Earl of Shortlands a signal service, and one which he will never forget. Years hence, when he drops in at the House of Lords, he will find himself chatting with other earls—and no doubt a few dukes—and the subject of selfless devotion will come up. Stories will be swapped, here an earl speaking of some splendid secretary or estate agent, there a duke eulogizing his faithful dog Ponto, and then Lord Shortlands will top the lot with his tale of you. 'Let me tell you about Augustus Robb,' he will say, and the dukes and earls will listen spellbound. 'Coo!' they will cry, when he has finished. 'Some fellow, that Augustus Robb. I'd like to meet him.' "
Augustus Robb took off his horn-rimmed spectacles and polished them. His head was swimming more than ever, and his chest had begun to heave. His was a life passed mainly in the society of men who spoke what came into their simple minds, and the things that came into their simple minds were nearly always rude. It was not often that he was able to listen to this sort of thing.
"In a nutshell," said Mike, "Lord Shortlands is being beset by butlers. Have you met the butler here, the man Spink?"
A shudder ran through Augustus Robb.
"Yus," he said. "Have you?"
"I have indeed."
"And prayed for him?"
"No, I haven't got around to that yet."
"I'm surprised to hear it. I wouldn't have thought you could have been in his presence five minutes without being moved to Christian pity."
"You find him a hard nut?"
"A lost scoffer," said Augustus Robb severely, "whose words are as barbed arrows winged with sinfulness. If ever there was an emissary of Satan with side whiskers, it's him."
He had got what is called in Parliamentary circles the feeling of the House. It would scarcely have been possible for these words to have gone better. Lord Shortlands snorted rapturously. Stanwood said " 'At's the stuff!" Terry lit up the speaker's system with a dazzling smile, and Mike patted him on the back.
"That's great," said Mike. "If that's the way you feel, we can get down to cases."
In Augustus Robb's demeanour, as he listened to the story of the stamp,

there exhibited itself at first only a growing horror. Three times in the course of the narrative he said "Coo!" and each time, as the inkiness of the butler's soul became more and more plain to him, with a greater intensity of repulsion. There seemed no question that Mike was holding his audience, and had its sympathy.

But when, passing from his preamble, he went on to outline what it was that Augustus Robb was expected to do, the other's aspect changed. It was still instinct with horror, but a horror directed now not at Mervyn Spink but at one whom it was evident that he had mentally labelled as The Tempter. He rose, swelling formidably.

"What! You're asking me to bust a pete?"

"A safe," corrected Lord Shortlands deferentially.

"Well, a pete is a safe, ain't it?"

"Is it?"

"Of course it is," said Mike. "Safes are always called petes in the best circles. Yes, that's the scheme, Augustus. How about it?"

"No!"

Mike blinked. The monosyllable, spoken at the fullest extent of a good man's lungs, had seemed to strike him like a projectile.

"Did you say No?"

"Yus, no."

"But it'll only take a few minutes of your time."

"No, I tell you. A thousand times no."

"Not even to oblige an earl?"

"Not even to oblige a dozen ruddy earls."

Mike blinked again. He glanced round at his colleagues, and drew little comfort from their deportment. Lord Shortlands was looking crushed and desolate. Terry's eyes were round with dismay. Stanwood Cobbold seemed to be grinding his teeth, which of course is never much use in a crisis of this sort.

"I had not expected this, Augustus," said Mike reproachfully.

"You knew I was saved, didn't you?"

"Yes, but can't you understand that this is a far, far better thing that we are asking you to do than you have ever done? Consider the righteousness of our cause."

"Busting a pete is busting a pete, and you can't get away from it."

"You aren't forgetting that Lord Shortlands' ancestors came over with the Conqueror?"

For an instant Augustus Robb seemed to waver.

"This won't please the Foster-Frenches."

The weakness passed. Augustus Robb was himself again.

"That's enough of that. Stop tempting me. Get thou behind me, Satan, and look slippy about it. Why don't you get behind me?" asked Augustus Robb peevishly.

"And how about the Byng-Brown-Byngs?" said Mike.

Stanwood exploded like a bomb. For some moments he had been muttering to himself, and it had been plain that he was not in sympathy with the conscientious objector.

"What's the good of talking to the fellow? Kick him!"

Mike started. It was a thought.

"Egad, Stanwood, I believe you've got something there."

"Grab him by the scruff of the neck and bend him over and leave the rest to me."

"Wait," said Mike. "Not in thin evening shoes. Go and put on your thick boots. And you, Terry, had better be leaving us. The situation is one which strong men must thresh out face to face. Or, perhaps, not face to face exactly——"

Augustus Robb had paled. He was essentially a man of peace.

"If there's going to be verlence——"

"There is."

It was Stanwood who had spoken. In his manner there was no trace now of his former meek obsequiousness. It had all the poised authority which had been wont to mark it in the days when, crouched and menacing, he had waited to plunge against the opposing line.

"You betcher there's going to be verlance. I'll give you two seconds to change your mind."

Augustus Robb changed it in one.

"Well, right ho," he said hastily. "If you put it that way, chum, I suppose I've no option."

"That's the way to talk."

"Well spoken, Augustus."

"But you're overlooking something. It's years since I bust a pete."

"No doubt the old skill still lingers."

"As to that, I wouldn't say it didn't. But what you've omitted to take into account, cockies," said Augustus Robb with gloomy triumph, "is me nervous system. I'm not the man I was. I wouldn't 'ave the nerve to do a job nowadays without I took a gargle first. And I can't take a gargle, because gargling's sinful. So there you are. It's an am-parce."

Terry smiled that winning smile of hers.

"You wouldn't mind taking a tiny little gargle to oblige me, Mr. Robb?"

"Yus, I would. And it wouldn't be tiny, either. I'd need a bucketful."

"Then take a bucketful," said Lord Shortlands.

It was a good, practical suggestion, but Augustus Robb shook his head.

"Those boots, Stanwood," said Mike. "Be as quick as you can."

Augustus Robb capitulated. He had never actually seen Stanwood on the football field, but his imagination was good and he could picture him punting.

"Well, all right. 'Ave it your own way, chums. But no good's going to come of this."

"Splendid, Augustus," said Mike. "We knew you wouldn't fail us. How about tools?"

"I'll have to go to London and fetch 'em, I suppose."

"You still have the dear old things, then?"

"Yus. I 'adn't the 'eart to get rid of 'em. They're with a gentleman friend of mine that lives in Seven Dials. I'll go and get 'em. More trouble," said Augustus Robb, and, moving broodingly to the door, was gone.

"Stanwood!" cried Terry. "You're marvellous! How did you think of it?"

"Oh, it just came to me," said Stanwood modestly.

"In these delicate negotiations," explained Mike, "it often happens that where skilled masters of the spoken word fail to bring home the bacon, success is achieved by some plain, blunt, practical man who ignores the niceties of diplomacy and goes straight to the root of the matter. The question now arises, How do we procure the needful? We can't very well raid the cellar. It seems to me that the best plan will be for me to run up to London tomorrow with Augustus and lay in supplies."

"Get plenty," advised Stanwood.

"I will."

"And of all varieties," added Lord Shortlands, who in matters like this was a farseeing man. "There's no telling what the chap will prefer. Many people, for instance, dislike the taste of whiskey. I have never been able to see eye to eye with them, but it is an undoubted fact. Get a good representative mixed assortment, my boy, and put it in my room. He will need a quiet place in which to prepare himself. And anything that's left over," said Lord Shortlands, a sudden brightness coming into his eyes, "I can use myself."

15

IN EVERY human enterprise, if success is to be achieved, there must always be behind the operations the directing brain. In the matter of breaking open the library safe at Beevor Castle and abstracting the Spanish 1851 *dos reales* stamp, blue unused, it was Mike who had framed the plan of campaign and issued the divisional orders.

These were as follows:

1. Zero hour to be 1.30 A.M.

Start the attack earlier, Mike had pointed out, and it might find members of the household awake. Start it later, and it cut into one's night too much. He wanted his sleep, he said, and Lord Shortlands said he wanted his, too.

2. All units to assemble in the study at one-fifteen.

Because they had to assemble somewhere, and it would be wisest if

Augustus Robb, before repairing to the library, were to remove a pane of glass from the study window and make a few chisel marks on the woodwork, thus conveying the suggestion that the job had been an outside one. This ruse was strongly approved of by Lord Shortlands, who did not conceal his opinion that the more outside the job could be made to look, the better.

3. Lord Shortlands to be O. C. Robbs.

His task was to smuggle Augustus Robb into his bedroom and there ply him with drink until in his, Augustus's, opinion his nerve was back in the midseason form of the old days. He would then conduct him to the study, reporting there at one–fifteen. This would allow five minutes for a pep talk from the general in charge of operations, eight minutes for the breaking of the window and the chisel marks and two for getting upstairs. A margin would also be left for kicking Augustus Robb, should he render this necessary by ringing in that conscience of his again.

4. Stanwood was to go to bed.

And darned well stay there. Because, though it was impossible to say offhand just how, if permitted to be present, he would gum the game, that he would somehow find a way of doing so was certain.

5. Terry was to go to bed, too.

Because in moments of excitement she had the extraordinary habit of squeaking like a basketful of puppies, and in any case in an enterprise of this kind girls were in the way. (Seconded by Lord Shortlands, who said that in the mystery thriller which Desborough Topping had given him for his birthday the detective had been seriously hampered in his activities by the adhesiveness of a girl named Mabel, who had hair the color of ripe wheat.)

6. Terry was to stop arguing and do as she was told.

Discussion on this point threatened for a time to become acrimonious, but on Mike challenging her to deny that her hair was the color of ripe wheat she had been obliged to yield.

Nevertheless, as the clock over the stable struck the hour of one, Terry was lying on the sofa in the study, reading the second of the three volumes of a novel entitled *Percy's Promise,* by Marcia Huddlestone (Popgood and Grooly, 1869). She had found it lying on the table and had picked it up for want of anything better. She was looking charming in pajamas, a kimono and mules.

At three minutes past the hour Lord Shortlands entered, looking charming in pajamas, a dressing gown and slippers. His eyes, as always in times of emotion, were protruding, and at the sight of his daughter they protruded still further.

"Good Lord, Terry! What are you doing here?"

"Just reading, darling, to while away the time."

"But Cardinal said you were to go to bed."

"So he did, didn't he? Bless my soul, what a nerve that young man has, to be sure. Bed, indeed! Well, you certainly have got a frightful collection of books, Shorty. There wasn't anything in your shelves published later than 1870."

"Eh? Oh, those aren't mine," said Lord Shortlands. He spoke absently. While he deplored his child's presence, it had just occurred to him what an admirable opportunity this was for speaking that word in season. "My old uncle's."

"Did he like Victorian novels?"

"I suppose so."

"I believe you do, too. This one was lying on the table, obviously recently perused."

"Young Cardinal borrowed it, and returned it this afternoon. He said it had given him food for thought. I don't know what he meant. Terry," said Lord Shortlands, welcoming the cue, "I've been thinking about young Cardinal."

"Have you, angel? He rather thrusts himself on the attention, doesn't he?"

"He's a smart chap."

"Yes. I suppose he would admit that himself."

"Look at the way he baffled Spink."

"Very adroit."

"Brave as a lion, too. Faces Adela without a tremor."

"What's all this leading up to, darling?"

"Well, I was—er—wondering if by any chance you might be beginning to change your mind about him."

"Oh, I see."

"Are you?"

"No."

"Ho," said Lord Shortlands, damped.

There was a pause. The thing was not going quite so well as the fifth earl had hoped.

"Why not?"

"There's a reason."

"I'm dashed it I can see what it is. I should have thought he would have been just the chap for you. Rich. Good-looking. Amusing. And loves you like the dickens. You can tell that by the way he looks at you. Its's a sort of—how shall I describe it?"

"A sort of melting look?"

"That's right. You've got it first shot. A sort of melting look."

"And your complaint is that it doesn't melt me?"

"Exactly."

"Well, I'll tell you something, Shorty. I am by no means insensible, as the heroine of *Percy's Promise* would say, to this look you mention. It may interest you to know that it goes through me like a burning dart."

"It does?" cried Lord Shortlands, greatly encouraged. This was more the sort of stuff he wanted to hear.

"It seems to pump me full of vitamines. It makes me feel as if the sun was shining and my hat was right and my shoes right and my frock was right and my stockings were right and somebody had just left me ten thousand a year."

"Well, then."

"Not so fast, my pet. Wait for the epilog. But all the same I'm not going to let myself fall in love with him. I don't feel that I have exclusive rights in that look of his."

"I don't follow you."

"I fancy I have to share it with a good many other girls."

"You mean you think he's one of these—er—flippertygibbets?"

"Yes, if a flippertygibbet is a man who can't help making love to every girl he meets who's reasonably pretty."

"But he says he's loved you since you were fifteen or whatever it was."

"He has to say something, to keep the conversation going."

"But what makes you feel like that about him?"

"Instinct. I think young Mike Cardinal is a butterfly, Shorty; the kind that flits from flower to flower and sips. I strongly suspect him of having been flitting and sipping this afternoon. Did you see him when he came back from the great city?"

"No. I was giving Whiskers his run."

"Well, I did. We had quite a chat. And the air for yards about him was heavy with some strange, exotic scent, as if he had been having his coat sleeve pawed at for hours by some mysterious, exotic female. I'm not blaming him, mind you. It's not his fault that he looks like a Greek god. And if women chuck themselves at his feet, it's only natural that he should pick them up. Still, you can understand my being a little wary. He thrills me, Shorty, but all the time there's a prudent side of me, a sort of Terry Cobbold in spectacles and mittens, that whispers that no good ever comes of getting entangled with Greek gods. I mistrust men who are too good-looking. In short, my heart inclines to Mike Cardinal, but my head restrains me. I suppose I feel about him pretty much as Mrs. Punter feels about Spink."

Lord Shortlands puffed unhappily.

"Well, I think you're making a great mistake."

"So do I—sometimes."

"About that scent. He probably rubbed up against some woman."

"That is what I fear."

"You ought to marry him."

"Why do you want me to so much?"

"Well, dash it, I like the chap."

"So do I."

"And have you considered what's going to happen after this fellow Robb has got that stamp? I get married and go off and leave you here alone with Adela—if, as you say, and I think you're right, Clare's going to collar Blair. You'll hate it. You'll be miserable, old girl. Why don't you marry the chap?"

The picture he had drawn of a Shorty-less Beevor Castle had not failed to make its impression on Terry. It was something she had not thought of. She was considering it with a frown, when the door opened and Mike came in.

Mike was looking tense and solemn. He was a young man abundantly equipped with what he called *sang-froid* and people who did not like him usually alluded to as gall, but tonight's operations were making him feel like a nervous impresario just before an opening. In another quarter of an hour the curtain would be going up, and the sense of his responsibility for the success of the venture weighed upon him. At the sight of Terry and of a Lord Shortlands unaccompanied by Augustus Robb he started visibly.

"What are you doing here?" he demanded sternly. "You're supposed to be in bed."

"I know. I got up. I want to watch. I've never seen a pete busted before."

"One wishes to keep the women out of this."

"Well, one won't."

"Now I know what the papers mean when they talk about the headstrong modern girl."

"Avid for sensation."

"Avid, as you say, for sensation. Well, it's lucky you're going to get an indulgent husband."

"Am I?"

"I think so. I've got a new system. Where's Augustus?"

"Up in Shorty's room, I suppose."

"Then why aren't you with him, Shorty? Staff work, staff work. We must have staff work."

Lord Shortlands spoke plaintively.

"He told me to go away. I didn't want to, but he said my watching him made him nervous. He seems a very high-strung sort of chap."

"How was he getting on?"

"All right, it seemed to me."

"Well, you had better go and fetch him."

"Can't you?"

"No. I want to have a word with Terry."

Lord Shortlands, on whom the strain was beginning to tell, ran a fevered hand through his grizzled hair, and whispered something about wishing he could have a drink.

This surprised Mike.

"Haven't you had one? Didn't you share Augustus's plenty?"

"He wouldn't let me. He said it was sinful. And when I pressed the point, he threatened to bounce a bottle on my head. I would give," said Lord Shortlands spaciously, "a million pounds for a drink."

"I can do you one cheaper than that," said Mike. "Skim up to my room, feel at the back of the top right-hand drawer of the chest of drawers, and you will find a flask full of what you need. Help yourself and leave twopence on the mantelpiece."

He went to the door and closed it after his rapidly departing host.

"Alone at last," he said.

Terry's gentle heart had been touched by a father's distress.

"Poor old Shorty!"

"Yes."

"He really isn't fit for this sort of thing."

"No."

"His high blood pressure——"

Mike took her gently by the elbow and led her to a chair. He deposited her lovingly in its depths and seated himself on the arm.

"When I said 'Alone at last,' " he explained, "I didn't mean that now was our chance to discuss Shorty's blood pressure. The time to do that will be later on, when we are sitting side by side before the fire in our little home. 'Let's have a long talk about Shorty's blood pressure,' you will say, and I shall reply 'Oh, goody! Yes, let's.' But for the moment there are weightier matters on the agenda paper. When I came into the room just now, I overheard your father make a very pregnant remark."

"Eavesdropping, eh?"

"I see no harm in dropping a few eaves from time to time. People do it behind screens on the stage, and are highly thought of. He was saying 'Why don't you marry the chap, you miserable little fathead?' "

"He didn't call me a fathead."

"He should have done. Was he alluding to me?"

"He was."

"What a pal! How did the subject come up?"

"He had been asking me why I wouldn't marry you."

"Now, there's a thing I've been trying to figure out for weeks, and I believe I've got it. I see you've been reading *Percy's Promise*. I skimmed through it last night, and it has given me food for thought. It has suggested to me this new system of which I spoke just now. I see now that I have not been handling my wooing the right way."

"No?"

"No. I have been too flip. Amusing, yes. Entertaining, true. But too flip. They did these things better in 1869. Have you got to the part where Lord Percy proposes to the girl in the conservatory?"

"Not yet."

"I will read it to you. Try to imagine that it is I who am speaking, because he puts in beautiful words just what I want to say. Ready?"

"If you are."

"Then here we go. 'It has been with a loving eye, dearest of all girls, that I have watched you grow from infancy to womanhood. I saw how your natural graces developed, and how by the sweetness of your disposition you were possessing yourself of a manner in which I, who have seen courts, must be allowed to pronounce perfect. It is not too much to say that I am asking a gift which any man, of whatever exalted rank, would be proud to have; that there is no position, however lofty, which you would not grace; and that I yield to no one in the resolution to make that home happy which it is in your power to give me. Your slightest wish shall be gratified, your most trifling want shall be anticipated.' How's that?"

"It's good."

"Let's try some more. 'Dearest, you are breaking a heart that beats only for you. I know that I am not one for whom nature has made a royal road to the hearts of women. You would feel for me if you knew the envy with which I regard those who are so favored. If I do not look, if I do not speak as a lover ought to do, it is not, heaven knows, because love is wanting. The pitcher may be full of good wine, but for that very reason it flows with difficulty. It is hard indeed that eloquence should be denied to one who is pleading for his very life. I love you, I love you, I love you. Dearest, can you never love me?' I don't know why he beefed about not being eloquent. Some steam there. How's it coming? Are you moved?"

"Not much."

"Odd. Percy's girl was. It was at that point that he swung the deal. 'You do not answer,' he cried, drawing her close to him, 'but your silence speaks for you as sweetly as any words. May I take my happiness for granted, love? Your cheek is white, but I will change that lily to a rose.' So saying, he pressed his lips to hers and she, with a low, soft cry, half sigh, half sob, returned his kiss. And thus they plighted troth. You can't get around a definite statement like that. Boy got girl. No question about it. But in my case Boy doesn't?"

"No."

"You didn't give a low, soft cry, half sigh, half sob, without my noticing it?"

"No."

"Then I think I see where the trouble lies. Percy, according to the author, had 'a flowing beard,' which he appears to have acquired—honestly, one hopes—at the early age of twenty-four. We shall have to wait till I have a flowing beard. It would seem to be an essential. I'll start growing one tomorrow."

"I wouldn't. Shall I tell you why I'm not moved?"

"It's about time you made some official pronouncement."

"Well . . . Have you got to sit on the arm of this chair?"

"Not necessarily. I just wanted to be handy, in case the moment arrived for changing that lily to a rose. However, I will move across the way. Now, then."

Terry hesitated.

"Proceed," said Mike encouragingly.

"It's going to sound rather crazy, I'm afraid."

"Never mind. Start gibbering. Why won't you marry me?"

"Well, if you really want to know, because you're too frightfully good-looking."

"Too—what?"

"Too dazzlingly handsome. I told you it was going to sound crazy."

There was a long silence. Mike seemed stunned.

"Crazy?" he said at length. "It's cuckoo. Girls have been slapped into padded cells for less. You wouldn't call me handsome?"

"You're like something out of a super-film. Haven't you noticed it yourself?"

"Never. Just a good, serviceable face, I should have said."

"The face that launched a thousand ships. Go and look in the glass."

Mike did so. He closed one eye, peered intently and shook his head.

"I don't get it. It's a nice face. A kind face. A face that makes you feel how thoroughly trustworthy and reliable I am. But nothing more."

"It's the profile that stuns. Look at yourself sideways."

"What do you think I am? A contortionist?" Mike moved away from the mirror. His air was still that of a man who is out of his depth. "And that's really why you won't marry me?"

"Yes."

"Well, I was expecting something pretty unbalanced, but nothing on this stupendous scale. You surpass yourself, my young breath-taker. I think I see what must have happened. Leaning out of that schoolroom window during your formative years, you overbalanced and fell on your fat little head."

"It's nice of you to try to find excuses."

"It's the only possible explanation. My child, you're *non compos.*"

"It isn't non composness. It's prudence."

"But what have you got against good-looking men?"

"I mistrust them."

"Including me?"

"Including you."

"Then you're a misguided little chump."

"All right, I'm a misguided little chump."

"My nature is pure gold, clear through."

"That's your story?"

"And I stick to it. You won't change your mind?"

"No."

Mike breathed a little stertorously.

"I suppose it would be a breach of hospitality if I socked my hostess's sister in the eye?"

"The county would purse its lips."

"Darn these hidebound conventions. Well, how much of a gargoyle has a man got to be before you will consider him as a mate? If I looked like Stanwood——"

"Ah!"

"Well, I don't suppose I shall ever touch that supreme height. But if I pursue the hobby of amateur boxing, to which I am greatly addicted, it is possible that some kindly fist may someday bestow on me a cauliflower ear or leave my nose just that half inch out of the straight which makes all the difference. If I come to you later with the old beezer pointing sou'-sou'west, will you reconsider?"

"I'll give the matter thought."

"We'll leave it at that, then. All this won't make any difference to my devotion, of course. I shall continue to love you."

"Thanks."

"Quite all right. A pleasure. But I do think Shorty ought to kick in three guineas and have your head examined by some good specialist. It would be money well spent. Ah, Shorty," said Mike, as the fifth earl entered, looking much refreshed. "Glad to see you once more, my dear old stag at eve. Do you know what your daughter Teresa has just been telling me? She says she won't marry me because I'm too good-looking."

"No!"

"Those were her very words, spoken with a sort of imbecile glitter in her eyes. The whole thing is extraordinarly sad. But why are you still alone? What have you done with Augustus?"

"I can't find him."

"Wasn't he in your room?"

"No. He's gone."

"Perhaps he went to the library," suggested Terry.

Mike frowned.

"I guess he did. I never saw such an undisciplined rabble in all my life. I wish people would stick to their instructions and not start acting on their own initiative."

"Too bad, Sergeant-Major."

"Well, what's the good of me organizing you, if you won't stay organized? Let's go to the library and look."

Terry's theory was proved correct. The missing man was in the library. He was tacking to and fro across the floor with a bottle of crème de menthe in his hand.

He greeted them, as they entered, with a rollicking "Hoy!"

16

"ROLLICKING," INDEED, was the only adjective to describe Augustus Robb's whole deportment at this critical moment in his career. That, or its French equivalent, was the word which would have leaped to the mind of the stylist Flaubert, always so careful in his search for the *mot juste*. His face was a vivid scarlet, his eyes gleaming, his smile broad and benevolent. It needed but a glance to see that he was full to the brim of good will to all men.

"Come in, cockies," he bellowed, waving the bottle spaciously, and the generous timbre of his voice sent a chill of apprehension through his audience. In the silent night it had seemed to blare out like the Last Trump.

"Sh!" said Mike.

"Sh!" said Lord Shortlands.

"Sh!" said Terry.

A look of courteous surprise came into the vermilion face of the star of the night's performance.

" 'Ow do you mean, Sh?" he asked, puzzled.

"Not so loud, Augustus. It's half-past one."

"What about it?"

"You'll go waking people."

"Coo! That's right. Never thought of that," said Augustus Robb. He put the bottle to his lips, and drank a deep draft. "Peppermint, this tastes of," he said. This was the first time he had come in contact with crème de menthe, and he wished to share his discoveries with his little group of friends. "Yus, pep-hic-ermint."

It had become apparent to Mike that in framing his plans he had omitted to guard against all the contingencies which might lead to those plans going awry. He had budgeted for an Augustus Robb primed to the sticking point. That the other, having reached his objective, might decide to push on further he had not foreseen. And it was only too manifest that he had done so. Augustus Robb, if not actually plastered, was beyond a question oiled, and he endeavoured to check the mischief before it could spread.

"Better give me that bottle, Augustus."

"Why?"

"I think you've had enough."

"Enough?" Augustus Robb seemed amazed. "Why, I've only just started."

"Come on, old friend. Hand it over."

A menacing look came into Augustus Robb's eyes.

"You lay a finger on it, cocky, just as much as a ruddy finger, and I'll bounce it on your head." He drank again. "Yus, peppermint," he said. "Nice taste. Wholesome, too. I always liked peppermints as a nipper. My old uncle Fred used to give me them to stop me reciting 'Oh, what a tangled web we weave, when first we practised to deceive!' Which is what you're doing, chum," said Augustus Robb, regarding Mike reproachfully. "Acting a lie, that's what it amounts to. Ananias and Sapphira."

Lord Shortlands plucked at Mike's elbow. His manner was anxious.

"Cardinal."

"Hullo?"

"Do you notice anything?"

"Eh?"

"I believe the fellow's blotto."

"I believe he is."

"What shall we do?"

"Start operations without delay, before he gets worse. Augustus."

"'ULLO?"

"Sh," said Mike.

"Sh," said Lord Shortlands.

"Sh," said Terry.

Their well-meant warnings piqued Augustus Robb. That menacing look came into his eyes again.

"What you saying Sh for?" he demanded, aggrieved. "You keep on saying Sh. Everybody says Sh. I've 'ad to speak of this before."

"Sorry, Augustus," said Mike pacifically. "It shan't occur again. How about making a start?"

"Start? What at?"

"That safe."

"What safe?"

"The safe you've come to open."

"Oh, that one?" said Augustus Robb, enlightened. "All right, cocky, let's go. 'Ullo."

"What's the matter?"

"'Where's me tools?"

"Haven't you got them?"

"Don't seem to see 'em nowhere about."

"You can't have lost them."

Augustus Robb could not concede this.

"Why can't I have lost them? Plumbers lose their tools, don't they? Well, then. Try to talk sense, chum."

"Perhaps you left them in Shorty's room, Mr. Robb," suggested Terry.

"No, don't *you* go making silly remarks, ducky. I've never been there."

"My father's room."

Augustus Robb turned to the fifth earl, surprised.

"Is your name Shorty?"

"Shorty is short for Shortlands," Mike explained.

"Shorty short for Shortlands," murmured Augustus Robb. Then, as the full humour of the thing began to penetrate, he repeated the words with an appreciative chuckle rather more loudly; so loudly, indeed, that the fifth earl rose a full six inches in the direction of the ceiling and, having descended, clutched at Mike's arm.

"Can't you stop him making such a noise?"

"I'll try."

"Adela is not a heavy sleeper."

Mike saw that he had overlooked something else in framing his plans. Lady Adela Toppping should have been given a Micky Finn in her bedtime glass of warm milk. It is just these small details that escape an organizer's notice.

"I think he's subsiding," he said. And indeed Augustus Robb, who had been striding about the room with an odd, lurching movement, as if he were having leg trouble, had navigated to a chair and was sitting there, looking benevolent and murmuring "Shorty short for Shortlands" in a meditative undertone, like a parrot under a green baize cloth. "Rush along and see if those tools are in your room."

Lord Shortlands rushed along, and a strange silence fell upon the library. Augustus Robb had stopped his soliloquy, and was sitting with bowed head. As he raised it for a moment in order to refresh himself from the bottle, Terry touched Mike's arm.

"Mike."

"Yes, love?"

"Look," whispered Terry, and there was womanly commiseration in her voice. "He's crying!"

Mike looked. It was even as she had said. A tear was stealing down behind the horn-rimmed spectacles.

"Something the matter, Augustus?" he asked.

Augustus Robb wiped away the pearly drop.

"Just thinking of 'Er, cocky," he said huskily.

"'Er?"

"The woman I lost, chum."

Mike felt profoundly relieved.

"It's all right," he whispered to Terry. "The quiet, sentimental stage."

"Oh, is that it?"

"That's it. Let us hope it persists, because the next one in rotation is the violent. I didn't know you'd lost a woman, Augustus. Where did you see her last?"

"I didn't. She wasn't there."

"Where?"

"At the blinking registry office. I suppose it's never occurred to you, cocky, to ask yourself why I'm a solitary chip drifting down the river of life, as the saying is. Well, I'll tell you. I was once going to marry a good woman, but she didn't turn up."

"That was tough."

"You may well say it was tough."

"What a shame, Mr. Robb."

"And *you* may well say 'What a shame, Mr. Robb,' ducky. No, she didn't turn up. I'd confessed my past to her the night before, and she had seemed to forgive, but she must have slep' on it and changed her mind, because the fact remains that I waited a couple of hours at the Beak Street registry office and not a sign of her."

"An unpleasant experience. What did you do?"

"I went and had a sarsaparilla and a ham sandwich and tried to forget. Not that I ever 'ave forgot. The memory of her sweet face still gnaws my bosom like a flock of perishing rats."

Mike nodded sympathetically.

"Women are like that."

The slur on the sex offended Augustus Robb's chivalry.

"No, they aren't. Unless they are, of course," he added, for he was a man who could look at things from every angle. "And yet sometimes," he said, finishing the crème de menthe thoughtfully, "I wonder if maybe she wasn't a mere tool of Fate, as the expression is. You see, there's a Beak Street registry office and a Meek Street registry ofice and a Greek Street registry office, and who knows but what she may have gone and got confused? What I mean, how am I to know that all the time I was waiting at Beak Street she mayn't have been waiting at Meek Street?"

"Or Greek Street."

"R. It's the sort of thing might easily happen."

"Didn't you think of asking her?"

"Yus. But too late. The possibility of there having been some such what you might call misunderstanding didn't occur to me till a week or two later, and when I nipped round to her lodging she'd gorn, leaving no address. And a couple of days after that I had to go to America with an American gentleman who I'd took service with, so there we were, sundered by the seas. Sundered by the ruddy seas," he added, to make his meaning clearer. "And I've never seen her since."

A silence fell. Mike and Terry, disinclined for chatter after the stark human story to which they had been listening, sat gazing at Augustus Robb in mute sympathy, and Augustus Robb, except for an occasional soft hiccough, might have been a statue of himself, erected by a few friends and admirers.

Presently he came to life, like a male Galatea.

"Broke my blinking 'eart, that did," he said. "If I was to tell you how that woman could cook steak and kidney pudding, you wouldn't believe me. Melted in the mouth."

"It's a tragedy," said Terry.

"You're right, ducky. It's a tragedy."

"You ought to have told it to Shakespeare," said Mike. "He could have made a play out of it."

"R.," said Augustus Robb moodily. He removed his horn-rimmed spectacles in order to wipe away another tear, and, replacing them, looked at his young companions mournfully. "Yus, it's a tragedy right enough. Lots of aching 'earts you see around you these days. Something chronic. Which reminds me. 'Ow's your business coming along, Mr. Cardinal? You and this little party. Thought quite a bit about that, I 'ave. Ever tried kissing her? I've known that to answer."

Terry started, and there came into her face a flush which Mike found himself comparing, to the latter's disadvantage, to the first faint glow of pink in some lovely summer sky. He asked himself what Lord Percy would have done at such a moment. The answer came readily. He would have spared the loved one's blushes, turning that rose back again to a lily.

"Let's talk about something else," he suggested.

Augustus Robb's brow darkened. He twitched his chin petulantly.

"I won't talk about something else. I don't want any pie-faced young Gawd-'elp-uses tellin' me what to talk about."

"Read any good books lately, Augustus?"

"Whippersnappers," said Augustus Robb, after a pause, as if, like Flaubert, he had been hunting for the *mot juste*, and was about to dilate on the theme when Lord Shortlands re-entered, announcing that he had been unable to find the tools.

Augustus Robb turned a cold eye upon him.

"What tools?"

"Your tools."

Augustus Robb stiffened. It was plain that that last unfortunate dip into the crème de menthe bottle had eased him imperceptibly from the sentimental to the peevish stage of intoxication, accentuating his natural touchiness to a dangerous degree.

He directed at Lord Shortlands a misty, but penetrating, stare.

"You let me catch you messing about with my tools, and I'll twist your head off and make you swallow it."

"But you told me to go and look for them," pleaded Lord Shortlands.

"I never!"

"Well, he did," said Lord Shortlands.

Augustus Robb transferred his morose gaze to Mike.

"What's it got to do with him, may I ask?"

"I thought it wisest to start hunting around, Augustus. We want those tools."

"Well, we've got 'em, ain't we? They're under the sofa, where I put 'em, ain't they? Fust thing I done on enterin' this room was to place my tools neatly under the sofa."

"I see. Just a little misunderstanding."

"I don't like little misunderstandings."

"Here you are. All present and correct."

Augustus Robb took the bag of tools absently. He was glaring at Lord Shortlands again. For some reason he seemed to have taken a sudden dislike to that inoffensive peer.

"Earls!" he said disparagingly, and it was plain that by some process not easily understandable the crème de menthe had turned this once staunch supporter of England's aristocracy into a republican with strong leanings towards the extreme left. "Earls aren't everything. They make me sick."

"Earls are all right, Augustus," said Mike, trying to check the drift to Moscow.

"No, they ain't," retorted Augustus Robb hotly. "Swanking about and taking the bread out of the mouths of the widow and the orphan. And, what's more, I don't believe he's a ruddy earl at all."

"Yes, he is. He'll show you his coronet tomorrow, and you can play with it, Augustus."

"Mr. Robb."

"I'm sorry."

"You well may be. Augustus, indeed! If there's one thing I don't 'old with, it's familiarity. I've had to speak to young Cobbold about that. I may not be an earl, but I have my self-respect."

"Quite right, Mr. Robb," said Terry.

"R.," said Augustus Robb.

Lord Shortlands, as if feeling that it had taken an embarrassing turn, changed the conversation.

"I stopped outside Adela's door and listened," he said to Mike. "She seemed to be asleep."

"Good."

"Who's Adela?" asked Augustus Robb.

"My daughter."

Augustus Robb frowned. He knew that for some reason his mind was slightly under a cloud, but he could detect an obvious misstatement when he heard one.

"No, she ain't. This little bit is your daughter."

"There are three of us, Mr. Robb," explained Terry. "Three little bits."

"Ho," said Augustus Robb in the manner of one who, though unconvinced, is too chivalrous to contradict a lady. "Well, let's all go up and 'ave a talk with Adela."

"Later, don't you think?" suggested Mike, touched by Lord Shortlands' almost animal cry of agony. "After you've attended to the safe. It's over by the window."

"To the right of the window," said Terry.

"Over there by the window, slightly to the right," said Lord Shortlands, clarifying the combined message beyond the possibility of mistake.

"R.," said Augustus Robb, comprehending. "If you'd told me that before, we shouldn't have wasted all this . . . OUCH!"

His three supporters leaped like one supporter.

"Sh!" said Mike.

"Sh!" said Lord Shortlands.

"Sh!" said Terry.

Augustus Robb glared balefully.

"You say 'Sh' again, and I'll know what to do about it. Touch of cramp, that was," he explained. "Ketches me sometimes."

He heaved himself from his chair, the bag of tools in his hand. After doing a few simple calisthenics to prevent a recurrence of the touch of cramp, he approached the safe and tapped it with an experimental forefinger. Then he sneered at it openly.

"Call this a safe?"

The loftiness of his tone encouraged his supporters greatly. Theirs was the lay outlook, and to them the safe appeared quite a toughish sort of safe. It was stimulating to hear this expert speak of it with so airy a contempt.

"You think you'll be able to bust it?" said Mike.

’   Augustus Robb gave a short, amused laugh.

"Bust it? I could do it with a sardine opener. Go and get me a sardine opener," he said, jerking an authoritative thumb at Lord Shortlands, whom he seemed to have come to regard as a sort of plumber's mate. "No, 'arf a mo'." He scrutinized the despised object more closely. "No, it ain't sporting. Gimme a hairpin."

Lord Shortlands, frankly unequal to the situation, had withdrawn to the sofa, and was sitting on it with his head between his hands. Mike, too, was at a loss for words. It was left to Terry to try to reason with the man of the hour.

"Don't you think you had better use your tools, Mr. Robb?" she said, smiling that winning smile of hers. "It seems a pity not to, after you went to all the trouble of going to London for them."

Augustus Robb, though normally clay in the hands of pleading Beauty, shook his head.

"Gimme a hairpin," he repeated firmly.

There came to Mike the realization of the blunder he had made in not permitting Stanwood Cobbold to take part in these operations. With his direct, forceful methods, Stanwood was just the man this crisis called for. He endeavoured to play an understudy's role, though conscious of being but a poor substitute.

"That'll be all of that," he said crisply and authoritatively. "We don't want any more of this nonsense. Cut the comedy, and get busy."

It was an error in tactics. The honeyed word might have softened Augustus Robb. The harsh tone offended him. He drew himself up haughtily.

"So that's the way you talk, is it? Well, just for that I'm going to chuck the ruddy tools out of the ruddy window."

He turned and raised the hand that held the bag. He started swinging it.

"Mike!" cried Terry.

"Stop him!" cried Lord Shortlands.

Mike sprang forward to do so. Then suddenly he paused.

The reason he paused was that he had heard from the corridor outside a female voice, uttering the words "Who is there?" and it had chilled him to the marrow. But it was an unfortunate thing to have done, for it left him within the orbit of the swinging bag. Full of hard instruments with sharp edges, it struck him on the side of the face, and he reeled back. The next moment there was a crash, sounding in many of its essentials like the end of the world. Augustus Robb had released the bag, and it had passed through the window with a rending noise of broken glass. A distant splash told that it had fallen into the moat.

"Coo!" said Augustus Robb, sobered.

Terry gave a cry.

"Oh, Mike! Are you hurt?"

But Mike had bounded from the room, banging the door behind him.

17

To THE little group he had left in the library this abrupt departure seemed inexplicable. Intent on their own affairs, they had heard no female voice in the corridor, and for some moments they gazed at each other in silent bewilderment.

Lord Shortlands was the first to speak. More and more during the recent proceedings he had been wishing himself elsewhere, and now that the chief executive had created a deadlock by recklessly disposing of his tools there seemed nothing to keep him.

"I'm going to bed," he announced.

"But what made him rush off like that?" asked Terry.

Augustus Robb had found a theory that seemed to cover the facts.

"Went to bathe his eye, ducky. Nasty one he stopped. Only natural his first impulse would be to redooce the swelling. Coo! I wouldn't have had a thing like that happen for a hundred quid."

"Oh, Shorty, do you think he's hurt?"

Lord Shortlands declined to be drawn into a discussion of Mike's injuries. He liked Mike, and in normal circumstances would have been the first to sympathize, but there had just come to him the stimulating thought that, even after Augustus Robb had had his fill, there must still be quite a bit of the right stuff in his room, and he yearned for it as the hart yearns for the waterbrooks. With the golden prospect of a couple of quick ones before him, it is difficult for an elderly gentleman with high blood pressure, who has been through what the fifth Earl of Shortlands had so recently been through, to allow his mind to dwell on the black eyes of young men who are more acquaintances than friends.

"Good night," he said, and left them.

Augustus Robb continued to suffer the pangs of remorse.

"No, not for a thousand million pounds would I 'ave 'ad a thing like that 'appen," he said regretfully. "When I think of all the blokes there are that I'd enjoy dotting in the eye, it do seem a bit 'ard that it 'ad to be Mr. Cardinal who copped it. A gentleman that I 'ave the highest respect for."

Terry turned on him like a leopardess.

"You might have killed him!"

"I wouldn't go so far as to say that, ducky," Augustus Robb demurred. "Just a simple slosh in the eye, such as so often occurs. 'Owever, I'm glad to see you takin' it to 'eart so much, because it shows that love has awakened in your bosom."

Terry's indignation had waned. Her sense of humour was seldom dormant for long.

"Does it, Mr. Robb?"

"Sure sign, ducky. You've been acting silly, trying to 'arden your heart to Mr. Cardinal like Pharaoh in the Good Book when all those frogs come along." He raised the crème de menthe to his lips and lowered it disappointedly. " 'Ullo, none left."

"What a shame."

"Peppermint," said Augustus Robb, sniffing. "Takes me back, that does. Years ago, before you were born or thought of, my old uncle Fred——"

"Yes, you told me."

"Did I? Ho. Well, what was we talking about?"

"Frogs."

"We wasn't, neither. I simply 'appened to mention frogs in passing, like. We was talking about 'ardening 'earts, and I was saying that love had awakened in your bosom. And 'igh time, too. Why don't you go after Mr. Cardinal and give him a nice big kiss?"

"That would be a good idea, you think?"

"Only possible course to pursue. He loves you, ducky."

"What a lot you seem to know about it all. Did he confide in you? Oh, I was forgetting. You read that letter of his."

"That's right. Found it lying on his desk."

"Do you always read people's private letters?"

"Why, yus, when I get the chanst. I like to keep abreast of what's going on around me. And I take a particular interest in Mr. Cardinal's affairs. There's a gentleman that any young woman ought to be proud to hitch up with. A fine feller, Mr. Cardinal is. What they call in America an ace."

"Did you like America, Mr. Robb?"

"Why, yus, America's all right. Ever tasted corn-beef hash?"

"No."

"You get that in America. And waffles."

"Tell me all about waffles."

"I won't tell you all about waffles. I'm telling you about Mr. Cardinal. The whitest man I know."

"Do you know many white men?"

Augustus Robb fell into a brief reverie.

"And planked shad," he said, coming out of it. "You get that in America, too. And chicken Maryland. R., and strorberry shortcake."

"You seem very fond of food."

"And I'm very fond of Mr. Cardinal," said Augustus Robb, not to be diverted from his theme. "I keep tellin' young Cobbold he ought to try and be more like 'im. Great anxiety that young Cobbold is to me. His pop put him in my charge, and I look upon him as a sacred trust. And what 'appens? 'Arf the time he's off somewhere getting a skinful, and the other 'arf he's going about allowing butlers to persuade him to say his name's Rossiter."

"I didn't know Stanwood drank so very much."

"Absorbs the stuff like a thirsty flower absorbs the summer rain, ducky. Different from Mr. Cardinal. Always moderate 'e is. You could let Mr. Cardinal loose in a distillery with a bucket in 'is hand, and he'd come out clear-eyed and rosy-cheeked and be able to say 'British Constitution' without 'esitation. Yus, a splendid feller. And that's what makes it seem so strange that a little peanut like you keeps giving him the push."

"Aren't you getting rather rude, Mr. Robb?"

"Only for your own good, ducky. I want to see you 'appy."

"Oh? I beg your pardon."

"Granted. You'd be very 'appy with Mr. Cardinal. Nice disposition he's got."

"Yes."

"Always merry and bright."

"Yes."

"Plays the ukulele."

"You're making my mouth water."

"*And* kind to animals. I've known Mr. Cardinal pick up a pore lorst dog in the street and press it to his bosom, like Abraham—muddy day it was, too—and fetch it along to young Cobbold's apartment and give it young Cobbold's dinner. Touched me, that did," said Augustus Robb, wiping away another tear. "Thinkin' of bein' kind to dorgs reminds me of 'Er," he said, in explanation of this weakness. "She was always very kind to dorgs. And now 'ow about going after him and giving him that kiss and telling him you'll be his?"

"I don't think I will, Mr. Robb."

"Aren't you going to be his?"

"No."

"Now, don't you be a little muttonhead, ducky. You just 'op along and . . . Oh, 'ullo, Mr. Cardinal."

Terry gave a cry.

"Oh, Mike!"

And Augustus Robb, with a sharp "Coo!", stared aghast at his handiwork. Mike's left eye was closed, and a bruise had begun to spread over the side of his face, giving him the appearance of a man who has been stung by bees.

"Coo, Mr. Cardinal, I'm sorry."

Mike waved aside his apologies.

"Quite all right, Augustus. Sort of thing that might have happened to anyone. Where's Shorty?"

"Gone to bed," said Terry. She was still staring at his battered face, conscious of strange emotions stirring within her. "Why did you rush off like that?"

"I heard your sister Adela out in the corridor."

"Oh, my goodness!"

"It's all right. I steered her off."

"What did you say to her?"

"Well, I had to think quick, of course. She was headed for the scene of disturbance, and moving well. She asked me what went on, and, as I told you, I had to think quick. You say Shorty's gone to bed? I'm glad. Let him be happy while he can. Poor old Shorty. The heart bleeds."

"Do go on. What did you say?"

"I'll tell you. I mentioned, I believe, that I had to think quick?"

"Yes, twice."

"No, only once, but then, like lightning. Well, what happened was this. It seemed to me, thinking quick, that the only way of solving the am-parce was to sacrifice Shorty. Like Russian peasants with their children, you know, when they are pursued by wolves and it becomes imperative to lighten the sledge. It would never have done for your sister to come in here and find Augustus, so I told her that Shorty was in the library, as tight as an owl and breaking windows. 'Look what he's done to my eye,' I said. I begged her to leave the thing to me. I said I would get him to bed all right. She was very grateful. She thanked me, and said what a comfort I was, and pushed off. You don't seem very elated."

"I'm thinking of Shorty."

"Yes, he is a little on my mind, too. I told you that my heart bled for him. Still, into each life some rain must fall. That's one of Spink's gags. Another is that you cannot make an omelette without breaking eggs."

"I suppose not. And, of course, you had to think quick."

"Very quick. I feel sure that Shorty, when informed of all the circumstances, will applaud."

"If not too heartily."

"If, as you say, not too heartily. He will see that I acted for the best."

"Let's hope that that will comfort him when he meets Adela tomorrow. And now what do we do for that eye of yours?"

"I was about to take it to bed."

"It wants bathing in warm water."

"It wants 'avin' a bit of steak put on it," said Augustus Robb with decision. His had been a life into which at one time injured eyes had entered rather largely. "You trot along to the larder, ducky, and get a nice piece of raw steak. Have him fixed up in no time."

"I think you're right," said Mike.

"I know I'm right. You can't beat steak."

"Cruel Sports of the Past—Beating the Steak. I hate to give you all this trouble."

"No trouble," said Terry, and departed on her errand of mercy.

Augustus Robb surveyed the eye, and delivered an expert's verdict.

"That's a shiner, all right, chum."

"It is, indeed, Augustus. I feel as if I'd got mumps."

"Pity it 'ad to come at a time like this."

"You consider the moment ill chosen?"

"Well, use your intelligence, cocky. You want to look your best before 'Er, don't you? Women don't like seein' a feller with a bunged-up eye. Puts them off of him. May awake pity, per'aps, but not love. I could tell by the way the little bit of fluff was talkin' just now——"

"By 'little bit of fluff' you mean——"

"Why, 'Er."

"I see. Would it be possible for you, Augustus, in speaking of Lady Teresa Cobbold, not to describe her as a little bit of fluff?"

"Well, if you're so particular. So what was I saying? Ho, yus. When I suggested to her that she should . . . Coo! That eye's getting worse. Deepenin' in colour. Reminds me of one a feller give me in our debating society once, when I was speaking in the Conservative interest, him being of Socialistic views . . . Where was I?"

"I don't know."

"I do. I was starting to tell you the advice I give that little bit of fluff."

"Augustus!"

"Mind you, I can fully understand your being took with 'er. Now I've seen 'er, I can appreciate those sentiments of yours in that letter. She's a cuddly little piece."

Mike sighed. He had hoped to be able to get through the evening without recourse to Stanwood Cobbold methods, but it was plain that only these methods would serve here.

"Augustus," he said gently.

" 'Ullo?"

"Doing anything at the moment?"

"No."

"Then just turn around, will you?"

"Why?"

"Never mind why. I ask this as a favor. Turn around, and bend over a little."

"Like this?"

"That's exactly right. There!" said Mike, and kicked the inviting target with a vigour and crispness of follow-through which would have caused even Stanwood to nod approvingly.

"Hoy!" cried Augustus Robb.

He had drawn himself to his full height, and would probably have spoken further, but at this moment Terry came in, carrying a bowl of warm water and a plate with a piece of steak on it.

"Here we are," she said. "You look very serious, Mr. Robb."

Augustus Robb did not reply. His feelings had been wounded to the quick, and he was full of thoughts too deep for utterance. Adjusting his horn-rimmed spectacles and giving Mike another long, silent, reproachful look, he strode from the room. Terry gazed after him, perplexed.

"What's the matter with Mr. Robb?"

"I have just been obliged to kick him."

"Kick him? Why?"

"He spoke lightly of a woman's name."

"No!"

"I assure you."

"How is he as a light speaker?"

"In the first rank. He sullied my ears by describing you as a cuddly little piece."

"But aren't I?"

"That is not the point. If we are to be saved from the disruptive forces that wrecked Rome and Babylon, we cannot have retired porch climbers speaking in this lax manner of girls who are more like angels than anything. It strikes at the very root of everything that makes for sane and stabilized government. 'Cuddly little piece,' indeed!"

"Bend your head down," said Terry. She dabbed at his eye with the sponge. "You know, you're going to be sorry for this."

"Not unless you drip the water down my neck."

"For kicking poor Mr. Robb, I mean. He's your staunchest friend and firmest supporter. Before you came in, he was urging me to marry you."

"What!"

"I told you you would be sorry."

"I'm gnawed by remorse. How can I ever atone? Tell me more."

"He was very emphatic. He said you were the whitest man he knew, and expressed himself as amazed that a little peanut like me should spurn your suit."

"God bless him! To think that foot of mine should have jolted that golden-hearted trouser seat. I will abase myself before him tomorrow. But isn't it extraordinary——"

"Don't wiggle. The water's going down your neck."

"I like it. But isn't it extraordinary how everyone seems to want you to marry me? First Shorty, and now Augustus. It's what the papers call a widespread popular demand. Don't you think you ought to listen to the Voice of the People?"

"Now the steak. I'll tie it up with your handkerchief."

Mike sighed sentimentally.

"How little I thought in those lonely days in Hollywood that a time would come when I would be sitting in your home, with you sticking steak on my eye!"

"Were you lonely in Hollywood?"

"Achingly lonely."

"Odd."

"Not at all. You were not there."

"I mean, that isn't Stanwood's story. He said you were never to be seen without dozens of girls around you, like the hero of a musical comedy."

Mike started.

"Did Stanwood tell you that?"

"Yes. He said that watching you flit through the night life of Hollywood always brought to his mind that old song 'Hullo, hullo, hullo, it's a different girl again!' "

There came to Mike, not for the first time, the thought that Stanwood Cobbold ought to be in some kind of home.

"Wasn't he right? Didn't you ever go out with girls?"

It is difficult to look dignified with a piece of steak on your left eye, but Mike did his best.

"I may occasionally have relaxed in feminine society. One does in those parts. But what of it?"

"Oh, nothing. I just mentioned it."

"Hollywood is not a monastery."

"No, so I've heard."

"It's a place where women are, as it were, rather thrust upon you. And one has to be civil."

"There. That's the best I can do. How does it feel?"

"Awful. Like some kind of loathsome growth."

"I wish you could see yourself in the glass."

"You're always wanting me to see myself in the glass. Do I look bad?"

"Repulsive. Like a wounded gangster after a beer war."

"Then now is obviously the moment to renew my suit. You said, if you remember, that if ever there came a time when my fatal beauty took a toss——"

"It's only temporary, I'm afraid. Tomorrow, if you keep the steak on, you'll be just as dazzling as ever. I'll say good night."

"You would say some silly thing like that at a moment like this. I'm going to keep you here till breakfast time, unless you're sensible."

"In what way sensible?"

"You know in what way sensible. Terry, you little mutt, will you marry me?"

"No."

"But why not?"

"I told you why not."

"I wrote that off as pure delirium. Girls don't turn a man down just because he has regular features."

"This one does."

"But you know I love you."

"Do I?"

"You ought to by this time. You're the only girl in the world, as far as I'm concerned."

"Not according to Stanwood. He was most explicit on the point. Dozens of them, he told me, night after night, each lovelier than the last and all of them squealing 'Oh, *Mike,* darling!' "

"Curse Stanwood! The sort of man who ought to be horsewhipped on the steps of his club."

"The only trouble is that if you horsewhipped Stanwood on the steps of his club, he would horsewhip you on the steps of yours."

"I know. That's the catch. It's all wrong that fellows who talk the way Stanwood Cobbold does should be constructed so large and muscular. It doesn't give the righteous a chance."

"Tell me about these girls."

"There's nothing to tell. I used to go dancing with them."

"Ah!"

"You needn't say 'Ah!' If you want to dance, you've got to provide yourself with a girl, haven't you? How long do you think it would take the management at the Trocadero to bounce a fellow who started pirouetting all over the floor by himself? They're extraordinarily strict about that sort of thing."

"What's the Trocadero?"

"A Hollywood haunt of pleasure."

"Where you took your harem?"

"Don't call them my harem! They were mere acquaintances; some merer than others, of course, but all of them very mere. I wish you would expunge Stanwood's whole story from your mind."

'Well, I can't. I think perhaps I had better tell you something."

"More delirium?"

"No, not this time. It's something that may make you understand why I'm like this. You asked me yesterday what I had got against men who were too good-looking, and I said I mistrusted them. I will now tell you why. I was once engaged to one."

"Good Lord! When?"

"Not so long ago. When I was in that musical comedy. He was the juvenile. Geoffrey Harvest."

Mike uttered a revolted cry.

"My God! That heel? That worm? That oleaginous louse? Whenever I went to the show, I used to long to leap across the footlights and crown him."

"You can't deny that he was handsome."

"In a certain ghastly, greasy, nausea-promoting way, perhaps."

"Well, that's the point I'm trying to make. I thought him wonderful."

"You ought to be ashamed of yourself."

"I am."

"A juvenile! You fell for a juvenile! And not one of those song-and-hoofing juveniles, whom you can respect, but the kind that looks noble and sings tenor. I am shocked and horrified, young Terry. Whatever made you go and do a fatheaded thing like that?"

"I told you. His beauty ensnared me. But the scales fell from my eyes. He turned out to be a flippertygibbet."

"A what was that once again?"

"Shorty's word, not mine."

"Where does Shorty pick up these expressions?"

"It means a man who can't resist a pretty face. After I had caught him not resisting a few, I broke off the engagement. And I made up my mind that I would never, never, never let myself be swept off my feet by good looks again. So now you understand."

Mike was struggling with complex emotions.

"But what earthly right have you coolly to assume that I'm like that?"

"Just a woman's intuition."

"You're all wrong."

"Perhaps. But there it is. I can't risk it. I couldn't go through it all again. I simply couldn't. You've no idea how a girl feels when she falls in love with a man who lets her down. It's horrible. You suffer torments, and all the while you're calling yourself a fool for minding. It's like being skinned alive in front of an amused audience."

"I wouldn't let you down."

"I wonder."

"Terry! Come on. Take a chance."

"You speak as if it were a sort of game. I'm afraid I'm rather Victorian and earnest about marriage. I don't look on it as just a lark."

"Nor do I."

"You seem to."

"Why do you say that?"

"Well, don't you think yourself that your attitude all through has been a little on the flippant side?"

Mike beat his breast, like the Wedding Guest.

"There you are! That's it! I felt all along that that was the trouble. You think I'm not sincere, because I clown. I knew it. All the time I was saying to myself 'Lay off it, you poor sap! Change the record,' but I couldn't. I had to clown. It was a kind of protective armour against shyness."

"You aren't telling me you're shy?"

'Of course I'm shy. Every man's shy when he's really in love. For God's sake don't think I'm not serious. I love you. I've always loved you. I loved you the first time I saw you. Terry, darling, do please believe me. This is life and death."

Terry's heart gave a leap. Her citadel of defence was crumbling.

"If you had talked like that before——"

"Well, it's not too late, is it? Terry, say it's not too late. Because it will be, if you turn me down now. This is my last chance."

"What do you mean?"

"I've got to go."

"Go?"

"Back to Hollywood."

A cold hand seemed to clutch at Terry's heart. She stared at him dumbly. He had been striding about the room, but now he was at her side, bending over her.

"Oh, Mike," she whispered.

"Next week at the latest. I found a cable waiting for me in London this afternoon. They want me at the office. The head man's ill, and I've got to go back at once. We shall be six thousand miles apart, and not a chance of ever getting together again."

"Oh, Mike," said Terry.

Into Mike's mind there flashed a recent remark of Augustus Robb's. Turning the conversation to the affairs of him, Mike, and what he described as "this little party," Augustus Robb had asked the pertinent question "Ever tried kissing her?", adding the words "I've known that to answer."

True, Augustus Robb had been considerably more than one over the eight when he had thrown out this *obiter dictum,* but that did not in any way detract from the value of the pronouncement. Many a man's brain gives of its best and most constructive only when it has been pepped up with crème de menthe, and something seemed to tell Mike that in so speaking the fellow had been right.

"Terry, darling!"

He took Terry in his arms and kissed her, and it was even as Augustus Robb had said.

It answered.

BOOK THREE

18

Stanwood Cobbold sat up in bed and switched on the light. He looked at his watch. The hour was some minutes after two.

Stanwood was a young man whom prolonged association with football coaches had trained to obey orders, and when Mike had told him to go to bed and stay there he had done so without demur. It had pained him to be excluded from the night's doings, but he was fair-minded and could quite appreciate the justice of his friend's statement that, if permitted to be present, he would infallibly gum the game. Looking back on his past, he realized that he always had gummed such games as he had taken part in, and there seemed no reason to suppose that he would not gum this one.

But now that he had woken at this particular moment, he could see no possible harm in getting up and stepping along to the library in order to ascertain if all had gone according to plan. By now, if they had run to schedule, the operations must be concluded, and he was consumed with curiosity as to how it had all come out. He also wanted to get a flash of Augustus Robb. A lit-up Augustus Robb should, he considered, provide a spectacle which nobody ought to miss.

He knew where the library was. It was thither that the little guy with the nose glasses had taken him after dinner to talk about stamps. Slipping on a dressing gown, he made his way down a flight of stairs and along a passage. A chink of light beneath the door told him that the room was still occupied, and he entered expecting to find a full gathering—a little apprehensive, too, lest that full gathering might turn on him and give him hell for intruding. His mental attitude, as he went in, resembled that of a large, wet dog which steals into a drawing room, unable to resist the gregarious urge to join the party but none too sure of its welcome.

He was relieved to find only Terry present. She was sitting in a deep chair, apparently wrapped in thought.

"Hiya," he said in what, if questioned, he would have described as a cautious whisper.

Terry came out of her meditations with a leap and a squeak. She had stayed on after Mike had left to take the basin and plate back to the kitchen.

397

She had promised him that she would go to bed immediately, but she had not done so, for she was loth to break the magic spell which was upon her. Stanwood's voice, which was like the sudden blaring of a radio when you turn the knob too far, gave her a painful shock.

"Stanwood!" she said severely. "What do you mean by yelling like that?"

"I was whispering," said Stanwood, aggrieved.

"Well, whisper a bit more piano. Come and sit on the sofa and murmur in my ear."

Stanwood tripped over a rug and upset a small table and came to rest at her side.

"Everything okay?" he murmured hoarsely.

"Yes, wonderful," said Terry, with shining eyes.

Stanwood was well pleased. The success or non-success of the expedition could not affect him personally, but it had had his sympathy and support.

"That's good. Then Augustus brought home the bacon all right?"

"What?"

"He got the stamp?"

"Oh, the stamp?" It came to Stanwood as a passing thought that his companion seemed a little distrait. "No, he didn't. There was a hitch."

"A hitch?"

"Yes: You see that broken window? Mr. Robb threw his tools through it, and they are now at the bottom of the moat."

Stanwood inspected the window. He had been thinking he felt a draft, but had put it down to his imagination.

"What made him do that?" he asked, interested.

"Fretfulness. Mike spoke crossly to him, and it hurt his feelings."

"Gee! He must have been sozzled."

"He was."

"I wish I'd seen him."

"It was a very impressive spectacle."

Stanwood found a variety of emotions competing for precedence within him—pity for Lord Shortlands, who had not got his stamp; regret that he himself should have come too late to see Augustus Robb with so spectacular a bun on; but principally bewilderment. He could not square this record of failure with the speaker's ecstatic mood and her statement that conditions were wonderful.

"But you said everything was okay."

"So it is. Have you ever felt that you were floating on a pink cloud over an ocean of bliss?"

"Sure," said Stanwood. This illusion had come to him twice in his life: once when Eileen Stoker, knocking the ash off her cigarette, had told him that she would be his, and once, a few years earlier, on the occasion when his inspired place kick had enabled his university to beat Notre Dame 7–6 in the last half minute.

"Well, that's how I'm feeling. I'm going to marry Mike, Stanwood."

"You are? But I thought——"

"So did I. But I changed my mind."

"Good for you."

"You're pleased?"

"You betcher."

There was silence. Terry, floating on that pink cloud, was thinking her own thoughts with a light in her eyes and a smile on her parted lips, and Stanwood was experiencing once again the surge of relief which had swept over him on the morning when Augustus Robb had first revealed Mike Cardinal's love for a girl who was not Eileen Stoker. As then, he felt that a great weight had been removed from his mind.

"I'm tickled to death," he said, resuming the conversation after time out for silent rejoicing. "And I'll tell you why. This removes old Mike from circulation. Great relief, that is."

"What do you mean?"

"Well, you know how it is when a guy that's as good-looking as he is is knocking around. You get uneasy."

"Why?"

"Well, you never know what may not happen, I had the idea that he was making a play for Eileen."

The pink cloud failed to support Terry. It shredded away beneath her, and she plunged into the ocean. And it was not, as she had supposed, an ocean of bliss, but a cold, stinging ocean, full of horrible creatures which were driving poisoned darts into her.

"Don't be an idiot," she said, and her voice sounded strange and unfamiliar in her ears.

Stanwood proceeded. He was feeling fine.

"It was at that party of mine that I first got thinking that way. I gave a party for Eileen when she hit London, and Mike was there with his hair in a braid, and he seemed to me to be giving her quite a rush. I don't know if you've ever noticed that way he's got of looking at girls? I'd call it a sort of melting look . . . Yes?"

"Nothing."

"I thought you spoke."

"No."

"Well, he seemed to me to be giving her that look a good deal during the doings, and I didn't like it much. Of course he had known her in Hollywood—"

"Were they great friends?"

"Oh, sure. Well, that was that, and when she sprang that thing on me—"

"What thing?" said Terry dully.

"Didn't I tell you about that? Why, no, of course, I didn't get the chance. She suddenly told me she wasn't going to marry me unless I could get me some money. Said she'd tried it before, marrying guys with no money, and it hadn't worked out so good. So it was all off, she said, if I couldn't deliver. Well, that sounded straight enough, but tonight, as I was dropping off to sleep, it suddenly struck me that maybe it was just a bit of boloney."

"Boloney?"

"The old army game," explained Stanwood. "I thought she might be simply playing me up. You see, I remembered her and Mike at that party, and I knew what Mike's like with girls, and I sort of wondered if they mightn't have fallen for each other and this was just her way of easing me out. That's why it's so great to hear that you and he have fixed it up. Because if he's that way with you, he can't be that way with her, can he?"

Terry found herself unable to subscribe to this simple creed. It appeared to satisfy Stanwood, who had an honest and guileless mind, but she shivered. There had risen before her eyes the wraith of Geoffrey Harvest, that inconstant juvenile. He, though ostensibly "that way" with her, had never experienced the slightest difficulty in being "that way" with others. Something seemed to stab at her heart, and with a little cry she buried her face in her hands.

"Here! Hey!" said Stanwood. "What goes on?"

The minds of men like Stanwood Cobbold run on conventional lines. Certain actions automatically produce in them certain responses. When, for instance, they find themselves in the society of an old crony of the opposite sex and that crony suddenly gives a gurgle like a dying duck and buries her face in her hands, the Stanwood Cobbolds know what to do. They say "Here! Hey! What goes on?", and place their arm in a brotherly fashion about her waist.

It was as Stanwood was adjusting this brotherly arm that a voice spoke in his rear.

"Mr. ROSSITER!"

Lady Adela Topping was standing in the doorway, surveying the scene with what was only too plainly a disapproving eye.

When a woman of strict views comes into her library at half-past two in the morning to inspect the damage created there by a supposedly inebriated father and finds her youngest sister, towards whom she has always felt like a mother, seated on the sofa in pajamas and a kimono with a young man in pajamas and a dressing gown; and when this young man has his arm, if not actually around her waist, as nearly so as makes no matter, it is understandable that she should speak like Mrs. Grundy at her most censorious. It was thus that Lady Adela had spoken, and Stanwood, who until her voice rang out had been unaware that she was a pleasant visitor, rose from his seat as if a charge of trinitrotoluol had been touched off under him.

"Gosh!" he exclaimed.

It was a favorite monosyllable of his, but never had he spoken it with such a wealth of emphasis. His emotions were almost identical with those which he had experienced one November afternoon when an opposing linesman, noticing that the referee was looking the other way, had driven a quick fist into his solar plexus. For an instant he was incapable of further speech, or even of connected thought. Then, his brain clearing, he saw what he had to do.

In the code of the Stanwood Cobbolds of this world there is a commandment which stands out above all others, written in large letters, and those letters of gold. It is the one that enacts that if by his ill-considered actions the man of honour has compromised a lady he must at once proceed, no matter what the cost, to de-compromise her.

He did not hesitate. Tripping over the skirt of his dressing gown and clutching at a pedestal bearing a bust of the late Mr. Gladstone and bringing pedestal and bust with a crash to the ground, he said with quiet nobility:

"It's all right, ma'am. We're engaged!"

As a general rule, given conditions such as prevailed in the library of Beevor Castle at two-thirty on this May morning, no better thing than this can be said. Such a statement clears the air and removes misunderstandings. It smoothes the frown from the knitted brow of censure and brings to the tightened lips of disapproval the forgiving smile. But on this occasion something went wrong with the system, and what caused this hitch was Lady Adela's practical, common-sense outlook.

"Engaged?" she echoed, not in the least soothed; in fact, looking more like Mrs. Grundy than ever. "Don't talk nonsense. How can you be engaged? You met my sister for the first time at dinner tonight."

Then, suddenly, as she paused for a reply, there came to her the recollection of certain babblings which Desborough had inflicted upon her in the privacy of her bedroom that night, while she was creaming her face. Some story about this Mr. Rossiter of Spink's being an impostor; a view, if she recollected rightly, which he had based on the fact that the other had displayed an ignorance about stamps.

At the time she had scouted the notion, it being her habit to scout practically all her husband's notions. But now, gazing at Stanwood, she found herself inclining to a theory which at the time when it was placed before her she had dismissed as absurd. A moment later she was not merely inclining, she had become that theory's wholehearted supporter. Foreign though it was to her policy to admit that Desborough could ever be right about anything, she knew that in this single instance he had not erred.

Nearly a year had passed since, in exile at Harrogate, she had read the second of those reports which she had ordered Mervyn Spink to send her each month, telling of the progress of events at the castle during her absence, but now a sentence in it came vividly to her mind. Mervyn Spink, in his running commentary, had stated that, owing to having broken his spectacles and so rendered it difficult for him to see where he was going, young Mr. Rossiter had had the misfortune to collide with and destroy the large Chinese vase in the hall.

His spectacles!

She fixed Stanwood with a burning eye, which, much as he would have preferred to do so, he could not avoid.

"Where are your spectacles?" she demanded.

"Ma'am?"

"Do you wear spectacles?"

"No, ma'am."

"Then WHO ARE YOU?"

"Stanwood Cobbold, ma'am," said Stanwood, even as Mike had predicted. Beneath that eye he was incapable of subterfuge.

Lady Adela gasped. Whatever she had expected to hear, it was not this.

"Stanwood Cobbold?"

"Yes, ma'am."

Lady Adela, as so often happens in these knotty cases, decided to take a second opinon.

"Is this Mr. Cobbold, Terry?"

"Yes."

"Then who—WHO—is the other one?"

"He is a friend of Stanwood's. His name is Cardinal."

A bright flush came into Lady Adela's face. No hostess can be expected to enjoy this sort of thing, and she was the type of hostess who enjoys it least.

"Then why did he come here, saying he was you?" she demanded, turning that incandescent eye upon Stanwood again.

Stanwood cleared his throat. He untied the knot of the cord of his dressing gown and retied it. He passed a hand over his chin, then ran it down the back of his head.

"Well, it was this way——" he began, and so evident was it to Terry that he was about to relate in full detail the story of Lord Shortlands and his cook that she intervened hurriedly.

"Stanwood had some very important business that kept him in London——"

"Yay," said Stanwood, grateful for this kind assistance.

"—so he couldn't come, and—Mr. Cardinal made a sort of bet that he could come instead——"

"Yay," said Stanwood, well pleased with the way the story was shaping.

"—and not be found out . . ."

She paused. It may have been owing to Stanwood's interpolations, but the story sounded to her thin. She passed it under swift review. Yes, thin.

"It was a sort of joke," she said lamely.

Earls' daughters do not snort, but Lady Adela came very near to doing so.

"A joke!"

"And then Stanwood found that he was able to come, after all . . ."

Terry paused again.

"So he came," she said.

To her amazement she saw that her sister's stony gaze was softening. It was

as if a sweeter, kindlier Lady Adela Topping had been substituted for that
forbidding statue of sternness and disapproval. The chatelaine of Beevor
Castle was actually smiling.

"I think I can guess why he did that," she said archly, and again Terry
marvelled. She had never seen Adela arch before. "You found you couldn't
keep away from Terry, Mr. Cobbold? Wasn't that it?"
that it?"

Stanwood was in poor shape, but he was still equal to saying "Yay," so he
said it.

"And Spink suggested your pretending to be Mr. Rossiter?"

"Yay."

"I shall speak to Spink in the morning," said Lady Adela, with a return of
her earlier manner. "And this Mr. Cardinal, too. Well, I ought to be very
angry with you, Mr. Cobbold."

"Yay."

"But I feel I can't be. And now you had better go to bed."

"Yay."

"I would like a word with Terry. Good night."

"Yay," said Stanwood, and withdrew in disorder.

The word his hostess had with Terry was brief.

"Well, really, Terry!" she said.

Terry did not speak.

"You are the most extraordinary girl. Behaving like this. Still, I won't scold
you. I'm so delighted."

Lady Adela folded her sister in a loving embrace. She gave her a long,
lingering, congratulatory kiss.

"Desborough says his father's worth MILLIONS!" she said.

19

THE SUNSHINE of another balmy day gilded the ancient walls of Beevor
Castle. Nine mellow chimes sounded from the clock over the stables. And
Lord Shortlands, entering the breakfast room, heaved a silent sigh as he saw
Desborough Topping seated at the table. He had hoped for solitude. Sombre
though his thoughts were, he wanted to be alone with them.

"Oh, hello," said Desborough Topping. "Good morning."

"Good morning," said Lord Shortlands.

He spoke dully. He was pale and leaden-eyed and looked like a butler who
has come home with the milk, for he had had little sleep. Few things are less
conducive to slumber than the sudden collapse of all one's hopes and dreams
round about bedtime, and when Augustus Robb in that unfortunate moment

of pique had hurled his bag of tools into the moat, he had ruined the fifth earl's chances of a good night's rest. From two o'clock onwards the unhappy peer had tossed on his pillow, dozing only in snatches and waking beyond hope of further repose at about the hour when the knowledgeable bird is starting wormwards.

"Nice day," said Desborough Topping. "Don't touch the bacon," he advised. "That girl's scorched it again."

"Oh?" said Lord Shortlands. A tragedy to his son-in-law, who liked his bit of bacon of a morning, the misadventure left him cold.

"To a cinder, darn her. Thank goodness Mrs. Punter comes back this afternoon."

A look of infinite sadness came into Lord Shortlands' eyes. He was aware of Mrs. Punter's imminent return, and last night had hoped to have been able to greet her with the news that he had become a man of capital. Augustus Robb had shattered that dream. He helped himself to coffee—black coffee, but no blacker than his thoughts of Augustus Robb.

Breakfast at Beevor Castle was a repast in the grand old English manner, designed for sturdy men who liked to put their heads down and square their elbows and go to it. It was open to Lord Shortlands, had he so desired, to start with porridge, proceed to kippers, sausages, scrambled eggs and cold ham, and wind up with marmalade: and no better evidence of his state of mind can be advanced than the fact that he merely took a slice of dry toast, for he was a man who, when conditions were right, could put tapeworms to the blush at the morning meal. His prowess with knife and fork had often been noted by his friends. "Shortlands," they used to say, "may have his limitations, but he *can* breakfast."

He finished his coffee and refilled his cup. Desborough Topping, who had been fortifying himself with scrambled eggs, rose and helped himself to ham from the sideboard.

"Young Cobbold just left," he said, returning to the table.

"Oh?"

"Yes. Hurried through his breakfast. Said he had to get in to London early."

"Oh?"

"Probably wanted to have that eye of his seen to."

Lord Shortlands was not a quick-witted man, but even he could see that he must know nothing of Mike's eye.

"What eye?"

"He has a black eye."

"How did he get that?"

"AR, that's what I'd like to know, but he didn't tell me. I said to him 'That's a nasty eye you've got,' and he said 'Into each life some nasty eye must fall.' Evasive."

"Perhaps he bumped into something."

"Maybe."

Desborough Topping applied himself to his ham in silence for a space.

"But what?"

"What?"

"That's what I said—What? What could he have bumped into?"

Lord Shortlands tried to think of some of the things with which a man's eye could collide.

"A door?"

"Then why not say so?"

"I don't know."

"Nor me. Mysterious."

"Most."

"There's a lot of things going on in this house that want explaining. Did you hear a crash in the night?"

"A crash?"

"It woke me up."

Lord Shortlands was in a condition when he would have found any breakfast-table conversation trying, but he found this one particularly so.

"No. I—ah—heard nothing."

"Well, there was a crash. Around two in the morning. A sort of crashing sound, as if something had—er—crashed. I heard it distinctly. And that's not the only thing I'd like to have explained. Look," said Desborough Topping, peering keenly through his pince-nez like Scotland Yard on the trail, "what do you make of that guy that calls himself Rossiter?"

Lord Shortlands licked his lips. This is a phrase that usually denotes joy. In this instance, it did not. He prayed for something to break up this tête-à-tête, and his prayer was answered. The voice of Cosmo Blair, raised in song, sounded from without. The door opened, and Clare entered, followed by the eminent playwright.

"Ah, my dear Shortlands."

"Good morning, Father."

"Good morning," said Lord Shortlands, feeling like the man who, having got rid of one devil, was immediately occupied by seven others, worse than the first. When he had prayed for something to interrupt his chat with Desborough Topping, he had not been thinking of Cosmo Blair.

His spirits drooped still further. Those of Cosmo Blair, on the other hand, appeared to be soaring. Lord Shortlands had never seen the fellow so effervescent.

"Did you hear a crash last night?" asked Desborough Topping.

"I am in no mood to talk of crashes, my dear Topping," said Cosmo Blair. "This, my dear Topping and my dear Shortlands, is the happiest day of my life." He advanced to the table, and rested his hands on the cloth. "My lords, ladies and gentlemen, pray silence. Charge your coffee cups and drink to the health of the young couple."

"Cosmo and I are engaged, Father," said Clare in her direct way.

"My God!" said Lord Shortlands. "I mean, are you?"

Cosmo Blair placed a reassuring hand on his shoulder.

"I think I know what is in your mind, my dear Shortlands. You fear that you are about to lose a daughter. Have no anxiety. You are merely gaining a son."

"We're going to live at the castle," explained Clare.

"So that's all right," said Cosmo Blair. He was a kindly man at heart, and it gave him pleasure to relieve his future father-in-law's apprehensions. "We shall both be with you."

There came upon Lord Shortlands an urgent desire to get away from it all. Cosmo Blair's society often had this effect on him. He yearned for Terry. A moment before, he had been thinking of having a third cup of coffee, but now he decided to lose no time in going to her room, where he presumed her to be breakfasting. Terry was always the best medicine for a bruised soul.

He rose, accordingly, and Desborough Topping cocked a surprised eye at him.

"Finished?"

"Yes."

"Not going to eat anything?"

"No appetite."

"Too bad."

"A liver pill, my dear Shortlands," said Cosmo Blair. "That's what you want. Take it in a little water."

"Oh, by the way, Father," said Clare, "Adela would like a word with you later on."

Lord Shortlands started.

"Adela? What about?"

"She didn't say. I just poked my head in at her door and said Cosmo and I were engaged, and she told me to tell you."

It was a pensive Lord Shortlands who made his way to Terry's room. The news that he was to have Cosmo Blair with him for apparently the rest of his life had shaken him deeply, but not more so than the announcement that Adela wanted a word with him. It too often happened that, when his eldest daughter had a word with him, that word stretched itself into several thousand words, all unpleasant, and in his present low state of mind he felt unequal to anything but the kindest and gentlest treatment.

But he quickly recovered his poise. On occasions like this what a man needs above all else is a clean conscience, and his, on examination, proved to be as clean as a whistle. Except for wanting to marry her cook, introducing impostors into her home and inciting ex-burglars to break open her safe, of all of which peccadilloes she was of course ignorant, he had done absolutely nothing to invite Adela's censure. If Adela wanted a word with him, he told himself, it was no doubt on some trifling matter of purely domestic interest.

As he knocked on Terry's door, he was conscious of that moral strength which comes to fathers on whom their daughters have not got the goods.

Desborough Topping, meanwhile, had finished his ham and had gone up to see his wife, his dutiful habit at this time of day. He found her propped up among the pillows with a bed table across her knees, and was pleased to note that she seemed in excellent humour.

"Good morning, honey."

"Good morning, dear. Have you seen Clare?"

"Just left her. You mean this engagement of hers? She was telling me about that. You're pleased, I guess."

"Delighted. I like Cosmo so much."

"Got the stuff, too."

"Yes. And isn't it extraordinary that the two things should have happened almost at the same time?"

"Eh?"

"Don't you know? Terry's engaged to Stanwood Cobbold."

"You don't say!"

"Yes. It's really wonderful. He seems so nice, and of course Mr. Cobbold has millions."

"Yes, old Ellery's well fixed. When did it happen?"

"I heard about it early this morning."

"Funny he didn't say anything to me about it. He came in and rushed through his breakfast and dashed off. So they're engaged, are they? He looks as if he'd been having a barroom scrap instead of getting engaged. Got a peach of a black eye. I'd like to know who gave him that."

An austere look came into Lady Adela's face.

"I can tell you. It was Father."

"Father?"

"He was disgracefully intoxicated last night. I went to his room this morning, and it was littered with bottles."

Desborough Topping was visibly impressed. He had never supposed his father-in-law capable of such spirited behaviour. He also learned with surprise that he packed so spectacular a punch.

"Gee!" he said feelingly. "I'm glad he didn't take it into his head to haul off and sock *me*. I thought he looked a little peaked this morning. Well, say, he must have been pretty bad. I was discussing Cobbold's eye with him, just now, and he'd forgotten all about it."

"I will refresh his memory," said Lady Adela coldly. "But that wasn't Stanwood Cobbold that Father hit. It was a friend of his, a Mr. Cardinal. Mr. Rossiter is really Stanwood Cobbold."

Desborough Topping sat down on the bed. His air was that of one who is being tried too high.

"I don't get this."

"Well, I must admit that I am not very clear about it all myself. According to Terry, Stanwood found himself unable to come here, and this Mr. Cardinal made a bet that he could come instead of him and not be found out."

"Sounds crazy."

"Very. I intend to have a word with Mr. Cardinal."

"He's gone to London."

"When he gets back, then."

"But you say Cobbold couldn't come, and he did come."

"Oh, that part of it is easy enough to understand. After a day or two he found he was able to, and he couldn't keep away from Terry. So he came to the inn, and I suppose Spink told him he could get into the castle by pretending to be Mr. Rossiter."

Desborough Topping whistled.

"Then Spink——"

"Exactly. It was a deliberate plot on Spink's part to get possession of that stamp. I shall give him notice immediately."

"I would. The guy's a crook. These thriller fellows are right. Butlers want watching. I remember in *Murder at Murslow Grange* ... What are you planning to do with the stamp?"

"I've been thinking about that. We shall never know now whom it really belongs to. I think you had better have it."

"Me?"

"Well, nobody claims it, and it's about time you had some sort of return for all you've done for us. After all, you have been supporting the whole family for years."

Desborough Topping was moved. He bent over and kissed his wife.

"I call that mighty good of you, honey. I'll add it to my collection. It isn't every day that one gets the chance of laying one's hands on a Spanish *dos reales* unused, with an error in colour. But tell me more about the old man. Sozzled, was he?"

"Disgustingly."

"Did you see him?"

"No, I did not actually see him. I heard a crash in the early morning——"

"Oh, there was a crash? I thought so."

"It seemed to come from the library, so I started to go there, and I had nearly reached the door when Mr. Cardinal came rushing out with his eye all swollen. He told me that Father was in there in a terrible state. He said he had broken a window and hit him in the eye, but that I wasn't to worry, because he could get him to bed all right."

"Gee!"

"So I decided to leave everything to him. I am very angry with Mr. Cardinal, but I must say he seems a capable young man. He must have managed, for I heard nothing else. Then, some time later, I thought I would go to the library again and see what damage had been done, and there was

Terry sitting on the sofa with Stanwood Cobbold. At half-past two in the morning!"

"Gosh!"

"He had his arm around her waist."

"Well, I'll be darned!"

"When he saw me, he jumped up, of course, and it suddenly struck me that he was not wearing spectacles."

"Eh?"

"What you had told me of your suspicions had made me doubtful about him, and then I remembered that Spink in one of his letters, when the Rossiters had the castle, had mentioned that the son wore spectacles. So I asked him who he was, and he said he was Stanwood Cobbold. And then he told me that he and Terry were engaged."

"But what were they doing in the library?"

"I suppose they both heard the noise and went to see what had happened, and then they sat down for a talk before going to bed again. Just imagine! At half-past two in the morning! Terry really is the most reckless child. Thank heaven she's going to be married."

"And to a fellow who'll have all the money on earth, if his father loosens up. Which he will, of course. Old Ellery will be tickled stiff about this."

"You had better send him a cable, telling him what has happened. A nice, cordial cable, coming from an old friend. Go and do it now."

"Yes, dear."

"And find Father and tell him I want to see him."

"You wouldn't let him have his hangover in peace?"

"Certainly not."

"Just as you say, dear."

It was some little time before Desborough Topping returned.

"I've sent the cable. I said, 'Well comma Ellery comma old socks comma how's every little thing stop. Your son Stanwood just got engaged to Lady Teresa Cobbold stop. Charming girl stop. Congratulations and all the best stop.' Was that all right?"

"Splendid. Did you find Father?"

"I hunted everywhere. That's what kept me. But I couldn't locate him. Then I met Clare, and she told me that he and Terry had gone off to London. She met them starting out to make the train. She said they were planning to lunch somewhere."

"But Father hasn't any money. I gave him five pounds on his birthday, but he must have spent that when he went to London to meet Stanwood. Where could he have got any more?"

"Ah," said Desborough Topping guardedly. "There's an interesting piece in the paper this morning about the Modern Girl," he said, hastily changing a subject that threatened to become embarrassing. "I'll fetch it for you."

LORD SHORTLANDS' decision to visit London that morning had been one of those instantaneous decisions which men take in sudden crises. No sooner had he learned from Terry of the ingenious ruse whereby Mike some seven hours earlier had succeeded in checking his daughter Adela's advance on the library than the idea of absenting himself from Beevor Castle for a while had come to him in a flash.

It was with mixed feelings that he had listened to her story. A fair-minded man, he admitted that it had been essential for Mike, confronted with that menacing figure, to say something that would ease the strain, but he made no secret of his regret that he had not said something else. Within thirty seconds of the conclusion of the recital he was urging Terry to get dressed as quickly as possible and accompany him to the metropolis while the going was good.

This craven flight would, of course, merely postpone the impending doom, but he had a feeling that he would be able to face Adela with more hardihood after a lunch at Barribault's or some similar establishment, and he had not forgotten that he still had in his possession the greater part of the ten pounds which Desborough Topping had given him on his birthday. His frame of mind was somewhat similar to that of the condemned man who on the morning of his execution makes a hearty breakfast.

They took the eleven-three train, stopping only at Sevenoaks, and their arrival at the terminus found the fifth earl still gloomy and, in addition, extremely bewildered. It may have been because his mind, with so much on it, was not at its brightest, but he had found himself quite unable to follow Terry's tale of her matrimonial commitments. There were moments when he received the impression that she was going to marry young Cardinal, others when it seemed that she was going to marry Stanwood Cobbold, and still others when she appeared to be contemplating marrying both of them.

All very obscure and involved, felt Lord Shortlands, and not at all the sort of thing which a dutiful daughter should have inflicted on a father who had had about an hour and half's sleep. The one fact that emerged clearly was that if ever there was a time for hastening to his club and calling for the wine list, this was it, and he proceeded to do so, arranging with Terry, as before, to meet him in the lobby of Barribault's Hotel at one-thirty. This done, he sped like an arrow to the Senior Buffers.

Terry, for her part, went off to saunter through the streets, to eye the passers-by, to think opalescent thoughts and to pause from time to time to breathe on the shopwindows, particularly those which displayed hats, shoes, toilet soaps and jewellery. All these things she did with a high heart, for she was feeling—and, in the opinion of many who saw her, looking—like the Spirit of Springtime. She lacked the money this time to buy a new hat, but found in her crippled finances no cause for dejection. Hers was a mood of effervescent happinesss which did not require the artificial stimulus of new hats. She floated through a world of sunshine and roses.

Joy, it has been well said, cometh in the morning. Whatever doubts and misgivings may have disturbed Terry in the darkness, they had vanished in the light of the new day. She was now able to appraise at their true value those babblings of Stanwood Cobbold which had seemed so sinister in the small hours. After what had passed between her and Mike in the library last night, it was ridiculous to suppose for an instant that he did not love her, and her alone. Stanwood Cobbold, in suggesting that his fancy might rove towards motion-picture stars, had shown that he simply had no grasp of his subject.

She found herself blaming Stanwood Cobbold. Nobody, of course, who enjoyed the pleasure of intimacy with him, expected him to talk anything but nonsense, but he need not, she felt, have descended to such utter nonsense as that of which he had been guilty last night. She had just decided that she would be rather cold to him on her return, when she saw that there would be no need to wait till then.

An hour's aimless rambling through London's sunlit streets had taken Terry to Berkeley Square, and she had paused to survey it and to think with regret how they had ruined this pleasant oasis with their beastly Air Ministries and blocks of flats, when she was aware of a bowed figure clumping slowly towards her on leaden feet. It was Stanwood in person, and so dejected was his aspect that all thought of being cold left her.

"Stanwood," she cried, and he looked up like one coming out of a trance.

"Hiya," he said hollowly.

He made no reference to the circumstances of their last meeting. Presumably he had not forgotten them, but more recent happenings had relegated them to the category of things that do not matter. He gazed at Terry dully, like a hippopotamus that has had bad news.

"Hello," he said. "What are you doing here?"

"Shorty and I broke out of the Big House and came in to have lunch. What are you?"

Stanwood's attention seemed to wander. A blank expression came into his eyes. It was necessary for Terry, in order to recall him to the present, to kick him on the ankle.

"Ouch!" said Stanwood. He passed a hand across his forehead. "What did you say?"

"I asked what you were doing in London."

A look of pain contorted the young man's face.

"I came to see Eileen."

"How is she?"

"I don't know. I haven't seen her."

"Oh? What train did you catch?"

"I came by car. Hired it at the inn. Terry, I'm feeling shot to pieces."

"Poor old Stanwood. Has something gone wrong?" Terry looked at her watch. "Hullo, I must be getting along. I'm meeting Shorty at Barribault's at half-past one. I'd ask you to join us, but I know he wants to be alone with me. He's feeling rather low today."

"I'll bet he's not feeling as low as I am. A worm would have to pin its ears back to get under me. I couldn't lunch, anyway. Simply couldn't swallow the stuff."

"Well, walk along with me, and tell me all about it. What's the trouble?"

"It started with this letter," said Stanwood, falling into step at her side. "This letter from Eileen that I found at the inn."

"Addressed to you?"

"Yay."

"You mean you registered at the inn under your own name?"

"Sure."

"God bless you, Stanwood! Not that it matters now, of course."

"Nothing matters now," said the stricken man.

It seemed to Terry ironical that on this day of days it should be her fate to associate with none but the crushed in spirit, and she found herself thinking wistfully of Mike. Mike might have his faults—her sister Adela by now had probably discovered dozens—but he was not depressing.

"Cheer up," she urged.

"Cheer up?" said Stanwood, with a hollow, rasping laugh. "Swell chance I've got of cheering up. For two pins I'd go and bump myself off."

They walked on in silence. Stanwood seemed to be enveloped in a murky cloud, and his gloom, for misery is catching, was communicating itself to Terry. In spite of herself, those doubts and misgivings were beginning to vex her once more. There was about Stanwood in his present mood something that chilled the spirit and encouraged morbidity of thought. It was as if she had had for a companion the Terry Cobbold in mittens and spectacles of whom she had spoken to Lord Shortlands, and that this mittened Terry Cobbold were whispering, as she had so often whispered, that no good ever comes of getting entangled with Greek gods.

"All alike," this Prudent Self seemed to be murmuring. "They're all alike, these good-looking young men. Remember how you felt about Geoffrey Harvest at the beginning. You thought him perfect. And what a flippertygibbet *he* turned out to be!"

She wrenched her mind free from these odious reflections. She refused to think of Geoffrey Harvest of abominable memory. Mike was not Geoffrey Harvest. She could trust Mike.

"Well, tell me about the letter," she said. "Why was it so shattering?"

"It was in answer to one I had written her, begging her for Pete's sake to tie a can to that crazy notion of hers about not marrying me because I've no money. I told you about that?"

"Yes, I remember."

"She said she still stuck to it."

"But didn't you expect her to? She wouldn't change her mind right away. I don't see why that letter should worry you. Why did it?"

"Because I read between the lines. There's more to it than meets the eye. Have a look at it," said Stanwood, and thrust a hand into his breast pocket. "You'll see what I mean."

There was nothing of Augustus Robb about Terry. She had no desire to read other people's letters even when invited to, and she was just about to say so when the hand emerged, brandishing before her face a large white envelope, and there floated to her nostrils a wave of scent.

There are certain scents which live up to the advertiser's slogan "Distinctively individual." That affected by Miss Eileen Stoker was one of these. It was a heavy, languorous, overpowering scent, probably answering to one of those boldly improper names which manufacturers of perfume think up with such deplorable readiness, a scent calculated to impress itself on the least retentive memory. It had impressed itself on Terry's memory the day before, when she had first made its acquaintance on Mike's sleeve. They had turned into Duke Street now, and Barribault's Hotel loomed up before them, a solid mass of stone and steel, but not so solid that it did not seem to sway drunkenly before Terry's eyes.

As if in a dream she heard Stanwood speaking.

"Remember what I was saying last night about the old army game? How I thought all that boloney about the money was just Eileen's way of easing me out because she was stuck on someone else? And remember what I told you about Mike and her at that party of mine? Remember me saying I thought he was making a play for her? Well, look. When I got to London, I called her, and she hung up before I'd had time to say a couple of words. And when I rushed around to her hotel, she wouldn't see me. And that's not the half of it. Listen. You've not heard anything yet. I was in the small bar at Barribault's just now, and Aloysius McGuffy told me that she and Mike were lunching there yesterday. What do you know about that?"

Terry forced herself to speak. Her voice sounded strange to her.

"There's no harm in people lunching together."

Stanwood was not prepared to accept this easy philosophy.

"Yes, there is."

"I used to lunch with you."

"That's not the same thing. There are lunches and lunches."

"It doesn't mean anything."

"Yes, it does. It means that they're that way."

"Why?" said Terry, fighting hard.

They had reached the sidewalk outside Barribault's Hotel, and Stanwood halted. His face was earnest, and he emphasized his words with wide gestures.

"I look on that lunch as a what-d'you-call-it; a straw showing which way the wind is blowing. If it wasn't, why was Mike so cagey about it? Did he mention it to you? Of course he didn't. Nor to me. Not a yip out of him. Kept it right under his hat. And why? Because it was a——"

Stanwood paused. A light wind had sprung up, and a straw which showed which way it was blowing had lodged itself in his throat, momentarily preventing speech. And before he could remove this obstacle to eloquence and resume his remarks, there occurred an interruption so dramatic that he could only stand and stare, horror growing in his eyes.

On the sidewalk outside the main entrance of Barribault's Hotel there is posted a zealous functionary about eight feet in height, dressed in what appears to be the uniform of an admiral in the Ruritanian navy, whose duty it is to meet cars and taxis, open the door for their occupants and assist them to alight. This ornamental person had just swooped down upon a taxi which was drawing up at the curb.

In addition to being eight feet high, the admiral was also some four feet in width, and his substantial body for a moment hid from view the couple whom he was scooping from the cab's interior. Then, moving past him, they came in sight.

No member of the many Boost for Eileen Stoker clubs which flourished both in America and Great Britain would have failed to recognize the female of the pair, and neither Terry nor Stanwood had any difficulty in identifying her escort. Mike Cardinal passed them without a glance, his whole attention riveted on his fair companion. He was talking earnestly to her in a low, pleading voice, one hand on her arm, and as they paused for an instant at the swing door his eyes met hers and he gave her a Look. Lord Shortlands, had he been present instead of at the moment turning the corner of the street, would have been able to classify that look. It was of the kind known as melting.

Duke Street swam about Terry, wrapped in a flickering mist. From somewhere in the heart of this mist she was vaguely aware of the hoarse cry of a strong man in his agony, and when some little while later the visibility improved she found that she was alone.

She stood where she was, pale and rigid. The life of London went on around her, but she gave it no attention. "Fool!" she was saying to herself. "Fool!" And the Terry Cobbold in spectacles and mittens sighed and said "I told you so."

She was aware of a voice speaking her name.

"Ah, there you are, Terry. Not late, am I?"

It was a new and improved edition of Lord Shortlands that pawed the sidewalk outside Barribault's Hotel with his spatted feet. His childlike faith in his club's champagne had not been betrayed. He had trusted it to buck him up, and it had done so. His manner now was cheerful, almost exuberant. He had no reason to suppose that the meeting with his daughter Adela, when at length he returned to the castle, would be in any sense an agreeable one, but he faced it with intrepidity. This was due not merely to the champagne, which had been excellent, but to the fact that he had just had an inspiration, and that had been excellent, too.

If Terry was going to marry this young Cardinal, he told himself—and a careful review of their conversation in the train had left him with the conclusion that this was what she had said she was going to do—why should not young Cardinal, admittedly a man of substance, lend him that two hundred pounds?

Lord Shortlands, as a panhandler, was a man who had his code. It was a code which forbade the putting of the bite on those linked to him by no close ties. Acquaintances were safe from the fifth earl. They could flaunt their bank rolls in his face, and he would not so much as hint at a desire to count himself in. But let those acquaintances become prospective sons-in-law, and only by climbing trees and pulling them up after them could they hope to escape him. Unless, of course, like Desborough Topping, they had taken the mad step of having joint accounts with Adela. He regarded the financial transaction which he had sketched out as virtually concluded, and this gave to his deportment a rare *bonhomie*.

"Come along," he said jovially. Abstention from breakfast had sharpened his appetite, and he was looking forward with keen pleasure to testing the always generous catering of Barribault's Hotel.

Terry did not move.

"Let's go somewhere else, Shorty."

"Eh? Why?"

"I'd rather."

"Just as you say. The Ritz?"

"All right."

"Hey, taxi," said Lord Shortlands, and the admiral sprang to do his bidding. "Ritz," said Lord Shortlands to the admiral.

"Ritz," said the admiral to the chauffeur.

"Ritz," said the chauffeur, soliloquizing.

Lord Shortlands produced largesse. The admiral touched his hat. The chauffeur did grating things with his gears. The cab rolled off.

"Terry," said Lord Shortlands.

"Shorty," said Terry simultaneously.

Lord Shortlands, who had been about to say "Do you think that young man of yours would lend me two hundred pounds?", gave way courteously.

"Yes?"

"Oh, sorry, Shorty, you were saying something?"

"After you, my dear."

Thus generously given precedence, Terry hesitated. She had an idea that what she was about to say might cast a cloud on her companion's mood of well-being. Shorty, she knew, thought highly of Mike.

"I've made a mistake, Shorty."

Lord Shortlands looked sympathetic. He often made mistakes himself.
"A mistake?"
Terry forced herself to her distasteful task.
"I'm not going to marry Mike."
"What!"
"No," said Terry.
Lord Shortlands sank back in his seat, a broken man. The day was still as fair as ever, but it seemed to him that the sun had suddenly gone out with a pop.

21

BUTLERS, LIKE clams, hide their emotions well. In the demeanour of Mervyn Spink, as he drooped gracefully over the telephone in Lord Shortlands' study at four o'clock that afternoon, there was nothing to indicate that vultures were gnawing at his bosom. Sherlock Holmes himself could not have deduced from his deportment that he had recently been deprived of his portfolio after a scene which—on the part, at least, of Lady Adela Topping, his employer—had been stormy and full of wounding personalities. Outwardly, he remained his old calm elegant self, and his voice, as he spoke into the instrument, was quiet and controlled.

"Hullo?" he said. "Are you there? The office of the Kentish *Times?* Could you inform me what won the three-thirty at Kempton? . . . Thank you."

He hung up, his face an impassive mask. It was impossible to tell from it whether the news he had received had been good news or bad news. He left the study, and made his stately way to the hall. There was always some little task to be done in the hall—ash trays to be emptied, papers to be put tidy and the like—and though under sentence of dismissal, he was not the man to shirk his duties. "You leave tomorrow!" Lady Adela had said, putting a good deal of stomp into the words, and he was leaving tomorrow. But while he remained on the premises, his motto was Service.

As a rule, at four in the afternoon he could count on having the hall to himself and being able to scrounge his customary half dozen cigarettes from the silver box on the centre table, but today it had two occupants. Lord Shortlands, looking as if the rescue party had dumped him there after a train accident, was reclining bonelessly in one of the armchairs. Terry sitting in another. She looked up as the butler entered. Her face was pale and set.

"Is Mr. Cobbold back, Spink?"
"Yes, m'lady. I fancy he is in his room."
"Will you give him this note, please."
"Very good, m'lady."

Lord Shortlands came to life.

"Spink."

"M'lord?"

"Has—ah—has Mrs. Punter arrived?"

"Yes, m'lord."

"Ha!"

Mervyn Spink waited respectfully for further observations but, finding that the other had gone off the air, withdrew, and Lord Shortlands turned to Terry. His voice was low and hoarse, like that of a bandit in an old-fashioned comic opera.

"Terry!"

"Yes?"

"Did you notice anything?"

"How do you mean?"

"About that viper. The man Spink. Did you see a sort of gleam in his eye?"

"No."

"I did. A distinct gleam. As if he had got something up his sleeve. You heard what he said? Mrs. Punter's back."

"Yes."

"Horrible gloating way he said it. I suppose he's been smarming round her ever since she arrived. That's where he scores, being a butler. No barriers between him and the cook. There he is, right on the spot, able to fuss over her to his heart's content. Probably told her she must be feeling tired after her journey, and insisted on her having a drop of sherry. Just the sort of little attention that wins a woman's heart. Not that it matters much now," said Lord Shortlands heavily. "If you aren't going to marry this young Cardinal, I'm dished, anyway."

Terry sighed. At lunch and during the return in the train and subsequently while she was writing that note, the fifth earl had gone into the matter of her broken engagement rather fully, and it seemed that the topic was to come up again.

"I'm sorry," she said.

"I still can't understand why you're giving the chap the push."

"I explained."

"Well, I don't see it. Why shouldn't he lunch with this woman? Old friends, apparently."

"I told you. It was the way he looked at her."

"Pooh!"

"And after what I went through with Geoffrey——"

"Pooh, pooh!"

A single "Pooh!" is trying enough to a girl whose heart is feeling as if it had been split in half, but Terry, by clenching her fists and biting her lip, had contrived to endure it. The double dose was too much for her.

"Oh, for goodness sake do let's stop talking about it, Shorty."

Lord Shortlands heaved himself out of his chair. He could make allowances for a daughter's grief, but her tone had hurt him.

"I shall go for a stroll," he said.

"Yes, do. Much better than sitting here, waiting."

At the thought of what he was waiting for, Lord Shortlands shivered.

"I shall go for a stroll around the moat. The moat!" he said broodingly. "Might drown myself in it," he went on, brightening a little at the thought. But the animation induced by this reflection soon waned. "I wonder where Adela's got to."

"She's probably gardening."

"Well, this suspense is awful. I'm in such a state of mind that I almost hope I'll run into her," said Lord Shortlands, and went out, and a few moments later Terry was aroused from her thoughts by the entry of Stanwood Cobbold. Stanwood was looking tense and grave, as became a man whose heart was broken. To him, as to Terry, that glilmpse of Mike and Eileen Stoker at the door of Barribault's Hotel had come as a shattering blow, withering hopes and destroying dreams.

"Oh, there you are," he said sepulchrally. "Spink gave me your note."

"What! But it was meant for Mike."

"Sure, I know. But Spink got mixed. You can't blame him. He's just been fired, he tells me, and I guess it's preying on his mind. So you've given Mike the razz?"

"Yes."

"Quite right," said Stanwood warmly. "Show him where he gets off. Later on, when I'm feeling sort of brighter, I'm going to write Eileen a letter, telling her where *she* gets off. Who was that female in the Bible whose work was always so raw?"

"Delilah?"

"Jezebel," said Stanwood, remembering. "I've heard Augustus Robb mention her. That's how I shall begin. 'Jezebel!' I shall begin. That'll make her sit up. And there's a Scarlet Woman of Babylon that Augustus sometimes wisecracks about. I shall work her in, too. The great question now is, Do I or do I not poke Mike in the snoot?"

"No!"

"Maybe you're right," said Stanwood.

He relapsed into a brooding silence. Terry was wishing that he would go away and leave her to her misery, but as it was evident that he was determined to remain and talk, she sought in her mind for something to talk about which would not make her feel as if jagged knives were being thrust through her heart.

"Have you seen Adela?" she asked.

"Her Nibs? No. Why?" said Stanwood, in sudden alarm. "Is she looking for me?"

"Not that I know of."

"Thank God! If I never meet that dame again, it'll be soon enough for me. Why did you ask if I'd seen her?"

"I don't know."

"Well, I wish you wouldn't. You gave me goose prickles. Some party, that, last night."

"Yes. I never knew you had such ready resource."

"Eh?"

" 'It's all right, ma'am. We're engaged.' "

"Oh, that? Well, I had to say something."

"I suppose so."

"And it worked. Gosh!" said Stanwood, starting. It was plain that an idea of some kind had agitated the brain behind that brow of bone. "Golly! You've given me a thought there. Look! Why shouldn't we?"

"Why shouldn't we what?"

"Be engaged."

Terry gasped.

"You mean really?"

"Sure."

"Are you choosing this moment to ask me to marry you?"

"You betcher, and I'll tell you why. You want to show Mike where he gets off. I want to show Eileen where she gets off. You're feeling licked to a splinter. I'm feeling licked to a splinter. Let's merge."

"Oh, Stanwood!" said Terry, and began to laugh.

Stanwood eyed her askance. He did not like this mirth. Her laughter was musical, but he soon began to entertain the idea that there was something of hysteria in it, and at the thought of being alone with a hysterical girl his stout soul wilted. He was none too sure of the procedure. Did you burn feathers under their noses? Or just slap them on the back?

"Hey!" he cried. "Pipe down!"

"I can't. It's too funny."

Stanwood began to be conscious of a certain pique. He had offered this girl a good man's—well, not love, perhaps, but at any rate affection, and he could see no reason why a good man's affection should be given the horse's laugh. His manner became stiff.

"I can't see what's so darned funny about it."

And Terry, suddenly sobered, found that she, too, was unable to do so.

"I'm sorry I laughed," she said. "But you startled me. You'll admit you were a little sudden. Are you really serious?"

"Sure."

Terry was looking at Stanwood, thoughtfully, weighing him up. She liked him, she told herself. She had always liked him. He made her feel motherly. And he was a man you could trust. She could think of many worse things that the future could hold than marriage with Stanwood Cobbold. To marry Stanwood would be to put into snug harbour out of the storm. Perhaps this was what Fate had designed for her from the start, a quiet, unromantic union with no nonsense about it, solidly based on friendship.

It would mean, too, that she would be able to leave the castle, to go out into the wide world where there might be a chance of forgetting, and she realized now how vitally this mattered to her. I can't do it, she had been saying to herself in a hopeless, trapped way. I can't go on living all alone in this awful place where everything will always remind me of Mike. She saw that she was being offered release from prison.

"If it's the money end you're worrying about," said Stanwood, "that's all right. Father will cough up, when he hears it's you I'm marrying."

"I'm not worrying about that, my pet," said Terry. "I'm worrying about you and what you're letting yourself in for."

"If it's okay by you, it's okay by me."

"Sure?"

"Sure."

"Quite sure?"

"Absolutely sure. You betcher. Why not?"

"I'm afraid I shall always love Mike," said Terry, with a little choke in her voice.

"And I shall always love Eileen, darn her gizzard. But what does it matter? Don't talk to me about love," said Stanwood, plainly contemptuous of the divine emotion. "Love's a mess. Look at all the bimbos you see that start out thinking they're crazy about each other. For the first couple of months they can't quit holding hands and feeding each other with their spoons, and after that they're off to the lawyer to fix up the divorce so quick you can't see them for dust. To hell with love. Feed it to the birds. I want no piece of it."

"Friendship is the thing, you think?"

"Sure. If a fellow and a girl are just buddies, they stay buddies."

"There's something in that."

"And we've always got along together like a couple of gobs on shore leave. We'll have a swell time. It's like that song I remember—'Tumty tumty tumty tumty, I was looking for a pal like you.' "

Terry sighed.

"Well, all right, Stanwood."

"Check?"

"Yes."

"Swell. I'll kiss you, shall I?"

He did, and there followed a silence not untinged with embarrassment. To each of the plighted pair it seemed a little difficult to know what to say next. It was a relief to both when Lord Shortlands reappeared, back from his stroll round the moat.

The moat, as always, had lowered his spirits dangerously. It was a sheet of water on which he never looked without despondency. His manner was so dejected that Terry lost no time in imparting news which she felt sure would bring the sparkle back to his eyes.

"Adela has given Spink the sack, Shorty."

For an instant, as she had foreseen, the words acted as a tonic. But, like the one which Stanwood was accustomed to imbibe in his dark hours, its effects, powerful at first, were evanescent. What did it profit, Lord Shortlands was asking himself, that Beevor Castle should be freed from Spinks, if he himself remained unable to acquire that two hundred pounds?

"And Stanwood and I are engaged," said Terry.

The fifth earl clutched his forehead. That feeling of bewilderment, of having an insufficient grasp on the trend of things, which had come to him in the train, was troubling him once more.

"You and Stanwood?"

"Yes."

"Not you and young Cardinal?"

"No."

"But you and Stanwood?" said Lord Shortlands, feeling his way carefully. "Yes."

Lord Shortlands' face cleared. He had got it at last.

"I hope you'll be very happy," he said. "Stanwood, my boy, I have only this to say—Be good to my little girl, and can you lend me two hundred pounds?"

If Stanwood was surprised, he did not show it.

"Sure," he said agreeably.

"My dear fellow!"

"At least, when I say 'Sure,' " said Stanwood, correcting himself. "I mean I can't."

"You can't?" moaned Lord Shortlands, in the depths.

"Not yet, what I mean. I don't have it. Father cabled me a thousand bucks the other day, but most of it's gone, so you'll have to wait till I can pop it across him again."

Hope stirred feebly in Lord Shortlands' bosom.

"And when do you anticipate that you will be able to—ah—pop it across him?"

Stanwod reflected.

"Well, I usually find it best to give him about a month to sort of simmer."

"A month?" With Mervyn Spink out of the place and unable to exert his fatal fascination, a month seemed to Lord Shortlands no time at all. "Why, that will be admirable. In a month from now, you think——"

"Oh, sure. Maybe less."

Lord Shortlands closed his eyes. As on a former occasion, he seemed to be praying. When he opened them again, it was to observe that Spink had shimmered silently in.

"New York wishes to speak to you on the telephone, sir," he said, addressing Stanwood.

"New York?"

"Yes, sir."

"Gosh, that must be Father," said Stanwood, and hurried out.

Lord Shortlands found himself filled with an ungenerous desire to triumph over a fallen rival.

"I hear you're leaving us, Spink," he said, with unction.

"Yes, m'lord."

"Too bad."

'Thank you, m'lord. I shall be sorry to terminate my association with the castle. I have been extremely happy here."

"Made some nice friends, eh?"

"Yes, m'lord."

"You'll miss them."

"Yes, m'lord. But there are consolations."

"Eh?"

"I have been fortunate in a recent investment on the turf, m'lord. Silver King in the three-thirty race at Kempton Park this afternoon at a hundred to eight. What a beauty!" said Mervyn Spink, momentarily allowing his human side to come uppermost, a thing which butlers seldom do unless they are leaving tomorrow.

Lord Shortlands' jaw had begun to droop slowly, as if pulled by an invisible spring. He spoke in a hushed voice, in keeping with the solemnity of the moment.

"How much did you have on?"

"Fifty pounds, m'lord."

"Fifty *pounds!* At a hundred to eight?"

"I felt that it was not a moment for exercising caution, m'lord. I invested my entire savings."

Mervyn Spink withdrew, unnoticed as far as Lord Shortlands was concerned, for the latter had leaped to the writing table and was doing sums with a pencil and a piece of paper.

Presently he raised an ashen face.

"Six hundred and twenty-five quid! That viper has trousered six hundred and twenty-five quid! I told you that one of these days he would strike a long-priced winner, but you wouldn't listen to me." He paused, and mopped his furrowed brow. "I'm going to the library to lie downl" he said. "Adela won't think of looking for me there. If you meet her, tell her you haven't seen me."

He tottered out. He had been gone perhaps two minutes, when there was a cheerful sound of whistling without, and Mike came in.

22

FROM THE first moment of his entry it was abundantly evident that Mike was feeling pleased with himself. His whistling had suggested this, and his attitude confirmed it. He exuded lightheartedness and *bien-être,* and the thought of anyone being pleased with Mycroft Cardinal, the Emperor of the flippertygibbets, was so revolting to Terry that she stiffened and drew herself up coldly. Her bearing, as she faced him, was that of a Snow Queen. Icicles seemed to be forming on her upper slopes.

This, however, appeared to have escaped Mike's notice, for, swooping down on her, he kissed her fondly; then, placing a hand on either side of her waist, picked her up and waved her about for a while, concluding by lowering her into her chair and kissing her again. His manner was entirely free from any suggestion of diffidence or uncertainty as to his welcome.

"My angel! My seraph! My dream kitten!" he said. "I feel as if I hadn't seen you in years. And yet you don't look a day older."

Terry did not reply. It is not easy for a girl who has been intending to be distant and aloof to think of anything good to say under such conditions.

"Notice the eye?" said Mike.

Terry directed what she had hoped was a chilling and indifferent glance at the eye. She had already observed that its sombre hues had vanished.

"I had it painted out at a painting-out shop. For your sake. Augustus Robb warned me that girls didn't like men with bunged-up eyes, and you can always go by him. And now, my child, I have news. Where's Shorty?"

"In the library, I believe."

"I have tidings for him that will bring the sparkle back to his eyes and make him skip like the high hills. Augustus is in again!"

Terry did not understand him, and signified this by raising her eyebrows coldly.

"Yes, Augustus has started functioning once more. He is going to carry on from where he left off last night. I sought him out this morning and grovelled. I said that it was merely strained nerves that had caused me to kick him, and begged him to take the big, broad view. His manner was a little stiff at first, but eventually he relented. If I would go to his gentleman friend in Seven Dials and borrow his tools, he said, he would do the rest. 'Tell him,' he said, 'that Gus wants the old persuaders.' So I called on the gentleman friend—a charming fellow, whose only fault, if you call it a fault, was that his eyes were a bit close together—and gave him the password, and I've just seen Augustus and handed over the old persuaders. He promised to get to work immediately. Your sister Adela, I have ascertained, is out in the garden, no doubt making the lives of the local snails a hell on earth, and Desborough Topping is in his room, having an indoor Turkish bath for his lumbago, so the coast is clear. If Shorty's in the library, he's probably caddying for Augustus at this very moment with a song in his heart, realizing, as you will have realized, that he will soon be sitting on top of the world. Augustus guarantees to bust that pete in five minutes.

He paused. A duller man than he would have noted that Terry was not responsive.

"I had anticipated a certain amount of girlish joy," he said.

"Oh, I'm delighted."

"Then why aren't you squeaking? I should have thought such news would have been well worth a squeak or two." Mike paused again, and sniffed. "Odd smell in here," he said. "Can it be I?"

Terry's lip curled. The smell to which he alluded had not escaped her.

"You've probably not noticed it," she said coldly, "but you are reeking of scent."

"Am I? So I am. Tut, tut."

His reaction to a discovery which should have bathed him in shame and confusion seemed to Terry entirely inadequate. Would nothing, she was asking herself, stir this man's conscience?

"And I'm not surprised," she said bitterly. "Did you enjoy your lunch?"

Mike seemed perplexed.

"How have we got on to the subject of lunch? We were talking of scent."

Terry bit her lip. It was showing a disposition to tremble, and she would have preferred to die the most horrible death rather than shed tears.

"Why lunch?" asked Mike.

"I happened to see you going to lunch today."

"I didn't know you were in London."

"No."

"Were you at Barribault's?"

"I was on the pavement outside."

"And you saw me going in?"

"Yes."

"Then you saw me at my best," said Mike. "Yous saw me in the act of giving a prospect the works, and that is the moment to catch me."

"What do you mean?"

"I've got La Stoker signed up on the dotted line. From now on, for a period of five years, the dear old firm will peddle her at ten per cent of her stupendous salary. It's an ironclad contract, and if she attempts to slide out of it she'll get bitten to death by wild lawyers. And I did it. I, Cardinal. I'm good, I tell you. Good, good, good!"

Terry gasped. Her heart, which she had supposed crushed and dead, gave a sudden leap. There shot through her a suspicion, growing with the moments, that the Lady Teresa Cobbold had made a fool of herself. And at the same time, tentatively at first but rapidly gaining in strength as the purport of his words came home to her, soft music began to play in the recesses of her soul.

"Oh, Mike!" she said.

"I should have begun by telling you that in that cable of his recalling me to the office my boss mentioned that La Stoker had severed relations with her agent before leaving Hollywood and had made no new commitments, and he urged me to get in touch with her and secure her custom. 'Give her the old oil,' he pleaded, in effect, and I gave it her abundantly. I laid the foundations of my brilliant campaign yesterday with a lunch which set the office back about twenty bucks and had her rocking on her French heels, and today I took her out again and polished her off. But it was in no sense a walkover. The Stoker is one of those dumb females whose impulse, if you ask them to do something, is to say 'Well, I dunno' and do the opposite, and there were times, I confess, when I felt like giving the thing up and getting what small consolation I could from beating her over the head with a bottle. Still, I triumphed in the end, and why on earth you're not leaping about and fawning on me is more than I can understand. What's the matter with you?"

Terry choked. Odd things were happening inside her. Carried away, no doubt, by that soft music, her heart appeared now to have parted completely from its moorings and to be going into a sort of adagio dance.

"Was that really it?"

"Was what really what?"

"Was it really just a business lunch?"

"Strictly business."

"Oh, Mike!"

"You may well say 'Oh, Mike!' I was superb. I played on that goofy dame as on a stringed instrument. I gave her everything I'd got: the whispered compliment, the gentle pressure of the hand, the smile that wins, the melting look——"

Terry laughed shakily.

"I saw the melting look."

"You did? Good Lord, I hope you didn't think——"

"That's exactly what I did think. I thought it was Geoffrey Harvest all over again. Well, you never said a word to me about it," said Terry defensively.

"The Cardinals don't talk. They act."

"And you sneaked off at dawn——"

"It wasn't at dawn. I took the nine-forty-five. And I didn't sneak off. I strode from the house with my chin up and my chest out, twirling my clouded cane. So you thought I was a flippertygibbet?"

"Yes. Flitting from flower to flower."

"Is that what flippertygibbets do?"

"Yes. They're very like butterflies in their habits. And it's no good looking at me in that reproachful way, as if you were King Arthur and I was Guinevere——"

"It isn't exactly reproachful. Sadness was what I was trying to register. You must know that you're the only girl in the world I could possibly love, and that only an absolute nitwit would go flitting elsewhere if he'd got you. Don't you ever look in the glass?"

"Well, I stick to it that it was a perfectly natural mistake to make. There were you, devouring this woman with your eyes——"

"I was thinking of that ten per cent."

"—and generally behaving like Great Lovers through the Ages. Anyone would have been misled. Stanwood was."

"Stanwood."

"He was among the spectators."

"Egad! What did he think?"

"The worst. Well, when I tell you that he spoke of writing a letter to Miss Stoker calling her the Scarlet Woman of Babylon——"

"Where on earth did Stanwood ever hear of the Scarlet Woman of Babylon?"

"Apparently Mr. Robb chats with him about her sometimes. And then he came to me and asked me to marry him."

"To—what?"

"To marry him. And I said I would."

Mike tottered.

"You said you would?"

"Yes. It was his idea. He said it would show you where you got off."

Mike drew a deep breath.

"If Shorty kicks at paying three guineas to have your head examined," he said feelingly, "I'll put up the money myelf. Let me tell you something for your files. You're not marrying any blasted Stanwoods. You're marrying me."

"Yes, I see that now."

"Got it quite clear in your little nut, have you?"

"Quite."

"It's a pity you were ever uncertain on the point, for look what you have done. Playing with hearts, I call it. Now I have the unpleasant task of telling an old friend that if he doesn't lay off, I'll push his face in. And what makes it so extremely awkward is that I don't believe I can push Stanwood's face in, unless I seize a happy moment when he's looking the other way."

"Will you really tell him?"

"Of course."

"Oh, Mike, how noble of you. I was wondering how I could do it."

"Where is this home-wrecker?"

"Telephoning. His father rang him up from New York."

"Well, here's something that may comfort you. I doubt if we shall have much moaning at the bar when we break it to him that the deal is off. Towards the end of lunch, when the main business details had been settled, I worked like a beaver in his interests, and La Stoker is now prepared to marry him any time he says the word. I might perhaps have mentioned that earlier."

"You might."

"My old trouble. Playing for suspense. But let's not talk about Stanwood. His romance is merely a side issue. Ours is what matters."

"Yes."

"Have you any objection to getting married like lightning?"

"Not if it's to you."

" 'At's the way to talk! It will be. I'll see to that. Well, that's what we'll have to do, because time is running short. I've got to sail next week."

"How pleased all the girls in Hollywood will be to see you again."

"Are there girls in Hollywood?"

"Stanwood says so."

"I don't suppose I shall so much as notice them."

"How about if they come squealing 'Oh, *Mike,* darling'?"

"There is such a thing as police protection, I presume. But I was saying. About getting swiftly off the mark. It must be a simple ceremony at the registry office for us."

"Beak Street?"

"Or Greek Street. For goodness' sake don't go to the wrong place, like Augustus Robb's girl. And now to tackle Stanwood. Ah," said Mike, as a thunder of large feet approached along the corridor, "here, if I mistake not, Watson, is our client now."

Stanwood Cobbold came charging into the room, as if bucking an invisible line.

23

THAT HIS conversation on the telephone had been one fraught with interest and of the most agreeable nature was manifest at once in Stanwood's whole appearance. His eyes were starting, his hair ruffled where he had clutched it with an excited hand and his face as nearly like the Soul's Awakening as it was possible for it to look. Picture a hippopotamus that has just learned that its love is returned by the female hippopotamus for which it has long entertained feelings deeper and warmer than those of ordinary friendship, and you have Stanwood Cobbold at this important moment in his life.

"S-s-s-s——" he began, like a soda-water syphon, and Mike rapped the table, calling for order. One has to be pretty sharp on this sort of thing at the outset.

"Spit," he advised.

Stanwood did not spit; but he swallowed once or twice, and seemed to get a grip on his emotion. His voice, when he started again, was calmer.

"Say, I've just been talking to Eileen."

"It's a small point, but you mean your father."

"No, I don't mean my father. I mean Eileen. I called her up after I was through with Father. It's all right. She's going to marry me."

"Marry you?"

"Sure."

Mike frowned.

"Just a minute."

"Can't stop," said Stanwood, exhibiting restiveness. "I've got to rush to the inn and hire that car again and go in and see her."

"Nevertheless," said Mike, "I repeat. Just a minute. You say you're going to marry La Stoker?"

"Sure."

"That wasn't the story I heard. The way I got it was that you were going to marry Terry."

"Oh, gosh!" said Stanwood, pausing. He seemed disconcerted. It was plain that Terry had to some extent slipped his memory.

"Yes, what about me?" said Terry. "Are you proposing to throw this eager heart aside like an old tube of tooth paste?"

Stanwood reflected. It was not long before he reached his decision.

"You betcher. You don't mind, do you?"

"Not a bit," said Terry.

"Swell," said Stanwood.

"It's just as well that you've got that settled," said Mike, "because Terry is going to marry me, and the last thing we wanted was you clumping up the aisle, shouting 'I forbid the banns!' "

Stanwood gaped.

"She's going to marry you?"

"Yes."

"What, even after—"

"Mike has explained everything, Stanwood," said Terry.

A look of awe came into Stanwood's face. He regarded his friend with reverence. If Mike had explained everything, that look seemed to say, then Mike, as the latter had so often had occasion to point out himself, was good. He shook Mike's hand, and said that that was dandy.

"He turns out to be as pure as the driven snow."

"Rather purer, if anything," said Mike. "Your foul suspicions were entirely unfounded, my dear Stanwood. Ask your girl friend, when you see her, and she will tell you that I was merely signing her up in my capacity of junior partner in the firm of Schwartz and Cardinal, ham purveyors of Hollywood. The whole thing was a simple business transaction, entirely free from all taint of sex. There is absolutely nothing between your darned Stoker and me, and there never has been anything. For your information, I wouldn't touch her with a barge pole."

"Oh, say," said Stanwood, wounded, and Terry asked if that was not a little severe. Mike considered.

"Yes," he agreed. "I'm sorry. I went too far. I *would* touch her with a barge pole, provided it was a good long one."

"Thanks, o' man."

"Not at all."

"So that's all right," said Terry. "I'm so glad everything's settled, Stanwood."

"Yes," said Mike. "One likes to see the young folks happy."

"How sensible of her not to mind about you having no money."

"Eh?" said Stanwood. "Oh, but I do have some money. I forgot to tell you. Seems that the little guy with the nose glasses cabled Father that I was engaged to you, and Father was so tickled that he's deposited a hundred and fifty thousand smackers to my account. That's what he called up about. So I'm nicely fixed," said Stanwood, and without further words dived through the door, en route for the inn and the car that was for hire.

He left behind him a rather stunned silence.

"Well!" said Terry, and Mike agreed that "Well!" about summed it up.

"I hope he'll be happy," said Terry doubtfully.

"As a lark," said Mike. "Not in the sense that we shall be, of course. Nobody could be. But I see quite a bright and prosperous future for the lad. The Stoker's all right. A little apt to turn the conversation to the subject of her last picture, but he'll enjoy that."

"I don't like the scent she uses."

"Stanwood does. He often told me so."

"She isn't a flippertygibbet?"

"Not in the least. A quiet little homebody, never happier than among her books. I've read interviews with her that stressed that. And she often puts on a simple gingham apron and cooks a bite of dinner for herself."

"I'd hate Stanwood to be unhappy."

"Don't you worry. They're the ideal mates. She's solid ivory from the frontal bone to the occiput, and so is Stanwood. Ah, my dear Shorty," said Mike, breaking off and addressing Lord Shortlands, who had just entered.

A glance was enough to tell that this was a very different Lord Shortlands from the crushed martyr who had tottered out to go and lie down in the library. It was a near thing, but he looked a little more like the Soul's Awakening than Stanwood Cobbold had done.

Terry glanced questioningly at Mike.

"Shall we tell him at once, or break it gently?"

"At once, I think."

"All right. Shorty, darling, shake hands——"

"Mitt."

"Yes, much better. Mitt Mr. Cardinal, Shorty. We're going to be married."

The unmistakable look of the man who feels that the strain is becoming too much for him came into Lord Shortlands' face. He gave the impression of having definitely given up the attempt to cope with things.

"Married?" he said feebly.

"Yes."

"You and Cardinal?"

"Yes."

"Not you and Stanwood?"

"No."

"But you and Cardinal?"

"Yes."

"My God!" murmured Lord Shortlands, passing a hand across his brow.

"The fact is, my dear Shorty," said Mike, "things have been getting a little mixed, and it has taken some time to straighten them out. There had been mistakes and misunderstandings, not unlike those which occured in Vol. Two of *Percy's Promise*, a work which you may or may not have read. By Marcia Huddlestone (Popgood and Grooly, 1869). These, however, are now at an end, so brush up the old top hat and get ready for the wedding. The bells of the little village church—or, rather, the little Beak Street registry office—are soon to peal out in no uncertain manner. You may take this as official. Have you seen Augustus?"

The Soul's Awakening expression, which had been temporarily erased, came back into Lord Shortlands' face. After what had occurred on the previous night, he had never expected the name of Augustus Robb to be music to his ears, but this was what it now was. Augustus Robb stood very high on the list of men he liked and respected.

"I have, indeed. I've just left him."

"Why didn't you stay and watch?"

"He wouldn't let me. Said it made him nervous. Very temperamental chap. I told him he would find me here when he was finished."

"How was he coming along?"

"He appeared entirely confident."

"Then very shortly . . . Ah!"

Augustus Robb had come into the room, jauntily, like an artist conscious of having done a good piece of work. He had an excellent reception.

"Augustus!" cried Mike.

"Mr. Robb!" cried Terry.

"Did you get it?" cried Lord Shortlands.

" 'Ullo, cocky. 'Ullo, ducky. Yus, chum, I got it," said Augustus Robb, replying to them in rotation. "But——"

An unforeseen interruption forced him to leave the sentence uncompleted. "Ah!" said a voice, and they turned to see Lady Adela in the doorway.

Lady Adela was wearing gardening gloves and carrying the shears which had so intimidated Mike at their first meeting. Her eyes, as they rested upon Lord Shortlands, had in them the stern gleam that is seen in those of a tigress which prepares to leap upon the goat which it has marked down for the evening meal. Her righteous indignation, denied expression by his craven flight to London, had been banking up within her since half-past nine that morning, and it was plain that she welcomed the imminent bursting of the dam.

"Ah!" she said. "I would like to speak to you, Father." She looked at the assembled company, and added the word "Alone." What she had to say was not for the ears of others.

Augustus Robb was always the gentleman. His social sense was perfect. Besides, he intended to listen at the door.

"Want us to shift, ducky?" he said agreeably. "Right ho."

Lady Adela, who had never been called "ducky" before and did not like the new experience, raised her eyebrows haughtily. It began to seem as if Augustus Robb was going to get his before Lord Shortlands.

"Who are you?" she asked.

"Name of Robb, dearie. Augustus Robb."

"He's Stanwood's valet," said Terry.

"Oh?" said Lady Adela, and left unspoken the words that had been trembling on her lips. Vassals and retainers of Stanwood Cobbold were immune from her wrath. Later on, perhaps, she would suggest to the dear boy that his personal attendant was a little lacking in the polish which one likes to see in personal attendants, but for the moment this chummy servitor must be spared. All she did, accordingly, was to catch his eye.

It was enough. Blinking, as if he had been struck by lightning, Augustus Robb withdrew, followed by Mike and Terry, and Lady Adela turned to Lord Shortlands.

"Father!" she said.

"Well?" said Lord Shortlands.

In the word "Well?", as inscribed on the printed page, there is little to cause the startled stare and the quick catch of the breath. It seems a mild and innocuous word. But hear it spoken in a loud, rasping, defiant voice by a man with his chin protruding and his thumbs in the armholes of his waistcoat, and the effect is vastly different. Proceeding like a bullet from Lord Shortlands' lips, it left Lady Adela silent and gaping, her feelings closely resembling those which would have come to the above-mentioned tigress had the goat on the bill of fare suddenly turned and bitten it in the leg.

Of all moral tonics there is none that so braces a chronically impecunious earl as the knowledge that he is fifteen hundred pounds on the right side of the ledger. Lord Shortlands had Augustus Robb's assurance that that stamp, for which he had gone through so much, was now as good as in his pocket, and the thought lent him a rare courage. Ancestors of his had been tough nuts on the field of Hastings and devils of fellows among the paynim, and their spirit had descended upon him. He seemed to be clad in mail and brandishing a battle-ax.

"Well? What is it? It's no good you trying to come bullying me, Adela," he said, though perhaps Flaubert would have preferred the word "thundered." "I've put up with that sort of thing long enough."

Lady Adela was a woman of mettle. She tried hard to shake off the illusion that somebody had hit her between the eyes with a wet fish.

"Father!"

Lord Shortlands snorted. One of the main planks in the platform of those ancestors, whose spirit had descended upon him, had always been a rugged disinclination to take any lip from their womenfolk.

"Don't stand there saying 'Father!' No sense in it. I tell you I'm not going to put up with it any longer. I may mention that I have very much disliked your manner on several occasions. In my young days daughters were respectful to their fathers."

This would, of course, have been a good opportunity for Lady Adela to say that they had probably had a different kind of father, but that strange, sandbagged sensation held her dumb, and Lord Shortlands proceeded with his remarks.

"I've decided to leave this bally castle," he said. "Leave it immediately. I have been able to lay my hands on a large sum of money, and there's nothing to keep me. I'm sick and tired of seeing that damned moat and that blasted wing built in 1259 and all the rest of the frightful place. If it interests you to hear my plans, I'm going to buy a public house."

"Father!"

"Will you *stop* saying 'Father!' Are you a parrot?"

Lady Adela's mind was now so disordered that she could scarcely have said what she was. Whatever it might be, it was something with a swimming head. The only point on which she was actually clear was that she had been swept into the vortex of an upheaval of the same nature as, but on rather bigger lines than, the French Revolution.

"Oh, and by the way," added Lord Shortlands, "I'm going to marry Mrs. Punter."

It is proof of the chaotic condition to which Lady Adela's faculties had been reduced that for an instant the name suggested nothing to her. Mrs. Punter? she was asking herself dazedly. Did she know a Mrs. Punter? A member of the Dorsetshire Punters, would it be? Or perhaps one of the Essex lot?

"Punter?" she whispered.

"Yes, Punter, Punter, Punter. You know perfectly well who Mrs. Punter is. The cook."

"The cook?" screamed Lady Adela.

"Yes, the cook," said Lord Shortlands. "And don't shout like that."

When she spoke again, Lady Adela did not shout. Horror made her words come out in a dry whisper, preceded by an odd, crackling sound which it would have taken a very sharp-eared medical man to distinguish from a death rattle.

"You can't marry the cook, Father!"

"Can't I?" said Lord Shortlands, thrusting his thumbs deeper into the armholes of his waistcoat and waggling his fingers. "Watch me!"

It seemed to Lady Adela, for it was evident that nothing was to be gained by arguing with this unbridled man, that the only course open to her was to fly to Mrs. Punter, whom she had always found a reasonable woman, and appeal to her sense of what was fitting. She proceeded to put this plan into action with such promptness that she was gone before Lord Shortlands realized that she had started. One quick leap, a whizzing sound, and she had vanished. And a moment later Augustus Robb re-entered, wearing the un-mistakable air of a man who has had his ear to the keyhole.

"Coo, m'lord," said Augustus Robb admiringly. "That was telling her!"

"Ha!" said Lord Shortlands, still very much above himself. He strode masterfully about the room, waggling his fingers.

"And I've got something to tell *you*, chum," said Augustus Robb. "It's like this."

He broke off, for Mike and Terry had come in. Terry seemed a little agitated, and Mike was patting her hand.

"Your daughter Teresa," he said, "has been suffering a good deal of filial agony on your behalf, my dear Shorty. She was offering me eight to one that we should find you chewed into fragments, and I must say I was anticipating that I should have to dig down for the price of a wreath and a bunch of lilies. But at a hasty glance you appear to be still in one piece."

Lord Shortlands said that he was quite all right, never better, and Augustus Robb endorsed the statement.

"He put it all over her. Ticked her off, he did. Proper."

Terry was amazed.

"Shorty! Did you?"

"Certainly," said Lord Shortlands, and if there was in his manner a touch of pomposity, this was only to be expected after so notable a victory. Wellington was probably a little pompous after Waterloo. "I have been too lenient with Adela in the past, far too lenient, and she has taken advantage of my good nature. It was high time that I asserted myself. As Mr. Robb so rightly says, I—ah—ticked her off proper. She's gone away with a flea in her ear, I can assure you. Ha! You should have seen her face when I said I was going to marry Alice Punter."

The man was lost to all shame.

"You said that?"

"Certainly."

"To *Adela?*"

"You betcher. 'Oh, and by the way,' I said, 'I'm going to marry Mrs. Punter.' "

"But you ain't, chum," said Augustus Robb mildly. "That's what I was starting to tell you."

"Eh?" Lord Shortlands glared formidably. He was under an obligation to this buster of petes, but gratitude was not going to make him put up with this sort of thing. "Who says so?"

Augustus Robb removed his horn-rimmed spectacles, gave them a polish and replaced them.

"Well, I do, cocky, for one, and she does, for another. Because the 'ole thing is, you see, she's going to marry *me*."

"What!"

"Yus. It's a long story," said Augustus Robb. "I was telling Mr. Cardinal and his little bit about it last night. We ought to have got married years ago, only she inadvertently went and waited for me at the Meek Street registry office when I was waiting for 'er at the Beak Street registry office. Shouldn't wonder if that sort of thing didn't often occur."

Terry gasped.

"Then—"

"Yus, ducky. She's the woman I loved and lorst. You could have knocked me down with a feather," said Augustus Robb. "I come out of that library after getting that there stamp, and I was doing a quiet shift-ho to my room to hide the blinking thing, when I see someone coming along the passage, and it was 'Er!"

"Good heavens!"

"You may well say 'Good heavens!', ducky. It was a fair staggerer. 'Alice!' I says, knocked all of a heap. 'Gus!' she says, pressing of a 'and to 'er 'eart. 'Is it you?' I says. 'Yus, it is,' she says, 'and you're a nice cup of tea, you are,' she says. 'What 'ave you got to say for yourself?' she says. Whereupon explanations ensued, as the expression is, and the upshot of it all is that we're off to Beak Street registry office next week—together, this time."

"You'll probably find us in the waiting room," said Mike. "My heartiest congratulations, Augustus."

"Thanks, cocky."

"If there's one thing I like, it is to see two loving hearts come together after long separation, particularly in springtime. But have you considered one rather important point? Mrs. Punter's ideals are pretty high. The man who wins her must have two hundred pounds to buy a pub."

"I've got it, and more."

"Been robbing a bank?"

"No, I 'ave not been robbing a bank. But there's a little bit of money coming to me from a source I'm not at liberty to mention. I could buy 'er 'arf a dozen pubs."

A faint groan greeted this statement. It proceeded from Lord Shortlands, who at the beginning of the recital had sunk into a chair and was lying in it in that curious boneless manner which he affected in moments of keen emotion. Terry looked at him remorsefully. Augustus Robb's human-interest story had caused her to forget that what was jam for him was gall and wormwood to a loved father.

"Oh, Shorty, darling!" she cried. "I wasn't thinking of you."

"It's all right," said Mike. "He still has us."

"Yes, Shorty, you still have us."

"And the stamp," said Mike.

Lord Shortlands stirred. He half rose in his chair like a corpse preparing to step out of the coffin. He had forgotten the stamp. Reminded of it, he showed signs of perking up a little.

"Gimme," he said feebly.

"Give him the stamp, Augustus," said Mike.

Something in the trend events had taken seemed to be embarrassing Augustus Robb. He shifted from one foot to the other, looking coy.

"Now, there's something I was intending to touch on," he said. "Yus, I was going to mention that. I'm sorry to tell you, chums, that there's been a somewhat regrettable occurrence. You see, when I come out of that liberry, I put that there stamp in me mouth, to keep it safe like, and what with the excitement and what I might call agitation of meeting 'Er, I——"

"What?" cried Lord Shortlands, for the speaker had paused. He had risen completely from his chair now, and was pawing the air feverishly. "What?"

"I swallered it, cocky," said Augustus Robb, and Lord Shortlands' blood pressure leaped to a new high as if somebody had cried "Hoop-la!" to it. "Last thing I'd 'ave wanted to 'ave 'appen, but there you are. That's Life, that's what that is. Well, good-bye, all," said Augustus Robb, and was gone. Lady Adela herself had not moved quicker.

The first of a stunned trio to comment on the situation was Lord Shortlands.

"It's a ramp!" he shouted passionately. "It's a swindle! I don't believe a word of it. He's gone off with the thing in his pocket."

Mike nodded sympathetically. The same thought had occurred to him.

"I fear so, Shorty. One should have reflected, before enlisting Augustus's services, that he is a man of infinite guile. One begins to see now why he spoke so loftily about having enough money to buy half a dozen pubs."

"I'll sue him! I'll fight the case to the House of Lords!"

"H'm," said Mike. And Lord Shortlands, on reflection, said "H'm" too.

A moment later he was uttering a cry so loud and agonized that Terry leaped like a jumping bean, and even Mike was disconcerted. The fifth earl was staring before him with bulging eyes. He reminded Mike of a butler discovering beetles in his glass of port.

"What the devil am I to do?" he wailed, writhing visibly. "I've gone and told Adela about Mrs. Punter!"

"So you have!" said Mike. "If I may borrow Augustus's favorite expression, Coo! But have no alarm——"

"She'll make my life a hell! I'll never have another peaceful moment. My every movement will be watched for the rest of my life. Why, dash it, it'll be like being a prisoner in a bally chain gang."

Terry's eyes grew round.

"Oh, Shorty!" she cried, but Mike patted him on the back.

"It's quite all right," he said. "You heard me say 'Have no alarm.' Will the public never learn that if they have Mycroft Cardinal in their corner, Fate cannot touch them?"

"You have a plan?" said Terry.

"I have a plan. Shorty will accompany us to Dottyville-on-the-Pacific."

"Of course!"

"I must try to break you of that habit of yours of saying 'Of course!' when

I put forward one of my brilliant solutions, as if you had been on the point of thinking of it yourself."

"Sorry, my king."

"Okey-doke, my queen."

"Where is Dottyville-on-the-Pacific?" asked Lord Shortlands.

"A little west of Los Angeles," said Mike. "It is sometimes known as Hollywood. We shall be starting thither almost any day now. Just got to get married and fix up your passport and so on. Pack a few necessaries and sneak off to your club and wait there for further instructions. I will attend to all the financial arrangements."

"My dear boy!"

"What an organizer! He thinks of everything, doesn't he?" said Terry.

"He does, indeed," said Lord Shortlands.

"And when we get to Hollywood," said Mike, "if you feel like making a little spending money, I think I can put you in the way of it. I don't know if you ever noticed it, my dear Shorty, but you are a particularly good butler type."

"A butler type?"

Terry squeaked.

"All these years," she said, "I've been trying to think what Shorty reminded me of, and now I know. Of course, darling, you look exactly like a butler."

"Do I?" said Lord Shortlands.

"Exactly," said Terry.

"And for such," proceeded Mike, "there is a constant demand. I cannot hold out hope of stardom, of course; just a nice, steady living. Say 'Very good, m'lord.' "

"Very good, m'lord."

"Perfect. What artistry! You will be a great asset to the silver screen. And now we must leave you. My future wife wishes to show me the rose garden."

"Haven't you seen it?"

"Not with her," said Mike.

For some moments after he found himself alone, Lord Shortlands stood motionless, gazing into the golden future. Then, walking jerkily, for he was still enfeebled, he moved to the mirror and peered into it.

"Very good, m'lord," he said, extending his elbows at right angles. "Very good, m'lord."

A look of satisfaction came into his face. Butler parts would be pie.

Mervyn Spink came silently in, and Lord Shortlands, seeing him in the mirror, turned. As these two strong men, linked by the bond of thwarted love, faced each other, there was a silence. Mervyn Spink was feeling that Lord Shortlands was not such a bad old buster, after all, and Lord Shortlands was feeling strangely softened towards Mervyn Spink.

"You have heard, m'lord?"
Lord Shortlands nodded.
"A nasty knock, m'lord."
"Very nasty."
"We must face it like men, m'lord."
"You betcher. Be British."
Mervyn Spink coughed.
"If your lordship would care for a drop of something to take your lordship's mind off it, I have the materials in my pantry."
Lord Shortlands moistened his lips with the tip of his tongue. The suggestion was a very welcome one. It astounded him to think that he could ever have disliked this St. Bernard dog among butlers.
"Lead me to it, Spink."
"This way, m'lord."
"Don't call me 'm'lord.' "
"This way, Shortlands."
"Don't call me 'Shortlands,' " said the fifth earl. "Call me Shorty."
He put his hand in his new friend's arm, and they went out.

The Butler Did It

1

THE DINNER given by J. J. Bunyan at his New York residence on the night of September the tenth, 1929, was attended by eleven guests, most of them fat and all, except Mortimer Bayliss, millionaires. In the pre-October days of the year 1929 you seldom met anyone in New York who was not a millionaire. He might be a little short of the mark when you ran into him on Monday morning, but by Friday afternoon he would have got the stuff all right and be looking around for more. Not one of those present but had made his hundred thousand dollars or so in the past few hours, and no doubt Keggs, Mr. Bunyan's English butler, and the rest of the Park Avenue staff had added appreciably to their savings, as in all probability had the two chauffeurs, the ten gardeners, the five stablemen and the pastry cook down at Meadowhampton, Long Island, where Mr. Bunyan had his summer home.

For the bull market was booming and the golden age had set in with a roll of drums and a fanfare of trumpets. About the only problem worrying people in those happy days was what to do with all the easy money which a benevolent Providence kept pouring so steadily out of its cornucopia all the time.

It was to this subject that the company's attention had turned when dinner was over and Keggs had withdrawn his stately presence and left them to their cigars and coffee, and the debate was in full swing when Mortimer Bayliss intervened in it. For the last ten minutes he had been sitting hunched up in his chair, scowling silently and curling a scornful lip.

Mortimer Bayliss was the curator of the world-famous Bunyan picture collection. Mr. Bunyan liked having him as a guest at these otherwise all-financier dinners, partly because he felt he lent an intellectual tone but principally because he made a specialty of being abominably rude to everyone except his employer, which appealed to the latter's primitive sense of humor. Mortimer Bayliss was a tall, thin, sardonic man who looked like a Mephistopheles troubled with ulcers, and he had the supercilious manner which so often renders art experts unpopular. He considered his fellow diners clods and Philistines and their foolish babble offended him.

"Yachts!" he said. "Palaces on the Riviera! Oh God, oh Montreal! Have you wretched embryos no imagination? Get some fun out of your beastly wealth, why don't you?"

"How do you mean, fun?" asked one of the stouter millionaires.

"I mean do something that will give you an interest in life." Mortimer Bayliss flashed a black-rimmed monocle about the table and glared through it at a harmless little man who looked like an overfed rabbit. "You!" he said. "Brewster or whatever your name is. Ever heard of Tonti?"

"Sure. He wrote a song called 'Good-by.' "

"That was Tosti, my poor oaf. Tonti was an Italian banker who flourished in the seventeenth century and in the intervals of telling people that it would be impossible in the circumstances to sanction an increase in their overdraft invented the tontine. And if you want me to tell you what a tontine is—"

"I know that," said J. J. Bunyan. "It's where a bunch of guys put up money and found a trust and the money goes on accumulating till they all die off and there's only one fellow left in, and he takes the lot. Right?"

"Correct in every detail, J. J. You and I are educated men."

"Somebody once wrote a story about a tontine."

"Robert Louis Stevenson. Title, 'The Wrong Box.' "

"That's right. Remember enjoying it as a kid."

"You had good taste. Have any of you untutored peasants read 'The Wrong Box'? No? I thought as much. I don't suppose you read anything except the *Wall Street Journal* and *Captain Billy's Whizz Bang*. Just a mob of barely sentient illiterates," said Mortimer Bayliss, and helped himself to another glass of the cognac which his medical adviser had warned him on no account to touch.

"What made you bring Tonti up, Mort?" said J. J. Bunyan. "Are you suggesting that we start a tontine?"

"Why not? Don't you think it would be fun?"

"It might, at that."

The man who had been addressed as Brewster wrinkled his brow. It always took him some time to assimilate anything not having to do with figures.

"I don't get the idea, J. J. What happens? Suppose we each put up a thousand dollars—"

"A thousand?" Mortimer Bayliss snorted. "Fifty thousand is more like it. You want to make it interesting, don't you?"

"All right, fifty thousand. Then what?"

"You die—a task well within the scope of even your abilities. You die off one by one, and when you've all died except one, that one scoops the kitty. J. J. explained it a moment ago in his admirably lucid way, but apparently it did not penetrate the concrete. That's the worst of these cheap imitation heads, they're never satisfactory."

A millionaire with high blood pressure took a dim view of the suggestion. He said it sounded to him like waiting for dead men's shoes, and Mortimer Bayliss said that that was precisely what it was.

"I don't like it."

"Tonti did."

"Sounds sort of gruesome to me. And another thing. The winner wouldn't collect till he was about ninety, and what use would the money be to him then? Silly, I call it."

Six other millionaires said it seemed silly to them, too.

"The voting appears to be against you, Mort," said J. J. Bunyan. "Try again."

"How about your sons?"

"How do you mean, how about them?"

"You've all got sons, and pretty repulsive most of them are. Start a tontine for them. No, wait," said Mortimer Bayliss, a finger to his forehead. "Here's a really bright idea. Just came to me, born no doubt of this potent brandy. Start a tontine for your revolting offspring, but fix it that the cash goes to the one that's the last to get married. Same thing, really. Death or marriage, what's the difference?" said Mortimer Bayliss, who had been a bachelor for forty-three years and intended to remain one.

This time his audience was far more responsive. There were murmurs of interest and approval. Quick-witted millionaires could be heard explaining the thing to neighbors whose brains moved more slowly.

"If you each put in fifty thousand, that's over half a million to begin with, and—"

"Compound interest," said J. J. Bunyan, rolling the words round his tongue like vintage port.

"Exactly. There will be the interest piling up over the years. By the time the money's paid out it should come to close on a million. Worth having, that, and the most you stand to lose is your original stake, which you're going to lose anyway when this bull market explodes, as it most certainly will. What was it someone said of the Roman Empire in the days of Tiberius? 'It is too large, a bubble blown so big and tenuous that the first shock will disrupt it in suds.' That's what's going to happen here. There's a crash coming, my hearties, a crash that'll shake the fillings out of your back teeth and dislocate your spinal cords."

Shocked voices rose in protest. Mortimer Bayliss was a licensed buffoon, but this was carrying buffoonery too far. Even J. J. Bunyan pursed his lips.

"Really, Mort!"

"All right. I'm just telling you. Shoot, if you must, this old gray head, but these things will come to pass. I have read it in the tea leaves. My little bit of money is safely tucked away in government bonds, and I advise you to put yours there. With every stock on the list quoted at about ten times its proper value, there's got to be a crash sooner or later. That's why I suggest that you start this tontine for your progeny. Then at least one of the unfortunate little tykes won't have to end his days selling pencils in the street. Of course, there's just one thing. I don't know how far you superfatted plutocrats trust one another—not an inch, I imagine, and very sensible of you, too—but I have heard that you do observe gentlemen's agreements. Correct, J. J.?"

"Of course it's correct. Nobody here would dream of breaking a gentlemen's agreement."

"Well, it's obvious that you will have to have a solemn gentlemen's agreement to keep the thing under your hats. Tip the lads off to what they're going to lose by entering the holy state, and you'll have eleven permanent celibates on your hands. Henry the Eighth and Brigham Young would have stayed single if they had known that listening to the voice of love was going to set them back a million bucks. Well, there you are, that's the best I can do for you," said Mortimer Bayliss, and, having directed a stare of scorn and loathing at the company through his black-rimmed monocle, refilled his glass and sat back, looking like a Mephistopheles who has just placed before a prospective client an attractive proposition involving the sale of his soul.

His words were followed by a silence in which you could have heard a stock drop. It lasted till J. J. Bunyan spoke.

"Boys," said J. J. Bunyan, "I think our friend Mort has got something."

2

THE SUNSHINE of a fine summer morning was doing its best for the London suburb of Valley Fields, beaming benevolently on its tree-lined roads, its neat little gardens, its rustic front gates and its soaring television antennae.

It was worth the sun's while to take a little trouble over Valley Fields, for there are few more pleasant spots on the outskirts of England's metropolis. One of its residents, a Major Flood-Smith, in the course of a letter to the *South London Argus* exposing the hellhounds of the local Gas, Light and Water Company, once alluded to it as "a fragrant oasis." He gave the letter to his cook to mail, and she forgot it and found it three weeks later in a drawer and burned it, and the editor would never have printed it anyway, it being diametrically opposed to the policy for which the *Argus* had always fearlessly stood, but—and this is the point we would stress—in using the words "fragrant oasis" the Major was dead right. He had rung the bell, hit the nail on the head and put the thing in a nutshell.

Where other suburbs go in for multiple stores and roller-skating rinks and Splendide Cinemas, Valley Fields specializes in trees and grass and flowers. More seeds are planted there each spring, more lawn mowers pushed, more garden rollers borrowed and more patent mixtures for squirting green fly purchased than in any other community on the Surrey side of the river Thames. This gives it a rural charm which—to quote Major Flood-Smith once more—makes it absolutely damned impossible to believe that you are only seven miles from Piccadilly Circus. (Or, if a crow, only five.) One has the feeling, as one comes out of its olde-worlde station, that this is where Tennyson must have got the idea of the island valley of Avilion, where falls not hail or rain or any snow, nor ever wind blows loudly.

Of all the delectable spots in Valley Fields (too numerous to mention), it is probable that the connoisseur would point with the greatest pride at Mulberry Grove, the little cul-de-sac, bright with lilac, almond, thorn, rowan and laburnum trees, which lies off Rosendale Road, and it was here that the sun was putting in its adroitest work. At the house which a builder with romance in his soul had named Castlewood its rays made their way across the neat garden and passed through French windows into a cozy living room, where they lit up, among other interesting objects, an aspidistra plant, a cuckoo clock, a caged canary, a bowl of goldfish, the photograph in a silver frame of a strikingly handsome girl, inscribed "Love, Elaine," and another photograph similarly framed—this one of an elderly gentleman with a long upper lip and beetling eyebrows, who signed himself "Cordially yours, Uffenham." Finally, reaching the armchair, they rested on the portly form of Augustus Keggs, retired butler, who was reading the *Times*. The date on the paper was June 20, 1955.

The twenty-five years and nine months which had elapsed since J. J. Bunyan's dinner party had robbed the world of that dinner's host and most of his guests, but they had touched Keggs lightly. For some reason, probably known to scientists, butlers, as far at any rate as outward appearance is concerned, do not grow old as we grow old. Keggs, reclining in his chair with his feet on a footstool and a mild cigar between his lips, looked almost precisely as he had looked a quarter of a century ago. Then he had resembled a Roman emperor who had been doing himself too well on the starchy foods. His aspect now was that of a somewhat stouter Roman emperor, one who had given up any attempt to watch his calories and liked his potatoes with lots of butter on them.

So solidly was he wedged into the cushions that one would have said that nothing short of a convulsion of nature would have been able to hoist him out of them. This, however, was not the case. As the door opened and a small, fairhaired girl came in, he did not actually leap to his feet, but he heaved himself up in slow motion like a courtly hippopotamus rising from its bed of reeds on a riverbank. This was Jane Benedick, niece of the Lord Uffenham who, as stated on that photograph, was cordially his. Lord Uffenham, under whom he had served on his return from America in the early thirties, had been the last of his long list of employers.

"Good morning, Mr. Keggs."

"Good morning, miss."

Jane was a pretty girl—eyes blue, nose small, figure excellent—at whom most men would have cast more than a passing glance, but the really attractive thing about her was her voice, which was one of singular beauty. It sometimes reminded Lord Uffenham, who had his poetical moments, of ice tinkling in a highball glass.

"Good morning, Mr. Keggs. I wouldn't have disturbed you," said Jane, "but the big shot is screaming for breakfast, and I can't find his *Times* anywhere. Did you pinch it?"

A touch of embarrassment crept into Keggs's manner.

"Yes, miss. I am sorry. I was glancing at the marriage announcements."

"Any hot news?"

"There was an item of interest to me, miss. I see that Mr. James Brewster was married yesterday."

"Friend of yours?"

"The son of a friend of the gentleman in whose employment I was many years ago in New York."

"I see. Belonging to your early or American period."

"I make something of a hobby of following the matrimonial ventures of the sons of Mr. Bunyan's friends. Sentiment, I suppose."

"Does you credit. Bunyan? Any relation of the Roscoe Bunyan who's taken Shipley?"

"His father, miss. A very wealthy gentleman. Like so many others, he lost a great deal of money in the market crash of 1929, but I believe the younger Mr. Bunyan inherited a matter of twenty million dollars after paying death duties."

"Golly! And Uncle George says he haggled about the rent like a shopkeeper in an Oriental bazaar. He isn't married, is he?"

"No, miss."

"A bit of luck for some nice girl."

"I have the same feeling, unless he has greatly changed from the days when I was in his father's service. I remember him as a most unpleasant boy."

"So do I, by golly. What I could tell you about Roscoe Bunyan!"

"You, miss? When did you meet Mr. Roscoe?"

"During my early or American period. Didn't you know that I was sent off to America at the beginning of the war with a lot of other children?"

"No, miss. I had retired and was no longer with his lordship some years before hostilities broke out."

"Well, I was. Uncle George exported me, and I was taken over for the duration by some kind people who went for the summer to a place called Meadowhampton on Long Island. The Bunyan country house was there. Did they have it in your time?"

"Oh, yes, miss. We were at Meadowhampton every year from the middle of June to Labor Day. A charming spot."

"I'd have liked it a lot better if it hadn't been for Roscoe. He made my life hell, the little brute. Or he did till one of the other boys stopped him. He had a foul habit of ducking me in the pool down on the beach where we all went, and one day after he had held me under water till I swelled like a gasometer and my whole life seemed to pass before my eyes this angel boy told him that if he didn't desist he would knock his block off. So he desisted. But I still dream about him in nightmares. And now after all these years he has popped up in England and evicted me from my childhood home. It's a strange world, Mr. Keggs."

"Most extraordinary."

"Still, too late to do anything about it now, I suppose," said Jane. "Hullo, who's this?"

"Miss?"

Jane was roaming about the room, and had come to the table in the corner. "This 'Love, Elaine' thing. New, isn't it?"

"Yes, miss. I received it yesterday."

"Who is it?"

"My niece Emma, miss."

"It says Elaine."

"She acts under the name of Elaine Dawn."

"Oh, she's on the stage? I don't wonder, with a face like that. She's beautiful."

"I believe she is generally admired."

"Emma Keggs?"

"Billson, miss. Her mother, my sister Flossie, is Mrs. Wilberforce Billson."

As Jane stood there, silenced by the revelation that this superman had a sister called Flossie, and wondering if she called him Gus, there came from outside the sound of ponderous footsteps.

"Uncle George up and about," she said. "I must be going and getting that breakfast."

A shadow flitted across Keggs's ample face. He was able to bear up bravely at the thought of Lord Uffenham, his circumstances reduced by postwar conditions, economizing by living in lodgings in a London suburb, but he had never been able to reconcile himself to the fact of his lordship's niece soiling her hands in the kitchen. Though so much of his butlerhood had been passed in the United States, Augustus Keggs had never lost his ingrained reverence for the aristocracy of his native land.

"I don't like to think of your doing the cooking, miss."

"Somebody had to take it on when your Mrs. Brown became sick of a fever. And you can't say I don't do it well."

"You do it admirably, miss."

"I got a lot of practice at home. We always seemed to be a cook short."

Keggs heaved a nostalgic sigh.

"When I was at Shipley Hall, his lordship had a staff of ten."

"And now look at him. These are the times that try men's souls."

"They are indeed."

"Still, we're snug enough here. Ought to consider ourselves jolly lucky, finding a haven like this. If it isn't Shipley, it's the next best thing. You can almost feel you're in the country. All the same, I wish we had a bit more money."

"It may come from the sale of his lordship's pictures, miss."

"Oh, you've heard about those?"

"His lordship was telling me last night, as we walked back from the Green Lion. He hopes they will restore the family fortunes."

"No harm in hoping," said Jane, and went off to scramble eggs.

For some moments after she had left, Keggs remained wrapped in thought. Then, going to the writing table, he took from a drawer a leather-covered notebook and turned to a page that contained a list of names. Unscrewing his fountain pen, he proceeded to put a tick against one of them. It was the name of James Barr Brewster, only son of the late John Waldo Brewster of New York City, who on the previous day had been united in matrimony to Sybil, daughter of Colonel and Mrs. R. G. Fanshawe-Chadwick of The Hollies, Cheltenham.

Only two names on the list now remained unticked.

He went to the telephone. He had no need to ask Information for the number he required. It was graven on his memory.

"Shipley Hall," said a fruity voice. "Mr. Roscoe Bunyan's residence."

"Good morning. Could I speak to Mr. Bunyan? This is Mr. Keggs, his father's former butler."

The voice at the Shipley end became warmer. Deep was calling to deep, butler to butler.

"Mr. Bunyan is in London at the moment, Mr. Keggs. He went up yesterday to attend a party. Would you care to speak to Mr. Bayliss?"

"No, thank you. It is a personal matter. Mr. Mortimer Bayliss, would that be?"

"That's right."

"He is in England, then?"

"Been staying here about a week. And a weird old duck he is, too."

Keggs did not encourage this lapse into criticism of an employer's guests. He had his code.

"When," he asked, with a touch of formal coldness, "will Mr. Bunyan be returning?"

"This morning, he said."

"If I were to call about eleven?"

"You'd catch him then, I think."

"Thank you, Mr.—"

"Skidmore."

"Thank you, Mr. Skidmore," said Keggs, and hung up.

3

OUT IN the garden under the shade of a spreading tree, Lord Uffenham, having bathed, shaved and done his Daily Dozen, had seated himself at a rustic table and was waiting for the ravens to feed him. Beside him on the grass lay a fine bulldog, sunk at the moment in sleep but ready to become alert at the first signs of breakfast. At these alfresco meals he usually found the pickings good.

George, sixth Viscount Uffenham, was a man built on generous lines. It was as though Nature had originally intended to make two viscounts, but had decided halfway through to use all the material at one go, and get the thing over with. In shape he resembled a pear, being reasonably narrow at the top but getting wider all the way down and culminating in a pair of boots of the outsize or violin-case type. Above his great spreading steppes of body there was poised a large and egglike head, the bald dome of which rose like some proud mountain peak from a foothill fringe of straggling hair. His upper lip was very long and straight, his chin pointed. Two huge unblinking eyes of the palest blue looked out from beneath rugged brows with a strange fixity. His air was that of a man perpetually thinking deep thoughts, and so indeed he was. His mental outlook closely resembled that of the White Knight in *Through the Looking Glass*, who, it will be remembered, frequently omitted to hear what was said to him because he was thinking of a way to feed oneself on batter and so go on from day to day getting a little fatter.

"There you are," said Jane, arriving with laden tray. "Scrambled eggs, all piping hot, coffee, toast, butter, marmalade, the *Times* and a couple of biscuits for the hound. Well, what's on your mind, baby?"

"Hey?"

"I heard a whirring sound as I approached, and knew it must be your brain working. I hope I haven't derailed a train of cosmic thought."

"Hey?"

Jane sighed. Conversing with the head of the family often tended to try the patience of his loved ones, for when some matter of import engrossed him he had an annoying habit of going off into a trance and becoming remote. Concentrated now on whatever it was that had engaged his interest, he gave the impression that it would be possible to get into communication with him only on the ouija board. But Jane was a resourceful girl. She took the coffeepot and pressed it firmly on his hand, and he came out of his coma with a yelp of anguish.

"Hey! What's the idea? Lord love a duck, are you aware that that pot is slightly hotter than blazes?"

"Well, I wanted to rouse you. What were you musing about?"

"Hey? Musing? Oh, yer mean musing? I was musing, if yer must know, on Keggs. I've come to the conclusion that Keggs is deep and dark."

"How do you mean, deep and dark?"

"Subtle. Sinister. Machiavellian. Never suspected it when he was with me at Shipley, no doubt because butlers wear the mask, but now I find myself eying him askance and wondering what he'll be up to next. Take that episode at the pub."

"What episode was that?"

"And look at this Mulberry Grove place. Three houses in it—Castlewood, Peacehaven and The Nook—each with its summerhouse, each with its bird bath, and all Keggs property. How, I ask myself, did Augustus Keggs accumulate the money to buy this vast estate? You don't get summerhouses and bird baths for nothing."

"He bought them with his savings, chump."

"But how did he acquire those savings?"

"He was years in America before he came to you, working for Mr. Bunyan, the father of the frightful young man who's taken Shipley. I suppose the Bunyan home was always full of guests at weekends, and American weekend guests never tip the butler less than a thousand dollars."

Lord Uffenham considered this.

"I see what yer mean. Yerss, as you say, that might account for his opulence. Nevertheless, I still maintain, after what happened at the pub, that the blighter is slippery. A twister, if ever there was one."

"What was it that happened at the pub? You didn't tell me."

"I did."

"You didn't."

"Oh, didn't I? Fully intended to. Must have slipped my mind. It was at the Green Lion in Rosendale Road. He and I looked in there last night for a quick one, and almost before we'd had time to blow the froth off he was chiseling the aborigines out of their hard-earned cash by means of . . . what's the word?"

"What's what word?"

"The word I'm trying to think of. Chick something."

"Chicanery?"

"That's right, chicanery. You ever been in a pub?"

"No."

"Well, you all sit around and swig yer beer and discuss whatever subject happens to come up, and it wasn't long before Keggs turned the conversation to boxing. It's a thing he's interested in. His sister married a boxer, he tells me. Feller of the name of Billson. Battling Billson I believe he was called. Retired now, runs a pub somewhere. Lots of these fellers run pubs when they leave the ring. Where was I?"

"Sitting around and swigging yer beer."

"That's right, and, as I say, Keggs brought up the subject of boxing, deploring the way it had deteriorated. The chaps fighting now, he claimed, weren't a patch on the old-timers. 'Ah,' he said, shaking his bally head in a mournful sort of way, 'we haven't any nippy welterweights like Jack Dempsey today.' "

"But wasn't Jack Dempsey a heavyweight?"

"Of course he was, and so a dozen voices told him. But he would stick to it that he only weighed ten stone four, and bobs were produced on every side by those who thought they were on a safe thing and placed in the custody of the landlord, who was appointed arbiter. 'I'm sorry, Mr. Keggs,' he said, 'but I'm afraid I must decide against you. Jack Dempsey weighed over thirteen stone when he won the heavyweight championship from Jess Willard.' And was Keggs taken aback? Not a bit. Did he exhibit pique? Or chagrin? Not a trace. 'Oh, *that* Jack Dempsey?' he said with one of those faint, tolerant smiles. 'His name was William Harrison Dempsey. I was not referring to him. Naturally I meant the original Jack Dempsey, the Nonpareil.' And he pulled out a book—yerss, he had it in his pocket—and read out where it said about how it is interesting to remember that the fighting weight of Jack Dempsey the Nonpareil was only a hundred and forty-four pounds with tights on. Well, there was a pretty general outcry, as you can imagine, with those present hotly demanding their bobs back, but the landlord had no option but to award the stakes to Keggs, and he cleaned up as much as fifteen shillings and sixpence. He told me, when we were walking home, that he had made a steady income for thirty years out of that piece of chicanery. So now perhaps you'll agree that he's deep and dark and wants watching."

"I think he's a sweetie-pie."

"A sweetie-pie, no doubt, in many respects, but a slippery sweetie-pie, the sort of sweetie-pie apt at any moment to be up to something fishy. I wouldn't trust him as far as I could throw—" Lord Uffenham looked about him for an illustration—"as far as I could throw that ruddy statue," he concluded.

The statue in question, standing on the lawn of Peacehaven, the house next door, was what is known in the trade as a colossal nude, and it was the work of a young sculptor named Stanhope Twine, who lived there. Jane—possibly because she was engaged to be married to him—admired it. Lord Uffenham did not. He disliked the statue, and he had no use whatever for Stanhope Twine. The Supreme Being, he presumed, would not have created Stanhope Twine without some definite purpose in view, but as to what that purpose could have been Lord Uffenham frankly confessed himself fogged. He resented being called on to share the same planet with a herring-gutted young son of a what-not who marcelled his hair, wore yellow corduroy trousers and, when he met his elders and betters, said "Ah, Uffenham" to them in an insufferably patronizing tone of voice. Jane always wanted to stroke Stanhope Twine's head. Lord Uffenham would have preferred to beat it in with a hatchet. He looked down with a reproachful eye at the bulldog, whose name, like his own, was George. This otherwise excellent animal had more than once given signs of wanting to fraternize with Stanhope Twine. He had that defect, so common in bulldogs, of liking everyone, from the highest to the lowest.

Jane was looking at the statue.

"Stanhope thinks it's the best thing he's done," she said.

"Stanhope!"

"Don't say 'Stanhope!' "

"I only said 'Stanhope!' "

"But in a cold, soupy voice as if it revolted your lips to frame the word."

This was precisely how Lord Uffenham's lips had felt about it, but he lacked the nerve to say so. Though a courageous man with a fine military record in his younger days, he feared his niece's wrath. Jane, when the tigress that slept within her was roused, had a nasty way of telling him that something had gone wrong with the kitchen range and there would be only bread and cheese for dinner. Changing the subject tactfully, he said, "Hey!"

"Yes, m'lord?"

"Did you go that gallery place about my pictures?"

"I did, and saw Mr. Gish in person. He seemed intrigued."

"Good."

"I'm going to ring him up soon and ask how things are coming along."

"Excellent. Keep after the blighter. If I can sell those pictures, I'll be able to live at Shipley again."

"And I'll be able to marry Stanhope."

"Ugh!"

"What did you say?"

"I didn't say anything."

"You said 'Ugh!' "

"Nothing of the kind."

"It sounded like 'Ugh!' "

"Very possibly. Many things do. But don't bother me now, my dear girl. I'm doing my crossword puzzle, and it's a stinker this morning. Run and ask Keggs what the dickens 'Adventurer goes in for outrageous road-speed' is supposed to signify. Tell him it's urgent. And I want some more coffee."

"You drink too much coffee."

"Yer can't drink too much coffee. It bucks you up. It stimulates the mental processes."

"All right. I'll get you some. What a lot of trouble you do give, to be sure." Jane returned with the coffee.

"I've made just one cup," she said. "I disapprove of your poisoning your system with caffeine. And that 'road-speed' thing is an anagram, Mr. Keggs says, and the answer is 'desperado.' Bung it down."

"I will. Desperado, eh? Capital. Now, go and ask him what the devil 'So the subordinate professional on trial gets wages in advance not without demur' means."

"He's not here."

"Don't be an ass. Of course he's here. He lives here, doesn't he?"

"He does. But at the moment he's off somewhere in his little car, going in for outrageous road-speed. I caught him just as he was leaving. Adieu, he cried, and waved his lily hand, and then he shot out into Mulberry Grove and headed for the great open spaces. You'll have to wait till he gets back," said Jane, and went about her domestic duties.

And Lord Uffenham, returning to his crossword puzzle, was wondering what sort of mind a man could have who was capable of springing a thing like "So the subordinate professional on trial gets wages in advance not without demur" on a sensitive public, when from the corner of his eye he observed Stanhope Twine coming out of the back door of Peacehaven, his intention apparently to take a refreshing look at his masterpiece.

He rose in a marked manner and went into the house. He was in no mood to have "Ah, Uffenham" said to him.

4

AT ABOUT the moment when Lord Uffenham was downing his first forkful of scrambled egg and the dog George the first of his two biscuits, the Roscoe Bunyan whom Jane Benedick disliked so much was standing beside his Jaguar outside a studio in St. John's Wood, preparing to drive back to Shipley Hall and get some sleep. The party which he had gone up to London to attend had been one of those bohemian parties which last all night, terminating in a flurry of eggs and bacon as the postman is making his first delivery of the morning.

There was rather a lot of Roscoe Bunyan. As a boy, he had been a large, stout boy, inclined to hot dogs, candy and ice cream sodas between meals, and he was no fonder of diet systems now than he had been in his formative years. Most of his acquaintances would have preferred far less of this singularly unattractive young man, but he had insisted on giving full measure, bulging freely in all directions. His face was red, the back of his neck overflowed his collar, and there had recently been published a second edition of his chin. It is not surprising, therefore, that such passers-by as had a love for the beautiful should have removed their gaze from him after a brief glance and transferred it to the girl who was standing beside him.

Elaine Dawn unquestionably took the eye. Nobody, looking at her, would have supposed her to be the daughter of a Shoreditch public-house proprietor who had formerly been a heavyweight boxer. It often happens that fathers, incapable themselves of finishing in the first three in a seaside beauty contest, produce offspring who set the populace whistling, and this had occurred in the case of Elaine's parent, Battling Billson. He himself, partly because Nature had fashioned him that way and partly as the result of the risks of his profession, looked like a gorilla which had been caught in machinery of some sort, but his child was a breath-taking brunette of the Cleopatra type. One felt that she would have got on well with Marc Antony.

Eying her as she stood there, Roscoe could understand why he had made that impulsive proposal of marriage in the later stages of another of those all-night parties two weeks before. She had what it takes to unsettle the cool judgment of the most levelheaded young man.

The engagement had not been announced. Roscoe in an expansive moment had mentioned it to his guest Mortimer Bayliss, but Elaine had maintained a discreet silence about it. She thought it better so. A girl with parents like hers does not want those parents coming around to say Hello to their future son-in-law till it is too late for that son-in-law to realize the sort of family he is marrying into. Emma Billson loved and respected her father and mother, but she was a sensible girl, prudent and practical, and none realized more clearly than she that they were not everybody's money. Roscoe, some instinct told her, would not find them an encouraging spectacle. Time enough to confront him with them on the return from the honeymoon.

"Well," said Roscoe, yawning cavernously, "I'm off to grab some sleep. You'll get home all right?"

Miss Dawn lived out Pinner way, which is distant several miles from St. John's Wood, and in a direction diametrically opposite to Shipley Hall. It speaks well for Roscoe's sturdy good sense that the idea of driving her there had never occurred to him. He, like his betrothed, was prudent and practical.

"Take a cab or something," he said helpfully, and climbed into his Jaguar and was gone.

It was an hour and a quarter's drive from London to Shipley Hall, but Roscoe, who from earliest youth had been the sort of charioteer of whom traffic policemen inquire the locality of the fire, did it in forty-six minutes. Arriving and passing drowsily up the stairs to his bedroom, he was intercepted by Skidmore.

"Excuse me, sir," said Skidmore. "A Mr. Keggs has called."

Roscoe frowned.

"Keggs? I don't know any Keggs."

"He tells me that he at one time held the post of butler to your father, sir."

"Oh, that guy?" Out of the dead past there emerged slowly before Roscoe's mental eye a moonfaced figure with a Limey accent and a spreading waistline. "What does he want?"

"He did not say, sir, except to urge that the matter was important."

"Where is he?"

"In my pantry, sir."

Roscoe mused. Important? To whom? Oh, well, better see the man, perhaps, and get it over.

"All right, bring him into the smoking room," he said, and presently Keggs entered, bearing the derby hat without which no butler, however ex, ever stirs abroad.

"Good morning, sir," he said. "I trust that you remember me, sir? I had the honor to serve the late Mr. Bunyan, Senior, many years ago in the capacity of butler." His gooseberry eyes roamed to and fro, and he wheezed sentimentally for a moment. "It seems strange to be in this room once more," he observed genially. "After returning from America, I was for some time in the service of Lord Uffenham at Shipley Hall. Revisiting it brings tears to my eyes."

Roscoe was not interested in Keggs's eyes, though inclined, for he was of an impatient spirit and needed his sleep, to damn them.

"Get on," he said curtly. "What do you want?"

Keggs was silent for a moment, seeming to be marshalling his thoughts with a view to selecting the right opening. He looked at the derby hat, and appeared to draw inspiration from it.

"You are a rich man, Mr. Bunyan," he began, and Roscoe started as though the Shipley Hall ghost had confronted him.

A faint, indulgent smile flitted for an instant across Keggs's face. He had interpreted that start.

"No, sir," he went on. "I have not come to borrow money. I was about to say that, though a rich man, you have probably no objection to becoming richer. Coming without further preamble to what I may call the *res*, sir, I am in a position to put you in the way of obtaining a million dollars."

"What!"

"I speak in rough figures, of course. But I think it may be estimated at a million."

It had frequently been said of Roscoe Bunyan by those who knew him that, though loaded down above the Plimsoll line with money, he would at no time refrain from walking ten miles in tight shoes to pick up a penny someone had dropped. He loved money as dearly as he loved food. When, therefore, retired butlers announced that they could put him in the way of obtaining a million dollars, they touched the deeps in him, and his whole soul, such as it was, became electrified. He stared at this derby-hatted Santa Claus in much the same way as on another occasion stout Cortez—though some say stout Balboa—stared at the Pacific. The suspicion that stout Keggs might be inebriated he dismissed instantly. The man's whole aspect radiated sobriety.

A sudden displeasing thought struck him. It was that his visitor was going to try to get him to put up money for something. He had some invention, possibly a patent corkscrew, for which he required financial backing, or, still worse, had in his possession the map, yellowed by the years, which showed—spot marked X—where Captain Kidd had buried his treasure. He snorted slightly, feeling that any such project must be nipped in the bud.

Keggs was just as good at interpreting snorts as at probing the inner meaning of starts. He raised a paternal hand, looking like a high priest rebuking an inferior priest for some lapse from the priestly standard.

"I think I divine what you have in mind, sir. Your are under the impression that I wish you to finance a commercial venture of some nature."

"Don't you?"

"No, sir. I have only information to sell."

"Sell?" It was a verb that grated on Roscoe.

"Naturally I am desirous of receiving a certain emolument in return for my information."

Roscoe chewed a dubious lip. He hated giving other people emoluments. All his life the money in his purse had been earmarked for the exclusive use of R. Bunyan. Still, if it was really true about that million dollars. . . .

"Well, all right. Shoot."

"Very good, sir. I must begin," said Keggs in a professional manner, " by asking if the name of Tonti is familiar to you?"

"Never heard of him. Who is he?"

" 'Was,' sir, not 'is.' Tonti is no longer with us," said Keggs, as who should say that all flesh is grass. "He was an Italian banker who flourished in the seventeenth century, and originated what is known as the tontine, the nature of which I will explain. And now," he concluded, having done so, "if I may have your attention, sir, I will relate a brief story."

He consulted the derby hat again, and began.

"On the tenth of September, 1929, sir, your late father entertained at dinner at our Park Avenue residence eleven guests, all, with the exception of Mr. Mortimer Bayliss, well-known financiers like himself. This, I need not remind you, was some weeks before the disastrous financial crash of the year 1929 occurred, and what is termed the bull market was at its height. All the gentlemen present had made and were making very large fortunes, and at the conclusion of the meal there was an exchange of views as to what should be done with all the money that was accruing daily in that era of frenzied speculation."

Here Keggs, whom the passage of years had left a little touched in the wind, paused for breath, and Roscoe took advantage of the momentary silence to ask him if he could not for God's sake to speed it up a little. Would it not be possible for him, inquired Roscoe, to put a stick of dynamite under himself and come to the point?

"I was about to do so, sir," said Keggs equably. "The gentlemen, as I say, were discussing what would be the most amusing way of spending their money, and Mr. Mortimer Bayliss, always fertile with suggestions, proposed a tontine. But a tontine differing from the one I was describing to you a moment ago. The idea of the scheme as originated by Tonti—of death gradually eliminating all the competitors but one—made no appeal to the gentlemen, most of whom suffered from high blood pressure, and it was then that Mr. Bayliss offered this alternative proposal. It was, in a word, that Mr. Bunyan and each of his guests should contribute fifty thousand dollars to a fund or pool, and that the entire sum—with compound interest over the years—should be paid to whichever of the contributors' sons was the last to become married. You spoke, sir?"

Roscoe had not spoken, he had snorted. But the snort he snorted now was

a very different snort from the snort he had snorted when snorting previously.
Then he had been cold and on his guard, alert to nip in the bud anything that
could be classed under the heading of funny business or rannygazoo. Now he
was eager, ardent, enthusiastic, and he expressed his emotion in an awestruck
"Gosh!"

"The last to get married?"

"Yes, sir."

"*I'm* not married."

"No, sir."

Golden visions rose before Roscoe's eyes.

"You're sure my father was in this?"

"Yes, sir."

"He never said a word to me about it."

"Secrecy and silence were of the essence, sir."

"And this was in 1929?"

"Yes, sir."

"Then—"

"Precisely, sir. In the course of the past twenty-five years the field, if I may
employ a sporting expression, has thinned out. Several of the young gentlemen were eliminated in the recent global hostilities, while others have
married. My *Times* informs me that Mr. James Brewster, son of the late Mr.
John Brewster, became married yesterday. Until then he, yourself and one
other gentleman were the sole survivors, as one might describe them."

"You mean now there are only two of us?"

"Exactly, sir, only yourself and this other contestant. Who—" here Keggs
paused significantly—"is affianced—"

"Gosh!"

"And—" Keggs paused again—"of straitened means."

The glow which had warmed Roscoe at the word "affianced" faded.

"Then he isn't likely to get married," he said morosely. "Darn it, he may
not marry for years."

Keggs coughed.

"Unless encouraged to do so by a little financial assistance from somebody
more happily situated. As it might be yourself, sir."

"Eh?"

"If you were to give the young gentleman financial assistance, it would
quite possibly turn the scale. He would feel emboldened to take the plunge.
Leaving you in possession of what, if you will pardon the argot, I might term
the jackpot."

Roscoe plucked at his double chin, debating within himself what to do for
the best. And as he sat there at a young man's crossroads, Mortimer Bayliss
sauntered in.

The years, which had dealt so gently with Augustus Keggs, had been
rougher with Mortimer Bayliss, withering him till he now resembled

something excavated from the tomb of one of the earlier Ptolemies. Seeing the visitor, he halted, raking him with the black-rimmed monocle which the passage of time had not succeeded in dislodging from his eye.

"Keggs!" he cried, astounded.

"Good morning, Mr. Bayliss."

"Aren't you dead yet? I thought we'd seen the last of you years ago. You're fatter than ever, my obese butler. *And* uglier. What on earth are you doing here?"

"I came to see Mr. Bunyan on a matter of business, sir."

"Oh, you're talking business? Then I'll leave you."

"You won't!" said Roscoe, starting into life. "You're just the man I want. Is it true what Keggs has been telling me?"

"Mr. Bunyan is alluding to my account of what occurred at his father's dinner table on the night of September the tenth, 1929, Mr. Bayliss. Your suggestion of the matrimonial tontine, sir."

It was not easy to disconcert Mortimer Bayliss, but at these words the monocle fell from his eye, and he stared incredulously.

"You know about that? For heaven's sake! Where were you? Under the table? Lurking in a corner, disguised as a potted palm?"

"No, sir, I was not present, except in spirit. But I had made a daily practice, from the very early beginnings of the bull market, of concealing a dictaphone behind the portrait of George Washington over the mantelpiece in the dining room. I thought it might prove helpful to me in making my investments."

"You mean you got a recording of every word spoken at those dinners of J. J.'s? You must have collected some pretty good market tips."

"I did, sir. But none more profitable than yours, of selling my holdings and investing my money in government bonds."

"You had the sense to do that?"

"I sold out next day, sir. I have always felt extremely grateful to you, Mr. Bayliss. I look upon you as the founder of my fortunes."

Roscoe, who had been listening with mounting impatience to these amiable exchanges, broke in on them petulantly.

"Never mind all that. To hell with your fortunes. Is it true about this tontine thing, Bayliss?"

"Quite true. It was one of my brightest ideas."

"There really is this money coming to the son who's the last to marry?

"Yes, it's all there, waiting."

"And it works out at a million?"

"About that, I should imagine, by this time. Half a million was the original sum put up. One of the eleven—"

"Twelve."

"Eleven, fool. You don't suppose a sonless bachelor like myself was going to contribute, do you? There was J. J., and there were ten of his guests, making eleven in all. And, as I was about to tell you when you interrupted me with your fatuous remark, one of that eleven changed his mind in the calmer atmosphere of the morning after, and backed out. So there were ten starters at fifty thousand a head."

"And only two of us left in now, Keggs says."

"Indeed? I hadn't been following the race. Who's the other fellow?"

"I don't know yet."

"And when you do know?"

"I'm going to fix him."

"In what sense do you use the word 'fix'?"

"Keggs says he wants to get married, but can't afford to. So I slip him something—"

"—and push him over the edge. I follow the train of thought. Nobbling the other horse. A thoroughly dirty trick. Whose idea was that?"

"Keggs's."

"Oh? Well, you might not think it to look at me, Keggs, but I am blushing for you. Between the two of you, you seem to have turned what started out as a nice clean sporting contest into the lowest kind of ramp. And how about the wages of sin? I take it that Keggs expects a return of some sort for his skulduggery. What are you going to give him?"

Roscoe reflected for a moment.

"Fifty pounds," he said, and Keggs, who had been fondling the derby hat, started as if it had bitten him.

"Fifty pounds, sir?"

"What's wrong with fifty pounds?"

"I had expected rather more, sir."

"You won't get it," said Roscoe.

There was a silence. It was plain that Keggs had been cut to the quick and that the dream castles he had been building were shattered and lying about him in ruins. A butler never displays emotion, but he was an ex-butler, and he displayed quite a good deal. But presently the tempest within him became stilled. Calm returned to his moon-like features.

"Very good, sir," he said, showing himself one of those stouthearted men who can meet with triumph and disaster and treat those two impostors just the same, as recommended by Mr. Kipling.

"Right," said Mortimer Bayliss. "So we can get on with it. Who is the mysterious unknown?"

"The name is Twine, sir.

"Twine?" Roscoe turned to Mr. Bayliss. "I don't remember a friend of my father's called Twine. Do you?"

Mortimer Bayliss shrugged his shoulders.

"Why should I? Are you under the impression that the late J. J.'s loathsome associates were as a string of pearls to me and that I used to count them over, every one apart, my rosary, my rosary? Tell us about this Twine, Keggs."

"He is a sculptor, sir. He resides next door to me."

"Odd coincidence."

"Yes, sir. It is a small world, I often say."

"And who is he engaged to?"

"A Miss Benedick, sir, niece of the Lord Uffenham in whose service I was at one time. The young lady and his lordship reside at Castlewood."

"Eh?"

"My house, sir. The address is Castlewood, Mulberry Grove, Valley Fields. Mr. Twine is at Peacehaven."

"Where he sculps?"

"Yes, sir."

"But not with great success, I gather?"

"No, sir. I should describe Mr. Twine as fiscally crippled. This constitutes an obstacle in the way of his becoming united to the young lady."

"Poverty is the banana skin on the doorstep of romance."

"Precisely, sir."

"And you suggest that Mr. Bunyan should correct this state of things?"

"Yes, sir. I feel sure that Mr. Twine would embark on matrimony immediately, if Mr. Bunyan were to give him twenty thousand pounds."

Roscoe quivered from stem to stern, his eyes popping from their sockets.

"Are you crazy?" he gasped. "Twenty thousand pounds?"

"Sprat to catch a whale," said Mortimer Bayliss. "Don't spoil the ship for a ha'porth of tar, or, putting it another way, if you don't speculate, you can't accumulate."

Roscoe ran a hand feverishly through his hair. Though he could see that there was sense in these platitudes, nothing was going to make them attractive to him.

"But how could I do it? You can't walk in on a man you've never met and give him money."

"No, that's true. Any suggestions, Keggs?"

"It could be very simply arranged, sir. There is a statue of Mr. Twine's in the garden of Peacehaven. A day or two ago, if I might suggest it, Mr. Bunyan, calling on his father's former butler to talk of old times, happened to glance over the fence—"

"—and saw the masterpiece and was struck all of a heap? Of course. How right you are. You get the idea, Roscoe? 'Egad!' you said, addressing yourself. 'An undiscovered genius.' And you decided to pop in on him with your checkbook."

"And offer him twenty thousand pounds for a statue? He'll think I'm dippy."

"How do you get around that, Keggs?"

"Quite easily, sir. I was perusing not long ago the autobiography of an eminent playwright, in which he relates how, when merely a young man of promise, he was approached by a financial gentleman who offered him an annual income for a number of years in return for one-third of his, the playwright's, future earnings."

"Did he accept it?"

"No sir, but I am sure that Mr. Twine would accept a similar offer from Mr. Bunyan."

"Of course he would, especially if the offer was twenty thousand pounds cash down. You can't miss, Roscoe. He'll start getting measured for the wedding trousers five minutes after he banks the check. And I'll tell you what I'll do. I'll handle the whole business for you. You need not appear except as a benevolent figure in the background. What's this Twine's telephone number, Keggs? I'll go and talk to him now."

Some minutes had passed before he returned, minutes occupied by Roscoe in gazing bleakly into space, by Keggs in fondling the derby hat. A tentative remark by the ex-butler dealing with the continued fineness of the June weather was poorly received. Roscoe was not in conversational mood.

"I've talked to him," said Mortimer Bayliss, "and his reception of my name was, I must say, extremely gratifying. 'Not *the* Mortimer Bayliss?' he gurgled. 'None other,' I replied, blushing prettily. And then I told him how you had seen the statue and been greatly impressed by it and wanted me to give my expert opinion of it and his other works, which are probably too foul for words, eh, Keggs?"

"I do not admire them myself, sir."

"And the upshot of it all is that he has invited me to dinner tonight at Wee Holme. Or is it Kozy-Kot?"

"Peacehaven, sir."

"Just as bad, if not worse. I suppose I shall get the usual loathsome suburban dinner."

"No, sir. Mr. Twine has an excellent cook."

"He has? Well, that's something. It will help me to endure what will undoubtedly be a ghastly evening, for if there is one thing I hate, it is busts in any quantity. J. J. was always trying to make me buy him busts. He had a morbid passion for them. So much, then, for this evening. Tomorrow I shall allow him to simmer and the day after give him lunch at my club and spring the proposition on him. I had better take your check with me, so that I can flutter it before his eyes. And you ought to thank Keggs for his shrewd suggestion."

Roscoe gulped. He was suffering as only a parsimonious multimillionaire can suffer when faced with the prospect of becoming separated from twenty thousand pounds. But he could see that the investment was a sound one. A sprat, as Mortimer Bayliss had said, to catch a whale. Nevertheless, as he spoke, his voice was hollow.

"Thank you, Keggs."

"Not at all, sir. A pleasure. Good morning, sir. Good morning, Mr. Bayliss."

"You leaving us?"

"I ought to be getting back, sir."

"Train?"

"I have my car."

"I'll see you to it. Keggs," said Mortimer Bayliss, closing the door behind them and halting before him with monocle poised and a look on his mummified face like that of a district attorney about to cross-examine the stuffing out of a rat of the underworld, "a word with you, my fishy major-domo. What's the game?"

"Sir?"

"Wipe that blasted saintly expression off your fat face, moron. What, I asked, is the game, and I should like a categorical answer. Come clean, you derby-hatted hellhound. You know as well as I do that J. J. Bunyan never had a friend called Twine."

It would be too much to say that Keggs giggled. Butlers, even when retired, do not giggle. But he came very near to giggling.

"I was asking myself if that point had struck you, sir."

"Well, tell yourself it did."

"I feared for a moment that you were about to expose my little deception."

Mortimer Bayliss raised his eyebrows.

"My good Keggs, when I see a situation developing which promises to culminate in Roscoe Bunyan's paying out twenty thousand pounds for nothing, I allow it to develop. I don't spoil the fun by exposing little deceptions. Heaven knows there aren't too many chances of getting a good laugh these days."

"No, indeed, sir."

"A benevolent Providence has been saving up something like this for Roscoe for years. He's far too fond of money. Very bad for his soul. It is doing him a kindness to take some of it off him from time to time. You felt that, eh?"

"Very strongly, sir."

"Yes, I could see you feeling it when he spoke of rewarding you for your services with fifty pounds in full settlement."

"The offer did seem to me in the circumstances somewhat inadequate, I confess."

"So you gave him what is called the wrong steer by way of getting back at him?"

"I was also actuated by a genuine desire to be of service to Miss Benedick, sir. A charming young lady. I would not say that I consider Mr. Twine an ideal mate for Miss Benedick, but she appears to be in favor of the union, so I am only too happy to be instrumental in bringing it to fruition."

"Golly!"

"Sir?"

"Nothing. I was only admiring the way you talk. Has anyone ever called you the Boy Orator of Valley Fields?"

"Not to my knowledge, sir."

"Posterity will. And now, my dear Keggs, tell me—briefly, if you can manage it—who is the real McCoy?"

"Sir?"

"The genuine one, fathead. The true claimant, ass. Roscoe's rival."

"Oh, I beg your pardon, sir. You misled me for a moment by alluding to him as McCoy. His name is Hollister."

"What!" The information seemed to surprise Mortimer Bayliss. "You mean Joe Hollister's son?"

"I believe Mr. Hollister, Senior's name was Joseph."

"I know darned well it was. He was my best—I might say my only—friend. Why, it is impossible to say, but I have never been a popular man. What's young Bill Hollister doing these days? The last I heard of him, he was going to learn painting in Paris."

"Mr. Hollister, Junior, is at present employed as an assistant at the well-known Gish Galleries in Bond Street."

"That den of thieves! And he's engaged to be married, you say?"

"To a Miss Angela Murphrey, sir, a lady who studies the violin at the Royal College of Music."

"How the devil do you know all this?"

"Through the good offices of the investigation bureau which I have been employing, sir."

"Good God! You put a private eye on to him?"

"It was the simplest method of keeping myself *au courant* with his affairs."

"God bless you, Keggs! You ought to be head of the secret police in Moscow."

"I doubt if I would care for residence in Russia, sir. The climate. Would there be anything further, Mr. Bayliss?"

"No, I think that about winds up the agenda. God bless you again, my Keggs, making twice in all."

Mortimer Bayliss went back to Roscoe. A more cheerful Roscoe now, for he had been thinking things over and had adjusted himself to the high cost of sprats.

"Keggs gone?" he said.

"Yes, he has departed, and in what looked to me like dudgeon. Fifty pounds, Roscoe! Not much of a tip, considering everything. Have you no regrets?"

"Of course I haven't."

"You may ere long."

"What do you mean?"

"Oh, nothing. You know," said Mortimer Bayliss, "there's one thing about this business that you appear to have overlooked."

"Eh?"

"How about your own wedding? I seem to remember your telling me you were engaged."

"Oh, that? I'll break it off, of course."

"I see. Break it off. And what about breach of promise actions? I suppose you've written her letters?"

"One or two."
"Mentioning marriage?"
"Yes, I did mention marriage."
"Then you'd better start worrying."
"No need to worry. It's all right."
"Why—I am a child in these matters—is it all right?"
"I know an excellent man called Pilbeam, who runs the Argus Enquiry Agency. He'll get those letters for me. I gave him the same sort of job about a year ago, and he did it without a hitch. He's always doing that sort of thing. Of course, I won't break off the engagement till I've got them."

Mortimer Bayliss threw his head back, and the room rang with the cackling laughter which twenty-six years ago had too often rasped the nerves of J. J. Bunyan's guests.

"The last of the Romantics! What a rare soul you are, Roscoe. You remind me of Sir Galahad."

5

THE SUN was high in the sky above London's West End and all good men had long since buckled down to the day's work at their shops and offices, when a young man with a headache turned out of Piccadilly and started to walk up Bond Street—a square-jawed, solidly built young man who looked less like the art gallery assistant he actually was than a contender for the middleweight championship who has broken training for a while. His name was Bill Hollister, and the headache from which he was suffering was due to the fact that he, like Roscoe Bunyan, had been one of the revelers at that all-night party at the St. John's Wood studio.

But though an unseen hand had begun at brief intervals to drive red-hot spikes rather briskly through his temples, his heart was light and he was in two minds about whistling a gay tune. Like the heroine of the poet Browning's "Pippa Passes," he was of the opinion that God was in His heaven and all right with the world. Indeed, if Pippa had happened to pass at that moment, he would have slapped her on the back and told her he knew just how she felt.

It has been well said—among others by Lord Uffenham, who in his salad days was always having trouble through getting engaged to the wrong girl—that there is no ecstasy so profound as that which comes to a young man who is unexpectedly given his freedom by a fiancée for whom he has never much cared, to whom he proposed in what, he feels, must have been one of those moments of madness, sheer madness, which people are always having on radio and in television. And this had happened to Bill. Uneasily betrothed for the past month to the Miss Angela Murphrey of whom Keggs had spoken to Mortimer Bayliss, he had found awaiting him on his return from the St. John's Wood party a letter from her, formally severing their relations, and it had acted on him like Benzedrine.

It had not come wholly as a surprise, this letter, for Miss Murphrey had for some little time been throwing out hints that suggested that she might be dubious as to his suitability as a life partner. She was one of those forceful girls who do not shrink from speaking their minds when they detect flaws in their chosen mates. "Why don't you brush your hair?" she would say to her William. "You look like a sheep dog." Or, again, "Why do you wear that awful cutaway coat and those striped trousers? You look like an undertaker." Useless to tell her that the cross he had to bear was that every time he brushed his hair it sprang out of shape again the moment the brush was removed. Equally useless to plead that he was compelled to wear a cutaway coat and striped trousers because they were the uniform of his guild, and to explain that if an assistant of his were to show up at the Gish Galleries in mufti, Mr. Gish would have him shot at sunrise. A melancholy silence was his only course.

Coming right down to it, then, practically all Bill Hollister had got out of his association with Miss Murphrey was the discovery that his personal appearance was that of a shaggy dog, expert at herding sheep, which had taken up mortician work in its spare time, and surely, he felt, a marriage of true minds should have produced something a little warmer. The thought that from now on Miss Murphrey would take the high road while he took the low road, and that neither on the bonnie bonnie banks of Loch Lomond nor elsewhere would they ever meet again, was a very stimulating one. An assistant who worked at the Gish Galleries was supposed to be at his post by nine-thirty, but though the hour was now eleven forty-five and he knew that behind those portals Leonard Gish must be crouching to spring, a Leonard Gish whose bite might well be fatal, he refused to allow the shape of things to come to diminish his feeling of *bien être*. Arriving at his destination, he beamed on the young woman who sat in the outer office, a Miss Elphinstone, and greeted her exuberantly, as one who after much searching has found an old friend.

"Good morning, Elphinstone, good morning, good morning, good morning. Everything under control?"

In Miss Elphinstone's gaze there was no answering exuberance, only austere rebuke and a chilly disapproval. There had always been something Murphreyesque about this lady receptionist, as she liked to describe herself, and many a time had Bill urged her to take the lemon out of her mouth and look on the bright side, stressing the fact that the world was so full of a number of things that he was sure we should all be as happy as kings.

"Ho!" she said.

"Ho to you," responded Bill civilly.

"Well, if I'd known you were coming, I'd have baked a cake," said Miss Elphinstone. "This is a nice time to be starting work."

"I would prefer not to hear that word 'work' mentioned," said Bill with a touch of stiffness. "It does something to me this morning."

"Coming here at twelve o'clock."

"Ah, now I get you. A little late, you feel? Yes, possibly you're right. I was at a party last night and got home with the milk. A photo finish. Sinking into a chair, I dozed off, and who more surprised than I to find on waking that it was past eleven. Elphinstone," said Bill, eying her closely, "I don't like that yellow make-up you're using this morning. And why do you flicker at the rims? It's a most disturbing spectacle."

"You'll flicker when Mr. Gish sees you. He's been jumping around like a cat on a hot shovel."

"You probably mean a pea in that painful position, but I take your point. Cross, is he? I'm sorry to hear that, for this morning I want to have smiling faces about me. You see me today, Elphinstone, sitting on top of the world with a rainbow round my shoulder and my hat on the side of my head. You don't understand why, not knowing the facts, but I feel like a caged skylark that has been freed and permitted to soar into the empyrean with a song on its beak. If Shelley were to see me now, he would say 'Hail to thee, blithe spirit,' and he would mean it. I feel . . . but as something in your manner tells me that you don't give a hoot how I feel, and as Pop Gish no doubt wishes to have speech with me, I will be getting in touch with him."

"He's gone."

"Already? Before lunch?"

"He's gone to the country to the sale of some old furniture."

"Oh, I see." The stern look faded from Bill's face. "I feared for a moment that he had turned into a clockwatcher and was not giving his all to the dear old gallery. Well, if you had mentioned this sooner, I would have been spared considerable nervous tension. I was picturing him in there all ready to attack me with tooth and claw. Did the fine old man leave any little messages for me?"

'He said tell you that if you want to jump into the river with a pound of lead in each hand, it will be all right with him."

"That was not the true Leonard Gish speaking. He will be sorry for those harsh words later on, when he has had time to reflect. Any further instructions? Remember that my motto is Service."

"Yes, there was something about some pictures at some house down in Kent. You'll find the address on his desk. He wants you to go and look at them this afternoon."

"No," said Bill. Here he felt he had to be firm. "I'll do anything in reason, but I won't go anywhere this afternoon. Make it tomorrow."

"Suit yourself. It's no skin off *my* nose."

"What deplorably vulgar expressions you use, Elphinstone. I sometimes feel all the trouble I have taken to educate you has been thrown away. Very disheartening. And stop *flickering,* woman. I've had to speak to you about this before. Anything else?"

"Yes, he said ... wait a minute, he wrote it down.... He said if Mrs. Weston-Smythe comes in, you're to show her first The Follower of El Greco, then the Diaz Flower Piece, then the Pupil of the Master of the Holy Kinship of Cologne, and then the Bernardo Daddi."

"My heart belongs to Daddi."

"And be sure to get them in the right order. Does that mean anything to you?"

"Clear as mud. It is what is known as easing the sucker into it. It's like when you tell a story that's leading up to a smashing finish and make the early stages of it as dull as possible so as to heighten the effect of the final snapperoo. The one we want to sell her is the Daddi, so we pave the way with The Follower and the Flower Piece and the Pupil, each lousier than the last. These you might describe as the come-ons. They are designed to lower the spirits of Mrs. Weston-Smythe and make her feel that this is what she gets for belonging to the human race. Then, while she is still wallowing in the depths, wondering what she can do to shake off this awful depression, we flash the Daddi at her. Naturally, after all that build-up, it looks to her like the picture of her dreams, and she buys it. Psychological stuff."

Miss Elphinstone regarded him with a novel respect.

"I call that clever. I had no idea you really knew anything about this business. I thought you were—"

"Just one of the sheep dogs? Far, far from it. My diffident manner misleads people. Anything else?"

"Oh, yes. There was someone on the phone for you just now. Spine, he said his name was."

"Not Spine. Twine. A club acquaintance, and between ourselves something of a pill. What did he want?"

"How should I know?"

"Well, I'm glad I didn't have to talk to him, for I am in no condition for telephone conversations as of even date. It's curious, the way I'm feeling this morning. Spiritually, I am right up there with the Cherubim and Seraphim and likely at any moment to start singing hosanna, but physically you see me not at my superb best. My head aches and a drowsy numbness pains my sense, as though of hemlock I had drunk or emptied some dull opiate to the drains one minute past and Lethe-wards had sunk. Keats had the same experience. You are a young girl starting out in life, Elphinstone, so I'll give you a word of advice which will be useful to you. Stay away from bohemian revels in artists' studios. And if you feel you must go in for bohemian revels, insist on being served barley water. Only so in the cold gray light of the morning after will you escape having a head that feels as if it had been blown up with a bicycle pump to approximately three times its proper size."

It was some minutes later, as Bill was resting the head of which he had spoken against the telephone in the hope of cooling it, that the instrument suddenly jerked him out of his repose by ringing. Wearily lifting the receiver, he found his ear assaulted by a high-pitched voice.

"Hullo," it said. "Hullo. Are you there?"

"No," said Bill, "I'm not. Go away."

"Is that you, Hollister? This is Twine. Listen, Hollister, didn't you tell me once that you knew Mortimer Bayliss?"

"When I was a boy. He used to come and play chess with my father, and curse me for peering over his shoulder. Why?"

"I'm giving him dinner tonight."

"Then you'd better make it a good one. Because he's extremely apt, if anything goes wrong with the catering, to stab you with a fish fork. A testy character, this Bayliss, a human snapping turtle. How did you get mixed up with him?"

"It's rather extraordinary. Do you know a man called Bunyan at the club?"

"Roscoe Bunyan? Land sakes, honeychile, I've known him since we were both so high. We were boys together. How does he come into it?"

"Apparently he's seen some of my things and liked them, and he's told Bayliss to look at them and give his opinion. So I asked him to dine tonight, and I was wondering if you would come along."

"You want me to give you moral support?"

"Yes, I do. You know him, and you've got the gift of the gab."

"I would prefer to be called an entertaining conversationalist."

"You can talk to him at dinner. Then after dinner you just clear out and leave me to show him my things."

"I see."

"You will come, won't you?"

There was a pleading note in Stanhope Twine's voice which it was not easy for one of Bill's amiability to resist. He was not particulary fond of Stanhope Twine, whom actually he knew only very slightly through meeting him occasionally at the club to which they both belonged, but he could appreciate that this was a big opportunity for him and it would, he felt, be churlish to withhold his aid in helping things along. There had always been something of the Boy Scout about Bill Hollister.

He was, moreover, looking forward to meeting Mortimer Bayliss again. He had described him to Stanhope Twine as a human snapping turtle, and a human snapping turtle, unless the years had mellowed him, turning him into a kindly old gentleman with a fondness for the society of his juniors, he no doubt still was. But Bill knew him to be one of those snapping turtles which beneath rough exteriors conceal hearts of gold. He had learned from his late father that when the crash of 1929 had wiped out the Hollister fortune, it was Mortimer Bayliss who had come to the rescue, full of strange oaths but bearing a checkbook and fountain pen and offering to write a check for any amount his old friend might require to see him through the bad times. You might have to dig for the rich ore in Mortimer Bayliss, but it was there.

"All right," he said. "I was rather thinking of staying at home and quietly passing beyond the veil, but I'll be with you."

"Good. Peacehaven, Mulberry Grove, Valley Fields, is the address. You know how to get to Valley Fields?"

"My native guide 'Mbongo will find the way. Most capable fellow."

"Somewhere around seven."

"Right."

Bill replaced the receiver and looked at his watch. Yes, as he had supposed, time for lunch. He found his hat, gave Miss Elphinstone a friendly pat on the back hair, and started out to see if he could toy with a little something.

6

PREPARATIONS FOR Stanhope Twine's dinner party began immediately after Mortimer Bayliss had concluded his telephone call, and Mulberry Grove was astir. Stanhope Twine told the news to Jane over the fence, and Jane lost no time in seeking out her Uncle George, to inform him that he would have to take the evening meal elsewhere tonight. She found him in his study having difficulties with "Tree gets mixed up with comic hat in scene of his triumphs," and for a while listened sympathetically while he spoke his mind on the subject of the smart alecks who compose crossword puzzles these days. Lord Uffenham had been brought up in the sound old tradition of the Sun god Ra and the large Australian bird Emu, and he resented all this newfangled stuff about subordinate professionals and comic hats. It made him sick, he said, and Jane said she didn't wonder.

"And now touching on dinner tonight. Would you like caviar to start with, followed by clear soup, roast chicken with bread sauce and two veg, poires Hélène and a jam omelette?"

"Capital."

"Well, you won't get them," said Jane brutally. "Tonight's the night of Stanhope's big dinner party, and I shall be over at Peacehaven, cooking for it. We're doing things in style, to impress Mr. Bayliss."

"Hey?"

"Mortimer Bayliss. Very celebrated old gentleman, I gather, and no fault of his that I've never heard of him in my life. Apparently he's something very big and important in the art world, and he's coming to look at Stanhope's busts and things. I do hope he'll like Stanhope."

"Did yer say like *Stanhope* ?"

"I did."

"I see. Puzzled me for a moment. However," said Lord Uffenham, skill-fully evading the danger point, "that is neither here nor there. The point to keep the eye on is that there won't be any dinner for me. All right, I'll get a chop at the local. I'll take Keggs along."

"You won't. Mr. Keggs has promsied to come out of his retirement and buttle. I told you we were doing things in style. We plan to knock this Bayliss' eye out."

And so it came about that the first thing on which Bill Hollister's eye rested, when the front door of Peacehaven opened at seven o'clock that night, was Augustus Keggs, looking like something out of an Edwardian drawing-room comedy. The spectacle rocked him back on his heels. The last thing he had expected to encounter in this remote suburb was a vintage butler of obviously a very good year.

"Mr. Twine?" he said, recovering.

"Mr. Twine has had to step out to purchase cigarettes, sir. He will be returning shortly. If you would take a seat."

Bill took a seat, but it was not long before the beauty of the evening drew him out into the garden. Like those of The Nook to the left and Castlewood to the right, it was on the small side, and its features of interest were soon exhausted. Having admired the summerhouse and the bird bath and winced away from the statue, he glanced over the right-hand fence in the hope of finding something more intriguing there, and was rewarded with the specta-cle of a large, pear-shaped man of elderly aspect, who was digging in a flower bed with a spade.

Digging is strenuous work, and if you are past your first youth, you cannot do it for long without getting a crick in the back. Presently Lord Uffenham straightened himself, and seeing Bill came lumbering toward him. He always welcomed the opportunity to exchange ideas with his fellow men.

"Nice evening," he said.

"Very," said Bill.

"Ever do crossword puzzles?"

"Sometimes."

"Don't happen to know what the answer to 'Tree gets mixed up with comic hat in scene of his triumphs' would be, do yer?"

"I'm afraid not."

"Thought yer probably wouldn't. Well, what the hell? These bally cross-word puzzles are just a waste of time. Forget the whole thing, I say."

"The right spirit."

"Life's too short."

"Much too short," agreed Bill.

Lord Uffenham removed a segment of soil from his jutting chin, and prepared to change the subject. Over his tea and buttered toast that afternoon he had read an item in the evening paper that had made a deep impression on him. He was always reading things in the papers that brought him up with a round turn.

"Hey!" he said.

"Yes?" said Bill.

"Tell yer something that'll surprise yer," said Lord Uffenham. "Know how many people are born every year?"

"Down here, do you mean?"

"No, all over the bally place. England, America, China, Japan, Africa, everywhere. Thirty-six million."

"You don't say?"

"Fact. Every year there are thirty-six million more people in the world. Makes yer think a bit, that."

"It does indeed."

"Thirty-six million. And half of them probably sculptors. As if there weren't enough ruddy sculptors in the world already."

"You don't like sculptors?"

"Scum of the earth."

"Yet sculptors are also God's creatures."

"In a sense, yerss. But they've no right to leave things like that lying about the place."

Bill glanced at the colossal nude.

"It does take up space which might be utilized for other purposes," he assented. "But no doubt Twine admires it."

"He a friend of yours?"

"We belong to the same club."

"Must be an easy club to get into . What d'yer make the time?"

"Seven-twenty."

"Late as that? I must be getting off to that chop."

"What chop would that be?"

"I'm having dinner at the pub."

"May good digestion wait on appetite."

"Hey? Oh, yerss. Yerss, I see what yer mean. Very well put. Good evening to yer, sir," said Lord Uffenham, and lumbered off. And Bill, greatly uplifted, as anyone would have been, by these intellectual exchanges with what was evidently one of Valley Fields's best minds, was making his way to the house, when Mortimer Bayliss came out of it.

"Oh, hello, Mr. Bayliss," said Bill. "You probably won't remember me. Bill Hollister."

He was thinking, as he spoke, how incredibly ancient the other looked. But though he gave the impression that he would never see a hundred and four again, it was plain that there still lingered in the curator of the Bunyan collection the fire which in the old days had caused him so seldom to be invited twice to the same house.

"Bill Hollister? Yes, I remember you. A loathsome little blot you were, too. You used to breathe down the back of my neck when I came to play chess with your father. An ugly gingerheaded brute of a boy with a revolting grin and, as far as I was able to ascertain, no redeeming qualities of any sort. Did you know that when you were born, it was only by maintaining an iron front that I avoided becoming your godfather? Phew! That was a narrow escape."

A feeling of warm affection for Mortimer Bayliss had come over Bill.

"You missed a good thing," he said. "You might have been the envied of all. People are always coming up to me in the street and saying, 'I wish you were my godson.' I've improved enormously since those early days."

"Nonsense. I should say you were probably, if anything, more loathsome than ever. Extraordinary that you should have got any girl to look at you. Yet somebody told me you were engaged to be married."

"Who?"

"Never you mind. I have my sources of information. Are you?"

"No longer."

"Had the sense to get out of it, did you? Good. And I hear you work for old Gish."

"Yes. If you ask him, he'll probably say I don't, but I do."

"You didn't keep on with your painting, then?"

"I couldn't make a go of it."

"Too good for the rabble?"

"That's what I've always thought."

"And it suddenly struck you, I suppose, that you had to eat?"

"Exactly. And thanks to Gish this can be arranged. On a modest scale, of course, nothing elaborate. But how did you know I had ever tried to be a painter?"

"The last time I saw your father, a year or two before he died, he told me you were going to study in Paris," said Mortimer Bayliss, omitting to mention that it was he who had given the late Mr. Hollister the money to pay for Bill's studies. "I had dreams of being a painter myself, at one time, but I woke up. Much simpler, I found, to tell other people how to paint." He cocked his monocle at a willowy form that had emerged from the house and was hurrying down the garden path toward them. "What bloody man is this?" he asked, becoming Shakespearean.

"That is our host, Stanhope Twine."

"Looks a bit of a poop."

"And is. Hello, Stanhope."

Stanhope Twine was all high voice and agitation.

"Hullo, Hollister. I'm terribly, terribly sorry I wasn't here when you arrived, Mr. Bayliss. I went out to get some cigarettes for you."

"Never smoke the filthy things," said Mortimer Bayliss cordially. "And if you're going to offer me a cocktail, don't. I never touch them."

"Do you drink sherry?"

"I don't drink anything. Gave it up years ago."

"You do eat, don't you?" asked Bill with some concern. "We want this thing to be a success."

Mortimer Bayliss eyed him coldly.

"Are you being funny?"

"Trying to be."

"Try harder," Mortimer Bayliss advised.

"Dinner is served, sir," said Keggs, materializing out of thin air at their side, as is the way with the best butlers. You think they aren't there, and then you suddenly find they are.

7

OBEDIENT TO his host's instructions, Bill detached himself from the party reasonably soon after Keggs had served the coffee, and at nine-thirty was out in the garden again, reclining in a deck chair and gazing up at the stars.

It had been an unexpectedly enjoyable evening, for Mortimer Bayliss had tapped a vein of geniality of which his best friends—if any—would not have believed him capable. Softened by a superb dinner superbly served by a butler who had—no easy feat—in his day satisfied J. J. Bunyan, he conveyed the impression that a child could have played with him and, furthermore, that had such a child been present, he would have patted its head and given it sixpence. His table talk, with its flow of anecdote about shady millionaires and shadier Rumanian art dealers, had been gay and sparkling, and Bill would gladly have had more of it. But he could understand Stanhope Twine, the ice broken, wanting to have this mellowed and influential man to himself, so had withdrawn as per gentlemen's agreement.

The garden, which had been so pleasant at seven-twenty, was even pleasanter at half past nine, for it was wrapped now in the velvet stillness of the summer night. Though stillness is, of course, a relative term. Bill, relaxed in his chair, was in a position to hear a pianist, who appeared to be of tender years and to have learned his art through the medium of a correspondence course, playing what sounded like "Tinkling Tunes for the Tots" at The Nook next door and, further afield, the blare of the television set at Balmoral in the adjoining road, while at another house in the same neighborhood—Chatsworth—somebody whose voice would have been the better for treatment with sandpaper was rendering extracts from the works of Gilbert and Sullivan.

Nevertheless, though he wished the Balmoral bunch would turn down that TV set a bit and the virtuoso at The Nook give up the unequal struggle and go to bed, he found Valley Fields by night very soothing, and quickly surrendered to its gentle magic. Like Major Flood-Smith, he had difficulty in believing that only a few miles separated him from the roar and bustle of the metropolis, and it is possible that he would shortly have fallen into a restful sleep, had not his attention at this moment been drawn to a singular—it would not be too much to say sinister—spectacle. On the lawn, only a few yards from where he sat, a light was flickering to and fro. Some creature of the night had invaded the privacy of Peacehaven with an electric torch.

When you are a man's guest, even if that man is one for whom you feel no great affection, you cannot ignore the presence in his garden of prowlers. His bread and salt have placed you under an obligation. Bill, obeying this unwritten law, rose noiselessly and advanced with stealth on the intruder, modeling his technique on that of those Fenimore Cooper Indians who were accustomed to move from spot to spot without letting a twig snap beneath their feet. Arriving behind a dark figure and feeling that he could not do better than borrow from the vocabulary of Miss Elphinstone, he said, "Ho!" and Lord Uffenham, for it was he, spun round with a loud snort.

It is always difficult to pin down to an exact point in time the birth of an inspiration, for one never knows how long it may not have been lurking unnoticed in the subconscious. Quite possibly the idea of climbing the fence into Stanhope Twine's garden, armed with a pot of black paint, and painting on the chin of his colossal nude a small imperial beard of the type worn by ambassadors had been burgeoning within Lord Uffenham for weeks. But it was only as he walked back from the Green Lion in Rosendale Road after his frugal dinner that the thought stole into the upper reaches of his mind that a small imperial beard was just what the colossal nude needed and that he would never have a better opportunity of applying it than now. His niece Jane was in the Peacehaven kitchen. Augustus Keggs was busy buttling. And Stanhope Twine and his guests were safely indoors. Conditions, in a word, could scarcely have been improved upon.

So reasoned Lord Uffenham, and it was consequently a most unpleasant shock to him when that "Ho!" came at him out of the darkness, indicating that others besides himself were abroad in the night. To the fact that he would tomorrow be closely grilled by his niece he had steeled himself. A man with a mission can face these unpleasantnesses. But he had not bargained for fellow travelers. Their presence disturbed him, especially when they said "Ho!" like that. And now, adding to his discomfort, a clutching hand grasped his nose, twisting it in the manner of a hand that intended to stand no nonsense. The pain was considerable, and his agonized "Hey" nearly drowned the television set at Balmoral.

Anyone who had once heard Lord Uffenham say "Hey!" was able ever afterward to recognize his distinctive note, and Bill, it will be recalled, had enjoyed that experience. This, he realized, could be no other than his predinner acquaintance who had spoken so searchingly of sculptors.

"Oh, it's you," he said, releasing the nose, and there was a moment of silence. Then the wounded man spoke in a voice vibrant with feeling.

"If yer know me a thousand years," he said, "never do that again. I thought it was coming off at the roots."

"I'm sorry."

"No good being sorry now."

"I took you for a midnight marauder."

"How d'yer mean, midnight? It's only ten."

"Well, a ten-oclock marauder. It seemed odd that you should be prowling about Twine's garden with a flashlight."

Lord Uffenham had recovered his poise. He was his old self again now, the fine sturdy old gentleman who had so often looked his niece Jane in the eye, stoutly denying all charges and generally managing to get away with it.

"Lord love a duck," he said. "Aren't you familiar with life in the suburbs?"

"Not very. I'm more the metropolitan type."

"Well, we're like one great big family down here. I stroll in your garden, you stroll in mine. You borrow my roller, I borrow yours."

"Wholesome give and take."

"Exactly. Tomorrow in all probability I shall look out of window and see Stanhope Twine on my lawn. 'Ah, Twine,' I shall say, and he will reply, 'Good morning, good morning.' All very pleasant and neighborly. Still, it might be as well if yer didn't mention to him that yer found me here. He's a little nervous just now about people coming into his garden, because he's afraid they may leave finger marks on that statue of his. There are some children at The Nook next door, who occasionally pot at it with catapults, and this makes him sensitive. So just forget yer saw me."

"I will."

"Thank yer, my boy. I knew you'd understand. You're the feller I was talking to before dinner, aren't yer?"

"That's right. How was the chop?"

"What chop?"

"Your chop."

"Oh, that chop? There wasn't any chop. Had to have liver and bacon."

"Tough."

"Yerss, it was, rather. But I can rough it. You been dining with Twine?"

"Yes."

"How did yer get away?" asked Lord Uffenham, rather in the manner of a Parisian of pre-Revolutionary days addressing a friend who, when last heard of, had been in the Bastille.

"I was driven out into the snow. Twine wanted to be alone with his other guest, a man who is interested in his work."

"Interested in *Twine's* work? He must be potty. Well," said Lord Uffenham, suddenly realizing that time was flying and that his niece Jane would be heading for home ere long, "can't stop here talking to you all night, much as I've enjoyed seeing yer again. If yer'll give me a hand over the fence, I think I'll be getting back."

When Jane returned, he wanted her to find him in his study with a good book, curled up in an armchair and not having stirred from it for hours.

8

THE COMING of a new day found George, sixth Viscount Uffenham, who on the previous night had sown the wind, reaping the whirlwind. One glance at his niece Jane as she entered the study where he sat trying to ascertain what the composer of his crossword puzzle meant by the words "Spasmodic as a busy tailor," had been enough to tell his practiced eye that she was ratty, hot under the collar and madder than a wet hen.

"Uncle George," she said, and musical though her voice was, Lord Uffenham did not like it. "Was it you who painted that mustache on Stanhope's statue?"

It was most fortunate that she should have worded her inquiry thus, for it enabled Lord Uffenham to deny the accusation with a clear conscience. What he had painted on Stanhope Twine's statue, it will be recalled, was a small imperial beard.

"Certainly not," he said with a dignity that became him well. "Wouldn't dream of doing such a thing."

"It must have been you."

"Ridiculous."

"Who else could it have been?"

"Hey?"

"It's no use pretending to go into one of your trances. You heard what I said."

"Yerss, I heard what you said, and it shocked me. Let's get this thing straight. Someone, you say, has been painting a mustache on that Ladies' Night in a Turkish Bath eyesore of Twine's. Well and good. Just what it needed. But if you think it was me—"

"I do."

"Then ask yerself one question."

"What question?"

"I'll tell yer what question. Ask yerself if it's likely that a busy man like me, a man with a hundred calls on his time, would go about the place painting mustaches on statues. Lord love a duck, you'll be saying next . . . I don't know what you'll be saying next," said Lord Uffenham, frankly giving the thing up. "Changing the subject, it says here in my crossword puzzle 'Spasmodic as a busy tailor,' and if yer can tell me what the hell that means—"

"I don't propose to change the subject."

"Oh, all right, let's go on threshing it out, though I doubt if we'll get anywhere. Waste of time, if yer ask me. How's Twine? Is he ratty?"

"He's furious," said Jane, and was conscious of a slight discomfort as she remembered how shrill her betrothed had become in his hour of travail. Stanhope Twine was one of those men who are not at their best when upset.

"Well, it's no good his trying to fasten it on me. The charge won't stick. It was probably one of those kids at The Nook," said Lord Uffenham, like Doctor Watson saying, 'Holmes, a child has done this horrid thing!' There are three of them, each capable of painting a hundred mustaches on a

476

hundred statues. Twine should watch them closely and be on the alert for clues. Not that he'll get any. Impossible of proof, the whole thing. How's he going to bring it home to anyone? Answer me that."

It was precisely this that was giving Jane that feeling of bafflement and frustration. She was in the position of the Big Four at Scotland Yard when they know perfectly well that it was Professor Moriarty who put the arsenic in the Ruritanian ambassador's soup but have no means of proving it to the satisfaction of a jury. On such occasions the Big Four knit their brows and bite their lower lips, and Jane knit and bit hers. A momentary urge to bang her uncle on the head with the coffeepot came and passed. It is at such times as these that breeding tells.

But she had other weapons in her armory.

"Did I tell you the kitchen range had gone wrong again?" she asked casually.

"No, has it?"

"You'll have to lunch on sardines."

Lord Uffenham snorted militantly. The consciousness of having won a moral victory made him strong.

"Like blazes I'll lunch on any bally sardines. Yer know what I'm going to do with you? I'm going to take yer up to London and fill yer to the brim with rich food at Barribault's. We'll go on a regular bender. And after lunch you can saunter down Bond Street, rubbing your nose on the jewelers' windows."

He could have said nothing more calculated to soothe a fermenting niece. Jane did not often nowadays get a treat like lunch at Barribault's Hotel, that haunt of Texas millionaires and visiting maharajahs. And if there was one thing she enjoyed, it was window-shopping. Ceasing to be the governess grilling a juvenile suspect, she kissed Lord Uffenham on the top of his bald head.

"That'll be wonderful. I'll have to get back fairly early, though, because I'm having tea with Dora Wimpole. All right, then, we'll leave it that the outrage was the work of an international gang."

"Yerss, always up to something, those international gangs. Noted for it."

Well content with this happy ending to an episode which at the outset had threatened to be a bit sticky, Lord Uffenham turned to his *Times*. But having discovered that one of the clues in his crossword puzzle was "The ointment in short has no point" and another "No see here, it's a sort of church with a chapter," both beyond the powers of even a Keggs to solve, cast the beastly thing from him and prepared for further conversation.

"What's Twine doing about it?"

"He's rubbing it with turpentine."

"That'll take it off, will it?"

"He hopes so."

"Yerss, turpentine ought to do it. That'll be one in the eye for those Nook kids. They won't know which way to look. All their trouble for nothing."

"I thought we had agreed that it was an international gang that had done it."

"Or, as you say, one in the eye for the international gang. *They* won't know which way to look. So he was furious about it, was he? I thought I heard him. It sounded like a pig being killed. I will say for Stanhope Twine that whatever his other defects—and they are numerous—they pale into insignificance beside his revolting voice. How yer can stand the feller beats me. Let alone wanting to marry him."

Usually when the subject of Stanhope Twine came up and the conversation reached this point it was Jane's practice to say her say in no restrained fashion, but today the prospect of lunch at Barribault's had softened her, and it was quite mildly that she suggested that as they had discussed all that before, there was no need to go into it again.

Lord Uffenham was not to be put off. He considered himself *in loco parentis* to this girl, and her welfare was very near his heart.

"There is every need. I want to save yer from yerself, my good wench. And I want to save myself from having a nephew foisted on me, the mere contemplation of whose bally face gives me a rising sensation of nausea. Lord love a duck, when you get hitched up, I want yer old man to be someone I can drop in on and smoke a pipe with and generally nurse in my bosom. Like young Miller, who married yer sister Anne. I was always in and out of their place, and it has been a lasting grief to me that they pushed off to America and settled there. I miss Walter."

"You mean Jeff."

"Is his name Jeff?"

"That's the story he tells."

"Jeff, yerss, of course. I'm bad at names. I remember, back in the year 1912, getting the push from a girl called Kate because I wrote her a letter beginning 'My own darling Mabel.' But I was saying . . . What was I saying?"

"That you want me to marry someone you can nurse in your bosom."

"That's right. Not much to ask of one's niece, I should have thought. But what happens? You come and lay this marble-chipping Gawd-help-us on the mat with a cheery 'Hi, everybody, look what I've found.' You ought to have more consideration for others, my girl."

"Nieces can't marry just to give uncles something to nurse in their bosom. They have to think of themselves."

"Not if they've got the right stuff in them. Did I think of myself? No! I said to myself, 'This girl isn't yer niece Jane's cup of tea, Uffenham, and you must put Jane's feelings first. Wash her out, my boy, wash her out.' "

"Uncle George."

"Yerss?"

"What on earth are you talking about?"

"I'm talking about my late fiancée."

"Your *what?*"

"Lord love a duck, you now what a fiancée is. You're one yerself, God help yer. Yerss, I don't mind telling yer, now that the thing's all blown over, that as recently as a couple of weeks ago I was engaged to be married to an usherette called Marlene at the Rivoli Cinema at Herne Hill. But I knew she wasn't the sort of girl you would cotton to, so I broke it off."

Here Lord Uffenham permitted himself a little license. It was not he but his betrothed who had broken the engagement, she having met a commercial traveler who in looks, dress and general *espièglerie* left his lordship simply nowhere. It had been a great relief to the elderly peer.

Not that he thought of himself as elderly. Except for an occasional twinge of rheumatism when the English summer was more than ordinarily severe, Lord Uffenham still felt like the gay young Guardee he had been in 1912. It was not the fact that he was a little older than he had been forty years ago that had sown doubts in his mind during the period of his betrothal, but the revelation that his affianced was a girl of expensive tastes. It is disquieting for a man who is living on a meager annuity to discover that he is expected to come through every other day with bottles of scent and boxes of chocolates. A man in such circumstances hears the voice of prudence whispering in his ear and knows that it is talking sense.

"Yerss," he said, "I broke it off. She wasn't a girl you'd have cared for, so I sacrificed myself."

Jane was still gasping.

"Well! "she said.

"Quite all right," said Lord Uffenham, looking like Sidney Carton. "Got to do the square thing. *Noblesse oblige.*"

"So that's what happens when I let you go for a run by yourself! I shall keep you on a lead in future. Fancy at your age—"

"What d'yer mean, my age?"

"—sneaking off—"

"I resent that word 'sneaking' "

"—and getting engaged to usherettes."

"Not half as bad as getting engaged to sculptors."

"What on earth made you do such a chuckleheaded thing?"

Actually what had caused Lord Uffenham to plight his troth had been that lifelong habit of his of proposing marriage to girls whenever the conversation seemed to be flagging a bit and a feller felt he had to say *something*. It had got him into trouble before—notably in the years 1912, 1913, 1920 and 1921—and he saw now that it was a mistake. But he did not mention this to Jane, for he had seen his opportunity to speak the word in season.

"I'll tell yer what made me do it. She was the first pretty girl I'd had a chance of talking to since I came to live down here, so she bowled me over. I was corn before her sickle. And exactly the same thing has happened to you. Yer wouldn't have looked twice at a feller like Twine if yer hadn't been cooped up in a London suburb with nobody else in sight."

Jane gave a little start. It is always disconcerting when someone else puts into words a thought that has been hovering at the back of one's own mind.

"Nonsense," she said, but she spoke uncertainly.

Lord Uffenham pressed his attack like a good general. That touch of uncertainty had not escaped him.

"I'll prove it to yer from my own case history. Do you remember your Great-aunt Alice? No, she died three years before you were born, so I doubt if you'd ever have met her. She lived in a godforsaken little village on the Welsh border in Shropshire, and my old guv'nor made me go and stay with her one summer. Said there might be money in it. There wasn't, as it turned out, because she left it all to the Society for the Propagation of the Gospel in Foreign Parts, but the point I'm making is that I hadn't been there a week when I got engaged to the sister-in-law of a woman called Postlethwaite, who bred Siamese cats. Purely as the result of ennui and by way of filling in the time somehow. Yours is a parallel case, and I feel it my duty, as an older man than you, to warn yer. Don't dream of marrying that monumental mason just to relieve the monotony of suburban life. If yer do, there'll be a bitter awakening," said Lord Uffenham and having delivered this valuable lecture on what a young girl ought to know picked up his *Times* and bent his fine mind to the solving of the clue "Naked without a penny has the actor become." And Jane, seeing that he was now beyond the reach of the human voice, went to her room to select a frock which would do the family credit at Barribault's,

Her air was that of a girl who has been given food for thought.

9

AT ABOUT the same moment, up in London, Bill Hollister was entering the Gish Galleries.

"Punctual to the dot, you observe, Elphinstone," he said, "if you'll excuse a slight touch of smugness. I turned in early last night and got my full eight hours. Hence the sparkling eyes, elastic walk and rosy cheeks, and hence, no doubt, the fact that you look to me once more your own bonny self and not, as was the case yesterday, like a Chinaman with a combination of jaundice and ague. Elphinstone, I've come to the conclusion that we are saps, you and I. We don't know what's good for us. Where do you live?"

"I live with an aunt in Camden Town."

"If you can call that living. And I hang out off the King's Road. Chelsea. That is why I say that we are saps. We ought both to move to Valley Fields. In that favored spot you can maintain an establishment on the general lines of that of an oriental monarch of the better type on next to nothing. I ascertained this last night by personal observation. I was dining there."

"You do get around, don't you?"

"Yes, I suppose I am something of a social pet. It's probably my affability that does it. I was dining with my club acquaintance Twine, or Spine as you prefer to call him, a man who I should have said was about as impecunious as, if you will pardon the expression, dammit, and I had scarcely crossed the threshold when platoons of butlers sprang out at me from every nook and cranny. You wouldn't be far out in saying that Twine dwells in marble halls with vassals and serfs at his side. And, what is more, he has a cook who is a veritable cordon bleu."

"Eh?"

"I thought that would be above your head, young dumbbell. I mean that she is a consummate artist. The dinner she dished up last night was of the kind that melts in the mouth and puts hair on the chest. It's a little hard. There is Twine, a mere cipher in the body politic, with a cook like that cooking her head off for him, while I, holding an important executive position in a famous art gallery, and looked up to from one end of Bond Street to the other, dine on leftovers and lunch on bread and cheese."

"You won't have to have bread and cheese today. Mr. Gish said to tell you you're to take someone to lunch."

"Who?"

"I don't know. One of the customers."

"Clients, girl, clients. Well," said Bill, not surprised, for Mr. Gish, whose digestion had ceased to function satisfactorily in 1947, always preferred to let his assistant entertain the victims for whom he was spreading his net, "that's fine. I shall enjoy that. I hope the venue will be Barribault's. I haven't been to Barribault since the day when Pop Gish, coming all over Dickensy as the result of selling a Matisse for six times its proper value, invited me there to celebrate with him. Would this, do you suppose, be a client important enough to justify a Barribault's orgy?"

"You'd better ask him. He wants to see you."

"Who wouldn't? Well, I think I can give him five minutes. But you realize what this means, Elphinstone? It means that you will have to do without me for a while. Come, come, woman, stop crying like that. When the fields are white with daisies, I'll return."

In the main gallery Mr. Gish, small, dark and irascible, in appearance and temperament rather like a salamander, was standing before the statuette of a nude lady who appeared to be practicing some sort of dance step. He was flicking at it with a feather duster, and Bill raised his hat, always the chivalrous gentleman.

"Is this man annoying you, madam?" he asked courteously.

The sound of that familiar voice seemed to affect the proprietor of the Gish Galleries like an unexpected alligator bite in the lower limbs. He spun on his axis, eyes blazing through their horn-rimmed spectacles, and, like Miss Elphinstone on a similar occasion, said "Ho!

"So you've condescended to come here, have you?"

"And right on time, chief, as you may have noticed."

"Where the devil were you yesterday?"

Bill raised a hand.

"Never mind yesterday. As the poet says, 'Every day is a fresh beginning. Every morn is the world made anew. Yesterday's errors let yesterday cover.' Today is another day, and here I am, alert, keen-eyed and on my toes, all eagerness to learn what's cooking."

As so often happened when he found himself in conference with his young assistant, two conflicting emotions were warring within Mr. Gish—one an imperious urge to fire him on the spot, the other an uneasy feeling that to do so would be to label himself an ingrate. Twenty-six years ago, in the spacious days of 1929, Bill's father, who had more money then than he knew what to do with, had given Mr. Gish some of it to start this business of his, and a conscientious man cannot lightly ignore such an obligation. Bill, too, was a good assistant, if you could stand his affability, a definite improvement on some of the wooden-headed morons whom Mr. Gish had employed in his time. If you told him to do something, he did not gape at you like a weak-minded fish, he went and did it—and did it, moreover, without messing everything up. He had a good picture-side manner, and clients liked him. There was something about his honest, open face and the cauliflower ear which had accrued to him as the result of his amateur boxing that inspired trust.

Weighing these things, Mr. Gish decided not to cleanse his bosom of the perilous stuff that was weighing on his heart, and Bill proceeded.

"I hear you want me to give one of the local lepers lunch. Who is it this time?"

"He's a big paint and enamel man. His name's McColl. I've sold him my Boudin, and I'm hoping he'll buy my Degas."

"He will if the suavity of my small talk and a hell of a good lunch can swing it. I think nothing meaner than Barribault's for a big paint and enamel man, don't you?"

"Yes, take him to Barribault's. Tell Miss Elphinstone to book a table."

"I will. And while on the subject of Elphinstone, she was saying something about your wanting me to go and look at some pictures."

"Oh, those pictures, yes. Were they any good?"

"I have yet to see them."

Mr. Gish started.

"What do you mean? Didn't you go?"

"I couldn't. I was feeling much too frail. I think I may have been over-working lately. Tell me about them."

For an instant it seemed that the man at the helm of the Gish Galleries was about to forget his obligations to Mr. Hollister, Senior, but his better self rose to the surface, and with a strong effort he succeeded in suppressing the words that rose to his lips.

"They belong to Lord Uffenham. There was a girl in here the day before yesterday—"

"They can't keep away from you, can they, poor fluttering moths."

"A Miss Benedick. Lord Uffenham's niece. She says he wants me to sell these pictures for him. They are down at his place in the country, Shipley Hall, near Tonbridge."

"No, there, with the deepest respect, me lud, you're wrong. Shipley Hall is the rural seat of my old buddy, Roscoe Bunyan. I heard him telling someone so at our mutual club the other day. You don't know Roscoe, do you? He looks like a cartoon of Capital in the *Daily Worker*. Country butter, no doubt. He probably eats it by the pound at Shipley Hall, which, as I said before, belongs to him and not to this Lord Uffenham of whom you speak."

"Lord Uffenham has let Shipley Hall to him."

"Oh, I see. That throws a different light on the matter."

"After you've given McColl lunch, go there and look at those pictures."

"Why don't you?"

"I have to go to Brighton."

"Always off on a jaunt somewhere, aren't you? It's always the way. Everybody works but Father."

Mr. Gish counted ten slowly. Once again his better self had attempted to get away from him.

"To a sale," he said coldly.

"Oh, to a sale?"

"Yes, to a sale."

"Well, it makes a good story," said Bill a little dubiously. "All right, while you are out with the boys, burning up Brighton, I will kiss McColl good-by and drive to this Shipley Hall of which I have heard so much. Where do I find you, to communicate with you?"

"I shall be at the Hotel Metropole from four o'clock on."

"I see. In the bar, of course."

"In the *lounge*. I am having tea with a client."

"Female, one presumes. What, I ask myself, is the secret of this mysterious attraction? Very well, I will give you a buzz as soon as I have formed an opinion of these pictures. And may I say how gratified I am that you should be entrusting me with this important commission. Bless my soul, you must have great confidence in me."

"I haven't any confidence in you. And I don't want you to form an opinion, as you call it. All you have to do is to ask Mortimer Bayliss what he thinks of them."

"Mortimer Bayliss? Is he at Shipley Hall? I ran into him last night."

"Well, you'll run into him again this afternoon. Ask him what he feels about them. There isn't a better judge of pictures in the world."

"And what a beautiful world it is, is it not? Let me tell you how it strikes me. I look about me, and I say to myself—"

But Mr. Gish, never able to stay in one place for long, particularly if it involved conversing with his affable assistant, had vanished.

The morning's work proceeded much as on other mornings. Mrs. Weston-Smythe came in, saw—in the order named—The Follower of El Greco, the Diaz Flower Piece and the Pupil of the Master of the Holy Kinship of Cologne, and then, when her spirits were at their lowest ebb, was shown the Bernardo Daddi, which she bought. At one o'clock Bill took hat in hand, gave his cutaway coat a flick with the whisk broom, and prepared to make his way to Barribault's, greatly stimulated by the thought of the slap-up lunch that admirable eating house was going to give him at the firm's expense.

In the outer office Miss Elphinstone was at the telephone.

"Oh, just a minute," she said as she saw Bill. She put a hand over the mouthpiece. "It's a girl."

"And I had always wanted a boy. Too bad."

"Do you know anything about some pictures?"

"I know everything about all pictures."

"It's a Miss Benedick about some pictures she says she saw Mr. Gish about them the day before yesterday belonging to her uncle, Lord Buffenham."

"Ye gods, child, your syntax! What you mean, I presume, is that a Miss Benedick is calling with reference to certain paintings at present the property of her uncle, Lord Uffenham—not Buffenham—concerning which she has been in conference with my employer with a view to his selling them. Yes, I've been briefed about those. Out of the way, Elphinstone, let me grapple with this. Hello? Miss Benedick?"

"Oh, good morning. I'm speaking for my uncle, Lord Uffenham," said a voice, and Bill nearly dropped the receiver.

For the voice was a voice in a million, a voice that cast a spell and wooed the ear to listen, a voice that stole into a man's heart and stirred him up as with a ten-foot pole. He had never in his life heard anything that made so instant an appeal to him, and strange thrills ran up his spine and out at the roots of his hair.

With difficulty he contrived to speak.

"Was . . . was it about those picures of Lord Uffenham's?"

"Yes."

"Down at Shipley Hall?"

"Yes."

"You called here about them the other day."

"Yes."

Bill wished that she would not confine herself to monosyllables. He wanted long, lovely sentences.

"I'm going to Shipley Hall this afternoon to look at them."

"Oh, good. Who are you?"

"Mr. Gish's assistant. Ah, shut up, woman."

"I beg your pardon?"

"I'm sorry. I was addressing the fatheaded lady receptionist at my elbow. She said she betted I couldn't say 'Mr. Gish's assistant' ten times quick."

"And can you?"

"I'm not sure."

"Well, do try. And thank you ever so much. I'll tell my uncle."

Bill replaced the receiver dazedly. He was feeling as if he had passed through some great emotional experience, as indeed he had. It amazed him that Miss Elphinstone, who also had had the privilege of hearing that lovely voice, should be sitting there calm and unmoved, and not only calm and unmoved but chewing gum.

Bill Hollister was unusually sensitive to beauty in the human voice. One of the reasons why he preferred not to see too much of Stanhope Twine was that the latter, when he felt strongly on any subject, was inclined to squeal and gibber like the sheeted dead in the Roman streets a little ere the mightiest Julius fell. And he could, he sometimes thought, have borne with more equanimity Miss Murphrey's comparison of him to a sheep dog operating a funeral parlor as a side line, had her vocal delivery less closely resembled that of a peahen.

The voice to which he had been listening and which was still echoing down the corridors of his soul, had been a magic voice, a round, soft, liquid voice, a voice to appease a traffic policeman or soothe an inland revenue official. He felt as if he had been in telephonic communication with an angel, one probably the mainstay of the celestial choir, and there rose before his mental eye a picture. The scene was a church, and he, in a cutaway coat and striped trousers, was walking down the aisle with this silver-voiced girl on his arm while the organ played "Oh, Perfect Love" and the spectators in the ringside pews whispered "What a charming couple!" A bishop and assistant clergy had done their stuff, the returns were all in, and she was his . . . his . . . his . . . for better and for worse, in sickness and in health, till death did them . . .

At this point it occurred to him that he had not the pleasure of her acquaintance, or any reasonable hope of making it. There was, he reflected, always something. Moodily he passed out into Bond Street and, directing his steps eastward, was presently seated with Mr. McColl at a table in Barribault's glittering dining room.

The lunch was not one of those festive lunches, though Barribault's, as always, spared no effort to make it go. Bill had no means of knowing what was the norm or average of sprightliness among big paint and enamel men, but an hour spent in his society inclined him to think that Mr. McColl was below rather than above it. He was a strong silent paint and enamel man, who tucked into his food with a fine appetite, but contributed little or nothing to the feast of reason and the flow of soul beyond an occasional grunt, seeming to be brooding on the last lot of enamel or yesterday's consignment of paint. Bill in consequence had had to work a good deal harder than he could have wished, especially at a moment when his spirits were low and his mind preoccupied. It was a relief to him when his guest rose to go and he was able to escort him to the swing doors and leave him there in the care of the Ruritanian Field Marshal who gets taxis for Barribault's clientele.

As he turned back into the lobby, his spirits were still low, nor, despite the fact that he had seen the last of Mr. McColl, is this to be wondered at. It is generally supposed that the depths of human frustration are plumbed by the man who is all dressed up and no place to go, and few, contemplating such a man, are so callous as not to heave a sigh and drop the tear of pity. But though that dressy unfortunate is unquestionably in a nasty spot and entitled to beat his breast like the wedding guest when he heard the loud bassoon, his sufferings are a good deal less acute than those of one who, all eagerness to pour out the treasures of a rich nature on the girl he loves, is debarred from doing so by the circumstance that he does not know where she lives or what she looks like.

A consuming desire to smoke came upon Bill. He reached for his cigarette case and found it was not there. He must, he supposed, have left it on the table, and he hurried back to the restaurant to retrieve it before some maharajah who liked nice things saw and pocketed it.

To get to the table which he had been occupying he had to pass one where there was sitting a small, fairhaired girl, at whom he cast a fleeting glance. And he was moving on, having classified her mentally as "rather pretty," when she spoke, addressing a passing bus boy.

"Will you ask the headwaiter to come here, please," she said, and Bill, having started convulsively as if the management of Barribault's had thrust a skewer into the fleshy part of his leg, not that they would, became as rigid as ever Lord Uffenham had become when falling into one of his trances. He had the momentary illusion that the management of Barribault's, however foreign to their normal policy such an action would have been, had hit him over the head with a sock full of wet sand.

10

IN THE actual line "Will you ask the headwaiter to come here, please" there is nothing, one would say, calculated to stun the senses and cause the hearer to stiffen in every limb. It is the sort of throw-away line a dramatist would give to one of his minor characters at the beginning of the Act Three supper scene to cover the noise of the customers stumbling back into the auditorium after the intermission and tripping over other people's feet. It misses the Aristotelian ideal of pity and terror by a wide margin.

What had congealed Bill where he stood had not been the words themselves but the voice that had spoken them. He refused to believe that in a smallish city like London there could co-exist two such magic voices. With eyes protruding to their fullest extent he stared at this fairhaired, rather pretty girl, and noted that her charms had become enhanced by a flush which, in his opinion, was most attractive. Many girls, even in these sophisticated days, find themselves flushing when human snails halt beside the table where they are lunching and stand goggling at them with their eyes sticking six inches out of the parent sockets. Giving this snail-impersonator a look such as a particularly fastidious princess might have given the caterpillar which she had discovered in her salad, Jane averted her gaze, and was continuing to avert it, when the uncouth intruder spoke.

"Miss Benedick?" he said, in a low, hoarse voice which would have interested a throat specialist, and Jane turned like a startled kitten, her flush now the blush of shame and embarrassment. For the first time in the last quarter of an hour she was thankful that her Uncle George was not with her, for he was a stern critic of this sort of thing. "Hell's bells," her Uncle George had often said to her, waggling his eyebrows to lend emphasis to his words, "yer've *got* to remember *peo*ple, my girl, or yer'll be about as popular as a ruddy ant at a picnic. Nothing makes fellers rattier than having wenches not know them from Adam next time they meet."

And now that she looked at this young man, seeing him steadily and seeing him whole, there did come to her a faint glimmering of a recollection of having met him before somewhere . . . at some long-ago Hunt Ball, perhaps, or some distant garden party, or possibly in some previous existence. That hair of his, ginger in color and looking as if he had brushed it a week ago last Wednesday, seemed somehow to strike a chord, as did his eyes, which, she now saw, were very pleasant eyes. She was goading her memory to dredge from its depths a name, and memory, as always on these occasions, was shrugging its shoulders and giving the thing up as a bad job, when he spoke again.

"We were talking on the telephone this morning. About Lord Uffenham's pictures. I'm at the Gish Galleries."

A wave of relief swept over Jane. No girl can be expected to remember people, if they have simply been anonymous voices on the telephone. She had not failed that male Emily Post, her Uncle George, after all, and this healing thought lent such animation to her manner that Bill's interior organs were for the second time stirred up by that invisible ten-foot pole. He was wondering how he could ever have labeled this girl in his mind as "rather pretty." It was as though some traveler, seeing the Taj Mahal by moonlight for the first time, had described it in a letter home as a fairly decent-looking sort of tomb.

"Of course! You're Mr. Gish's assistant. Do sit down," said Jane.

Bill sat down, glad to do so, for he was feeling a little dizzy. Her last words had been accompanied by a smile, and the effect of it had been devastating. His only coherent thought, as he took his seat, was that a lifetime devoted to waiting and watching for that smile would be a lifetime well spent.

Jane was puzzled.

"But how," she asked, "did you know who I was?"

"I recognized your voice."

"Recognized my voice?" Jane stared. "After half a dozen words on the telephone?"

"One would have been ample," said Bill. He had now got over his initial nervousness and was feeling his affable self once more. "It is a lovely, unique voice, in a class of its own and once heard never forgotten, limpid as a woodland brook and vibrant with all the music of the spheres. When you asked that child in the apron with the gravy spots on it to send the headwaiter along, one could fancy one was listening to silver bells tinkling across the foam of perilous seas in faery lands forlorn."

"Seas *where*?"

"In faery lands forlorn. Not my own. Keats."

"Oh? Well, that's good, isn't it?"

"Couldn't be better," agreed Bill cordially.

Jane had become conscious of a certain uneasiness. Usually an adept at keeping ardent youth at a safe distance, she had begun to wonder if her technique would be sound enough to serve her here. Many young men in their time had said nice things to her, but none with the ecstatic fervor which had animated the remarks of this one. He gave the impression of speaking straight from the heart, and a large, throbbing heart at that. A well-read young man, too. Keats and everything. She remembered another of her Uncle George's obiter dicta. "When they start talking poetry at yer," that deep thinker had once warned her, "watch yer step like billy-o, my girl."

And what was making her uneasy was that she was not at all sure that she wanted to watch her step. She was feeling strangely drawn to this man who had come crashing into her life and who had now for some moments been gazing at her with the uninhibited enthusiasm of a small boy confronted with a saucer of ice cream. She liked his hair, though not blind to the fact that it could have done with a couple of licks from a pair of military brushes. She liked his eyes, which were as friendly and honest as any eyes she had ever looked into. She liked everything about him . . . and far more warmly, her conscience told her, than a girl who was engaged to Stanhope Twine ought to be doing. A girl engaged to Stanhope Twine should, it pointed out, experience this odd sensation of breathlessness only when it was Stanhope Twine who had induced it. That a gingerheaded young man, whom she had never seen till five minutes ago, should be causing her to feel as if she were floating on a pink cloud and listening to the music of a particularly good orchestra was, her conscience suggested in that unpleasant way which consciences have, all wrong.

With a feeling that there was much in what it said and that the emotional content of the conversation should without delay be reduced, she turned it to a safer subject.

"So you're really going to Shipley this afternoon to see those pictures of

Uncle George's?" she said. "I must say I envy you. It's a lovely place, especially at this time of year. I miss it terribly."

"You've not been there lately?"

"Not for ages."

"You were there as a child?"

"All the time."

Bill's eyes closed in a sort of ecstasy.

"How wonderful it will be, seeing all the little spots and nooks where you wandered as a child," he said devoutly. "I shall feel I am on holy ground."

Jane perceived that in supposing that she had found a safer subject she had erred. She tried another.

"That headwaiter seems a long time coming," she said.

Bill, who had intended to speak further and at some length, blinked as if he had been sauntering down the street and had walked into a lamp post. It pained him that she should wish to talk of headwaiters, for it lowered the conversation to a prosaic plane which he deprecated, but if such was her desire, he must indulge it.

"Oh, yes, you want to see him, don't you?"

"Actually I don't in the least, but I'm afraid I've got to."

"What's the trouble?"

"I can't pay the bill."

"Lost your purse?"

"No, I've got my purse, but there's nothing in it. Would you care to hear my story?"

"I'm all agog."

"My uncle invited me to lunch . . ."

"According to Nancy Mitford, you should say 'luncheon,' but go on."

"The arrangement was that he would look in at his club and meet me here at one, and we would then luncheon together at his expense. When he hadn't turned up by half past, I couldn't hold out any longer. So I came in and luncheoned by myself."

"Paying no attention to the prices in the right-hand column?"

"Ignoring them completely. I thought it would be all right and that he was bound to arrive, but he hasn't. I know just what has happened. He has got talking with the boys, as he calls them, and forgotten all about me."

"Absent-minded?"

"Not exactly absent-minded, but he gets absorbed in things. He's probably deep in a discussion of the apostolic claims of the church of Abyssinia or something. Or else he's telling them why greyhounds are called greyhounds. He found that out in the evening paper yesterday, and it thrilled him."

"Why are they?"

"Because grey is the old English word for badger, and greyhounds were used in hunting the badger."

"I thought they hunted electric hares."

"Only when they can't get badgers. And anyway, however they pass their time, it doesn't alter the fact that here I am, penniless. Well, not quite penniless, but certainly two pounds fiveless."

"You think that is what the bruise will amount to?"

"About that. I rather let myself go."

"Quite rightly. It's a poor heart that never rejoices, and one's only young once, I often say. Then all is well. I can manage two pounds five."

"You? But you can't pay for my lunch."

"Of course I can pay for your luncheon. Who's to stop me?"

"Not I, for one. You've saved my life."

"Just the Gish Galleries service."

The magnificent form of the headwaiter materialized at their side. Bill gave him a lordly look.

"*L'addition*," he said haughtily.

"Yes, sir," said the headwaiter.

Jane drew a reverent breath.

"Just like that!" she said. "And in French!"

"One drops into it, I find. Unconsciously, as it were."

"Do you speak it fluently?"

"Very, what I know of it. Which is just that word '*l'addition*' and, of course, '*Oo la la!*' "

"I can't remember even as much as that. And I had a French governess. Where did you study?"

"In Paris, when I was learning to paint."

"Oh, so *that's* why you don't brush your hair."

"I beg your pardon?"

"I mean because you're an artist."

"I'm not an artist. Not now. My soul belongs to Pop Gish of the Gish Galleries."

"What a shame!"

"Oh, it's not a bad life. I like Gish. What Gish thinks of me, I couldn't tell you. From time to time I seem to sense something in his manner that suggests that he may be feeling the strain a little."

"How did you come to get into a job like that?"

"It's a long story, but I think I can condense it into a short-short. I was in London a good deal during the war as a G.I. and got very fond of it, and after I had gone home and worked at various things and saved a bit of money I came back on a sort of sentimental pilgrimage. When my money ran out, which was considerably sooner than I had foreseen, I had to find a job, and your choice of jobs when you are in a foreign country without a labor permit is rather limited. You don't get the cream of what's going."

"I suppose not."

"So when I ran into Gish, who was an old friend of my father's, and he offered me sanctuary in his thieves' kitchen, I jumped at it."

"How did you run into him?"

"In the process of hawking my pictures around every gallery in town. His was about the forty-seventh I visited. He took me on, and I've been working there ever since."

"But you'd rather be painting?"

"If I had lots of money, I'd do nothing else. What would you do if you had lots of money?"

Jane reflected.

"Well, I'd start by fixing up Uncle George at Shipley again. He does hate it so, not being able to live there. After that . . . I think I'd come and luncheon at Barribault's every day."

"Me, too. It's a great place."

"Yes."

"Wonderful cooking."

"Marvelous. And one mets such interesting people. Ah!"

"Yes?"

"A waiter is sneaking up behind you with a little tray in his hand. No doubt containing the bad news."

"Or the kiss of death, as I sometimes call it."

"Are you sure you can pay it?"

"Just this once. You mustn't rely on me as a general thing. There," said Bill, as the waiter withdrew. "*Oo la la!* The shadow has passed."

"And a great weight has rolled from my mind. I don't know how to thank you. My preserver! What do you think would have happened if you hadn't come riding up on your white horse? What would they have done to me?"

"It's difficult to say. I don't know how they handle these things in a place like Barribault's. My only experience of a similar nature has been in a rather more rugged establishment, many years ago when I was a slip of a boy. I boyishly slipped the bad news to the management after a hearty meal of hot dogs and ice cream that I was unable to meet my financial obligations, and a fellow in shirt sleeves of about the build of Rocky Marciano grabbed me by the scruff of the neck and kicked me fourteen times. I was then set to washing dishes."

"How awful!"

"But educative. Tried in the furnace, I came out of that kitchen a graver, deeper boy."

"Where was this?"

"At a joint called Archie's Diner, Good Eats, over in America, not far from a place of the name of Meadowhampton."

"What! Did you say Meadowhampton?"

"Yes. It's on Long Island."

"But how extraordinary!"

"Why?"

"It's my home town."

Bill looked at her incredulously.

"You mean you *know* Meadowhampton? This is astounding. I wouldn't have thought anyone outside America had ever heard of it. When were you there?"

"Ages ago. When I was a slip of a girl. I was sent over to America at the beginning of the war."

"Oh, I see."

"I remember every bit of it. Straw's paper shop, the Patio Inn, the drug-store, the movie house, the library, the Swordfish Club . . . I loved Meadow-hampton. It seems so odd that it should have pursued me to England."

"Would you call it pursuing?"

"Oh, I don't mean you. Someone from there has taken Shipley."

"Roscoe Bunyan."

"That's right. So you know him? What a pity. I wanted to say all sorts of unpleasant things about him. But if he's a friend of yours—"

"I wouldn't say exactly a friend. We belong to the same club and exchange a word or two occasionally, but we are not social equals. He's rich. I'm just one of the dregs. He isn't such a bad fellow, though. I rather like him."

"Then you must like everybody."

Bill thought this over. It was a novel idea, but there was truth in it.

"I suppose I do."

"I see. Just another George."

"Another who?"

"Our bulldog."

"Is he a glad-hander?"

"Very much so. If we ever have a burglar, George will put him at his ease in a moment. The perfect host. But you can't really like Roscoe Bunyan?"

"I don't dislike him. I did as a boy, I remember."

"I'm not surprised. He was a loathsome boy."

"He was, wasn't he? Very much the Bunyan heir. I nearly beat him up once."

"How wonderful. Why was that? Did he steal your all-day sucker?"

"We differed on a point of policy. There was a wretched little rat of a girl spending the summer at Meadowhampton, and Roscoe thought the done thing was to hold her under water in the swimming pool till her eyes popped. I took a conflicting view and told him—speaking sternly—that if he ever did it again . . ."

Barribault's restaurant is solidly built, but to Jane it seemed that it had suddenly begun to float about her. The headwaiter, passing at the moment, had the aspect of a headwaiter dancing the shimmy.

"It can't be!" she cried. "I don't believe it! It isn't really *you*?"

Bill could make nothing of this. She was leaning forward, her eyes shining.

"Don't tell me you're Bill Hollister!"

"Yes, but—?"

"I'm the rat," said Jane.

11

BILL BLINKED.

"The rat?"

"The wretched little rat."

"You?"

"Yes."

"You mean . . . *you* are?"

"That's right. The one who was forever blowing bubbles . . . when Roscoe Bunyan held her under water."

Bill stared across the table. He looked at her fixedly for a moment, and shook his head.

"No," he said. "It doesn't make sense. The rat to whom you allude . . . What was her name?"

"Jane."

"That's right. As I recall her, she had a face that would have stopped a clock."

"I stopped dozens in my prime. I didn't know my own strength."

"Her mouth looked like the back of a telephone switchboard."

"I had to wear braces on my teeth, to straighten them."

"She was heavily spectacled."

"Until my twelfth year, glasses were prescribed to correct a slight strabismus."

"And why do I remember nothing of that divine voice?"

"I don't suppose it was divine then. Probably squeaky."

Bill continued dazed.

"This," he said, "has come as a great surprise."

"I thought it might."

"Do you mind if I have a small beaker of brandy?"

"Go ahead."

"And for you?"

"Nothing, thanks."

Bill caught the waiter's eye and gave his order.

"I'm rather shaken," he explained. "I still have a feeling you're pulling my leg."

"No, that's my story, and I stick to it."

"You really are . . . ?"

"Yes, really."

Bill drew a deep breath.

"But, good heavens, it's incredible. The mind boggles. I mean, look at you now. You're . . ."

"Yes?"

"You're beautiful . . . lovely . . . wonderful . . . marvelous . . . a radiant vision. The child Jane could have made good money scaring crows in the cornfields of Minnesota, and you . . . why, you begin where Helen of Troy left off."

"All done with mirrors."

The waiter brought the brandy, and Bill drained it at a gulp.

"You should sip it," said Jane maternally.

"Sip it? When my whole nervous system is doing buck-and-wing dances? A weaker man would have called for the cask."

"I'm afraid I've upset you."

"I wouldn't call it upsetting so much. It's more like . . . no, I don't know how to describe it."

"Has everything gone black?"

"Just the opposite. It is as if sunshine were pouring through the roof and all the waiters and bus boys singing close harmony at the top of their voices. I can't get over it that you should have remembered me all these years."

"How could I forget you? You were my dream boy. I adored you with a passion I cannot hope to express."

"You *did?*"

"I worshiped you. I used to follow you about, just gazing at you and wondering how anything so perfect could possibly exist. When you dived off the high board, I would look up at you from the shallow end and whisper 'My hero!' I would have died for one little rose from your hair."

Bill drew another deep breath.

"You might have mentioned it."

"I was far too modest. I deemed it best not to tell my love, but to let concealment like a worm i' the bud feed on my damask cheek. Not my own. Shakespeare. Besides, what would have been the use? You wouldn't have looked at me. Or if you had, it would have been with a shudder."

Bill was still having trouble with his breathing. He had become conscious of a marked respiratory embarrassment with an absence of endotracheal oxygenation. His voice, when he was able to speak, was husky. That throat specialist, had he been present, would have given him a sharp look, scenting custom.

"So that was how you felt about me! And here we are, meeting again like this. I'd call it Fate, wouldn't you?"

"Curious, anyway."

"No, it's Fate, and it's never any use trying to buck Fate. You aren't married, are you? No, of course you aren't. It was Miss Benedick, wasn't it? Fine! Capital! Splendid!"

"Why so pleased?"

"Because . . . Because . . . This is possibly going to seem a little sudden, so keep steadily before you the fact that the whole thing was destined from the beginning of time, and it is not for us to throw a spanner into the designs of destiny. Jane," said Bill, leaning forward and placing a hand on hers, "Jane . . ."

"Hello, hello, so there yer are," said a voice. There had loomed up beside the table something large and pear-shaped with heavy eyebrows and a guilty look. "Bit late, ain't I?" it said, speaking bluffly but avoiding its niece's eye. "I got talking to a chap at the club."

If this had been a picnic and Lord Uffenham the ant of which he had spoken in that powerful passage quoted on an earlier page, his intrusion could scarcely have been less welcome to the young man whose well-phrased speech he had interrupted. Bill turned, scowling darkly, and having turned sat gaping. *Distinctive* and *individual* were the adjectives that sprang to the lips of anyone wishing to describe Lord Uffenham's appearance, and he had no difficulty in recognizing his crony of last night. And the thought that if he had only fraternized with the man more heartily, leaving him no option but to ask him to come in and have a drink, he would have met Jane several hours earlier was so poignant as to deprive him of speech. Each Janeless hour was, in the opinion of William Hollister, an hour wasted and gone down the drain.

Jane, though the head of the family would have preferred it otherwise, had not been deprived of speech.

"Uncle George . . ." she said.

"About this new rabbit disease, this myx-whatever-its-dashed-name-is," proceeded Lord Uffenham, still avoiding the eye. "Absorbing subject. Did yer know that foxes, there being now a nation-wide shortage of rabbits, have taken to eating frogs? This club chap assures me it's a fact. They pursue them in packs all over the countryside."

Jane was not to be diverted into a discusison of the dietary arrangements of foxes. Foxes, as far as she was concerned, could eat cake.

"Uncle George," she said, and her voice was cold, "are you aware, you frightful old uncle, that if it had not been for Bill Hollister here, the management of Barribault's would have grabbed me by the scruff of the neck, kicked me fourteen times and set me to work washing dishes?"

"Lord love a duck! What would they do that for?"

"It's an old Barribault custom when girls eat large meals and can't pay for them. Fortunately Bill descended from a cloud in the nick of time, and saved me from the fate that is worse than death. You owe him two pounds ten. Fork out."

Lord Uffenham forked out.

"Thank yer, my boy," he said graciously. "Very civil of yer . . ."

His voice trailed away. He, too, had recognized his crony of last night, and the thought of how much depended on this crony's secrecy and silence sent his heart sinking into those substantial boots of his. He was up against that old business of "Where were you on the night of June the twenty-second?" that had so often undone members of the criminal classes to which he belonged. One word from this young man to the effect that they had met and conversed in the garden of Peacehaven on the night of the bearding of Stanhope Twine's statue, and his name would not be Uffenham, but mud. He caught Bill's eye and threw his whole soul into a glance of agonized appeal.

Bill, though mystified, did not fail him.

"Not at all," he said. "Only too glad I was able to help. It's very interesting meeting you, Lord Uffenham—"

"For the first time," interjected that underworld character hastily.

"For the first time," said Bill, "because I'm the man the Gish Galleries are sending down to look at your pictures."

"Really? Well, I'm dashed."

"He's Mr. Gish's assistant . . . Mr. Gish's assistant . . . Mr. Sish's . . . I knew it couldn't be done," said Jane. "Tell him about the pictures."

"Yes, I'd like to hear about the pictures," said Bill.

Lord Uffenham mused for a moment. His heart was back in its right place again and bursting with devotion and gratitude to this splendid young feller whose ready intelligence had saved him from the soup into which it had seemed that he must inevitably be plunged. He had never met a young feller he liked more. He had not supposed they made young fellers like that nowadays.

"Well, they're . . ." He paused, seeking the *mot juste.* "They're pictures, if yer know what I mean. When yer going to look at them?"

"Right away. I'm driving down."

"I'll come with yer."

"Splendid. You too?"

"No, sorry," said Jane. "I promised an old school friend I would have tea with her, and I can't put her off."

"Why not?"

"She's a very old school friend. Almost decrepit."

"And we don't want any bally girls around" said Lord Uffenham gallantly. "Give me a couple of minutes for a spot of lunch, my boy, and I'll be with yer."

"I'll go and get the car."

"Do. Yer'll find me waiting out in the street. Yer can't miss me. Yerss," said Lord Uffenham, "it's a fact. Foxes, no longer able to get the daily rabbit, now eat frogs. Like," he added, driving home his point, "a lot of ruddy Frenchmen."

12

As foreshadowed, Lord Uffenham was waiting in the street when Bill returned with the car. He was deep in conversation with the Ruritanian Field Marshal at the door. The chap at the club, so informative about rabbits, had also spoken at some length on the sister subject of eels, and Lord Uffenham, who believed in handing these things on, was bringing the Field Marshal abreast of the eel situation in the south of England, one fraught with interest.

"Yerss," he was saying, "according to this feller—Pargiter his name is, though I don't suppose yer know him—the streams down there are so full of the little blighters that the water has taken on the consistency of jelly."

"Coo," said the Field Marshal.

"Three inches long they are, and they have white stomachs."

"Cor," said the Field Marshal.

"Never been in the West Indies, have yer?"

The Field Marshal said he had not.

"Well, that's where they're born, and when they're old enough, they come to England. Though why the hell they should want to come to England, with a Labor Government likely to get in at any moment, is more than I can tell yer."

These unfortunately proved to be fighting words. The harmony which had been prevailing, until now perfect, was rudely jarred. The Field Marshal, stiffening and drawing himself up to his full height of approximately six feet eleven inches, informed Lord Uffenham that he invariably voted the Labor ticket—wishing, he explained, to save the land he loved from the domination of a lot of blinking Fascists, and Lord Uffenham said the Field Marshal ought to lose no time in having his head examined, because anybody with an ounce more sense than a child with water on the brain knew that those Labor blisters were nothing but a bunch of bally Bolsheviks. And the political argument that ensued—with Lord Uffenham accusing the Field Marshal of being in the pay of Moscow and the Field Marshal reminding Lord Uffenham that Mr. Aneurin Bevan had described him and the likes of him as lower than vermin—was beginning to verge on the heated, when it was interrupted by the tooting of Bill's klaxon.

It was a ruffled Lord Uffenham who climbed into the car and took his seat, causing Bill, at the wheel, to shoot some inches into the air. It was the sixth Viscount's practice, when intending to sit, to hover poised for a moment and then, relaxing limply, to come down with a bump, like an avalanche.

The opening stages of the drive were conducted in silence, for Bill was thinking of Jane and Lord Uffenham of all the good things he could have said to the Field Marshal, if only he had thought of them in time. But after a mile or so the agony of dwelling on what might have been abated, and it occurred to him that he had not yet expressed his gratitude to his young friend for having so intelligently refrained from spilling the beans at the recent get-together. He proceeded to repair the omission.

"Great presence of mind yer showed back there at Barribault's, my boy," he said. "When yer stated yer'd never seen me before," he explained. "Touch and go it was for a moment."

Bill was glad this mystery was going to be cleared up. It had been bothering him.

"Oh, yes. I was rather wondering about that. I read the message in your eye, but I couldn't understand it. Why were you so anxious to avoid any touch of auld lang syne?"

"I'll tell yer. Throw yer mind back. Remember that statue of Twine's, the one of the stout female with no clothes on?"

"Vividly."

"We agreed it was an eyesore?"

"We did."

"Well, when we ran into each other last night, I'd just been painting a beard on it."

"A beard?"

"A small imperial beard. With black paint."

"Oh, I see. Yes, very sensible. Most judicious."

"You approve?"

"Wholeheartedly."

"I thought yer would. You're broad-minded. But my niece Jane isn't, and if she'd found out I'd been in that garden, she'd have put two and two together and there'd have been hell to pay. Jane's a good girl—"

"She's an angel."

Lord Uffenham considered this.

"Yerss, I suppose yer could call her that, stretching the facts a little, but she's like all women, it's fatal to let her get the goods on yer. Women never forget. They're worse than elephants. If that statue job had been brought home to me, I'd never have heard the last of it. She'd have touched on it at intervals for the rest of her life. Her mother was that way. My sister Beatrice. I've known my sister Beatrice to bring up things that happened fifty years ago, when we were tots together in our mutual nursery. 'I wouldn't have a second helping of that fruit salad, if I were you, George,'" said Lord Uffenham, assuming for purposes of voice similitude a high falsetto. "'Yer know how weak yer stomach is. Remember how sick yer were at the Montgomerys' Christmas party in 1901.' That sort of thing. It's the kind of crisis one wants, if possible, to avoid. So I'm extremely grateful to yer, my boy."

"Only too glad to have done my bit. We men must stick together."

"Yerss. Solid front. It's the only way," said Lord Uffenham, and went into a trance. The impression he conveyed was that he had unhitched his mind and was giving it a complete rest, but that this was not the case was shown by his first words as—some miles later—he came to life again. Turning on his broad base and fixing his pale blue eyes on Bill, he said, "Angel, did yer say?"

"I beg your pardon?"

"Jane. I think I heard yer say she was an angel?"

"Oh, Jane? Yes, definitely an angel. No argument about that."

"Known her long?"

"We were tots together in America."

"Back in 1939?"

"Yes."

"Seen much of her since?"

"Nothing, until today."

"Yer met her for the first time today after fifteen years, and yer say she's an angel?"

"I do."

"Didn't take yer long to make up yer mind."

"One glance at that divine face was enough."

"She's pretty, of course."

"You understate it. How in the space of a few brief years she can have succeeded in converting herself from the gargoyle of 1939 into the radiant, lovely, glamorous, superlative girl she is today simply beats me. It's the nearest thing to a miracle I ever struck. It just shows what can be done if you have the right spirit and the will to win."

Lord Uffenham started. A sudden interest quickened his stare. The words he had just heard had been spoken, or he was dashed well mistaken, by the voice of love, and it seemed to him that this was a good thing and ought to be pushed along. Often he had dreamed wistfully of a Prince Charming who would some day pop up out of a trap and, if encouraged to play his cards right, take Jane's mind off Stanhope Twine before it was too late, and here, seated beside him, appeared to be the very man. He was about to probe and question, with a view to ascertaining the exact warmth of his companion's feelings, but at this moment Shipley Hall became visible through the trees, diverting his thoughts and sweeping him away on a wave of sentimentality.

Shipley Hall stood on a wide plateau, backed by rolling woodland, a massive white house set about with gay flower beds and spreading lawns. The sight of it, as the car turned in at the iron gates and rolled up the drive, drew from Lord Uffenham a low gurgle such as might have proceeded from the lips of his bulldog George on beholding a T-bone steak, and Bill, always sympathetic, knew how he was feeling. Some poignant stuff was written by the poet Thomas Moore in the nineteenth century descriptive of the emotions of the Peri who was excluded from Paradise, and those of the British landowner who is revisiting the old home which poverty has compelled him to let furnished to a rich American are virtually identical.

As if to underline and emphasize his state of exile, the Jaguar of the new owner was standing at the front door, and Lord Uffenham eyed it askance. He had overcome his momentary weakness, and his long upper lip was stiff once more.

"That feller Bunyan's here," he said.

"Yes, that's his car."

"If we go in, he'll want to show yer round the place as if it belonged to him."

Forbearing to twist the knife in the wound by pointing out that it did, Bill said, "We'll have to go in, if I'm to look at those pictures."

"Plenty of time for that. I want to show yer round myself. See that tree there? At the age of ten, concealed behind that tree, I once plugged an under-gardener in the seat of the pants with my bow and arrow. He was as sick as mud. See that rose garden?"

Bill saw the rose garden.

"Used to be a pond there. My niece fell into it when she was a kid, and just before she went down for the third time, was hauled out with leeches all over her."

Bill's heart stood still. True, the incident had occurred a long time ago, and she was presumably all right now, but he shuddered to the foundations of his being at the picture of Jane submerged in the inky depths. There floated into his mind the passing thought that the woman he loved had apparently spent most of her formative years under water.

"Good God," he cried, aghast.

"Sucking her blood like billy-o, they were. 'Lord love a duck, Anne,' I remember saying—"

"You mean Jane."

"No, this wasn't Jane. It was her sister Anne."

"Oh?" said Bill, immediately losing interest. He had no objection to leeches sucking blood—leeches will be leeches—provided they did not suck Jane's.

"I really ought to see those pictures," he said. "After all, it's what we came for."

This seemed to strike Lord Uffenham, after some thought, as reasonable.

"Yerss, there's something in that, no doubt. All right, let's go in. What I'm hoping," he said, as they made their way through paths with a history and shrubberies with a past, "is that they'll fetch a whacking great sum and enable me to get back Shipley and push this Bunyan off the premises. Makes yer feel sort of at a loose end, getting kicked out of yer boyhood home. There have been Uffenhams at Shipley since I don't know how long. I suppose there's a lot of money in pictures?"

"You'd be surprised. Pop Gish has a Renoir he's expecting to sell for a hundred thousand dollars."

"A hundred thousand dollars," said Lord Uffenham, "would be a great help. Here we are. We'll slip in at the side door. No need to stir up butlers and things."

The picture gallery at Shipley Hall was on the first floor, reached by way of a polished and slippery oak staircase— ("Came a hell of a purler down these stairs at the age of fifteen, trying to avoid my Uncle Gregory, who was after me with a hunting crop for some reason which has escaped my memory")— and was occupied at the moment of their entry by Mortimer Bayliss. He eyed them frostily. He hated to be interrupted when looking at pictures.

"Hello, Mr. Bayliss," said Bill. "A lovely afternoon, is it not?"

"Get out, you foul Hollister," said Mortimer Bayliss in his cordial way. "What do you think you're doing here?"

"In pursuance of my duties as Mr. Gish's assistant, I've come to look at Lord Uffenham's pictures."

"Oh? And who," asked Mr. Bayliss, indicating the sixth Viscount, whom the poignant emotions caused by revisiting his old home had thrown into a trance, "is your stuffed friend?"

"That's Lord Uffenham in person. He came along for the ride. Lord Uffenham!"

"Hey?"

"This is Mr. Mortimer Bayliss, who is longing to meet you. He's an art expert."

"What do you mean, *an* art expert?" said Mr. Bayliss, piqued.

"Sorry. I should have said 'the.' "

"You certainly should, you beardless oaf." Mr. Bayliss turned his black-rimmed monocle on Lord Uffenham, scrutinizing him, it seemed to Bill, with a touch of pity. "So you are the owner of these frightful daubs, are you?"

Bill started.

"Daubs?"

"No, I ought not to have called them that. Very good bits of work, some of them. But you realize, of course, that they're all forgeries?"

"What!"

"It might be a Rumanian art gallery. Somebody once said, 'If I were a forgery, where would I be?' and the answer was, 'In a Rumanian art gallery.' Yes, they're fakes, every one of them."

Lord Uffenham, who had been coming slowly out of his coma, emerged from it in time to hear these last words. He uttered an anguished "Hey! What was that you said? Fakes?"

"That was the gist of my remarks. I can tell you the artists' names, if you wish. This," said Mr. Bayliss, indicating the Gainsborough he had been examining, "is undoubtedly a Wilfred Robinson. He painted a beautiful Gainsborough. That Constable is a Sidney Biffen. His middle period, I should say. About this Vermeer I'm not so sure. It might be a Paul Muller or it might be a Jan Dircks. Their style is somewhat similar, due no doubt to the fact that they were both pupils of Van Meegeren. Ah," said Mr. Bayliss with enthusiasm, "there was a man, that Van Meegeren. Started out in a modest way forging De Hoochs, and then rose to Vermeers and never looked back. Sold the last one he did for half a million pounds. They don't make men like that nowadays. Still, Muller and Dircks are quite good, quite good. Not bad at all," said Mr. Bayliss tolerantly.

Lord Uffenham had the appearance of a man who has been struck by an unexpected thunderbolt. A faint "Lord love a duck" escaped him.

"Yer mean the bally things aren't worth *anything*?"

"Oh, they'd fetch a few hundreds, I suppose, if you had the luck to find the right mug." He looked at his watch. "Hullo, as late as that? Time for my afternoon nap. Well, glad to have been of help," said Mortimer Bayliss, and went out.

Bill, too, was feeling as if something hard and heavy had hit him. He had come to be very fond of Lord Uffenham, and it distressed him to see the stricken peer in his hour of travail. Lord Uffenham having reeled beneath the blow, had once more turned rigid, and was looking like a statue of himself subscribed for and erected by a few friends and admirers. Bill's heart bled for him.

It also bled for his employer. Mr. Gish, he presumed, had been hoping for big things in the way of commission from the sale of these pictures. It would now be his, Bill's, distasteful task to speak to him of Wilfred Robinson, of Sidney Biffen, of Paul Muller and Jan Dircks. With a compassionate glance at Lord Uffenham, who was still looking as if he had been hewn from the solid rock, he stole out, and a passing housemaid directed him to the telephone.

13

LORD UFFENHAM was a resilient man. He might totter when thunderbolts hit him, but it was never long before he threw off their ill effects and returned to normal. Two minutes after Bill had left him, he was perking up. He had become aware that, though the storm clouds had unquestionably gathered, there was a silver lining in them. What had happened, he was feeling, might after all be for the best.

It would have been pleasant, of course, he mused, following this train of thought, to have made a packet out of the ancestral pictures, but you had to look at these things from every angle. When your niece has madly plighted her troth to a bally sculptor and needs only the slightest encouragement to go and get hitched up with him, making a packet has its disadvantages. If, reasoned Lord Uffenham, he had become a man of substance with money to give away in large handfuls, it would scarcely have been possible to deny the misguided girl her cut, and then what? Why, first thing you knew, some clergyman would have been saying to her "Will yer, Jane, take this Stanhope?" and she would have been saying "Well, Lord love a duck, that's the whole idea. What d'yer think I bought this wedding dress for?" and there she would have been, tied for life to the frightful feller. There were aspects of the activities of the Messrs. Robinson, Biffen, Dircks and Muller at which one found oneself shaking the head a bit, but really, upon his soul, the clear-thinking peer told himself, things might have been a dashed sight worse.

It was consequently to a restored and revivified Lord Uffenham that Bill re-entered some ten minutes later. But as the other's rugged face seldom betrayed emotion of any sort, having much in common with that of a cigar-store Indian, his opening words were words of commiseration, the verbal equivalent of the silent handclasp and the sympathetic kneading of the shoulder blades.

"I'm awfully sorry," he said, speaking like one who stands beside a sickbed.

"Hey?"

"About the pictures."

"Oh, those? Dismiss them from yer mind and don't give 'em a thought," said Lord Uffenham buoyantly. "Bit of a sock in the jaw at the moment, I admit, but a feller has to take the rough with the smooth. Easy come, easy go, is the way I look at it. One can see how it happened, of course. What yer've got to bear in mind is that I'm not the first Viscount by a long chalk. I'm the sixth. That means that there were five ruddy Viscounts before me, all needing the stuff and seeing those pictures standing there just waiting to be cashed in on. Here was a handy way of raising the wind, so they raised it, and very sensible, too. I should say my Uncle Gregory, the one I inherited from, probably dipped into the till more freely than any of them. He never had a bean, and as it was a sort of obsession with him to back horses that finished sixth, he always had all the bookies after him like a pack of wolves every settling day. My old guv'nor used to say he wished he had a quid for every time he'd seen his brother Gregory running like the wind down Piccadilly with a high-up man from some turf accountant's firm in hot pursuit behind him. Kept him in wonderful condition, of course."

Bill was relieved. He had not expected this fine spirit, so different from that exhibited by Mr. Gish at their recent telephone conversation. Mr. Gish, receiving the bad news, had mourned and would not be comforted.

"Well, I'm glad you take such a philosophical view."

"Hey?"

"I was afraid you would be upset."

"No use getting upset about these things. All in the day's work. But Jane isn't going to like it, I'm afraid. She was counting on those pictures to restore the family fortunes. I'd better go and phone her."

"I'll come with you. I want to talk to Jane."

"To express sympathy?"

"No, to ask her to marry me."

"What an admirable idea! Lord love a duck! So I was right. You do love the wench?"

"I do."

"Quick work."

"That's the way we Hollisters are. We see, we love, we act. *Voilà!*"

"How d'yer mean, *voilà?*"

"A French expression, signifying 'There you have it in a nutshell.' I must remember to tell Jane that. She thinks all the French I know is *'l'addition'* and *'Oo la la!'* "

Standing beside the telephone while his companion rumbled on into it, Bill listened with growing impatience. Every minute that kept him from pouring out his soul to Jane was like an hour.

"So there yer are," said Lord Uffenham, summing up. "There yer have it in a nutshell. *Voilà!* . . . Hey? I said *voilà*. A French expression. Don't be silly, my girl, of course you got it. V for vermicelli, O for—"

Bill could endure it no longer.

"Here, give me that telephone."

"Oh, yerss, I was forgetting. Don't ring off, Jane. Here's someone wants to talk to yer."

Bill took the instrument, and Lord Uffenham whispered a word of warning.

"Pick yer words carefully, my boy, don't rush her."

"I won't. Jane? Bill speaking. Look, Jane, this is important. Will you marry me?"

"That's what I meant by rushing her," said Lord Uffenham, shaking his head reprovingly. "Reminds me of a poem my old guv'nor used to read me when I was a kid. About a feller named Alphonso and a wench called Emily. How did it go, now? Used to know it by heart once. Ah, yes, 'Alphonso, who for cool assurance all creation licks, he up and said to Emily, who has cheek enough for six—' "

Bill had replaced the receiver. There was a rather stunned look on his face.

" 'Miss Emily, I love yer. Will yer marry? Say the word,' and Emily said, 'Certainly, Alphonso, like a bird.' " He scanned Bill's face thoughtfully. "I take it from something in yer manner that that wasn't what Jane said?"

"She didn't say anything. She gave a sort of gasp, and hung up."

Lord Uffenham nodded sagely. In his younger days he had frequently heard girls gasp over the telephone, and it had always spelled trouble.

"I told yer not to rush her. See what's happened? You've made her ratty. She thought you were having a joke with her."

"Having a joke?"

"Making fun of her. Pulling her leg. Well, what would *you* think if you were a girl, and a feller you hardly knew from a hole in the ground suddenly bellowed at yer 'Hey! How about marrying me?' No tact, no leading up to the thing gracefully, just 'Hello there, let's get married,' as if yer were inviting her out to tea and shrimps or something."

How much more circumspectly, he was thinking, the great bustard would have comported itself in similar circumstances. The great bustard, as he had recently learned from his *Wonders of the Bird World*, when entertaining for a female bustard feelings deeper and warmer than those of ordinary friendship, does not shout proposals of marriage over the telephone. It ruffles its back feathers, inflates its chest and buries its whiskers in it, thus showing tact and leading up to the thing gracefully. And he was about to pass these nature notes on to Bill, when the latter spoke. There was, Bill had realized, something in what the other had said.

"I was abrupt, you think?"

"That's how it struck me."

Bill reflected.

"Yes, I suppose I was. It never occurred to me at the time."

"Always a mistake, anyway, proposing on the telephone. I remember in the year 1920, when I was potty about a girl called Janice, ringing her up and saying, 'I love yer, I love yer. Will yer marry me?' and she said, 'You betcher, of course I will.'"

"Wasn't that all right?"

"Far from it. Because I'd got the numbers in my little red book mixed up, and it wasn't Janice I was talking to, it was a girl called Constance, whom I'd never much liked. Took me quite a while adjusting that situation."

"Well, I've got to adjust this situation. Come on, let's get in that car and drive to your place. I'll have it out with her."

"She won't be there. She'll have gone off to that school friend of hers, and you know how it is when girls from the old school get together. She may not be home till midnight."

"But I must see her."

"Come and have a bite of dinner tomorrow. Seven o'clock. Don't dress."

Bill looked at Lord Uffenham with approval. The old gentleman might be an odd shape, but he got some good ideas.

"I will. Thank you very much."

"I can promise yer an excellent dinner. Jane's a superb cook."

"Does she cook?"

"Does she *cook*? Well, you ought to know. She did that dinner at Twine's that you were at last night. Good, wasn't it?"

"It was terrific. I was saying to somebody only this morning that it melted in the mouth. But what on earth was she doing cooking for Twine?"

"She's engaged to him."

"Engaged? What do you mean?"

"What d'yer think I mean?"

"She's going to *marry* him?"

"So she says."

It had sometimes happened to Bill, when indulging in his hobby of amateur boxing, to place the point of his jaw in a spot where his opponent was simultaneously placing his fist, and the result had always been a curious illusion that the top of his head had parted abruptly from its moorings. He experienced a similar sensation now. Tottering, he might have fallen, had he not clutched at something solid, which proved to be Lord Uffenham's arm. The latter uttered a yelp of the same nature as the one he had uttered in the garden of Peacehaven.

"Hey!"

Bill was still dazed.

"Oh, sorry,"he said. "Did I grab you?"

"You grabbed me like a ton of bricks right in the fleshy part. Hurt like sin. What's the matter? Feeling faint?"

"No, I'm all right now. It gave me rather a shock for a moment."

"I can well believe it. It gave *me* a shock, when she told me. When the wench breezed in one morning while I was doing my crossword puzzle and sprang it on me as calm as a halibut on ice that she was going to marry Stanhope Twine, I nearly swooned where I sat. 'What!' I said. '*That* young slab of damnation? Yer kidding.' But no. She stuck to it that it was all fixed up. Stuck stoutly."

Bill stood plunged in thought, and Lord Uffenham heaved a sigh.

"I don't mind telling you that the whole thing has come very near to breaking my ruddy heart. *Twine*, I'll trouble yer!"

"I know what you mean."

"A feller who marcels his hair."

"Yes."

"And wears yellow corduroy trousers."

"Yes."

"The last chap in the world one wants about the house."

"I quite agree with you. We can't have this sort of thing going on. We must put a stop to it at once."

"But how?"

"I shall talk to her and make her see the light."

"You won't rush her?"

"Certainly not. I shall be very calm and tactful and persuasive. I know just the tone to take."

"You think you'll be able to prize her away from him?"

"I think so."

"Well, best of luck, my dear boy. If you do, nobody will wave his hat and cheer more heartily than I. But I don't mind telling yer that so far the voice of reason has been powerless to drive sense into her fat head. Lord love a duck," said Lord Uffenham, heaving another sigh, "when I think of Jane wanting to marry Stanhope Twine and remember that her sister Anne came within an ace of marrying an interior decorator, I ask myself if there may not be a touch of eccentricity in the family."

14

ON THE rare occasions when the weather was fine enough to permit of it, it was Roscoe Bunyan's custom to take his before-dinner cocktail on the terrace opening off the drawing room to Shipley Hall, from which one got a charming view of rolling parkland and distant woods, and it was here on the evening following the visit of Bill and Lord Uffenham to Shipley that he might have been observed giving a rather close imitation of an expectant father at a maternity home—sitting down, jumping up, pacing to and fro and generally behaving with the uneasy mobility usually associated with peas on shovels and cats on hot bricks. That morning Mortimer Bayliss had gone off to give Stanhope Twine lunch at his club and place the twenty thousand pound proposition before him, and at any moment now he would be returning from his mission, bringing the news of its success or failure.

That Roscoe, at first so reluctant to part with this substantial sum, should now be all of a twitter lest at the eleventh hour something should have gone wrong with the negotiations, preventing him from doing so, may seem peculiar. But in the period that had elapsed since the departure of Keggs the business sense which he had inherited from his father, the late J. J., had had time to work, and it had told him that, however keen the agony of bidding farewell to twenty thousand pounds, if he paid it out and in return secured a million dollars, he would be left with a most attractive profit. And attractive profits were meat and drink to him.

Presently Skidmore arrived with the cocktails, but it was only after his employer had had one quick and was starting on another rather slower that Mortimer Bayliss appeared, looking like an Egyptian mummy in need of a bracer.

"At last!" cried Roscoe.

Mr. Bayliss headed purposefully for the cocktail table, though only in quest of tomato juice. It was many years since his medical adviser had prohibited anything more in tune with modern enlightened thought. Like Jamshyd, the curator of the Bunyan collection had once gloried and drunk deep, but those brave old days were over.

"Were you expecting me earlier?" he said, sipping the hell-brew and wishing, as he so often wished, that it tasted a little less like a weak solution of old rubber overshoes. "I looked in at the Gish Galleries after lunch. It always amazes me that Leonard Gish is still a free man. I'd have thought that he would long since have been doing his bit of time at Wormwood Scrubbs or Pentonville. Negligence somewhere."

Roscoe was in no mood to discuss Mr. Gish.

"What happened?" he asked, quivering.

"He tried to get two hundred thousand dollars out of me for that Renoir of his. Worth at the most a hundred thousand. That's an art dealer for you."

Roscoe continued to impersonate a tuning fork. "At lunch, man! What happened at your lunch with Twine?"

"Oh, that? Everything went according to plan. I gave him your check, and he rushed off, without waiting for coffee, to deposit it."

Roscoe collapsed into a chair with a grunt of relief.

"I was afraid he might back out."

"There was never any chance of that. For a moment I thought he was going to kiss me. Sometimes," said Mortimer Bayliss, gazing with distaste at his tomato juice, "I am tempted to rebel, to tell these doctors where they can stick their medical advice and go back to the spacious times when I was known as Six-Martini Bayliss. Then I tell myself that it is not fair to the world to deprive it of its finest art expert. Yes, as of course one knew he would, Twine jumped at it."

"Swell!"

Mortimer Bayliss removed his monocle, polished it thoughtfully, replaced it in his eye and through it gazed at his companion in a way that would have struck a beholder more sensitive to impressions than Roscoe as enigmatic.

"Swell?" he said meditatively. "I wonder—"

"What do you mean?"

"I am not wholly convinced that everything is as rosy as you seem to imagine."

A disturbing thought struck Roscoe.

"Don't tell me he's not engaged?"

"He's engaged all right."

"Well, then?"

Mortimer Bayliss finished his tomato juice, put the glass on the table, shuddered a little and said that the Borgias could have learned a lot, if they had lived today.

"Yes, he told me he was engaged, but something else he happened to mention made me ask myself if you are quite as much on velvet as I am sure we should all like you to be. He was touching on the parental opposition to his artistic career. His father disliked the idea of his becoming a sculptor, he told me. I wasn't surprised. These hay, corn and feed merchants always want their sons to go into the business."

Roscoe could not follow this.

"These what?"

"Twine's father is a prosperous hay, corn and feed man up in Liverpool. Twine and Bessemer is, I understand, the name of the firm."

Roscoe's bewilderment deepened.

"But he's an American."

"Twine? No, English. No connection with America at all."

"Keggs said—"

Mortimer Bayliss' face still had the impassivity of something that had died on the banks of the Nile five thousand years ago, but inwardly he was bubbling with merriment. He had no liking for the Roscoes of this world.

"Ah, that brings me to what I have been trying to break gently to you, my dear boy. What Keggs says, when he comes and hands you a million dollars on a plate with watercress round it and you reward him with a measly fifty pounds, is not evidence. His haughty spirit wounded, he told you Twine was the man, knowing well that Twine was not the man, thus getting his own back by making you pay twenty thousand pounds for nothing. From what I know of Keggs, and I used to study him rather closely in the old days, that sort of thing would appeal to his peculiar sense of humor. I don't want to rub it in, but I must say I have often felt that your thriftiness would get you into trouble some day."

The rolling parkland and the distant woods were flickering before Roscoe's eyes like an early silent motion picture. He rose, his face purple and his eyes gleaming.

"I'll wring the man's neck."

"Well, if you must, of course. But there's a law against it."

"I'll go and do it now."

"How about dinner?"

"I don't want any dinner."

"I do," said Mortimer Bayliss. "I need it sorely. But I can't miss seeing you wring Keggs's neck. I'll come with you. I'm one of those modern teen-agers you read about—avid for excitement."

15

IT WAS not often that Lord Uffenham entertained guests at his Mulberry Grove residence, for he preferred, when exercising hospitality, to do it at his club. But when he did so entertian, it was Augustus Keggs's kindly practice to buckle on his discarded armor, as he had done on the night of Stanhope Twine's dinner party, and leap into the breach, buttling as devotedly as in the old Shipley Hall days. Augustus Keggs, though retired and a capitalist, was still animated by the feudal spirit.

It was he, in consequence, who opened the front door of Castlewood to Bill on his arrival, and the latter, who had been subjected to a considerable strain these last few days, had a momentary feeling that he had cracked under it and was seeing things. Then a plausible solution suggested itself. Keggs, he decided, must be a specialist who, in return for some suitable fee, hired himself out for the evening when Valley Fields felt like making whoopee. He greeted him with the cordiality of an old friend.

"Hello," he said, "we're seeing a lot of each other these days, aren't we?"

"Yes, indeed, sir," Keggs agreed, smiling indulgently.

"You seem to pop from spot to spot like the chamois of the Alps leaping from crag to crag. I don't believe I gave you my name last time, did I? Well, there must be no secrets and reservations between old buddies like us. It's Hollister."

Respectful interest came into Keggs's gooseberry eyes.

"Indeed, sir? Might I inquire, if it is not a liberty, if you are the son of Mr. Joseph Hollister, formerly of New York City?"

"Yes, that's right. My father's name was Joseph. You knew him?"

"I was in the service of the late Mr. J. J. Bunyan many years ago, and Mr. Hollister, Senior, was a frequent dinner guest at our table. I was struck immediately by the resemblance. If you will step this way, sir. His lordship is in his study."

The study was a large, airy room, comfortably furnished in country-house style, for Lord Uffenham on being driven from his garden of Eden had been at pains to loot the place of all the chairs, rugs, pictures, books and personal belongings he liked best. On the walls hung photographs of him at every stage of his development—the schoolboy, the undergraduate, the guardsman, the boulevardier and the warrior of the battlefields of Loos and the Somme—and it would have interested Bill to examine these, to see if his host had always been that peculiar shape. But he was given no opportunity of doing so, for Lord Uffenham, who was looking grave as though he had recently received disturbing news, thrust him into a chair, handed him a cocktail and immediately began to speak.

"Holloway," he said.

Bill mentioned that the name was Hollister, and Lord Uffenham said Oh, was it, adding that the point was immaterial, for now that they had become such close friends, he proposed to address him as Augustus.

"Why?" asked Bill, interested.

"It's yer name."

"My name is not Augustus."

"*Not* Augustus?"

"No, not Augustus."

Lord Uffenham clicked his tongue.

"I see where I went wrong. Keggs's name is Augustus. That's what muddled me. I don't always get names right. My niece Anne, Jane's sister—"

"The one who fell into the pond?"

"That's right, and got leeches all over her. She got spliced to a young feller called Jeff Miller, and it was only after a considerable lapse of time that I was able to rid myself of the belief that his name was Walter Willard."

"I don't call that such a bad shot."

"No. But one likes to be accurate. Jane's always on at me about it."

"Where is Jane?"

"In the kitchen."

"Should I go and have a word with her?"

"I wouldn't advise it. Women hate to be interrupted when dishing up dinner, especially if already ratty. Yerss, Fred, she's still ratty, I'm sorry to say. Goes about in a sort of dream, looking like a dying duck, and doesn't answer when you speak to her. She's in shock."

"Oh, no, really."

"In shock," repeated Lord Uffenham firmly. "And why wouldn't she be, after the way you rushed her? Why, there was a girl I used to know in 1912 who got in shock once because I didn't like her new hat. Took a diamond sunburst to bring her round, I remember. You shook Jane to her bally foundations, my boy, and if you're going to make her cast off the spell of the hellhound Twine, you'll have to spit on yer hands and pull your socks up in no uncertain manner. Because a very serious situation has arisen. You know what she told me this evening just before going off to put the chicken in the oven? She told me that Twine has got his hooks on a whacking great sum of money."

Bill started.

"Twine has? How much?"

"Twenty thousand ruddy pounds. No less."

"What!"

"It's a fact. She had it direct from Keggs, who appears to have been present throughout the whole conversation between Bunyan and that art expert chap."

"Bayliss?"

"I'd have said Banstead."

"But what have he and Bunyan to do with it?"

"I'm telling yer. It seems that the feller Bunyan and the feller Banstead were talking about the feller Twine's statues, and the feller Banstead said the feller Twine was a genius or words to that effect, and the upshot of the whole thing is that Bunyan's given Twine twenty thousand pounds in return for a percentage of his future earnings. Must have been as tight as an owl, I should say, but there it is. So Twine, blister his insides, now has twenty thousand of the best in his hip pocket. You see what this means? It means that the only shield and safeguard we had against his marrying Jane—the fact that he couldn't afford to—no longer exists. He could marry fifty Janes. If," said Lord Uffenham, having reviewed his statement, "he were a Mormon. Not otherwise, of course. Yerss," he concluded, "that frightful young blot on the landscape has now got the stuff, and if you're going to accomplish anything constructive, Fred, yer'll have to look slippy."

His gravity had communicated itself to Bill. Until now, he had been inclined, even though Jane was engaged to him, to underestimate Stanhope Twine as a menace. But a Stanhope Twine whose corduroy trousers were bulging with Roscoe Bunyan's gold might well be a formidable rival. Unquestionably socks would have to be pulled up and hands spat on, not to mention stones turned and avenues explored.

"You're sure of this?" he said.

"I tell yer, Keggs was there."

"Where?"

"At Shipley, where the conversation took place."

"What was he doing there?"

"He'd gone to see Bunyan about something."

"Odd their discussing a thing like that in front of Keggs."

"He was probably listening at the keyhole."

"And another thing I don't understand is how Roscoe could ever have brought himself to risk twenty thousand pounds on the future of an unknown man. It doesn't sound like him."

Lord Uffenham saw that his young friend had got mixed up. He was quite patient about it. He knew that he sometimes got mixed up himself.

"It wasn't Roscoe. It was Bunyan."

"His name is Roscoe."

"No, it's not. It's Bunyan."

"His Christian name."

Enlightenment flooded on Lord Uffenham. He could be as quick as lightning at times.

"Oh, his *Christian* name. Now I've got yer. Now I follow yer."

"The thing seems absolutely incredible. Roscoe never parts. He's noted for it. He is known far and wide as the man with the one-way pockets."

Lord Uffenham was beginning to feel a little impatient. He spoke with some sharpness.

"Well, he's parted now."

"If the story's true."

"Of course it's true. Why would Keggs invent a yarn like that? You're wandering from the point, Fred. We mustn't waste precious time asking ourselves *why* Ronald Bunyan committed this rash act. We've got to put our heads together and decide what's to be done. Have another cocktail?"

"Thanks. I feel I need one."

"Two problems confront us," said Lord Uffenham, having refilled their glasses: "(a) how to stop Jane being ratty with yer and (b) how to prevent her charging off to the registrar's and getting spliced to the Twine excrescence. The first is the tricky one. Solve that, and you'll be in a position to handle Problem B for yerself. Because you aren't going to tell me you're not capable of cutting out a blister like Stanhope Twine. And you'll be relieved to hear, Fred, that I have the matter well in hand."

"You have?"

"Yerss, I see the way. We can get cracking. You ever read poetry?"

"Quite a good deal. Why?"

"I was thinking that once in a while those poets stumble on something that makes sense. Remember the feller who said that women were gosh-awful pains in the neck when things were going right with you, but turned into bally angels when yer had a hangover?"

" 'Oh, woman, in our hours of ease . . .' "

"That's the one. My old guv'nor used to recite it whenever he got a bit bottled. Well, there's a lot in it. Take Jane. At the moment ratty, but if pain and anguish were to wring yer brow, she'd be all over yer, I'm convinced of it. It was the same with her sister Anne."

"The one who married Walter Willard?"

Lord Uffenham tut-tutted.

"You want to watch yerself over names, Fred," he said rebukingly. "Miller I told yer he was called, Jeff Miller. Your trouble is yer don't retain. Yerss,

Jeff Miller, a fine young chap whom I looked on as a son, loved my niece Anne and kept pressing his suit; but the cloth-headed girl would have none of him, being under the extraordinary illusion that what she wanted was a putty-souled interior decorator named Lionel Green. When Jeff wooed her, it made her as sore as a gumboil. She wouldn't speak to him, and she had developed a habit, when they found themselves alone together, of whizzing from his presence as if shot from a gun. This made things difficult for Jeff."

"It must have done. Complex, you might say?"

"Very complex. He began to lose heart, feeling that he was making no solid progress. All this, I should mention, was taking place down at Shipley under my personal eye, and I don't mind telling yer that my flesh used to creep when I saw Anne giving Jeff the sleeve across the windpipe and realized that every minute brought closer the day when she would become the bride of this pestilential poop Lionel Green. I could see no hope of easing the tension and finding a formula, and I was trying to steel myself to the prospect of becoming the uncle of an interior decorator, when one evening by the greatest good luck a sweet little woman named Mrs. Molloy, who was staying at Shipley at the time, hauled off and walloped Jeff over the head with my tobacco jar."

It seemed to Bill that the home life of his host presented what Sherlock Holmes would have called certain features of interest.

"She did?"

"Bang on the occipital bone. It's a long story. She and her husband were crooks, and Jeff caught them trying to loot the house. He started hammering the stuffing out of Molloy, so Mrs. Molloy very naturally crowned him with the tobacco jar. And that, of course, made everything all right between him and Anne."

"All right?" Bill was conscious of a feeling, such as comes to all of us at times, of not being equal to the intellectual pressure of the conversation. "Why?"

"Hey?"

"Why was that the happy ending?"

"Because it opened Anne's eyes. It made her look into her heart and read its message. Seeing Jeff lying there with his toes turned up and giving every evidence of having handed in his dinner pail, she knew in a flash that he was the one she loved, and she flung herself on his prostrate form and started to kiss him, at the same time saying 'Oh, Jeff, darling' and all that sort of thing. Never gave Lionel Green another thought. Interesting story. Throws a light on feminine psychology."

"It must have been a solid tobacco jar."

"It was. I bought it when I went up to Cambridge. When you're a freshman, the first thing yer buy is a stone tobacco jar with the college arms on it. I'll show it to yer," said Lord Uffenham, lumbering across the room and returning with the blunt instrument. "Good value there," he said, regarding it affectionately. "Forty-odd years I've had it, and still unbroken. Jeff's head didn't even dent it. Lord love a duck, I can see the scene as plainly as if it had happened yesterday. There was Jeff squaring away at Molloy—unpleasant feller, he was. Going a bit bald on the top, I remember—and Mrs. Molloy —Dolly her name was, and, as I say, a sweet little woman, though of course with some defects—upped with the jar and let him have it. Like this," said Lord Uffenham, and lumbered to the door. "Jane," he called "Jay-un."

"Yes?"

"Cummere. Young Holloway's had an accident. I was showing him that tobacco jar of mine, and my hand slipped."

16

IT WAS some little time later that Bill, waking from a disordered nightmare in which strange and violent things had been happening to him, became aware that someone was standing at his side, offering him a glass of brandy.

"Take a sip of this, my boy," said Lord Uffenham, for it was he. The altruistic peer was wearing a look of smug satisfaction such as some great general might have worn after a famous victory. Wellington probably looked like that at Waterloo.

Bill took a sip, and found his head clearing. He fixed a bleary and accusing eye on his host.

"Was that you?" he said coldly.

"Hey?"

"Did you hit me with that tobacco jar?"

The smug expression on Lord Uffenham's face was rendered more repellent by a modest smirk. He seemed to be deprecating thanks. It was as though he were saying that it was nothing, nothing, that any man would have done what he had done.

"Yerss, that's right. Bring the young folks together, that's what I say. As I had anticipated, it worked. I take it you weren't noticing much at the time, so I'll give yer a brief outline of what occurred. I went to the door, shouted 'Jane! Jay-un!' and she shouted back 'What the hell's the matter now?' or words to that effect, no doubt being busy with the dinner and not wanting to have her mind taken off it. 'Cummere,' I said. 'Young Holloway's had an accident.' And up she comes and, seeing your prostrate form, flings herself on it and kisses yer. The usual routine."

Bill had not supposed that any human power would have been able to do anything to diminish the throbbing ache in a head which was feeling as if something of about the dimensions of Stanhope Twine's colossal nude had fallen on it from a seventh-floor window, but at these words the throbbing ceased to be, the ache was no more. In their place came a yeasty elation such as he had never experienced, not even when reading the letter from Miss

Angela Murphrey, freeing him of his honorable obligation. He felt like the uplifted gentleman in the poem who on honeydew had fed and drunk the milk of Paradise, and would not have been greatly surprised had Lord Uffenham said "Beware, beware! His flashing eyes, his floating hair!" and woven a circle round him thrice.

He drew one of those deep breaths which lately had become such a feature of his existence.

"She kissed me?" he said reverently.

"Like nobody's business. At the same time crying 'Oh, Bill, darling! Speak to me, Bill, darling! Lord love a duck, are yer dead, Bill, darling?' and so on and so forth. Odd that she should have called yer Bill, when yer name's Fred, but that's a side issue and probably without importance. The point to keep steadily before us is that she said 'Darling' and kissed yer. Weighing the evidence, Fred, I think we can say the thing's in the bag."

Bill rose and began to pace the room. Curiously, considering on how dashing, one might almost say fiery, lines his wooing had been conducted, his chief emotion, apart from that feeling of ecstasy which made him want to slap all mankind on the back, starting with Lord Uffenham, was a deep humility. He was weighed down with a sense of unworthiness, much as a swineherd in a fairy tale might have been, who found himself loved by the princess. How his personality could have cast such a spell he was unable to understand.

It was not as though he had been a sort of Greek god or movie star. There was a mirror over the fireplace in Lord Uffenham's study, and he paused for a moment to examine himself in it. It was just as he had supposed. An honest face, but nothing more. One formed a picture of Jane Benedick as one of those exceptional girls who do not go by the outer crust but burrow through till they have found the soul within.

Yet even this explanation scarcely held water. His soul, as he knew, having lived a lifetime with it, was a good enough soul, as souls went, but not by any means the kind you hang out flags about. It was probably entered in the celestial books as "Soul, gent's ordinary, one." But despite all this she had flung herself on his prostrate form and kissed him, at the same time saying "Oh, Bill, darling! Speak to me, Bill darling! Lord love a duck, are yer dead, Bill, darling?" It was all very mystifying, and if the story had not proceeded from a reliable source, his informant having been an actual eyewitness, he could hardly have believed it.

An intense desire to see her swept over him.

"Where is she?" he cried.

"She stepped out to get some cold water and a sponge, and," said Lord Uffenham, starting visibly, "I hear her coming back. I'll be moving along, I think."

Jane entered, bearing a basin, and as she saw the head of the family her eyes flashed fire.

"Uncle George," she said, speaking from between clenched teeth.

"Quite. Quite. But got one or two things to attend to just now, my dear. See yer later," said Lord Uffenham, and disappeared like a diving duck.

Jane put the basin down. The fire had died from her eyes, and they were moist.

"Oh, Bill!" she said.

He could not speak. Words—and this was a thing that rarely happened where he was concerned—failed him. He could but look at her in silence, wondering anew how this golden princess had ever brought herself to stoop to a man like himself—just one of the swineherds, as you might say, and not much of a swineherd at that. How lovely she was, he was thinking, though in forming this view he was in actual fact mistaken. A girl cannot stand over a kitchen stove on a warm June night, cooking a chicken and two veg, not to mention clear soup, and other delicacies, and remain natty. Jane's face was flushed and her hair disheveled, and across one cheek there was a smudge of what appeared to be black lead. Nevertheless, she seemed to him perfection. This, he told himself sentimentally, was how he must always remember her—with grubby face and an apron round her waist.

"Jane!" he whispered. "Oh, Jane!"

"This," said Jane some moments later, "can't be doing your head good."

"It's doing *me* good," Bill assured her. "For the first time I'm beginning to realize that there may be something in this, that I'm not just dreaming. Or am I?"

"No."

"You really—?"

"Of course I do. You're my Bill."

Once again Bill became conscious of that respiratory embarrassment and the absence of endotracheal oxygenation. He shrugged his shoulders, giving the thing up. But his soul was singing, and his heart was light.

"Well, it all seems most peculiar to me, you being what you are and I being what I am. I ask myself, 'What have you done to deserve this, William Quackenbush Hollister...?' "

"William *what* Hollister?"

"Not my fault, my godfather's. Don't let it put you off me. Think of me as Q. What, I was saying, have I done to deserve this? And the answer, as far as I have been able to work it out, is 'Not a damn thing.' Still, if you say so ... What are you doing with that sponge?"

"I'm going to bathe your head."

"Good God, this is no time for bathing heads. I want to tell you, if I can find words, how I feel about you. You're wonderful!"

"No, no. I'm just a simple little home body."

"You are *not*. You're lovely."

"You didn't always think so, did you?"

"You mean when we were tots? I was a boy then, incapable of spotting a good thing when I saw one. Tell me, by the way, about this loveliness of yours. When did you feel it coming on?"

"I believe I began to look fairly human when I was about fourteen. They had removed the telephone switchboard effects by then."

"And the spectacles?"

"And the spectacles. The strabismus had been corrected."

Bill heaved a sigh, thinking of all he had missed through not having seen her at the age of fourteen. They were sitting now in Lord Uffenham's armchair, a roomy affair well adapted to the reception of two young people who did not mind being fairly close together. From the wall above them a photograph of Lord Uffenham in some sort of Masonic uniform gazed down—benevolently, it seemed, as if he were saying, "Bless yer, my children."

"When you were fourteen, I must have been slogging through Normandy on my way to Paris with the army of liberation."

"Shouting '*Oo la la*'?"

"That and '*l'addition.*' Everybody said I was a great help. Don't wriggle."

"I'm not wriggling, I'm getting up. I'm going to bathe your head."

"I don't want my head bathed."

"But you've got an enormous lump."

"I ignore it. These things cannot affect us finally. I'm glad, though, that this didn't happen when my Lord Uffenham was younger and stronger."

The cold, stern look returned to Jane's face.

"Don't mention that man's name in my presence. He ought to be in Colney Hatch."

"Nonsense. I won't hear a word against Uncle George. He moves in a mysterious way, his wonders to perform, but he gets results. He brought the young folks together."

"Nevertheless, he ought to be skinned—very slowly—with a blunt knife and dipped in boiling oil. That would teach him. I do wish that the men who marry into our family didn't always have to be hit over the head with that tobacco jar."

"Have you no respect for tradition? But I see what you mean. One of these days, you feel, some suitor with a thin skull is going to land the old philanthropist in the dock on a murder charge."

"There won't be any more suitors, because there aren't any more Benedicks. It's like Uncle George's rabbits. The supply has given out."

"Well, I've got the Benedick *I* want."

"You ought to have seen the one that got away."

"Eh?"

"Anne."

"Ah yes, your plain sister."

"She isn't. She's the prettiest thing you ever saw."

Bill could not yield on this point.

"Any sister of yours—even it she were Cleopatra and Lillian Russell and Marilyn Monroe rolled into one—would be your plain sister. Anyway, I doubt if Anne would have appealed to me. All those leeches. Tell me, to settle a bet, is she Mrs. Jeff Miller or Mrs. Walter Willard?"

"The former."

"Had Jeff Miller known her long?"

"No."

"Then I am one up on him there. I am marrying my childhood sweetheart. Much more romantic."

"Childhood sweetheart? I like that. When we were at Meadowhampton, you never gave me a look."

"We went into all that. You were a gargoyle."

"So when you say you love me, it is for my looks alone?"

"It is not for your darned looks alone. We'd better get that straight before proceeding further. I'm marrying you for your cooking, and I shall keep a very sharp lookout for any falling off from the standard. And if we're digging up the dead past, what about you and Twine? Yes, I don't wonder you hang your head and shuffle your feet. I take my eye off you for half a minute—"

"Fifteen years."

"I take my eye off you for a mere fifteen years, and what happens? You leave me flat for a fellow who wears yellow corduroy trousers. And that brings me to a rather important item on the agenda paper. What do we do about Twine? He should be informed, I think. Scarcely humane to keep him in the dark till he gets his slice of wedding cake. What steps do we take?"

"Oh, Bill!"

"What's the matter? You're crying."

"No, I'm laughing."

"What's so funny?"

"Your saying about taking steps. We don't need to take any steps. He's taken them."

Bill stared.

"You mean he's given you the push?"

"He called it releasing me."

"Tell me all."

"There isn't much to tell. I thought his manner seemed a little strange this morning, when I was breaking it to him that there would be no money coming in from those pictures, and this evening, just before you arrived, I had a note from him. It was a beautiful note. He said he felt he had no right to—"

"Don't tell me. Let me guess. Take the best years of your life?"

"Yes. He said it was wrong to hold me to my promise when there was so little chance of his ever having enough money to marry on, so he thought it only fair to release me. It was touching."

"Doesn't he call twenty thousand pounds enough money?"

"He didn't know I knew about that."

"No, I imagine not."

"I can see how his mind worked. Did you ever hear the story about the man in the First War who enlisted in the infantry instead of the cavalry because—"

" 'When Ah run away, Ah don't aim to be hampered by no horse.' Yes, Mortimer Bayliss told me that one in one of his rare jovial moments, when I was a boy. How does it apply?"

"Well, Stanhope was always talking about how he ought to be traveling in Italy and France and all that, to broaden his mind and improve his art, and now that he's able to travel he don't aim to be hampered by no wife. Especially a wife without any money. He's rather a self-centered man."

"What did you ever see in him, you misguided little half-wit?"

"I suppose Uncle George's theory is the right one, though I wouldn't tell him so; it's bad for discipline. 'Yer wouldn't have looked twice at the feller,' he said, 'if yer hadn't been cooped up in a London suburb with nobody else in sight.' That must have been it. You get talking across the fence, and one thing leads to another."

"And those yellow trousers probably dazzled you. Well, all right, I'll overlook it this time, but don't let it occur again." Bill paused, listening. "Do you keep an elephant here?"

"Not that I know of. Though Uncle George has often talked of buying an ostrich, if the funds will run to it. He wants to see if it will really bury its head in the sand. Why do you ask?"

"I thought I heard one coming up the stairs."

It was not an elephant, it was the sixth Viscount Uffenham. He burst into the room, looking—for him—quite animated.

"Hey?" he said. "What's going on in the ruddy kitchen? Smoke's billowing out of it in clouds, and it smells to heaven."

Jane uttered a stricken cry.

"Oh, death and despair, the dinner! It must be burned to a cinder."

She darted out, and Lord Uffenham followed her with an indulgent eye.

"Women!" he said, with a short, amused laugh. "Well, Fred, how did things work out?"

"Fine, Uncle George. You are losing a niece, but gaining a nephew."

"Excellent. Couldn't be better."

"Well, actually, it could be a lot better, because I'm really much too poor to think of getting married. All I have is my pittance from the Gish Galleries."

"Nothing else?"

"Not a cent."

"Pity those pictures turned blue on us."

"Yes, but you've got to weigh this against that. If it hadn't been for them, I should never have met Jane."

"That's true. Oh, well, something'll turn up. Yes, Keggs?"

Keggs had floated in, looking grave.

"Miss Benedick desired me to step up and inform your lordship that she regrets that it will be impossible for her to provide dinner tonight," he said in a hushed voice.

Lord Uffenham waved dinner away with an airy gesture.

"Gone west, has it? Well, who cares? Keggs, I want yer to fill a glass and drink the health of the young couple."

"M'lord?"

"Young Fred Holloway here and my niece Jane. They're getting spliced.

"Indeed, m'lord? I am sure I wish you every happiness, sir."

Jane came in. She was dirty and dispirited.

"There won't be any dinner," she said. "It's a charred ruin. We'll have to go to that pub you and Mr. Keggs sneak off to in the evenings."

Lord Uffenham scoffed at this pedestrian suggestion.

"What?" he cried. "Go to the local on a night like this, when yer've seen the light and given that perisher Twine the heave-ho, and hitched on to a splendid young feller whom I can nurse in my bosom? Not by a jugful. We'll go to Barribault's, and you'd better wash yer face, my girl. It's a mass of smuts. Makes yer look as if yer'd blacked up to sing comic songs with a banjo from a punt at Henley Regatta.

17

THE DISCOVERY that a wolf in butler's clothing has with subtle chicanery tricked him out of twenty thousand pounds always affects the precision of a motorist's driving, and this is especially so if he is a motorist who sets as high a value on money as did Roscoe Bunyan. It was not long after setting out for Valley Fields that Roscoe, his thoughts elsewhere, ran his Jaguar into a telegraph pole, inflicting internal injuries so severe that he had to walk back to Shipley Hall and get the station wagon. It was consequently somewhat late when he and Mortimer Bayliss arrived at Castlewood and were admitted by Augustus Keggs.

Keggs showed no surprise at seeing them. It had occurred to him that he might shortly be receiving a visit from the son of his old employer. He admired and respected Mortimer Bayliss, but he knew him to be a man incapable of keeping a good joke to himself. The incursion of the Shipley Hall party found him, therefore, prepared, and he was all amiability and old-world courtesy, in sharp contradistinction to Roscoe, who resembled a volcano about to spread molten lava over the countryside while thousands flee. He conducted the visitors to his cozy living room, and put a green baize cloth over the canary's cage, so as to ensure an absence of background music, always so disturbing at anything in the nature of a board meeting. Nobody could have been more suave. Even when Roscoe, finding speech, called him six deleterious names, the mildest of which was "fat swindler," he continued to look like a particularly saintly bishop.

"I had anticipated a certain show of displeasure on your part, sir," he said equably, "but I am sure Mr. Bayliss will agree with me that nothing is to be gained by recrimination."

Mortimer Bayliss was in edgy mood. He resented being snatched away from the dinner to which he had been looking forward for several hours. He regarded Roscoe sourly, thinking, as he so often thought, what a degenerate scion he was of old J. J., whom in spite of numerous faults he had rather liked. J. J. Bunyan had been an old pirate, and his business ethics had often made the judicious grieve, but there had been a spaciousness about him reminiscent of some breezy buccaneer of the Spanish Main. There was nothing spacious about Roscoe. He was, in Mortimer Bayliss' opinion, a mean-souled young twerp.

"Quite right," he snapped. "This is a business conference."

Roscoe quivered in every chin.

"You expect me to be polite to the oily old thug after he's pulled a fast one like that?"

"You can't blame him for getting a bit of his own back. I told you you would be sorry for trying to fob him off with a measly fifty pounds. It hurt his feelings."

"It did indeed, sir," said Keggs, looking reproachfully at Roscoe, like a bishop who has found his favorite curate smoking marijuana. "Fifty pounds in return for all that I was doing for you, sir. It wounded me deeply."

"Well, now you've wounded him deeply, so you're all square and can start again from scratch. And for heaven's sake," said Mortimer Bayliss, "let's get a move on, because I want my dinner. I take it that you are now prepared to reveal the real name of the mystery man who is his fellow survivor in the Bayliss Matrimonial Tontine?"

Here Mr. Bayliss thought it advisable to give Augustus Keggs a long, steady look, a look that said as plain as whisper in the ear "Tell him you told me, and I'll strangle you with my bare hands." Much as he enjoyed baiting Roscoe, the nature of their relations made it injudicious to alienate him beyond hope of forgiveness, as must inevitably happen, were that thrifty young man to learn that a word from him, Bayliss, would have saved him twenty thousand pounds and that that word had not been spoken. Roscoe, whatever his shortcomings as a human being, was the owner of the Bunyan Collection and, as such, in a position to dispense with the services of its curator.

Keggs, already shown in this chronicle as an expert diagnostician of starts and snorts, was equally competent as an interpreter of long, steady looks. He had no difficulty in reading the message that was flashing from the black-rimmed monocle. If he had been a shade less dignified, one might have described the quick, slight flutter which disturbed his left eyelid as a wink.

"Certainly, sir," he said, "if suitable terms can be arranged."

"What's your idea of suitable terms?"

"A hundred thousand dollars, sir."

Roscoe had already drained the bitter cup so deeply that one might have supposed that an extra sip would not have affected him very much, but these words brought him out of his chair as if, in Lord Uffenham's powerful phrase, shot from a gun. His appearance and manner were those of a short-tempered whale which has just received a harpoon in a tender spot.

"What! Why, you—"

"Please, sir!" said Keggs.

"Please, Roscoe!" said Mortimer Bayliss. "We shall get nowhere, if you start interrupting. A hundred thousand dollars you think, Keggs? Cash down?"

"Oh, no, sir. What I had in mind was five thousand pounds in advance and the remainder when the proceeds of the tontine are in Mr. Roscoe's possession. I feel that I deserve some small recompense for my information."

A tremor ran through Roscoe, the sort of tremor that precedes a major earthquake.

"Small? SMALL? A hundred thousand dollars!"

"The customary agent's fee of ten per cent, sir."

"You—"

"Please, sir!"

"Please, Roscoe!" said Mortimer Bayliss. "Yes, I call that reasonable. If I'd been you, I'd have held out for halves. You do see, Roscoe, that he's got you in a cleft stick? Unless financially assisted, this other fellow won't get married for years and years, if ever. Who knows that he may not suddenly get a gleam of sense and realize that the only life is that of the bachelor? And you can't assist him financially if Keggs doesn't tell you who he is. You have your checkbook, I know, because you never move without it. Give him his five thousand."

"And have him tell me the wrong name again?" Roscoe laughed a mirthless laugh. "I see myself!"

Mortimer Bayliss nodded.

"One appreciates the difficulty. You get it, Keggs? If you tell him the name before you have the check, he'll double-cross you and give you nothing, and until you tell him, he won't part. It begins to look like an impasse."

"If I might be permitted to suggest a way out of the difficulty, sir. The name is one familiar to you, and you will recognize its authenticity. If I were to whisper it to you in confidence—"

"Excellent idea. Solves everything. Go ahead, Keggs. Whisper and I shall hear . . . *Really?*" said Mortimer Bayliss with an exaggerated show of interest, as he took out a cambric handkerchief and dried his ear. "Well, well, well! It's all right, Roscoe, this is the goods."

While Roscoe sat plunged in gloomy thought, this way and that dividing the swift mind, like Sir Bedivere, Keggs went to the writing desk and took from one of its pigeonholes a sheet of paper. Placing it on a salver, for old butlerian habits were still strong, he presented it to Mortimer Bayliss.

"Hoping that Mr. Bunyan might think well of my proposition, sir, I prepared a form of agreement, which only needs his signature to become legal. If you would care to glance at it?"

Mortimer Bayliss took the document, and screwed the monocle more firmly into his eye.

"You will see that it sets out quite clearly the circumstances and conditions, Mr. Bayliss."

"Very clearly. Is this a professional job?"

"No, sir, I did it myself with the assistance of *Every Man His Own Lawyer.*"

"Excellent bit of work. Come on, Roscoe. Out with the checkbook. But wait. I see the same objection we ran up against last time. How does he give Mr. X the money?"

"Very simply, sir. Mr. Bunyan is the owner of the Bunyan collection, of which you are curator. The young gentleman is in the art business."

"And so?"

"It would be perfectly understandable for Mr. Bunyan to offer him the post of assistant to yourself at a large salary, possibly with the proviso that he would prefer to employ a married man in that position. He might go so far as to hint that it would not be long before the young gentleman succeeded to your place as curator, you being old and past your work."

"Here!"

"Merely a ruse, sir."

"You may call it that. I call it blasphemy. Well, I get the idea, but it seems tough on the poor fish. He'll give up his job and get married, and then Roscoe will immediately fire him."

"No, sir. Obviously there would have to be a definite written agreement guaranteeing employment for a number of years."

"One of those *Every Man His Own Lawyer* things of yours?"

"Precisely, sir. Otherwise the young gentleman would not have the feeling of security necessary if he is to assume the responsibilities of matrimony."

"Or, in other words, feel safe in getting married?"

"Exactly, sir."

"You think of everything, don't you?"

"I endeavor to do so, sir."

Mortimer Bayliss waved a hand in the spacious gesture of the man who is disposing of somebody else's money.

"Come on, Roscoe. Upsy-daisy. Sign here."

"Eh?"

"Sign this paper, and you will hear who your rival is and all about him, and then perhaps for God's sake I'll be able to go off and get something to eat."

18

A PLEASANT time was had by all at Barribault's excellent grill room, Lord Uffenham, his spirits at their peak now that the dark menace of Stanhope Twine had been removed, being the life and soul of the party. From the opening slice of smoked salmon to the final demitasse he enchanted his audience, holding them spellbound with his tales of moving accidents by flood and field and hairbreadth 'scapes i' the imminent deadly breach in company with old Jacks and Joes and Jimmies of his distant youth. Though not all of them were 'scapes, for one of his best stories told how he and someone called old Sammy on Boat Race night of the year 1911 had been taken by the insolent foe and on the following morning fined forty shillings at Bosher Street police station.

It was getting late when the Uffenham-Hollister-Benedick group of revelers drew up in Bill's car outside the front gate of Castlewood, and their arrival coincided with the breaking up of the business conference. As they alighted, Keggs, having deposited check and contract in the drawer of his writing desk, was just escorting his visitors to the station wagon.

The well-nourished appearance of the Barribault trio gashed Mortimer Bayliss, who was now suffering the extreme of hunger, like a knife. It thrust on his mind thoughts of steaks and chops and juicy cuts off the joint, and in a rasping undertone he urged Roscoe, who was exchanging civilities with Lord Uffenham, for the love of Pete to cut it short and come along. But Roscoe had other views.

"Could I have a word with you, Hollister?" he said, and drew Bill aside.

Jane and Lord Uffenham went into the house. Mortimer Bayliss sat huddled in the station wagon, thinking of Hungarian goulash, and Roscoe spoke earnestly to Bill. And presently Lord Uffenham, curled up in his chair with his *Wonders of Bird Life,* saw his nephew-by-marriage-to-be enter, his face shining with a strange light.

"How right you were!" said Bill.

Lord Uffenham knew that he was always right about everything, but he was interested to learn to what particular exhibition of his rightness his young friend alluded.

"Which time was that?" he asked.

"When you said something would turn up. You saw Roscoe Bunyan buttonhole me just now?"

"Yerss, I saw him. Piefaced feller, that Bunyan."

"I wish you wouldn't call him piefaced."

"He *is* piefaced."

"I know, but I wish you wouldn't say so, for you are speaking of the man I love."

"He's a Tishbite."

Bill was always reasonable.

"I admit he *looks* like a Tishbite," he agreed, "but beneath that Tishbitten exterior there is a sterling nature. He's just given me the most stupendous job."

"Yer don't say?" Lord Uffenham was impressed. "Must be good in the blighter, after all. I withdraw the word Tishbite." He paused, reflecting. "But not the word piefaced," he added. "Howjer mean a job? What sort of job?"

"One of the very finest. Let me take you step by step through our conversation. He started by asking me if I had ever thought of leaving the Gish Galleries."

"To which yer replied?"

"That I had thought of it many a time and oft, but had always been deterred by the fear that, if I did, I might not be able to secure those three meals a day which are so essential to the man who wants to keep the roses in his cheeks. And then he tore off his whiskers and revealed himself as my guardian angel. Mortimer Bayliss, he said, is becoming senile and past his work, and how would I like to sign on as his assistant, eventually to take over the curatorship of the Bunyan collection."

"The what?"

"Roscoe's father, the late J. J. Bunyan, had one of the best collections of pictures in the world, and Roscoe inherited it. But let me tell you more. Having said this, he then named a salary—as a starter, mind you, just as a starter—which took my breath away. I'm rich!"

"Lord love a duck!"

"Rich enough, anyway, to support a wife who can do the cooking. I shall have to get busy, though. I've got to sail for America in a few days."

"With Jane?"

"Well, of course with Jane. Good heavens, you don't think I'm going to leave her behind. How soon can one get married?"

"Like a flash, I believe, if yer get a special license."

"I'll get two, to be on the safe side."

"I would. Can't go wrong, if yer have a spare." Lord Uffenham was silent for a moment. He seemed deeply moved. "Did yer know," he said at length, "that the herring gull, when it mates, swells its neck, opens its beak and regurgitates a large quantity of undigested food?"

"You don't say? That isn't a part of the Church of England marriage service, is it?"

"I believe not. Still," said Lord Uffenham, "it's an interesting thought. Makes yer realize that it takes all sorts to make a world."

Roscoe Bunyan and Mortimer Bayliss, meanwhile, having driven off in the station wagon, had stopped it—at the latter's request—outside the Green Lion in Rosendale Road and had gone into that hostelry's saloon bar to eat cold ham. Mortimer Bayliss would have preferred caviar *frais, consommé aux pommes d'amour, suprême de fois gras au champagne, timbale de ris de veau Toulousiane* and *diablotins,* but, like Lord Uffenham, he could, when necessary, take the rough with the smooth. It would perhaps be too much to say that when they resumed their journey to Shipley Hall, he was a ray of sunshine, but his mood had certainly changed for the better. He had leisure now to remember that Roscoe had just been separated from another five thousand pounds and had pledged himself legally to disburse a hundred thousand dollars, and this was a very stimulating thought. A little more of this, he was feeling, and the heir of the Bunyan millions would be growing so spiritual that his society would be a pleasure.

As they passed through the Shipley front door, Skidmore appeared.

"Excuse me, sir," said Skidmore. "Would you wish to speak to a Mr. Pilbeam?"

"Pilbeam?" Roscoe started. "Is he here?"

"No, sir. He rang up on the telephone while you were absent. He left his number."

"Get through to him," said Roscoe eagerly. "I'll take the call in the smoking room."

"Very good, sir."

"And bring me a cheese omelet and a pot of coffee and lots of toast and some of that fruit cake we had yesterday," said Mortimer Bayliss.

He was in the morning room, waiting for these necessaries, when Roscoe came in. His eye was bright, his manner animated.

"Pilbeam's got them," he announced.

"Oh?" said Mortimer Bayliss, wrenching his thoughts away from the coming meal. "Who is Pilbeam, and what has he got?"

"I told you about him. The fellow who runs the Argus Enquiry Agency. I hired him to get back those letters of mine."

"Ah, yes. From your fiancée Eulalie Morningside or whatever her name is?"

"Elaine Dawn."

"Is that her real name?"

"I suppose so."

"I don't. I'll bet it's Martha Stubbs or something. So he's got them, has he? And now, I take it, you will notify the unfortunate girl that it's all off?"

"Of course."

"Love's young dream!" he said. "We old bachelors will never understand it. You Romeos seem able to turn your affections on and off as if you were manipulating a faucet. It's only a week ago that you were raving to me about her. You said she was wonderful. Why the devil don't you marry the girl?"

"And lose that million?"

"What do you want with another million? You don't need it."

"Talk sense," said Roscoe.

Mortimer Bayliss forbore to press the point. The door had opened, and the cheese omelet had arrived.

19

THE ARGUS Enquiry Agency, whose offices are in the southwestern postal district of London, had come into being some years previously to fill a long-felt want—a want on the part of Percy Pilbeam, its founder, for more money. Starting out as editor of that celebrated weekly scandal sheet, *Society Spice*, he had wearied after a while of nosing out people's discreditable secrets for a salary, and had come to the conclusion that a man of his gifts would be doing far better for himself nosing out such secrets on his own behalf. Having borrowed some capital, he had handed in his portfolio, and was now in very good shape financially. It was the boast of the Argus that it never slept, and this, felt those who knew it, was, if it possessed a conscience, not surprising. Few would have been able to sleep with what the Argus Enquiry Agency had on its mind.

In engaging a private investigator, the prudent man sets more value on astuteness than on physical beauty, and in the case of the guiding spirit of the Argus this was fortunate, for though it was possible that there may have been more repellent human bloodhounds in London than Percy Pilbeam, they would have taken a considerable amount of finding. He was a small, weedy, heavily pimpled young man with eyes set too close together, whose flannel suit looked like a Neapolitan ice and whose upper lip was disfigured by a wispy and revolting mustache. The over-all picture he presented as Roscoe entered his office on the following morning was one calculated to jar on the sensitive eye, but to Roscoe, so profound was his relief that the fatal papers had been recovered, he looked quite attractive. He took the little packet of stationery with uplifted heart.

"Swell!" he said sunnily. "How did you manage to get them?"

Percy Pilbeam ran a pen airily through his brilliantined hair.

"Easy. She has to be at the theater every night. I waited till she had gone, got in, hunted around, found the letters and got out again. It was simple. Well, when I say simple," said Pilbeam, belatedly thinking of the bill he would be sending in, "it wasn't by any means. There was great risk involved. And of course the nervous strain."

"Oh, you wouldn't mind that," said Roscoe, also thinking of the bill. "Not a man of your experience. You told me you were always doing that sort of thing."

"Nevertheless . . . I beg your pardon?"

"Eh?"

"You said something."

This was inaccurate. Roscoe had not spoken, he had given a sudden gurgle, and he had gurgled suddenly because a thought had come like a full-blown rose, flushing his brow. It was not often that he received anything in the nature of an inspiration, for his brain moved as a rule rather sluggishly, but one had come to him now, and it had shaken him to the soles of his shoes.

Even the most stolid have their dreams, and ever since his visit to Castlewood visions had been rising before Roscoe's eyes of somehow getting that contract away from Keggs and tearing it up, thus drawing the subtle butler's fangs and rendering him no longer a force for evil. And he had thought of a capital way of doing this, plan complete in every detail. The only objection to it was that to carry it out called for nerve, and his own nerve was insufficient. He needed an ally, and it had suddenly occurred to him that in Pilbeam he had found one.

"Look," he said. "I want you to take on another job for me."

"What kind?"

"The same kind."

"You mean you've written some *more* letters?"

There was surprise in Pilbeam's voice, and also something not very far from awed admiration. This would make the third lot of compromising letters penned by this client, a so far undisputed record. Even baronets, so notoriously lax in their moral outlook, had been content with two.

Roscoe hastened to dispel the idea that he had been setting up a mark for all other takers of pen in hand to shoot at.

"No, no, it isn't letters this time. It's a paper, a document."

"The Naval Treaty?" said Pilbeam, who had his lighter moments.

"It's a sort of agreement."

Pilbeam began to understand.

"I see. Something you signed?"

"Yes."

"And you want to get out of it?"

"That's it. And the only way to get out of it is to—"

"Pinch it? Quite. Yes, I see that. And if I follow you correctly, you are suggesting that I do it?"

"Yes."

"H'm."

"It would be perfectly easy," said Roscoe persuasively. "The man who's got it is a fellow named Keggs. He used to be my father's butler years ago, and he's retired now and lives in Valley Fields. He owns some house property down there. All you would have to do is call on him and say you come from me and you're looking for a house and has he anything that would suit you. He'll probably be tickled to death, because I happen to know that the man who had one of his houses has just come into a lot of money and is sure to be leaving. Well, that gets you into the place, and when he brings out the drinks—he's bound to bring out drinks—you slip a kayo drop into his, and there you are. Simple as falling off a log," said Roscoe encouragingly. He looked at the other in rather a pained way. "Why," he asked, "do you say 'H'm'?"

It took Pilbeam but an instant to explain why he had said "H'm."

"I was wondering why, if it's as simple as all that, you don't do it yourself," he said nastily.

Roscoe hesitated. The question had put him in something of a difficulty. His actual reason for not wishing to revisit Castlewood was one he preferred to keep from the man whom he was hoping to send there as his representative. At one point in the business conference which had culminated in the signing of the contract, a bulldog of ruffianly aspect had looked in at the door, coughed in a menacing way and gone out. It had seemed to Roscoe, who was timid with dogs, that the animal, just before withdrawing, had given him a look as menacing as its cough, and nothing would have induced him to risk encountering it again. (Actually, George had coughed to attract the attention of the occupants of the room in case any of them had cake to dispose of, had been told by his sixth sense that there was no hope of cake, and had gone off to try to find Jane, who was usually good for a handout. The menace of his parting look had existed purely in Roscoe's imagination.)

"He would be on his guard against me," he said, inspired. "I'd never get to first base. But he wouldn't dream there was anything wrong about you."

This was plausible, and Pilbeam recognized it as such. Nevertheless he shook his head. The scheme as outlined by Roscoe did not offend his moral sense, for he had not got one, but it struck him as too hazardous for comfort. At a never to be forgotten point in his search of Miss Dawn's apartment the doorbell had suddenly rung, and he had distinctly felt his heart leap from its base and crash into his front teeth. He shrank from a repetition of that experience.

He mentioned this to Roscoe. Roscoe pooh-poohed his qualms.

"But, good Lord, man, this wouldn't be like that. You wouldn't be breaking in. You'd just be paying an ordinary call."

Pilbeam continued to shake his head.

"Sorry . . ." he was beginning, when Roscoe went on.

"I'd be prepared to pay something special."

Pilbeam's head ceased to shake. He wavered. Just as Roscoe liked making another million, so did he enjoy being paid something special.

"What is this agreement you speak of ?" he asked, interested but refraining from committing himself.

"Oh, just an agreement," said Roscoe. His native prudence forbade him to tell all. The private investigator who learns that he is saving a client a hundred thousand dollars is a private investigator who puts his prices up.

"What does it look like?"

"It's just a paper. He put it in an envelope and wrote something on the outside—'Agreement' or 'Contract' or '*In re* R. Bunyan, Esquire,' I suppose, or something like that. And then he locked it away in a drawer of the writing table."

Pilbeam reflected. His sales resistance was weakening.

"So it would not mean a long search?"

"You would lay your hands on it in half a minute. Just break open the drawer. Nothing else to it."

"If I were caught breaking open a drawer in someone else's house, I'd be sent to prison."

"Rather pleasant places, prisons, these days, they tell me."

"*Who* tell you?"

"Oh, one hears it around. Movies, concerts, entertainments, all that sort of thing. Besides, who could catch you?"

"Who else is in the house?"

"Lord Uffenham and his niece."

"There you are, then."

Roscoe refused to admit that there he was.

"Perfectly easy to get rid of them. Make it Saturday, and I'll send the old boy a couple of tickets for a matinee. That'll fix it. Nobody ever refuses free theater tickets."

Pilbeam fondled his distressing little mustache for a moment. Then he asked the question Roscoe had been hoping he would not ask.

"How about dogs?"

Roscoe hesitated. Then he saw that there was nothing for it but to come clean. All might well be lost, were this private invesitgator to find himself, unprepared, confronted with that bulldog. He judged others by himself, and he himself, if he had been rifling a drawer in a strange house and a bulldog had happened along, would have dropped everything and run like the wind. Concealment was useless. Now it must be told.

"There is a dog," he admitted.

"What sort of dog?"

"A bulldog."

"H'm."

"Very friendly animals, bulldogs, I believe."

"If you believe that, you'll believe anything. I knew a man who got mixed up with a bulldog, and he had to have seven stitches."

Inspiration came to Roscoe for the second time that morning.

"I'll tell you what I'll do," he said. "If you will go and attend to this man Keggs on Saturday afternoon, I'll go there on Friday night and give the dog a chunk of doctored meat."

Pilbeam frowned. Stoutly though those who knew him would have denied it, he had certain scruples. He did not look human, but he was not without human feelings.

"I don't like poisoning dogs."

"Oh, I wouldn't *poison* him. Just give him something that would make him take to his bed next day. Any vet will tell me the right dose."

"How would you contact this dog?"

"No difficulty about that. He's sure to be out in the garden this fine weather. I know the man who lives next door. I'll go and see him and drop the stuff over the fence." He paused, eyeing his companion pleadingly. "So you will do it, won't you?"

Pilbeam sat plunged in thought. Almost Roscoe had persuaded him. He liked this dog sequence. Unquestionably it would make his path straight. And he knew Roscoe to be a man of many millions, well able to pay for his whims.

"I'll do it for a thousand pounds, cash down," he said, and a sharp pang shot through Roscoe, not unlike a twinge of sciatica.

"A thousand pounds?"

"Didn't I speak distinctly?" said Pilbeam coldly. His sensitive soul resented anything in the nature of haggling.

Once more, as had happened at the business conference, Roscoe found himself in the unpleasant position of sipping the bitter cup. He had no choice but to agree, but mentally he was totting up the roster of the sprats which he was being compelled to distribute in order to catch the whale, and their number and bulk appalled him.

"You wouldn't feel like doing it for a hundred, would you?" he asked wistfully.

Pilbeam said he would not.

"A thousand pounds is a lot of money."

"Quite," said Pilbeam, jauntily massaging the third pimple from the the left on his right cheek. "That's why I like it."

20

IN STATING that no one ever refused free seats for the theater, Roscoe Bunyan had shown a firm grasp of human psychology. The matinee tickets, arriving at Castlewood by the first post on Friday, were received with the utmost enthusiasm. Lord Uffenham, though abating no whit of his opinion that their donor was piefaced, commended him heartily for his kindly thought, saying that it was dashed civil of the young blighter, and even Jane had to admit that in the years that had passed since their mixed bathing days at Meadowhampton Roscoe must have improved out of all knowledge. Joy, in short, on the Friday might have been said to reign supreme.

But on Saturday morning the sun went behind the clouds, for tragedy hit the home. Lord Uffenham, going to George the bulldog's basket to rout him out for his pre-breakfast airing, found him inert, his nose warm, his manner listless, his stump of a tail with not so much as a quiver in it. The dullest eye could perceive that the dumb chum was seriously below par, and Lord Uffenham lost no time in summoning his colleagues for a consultation.

"Jayun!"

"Hullo?"

"Keggs!"

"M'lord?"

"Cummere. Something wrong with George."

Gravely the three gathered at the sickbed. Lips were pursed, heads shaken. "Oh, George, my precious angel!" cried Jane, and "Most extraordinary," said Keggs, as indeed it was, for until now the invalid's health had always been of the robustest. His reputation was that of a dog able to eat tenpenny nails and thrive on them.

Approving their concern but feeling that it did not go far enough, Lord Uffenham struck the practical note, and became executive.

"Keggs!"

"M'lord?"

"Where's the nearest vet?"

"Offhand I could not say, m'lord, but I could ascertain by consulting the classified telephone directory."

"Go and do it, my dear feller."

"And make it snappy," said Jane. "Of course," she went on, as Keggs departed on his errand of mercy, "this dishes our theater party."

"Hey? Why?"

"Well, we can't go off and leave poor George on a bed of pain. We'll have to scratch the binge."

"Nonsense. Can't waste theater tickets. You go, I'll stay with George. Go and give Fred Holloway a buzz—"

"Hollister."

"Holloway or Hollister, the point is immaterial. Get him on the phone and tell him to take you to this bally theater."

"But it seems so selfish."

"Hey?"

"Leaving you here. You were looking forward to your little treat."

"Not a bit of it. Just as soon stay at home with my book."

"Couldn't Mr. Keggs look after George?"

"Wouldn't be equal to it. George needs a father's care. He will have to be chirruped to, and I doubt if Keggs is any good at chirruping. You do as I tell you."

"Well, all right, if you say so."

"You'll enjoy an afternoon out with your young man."

"I shall," said Jane, with conviction.

The morning passed. The veterinary surgeon called, diagnosed George's complaint as stomachic, giving it as his opinion that he must have picked up something poisonous, and went away assuring them that rest and a light diet and the mixture every three hours would in time effect a cure. Bill arrived in his car and took Jane off to lunch and the theater. And Lord Uffenham and George settled down for the afternoon, the former in his chair with *Wonders of the Bird World,* the latter in his basket with a woolly rug over him. And all was quiet on the Castlewood front till about half past four, when a young man in a Neapolitan ice suit and blue suede shoes turned in at the front gate and rang the door bell. It was Percy Pilbeam, up and coming.

Right-minded people cannot, of course, but look askance at Percy Pilbeam, for his was a code of ethics that left much to be desired, and yet those of tender heart must surely, we think, find that heart bleeding a little for the unfortunate private investigator as he walks so gaily into this house of peril, supposing it to be unoccupied except for Augustus Keggs. As he stands there, waiting for the bell to be answered and stroking his regrettable mustache, no thought is in his mind of a two-hundred-and-ten-pound Viscount lurking on the premises.

Had all gone according to plan, here should have been a complete absence of two-hundred-and-ten-pound Viscounts, but as we have seen, all had not gone according to plan. It just proves, if proof were needed, that the best-laid plans of mice and men gang oft agley. The poet Burns, it will be remembered, has commented on this.

The door opened.

"Mr. Keggs?" said Pilbeam.

"Yes, sir."

"Good afternoon. I was sent by Mr. Bunyan, who tells me he is an old friend of yours. I am looking for a house down here, and he thought you might have one that would suit me."

"Yes, indeed, sir," said Keggs, who had learned that morning from Stanhope Twine that Peacehaven would no longer be required by him. "If you will step this way."

"Charming spot, Valley Fields," said Percy Pilbeam. "I ought to have come here years ago."

"The loss is ours, sir," said Augustus Keggs courteously.

For Lord Uffenham the afternoon had passed not unpleasantly. He had finished *Wonders of the Bird World,* done quite a bit of chirruping to George, smoked a mild cigar and dozed off for half an hour or so. At five o'clock, George having fallen into a refreshing sleep and seeming able now to carry on under his own steam without a father to watch over him, he wandered out into the garden for a breath of air.

Among the first things that met his eye in the garden was a handsome snail, and he stood staring at it with unblinking gaze, his always inquiring mind concentrated on the problem of how snails, handicapped as they are by having no legs, manage nevertheless to get from point to point at so creditable a rate of speed. The one under advisement, though not a Roger Bannister, was unmistakably on its way somewhere and going all out, and he sought in vain for an explanation of his nippiness. He was still brooding on the mystery when Mortimer Bayliss appeared.

Mortimer Bayliss, though inclined to be brusque with his fellow men, was not without his softer side, and he had taken a great liking to Lord Uffenham, who reminded him of an elephant on which, when a boy, he had often ridden at the Bronx Zoo. He wished him well and was sorry that he had had to tell him the bad news about those pictures. A nasty knock it must have been, he felt, for the poor old buster to learn that what he had in his gallery and had hoped to raise money on was not the work of Gainsborough and Constable but of Wilfred Robinson and Sidney Biffen. When, therefore, a more detailed inspection revealed some quite decent stuff that had unaccountably been overlooked by the previous five Viscounts, it was with something of the feeling of a Boy Scout about to do his day's act of kindness that he had climbed into Roscoe's Jaguar, now happily recovered from its ailments, and driven to Castlewood to bring him the welcome tidings.

"Oh, there you are," he said, coming into the garden. "I've been ringing the bell, but nothing happened. Is everybody dead in this lazar house?"

"Hey?" said Lord Uffenham, emerging from his trance. "Oh, hullo, Banstead. Ringing, did yer say? Odd Keggs didn't hear yer. Asleep, I suppose. He takes a nap in the afternoon. I've been watching a snail."

"Always watch snails," said Mortimer Bayliss approvingly. "It is the secret of a happy and successful life. A snail a day keeps the doctor away."

"You ever pondered on snails?"

"Only intermittently, if at all."

"I was wondering how they get around the way they do. Look at this one. Breezing along like a two-year-old with its chin up and its chest out. How does it do it without any legs?"

"Will power, I should imagine. You can't keep a good snail down. Well, you're probably wondering why I'm here, though no doubt delighted to see me. I came to tell you that things aren't as bad as I gave you to understand when I saw you at Shipley that day. Those pictures. Some of them, I find, are all right."

"Worth money?"

"Quite a good bit."

"Well, that's capital. That's excellent. Things are certainly looking up. My luck's in. Ever noticed how everything seems to go right, when yer luck's in? You met my niece the other night, didn't yer—?"

"For a moment. Charming girl."

"Yerss, not so dusty. Well, until that night she was all tied up with about the worst piece of cheese in Valley Fields. But no longer. She's seen the light and is now engaged to that splendid feller Holloway."

"Hollister."

"Everybody keeps saying Hollister. Suppose I've got the name wrong. I sometimes do. I remember now he's a friend of yours."

"I've known him all his life."

"Fine young chap."

"One of the best. I curse him for the good of his soul, but I love him like an uncle. Pity he's so hard up."

"But he isn't. That's what I was going to tell yer. That feller Bunyan's given him an excellent job."

"He has? Well, well, well! Very altruistic young man, Roscoe Bunyan. Always doing these kindnesses." A cackle escaped Mortimer Bayliss. "So he's given him a job, has he?"

"Yerss. Something to do with some picture collection he owns."

"Assistant to the curator?"

"That's right, and guaranteed him the curator job as soon as he can get rid of the present chap. The present chap's no good."

"No good, eh?"

"No. Gone all senile, I gather. Ah well, none of us get younger."

"Thank goodness."

"Hey?"

"What hell it would be, if we did. Think of the risks you run of getting married when you're young."

"That's true," said Lord Uffenham, who all through his early twenties had been in constant peril.

"No young man is safe. By the mercy of Providence I managed to stay single in my hot youth, but it was a near thing once or twice, and I wouldn't care to have to go through it again. How well I remember that awful, haunting fear that at any moment some unguarded word would land me in the Niagara Falls hotel with rice dropping off me. I am speaking, of course, of the days when I still had hair and teeth and was known as Beau Bayliss, the days when a flick of my finger meant a broken heart. Yes, I got through, but few are as lucky as I was. If I had my way, marriage would be forbidden by law."

"Wouldn't the human race die out?"

"Yes, and what a break that would be for everybody. Think of a world without any Bunyans in it."

"Yer don't like Ronald Bunyan?"

"I do not."

"Nor me. Bit of a gumboil, I should describe him as. He was down here yesterday evening. I saw him in the garden next door. He was chatting with George over the fence."

"Who's George?"

"My bulldog. He's not well today."

"Who would be after chatting with Roscoe Bunyan? I've had two weeks of him, and it has aged me a dozen years. It must sadden you to think of a fellow like that at Shipley."

"Yerss. Unpleasant, losing yer old home. Not that I'm not comfortable here."

"Odd that you should be living cheek by jowl with my friend Keggs."

"Not so particularly odd. He used to be my butler."

"Oh, I see. That would, of course, bring you very close together. How do you split up the house?"

"He has the ground floor, and Jane and I the upstairs. It's like two separate flats. Works very well. Come and have a look at his quarters. He'll be glad to show yer round. He's very proud of the way he's fixed himself up, and I don't blame him. He's as snug as a bug in a rug."

They went round the angle of the house. Mortimer Bayliss paused to pick a flower. Lord Uffenham, reaching the French windows, halted abruptly,

stared, his lips moving in a silent "Lord love a duck!" and came tiptoeing
back to his companion, who was putting the flower in his buttonhole.

"Hey!" he whispered.

"Got laryngitis?" asked Mortimer Bayliss.

"No, not laryngitis."

"Then why are you talking like a leaky cistern?"

Lord Uffenham put a warning finger to his lips.

"I'll tell yer why I'm talking like a leaky cistern," he said, still speaking in
that conspiratorial whisper. "There's a bally burglar in there!"

21

VERY FEW things were able to disconcert Mortimer Bayliss. The monocle in
his eye did not even quiver.

"A burglar, eh?" he said, as if he had ordered one from the stores and was
glad to learn that it had arrived safely.

"That's right. Keggs is lying on the floor, out like a light, and there's a
horrible bounder at the desk, going through his effects. I didn't know burglars
ever burgled in the daytime," said Lord Uffenham with the disapproval
which men of orthodox outlook always show when their attention is drawn to
any deviation from the normal. "Always had the idea they only came out
after dark."

"You're thinking of dramatic critics. What sort of burglar is it?"

Lord Uffenham found himself puzzled, as any man might be when called
on to supply a word portrait of a marauder.

"How d'yer mean, what sort?"

"Big? The large economy size?"

"No, small."

"Then come on," said Mortimer Bayliss with enthusiasm. There was a
spade beside the flower bed in which on the previous evening, wishing to
discpline his figure, Lord Uffenham had been doing a little digging. "What
are we waiting for? Let's go!"

And so it came about that Percy Pilbeam, in the act of thrusting into his
pocket a Manila envelope inscribed with the words "*In re* R. Bunyan, Esq.,"
experienced once more that unpleasant sensation of having his heart leap
into his mouth and loosen a front tooth. He had supposed himself to be
alone—except for Keggs, who hardly counted—and lo, of a sudden a voice,
sounding to his sensitive ear like that of Conscience, shattered the afternoon
stillness with a stentorian "Hey!" Just the sort of thing the voice of Conscience might have been expected to say.

He whirled on his axis, hastily gulping his heart down again. There, looming massively inside the French windows, stood the largest man he had ever seen and, accompanying him, a friend and well-wisher holding a substantial spade. The day was warm, but cold shivers ran down his spine. He felt, gazing upon these twain, that their attitude foreboded violence, and violence was a thing which, for he was not one of your tough Marlowes or Mike Hammers, he feared and disliked. In the hope of easing a difficult situation, he smiled what was intended to be an ingratiating smile, and said, "Oh, hullo."

It had the worst effect.

"Hullo to you, with knobs on," retorted Lord Uffenham curtly. He turned to Mortimer Bayliss as to one on whose sympathy he knew he could rely. "He grins," he said, a querulous note in his voice. "We catch him burgling the house, catch him red-handed, as the expression is, and he *grins*. He says 'Oh, hullo,' and GRINS. Like a ruddy Cheshire cat. Have that spade ready, Banstead."

Percy Pilbeam, as if about to have his photograph taken, moistened his lips with the tip of the tongue. His brow was wet with dishonest sweat.

"I'm not burgling," he bleated weakly.

Lord Uffenham clicked his tongue. He did not mind hearing people talk poppycock, but it must not be utter poppycock.

"Don't be silly. If yer don't call it burgling to sneak into a feller's sitting room and lay him out cold with a blunt instrument and loot his bally desk, there are finer-minded men who do. Stick tightly to the spade, Banstead, we may be needing it at any moment."

Mortimer Bayliss was bending over the form on the floor, examining it with an experienced eye. In what he had called his hot youth he had often seen fellow customers in saloons lying on floors like that, and he knew the procedure.

"Not a blunt instrument," he said. "The impression I get is that my old friend has been slipped a knockout drop."

"Hey?"

"I don't believe you see much of them in England, but in America, notably in New York down Eighth and Ninth Avenue way, and particularly on Saturday nights, you might say they are common form. Did you slip him a knockout drop, blot?"

"Answer the question," thundered Lord Uffenham, as the blot hesitated coyly. "Yes or no?"

"Er—yes."

Lord Uffenham snorted.

"You see! A full confession. What shall we do with him? Break him into little bits? Or shall I beetle round to the police station and gather in a constable or two?"

Mortimer Bayliss was silent for a space, weighing the question. Then he spoke, and his words were music to Percy Pilbeam's ears.

"I think we might let him go."

Lord Uffenham started. He stared incredulously. His bulging eye was like that of a tiger to whom the suggestion has been made that it shall part with its breakfast coolie.

"Let him *go*?"

"After a few simple preliminaries. I remember reading a story once," said Mortimer Bayliss, adjusting his monocle, "that has always stuck in my mind. It was about a burglar who burgled a house and the owner caught him and held him up with a gun and made him take all his clothes off and then showed him politely out of the front door. It struck me as an excellent idea."

"A most admirable idea," assented Lord Uffenham warmly. He was remorseful that for an instant he had wronged this splendid fellow in thought. "Nothing could be more suitable."

"Good for a laugh, I think?"

"Dashed amusing. Very droll. What was it you called this bounder just now?"

"A blot?"

"That's right. Off with your clothes, blot."

Percy Pilbeam quivered like an aspen. There rose before him the picture of Roscoe Bunyan assuring him that he would find this house unoccupied, and a wave of anti-Roscoe sentiment flooded over him. Few men with pimples have ever felt more bitter toward a man with a double chin.

"But—" he began.

"Did I hear you say 'But'?" said Lord Uffenham.

"Yes, don't say 'But,' " said Mortimer Bayliss. "We want willing service and selfless co-operation. The trousers first, I think."

Lord Uffenham was musing, a finger to his cheek.

"Here's a thought, Banstead. Why not paint him black?"

"Have you black paint?"

"Plenty."

"It would look very pretty," said Mortimer Bayliss thoughtfully. "Yes, I can see him with a coat of black paint."

"Could I have a drink?" said Percy Pilbeam.

He spoke pleadingly, and Lord Uffenham, though in stern mood, saw no reason why justice should not be tempered with mercy to this small extent. He waved hospitably at the table where the siphon and decanter stood, and Pilbeam tottered to it and poured himself a brimming beaker.

"Or green?" said Lord Uffenham, and was about to inform his friend that he possessed green paint as well as black and to ask him if he did not think Pilbeam would look better in green—snappier, dressier, better in every way—but at this moment his remarks were interrupted by the receipt between the eyes of two thirds of a long whisky-and-soda. It gave him the passing sensation of having been caught in an explosion at a distillery.

In delineating Percy Pilbeam, we have stressed that he was neither brave nor beautiful, but we have shown him also, we fancy, as a young man with plenty of brains and one capable of thinking quickly in an emergency. He had thought quickly now. To fling his beverage in Lord Uffenham's face and dart to the French windows had been with him the work of an inspired instant. A whirring noise, and he was out in the open and going like the wind.

Riper years and a chronic stiffness in the joints prevented Lord Uffenham and Mortimer Bayliss from answering his challenge with a similar burst of speed. They, too, passed into the open, but their progress, when there, could not have been compared to even the gentlest breeze. They moved slowly and jerkily, like rheumatic buffaloes, and it is not surprising that on arrival at the front gate, they should have found a total shortage of private investigators. Pilbeam had gone, leaving not a wrack behind. All they saw was Bill and Jane standing by Bill's car, gazing interestedly down the road.

"Who," Bill asked, becoming aware of their presence, "was the jack rabbit?"

"Something in a striped suit came whizzing past us," said Jane.

"Wearing pimples with a red tie," said Bill. "A mistake, I think. One or the other, but not both."

Jane gave a sudden squeak of concern.

"Uncle George! You're wet."

"I know I'm wet," said Lord Uffenham morosely. "Who wouldn't be, with burglars drenching them with whisky-and-sodas all the time? I'm going in to change. Might catch a nasty cold."

He went moodily into the house, and Jane turned to Mortimer Bayliss.

"Burglars?" she said. "Was there a burglar?"

"There was, indeed. I took up this spade to quell him. Now that he is no longer here to be quelled, I'll be putting it back," said Mr. Bayliss, and went off to do so.

"Burglars!" said Jane. "Just imagine."

"Valley Fields for excitement."

"You ought to be saying 'There, there, little woman' and putting your arms about me and telling me to fear nothing, for you are here."

"A very admirable suggestion," said Bill.

Behind them somebody coughed. Keggs was standing there, his face contorted with pain. He had a severe headache, and even that soft cough had accentuated it.

"Oh, hullo, Mr. Keggs," said Bill. "We were—er—just discussing the wedding arrangements."

"I should not advocate an immediate wedding, sir," said Keggs sepulchrally.

22

IN THE mind of Augustus Keggs when, waking like Abou ben Adhem from a deep dream of peace, he found that he had acquired the headache of a lifetime and lost the Manila envelope inscribed "*In re* R. Bunyan, Esq.," there had been at first not unnaturally a certain disorder, but from the welter of confused emotions two coherent thoughts stood out. One was the intention to go to the drugstore in Rosendale Road, if he could navigate so far, and get the most powerful pick-me-up the man behind the counter could provide; the other a stern resolve to be revenged upon Roscoe Bunyan for the outrage he had perpetrated, an outrage so dastardly that few international gangs, however tough, would have cared to include it in their programs.

For that the hidden hand behind both headache and robbery had been that of Roscoe he had not for an instant doubt. When a man with a mustache and pimples calls on a retired butler saying that he has been sent by Mr. Bunyan, and proceeds to doctor the retired butler's drink and purloin the contract whereby Mr. Bunyan has pledged himself to pay the retired butler a hundred thousand dollars, the retired butler, unless very slow at the uptake, is able to deduce and form his own conclusions. He sees in what direction the evidence points and in compiling his list of suspects knows where to look.

So now, with a view to foiling Roscoe's plans and aims, Keggs, though he would have preferred to go straight to Rosendale Road for that pick-me-up, halted on seeing Bill, and said, "I should not advocate an immediate wedding, sir."

And while Bill stared at him, his eyes narrowing as our eyes are so apt to do when we are confronted with a speaker whom we suspect of having had a couple, he added, "If I might have your attention for a moment, Mr. Hollister."

Both Shakespeare (William) and Pope (Alexander) have stressed the tediousness of a twice-told tale, and a thrice-told tale is, of course, even worse. At two points already in this chronicle the story of Mortimer Bayliss' matrimonial tontine has been placed before the reader, and anyone so intelligent must, one feels, by this time have got the idea. No need, accordingly, to report Keggs's words verbatim. Sufficient to say that on this occasion, though hampered by shooting pains that started at the soles of his feet and got worse all the way up, he placed the facts before Bill and Jane as lucidly as some days earlier he had placed them before Roscoe Bunyan. And he found an audience equally receptive. Bill, as the narrative proceeded, stared at him dumbly. So did Jane. Then, as he concluded his remarks, they stared at each other dumbly.

"You mean," said Bill, transferring his popeyed gaze to Keggs, "that if I get married, I lose a million dollars?"

"If at the time of your embarkation on matrimony Mr. Roscoe is still single, yes, sir."

"And he's not even engaged, as far as I know."

"No, sir."

It was some days since Bill had drawn one of those deep breaths of his, but he drew one now. A man to whom the skulduggery of a Roscoe Bunyan has been suddenly revealed in all its naked horror is entitled to draw a deep breath or two.

"So that was why he gave me that job! To put me out of the running."

"Exactly, sir. It was a ruse or scheme."

"The hound!"

"Yes, sir."

"The heel!"

"Yes, sir."

"The slimy, slithering serpent!"

"Precisely, sir," said Keggs, in cordial agreement with the view that Roscoe Bunyan shared the low cunning and general lack of charm of the reptile he had mentioned. "Mr. Roscoe sticks at nothing, as one might say. Even as a growing lad, so I am informed by friends who remained in the service of the late Mr. Bunyan, his behavior was characterized by the same lack of scruple. At the age of fifteen he was expelled from his school for lending money to his fellow students at ruinous rates of interest. The child," said Keggs, "is the father of the man."

"The child should have been drowned in a bucket at birth," said Bill severely. "Then he wouldn't have become a man. But will anyone adopt these simple home remedies nowadays? Oh, no. Old-fashioned, they say, and what's the result? Roscoe Bunyan. Eh?"

"I merely said 'Ouch!' sir. I have a somewhat severe headache. I was about to go to the chemist's in the hope of procuring some specific that might alleviate it."

Oh? Then we mustn't keep you. I know what it is to have a headache. This bombshell of yours has given me one. Off you go."

"Thank you very much, sir," said Keggs, and with a hand pressed to his throbbing brow passed painfully on his way, headed for Rosendale Road and its pick-me-ups.

He left behind him a stunned silence. It was Bill who finally broke it.

"Well, that's that," he said. "Too bad. I'd have liked a million dollars."

Jane looked at him, wide-eyed.

"Bill! What do you mean?"

"Well, wouldn't anyone?"

"You aren't going ahead with the wedding *now*?"

"Of course I am. I've got to take this job of Roscoe's. I turned in my resignation to Gish the day before yesterday. I have to sail to America on Wednesday."

"But you don't have to get married first."

Bill stared.

"Are you suggesting that I leave you behind?"

"It would only mean waiting a little."

"A *little?*" Bill barked derisively. "You don't know R. Bunyan. Now he's on to it that he'll lose a million dollars if he gets married, he won't get married till he's seventy, if then. Pretty silly we should look, going on year after year, you here, me in America, exchanging picture postcards and waiting hopefully for Roscoe to walk down the aisle with a gardenia in his buttonhole."

"But think of the plans we made, all the things we were going to do if we ever had money. Don't you remember, that day at Barribault's? You were going to take up your painting again, and I was going to get Shipley back for Uncle George."

"I know, I know. Well, I'll have to do without my painting, and Uncle George will have to do without Shipley. Good heavens, young fathead, what do you think would happen to me, if I went off to America and left you here? I'd go steadily crazy. I'd be thinking all the time of all the sons of bachelors who were flocking round you, trying to get you away from me."

"You know I'd never look at another man."

"Why not? I'm nothing special. Just one of the swineherds, and not the best of them by any manner of means."

"One of the *what?*"

"In the fairy stories you read as a child. Surely you used to read fairy stories where the princess fell in love with the swineherd? The point I am making is that there you would be, surrounded by princes, all doing their damnedest to de-swineherd you, and after a time you'd be bound to wonder if it was worth while going on waiting for William Hollister."

"You are speaking of William *Quackenbush* Hollister?"

"The same."

"Well, I wouldn't wonder anything of the sort. I'd wait for you through all eternity, Bill, you old ass, and you know it."

"Yes, you think that now, but would you feel the same at the end of the first five years, with Roscoe still sitting tight and cannily refusing offers of marriage on all sides? I see you weakening. I see you saying to yourself, 'Who is this bird Hollister, anyway? Where does he get off, expecting to—' "

" '—take the best years of my life'?"

"Exactly. No, sir! You'll come with me on Wednesday, like a good girl, and to hell with all tontines."

Jane's eyes were glowing.

"Oh, Bill! Am I really worth a million dollars to you?"

"More. Considerably more. Any man who gets a girl like you for a mere million bucks has driven a shrewd bargain."

"Oh, *Bill!*" said Jane, and Keggs, returning some minutes later from his travels, found himself compelled to cough once more.

23

BUT THIS time the cough brought no attendant anguish with it. It is pleasant to be able to record that Augustus Keggs's confidence in the man behind the counter at the Rosendale Road Drugstore had not been misplaced. The fellow knew his pick-me-ups. He was good. He had taken a little of this from one bottle, a little of that from another bottle, added dynamite and red pepper, and handed the mixture to his suffering client, and it was not long before the latter, reassured that a hydrogen bomb had not, as at the outset of the proceedings he had feared, been exploded in his interior, was able to return to his cozy living room almost as good as new.

He found Lord Uffenham there. In flannel trousers and a sweater which might have been built to order by Omar the Tent-maker, the now dry Viscount was brooding ponderously over the bowl of goldfish.

"Ants' eggs," he said, as Keggs entered. "Why ants' eggs? Hey?"

"M'lord?"

"I've been wondering how the dickens goldfish acquired a taste for ants' eggs."

"They like them, m'lord."

"I know they like them. What I'm saying is, How did they come to like them? In their natural, wild state I don't see how they could ever have established contact with ants. Lord love a duck, man, you don't suppose the ancestors of these goldfish used to come ashore and roam the countryside hoping to find an ant hill where they could help themselves to a dish of eggs, do you? Oh, well, there it is," said Lord Uffenham philosophically, and turned to another aspect of life among the ants. "Did yer know they run quicker in warm weather?"

"M'lord?"

"Ants. When the weather's warm, they run quicker."

"Indeed, m'lord?"

"So I read somewhere. In the summer months they clip quite a bit off their winter time and dash all over the place like billy-o. Which reminds me. There was someone on the phone for you just now. A Mrs. Billson. Name convey anything to you?"

"My sister, m'lord."

"Oh, your sister? I was forgetting yer had a sister. I had three at one time," said Lord Uffenham with modest pride. "Well, she wants you to call her."

During the rather lengthy period of Keggs's telephoning Lord Uffenham continued to brood, first over the goldfish and then over the canary in its cage. The canary was eating groundsel, a thing his lordship would not have done on a bet, and, absorbed in his meditations on the bird's peculiar tastes, he heard nothing of what was going on in the corner of the room where the instrument stood. Had he been at liberty to give the conversation his attention, he would have gathered that the speaker at the Valley Fields end was getting some disturbing news over the wire. A dark flush had come into Keggs's face, and the hand that held the receiver was shaking.

Presently Lord Uffenham, wearying of the canary—and no wonder, for it definitely lacked sustained dramatic interest—went back to the goldfish. And he was just thinking how extraordinarily like one of them was to that aunt of his in Shropshire at whose house his old guv'nor had once made him go and stay, when he was jerked from his meditations by a sharp exclamation, and turned, mystified. It seemed almost inconceivable that one of Augustus Keggs's poise and dignity should have used violent language, but that was what it had sounded like.

"What did yer say?" he asked, blinking.

"I said, 'Damn and blast his eyes,' m'lord," replied Keggs respectfully.

"Eh? Who?"

"Mr. Bunyan, m'lord."

"Oh, that feller? What's he been doing?"

Keggs struggled with his emotion for a space. Then he regained self-control. A butler, toughened by years of listening to employers telling the same funny story night after night at the dinner table, learns to master his feelings.

"It has come as a complete surprise to me, m'lord, but it appears that Mr. Bunyan was engaged to be married to my niece Emma." Here his feelings momentarily got the better of him again, and he added the words "Curse him!" "One of those secret betrothals, m'lord. Her mother learned of it only this morning."

Lord Uffenham was mystified. He could detect nothing in the news that might have been expected to cause so pronounced a spiritual upheaval in this uncle. Most uncles, it seemed to him, knowing that Roscoe Bunyan had a matter of twenty million dollars in the old sock, would have wished that they had half his complaint.

"Engaged to yer niece, is he? Well, sooner her than me, but I should have said it was a dashed good match for the girl. Piefaced though he is, he's well fixed. Surely you know that the feller has more money than you can shake a stick at?"

"Certainly, m'lord. Mr. Bunyan must be among our wealthiest bachelors."

"Then why are yer standing there blinding and stiffing about it?" asked Lord Uffenham, completely at a loss.

Once again the intensity of his emotions was almost too much for Augustus Keggs. It was impossible for a man of his build to sway like a daffodil in a March wind, but he unquestionably swayed to a certain extent. There was a dangerous light in his gooseberry eyes, and when he spoke it was with a guttural intonation rather like that of the bulldog George when he got a bone stuck in his throat.

"My niece Emma has just been in telephonic communication with her mother, m'lord, to inform her that Mr. Bunyan has broken the engagement."

Lord Uffenham saw all. He could understand now why this old employee of his was seething like a newly opened bottle of ginger pop. In the other's place he, too, would have seethed. His quick sympathies were aroused.

"The dirty dog. Let yer niece Emma down, has he? Gave your niece Emma the push, did he? Odd thing is, I didn't know yer *had* a niece Emma."

"I fancy that if I ever mentioned her to your lordship, it would have been by her nom de tayarter. She acts under the name of Elaine Dawn."

"Oh, I see. On the stage, is she?"

"Precisely, m'lord, and weighing the pros and cons, she came to the conclusion that as Emma Billson she would be handicapped in her career. Something more euphonious seemed indicated."

"Yerss, possibly she was right. Though there was Lottie Collins."

"Yes, m'lord."

"And Florrie Ford—and Daisy Wood. Simple enough names, those."

"Very true, m'lord, but the ladies you mention were singers in the music halls. Emma's art is of a more serious nature. She is in what theatrical journals term the legit. When Mr. Bunyan made her acquaintance, she was playing a small role in a translation from the Russian."

"Oh, my God! An aunt of mine once made me take her to one of those. Lot of gosh-awful bounders standing around saying how sad it all was and wondering if Ivan was going to hang himself in the barn. Don't tell me that Roscoe Bunyan, a free agent, goes to see plays translated from the Russian."

"No, m'lord. He did not witness Emma's performance. They met at a party."

"Ah, now your story becomes more plausible. I know what happens at parties. He asked her to marry him?"

"Yes, m'lord."

"Did he write her any letters to that effect?"

"Several, m'lord."

"Then what's she worrying about? Lord love a duck, my dear feller, she's on velvet. She can sue him for breach of promise and skin him for millions."

"No, m'lord." A brief spasm shook Keggs. Of all sad words of tongue or pen, he seemed to be saying to himself, the saddest are these—It might have been. "On going this morning to the drawer where she kept Mr. Bunyan's letters, she found they had disappeared."

"Weren't there, yer mean?"

"Precisely, m'lord. Obviously an emissary of Mr. Bunyan had obtained clandestine access to her apartment in her absence and purloined the communications in question."

It took Lord Uffenham some moments to work this out, but eventually he unraveled it and was able to translate it from the butlerese. What the man was trying to say was that some low blister, bought with Bunyan's gold, had sneaked into the girl's flat and pinched the bally things. His whole chivalrous nature was stirred to its depths by the outrage.

"The louse!"

"Yes, m'lord."

"The ruddy Tishbite!"

"Yes, m'lord."

"She mustn't take this lying down."

"It is difficult to see what redress the unhappy girl can have."

"She could dot him in the eye."

"It would be but a poor palliative for her distress of mind."

"Well, *someone* ought to dot him in the eye. Wait!" said Lord Uffenham, holding up a hamlike hand. "An idea's coming. Let me think." He paced the room for a while. It was plain that that great brain was working. "Hey!" he said, halting in mid-stride.

"M'lord?"

"Didn't yer tell me once that that brother-in-law of yours used to be a professional scrapper?"

"Yes, m'lord. He fought under the sobriquet of Battling Billson."

"Good, was he? Tough sort of bloke?"

"Very, m'lord. I have a photograph of him, if your lordship would care to glance at it."

He went to a closet under the window and returned with a large album. Turning pages adorned with photographs—here an impressionistic study of himself as a callow young footman, there a snapshot of a stout lady heavily swathed in the bathing costume of the eighteen-nineties, labeled "Cousin Amy at Llandudno"—he came at last to the one he sought.

It was plainly a wedding group. Beside a chair, dressed in billowy white, stood a buxom girl with hair like a bird's nest and barmaid written all over her. In her left hand she held a bouquet of lilies of the valley, her right she rested lovingly on the shoulder of the man who was sitting in the chair.

The first thing the beholder noticed about this man was his size. Lord Uffenham was no pigmy, but beside the bridegroom in this photograph he would have seemed one. The fellow bestrode the narrow chair like a colossus. Impressed by his bulk and turning to a closer scrutiny, the eye was then arrested by his face, which was even more formidable. He had a broken nose, his jaw was the jaw of the star of a Western B-picture registering Determination, and beneath that wedding frock coat one could discern the rippling muscles. He was sitting with a clenched fist on each thigh, bending forward slightly as if to get a better view of an opponent across the ring. The whole effect was that of a boxer waiting for the opening bell, with his manager—female in this case—giving him a last pep talk before he came out fighting. It impressed Lord Uffenham profoundly.

"That's him, is it? The wench's father?"

"Yes, m'lord."

"Then I see daylight," said Lord Uffenham. "I see where we go from here."

24

THE MORNING following Pilbeam's visit to Castlewood found Roscoe Bunyan in radiant spirits. A telephone call from the private investigator as he breakfasted had informed him that the latter's mission had been carried out according to plan, and it was with a light heart that he stepped on the accelerator of his Jaguar and started off for London.

Giving his name to the gentlemanly office boy in the outer room, he was ushered without delay into the Pilbeam sanctum, and found the proprietor of the Argus Enquiry Agency seated at his desk, busy with papers of private eyeful interest. He looked up as his visitor entered, but there was no reflection in his aspect of the sunniness which was filling Roscoe. He was austere and cold.

"Oh, it's you?" he said distantly.

"Yes, here I am," said Roscoe, marveling not a little that on this morning of mornings the pimpled bloodhound should not have got more of the holiday spirit.

"A nice thing you let me in for yesterday," said Pilbeam, shivering for a moment, as memory did its work. "You told me that house would be empty."

"Wasn't it?"

"No, it was *not*. Let me tell you what happened."

The ability to tell a good story well is not given to all, but it was one which his fairy godmothers had bestowed on Percy Pilbeam in full measure. Nothing could have been clearer or more dramatic than his *resumé* of the Saturday afternoon's doings in that house of terror, Castlewood, Mulberry Grove, Valley Fields. It was like something particularly vivid from the pages of Edgar Allan Poe. And though both Lord Uffenham and Mortimer Bayliss might have taken exception to his description of their physical peculiarities and their misbehavior, even they would have had to admit that the picture he drew was an impressive one.

When he had finished, Roscoe agreed that all that could not have been at all pleasant, and Pilbeam said No, it had not been. Thrice in the night, he said, he had woken up shaking like a jelly, having dreamed that the ordeal was still in progress.

"Still," said Roscoe, indicating the bright side, "you got the paper."

"I did," said Pilbeam. "*And* read it."

Roscoe started violently.

"You mean you opened the envelope?"

"That's what I mean."

"Well, you had no right to."

Percy Pilbeam lowered the pen with which he had been combing the eastern end of his mustache.

"Sue me," he said briefly.

There was a rather tense silence for a moment. But Roscoe was feeling too uplifted to brood for long on this lapse from professional etiquette.

"Oh, well, I don't suppose it matters," he said, remembering that the bill had already been paid. "Where is it?"

"In the safe."

"Gimme."

"Certainly," said Pilbeam, "as soon as you have given *me* your check for two thousand pounds."

Roscoe reeled.

"What!"

"You should buy one of these hearing aids. Two thousand pounds, I said."

"But I paid you.'

"And now you're going to pay me again."

"But you promised me you would do the job for a thousand."

"And you promised me," said Pilbeam coldly, "that there would be nobody in that house but Keggs and a sick bulldog. Sick bulldog, my left foot. The place was congested with hulking human hippopotami and men with spades, and they wanted to take my clothes off and paint me black. Naturally, our original agreement, made under the supposition that I would have a clear field, is null and void. The extra two thousand is for moral and intellectual damage, and I'm going to have it."

"That's what you think."

"That's what I know."

"You do, do you?"

"Yes, I do."

"I won't give you a cent," said Roscoe.

Pilbeam, who during these exchanges had suspended the curling of his mustache, took up the pen again and ran it meditatively through the undergrowth, attending this time to the mustache's western aspect. He looked at Roscoe reproachfully, and one could see that his trust in the fundamental goodness of human nature had been shaken.

"So after all I went through to save you from having to give Keggs a hundred thousand dollars," he said, "you refuse to pay me a measly two thousand pounds?"

"That's right," said Roscoe.

Pilbeam sighed, a disillusioned man.

"Well, suit yourself," he said resignedly. "I've no doubt Keggs will think the paper worth that to him."

The room swam before Roscoe's eyes. He seemed to be seeing the other through a flickering mist which obscured his outlines and made him almost invisible. But though anyone would have told him that that was much the pleasantest way of seeing Percy Pilbeam, he drew no comfort from this.

"You wouldn't do that?"

"Who says so?"

"You'd give it to Keggs?"

"*Sell* it to Keggs," corrected Pilbeam. "I'm sure I should find him a good customer. A levelheaded sort of man he seemed to me."

"This is blackmail!"

"I know. Criminal offense. There's the phone, if you want to call the police."

"Keggs'll do that. He'll have you arrested."

"And lose a hundred thousand dollars? He won't have me arrested. He'll lay down the red carpet for me."

Roscoe had shot his bolt. He had gone out of his class, he realized, and had come up against an intelligence so superior that he was as a child in its presence. There seemed to him nothing to do but to accept defeat as gracefully as possible.

Then there flashed into his mind a healing thought. Checks could be stopped.

"All right," he said, "you win." He drew out the checkbook which was his constant companion. "May I borrow your pen?"

Pilbeam removed the pen from the hair on top of his head, to which some moments ago he had transferred it.

"Here you are. And now," he said, taking the check, "I'll just ask you to come with me to the bank while I cash this. They won't pay a large sum like two thousand pounds across the counter without your okay. And then we'll come back and I'll give you that paper and we'll all be happy."

It would be an overstatement to say that Roscoe, as he drove back to Shipley Hall half an hour later, was happy, but by the time he turned in at the Hall's gates the bitter cup, to which his lips were becoming so accustomed these days, had begun to taste a little better. Nothing, of course, could make the expenditure of two thousand pounds actually enjoyable, but by concentrating his mind on the fact that the Keggs-Bunyan contract was now a little pile of ashes in Percy Pilbeam's wastepaper basket he was able to bear up. If all was not for the best in this best of all possible worlds, it was at any rate considerably better than it might have been. A glance at the score sheet showed him that he was well ahead of the game. He would have preferred not to have been compelled to go in quite so largely for sprats, but the salient point that emerged was that he had caught the whale.

He braked the Jaguar at the front door, and went into the house. Skidmore was in the hall.

"A Mr. and Mrs. Billson have called, sir," said Skidmore.

25

EVER SINCE rising from his bed that morning, Mortimer Bayliss had been feeling depressed and irritable. Most unwisely, when replacing the spade in the flower bed, he had dug a few tentative digs with it, and this had brought on an attack of lumbago, causing him to look on life with a jaundiced eye. It was one of those reminders, which came so frequently nowadays, that he was not as young as he had been, and he resented anything that interfered with his mental picture of himself as a sprightly juvenile. As he stood in the gallery at Shipley Hall, staring moodily at one of the works of Sidney Biffen's middle period, there floated into his mind the somber words of Walter Savage Landor:

> I warmed both hands before the fire of life.
> It sinks, and I am ready to depart

and suddenly there came upon him the realization that he could not endure another day of Roscoe Bunyan's society.

Business connected with the Bunyan collection had brought him to Shipley, but that business being now concluded there was no reason why he should continue to be cooped up with one whom he had disliked as a boy and disliked even more heartily now that a too tolerant world had permitted him to survive to the age of thirty-one. Everything about Roscoe offended him—his face, his double chin, his conversation and his habit of employing private investigators to the undoing of fiancées and ex-butlers.

For it was clear to him, now that he had had time to think it over, that the hand of Roscoe had been behind yesterday's incursion into Castlewood of that striped-suited marauder with the mustache. It had puzzled him at the time why any burglar, unless fond of goldfish and aspidistras, should have thought it worth while to burgle Keggs's living room, but if one assumed him to have been a minion of Roscoe's, hired by Roscoe to make away with that contract, his actions became intelligible.

Roscoe, he felt, was a man in whose presence it was impossible for a self-respecting art expert to go on breathing, and he was hobbling to the bell to ring it, with a view to starting his preparations for leaving, when Skidmore appeared.

"Excuse me, sir," said Skidmore. "Could you see Mr. Keggs?"

A flicker of interest lightened the gloom of Mortimer Bayliss' gnarled face. Augustus Keggs was the one person whose society at the moment he felt equal to tolerating. They had much to talk about together.

"Is he here?"

"He arrived some little while ago in his car, sir, with a lady and gentleman."

"Then send him up. And pack."

"Sir?"

"My belongings, oaf."

"You are leaving Shipley Hall, sir?"

"I am. It stinks, and I am ready to depart."

When Keggs entered, nursing his derby hat, his aspect smote Mortimer

Bayliss like a blow. Misery loves company, and he had been looking foward
to getting together with a fellow invalid with whom he could swap symptoms.
To see the man in glowing health—positively rosy, in fact—was a sad
disappointment.

"You seem to have recovered," he said sourly. "I should have thought you
would have had a headache this morning."

"Oh, no, sir."

"No headache?"

"No, sir, thank you. I am in excellent fettle."

"Too bad. Ouch!"

"You are feeling unwell, sir?"

"Crick in the back. Lumbago."

"A painful ailment."

"Most. But never mind about me. Nobody ever does. I have yet to meet the
man who gives a damn what happens to poor old Bayliss. If I were being torn
limb from limb by a homicidal gorilla and a couple of fellows who knew me
came along, one of them would say, 'Don't look now, but Mortimer Bayliss is
over there being torn limb from limb by a gorilla,' and the other would reply,
'You're absolutely right. So he is,' and they would go off to lunch. Well, what
brings you here, Keggs? Yesterday's excitement in the home?"

"My visit is connected with that, yes, sir."

"I suppose when you came out of your swoon, you found the contract gone
and realized that the boy friend had swiped it on behalf of Roscoe?"

"Immediately, sir."

"And now you have come to plead with him to do the square thing and
give you at least a little something of his plenty? Not a hope, my good Keggs,
not a hope. Conscience will never make Roscoe part with a nickel."

"So I had anticipated, sir. It was not with any intention of appealing to Mr.
Bunyan's better feelings that I made the journey here. I came to escort my
sister and her husband, who are now closeted with Mr. Bunyan in the
smoking room. It was Lord Uffenham's suggestion that I should bring them
here for a conference. They are the parents of the young woman to whom Mr.
Bunyan was until recently betrothed. My niece Emma."

"What on earth do you suppose they can do?"

"His lordship was sanguine that a visit from them would accomplish
something in the nature of a desirable settlement."

A kindly, almost tender look came into the eye behind Mortimer Bayliss'
black-rimmed monocle. He was feeling a gentle pity for this man who
seemed so completely out of touch with the facts of life.

"But, Keggs," he said, and there was a pleading note in his voice, the sort of
note that creeps into a man's voice when he is trying to reason with the
half-witted, "the minion who stole that contract of yours also stole the letters
Roscoe wrote to the girl, promising marriage. She's as helpless as you are."

Keggs shook his head, a thing which before visiting the wizard of Rosendale Road he could not have done without causing it to split into two equal halves and shoot up to the ceiling.

"His lordship was inclined to think not. He took the view that Wilberforce—"

"Eh?"

"My brother-in-law, sir. His lordship took the view that Wilberforce might conceivably persuade Mr. Bunyan to change his mind and do the right thing by our Emma. And he was not astray in his judgment. When I left them a moment ago, Mr. Bunyan had quite come round to the idea of an immediate wedding."

It took a good deal, as has been shown, to dislodge the monocle from Mortimer Bayliss' eye, but at these words it shot from its base and leaped at the end of its string like a lamb gamboling in springtime.

"He had . . . *what*?"

"Sir?"

"Come round to the idea of an immediate wedding, did you say? He's going to marry the girl?"

"By special license."

"In spite of having got back the letters?"

"Precisely, sir."

Mortimer Bayliss hauled in the slack and replaced the monocle in his eye. It was almost an unconscious reflex action, for he was feeling dazed.

"Your brother-in-law must be very eloquent," he said.

Keggs smiled a gentle smile.

"I would not call him that, sir. He seldom speaks. My sister Flossie does all the talking for the family. But Wilberforce was at one time a professional boxer, operating in the heavyweight division."

A gleam of light penetrated Mortimer Bayliss' darkness. Dimly he began to see.

"Battling Billson was the name under which he appeared in the roped arena. He is a little elderly now, of course, but still vigorous. At his public house in Shoreditch the clientele, as is so often the way with the proletariat in the East End of London, is inclined to become obstreperous toward closing time, and my sister tells me that Wilberforce thinks nothing of engaging in combat half a dozen or more costermongers or representatives of the Merchant Marine simultaneously, always with complete success. His left hook, I understand, still functions as effectively as in his prime. And no doubt his mere appearance carried weight with Mr. Bunyan."

"Formidable, is it?"

"Extremely, sir. If one may employ the vernacular, he looks a killer."

A feeling of quiet happiness was stealing over Mortimer Bayliss. For years, he was telling himself, Roscoe Bunyan had been asking for something along these lines, and now he had got it.

"So those wedding bells will ring out?"

"Yes, sir."

"When?"

"Immediately, sir."

"Well, that's fine. I congratulate you."

"Thank you, sir. I have never been fond of Mr. Roscoe myself, but it is pleasant to think that my niece's future is provided for."

"How much would you say Roscoe has? Twenty million?"

"About that, I should imagine, sir."

"Nice money."

"Extremely nice, sir. Emma will like having it at her disposal. And there was one other thing."

"What's that?"

"I have drawn up a fresh contract to take the place of the one purloined from my apartment. Flossie, when I left the smoking room, was just going into the matter with Mr. Bunyan and by this time I have no doubt will have overcome any reluctance on his part to sign such a document. If you would be kind enough to come to the smoking room and witness it, as before, I should be greatly obliged. It is possible," said Keggs, forestalling an anticipated objection, "that you may be thinking that, with Mr. Roscoe planning to enter upon matrimony at so early a date, the contract will be valueless, marriage automatically ruling him out of the tontine. But I have a suggestion which I fancy would make things satisfactory for all parties concerned."

"You have?"

"Yes, sir. Why should not Mr. Bunyan and Mr. Hollister agree to divide the proceeds of the tontine equally, irrespective of which is the first to marry?"

There was something in Mortimer Bayliss' aspect of the watcher of the skies when a new planet swims into his ken. He started, and for a moment sat in silence, as if savoring the suggestion.

"That never occurred to me," he said.

"Mr. Bunyan, as I see it, would have no option but to agree. No doubt Mr. Hollister is anxious to embark on matrimony at as early a date as possible, but he would scarcely be unwilling to postpone the ceremony for the few days which will elapse before Mr. Roscoe's wedding takes place. This could be pointed out to Mr. Roscoe."

"I'll point it out to him myself."

"It would be a simple matter to draw up a contract binding on both gentlemen."

"Perfectly simple."

"And each would find it equally advantageous. Really, sir, I can see no flaw. It seems to solve everything."

"It does. In the smoking room, did you say your loved ones were?"

"Yes, sir."

"Then let's join them. I am particularly anxious to see this brother-in-law of yours, whose mere aspect has had so hypnotic an effect on our Mr. Bunyan. I can hardly wait. Good Lord!"

"Sir?"

"I was only thinking that if this girl he's marrying is your niece, Roscoe will have to go through life calling you Uncle Joe or whatever it is."

"Uncle Gussie, sir."

Mortimer Bayliss flung his arms up in a gesture of ecstasy. The sudden movement gave him a nasty twinge in the small of the back, but he ignored it.

"This," he said, "is the maddest, merriest day of all the glad new year. I do believe in fairies! I do!"

26

THERE ARE clubs in London where talk is as the crackling of thorns under a pot and it is *de rigueur* to throw lumps of sugar across the room at personal friends, and other, more sedate clubs where silence reigns and the inmates curl up in armchairs, close their eyes and leave the rest to Nature. Lord Uffenham's was one of the latter. In its smoking room this afternoon there were present, besides his lordship and Mortimer Bayliss, some dozen living corpses, all breathing gently with their eyes closed and letting the world go by. A traveled observer, entering, would have been forcibly reminded of seals basking on rocks or alligators taking it easy in some tropical swamp.

The eyes of Lord Uffenham and his guest were at the moment open, but the eyelids were a little weary and both were feeling in need of rest and repose. It taxes the energies of elderly gentlemen to attend a wedding, kiss the bride, and stand waving as the receding car takes the young couple off on their honeymoon. Like the gardenias in their buttonholes, these two were more than a trifle wilted.

Lord Uffenham, moreover, in addition to being physically fatigued, was mentally in a state of turmoil. Recent happenings had left him dazed and bewildered. He was able vaguely to gather that young Fred Holloway, who had hitched up with his niece Jane, had become possessed of approximately half a million dollars, and that of course was all to the good, for he had been assured by Jane that he, Lord Uffenham, was to have his share of these pennies from heaven, but how this very agreeable state of affairs had come about he did not begin to understand. All day he had been bending his brain to the problem and trying to make sense of the explanations which had been given him by Jane, by Bill, by Keggs and by Mortimer Bayliss, and this had made him feel drowsy.

It was consequently only a fleeting attention that he was able to accord to the observations of his companion, who, though also conscious of a certain exhaustion, was talking as fluently as usual.

"Weddings," said Mortimer Bayliss, drawing thoughtfully at his cigar, "always cheer me up. Why is that, Bayliss? I'll tell you. They give me that feeling of quiet satisfaction which comes to an explorer in the jungle who sees the boa constrictor swallow the other fellow, and not him. I look at the bridegroom and I say to myself, 'Well, they've got that poor mutt, Mortimer, but they haven't got you, Mort, old sport,' and my heart leaps up as if I had beheld a rainbow in the sky. Are you awake?"

"M-m-m-m-m," said Lord Uffenham.

"Mind you, I am quite aware, of course, that there are eccentrics who enjoy getting married. The recent Hollister, for instance, was obviously feeling no qualms as they sprang the trap on him. He gloried in his predicament. But, as I was telling you the other day, I have always regarded the holy state with the gravest concern. As a young man, I would sometimes dream that I was being married, and would wake sweating. But each year that passes lessens the peril, and my mind is now tolerably easy. I look at myself in the mirror and I say, 'Courage! With a face like that you are surely safe, Mortimer.' It is a most consoling thought. Are you still awake?"

Lord Uffenham did not reply. He was breathing gently.

"Because, if so, I would like your ruling on a point which has been exercising my mind not a little. Bill Hollister. Would you say that he was one of those honorable young men with rigid ethical standards, not—in short—the sort of young man to stick to money to which he was not entitled, as would be the case with so many of us, like a mustard plaster?"

Lord Uffenham breathed gently.

"That is the impression he has always given me, and I cannot, therefore, but feel that it would be injudicious to let him know the true facts about that matrimonial tontine of mine—to wit, that his father was never in it. You amaze me, Bayliss, tell me more. Certainly. I was just going to. As I told Roscoe, when the whole thing started, one of those dining at J. J. Bunyan's table on that September night in the year 1929 changed his mind next morning and decided to include himself out. That one was Bill's late father. He said he thought the whole idea damned silly and nobody was going to get fifty thousand dollars of his money for nonsense of that sort. In other words, to make it clear to the meanest intelligence—I allude to yours, my dear Uffenham—Roscoe has paid out half a million dollars he didn't have to, in addition to a hundred thousand to Keggs, twenty thousand pounds to Stanhope Twine, and, I imagine, a princely sum to that minion with the pimples. A consummation devoutly to be wished, of course, for, as I have sometimes pointed out, it will make him more spiritual, and he is a man who needs all the spirituality he can get, but a state of affairs at which Bill Hollister, if I read him aright, would look askance. I consider it a certainty that the young sap, if apprised, will insist on handing the stuff back, so the view I take is that he must not be apprised. As the phrase is, he must never know. Sealed lips, I say. What do you say?"

Lord Uffenham did not say anything. He had begun to snore softly, and it became plain to Mortimer Bayliss that of all this nicely reasoned speech he had heard not a single word.

And better so, felt Mortimer Bayliss, far better so. This top secret was one to be locked, if possible, in a single bosom. Viscounts sometimes babble. When in their cups, for instance. He did not know if Lord Uffenham was ever in his cups, but it was quite possible that he might some day chance to get into them and with an unloosened tongue speak the injudicious word.

Sealed lips, thought Mortimer Bayliss, sealed lips. You can't beat sealed lips.

He laid down his cigar. He leaned back in his chair. His eyes closed. And presently his gentle breathing blended with Lord Uffenham's gentle breathing and the gentle breathing of all the other basking alligators in the Mausoleum Club's smoking room.

He slept, the good man taking his rest after a busy day.

The Old Reliable

1

THE SUNSHINE which is such an agreeable feature of life in and around
Hollywood, when the weather is not unusual, blazed down from a sky of
turquoise blue on the spacious grounds of what, though that tempestuous
Mexican star had ceased for nearly a year to be its owner and it was now the
property of Mrs. Adela Shannon Cork, was still known locally as the Carmen
Flores place. The month was May, the hour noon.

The Carmen Flores place stood high up in the mountains at the point
where Alamo Drive peters out into a mere dirt track fringed with cactus and
rattlesnakes, and the rays of the sun illumined its swimming pool, its rose
garden, its orange trees, its lemon trees, its jacaranda trees and its stone-
flagged terrace. Sunshine, one might say, was everywhere, excepting only in
the heart of the large, stout, elderly gentleman seated on the terrace, who
looked like a Roman emperor who had been doing himself too well on
starchy foods and forgetting to watch his calories. His name was Smedley
Cork, he was the brother of Mrs. Adela Cork's late husband, and he was
gazing in a sullen, trapped sort of way at an object which had just appeared
on the skyline.

This was a butler, an unmistakably English butler, tall, decorous and
dignified, who was advancing toward him carrying on a salver a brimming
glass that contained a white liquid. Everything in Mrs. Cork's domain spoke
eloquently of wealth and luxury, but nothing more eloquently than the
presence on the premises of this Phipps. In Beverly Hills, as a general thing,
the householder employs a 'couple,' who prove totally incompetent and leave
the following week, to be succeeded by another couple, equally subhuman. A
Filipino butler indicates a certain modest degree of stepping out. An English
butler means magnificence. Nobody can go higher than that.

"Your yoghurt, sir," said Phipps, like a benevolent uncle bestowing a gift
on a deserving child.

Lost in daydreams, as he so often was when he sat on the terrace in the
sunshine, Smedley had forgotten all about the yoghurt which his sister-in-law
compelled him to drink at this time of the day in place of the more conventional cocktail. He sniffed at the glass with a shrinking distaste, and gave it as
his opinion that it smelled like a motorman's glove.

The butler's manner, respectful and sympathetic, seemed to suggest that he agreed and that there existed certain points of resemblance.

"It is, however, excellent for the health, I believe, sir. Bulgarian peasants drink it in large quantities. It makes them rosy."

"Well, who wants a rosy Bulgarian peasant?"

"There is that, of course, sir."

"You find a rosy Bulgarian peasant, you can keep him, see?"

"Thank you very much, sir."

With a powerful effort Smedley forced himself to swallow a portion of the unpleasant stuff. Coming up for breath, he gave the campus of the University of Southern California at Los Angeles, which lay beneath him in the valley, a nasty look.

"What a life!" he said.

"Yes, sir."

"It shouldn't happen to a dog."

"The world is full of sadness, sir," sighed Phipps.

Smedley resented this remark, helpful though he realized it was intended to be.

"A fat lot you know about sadness," he said hotly. "You're a carefree butler. If you don't like it here, you can go elsewhere, see what I mean? I can't, see what I mean? You ever been in prison, Phipps?"

The butler started.

"Sir?"

"No, of course you haven't. Then you wouldn't understand."

Smedley finished the yoghurt and fell into a moody silence. He was thinking of the will of the late Alfred Cork and feeling how strange and tragic it was that different people should so differently interpret a testator's wishes.

That clause which Al had inserted, enjoining his widow to 'support' his brother Smedley. There you had a typical instance of the way confusion and misunderstanding could arise. As Smedley saw it, when you instruct a woman to support somebody, you mean that you expect her to set him up in an apartment on Park Avenue with an income sufficient to enable him to maintain the same and run a car and belong to a few good clubs and take that annual trip to Paris or Rome or Bermuda or wherever it may be, and so on and so forth. Adela, more frugal in her views, had understood the bequest as limiting her obligations to the provision of a bed, three meals a day and the run of the house, and it was on these lines that her brother-in-law's life had proceeded. The unfortunate man ate well and slept well and had all the yoghurt he wanted, but apart from that his lot these last few years had been substantially that of a convict serving a sentence in a penitentiary.

He came out of his reverie with a grunt. There swept over him an urge to take this kindly butler into his confidence, concealing nothing.

"You know what I am, Phipps?"

"Sir?"

"I'm a bird in a gilded cage."

"Indeed, sir?"

"I'm a worm."

"You are geting me confused, sir. I understood you to say that you were a bird."

"A worm, too. A miserable, downtrodden Hey-you of a worm on whose horizon there is no ray of light. What are those things they have in Mexico?"

"Tamales, sir?"

"Peons, I'm just a peon. Ordered hither, ordered thither, ground beneath the iron heel, treated like a dog. And the bitter part is that I used to have a lot of money once. A pot of money. All gone now."

"Indeed, sir?"

"Yes, all gone. Ran through it. Wasted my substance. What a lesson this should be to all of us, Phipps, not to waste our substance."

"Yes, sir."

"A fool's game, wasting your substance. No percentage in it. If you don't have substance, where are you?"

"Precisely, sir."

"Precisely, sir, is right. Can you lend me a hundred dollars?"

"No, sir."

Smedley had not really hoped. But the sudden desire which had come to him for just one night out in the brighter spots of Los Angeles and district had been so imperious that he had thought it worth while to bring the subject up. Butlers, he knew, salted their cash away, and he was a great believer in sharing the wealth.

"How about fifty?"

"No, sir."

"I'd settle for fifty," said Smedley, who was not an unreasonable man, and knew that there are times when one must make concessions.

"No, sir."

Smedley gave it up. He saw too late that it had been a mistake to dish out that stuff about wasting one's substance. Simply putting ideas into the fellow's head. He sat for a moment scowling darkly, then suddenly brightened. He had just remembered that good old Bill had arrived in this ghastly house yesterday. It altered the whole aspect of affairs. How he had come to overlook such a promising source of revenue, he could not imagine. Wilhelmina ('Bill') Shannon was Adela's sister and consequently his sister-in-law by marriage, and if there was anything in the theory that blood is thicker than water, she should surely be good for a trifling sum like a hundred dollars. Besides, he had known dear old Bill since he was so high.

"Where's Miss Shannon?" he asked.

"In the Garden Room, sir. I believe she is working on Mrs. Cork's Memoirs."

"Right. Thank you, Phipps."

"Thank you, sir."

The butler made a stately exit, and Smedley, feeling a little drowsy, decided that later on would be time enough for going into committee of supply with Bill. He closed his eyes, and presently soft snores began to blend with the humming of the local insects and the rustle of the leaves in the tree above him.

The good man taking his rest.

Phipps, back in his pantry, was restoring his tissues with an iced lemonade. He frowned as he sipped the wholesome beverage, and his air was tense and preoccupied. The household cat brushed itself insinuatingly against his legs, but he remained unresponsive to its overtures. There is a time for tickling cats under the ear and a time for not tickling cats under the ear.

When Smedley Cork, in their conversation on the terrace, had described James Phipps as carefree, he had been misled, as casual observers are so apt to be misled, by the fact that butlers, like oysters, wear the mask and do not show their emotions. Carefree was the last adjective that could fittingly have been applied to the sombre man as he sat there in his pantry, brooding, brooding. If he had had his elbow on his knee and his chin in his hand, he might have been posing for Rodin's *Penseur*.

It was on Wilhelmina Shannon that he was brooding, as he had been doing almost incessantly since he had admitted her at the front door on the previous afternoon. He was cursing the malignant fate that had brought her to this house and asking himself for the hundredth time what, now that she was here, the harvest would be. It was the old, old story. The woman knew too much. His future hung on her silence, and the question that was agitating James Phipps was, were women ever silent? True, the balloon had not yet gone up, which argued his secret was still unrevealed, but could this happy state of things persist?

A bell rang, and he saw that it was that of the Garden Room. Duty, stern daughter of the voice of God, said Phipps to himself, or words to that effect, and left his lemonade and made his way thither.

The Garden Room of the Carmen Flores place was the one next to the library and immediately below the projection room, a cheerful apartment with a large desk beside the French windows that looked on the swimming pool. It caught the morning sun, and for those who liked it there was a fine view of the oil wells over by the coast. Bill Shannon, seated at the desk with the tube of a dictaphone in her hand, was too busy at the moment to look at oil wells. As Phipps had indicated, she was forcing herself to concentrate on the exacting task of composing her sister Adela's *Memoirs*.

Bill Shannon was a breezy, hearty, genial woman in the early forties, built on generous lines and clad in comfortable slacks. Rugged was a term that might have been applied to her face with its high cheekbones and masterful chin, but large, humorous eyes of a bright blue relieved this ruggedness and rendered her, if not spectacularly beautiful like her sister Adela, definitely attractive. Her disposition was amiable, and as a mixer she was second to none. Everybody liked Bill Shannon, even in Hollywood, where nobody likes anybody.

She raised the mouthpiece of the dictaphone and began to speak into it, if 'speak' is not too weak a word. Her voice was a powerful contralto, and Joe Davenport, a young friend of hers with whom she had worked on the Superba-Llewellyn lot, had sometimes complained that she was apt to use it as if she were chatting with a slightly deaf acquaintance in China. It was Joe's opinion that, if all other sources of income failed, she could always make a good living calling hogs in one of the Western states.

"Hollywood!" boomed Bill. "How shall I describe the emotions which filled me on that morning when I first came to Hollywood, an eager wide-eyed girl of sixteen ... Liar! You were nearly twenty ... So young, so unsophisticated. Just a—"

The door opened. Phipps appeared. Bill held up a hand. "—timid little tot," she concluded. "Yes, Phipps?"

"You rang, madam."

Bill nodded.

"Oh, yes. I want to confer with you in your executive capacity, Phipps. What with one thing and another, it has suddenly been borne in upon me that if I don't get a quick restorative, I shall expire. Have you ever written the *Memoirs* of a silent film star?"

"No, madam."

"It is a task that taxes the physique to the uttermost."

"No doubt, madam."

"So will you bring me a fairly strong whisky and soda?"

"Yes, madam."

"You really ought to go around with a keg of brandy attached to your neck, like Saint Bernard dogs in the Alps. No delay that way. No time lag."

"No, madam."

Bill, who had been sitting with her feet on the desk, put them down. She swivelled around in her chair and fixed her bright blue gaze on the butler. This was the first opportunity she had had since her arrival of a private and undisturbed talk with him, and it seemed to her that they had much to discuss.

"You're very curt and monosyllabic, Brother Phipps. Your manner is aloof. It is as though you felt in my presence a certain constraint and embarrassment. Do you?"

"Yes, madam."

"I'm not surprised. It's your conscience that makes you feel that way. I know your secret, Phipps."

"Yes, madam."

"I recognized you the moment I saw you, of course. Yours is a face that impresses itself on the mental retina. And now I suppose you're wondering what I propose to do about it?"

"Yes, madam."

Bill smiled. She had a delightful smile which lit up her whole face as if some inner lamp had been switched on, and Phipps, seeing it, was conscious for the first time since three o'clock on the previous afternoon of a lessening of the weight that pressed upon his heavy soul.

"Not a thing," said Bill. "My lips are sealed. The awful truth is safe with me. So be of good cheer, Phipps, and unleash that merry laugh of yours, of which I hear such good reports."

Phipps did not laugh, for laughter is not permitted to English butlers by the rules of their Guild, but he allowed his lips to twitch slightly and gazed at this noble woman with something approaching adoration, an emotion which he had never expected to feel for a member of the jury which three years before had sent him up the river for what the Press of New York was unanimous in describing as a well-earned sentence. It was a moment or two before he was able to clothe his feelings in words.

"I am sure I am extremly grateful to you for your kindness, madam. You relieve my apprehensions. I am most anxious not to lose my position here."

"Why? You could get a job anywhere. Walk into any house in Beverly Hills, and they'll lay down the red carpet for you."

"Yes, madam, but there are reasons why I do not wish to leave Mrs. Cork's service."

"What reasons?"

"Personal reasons, madam."

"I see. Well, I won't give you away."

"Thank you very much, madam."

"I am only sorry that I have occasioned you alarm and despondency. It must have given you a nasty jolt when you opened that front door yesterday and I walked in."

"Yes, madam."

"You must have felt like Macbeth seeing Banquo's ghost."

"My emotions were somewhat similar, madam."

Bill lit a cigarette.

"Rather odd that you should have remembered me. But I suppose, in the position you were in when we met, you've nothing much to do except study the faces of the jury."

"No, madam. It passes the time."

"Too bad we had to send you up."

"Yes, madam."

"But we couldn't go against the evidence."

"No, madam. But might I beg of you to lower your voice, madam. Walls have ears."

"Walls have what?"

"Ears, madam."

"Oh, ears! That's right. They have, haven't they? What was it like in Sing-Sing?" whispered Bill.

"Not very agreeable, madam," whispered Phipps.

"No, I imagine not," whispered Bill. "Oh, hello, Smedley."

Smedley Cork, his siesta concluded, had appeared in the French window.

Phipps left the the room, followed by the austere and disapproving look which impecunious elderly gentlemen give a butler who has refused to lend them a hundred dollars, and Smedley took a seat on the sofa.

"I want to talk to you, Bill," he said.

"And so you shall, pal. What's on your mind? My God, Smedley," said Bill with the candour of a friend of twenty-five years standing, "you've aged terribly since I saw you last. I was shocked when I got here and observed what a museum piece you had become. Your hair's as grey as a badger."

"I'm thinking of having it touched up."

"It won't do any good. There's only one real cure for grey hair. It was invented by a Frenchman. He called it the guillotine. I suppose it's living with Adela that's done it. I can't imagine anything more calculated to produce silver threads among the gold than constant association with that sister of mine."

Her words were music to Smedley's ears. He basked in her sympathy. Good old Bill, he told himself, had always been sympathetic. So much so that once or twice only that instinct for self-preservation which saves Nature's bachelors in their hour of need had prevented him from asking her to marry him. Occasionally, in black moods, he regretted this. Then the black mood would pass. The mere thought of being married appalled Smedley.

"It's a dog's life," he agreed. "She oppresses me, Bill. I'd be better off in Alcatraz. At least I wouldn't have to drink yoghurt there."

"Does Adela make you drink yoghurt?"

"Every day."

"Inhuman. Of course, it's good for you."

Smedley held up a protesting hand.

"Just as a favour," he begged, "don't mention those Bulgarian peasants."

"Which Bulgarian peasants would those be?"

"The ones it makes rosy."

"Does yoghurt make Bulgarian peasants rosy?"

"So Phipps says."

A deep chuckle escaped Bill Shannon.

"Phipps! If my lips weren't sealed, I could tell you something about Phipps. Ever hear of still waters?"

"What about them?"

"They run deep. That's Phipps. What a man! I suppose you look on him as just the ordinary sort of stage butler. Let me tell you that Brother Phipps has quite another side to him. However, as I say, my lips are sealed, so it's no use you trying to institute a probe."

Smedley was perplexed.

"How do you know anything about Phipps? You only got here yesterday. Had you met him before?"

"I had, and in curious circumstances. But don't ask questions."

"I don't want to ask questions. I'm not interested in Phipps. I'm off Phipps for life. He has hurt and disappointed me."

"You don't say? What was the trouble?"

"I asked him for a small loan just now, and would you believe it," said Smedley, with honest indignation. "he refused. Turned me down flat. 'No, sir,' he said. And the fellow's probably rolling in money. Thank God for people like you, Bill. You wouldn't do that sort of thing. You're big-hearted. You're a pal, as true as steel. Good old Bill! Dear old Bill! Could you lend me a hundred dollars, Bill?"

Bill blinked. Well though she knew Smedley, she had not seen it coming.

"A hundred dollars?"

"I need it sorely."

"Are you planning to go on a toot?"

"Yes," cried Smedley passionately. "I am. The toot of a lifetime, if I can raise the necessary funds. Do you realize that I haven't had a night out for five years? It's as much as I can do to get the price of a packet of cigarettes out of Adela. I'm just a worm in a gilded cage. So you will let me have that hundred, won't you, Bill?"

A look of gentle pity had come into Bill's blue eyes. Her heart ached for this tortured soul.

"If I had a hundred dollars, my poor broken blossom," she said, "I'd give it you like a shot. I think a toot is just what you need, to bring the roses back to your cheeks. But I'm as fiscally crippled as you are. You don't suppose I'd be here, ghostwriting the story of Adela's unspeakably dull life, if I had cash in the bank, do you?" She patted his shoulder commiseratingly. "I'm afraid I've spoiled your day. I'm sorry. What a lot of succotash people talk about poverty making you spiritual," she proceeded, in moralizing vein. "All it's ever done to me is make me envious of the lucky stiffs who've got the stuff, like that boy who used to work with me on the Superba-Llewellyn lot. Did I tell you about him? Got fired, went back to New York, and the first thing you know he wins one of those big radio jackpots. Twenty-four thousand bucks, they said it was in the papers. Would that sort of thing ever happen to me? No, sir, not in a million years."

"Nor to me. But——"

Smedley paused. But looked cautiously over his shoulder. He looked cautiously over his other shoulder. Then he turned and looked cautiously behind him.

"But what?" said Bill, mystified by the manoeuvres.

Smedley lowered his voice to a conspiratorial whisper.

"I'll tell you something, Bill."

"Well, tell it louder. I can't hear a word."

"It isn't a thing you can shout from the house tops," said Smedley, still conspiratorial. "If Adela got to hear of it, phut would go any chance I have of becoming a rich man."

"You haven't any chance of becoming a rich man."

"That," said Smedley, "is where you're wrong. I have, if things pan out as I hope they will. Bill, do you know who this house used to belong to?"

"Of course I do. It's a landmark. Carmen Flores."

"Exactly. Adela bought it furnished from her estate. All her belongings are still here, just as they were the day when she was killed in that plane crash. Get that. All her belongings."

"So what?"

Smedley glanced over his shoulder again. He lowered his voice again. If in repose he had looked like a Roman Emperor, he now looked like a Roman Emperor talking over a prospective murder with his second vice-president in charge of assassinations.

"Carmen Flores kept a diary."

"Did she?"

"So everyone says. I'm looking for it."

"Why, are you thinking of writing her biography?"

"And if I find it, I'll be on velvet. Think, Bill. Reflect. You know what she was like. Always having violent affairs with all sorts of important characters—stars, studio bosses and what have you—and no doubt writing it up in her tablets at her leisure. Why, finding that diary would be like finding a deposit of uranium."

"You mean that some of the men up top would pay highly to suppress the little brochure?"

"Practically all the men up top."

Bill regarded him tenderly. She had always been devoted to Smedley, though far from blind to the numerous defects in his spiritual make-up. If there was a lazier man in the world than Smedley Cork, she had never met him. If there was one more refreshingly free from principles of any kind, she had still to make his acquaintance. He was selfish, idle and practically everything else that he ought not to be. Nevertheless, she loved him. She had loved him twenty years ago when he was a young man with money and one chin. She loved him now, when he was a portly senior with no money and two chins. Women do these things.

"In other words," she said, "you are hoping to cash in on a little blackmail."

"It isn't blackmail," said Smedley indignantly. "It's a perfectly ordinary, straightforward business transaction. They want the diary, I have it."

"But you haven't."

"Well, if I had, I mean."

Bill laughed indulgently. The proposition, as outlined, seemed to her pure Smedley. It did not weaken in the slightest for love for him. If someone had come to her and said: 'Wilhelmina Shannon, you are wasting your affection on a totally unworthy object,' she would have replied, 'Yessir. And I like it.' She was a one-man woman.

"You'll never make your fortune, Smedley, honestly or dishonestly. Now, I shall—I don't know how, but somehow. And when I do, I'm going to marry you."

Smedley quivered.

"Don't say such things, even in fun."

"I'm not being funny. I've given the matter a good deal of thought these last twenty years, and when I got here and saw what was left of you after living with Adela all this time, I made up my mind there was only one thing for me to do, and that was to make a quick couple of dollars and lead you to the altar and spend the rest of my life looking after you. Because if ever a man needed looking after, my God, it's you. And it beats me what you're making such a fuss about. You used to be crazy about me."

"I was young and foolish."

"And now you're old and foolish, but all the same you're the only man I've ever wanted. It's odd, that. How does that song go? Fish gotta swim, birds gotta fly, I gotta love one man till I die. Can't help——"

"Now, Bill. Please. Listen."

"I haven't time to listen. I'm lunching with my literary agent at the Beverly-Wilshire. He's in Hollywood for a couple of days. Who knows but what I might contrive to touch him for a hundred? In which case, I'll come back and lay it at your feet, my king."

Smedley, a correct and fastidious dresser, who even in captivity affected Palm Beach suits of impeccable cut and crease, cast a disapproving eye at the slacks.

"You aren't going to the Beverly-Wilshire dressed like that?"

"I certainly am. And don't forget what I said about marrying you. Go off into a corner and start practising saying 'I will,' against the moment when the minister taps you on the chest and says: 'Wilt thou, Smedley, take this Wilhelmina?' because you're for it, my lad."

She passed through the French window on her way to the garage where her jalopy was. Her voice came booming back to him.

"Fish gotta swim, birds gotta fly, I gotta love one man till I die. Can't help lovin' that man of mine."

Smedley Cork leaned limply against the back of the sofa, grateful for its firm support. Warm though the morning was, he shivered, as only a confirmed bachelor gazing into the naked face of matrimony can shiver.

2

JOE DAVENPORT was giving Kay Shannon lunch at the Purple Chicken down Greenwich Village way. He would much have preferred to take her to the Colony or the Pavillon, but Kay held austere views on the subject of young men wasting their substance in riotous living, even if they had recently won radio jackpots. Like her Uncle Smedley, she felt that there was no percentage in it. What Joe's stomach, which had high standards, considered a pretty revolting meal had drawn to its close, and only the last hurdle, the coffee, remained to be surmounted.

The waiter brought the coffee, breathed down the back of Joe's neck and withdrew, and Joe, who had been speaking of the lethal qualities of the management's spaghetti, abandoned the topic and turned to the one always uppermost in his mind on the occasions when he lunched with Kay.

"So much for the spaghetti theme," he said. "I will return to it later, if you wish. For the moment, there are weightier matters on the agenda paper. Don't look now," said Joe, "but will you marry me?"

Kay was leaning forward, her chin cupped in her hands and her eyes fixed on him with that grave, intent glance which always made him feel as if some hidden hand had introduced an egg whisk into his soul and started rotating it. It was this gravity of hers that had attracted him so strongly from the first. There was, he had begun to feel just before he met her, too much female smiling in this world, particularly in the cheesecake zone of Hollywood, in which until a short while before, he had had his being. It had sometimes seemed to him that his life, till Kay came into it, had become an inferno of flashing teeth and merry squeals.

"Marry you?"

"That's right."

"You do get the oddest ideas," said Kay.

She glanced over her shoulder. The Purple Chicken is one of those uninhibited Greenwich Village restaurants where the social amenities are not rigorously observed, and in the far corner a man who might have been a neo-Vorticist sculptor and a girl who looked as if she did bead work had begun to quarrel as loudly and cosily as if they had been at home. Turning back, she caught Joe's eye, and he frowned rebukingly.

"Don't pay any attention to those two," he urged. "Our marriage wouldn't be like that. They probably aren't married, anyway."

"He seems to be talking to her like a husband."

"Ours would be an unbroken round of bliss. Do you read Blondie? Then you will admit that the best husband in America is Dagwood Bumstead. Well, I have much in common with him—a loving heart, gentle nature, a fondness for dogs and a taste for exotic sandwiches. Marry me, and you will be getting a super-Dagwood. Never a harsh word. Never a cross-eyed look. Your lightest wish would be law. I would bring you breakfast in bed every morning on a tray and sit and smoke to you when you had a headache."

"It sounds wonderful. Tell me something," said Kay. "I notice that, when you give me lunch, you always wait till the coffee comes before proposing to me. Why is that? Just a habit?"

"On the contrary, it is very subtle stuff. Psychology. I reason that a girl full to the brim is more likely to be in softened mood than one in the process of staying the pangs of hunger. And I hate proposing with the waiters listening in and making bets in the background. Well, will you?"

"No."

"You said that last time."

"And I say it this time."

"You're really turning me down again?"

"I am."

"In spite of the fact that you are bursting with my meat?"

"I had spaghetti."

"It makes no difference. The moral obligation of a lady bursting with a gentleman's spaghetti to do the square thing by the gentleman is equally strong."

The sculptor and the bead worker had paid their check and left. Freed of their distracting influence, Joe felt better able to concentrate on the matter in hand.

"It really is extraordinary," he said, "this way you've got of saying no every time I offer you a good man's love. No . . . No . . . No . . . You might be Molotov. Not that it matters, of course."

"No?"

"There you go again. I believe you say it in your sleep."

"Why doesn't it matter, Mr. Bones?"

"Because you're bound to marry me eventually, if only for my money."

"How much have you got?"

"A thousand dollars."

"Is that all?"

"What do you mean, is that all? I know of many a poor man who would be glad of a thousand dollars. Many a poor woman, too. Your Aunt Bill, for one."

"I was going to say, Is that all you have left out of that jackpot?"

"Oh, well, money slips away. That has been my constant trouble as a bachelor, just as it has been Bill's constant trouble as a spinster. Have you heard from Bill lately?"

"No."

"I had a telegram from her this morning."

"What on earth was she telegraphing about?"

"She has some big scheme on."

"What scheme?"

"She didn't say. The communication was rather mystic. She just spoke of her big scheme."

"I'll bet it's crazy."

"I'll bet it isn't. Bill crazy? The Old Reliable? As shrewd a woman as ever ate Corned Beef Hash Betty Grable at a studio commissary. Bill's a woman with ideas. When we were co-workers on the Superba-Llewellyn lot, there was a traffic cop out on Cahuenga Boulevard who lurked beside his motor cycle in a dark corner and sprang on it and dashed out to pursue motorists and give them tickets. We used to watch him from our windows, and we all burned to do something to the man, but only Bill had the vision and intelligence to go out and tie a chain to his back wheel while he was in the drug store and fasten the other end to a hydrant, so that the next time he sprang on his machine and started off, he was brought up short and shot over the handlebars and looked about as silly as I ever saw a traffic cop look. There you have Wilhelmina Shannon in a nutshell. A woman who gets things done. But to return to what I was saying, as a bachelor I have found it difficult to keep the cash from melting away. It will be different when I am married and settled down."

"I'm not going to marry you, Joe."

"Why not? Don't you like me?"

"You're nice to lunch with."

"Nice is surely a weak adjective."

The waiter was hovering in a meaning manner, and Joe, reading his thoughts, asked him for the check. He looked across the table at Kay and felt, not for the first time, that life was very strange. You never knew what it was cooking up for you. When, as he was leaving Hollywood, Bill Shannon had told him to get in touch with her niece Kay in New York, where she was working in a magazine office, he had done so, he remembered, purely to oblige good old Bill. A young man who never lacked for feminine society, he had anticipated small pleasure or profit from adding one more to the list of telephone numbers in his little red book. But Bill had told him to get in touch, so he had got in touch. And from that simple, kindly act, had resulted all these emotional earthquakes which were upsetting him so deplorably.

"Bill ought to have warned me what I as coming up against," said Joe, pursuing this train of thought. " 'When you hit New York,' she said, 'go and say Hello to my niece Kay.' Like that. Casual. Offhand. Not a suggestion that she was introducing into my life a girl with a heart of stone who would disorganize my whole existence and turn me into a nervous wreck. Talk about La Belle Dame Sans Merci."

"Keats!" said Kay, surprised. "A well-read young man, this. I must try to get his autograph. I didn't know you went in for poetry."

"All the time. Whenever I have a spare half-hour, you will generally find me curled up with Keats's latest. 'Ah, what can ail thee, wretched wight, alone and palely loitering?' I tell you," said Joe, "if that wretched wight were to walk into this restaurant at this moment, beefing about La Belle Dame Sans Merci having him in thrall, I would slap him on the back and tell him I knew just how he felt."

"Though, of course, he was a lot worse off than you are."

"How do you make that out?"

"He didn't have a little red book of telephone numbers."

Joe started and, though most of his friends would have said that such a thing was impossible, blushed.

"What do you know about my little red book?"

"You left it on the table once when you went to speak to someone. I glanced idly through it. Who are they all?"

"Chunks of my dead past."

"M'm."

"Don't say M'm. Those girls mean nothing to me. Ghosts, that's what they are. Just so much flotsam and jetsam left stranded by the tide on the beach of memory. Bring any one of them to me on a plate with watercress around her, and I wouldn't so much as touch her hand. Nobody but you exists for me now. Don't you believe me?"

"No."

"That word again. By the beard of Sam Goldwyn, there are moments when I feel an almost overpowering urge to bean you with a bottle."

Kay raised her coffee spoon.

"Stand back. I am armed."

"Oh, it's all right. I"m not going to. I would only get hell from Emily Post."

The waiter brought the bill, and Joe paid it absently. Kay was looking at him again in that odd, speculative way of hers.

"It isn't the little red book that worries me," she said. "If you're a reformed Casanova, that's fine. Shall I tell you the reason why I won't marry you, Joe?"

"I wish you would. Clear up this historic mystery."

"I'll only be saying what you know already."

"That's all right. Just so long as you talk about me."

Kay took a sip of coffee, found that it had become cold and put the cup down. The restaurant had emptied, the waiters retired to some secret lair of their own. She could speak without being overheard.

"Well, then, it's because you're not what the French call an *homme sérieux.* If you know what that means."

"I don't."

"I'll try to explain. Let's just run through your case history. I had it from Bill. She said that when you and she were in New York, before you both went to Hollywood, you were doing quite well as a writer."

"For the pulps."

"Well, what's wrong with that? Half the best known writers to-day started on the pulps. But they stuck to it and worked."

"I don't like the way you said that."

"Then you got a job with Superba-Llewellyn and went to Hollywood. Then you got fired."

"It happens to everybody."

"Yes, but most people when they get fired don't ask for a personal interview with the boss of the studio and in the course of conversation throw a richly bound copy of the *Saturday Evening Post* at his head. What made you do that?"

"It seemed a good idea at the time. He had incurred my displeasure. Did Bill tell you about it?"

"Yes."

"Bill talks too much."

"So you got yourself blacklisted. Not very balanced behaviour, do you think?"

Joe patted her hand indulgently.

"Women don't understand these things," he said. "There comes a time in the life of every man placed in juxtaposition with Ivor Llewellyn when he is compelled to throw copies of the *Saturday Evening Post* at his head. It's why they publish the *Saturday Evening Post.*"

"Well, all right. I still think it was unbalanced, but if you say so, all right. We now come to the matter of that radio jackpot. When you get a lot of money by a miracle, winning a radio jackpot——"

Joe, though saddened by the turn the conversation had taken, was obliged to chuckle.

"I always get a hearty laugh out of that," he said. "I'm sitting in my squalid flat one rainy evening, feeling extremely dubious as to the whereabouts of my next meal, when the telephone tinkles and a hearty character at Station W.J.Z. asks me to listen to a Mysterious Voice on a record and see if I can identify it. And whose mysterious voice is it? None other than that of Mr. Ivor Llewellyn, which had been ringing in my ears ever since that episode to which you have alluded. Having identified it, I am informed by the hearty character that I have won the big jackpot and scooped in wealth beyond the dreams of avarice. It just shows that nothing is put into this world without a purpose, not even Ivor Llewellyn. But I interrupt you."

"You do."

"I'm sorry. Carry on. You were saying—?"

"I was saying that the first thing you do when by a miracle you get a lot of money is to stop writing and just loaf."

"You wrong me."

"Have you written a single story since you won that money?"

"No. But I've not been loafing. I've been looking about me, crouching for the spring. The view I take is that there must be something better for me to do than hammer out cowboy stories for the pulp magazines. Now that I have a bit of capital, I can afford to wait and study the market. That's what I'm doing, studying the market."

"I see. Well," said Kay, getting up, "I must be going. And I still stick to it that you're not an *homme sérieux.*"

A feeling of desolation swept over Joe. It had been there in a modified form all the time, but it was only now that he actually seemed to realize that in a few days he would be separated from this girl by three thousand miles of mountain and desert and prairie. And if ever there was a job that called for uninterrupted personal supervision, it was this job of breaking down Kay Shannon's customer's sales resistance.

"Oh, don't go yet," he said.

"I must. I've a hundred things to do."

"Heavy day at the office?"

"I'm packing. My vacation starts to-morrow."

"You never told me that."

"I suppose it slipped my mind."

"Where are you going?"

"Hollywood. What's the matter?"

"Nothing's the matter."

"You barked like a seal."

"I always bark like a seal at about his hour. So you're going to Hollywood?"

"Well, Beverly Hills. I'm going to stay with my aunt."

"Bill?"

"No, this is another one. Bill's sister. Much higher in the social scale than Bill. She's one of the old aristocracy of Hollywood. Adela Shannon."

"What, *the* Adela Shannon? The silent film star?"

"That's the one."

"I've heard Bill speak of her. Bill didn't seem to like her much."

"I don't like her much myself."

"Then why are you going to stay with her?"

"Oh, I don't know. One must go somewhere. She invited me."

"Where does she live?"

"Up in the mountains at the top of Alamo Drive. What used to be the Carmen Flores place. You probably know it."

"She owns that palace, does she? She must have plenty of money."

"She has. She married a millionaire."

"You'll be doing the same thing yourself, if I find my niche and really get going. Well, expect an early phone call from me."

"Expect a what?"

Joe laughed. His depression had vanished. The sun had broken through the clouds and all was for the best in this best of all possible worlds.

"Did you think to escape me by running off to Hollywood? Girl, you have been living in a fool's paradise. I'm going there myself in a couple of days."

"What! But you're blacklisted in Hollywood."

"Oh, I'm not going to work there. No doubt they will come begging me to, but I shall draw myself up and say: 'Not after what has occured.' And I shall say it stiffly. No, I'm going to confer with Bill about this scheme of hers. Rightly or wrongly, she seems to think that my co-operation is needed to make it a success. She was very emphatic that I must drop everything and come running. It's a pity we won't be able to travel together, but there are one or two things I have to do before I can leave the metropolis. However, you will be hearing from me in due season. In fact, you'll be seeing me."

"You aren't thinking of strolling in on Aunt Adela?"

"I might."

"I wouldn't."

"She can't eat me."

"I don't know so much. She's not a vegetarian."

"Well, we will see, we will see. And as regards the matter which we have been discussing, we will leave things as they are for the time being. I shall continue to love you, of course."

"Thanks."

"Not at all," said Joe. "A pleasure. It'll be something to do."

3

"HOLLYWOOD," SAID Bill Shannon, "is not the place it used to be. Hollywood," said Bill, "once a combination of Santa Claus and Good King Wenceslas, has turned into a Scrooge. The dear old days are dead and the spirit of cheerful giving a thing of the past."

She was sharing a pot of coffee with Joe Davenport in the main dining-room of the Beverly Hills hotel, and her resonant voice rang through it like rolling thunder. Listening to her, Joe felt as if he were a section of the voting public being harangued by a Senator of more than ordinary lung power.

"Why, look," said Bill. "There was a time when only a person of exceptional ability and determination could keep from getting signed by a studio. Top level executives used to chase you along the Strip, pleading pitifully with you to accept a contract. 'Come and write for us,' they begged, and when you told them you weren't a writer, they said: 'Well, come and be a technical adviser.' And when you said you didn't want to be a technical adviser, they said: 'Then come and be a vocal instructor.' So you said: 'Oh, all right, I'll be a writer. I shall want fifteen hundred a week.' 'Or two thousand?' they said. 'It's a rounder figure. Simplifies book-keeping.' And you said: 'Oh, very well, two thousand. But don't expect me to do any work!' And they said: 'Of course not, of course not. What an idea! We just want to have you around the place.' But all that is over. Now? Ha! Nowadays, if they sign you up at all, it's just to have the fun of firing you."

All this was in response to Joe's casual question 'Well, how's dear old Hollywood?' and he felt like someone who has thoughtlessly punched a hole in a dam. Overcoming the dazed sensation of being a twig tossed along on foaming waters, he found himself able to guess at the cause of his companion's emotion.

"Don't tell me they've handed you the black spot, Bill."

"That's what they've done. Driven me out into the snow. And I always thought they looked on me as the Little Mother around the place. A sort of studio mascot."

"When did this happen?"

"Last week. I dance into my office with my hat on the side of my head, singing 'I'm to be Queen of the May, mother, I'm to be Queen of the May,' and there on the desk the brusheroo in its little blue envelope. A most unpleasant shock, you can take it from me. I had to go off to the commissary and restore myself with a Malted Milk Bette Davis."

Joe nodded understandingly.

"It's this economy wave."

"False economy."

"I suppose Hollywood's in a pretty bad way these days?"

"Down to its last billion."

"One might have expected that something like that would happen when they let me go. A suicidal policy. What are you going to do?"

"For the moment, I'm staying with my sister Adela. I'm ghostwriting the story of her life. By the way. Kay clocked in a day or two ago. Did you see anything of her in New York?"

Joe laughed one of those hollow, mirthless laughs.

"Did I see anything of her in New York! The answer to your question, Wilhelmina, is in the affirmative. My misguided old friend, you little knew what you were letting me in for when you told me to go and say Hello to that girl. Lowered morale. Depression and debility. Night sweats and loss of appetite. I love her, Bill."

"You do?"

"I do."

"Well, I don't know that I blame you. She's an attractive young squirt."

"I would prefer that you did not allude to her as a squirt. An angel, if you like. A seraph, if you wish. But not a squirt."

"Just as you say. And how's it all coming along? Does she respond? Are you her dream man?"

"To use a favourite word of her own, no."

"She won't marry you?"

"That's her story."

"Ask her again."

"I have asked her again. How do you think I fill in the time? I've asked her twelve times. No, sorry, fourteen. I overlooked a couple of small ones. The score would be fifteen if I had been able to get her on the phone just now, but she was out. Bill, who would a Mrs. Cork be?"

"My sister Adela. She married a well-to-do millionaire of that name. Why?"

"I was just wondering. We exchanged a word or two over the wire. Well, that's how matters stand. I keep proposing to her, and she steadfastly continues to be a black frost in my garden of dreams. So now you know why I look pale and wan."

"You look like a particularly healthy tomato. And you're crazy if you pay any attention to a girl when she says no. I'm in love with a man who's been saying no for the last twenty years. But do I despair? Not by a jugful. I keep after him, and I think I'm softening him up. What are you goggling like that for?"

Joe hesitated.

"Well, I'm sort of surprised."

"Why?"

"I somehow didn't associate you with the tender passion."

"Why not?"

"Or, rather," said Joe, catching his companion's eye, which had begun to look menacing, "it astonished me that anyone could resist you for twenty years."

"That's better."

"I think you'll get him. Persevere, Bill."

"I will. And you persevere, too."

"Right. Let's all persevere."

"We'll make it a double wedding."

"That's the spirit."

"And now, for heaven's sake, let's change the subject and get down to business. We can't waste the whole day talking about love. You got my telegram?"

"That's why I'm here."

"And my letter, giving you full details of this scheme of mine?"

"I never got any letter."

"And I'll tell you why. I've just remembered I forgot to mail it. But I can supply you with all the facts now. My boy, we're on the eve of making a stupendous fortune. We've got a gold mine."

"Proceed, Bill. You interest me strangely."

Bill tapped his chest with an impressive finger.

"Has it ever occurred to you, Joe, that all these years you and I have been in this writing game on the wrong end?"

"How do you mean, the wrong end?"

"The loser's end. The sap's end. We've been perfect suckers. Where is it getting us, toiling for the pulps and being wage slaves in Hollywood? Nowhere."

"So—?"

"So we're going to be literary agents."

"Eh?"

"I should say authors' representatives. It sounds better. We're going to loll back and let the other fellows do the work and take our ten per cent like officers and gentlemen."

"What has given you that idea?"

"It came to me like a flash the other afternoon when I was lunching with my personal bloodsucker, who has been putting in a few days in Screwball Centre. I had noticed from the first that the man seemed nervous and depressed, and just after I had touched him for a couple of hundred dollars during the smoked salmon course he suddenly buried his face in his hands with a low groan and said that this was the finish. It couldn't go on, he said. He had got to retire, he said. He said he had reached a point where he never wanted to see an author again. He said authors did something to him. He said he supposed Providence had had some sort of idea at the back of its mind when it put authors into the world, but he had never been able to figure out what it was, and he pined for a quiet evening of his life in some remote spot like the Virgin Islands, where he could reasonably hope to be free from them. So, to condense a novelette into a short-short, I arranged with him to give me first refusal of the goodwill and effects, or whatever they're called. But we've got to act like lightning, because a week from now, if we haven't clinched the deal, he will go elsewhere. So now is the time for all good men to come to the aid of the party."

Joe found himself a good deal infected by her enthusiasm. The thought of becoming an authors' representative had not presented itself to him before, but he could see now that it was just the sort of thing he had been subconsciously looking for when studying the market. Like all writers, he had long held the view that of all the soft snaps in this modern civilization of ours that of the authors' representative was the softest. Given the modest intelligence necessary for putting a typescript in an envelope and licking the gum, a man could scarcely fail in that branch of industry. Whoever went around in patched clothes with holes in his shoes and had to skip a meal from time to time, it was not the authors' representative.

He had begun to weave an opalescent daydream in which Kay, learning that he had become one of that opulent little band who represent authors, flung herself weeping on his chest, remorseful that she had ever wronged him by failing to classify him as what the French call an *homme sérieux,* when Bill continued her remarks.

"He's asking twenty thousand."

Joe's daydream broke into fragments like a soup-plate coming apart in the hands of a careless scullery maid. He gave a soft gurgle, and when he spoke, spoke in a low, grating voice.

"Twenty thousand?"

"That's all. He started by talking some wild, visionary stuff about thirty, but I soon put a stop to that."

"You expect to get twenty thousand dollars?"

"Why not?"

"Which bank are you going to burgle?"

Joe shrank back in his chair. Wilhelmina Shannon was raising her voice again.

"What do you mean, which bank am I going to burgle? I'm looking to you to put up the capital. Aren't you putrescent with money?"

"I've a thousand dollars, if you call that putrescent."

"A thousand? What's become of that radio jackpot?"

"Gone with the wind."

"You dissolute young rat."

"High cost of living, taxes, and so on. And a thing you're overlooking, Bill, is that these radio jackpots aren't solid cash. Don't be misled by what you read in the papers. Most of mine was canned soup. Would this man of yours settle for eight thousand cans of mixed soups? Maybe he's fond of soup. I could do him tomato, asparagus, green pea, chicken gumbo . . ."

An old gentleman who was drinking something through a straw at a table at the other end of the room leaped convulsively and nearly swallowed the straw. This was because Bill was raising her voice still higher.

"So one more dream turns blue," said Bill. "Can you direct me to a good Old Women's Home?"

Her anguish touched Joe. His was a resilient nature, and already he had begun to recover from the gloom into which he had been plunged.

"Don't be a defeatist, Bill. Why shouldn't we raise the money somewhere?"

"Where?"

"There used to be a place called Perelli's down at Santa Monica where one could engage in games of chance. I presume it still exists. I might take my thousand and look in there to-night."

"Don't be a fool."

"Perhaps you're right. Well, why shouldn't we float a loan in some quarter? Hollywood must be full of rich sportsmen who would like a flutter."

"I've never met them."

"What about Mrs. Cork?"

"Adela? The slowest woman with a dollar west of Dodge City. No, this is the end. Doom, desolation and despair. Well, see you in the breadline," said Bill, and moved ponderously to the door, a female Napoleon retreating from Moscow.

For some minutes after she had left him, Joe sat musing on the capriciousness of fate, which lures you on with golden promises and then turns round and lets you have it on the base of the skull with the stuffed eelskin. But his, as has been said, was a resilient nature, and it was not long before there began to glimmer through the cloud wrack a small but distinct silver lining. It might be that he would have to postpone becoming a millionaire for a while, but money is not everything and the world, he reminded himself, though admittedly grey in spots, still contained the girl he loved. And by chartering a yellow taxi from the stand outside the Marion Hunter bookshop and going to the top of Alamo Drive, he could feast his eyes on the house where she was in residence. With a little luck, he might even catch a glimpse of her.

Twenty minutes later, seated in a yellow taxi, he was gazing out of the window at a broad gateway and a tree-lined strip of concrete drive which led to a house unfortunately invisible from where he sat. He felt like some pilgrim visiting a shrine, and mingled with his reverence was the earthier feeling that when Mrs. Adela Cork had taken a millionaire for a husband, she had picked a good one. The grounds, he could see, were spacious and expensive, and when there suddenly appeared, crossing the drive with a tray of cocktails, what was plainly an imported English butler, any doubt that he might have had as to this being one of the Stately Homes of Hollywood was dispelled.

It was probably the sight of those cocktails that suggested to him that it was about time to be getting back and making arrangements for dinner. The

California evening had mellowed to twilight, and his stomach, always inclined to the policy of Do It Now, was sending up peremptory messages to the front office. Reluctantly, for he regretted the necessity of yielding to his lower nature, he was about to notify the charioteer that the homeward journey might commence, when along the drive and out of the gate came toddling a large, stout, elderly gentleman who looked like a Roman Emperor who has been doing himself too well on the starchy foods, and so impressive was his exterior that it immediately occurred to Joe that here, first crack out of the box, he had found the very man of whom he was in search, one of those big shots who feed sums like twenty thousand dollars to the birds.

For to Joe, meeting him here, it was obvious who this was. It could be none other than the plutocrat Cork, the super-tax-paying mate of Kay's Aunt Adela. You had only to cast an eye on the man to see that he had the stuff in sackfuls. It is difficult to explain exactly, but there is something about these very rich men which marks them off from the common herd. They look different. The way they walk is different. They say: 'Hey, taxi!' differently.

This was what the other was now saying and for a moment Joe was puzzled that such a Croesus should be hailing taxis. Then he saw that the explanation was quite simple. Something—trivial, one hoped—must have gone temporarily wrong with the Lincoln, the Cadillac and the two Rolls-Royces in his garage.

His lightning mind perceived that here was a heaven-sent opportunity of fraternizing with this gilt-edged security and starting a beautiful friendship.

"I am going to Beverly Hills, sir," he said, poking his head out of the window, full of charm. "Could I give you a lift, sir?"

"Very kind of you, sir."

"Not at all, sir."

"Thank you, sir."

"Don't give it a thought, sir. Hop in, sir, hop in."

The taxi rolled off down the mountain-side, and Joe braced himself to be fascinating.

4

THE MIDDAY sun, pouring into the Garden Room on the following morning, found Bill Shannon seated at the desk, the dictaphone tube in her hand, a peevish frown on her face. One would have said that she was not enjoying working on the *Memoirs* of her sister Adela, and one would have been right. Bill in her time had been many things, crime reporter, sob sister, writer of stories for the pulp magazines, Press agent, minor actress and baby sitter, but this was the most uncongenial task which she had ever undertaken.

As far as she could ascertain from the voluminous notes which the heroine of the *Memoirs* had placed at her disposal, nothing had ever happend to Adela that was of the remotest interest to anyone except herself. She had apparently never done anything in all her years of silent stardom but eat, sleep, get married, and have her photograph taken. It was not easy to see how the Adela Shannon Story could be stretched to cover three hundred pages of entertaining reading for the American public.

But Bill was conscientious and resolved to give of her best, and it was with splended determination that she ignored the sunshine that was trying to lure her out into the open spaces.

"It was all so new and strange," she boomed into the mouthpiece, "and I was just a timid little tot . . . Oh, dammit, I've used timid little tot before . . . and I was so young, so unsophisticated, so dazzled and bewildered by the glitter and glamour of this world . . . No, we want some adjectives there . . . of this strange, new, magic world into which I had been plunged . . . Oh, blast it, I said new and strange a moment ago . . . of this marvellous, magical, fairy-land world into which I had plunged like a diver diving into some rushing, sparkling stream. Who could have dreamed—"

Phipps came shimmering through the door, in his capable hands a whisky and soda on a tray. She welcomed him with a glad cry like that of a diver diving into some rushing, sparkling stream who finds the water warmer than she had expected. No Israelite in the desert, watching manna descending from the skies just when he had been saying to himself how well a spot of manna would go down right now, if only he had it, could have shown a more instantaneous approval and enthusiasm.

"Phipps, you're a mind reader."

"I thought you might be in need of refreshment, madam. You have been working all the morning."

"And no interruptions, thank heaven. Where is everybody?"

"Mrs. Cork went to Pasadena, madam, to address a ladies' club on Some Recollections of the Silent Screen. Miss Kay and his lordship are playing golf."

"And Mr. Smedley?"

"I have not seen Mr. Smedley, madam."

"Probably around somewhere."

"No doubt, madam."

Bill took a sip and a swallow and composed herself for conversation. She had reached a point in her labours when she was glad of the interruption which would have irked her earlier, and she was particularly glad to be interrupted by Phipps. This butler intrigued her. Since their get-together of the previous day, she had been thinking not a little about his curious case.

"I wish you would explain something that's been puzzling me, Phipps."

"Certainly, madam, if it is within my power."

Bill addressed herself to the glass again. Its amber contents were cool and refreshing. She lit a cigarette and blew a puff of smoke at a fly which had wandered in and was circling about her head.

"It's this," she said, putting the question which she hoped would lead to a solution of the mystery which had been vexing her. "You remember—how shall I put it, always bearing in mind that walls have ears—you remember that lawsuit of yours?"

"Yes, madam."

"The one where I was a member of the jury."

"Yes, madam."

Bill discouraged the fly with another broadside.

"Well, here's where I can't get the thing straight. It seemed to me that on that occasion, and the rest of the boys and girls felt the same, that the gentleman who was digging up the details of your past and dishing them out to the intelligent twelve, of whom I was one, established rather clearly that you were an expert safeblower."

"Yes, madam."

"And it didn't take me long after I'd got here to see that you were certainly an expert butler."

"Thank you, madam."

"Well, which came first, the chicken or the egg?"

"Madam?"

Bill saw that she had not made herself clear.

"I mean, are you a safeblower——"

"An ex-safeblower, madam."

"You're sure you spell it with an ex?"

"Oh, yes, madam."

"Well, be that as it may, are you a safeblower magically gifted with the art of buttling, or a butler who has somehow picked up the knack of blowing safes?"

"The latter, madam."

"You aren't really Mike the Mugg or something like that, just posing as a butler for your own subtle ends?"

"Oh, no, madam. I have been in service from a very early age. Domestic service is a tradition in my family. I started my career as what is known as a hall boy in a large establishment in Worcestershire."

"Where the sauce comes from?"

"I believe the condiment to which you allude is manufactured in that locality, madam."

Phipps stood silent for a moment, his thoughts apparently back in those happy days when life had been simple and free from problems and complexities. Apart from having to carry logs of wood up stairs and deposit them in bedrooms, hall boys in English houses have it pretty soft.

"In due course," he proceeded, coming out of his reverie, "I rose to be an under footman, then a footman and finally a butler. And it was after I had achieved that position that I entered the employment of an American gentleman and came to this country. I had always had a desire to visit the United States of Northern America. That was some ten years ago."

"And when did you learn to bust safes?"

"About five years after that, madam."

"What gave you the idea?"

Phipps looked cautiously over his shoulder. Having done this, he directed a searching glance at Bill, as if he were weighing her in the balance. He seemed to be asking himself whether it would be wise and judicious to confide in a woman who, though of course they knew each other quite well by sight, was after all a stranger. Then the benevolence of his companion's rugged face overcame his doubts. There was that about Bill Shannon which always encouraged people to confide in her.

"It came to me quite unexpectedly one evening when I was reading a volume entitled *Three Dead At Midways Court,* madam. I have always been fond of that type of literature, and in the course of my perusal of these fictional works—known, I believe, as whodunits—I was struck by the frequency with which the butler proved to be the criminal."

"I know what you mean. It's always the butler. It's an occupational disease."

"What is termed the Heavy in *Three Dead At Midways Court* turned out to be the butler, and until the final chapter nobody had suspected him for a moment. It started a train of thought. I mused, madam. Butlers, I told myself, never are suspected for a moment, and it occurred to me that a butler in a wealthy household who had acquired the technique of opening safes would be very advantageously placed. There he would be, if you follow me, madam, with the valuables at his elbow, if I may use the expression, and it would be extremely simple for him, by leaving a window open, to invest his operations with the appearance of what is known as an outside job. So to cut a long story short, madam, I made cautious inquiries and eventually found a practitioner in Brooklyn who in return for a fee was willing to impart his skill to me."

"In twelve easy lessons?"

"Twenty, madam. At first I was not a very apt pupil."

"But you picked it up all right as you went along?"

"Yes, madam."

Bill drew a deep breath. She was no rigid moralist, her temperament being one that always inclined her to take a tolerant view of the straying from the straight and narrow path of those with whom she associated, but she had a rudimentary conscience. And though she had never been fond of her sister Adela, she could not but feel that a word of warning should be given that exasperating woman. The generosity of the late Albert Cork, combined with her personal and private fortune, the outcome of years of pulling down a huge salary in the days before there was any income tax to speak of, had left Adela with enough jewellery to equip half the blondes in Hollywood, and it seemed unfair to allow her to go on giving board and lodging to a butler who, as had been established in court, could open safes with a twiddle of his finger tips.

"I ought to tell Mrs. Cork," she said.

"There is no necessity, madam. I have put all that sort of thing behind me."

"Says you, if I may use a homely phrase indicating doubt and uncertainty."

"No, madam, I assure you. Apart from the moral aspect of the matter, I would not dream of taking upon myself the risks inseparable from my former activities. My experience of American prison life has left me with no desire to repeat it."

Bill's face cleared. This was sense.

"I see what you mean. I remember reading an article in the *Yale Review* about the Reformed Criminal. The writer pointed out that there is nobody with such a strong bias toward honesty as the man who has just come out of prison. He said that if someone had been laid up for a year in hospital as the result of going over Niagara Falls in a barrel, the one outdoor sport in which he would be reluctant to indulge on emerging would be going over Niagara Falls in a barrel. Or, putting it another way, the burned child fears the fire."

"Precisely, madam, though the actual quotation is 'A burned child dreadeth the fire.' It occurs in Lyly's *Euphues.*"

"Is that a favourite bedside book of yours?"

"I glanced through it, madam, when I was in the service of the Earl of Powick, in Worcestershire. There was very little else to read in his lordship's library, and it rained a good deal."

"I've come up against that sort of thing myself. I once went to Valparaiso as a stewardess on a fruit boat, and the only book on board was *The Plays of William Shakespeare,* belonging to the chief engineer. By the time the voyage was over, I knew them by heart. I suppose that's why I quote him a good deal."

"No doubt, madam. A very admirable writer."

"Yes, he wrote some good stuff. But tell me all about your college days, Phipps. What's it like in Sing . . . ?"

"Hist, madam."

"How do you mean, hist? Oh, I get you."

Outside the French window a voice had suddenly made itself heard, singing a gay melody. A moment later, a long, lean young man, who appeared to have giraffe blood in him, came in, carrying a bag of golf clubs. Phipps greeted him with respectful devotion.

"Good morning, m'lord."

"Good morning, Lord Topham," said Bill.

"Oh, good morning," said the young man. Then, as if to clarify his meaning, he added the words "Good morning, good morning, good morning!" He beamed at Bill and the butler. "Well, Miss W. Shannon," he proceeded, "and you, Phipps, this is the maddest, merriest day of all the glad new year. I say this to you without reserve, Phipps, and you, Miss W. Shannon. Not only the maddest, but also the merriest day of the glad new year. I broke a hundred this morning, a feat which has eluded my every effort since I first took driver in hand at the age of twenty. A whisky and soda would not come amiss, Phippsy. You might take it to my room."

"Very good, m'lord," said Phipps. "I will attend to the matter immediately."

Lord Topham gazed after him admiringly as he disappeared in the stately manner habitual with him.

"You know, that chap makes me feel homesick. Absolutely. I never expected to find an English butler in Hollywood."

"All sorts of English oddities turn up in Hollywood," said Bill. "Excuse me." She picked up the mouthpiece of the dictaphone and began speaking into it. "Who could have dreamed that in a few short years the name of Adela Shannon would have been known to the whole wide world from China to Peru? Who would have supposed that before I made my third picture, I would have become loved, worshipped, idolized by the prince in his palace, the peasant in his cot, the explorer in the jungle and the Eskimo in his frozen igloo? So true it is—so true——Ha!" said Bill. "So true it is that one touch of nature makes the whole world kin and that courage, patience and perseverance will always find a way. I will now describe my first meeting with Nick Schenk." She lowered the instrument. "Sorry," she said. "I have to jot these things down when the inspiration comes."

Lord Topham was impressed, as the layman always is when privileged to observe genius in the throes of composition.

"Oh, absolutely," he agreed. "What was that about glue?"

"Igloo. It's a sort of gloo they have up in the Arctic circle."

"I see."

"Stickier than the usual kind."

"Quite. What are you doing? Working on a picture?"

"Not on a picture, no. I'm ghostwriting the story of my sister Adela's life."

"How's it coming?"

"Not too smoothly."

"Pretty much of a somewhat ghastly sweat, I imagine. I couldn't write anything if you paid me, much less talk it into that sewing-machine thing. Mrs. Cork was a big pot in the silent films, wasn't she?"

"One of the biggest. They called her the Empress of Stormy Emotion."

"Must have made a lot of money."

"Quite a good deal."

"I mean, you don't get a house like this for nothing."

"No. But here she is, to give you all the figures, if you want them."

The door which led to the main portion of the house had opened, and a strikingly handsome woman of about Bill's age was sailing in with that air of confidence and authority which is so noticeable in Empresses of Stormy Emotion, even when the passage of time has made them ex-Empresses. Adela Cork was tall and stately, with large, dark, slumberous eyes which could and did, light up in a baleful blaze when things were not going exactly as she desired. She had something of the imperious look of those portraits of Louise de Quenouaille which make the beholder feel what a man of steely nerve King Charles the Second must have been to associate on terms of intimacy with anything so formidable. Formidable was the word to describe Bill's sister Adela. Each of her three husbands, even the late Alfred Cork, who was as tough a citizen as ever owned an oil well, had curled up before her like carbon paper: and directors who were getting on in years sometimes woke trembling in the night, having dreamed that they were back in the pre-talkie days arguing some technical point with the former Adela Shannon.

At the moment, her mood was reasonably benevolent, though she proposed later on to have a word with Bill about those slacks. Her lecture had been well received, and she was still in the gentle glow of amiabilty induced by the applause of two hundred intelligent Pasadena matrons.

"Good morning," she said. "Good morning, Lord Topham."

"Good morning, good morning, good morning, good morning."

"Hello, Adela," said Bill. "Lord Topham was just saying how much he admired this house."

Adela smiled rewardingly on this worthy guest. She was fond and proud of Lord Topham. She had been to great trouble to extract him from the clutches of a prehensile hostess who had seemed at one time to have acquired permanent possession, and her attitude toward him was a little like that of a collector toward a valuable piece of bric-à-brac which he has wrested from a rival connoisseur.

"It is nice, isn't it? I bought it just as it stood from the estate of Carmen Flores, the Mexican star who was killed in that plane crash last year."

Lord Topham was interested. He was a great reader of *Screen Topics, Screen Secrets* and other organs of that nature.

"Oh, really? Carmen Flores, what? Fancy that."

"You have heard of Carmen Flores?"

"Absolutely. Well, I mean to say, one would, wouldn't one? She, as it were, lives in legend and song. By way of being what Americans call a red-hot mother, was she not?"

"Absolutely," said Bill. "I have often thought that if walls had tongues as well as ears . . . Walls do have ears. Did you know that?"

"No, really?"

"Absolutely," said Bill. "I had it from a reliable source. Well, as I was saying, I have often thought that if walls could speak, these walls could say a mouthful. Not that what they said would ever get past the Johnston office."

"Absolutely not," said Lord Topham, nodding sagely. "So this is where she lived, is it? Well, well. Who knows but that on that very sofa——I forget what I was going to say."

"Just in time," said Bill. "Quickly changing the subject, tell Adela about your triumphs on the links this morning."

Lord Topham required no coaxing.

"Oh, ah, yes. I broke a hundred, Mrs. Cork. Do you play golf?" he asked, though a glance at his hostess should have told him that it was a foolish question. Women like Adela Cork do not lower themselves to these trivial pastimes. With a stretch of imagination one could picture Mrs. Siddons or the mother of the Gracchi playing golf, but not Adela.

"No," she said. "I do not."

"Oh! Well, the idea of the game is to bash the old ball round the course in a minimum of strokes, and anyone who can accomplish the enterprise in under a hundred bashes is entitled to credit and respect. I did it for the first time this morning, and the news will stun my circle of friends across the sea. If you'll excuse me, I'll be going and telling old Twingo about it."

"Twingo?"

"A pal of mine in London. May I use your telephone? Thanks awfully," said Lord Topham, and hastened out to shoot the hot news across the Atlantic.

Bill smiled sardonically.

"Pal of mine in London . . . May I use your telephone . . . Just like that."

Adela bridled. She resented criticism of her favoured guest.

"Very rich men don't bother about these trifles. Lord Topham is one of the richest men in England."

"I'm not surprised. His personal expenses must be very small."

"And I do wish, Wilhelmina," said Adela, changing the subject, "that you would dress decently when you are in a civilized house. Slopping about in those slacks. You look perfectly revolting. What do you suppose Lord Topham thinks?"

"Does he think?"

"Dungarees!" said Adela, wrinkling her nose with distaste.

Bill was one of the few people whom Adela Cork could not intimidate.

"Never mind about my dungarees," she said. "Just tell yourself that they cover a warm heart and let it go at that. How was your lecture? Did you massacre them?"

"It was a great success. Everybody most enthusiastic."

"You're back early. Couldn't you touch the girls for lunch?"

Adela clicked her tongue.

"My dear Wilhelmina, have you forgotten that I am giving a big luncheon party to-day? All sorts of important people are coming, including Jacob Glutz."

"Of Medulla-Oblongata-Glutz? The man who looks like a lobster?"

"He does not look like a lobster."

"Pardon me, he looks much more like a lobster than most lobsters do."

"Well, whatever he looks like, I don't want him mistaking you for one of the gardeners. I trust you intend to change into something reasonably respectable before he arrives."

"Of course. These are just my working clothes."

"Have you been working on the *Memoirs?*"

"All the morning."

"Where have you got to?"

"Your first meeting with Nick Schenk."

"No further than that?"

Bill felt that this sort of thing must be checked at the outset. It was bad enough being compelled by poverty to write those *Memoirs* at all, without having Adela biting at her heels and baying after her like a bloodhound. A pang shot through her as she thought of the literary agency, now gone beyond recall.

"My good woman," she said, "be reasonable. The story of your great career will be a very important contribution to American literature. It is not a task that can be hurried. One proceeds slowly. One chisels and polishes. You don't suppose Lytton Strachey raced through his *Life of Queen Victoria* like a Bowery bum charging into a saloon for a quick beer?"

"I see. Yes. I suppose you're right."

"You bet I'm right. I was saying to Kay yesterday——What's the matter?"

Adela had uttered an exclamation. She was looking cautiously over her shoulder. It seemed to Bill that her life these last days had been passed exclusively in the society of people who looked cautiously over their shoulders. She watched her sister, mystified, as she went to the door, opened it quickly and peered out.

"I thought Phipps might be listening," said Adela, closing the door and coming back into the room. "Wilhelmina, there is someting I want to ask you. About Kay."

"What about her?"

Adela sank her voice to a stage whisper.

"Has she ever spoken to you of anyone called *Joe?*"

"Joe?"

"I'll tell you why I ask. Yesterday afternoon the telephone rang as I was coming through the hall. I answered it, and a man's voice said 'Kay? This is Joe. Stop me, if you've heard this before, but will you marry me?' "

Bill clicked her tongue.

"The boy's crazy. That's no way to——"

"I said: 'You are speaking to Mrs. Cork,' and he said 'Oops! Sorry!' and rang off. Have you any idea who it could have been?"

Bill was able to supply the information.

"I can tell you who it must certainly have been. A young writer of my acquaintance named Joe Davenport. We were at Superba-Llewellyn together till he got fired. Shipped out to Hollywood at the same time in a crate of twelve. There is nothing surprising in the fact that he should have been asking Kay to marry him. I believe he does it every hour on the hour. He loves her with a fervour you don't often see off the Superba-Llewellyn lot."

"Great heavens!"

"Why? Don't you approve of young love in springtime?"

"Not between my niece and a Hollywood writer who hasn't even got a job."

"Joe may be out of a job, but he has a glittering future, if he can find some sporting soul to lend him twenty thousand dollars. If he had the capital, he could buy a lucrative Authors' Representativery. Would you care to lend him twenty thousand dollars?"

"I would not. Is Kay in love with this man?"

"Well, she gives a sort of rippling laugh, a kind of amused tee-hee, whenever I mention his name. Maybe that's a good sign. I must consult Dorothy Dix."

Adela bristled.

"What do you mean, a good sign? It would be a disaster if she became entangled with a man like that. I am hoping she will marry Lord Topham. That is why I invited her here. He is one of the richest men in England."

"So you told me."

"I went to endless trouble to get him away from the Gloria Pirbrights, just so that Kay could meet him. Gloria was sticking to him like flypaper. I shall speak to Kay very seriously. I am not going to have any nonsense."

"Why don't you get Smedley to speak to her?"

"Smedley!"

"I always think a man can do these things so much more impressively. Women are apt to get shrill. And Smedley is the brother of the husband of the sister of Kay's father. Puts him almost *in loco parentis*, you might say."

Adela uttered a sound which in a woman of less impressive beauty would have been a snort.

"As if he could do anything. Smedley is a poor sheep who can't say boo to a goose."

"Well, name three sheep who can."

"Oh!"

"Yes?"

Adela was looking at Bill accusingly. Her manner was austere. In a hundred silent pictures she had looked just like that at a hundred heavies who had attempted in their uncouth way not to do right by our Nell. It was plain that some thought had floated into her mind which was reducing sisterly love to a minimum.

"Smedley!" she said. "I knew there was something I wanted to ask you, but talking about Kay put it out of my head. Wilhelmina, have you been giving Smedley money?"

Bill had hoped that secrecy and silence might have been preserved on this point, but apparently it was not to be. She replied with as much nonchalance as she could manage on the spur of the moment.

"Why, yes, I did slip him a hundred dollars."

"You idiot!"

"I'm sorry. I couldn't resist his pleading eye."

"Well, you will be interested to hear that he was out all night on what I suppose was a drunken orgy. I went to his room after breakfast, and his bed had not been slept in. He must have sneaked off to Los Angeles with your precious hundred dollars."

Bill did her best to soothe.

"Well, why agonize? He hasn't had a night out for years. Where's the harm in an occasional bender? Boys will be boys."

"Smedley is not a boy."

"What I always say is that as we shall pass this way only once, it surely behoves us—if behoves is the word I want—to do whatever in us lies to increase the sum of human happiness and——"

"Bah! Stuff and nonsense."

"Yes, I suppose that is one way of looking at it."

Adela went to the bell and pressed it.

"The only bright side of the thing," she said, "is that he will probably not return in time for lunch, and if he does, he will be in no condition to be at the table, to bore Mr. Glutz with those interminable stories of his about Broadway in the 'thirties."

"That's right," said Bill. "Always look for the silver lining. What are you ringing for?"

"I am expecting my masseuse. Oh, Phipps," said Adela, as the door opened, "has the masseuse arrived?"

"Yes, madam."

"She is in my room?"

"Yes, madam."

"Thank you," said Adela coldly. "Oh, Phipps."

"Madam?"

Adela's face, which had hardened as she spoke of Smedley, grew harder.

"I wanted to see you, Phipps, to give you a piece of news which I think will be of interest to you."

"Yes, madam?"

"You're fired!" said Adela, allowing the stormy emotion of which she had been Empress to leap from her eyes and scorch the butler like a jet from a flame thrower.

5

BUTLERS, AS the chronicler has already had occasion to remark in his observations on these fauna, are trained to hide their emotions. Whatever the turmoil in their souls, outwardly they aim at the easy insouciance of the Red Indian at the stage, and it is consequently not often that anyone is privileged to see one of them look aghast. But Phipps was now looking definitely aghast. His jaw had fallen and his eyes were round and horror-stricken.

He cast a tortured glance at Bill. 'Have you betrayed your promise?' the glance said. Bill's eye met his. 'Good heavens, no,' said Bill's eye. 'I haven't said a word. This is something completely new, and nobody more surprised

than the undersigned.' Adela, having exploded her bomb, continuted to
ferment in silence.

"Fired, madam?" faltered Phipps.

"That's what I said."

"But, madam——"

Bill intervened in her robust way. As Roget would have put it in his
Thesaurus, she was surprised, astonished, perplexed, bewildered and at a
loss, but she was not the woman to accept this sort of thing with meek
detachment. She liked Phipps and wished him well, and he had told her that
he particularly desired to remain in Adela's employment. Why this should be
so, she could not imagine, but if that was how he felt, this totally unexpected
thunderbolt must have been devastating. He was probably, she reflected with
a pang, experiencing much the same sense of having been hit over the head
with a blunt instrument as had come to her the previous afternoon on
learning from Joe Davenport that his entire capital consisted of a few dollars
and eight thousand tins of mixed soups.

"What do you mean, Adela? You can't fire *Phipps*."

One would have said a moment before that it would have been impossible
for even an Empress of Stormy Emotion to look sterner and haughtier than
Adela Cork was looking. But at these words the proud severity of her manner
took on a still more repellent coldness.

"Can't I?" she said crisply. "Watch me."

Bill became vehement. There were moments—this was one of them—when
she had a nostalgic yearning to be back in the days of their mutual nursery, to
return to the golden age when, if Adela annoyed her, she had been in a
position to put a worm down the back of her neck or to smite her shrewdly
with one of those hard objects which lie about nursery floors.

"You're crazy. You're like the base Indian who threw a pearl away richer
than all his tribe. I haven't been long in this joint, but I've been here quite
long enough to have got Phipps taped as the Butler Supreme."

"Thank you, madam."

"He's terrific. He out-Arthurs Treacher. He lends lustre to the whole
establishment. That harsh, grating sound you hear from time to time is the
envious gnashing of the teeth of all the other Beverly Hills employers who
haven't got him. Fire him? Absurd. What on earth put a silly idea like that
into your head?"

Adela continued stony.

"Have you quite finished?"

"No. But go on."

"I am firing Phipps for a very good reason. Wouldn't you fire a butler who
spends his whole time sneaking around in your bedroom?"

"Doing *what?* "

"That's what Phipps does. A couple of days ago I found him in my room,
routing about in one of the closets. He said he had seen a spider."

"Madam—"

Adela silenced the wretched man with an imperious gesture. She went on speaking in a voice that rose and vibrated with stormy passion.

"Yesterday he was there again. He said he had seen a mouse. As if there was the slightest possibility that there could be mice and spiders in my bedroom. And if it had been brimming over with mice and spiders, what business was that of his? I told him that if he ever put his ugly nose in my room again, I'd fire him. And this morning, as I was leaving for Pasadena, I went back to get a handkerchief, and there he was, if you please, under the dressing-table, with his fanny sticking up like a mesa in the Mojave desert. You leave at the end of the week, Phipps. I trust," concluded Adela, her hand on the door handle, "that I am a broadminded woman, but I'm not going to share my bedroom with the butler."

The sound of a door vigorously slammed died slowly away, leaving silence behind it. Bill was endeavoring to adjust her faculties to these sensational happenings. Phipps was standing rooted to the spot to which he had been rooted since his late employer's opening remarks, still exhibiting all the symptoms of having received a powerful blow in the solar plexus.

"For heaven's sake, Phipps, what's all this?" said Bill.

The butler came slowly to life, like a male Galatea. His face was pale and drawn.

"Would you object if I took a sip of your whisky and soda, madam?" he said in a low voice. "I do not often indulge, but this has come as a shock."

"Help yourself."

"Thank you, madam."

"And now," said Bill, "supply a few footnotes." There was something of severity in her manner as she eyed the butler. "Does this mean that you have been going back to your old activities? I thought you told me you had put all that sort of thing behind you."

"Oh, no, madam, nothing like that."

"Then what were you doing, routing about in cupboards and crawling under dressing-tables?"

"I—er—I was looking for something, madam."

"I gathered that. But what?"

Once again the butler directed that searching glance at her. And, as before, the scrutiny apparently proved satisfactory. After the briefest of pauses, he replied, speaking in the hushed voice of the man who knows that walls have ears.

"The diary of the late Miss Flores, madam."

"Good God!" said Bill. "Isn't this where I came in?"

Phipps, having decided to be confidential, was now in the mind to hold nothing back.

"It was a remark of Mr. Smedley's that gave me the idea, madam. Mr. Smedley chanced to observe one night at dinner that it was highly probable that the late Miss Flores had kept a diary and that, in the event of her having done so, the volume was presumably somewhere on the premises. I was handing the potatoes at the moment, and the dish literally trembled in my grasp, madam. For the thought occurred to me immediately that the sort of diary kept by the sort of lady the late Miss Flores was would be worth a great deal of money to whoever found it."

Bill eyed him gravely.

"Have you ever had that odd feeling, when somebody tells you something, Phipps, that you've heard it all before somewhere? Like hearing the familiar strains of some grand old anthem to which you have listened in childhood?"

"No, madam."

"It happens sometimes. Well, go on."

"Thank you, madam. I was saying that such a diary would be extremely valuable. The late Miss Flores, madam, was hot stuff, if I may venture to use the expression. In one quarter or another there would be a ready market for any diary which she had kept."

"True. So you looked for it?"

"Yes, madam."

"But didn't find it?"

"No, madam."

"Too bad."

"Yes, madam. Thinking the matter over, I reached the conclusion that, if the last Miss Flores had kept a diary, she would have secreted it somewhere in her sleeping apartment, the room now occupied by Mrs. Cork."

"So you said to yourself, 'Yoicks! Tally ho!' ?"

"Not precisely that, madam, but I proceeded to institute a diligent search, confident that I would eventually succeed in discovering its whereabouts."

"That was why you were so anxious not to lose your job here?"

"Precisely, madam. And now I am leaving at the end of the week. It is very bitter, madam," said Phipps with a sigh that seemed to come up from the soles of his shapley feet.

Bill reflected.

"You've still got a couple of days."

"But Mrs. Cork will be on the alert, madam. I really could not go through the ordeal of being caught by her again."

"Was she emotional?"

"Yes, madam. It was like being apprehended by a tigress while in the act of abstracting one of its cubs, madam."

Bill shrugged her shoulders.

"Well, my heart bleeds for you, but I don't know what to advise."

"No, madam."

"It's a problem."

"Yes, madam."

"You might——"

Bill broke off. She had been about to suggest that the butler might slip into Adela's bedtime Ovaltine what is known as a knockout drop or Mickey Finn. She had one in her possession, the gift of a Third Avenue bartender with whom she was on cordial terms, and would have been delighted to lend it to him. But at this moment Kay came in through the French window, a bag of clubs over her shoulder, and the conference had to be suspended.

"Hi, Bill," said Kay.

"Good morning, my child."

"Good morning, Phipps."

"Good morning, miss."

Rosy with exercise, tanned by the Californian sun, Kay presented an attractive picture. Bill, looking at her, could follow Joe Davenport's thought processes and understand his habit of proposing to her every hour on the hour.

"You two look very serious," said Kay. "What goes on?"

"Phipps and I were discussing the situation in China," said Bill. "He has been holding me spellbound."

"Well, don't let me stop you."

"Quite all right. Some other time, eh, Phipps?"

"Any time that suits you, madam."

Kay threw her bag of clubs into a corner.

"Well, Bill. Working away?"

"Like a beaver."

"On the *Memoirs?*"

"On the *Memoirs.*"

"Are they interesting?"

"Not in the least. I never realized before what dull lives silent screen stars led. It's agony, debasing my God-given talents with such hack-work."

"It's a shame they let you go from the studio."

"The loss is theirs. I've just got an idea for the finest B. picture ever screened, and Superba-Llewellyn could have had it if they had not madly dispensed with my services. I shall write it up for *Horror Stories.* It's about a sinister scientist who gets hold of a girl and starts trying to turn her into a lobster."

"A lobster?"

"You know. Those things that look like studio executives. He collected a covey of lobsters and mashed them up and extracted the juice, and he was just going to inject the brew into the gal's spinal column with a hypodermic syringe when her betrothed rushed in and stopped him."

"Why did he do that?"

"He didn't want the girl he loved to be turned into something that looked like a studio executive. Isn't that good psychology?"

"I mean why did the sinister scientist act that way?"

"Oh, just a whim. You know what these sinister scientists are."

"Well, it sounds fine. Full of meat."

"Full of lobsters. Were you ever turned into a lobster, Phipps?"

"No, madam."

"You're sure? Think back."

"No madam. I have not had that experience."

"Well, go and ask the cook if she ever was."

"Very good, madam," said the butler courteously and left the room. He had resumed his professional mask, and not even Sherlock Holmes, looking at his impassive face, could have guessed what vultures were gnawing at the bosom beneath that form-fitting shirt.

"Why all this research?" asked Kay.

"I'm a conscientious artist. I like to get my stuff right. If I'm doing a gangster story, I get it vetted by a gangster. If it's a hydrogen bomb story, I consult the firm that makes hydrogen bombs. And so on."

"Yours must be very interesting work, Miss Shannon."

"Well, it has brought me into contact with a lot of interesting people. I suppose I know more yeggs and thugs and crooks socially than anyone else in the United States. They send me cards at Christmas."

"You're a disreputable old bird, aren't you, Bill. I wonder Aunt Adela has you in the house."

"I'm doing those *Memoirs* of hers cheap. She never could resist a bargain. And don't use that expression 'old bird.' Hoity-toity, what next? However, as a matter of fact, the real reason why I sent Phipps away to chat with the cook was that I wanted to take his mind off his troubles. Adela has just fired him."

"Fired Phipps? Why?"

"It's a long story, too long to tell now. We'll go into it later. How was your golf game?"

"Weak and sinful. Lord Topham trimmed me. He broke a hundred."

"Yes, he has just been releasing the story."

"So you've seen him? Where is he?"

"Still at the telephone, I imagine. He went off to put in a transatlantic call about it at Adela's expense to a friend of his in London called Bingo or Stingo or something. And, while on the subject of telephones, Adela informs me that your young man called up yesterday. She wants to discuss it with you."

"What young man?"

"Have you a dozen? Joe Davenport. Adela intercepted a proposal of marriage from Joe to you yesterday, and you wouldn't be far out in saying that she is exercised in her mind. She's hoping you'll marry that pleasant but quarterwitted ornament of the British peerage, Lord Topham."

"Really? I suppose that's why she invited me here."

"She specifically told me so."

"Well, of course, it would be wonderful to be the wife of a man who can break a hundred. On the other hand——"

"Exactly. On the other hand. Don't overlook the fact that if you marry Topham, you'll have half a dozen imbecile children saying 'Absolutely, what?' all the time in an Oxford accent."

"Really, Miss Shannon!"

"Just a sneak preview."

Phipps appeared.

"The cook desires me to say that she has never been turned into a lobster, madam."

"We must face it like men, Phipps. Stiff upper lip, eh?"

"Yes, madam. I wonder if you could inform me of Mrs. Cork's whereabouts, madam?"

"I imagine she's in her room. You know that room of hers. She was going to have a massage, if you remember."

"Ah, yes, madam."

"Do you want to see her?"

"Yes, madam."

"I wouldn't at the moment."

"No, madam."

"What was it you wanted to see her about?"

"I wished to notify Mrs. Cork that a Mr. Davenport has arrived, madam." Kay uttered a cry.

"What?"

"Yes, miss. He is in the garage, putting his car away. His suitcases are in the hall."

"His *suitcases?*"

"Yes, miss. I gathered from the gentleman that he passed the evening with Mr. Smedley last night and Mr. Smedley invited him to spend a few weeks with us. Thank you, miss."

Phipps bowed slightly, and withdrew.

6

BILL WAS the first to break the silence which followed his departure.

"Well, well," said Bill.

Kay did not speak. She was feeling a little breathless. Phipps's announcement had given her the curious illusion of being the heroine of one of the silent films popularized by her Aunt Adela, in which the great feature had always been the pursuit of virtue by something pretty tough in the way of male pursuers. She had known that Joe was a pertinacious young man, but she had never suspected that his pertinacity would have carried him to such lengths as this. Even the most licentious of clubmen or the most bearded of desperadoes might well have hesitated to bring himself and suitcases into the home of Mrs. Albert Cork on the invitation of her impecunious brother-in-law.

"Well, well," said Bill. "The soul of hospitality, Smedley. You would think he was a Southerner."

"He must be crazy," said Kay. "He can't invite people here. This isn't his house."

"As Adela will no doubt point out to him."

Another facet of the mystery engaged Kay's attention.

"And what did Phipps mean, he passed the evening with Joe? Uncle Smedley never goes out. He told me so."

"He did last night. He was on a toot."

"So that's why he wasn't at dinner. I thought he had a headache."

"He probably has."

Kay was agitated. She was very fond of her Uncle Smedley, and the thought of what lay before him as the result of his thoughtless bonhomie touched her gentle heart.

"Do you think Aunt Adela will give him the devil?"

"If you want to bet against it, five will get you ten. But let's not discuss Smedley," said Bill. "Let us rather turn to the sacred meeting due to take place in a moment or two. So we are to have your young man with us for a few weeks, are we? Well, well, well."

Kay had flushed. This may have been because Bill, her motion-picture training having taught her that a scene always goes better to a musical accompaniment, had begun to hum Mendelssohn's "Wedding March," putting a good deal of feeling into it.

"Don't call him my young man. And it's more likely to be for a few minutes."

"Do you think Adela will throw him out?"

"Don't you?"

"No. Not after I have pleaded his cause. I shall use all my eloquence on his behalf. We alumni of Superba-Llewellyn must stick together."

Phipps appeared in the doorway.

"Mr. Davenport," he announced, and Joe came in, bringing, in Bill's opinion, the sunshine with him. Though suffering from the slight headache inevitable on the morning after an evening passed in the society of Smedley Cork when that earnest reveller was making up leeway after five years of abstinence, he was plainly in radiant spirits. He beamed on Bill and Kay, particularly the latter, with an almost Tophamic exuberance.

"Hello, there," he said, and would no doubt, like Lord Topham, have added that this was the maddest, merriest day of all the glad new year, if he had happened to think of it. "Hello, Bill."

"Hello, Joe."

"And, as I live and breathe, if it isn't my favourite glamour girl, Kay. Hello, Kay."

"Good morning."

"Well, here I am. Where's my hostess?"

"Having a massage. Well, Joe, if I'd known you were coming, I'd have baked a cake. You could have knocked me down with a feather when Phipps told us you were to be to-day's big surprise for my sister Adela."

"Today's unpleasant surprise," said Kay.

Joe looked hurt. The wrong note, he seemed to be saying, the wrong note entirely. On this morning of mornings he wanted there to be smiling faces about him. And nobody, not even a reasonably modest young man, likes to be told that his arrival is going to cast a blight on the home.

"Is it my imagination," he said plaintively, "or am I getting a rather tepid reception? I haven't got leprosy, you know."

"You might just as well have," said Kay.

"You don't think Mrs. Cork will be pleased to see me?"

"You'll be lucky if you escape with a few flesh wounds. I warned you, you remember, that day at lunch."

Bill intervened. She, too, thought the conversation was taking too morbid a tone.

"Nonsense," she said. "You may expect a warm Southern California welcome from Adela. Wait till I have reasoned with her."

"Can anyone reason with Aunt Adela?"

"I can. I will play on her as on a stringed instrument. Don't you worry, Joe. I guarantee you will be treated as a ewe lamb. So you ran into our Smedley last night?"

"Yes."

"An odd coincidence."

"Not so very. I was outside the gate here in a taxi, and he came along and we fraternized."

"What were you doing outside the gate in a taxi?"

"Just gazing. I gave him a lift down the hill. And when we found that he was at a loose end and I was at a loose end, it seemed the sensible thing to join forces. We started off with a bite at Mike Romanoff's."

"And then?"

"We looked in at Mocambo. He began to unbend rather at Mocambo."

"I can imagine."

"After that we went on to Ciro's."

"Where he unbent still further?"

"A good deal further."

"That was when he invited you to come and stay here?"

"Yes."

Bill nodded.

"I think I can reconstruct the scene. First, he climbed on the table and took his coat off and announced that he could lick any two men in the room."

"Any three."

"Then his mood seemed to soften. He climbed down, put his coat on, cried a little and invited everybody present to come and stay at his mountain home. 'Particularly you, my dear fellow,' he said to you."

"You might have been there."

"A pity I wasn't. What happened after that?"

"Well, all of a sudden I lost him. One moment he was there, the next he wasn't. Did you ever see the Indian Rope Trick?"

"No, but I know what you mean. He vanished?"

"Like a pea from under the shell. I don't know where he went."

"Probably to one or more of the numerous joints on Ventura Boulevard. I know Smedley on these occasions. Eye-witnesses have informed me of his habits. He likes to get about and see fresh faces. The faces are always nice and fresh along the Ventura Boulevard, and no doubt he felt that he would be able to express and fulfil himself better if he were alone. I think, Kay, it might be as well if you whistled up the bloodhounds and started a search, to see if he got home all right."

"I think it might."

"We know that his bed was not slept in."

"What!"

"So Adela says. She inspected it after breakfast. He was out all night."

"Why does he do these things?"

Bill could answer that.

"Because he's a fathead. I have watched Smedley Cork burgeon from boyhood to man's estate. As a boy, he was a small fathead. He is now a large fathead. Tell me more," said Bill, as Kay hurried out. "Did Smedley do his imitation of Beatrice Lillie?"

"No, I don't remember that."

"He usually does on these occasions, I'm told. First, his imitation of Beatrice Lillie, then in response to gales of applause, Gunga Din by the late Rudyard Kipling. It's terrific, I believe. How did you pass the long hours?"

Joe's face, which had become a little grave as the result of the introduction of the Mrs. Cork motif, cleared. He began to beam again.

"Bill," he said, "I have tidings of great joy. You remember those characters who brought the good news from Aix to Ghent? Well, they weren't in my class, simply not in my class. I have good news that is good news. This is where you leap about and clap your little hands, my Wilhelmina. You ask me how we passed the long hours. Well, as soon as I thought the time was ripe, I started talking business."

Bill's eyebrows rose.

"Business? With Smedley?"

"Selling him our authors' representatives scheme. It wasn't easy going, because his attention seemed to wander a good deal. I would put the thing with crystal clarity, and he would just sit back, looking glassy-eyed, like a fish on a slab, and when I said: 'Well, how about it?' he was rather apt to spring to his feet and utter what I imagine were college yells of some prehistoric vintage. Putting the question aside, if you know what I mean. Which, of course, rendered it difficult for me to make a convincing sales talk. But I persevered, I kept at it, and you will be relieved to hear, pardner, that all is well. Snatching at a moment when he was having a comparatively lucid interval, I drove the thing home, and he's going to put up that twenty thousand we require as the first step up the ladder of wealth. For heaven's sake, woman," said Joe, amazed, "why aren't you leaping about and clapping your little hands? Haven't you been listening? Pop Cork has definitely promised to put up that twenty thousand we need to buy the agency."

A sad, pitying look had come into Bill's face, the look of a mother forced to notify a loved child that his chances of obtaining candy are but slim, if not non-existent.

"There is a snag," she said.

"Eh? What snag?"

"The fact that Smedley hasn't a cent in the world."

"What!"

"Not a cent."

Joe stared. He could make nothing of this.

"But you told me he was a millionaire."

"Never."

"You did. At the hotel yesterday. You said your sister married a millionaire."

Bill's sad, pitying look deepened.

"Smedley isn't Adela's husband, my poor misled young friend. Adela's husband is no longer with us. Up there," said Bill, pointing heavenwards. "The gentleman with the harp. Smedley is merely his brother, and, as I say, he hasn't a cent in the world. For I hardly suppose that after such a majestic bender as he appears to have been on last night, he has anything left of the hundred I slipped him yesterday."

Joe was rocking on his base.

"You mean that last night he was just kidding me?"

"I don't think intentionally."

"Purely accidental, eh?"

Bill sighed. She was feeling like a mother who, in addition to having to notify him that there is no candy, has been compelled to strike a loved child on the base of the skull with a stocking full of sand.

"It's like this, Joe. When under the influence, poor Smedley gets delusions of grandeur. He believes he's back in the days when he really did have a lot of money . . . before he fooled it all away on musicals which closed on Saturday and repertory companies nobody bought tickets for and Czechoslovak ballets and seasons of grand opera in English. He was at one time Broadway's leading angel. I suppose he backed more flops than any other two men in the business. Whenever there was anything more than ordinarily hopeless in the way of a dramatic opus knocking around, the cry immediately went up: 'Where's Smedley?' It couldn't last. Five years ago his last few thousands went into a sweet little whimsical comedy adapted from the French which ran from a Friday night till the end of the week, and since then he has been penniless and dependent for his three squares a day on the grudging bounty of my sister Adela."

She paused, and Joe, who had been clutching at the desk, slowly relaxed his grip.

"I see," he said.

"I'm afraid this is something of a blow."

"It is, rather. Yes, quite a disappointment. I believe I'll take a turn in the garden and brood on it a little."

"I wish I could have broken it more gently."

"Oh, that's all right," said Joe dully.

He passed through the French window with bowed head, and Adela, appearing simultaneously in the doorway, gazed after him in surprise.

"Who is that?" she asked.

"Eh?" said Bill absently. Her thoughts were still occupied with Joe and the collapse of his hopes and dreams.

"That strange young man who just went out."

Bill braced herself for combat.

"The young man to whom you allude," she said, "is not in the least strange. He is a perfectly normal, wholesome young man of the type which has made America what it is. That is Joe Davenport. You remember we were speaking of him not long ago."

Adela reeled.

"Davenport! That man. What is he doing here? Did you invite him?"

"Not I. Smedley."

Adela's beautiful eyes were bulging. She looked like Louise de Querouaille on one of her bad mornings. If some former associate of hers, with whom she had worked in the era when films were silent, had chanced to wander in at this moment and catch a glimpse of her face, he would have climbed the nearest jacaranda tree and pulled it up after him. Just so had she been wont to look in the old days when bursting in on a director in his office with the dreaded 'I should like a word with you, Mr. Marsupial!' on her lips.

"Are you telling me that Smedley—Smedley—has been inviting people to my house?"

"That's right. It appears that they ran into one another last night and hobnobbed, and Smedley insisted on him coming to take pot luck for a week or two. You'll like Joe. One of the best."

"Ha!"

Bill's manner became firm.

"Now listen, Adela," she said. "I had anticipated that you might be a little difficult about this, and I have formed my plans."

"And I have formed mine. I shall order Phipps to throw this person out."

"You will do no such thing. You will welcome him in and treat him like a ewe lamb. And when I say ewe lamb, I mean EWE LAMB. Adela, you and I were children together."

"I have been trying to live it down ever since."

"And when we were children together," proceeded Bill, her voice cold and hard, "I used, if you remember, to put worms down the back of your neck from time to time, when such a corrective to your insufferable behaviour seemed to be indicated. Persist in your refusal to become the genial hostess to my friend Joe Davenport, and I shall resume that practice."

"We are not amused."

"No, and you'll be still less amused after lunch when, as you show Jacob Glutz the rose garden, you find me sliding up behind you with a fistful of worms."

Adela gasped. Forty years of acquaintance with her sister Wilhelmina had left her with the unpleasant feeling that she was not a woman to be trifled with. There might be things which her sister Wilhemina would hesitate to do, but, she was forced to admit, not many.

"I believe you mean it!"

"Of course I mean it. Not one worm, mark you, but a bevy of worms. Large, fat, sticky worms, Adela. Slithery, writhing, wriggly worms. Cold, clammy——"

Adela capitulated.

"There is no necessity to labour your point," she said stiffly.

"You see reason?"

"I am prepared to be civil to this friend of yours."

"Good. Oh, Joe." called Bill, going to the French window. "Come here a minute, will you? Start practising that sunny smile of yours, Adela. I want to see it split your face from side to side. And when you address your guest, let your voice be like that of a turtle dove calling to its mate. Joe, I want you to meet your hostess. My sister, Mrs. Cork."

Joe's head was still bowed. Communing with nature, as represented by the orange trees, the lemon trees, the jacaranda trees and the rattlesnakes, had done little to alleviate the despondency which had him in its grip. Dully he was aware of something large and feminine confronting him, and he bowed in its direction.

"How do you do?" he said.

"How do you do?" said Adela with a visible effort.

"I have just been telling my sister that you are to be her house guest," said Bill. "She is overjoyed. Eh, Adela?"

There was a momentary silence.

"Yes," said Adela.

"She says yes. So you may take up residence with an easy mind. Your status, as I foreshadowed, will be that of a ewe lamb."

"Well, that's fine."

"Yes, I think you will enjoy it. Ewe lambs live the life of Reilly. Ah, Lord Topham," said Bill, as that gentleman entered with a brief What ho. "Come and shake hands with Joe Davenport."

"Hullo," said Lord Topham, doing so.

"Hello," said Joe.

"Hullo-ullo-ullo."

"Yes," said Joe.

There was another momentary silence.

"Perhaps you would show Mr. Davenport his room, Lord Topham," said Adela, seeming to speak with difficulty. "It is the one next to yours."

"Right ho," said Lord Topham, for the task was well within his scope. He led Joe out. Through the open door he could be heard starting to describe to this new friend of his how he had broken a hundred this morning.

Bill sighed the contented sigh of the woman who has got things done.

"Well, Adela," she said, "I really must congratulate you. You were superb. Just the right note of warmth but ladylike ecstasy. You might have been the Queen of Sheba welcoming King Solomon. But why do you look like that? Is there something on your mind?"

A wistful expression had come into Adela's face.

"I was only thinking," she said, "that a dozen times since you have been in this house I could have dropped something heavy on your head from an upper landing—and I didn't do it."

"Of all sad words of tongue and pen, the saddest are these, It might have been. Well, Kay? What luck?"

Kay had come in, looking worried.

"I can't find him anywhere. Good morning, Aunt Adela. I've been trying to find Uncle Smedley."

A whistling sound, like escaping steam, came from Adela's nostrils.

"I want to find Smedley myself," she said grimly. "I want to ask him what he means by inviting his revolting friends to my house."

Bill seemed surprised.

"Why, I thought you liked Joe. You were charming to him just now. Perhaps Phipps can help us," she said, as the butler came in bearing cocktail materials on a tray. "Phipps, have you seen Mr. Smedley?"

"Not since last night, madam."

"You don't know where he is?" said Kay.

"Oh, yes, miss," said the butler brightly. "He is in prison."

7

IT WAS not immediately that any of those present found themselves able to comment on this front page piece of news. Speech was wiped from their lips, and nothing left to them but the language of the eye, which is always unsatisfactory. Then Kay spoke.

"*Prison?*"

"Yes, miss. Mr. Smedley is in the hands of the constabulary. He spoke to me on the telephone from the jail this morning."

A shuddering cry broke from Adela's lips. Totting up the household expenses week by week and watching him at meals having twice of everything, she had sometimes—for she was a dreamer—aren't we all?—thought how nice it would be if her brother-in-law were a disembodied spirit, his mortal remains safely tucked away in the family vault, but she had never hoped that he would some day go to prison. Prison leads to publicity of the wrong sort, not only for the captive himself but for his relatives by marriage. KIN OF ADELA SHANNON JAILED. INSET-PHOTOGRAPH OF ADELA SHANNON—Adela Shannon was feeling, and the picture thus conjured up gave her an unpleasant, fluttering sensation internally, as if she had been swallowing butterflies.

"Oh, God!" she said.

"He suggested that I should come and take the requisite steps through the proper channels," proceeded Phipps. "But I was unable to leave my domestic duties."

"It didn't occur to you to mention this to anyone?" said Bill.

"No, madam. Mr. Smedley asked me to respect his confidence."

Adela was clenching and unclenching her hands, going through the movements as if she were gripping a brother-in-law's throat. The thought may have been passing through her mind that in omitting to throttle Smedley earlier she had been remiss. One keeps putting these things off and is sorry later.

"Did you learn any details?" asked Bill.

"Yes, madam. Mr. Smedley supplied me with the facts. While visiting a night club on the Ventura Boulevard last night, he stabbed the master of ceremonies with an oyster fork. The latter, visibly taken aback, summoned the management, who summoned the police, who removed Mr. Smedley to the station house. I hope it will not get into the papers, madam."

"I, too, Phipps. At the thought of what Louella Parsons would do with this the imagination boggles."

"Yes, madam. It boggles perceptibly."

"Phipps," said Adela in a strangled voice, "you may go."

"Very good, madam."

Relieved of the butler's presence, Adela was able to give full expression to the emotions surging within her. For some moments, she proceeded to speak of her brother-in-law in terms which could scarcely have been more severe if he had been a fiend with hatchet who had just slain six. It was almost a perfect character sketch of the absent man, and might have continued indefinitely had she not run out of breath. Bill, listening, was aware of an unwilling respect for a woman she had never liked. Adela, she felt, might have her faults, but you had to admire her vocabulary.

"Take it easy," she urged.

"Take it easy? Ha! So this is what happens when I stop watching Smedley for a single instant. He's incorrigible."

"A word I'll bet he couldn't have said last night."

Phipps appeared.

"I thought you would wish to know, madam," he said in a discreet, hushed voice, "that Mr. Smedley has just returned. He was entering the front door as I passed through the hall."

"He's not in prison?" said Kay.

"Apparently not, miss."

"How was he looking?"

"Not very roguish, miss."

Adela's eyes flashed fire. Indeed, there was a sort of incandescence about her whole person. A bystander, had one been present, would have felt that if he had slapped on the back, he would have burned his hand. Not that any bystander, unless exceptionally reckless, would have ventured to slap her on the back.

"Where is he?"

"He has gone to his room, madam, to shave."

"And have a bath, no doubt," said Bill.

"He has had a bath, madam. He was washed by the authorities."

"Phipps," said Adela, "you may GO."

"Very good, madam."

"You'd better run up and view the body, Kay," said Bill. "He'll be wanting someone to hold his hand."

Kay was looking apprehensively at Adela, who was staring before her with quivering nostrils.

"Bill, do something. She's working herself up."

"So I noticed," said Bill. "In moments of emotion, Adela always resembles those priests of Baal who gashed themselves with knives. But leave it to me. I'll attend to her."

"What a comfort you are, Bill."

"The Old Reliable."

"Bless you."

Kay hurried out, and Bill came back to Adela, who was now grinding her teeth.

"Now then, Adela," she said briskly, "simmer down. Come off the boil, will you please."

"Don't talk to me!"

"That's just what I'm going to do. Adela, you make me sick."

"Well, really!"

Bill, veteran of a hundred sisterly battles stretching back into the misty past of a mutual nursery, allowed her voice to rise. It was on these occasions that she was grateful to Providence for having equipped her with sound, healthy vocal cords. A situation like this could not have been handled adequately by a woman missing on one lung.

"Sick," she repeated. "Sitting there licking your lips at the prospect of tearing the stuffing out of poor old Smedley. What an infernal tyrant you are. You love harrying and torturing people. You're like Simon Legree, though you lack Simon Legree's charm of manner. I always maintain that you killed old Al Cork."

Adela, who had been about to take up the Simon Legree issue, decided to dispose of this charge first.

"My husband was run over by a sightseeing omnibus."

Bill nodded. There was, of course, something in what she said.

"That may have helped," she agreed, "but it was being married to you that really did it. But it's silly having these family fights," she went on, in milder vein. "I'm sorry if I was rude."

"You're always rude."

"Well, ruder than usual. But I'm fond of Smedley. I was fond of him when he was a boy of fifteen with pimples. I was fond of him in his middle period, when he was scattering his money on Broadway turkeys. And I'm fond of him now. Some sort of mental flaw in me, I guess. Maybe I ought to see a psychiatrist. Still, there it is. So won't you skip the red tape and treat him decently?"

Adela bridled.

"I was under the impression that I had 'treated him decently.' I have supported him for five years. And a great strain it has been."

"Strain be damned!"

"Must you curse and swear?"

"Of course I must. What do you expect me to do when you insult my intelligence by trying to put gobbledy-gook like that over on me? Strain, indeed! You could afford to support a dozen Smedleys. Al Cork left you enough money to sink a ship, not to mention specific instructions that you'd *got* to support Smedley. And whatever you spend on the poor devil, you get back in the gratification it affords your sadistic instincts to have him under your fat thumb. Am I being rude again?"

"You are."

"I thought I was. All right, let's let it go. But don't forget about the quality of mercy. It isn't strained, you know. No, sir! It droppeth as the gentle rain upon the place beneath. So they tell me."

"Quality of mercy? Stuff and nonsense."

"You'd better not let Shakespeare hear you saying that."

"I——"

Adela broke off, and stiffened. Her aspect had become that of a leopardess sighting its prey. Smedley was entering the room, followed by Kay.

"Ah!" she said.

Smedley, normally so dapper, was looking soiled and crumpled, like a Roman Emperor who has sat up too late over the Falernian wine. With the best intentions in the world, police officials, hustling a man out of a night club into the wagon and subsequently thrusting him into a cell, tend to spoil his crease. Smedley's Palm Beach suit looked as if it had been slept in, as indeed it had. But, oddly for a man with a criminal record and the appearance of a tramp cyclist, he was not slinking into the room with a shamefaced slouch, but striding in boldly in quite a dominant manner. His chin was up—both his chins were up—and in his bloodshot eye there gleamed defiance. It was as though from some inner source he had obtained courage and resolution.

Adela flexed her muscles.

"Well, Smedley?" she said.

"Well?" said Smedley.

"You rather had her there," said Bill.

Smedley blinked. He peered as if he found some difficulty in focusing his gaze.

"Why, hello, Bill."

"Hello, my old stag at eve."

"I didn't see you. For some reason my eyes aren't at their best this morning. Floating spots. You look very yellow."

"It's your imagination. I'm really a pretty pink."

Adela, who had seated herself at the desk, rapped it imperiously. One felt that she would have preferred to have had a gavel, but, like Phipps when operating on a safe, she could do a lot with her finger tips.

"Never mind how Wilhelmina looks," she said. "I am waiting for an explanation."

Bill raised her eyebrows.

"You feel that a man needs to explain why he stabbed a night club master of ceremonies? Just doin' what comes naturally, I'd say. But I should like to know why you aren't in prison, Smedley. Phipps gave us to understand that you were in a dungeon with dripping walls, being gnawed by rats. What happened? Did the jailer's daughter smuggle you in a file in a meat pie?"

"The judge let me off with a caution."

"You see," said Bill triumphantly. "The quality of mercy *isn't* strained. Perhaps you'll believe me another time."

Adela uttered a stricken moan, a moan of a good woman calling on heaven to witness her wrongs. Her voice shook and quivered as it would unquestionably have shaken and quivered in the days of her screen triumphs, had not her deeper emotions in that backward age had to be expressed in sub-titles.

"The shame of it!" she cried. "The brother-in-law of Adela Shannon thrown into prison with all the riff-raff of Los Angeles!"

Kay caught Bill's eye.

"I suppose the society *is* a bit mixed in those prisons," she said.

"Everything very informal, I believe," said Bill.

"Does one dress?"

"Just a black tie."

"PLEASE!!!" said Adela.

She turned to the prisoner again.

"Well, Smedley? I am still waiting for an explanation."

"Tell her it's a poor heart that never rejoices."

"Wilhelmina, please!"

"Well, it is," said Bill. "Ask anyone."

"Have you an explanation?"

A curious writhing movement of the upper part of his body seemed to suggest that Smedley was trying to square his shoulders.

"Certainly I have an explanation. A complete and satisfactory explanation. I was celebrating."

"Celebrating? Celebrating what?"

"The most amazing piece of good fortune that ever happened to a deserving man. I was telling Kay about it upstairs."

Kay nodded.

"It's a real romance," she said. "It would make a good B. picture."

Bill frowned.

"Don't mention B. pictures in my presence, girl. Would you twist the knife in the wound?"

"Oh, Bill, forgive me."

"Quite all right, my child. You did but speak thoughtlessly. Tell us more, Smedley."

Smedley swelled impressively. It was his moment. He was a man who as a rule found difficulty in getting himself listened to in the home cirlce. He had a fund of good stories, but Adela had a way of cutting them short in the opening stanzas. This was the first time in something like five years that he had actually been encouraged to hold the floor.

"Well, sir," he said, "it's like Kay was saying. It's a real romance. Yesterday evening I was out on the terrace, thinking of this and that, and suddenly my guardian angel whispered in my ear—"

"Oh, go and lie down," said Adela wearily.

Smedley gave her a haughty look.

"I will not go and lie down."

"No," said Kay. "I think you ought to hear about his guardian angel."

"I am always glad to hear about guardian angels, always," said Bill. "What did yours whisper in your ear?"

"It whispered 'Smedley, my boy, try the top of the wardrobe.' "

Adela closed her eyes. She may have been praying, but more probably not.

"I really cannot endure this much longer."

"I, on the other hand," said Bill, "could listen for ever. Proceed, Smedley. What wardrobe? Where?"

"The one in Adela's bedroom."

Adela started convulsively. Nor can she fairly be blamed for doing so. She was wondering if a woman's personal sleeping quarters had ever been so extensively invaded. First Phipps, and now Smedley. Was her bedroom her bedroom, she was asking herself, or was it the Grand Concourse of the New York Central Railroad terminal?

She shot a basilisk glare at the speaker.

"Have you been messing about in my room?"

"I went in there for a moment, yes. There was something I was trying to find."

Sudden enlightenment came upon Bill.

"Ye gods!" she said. "The diary?"

"Yup."

"You were after that?"

"Yup."

"Was it there?"

"Yup. Yessir, plumb spang on top of the wardrobe."

"You've got it?"

"In my pocket," said Smedley, patting it.

Adela was looking from Bill to Smedley, from Smedley to Bill, dangerously, exasperated by the mystic turn the conversation had taken. She disliked people who spoke in riddles in her presence, particularly if one of them was a jail bird who had brought disgrace on her home and the other a sister whom she wished she had never allowed to come into it. There were probably no two individuals in America who could have occasioned her more irritation by wrapping their meaning up in cryptic speech. Her resemblance to a peevish leopardess became more marked.

"What are you talking about? What diary? Whose diary?"

"Carmen Flores's," said Kay. "Uncle Smedley's been trying to find it for weeks."

Bill sighed. Hers was a feeling heart.

"Alas, poor Phipps," she said. "What made you think of the wardrobe, Smedley?"

"If a woman has anything to hide, that's where she puts it. Well-known fact. It's in all the detective stories."

"Don't you ever read Agatha Christie?" said Kay.

"Who is Agatha Christie?" asked Adela.

"My dear Adela!" said Bill.

Smedley gave a short, unpleasant laugh.

"Just a dumb bunny," he said.

Adela drew herself up and directed at her brother-in-law a look of the sort which Evil Eye Fleagle of Brooklyn would have described as a full whammy.

"Don't you call me a dumb bunny, you—you fugitive from a chain gang!"

Smedley, in his turn, drew himself up.

"And don't you call me a fugitive from a chain gang. The idea!"

"I called you a fugitive from a chain gang because that's what you are. Don't the police want you?"

"No, the police do not want me."

"How I sympathize with the police," sighed Adela. "I know just how they feel."

Smedley stiffened.

"Adela, I resent that crack."

"It doesn't matter what you resent."

"Oh, doesn't it?"

"I think it does, Adela," said Bill. "This has put Smedley in a very different position from what he was this time yesterday."

"I don't know what you mean."

"It's very simple."

Joe came in. He had seen his room, heard in pitiless detail the story of how Lord Topham had broken a hundred that morning, and he was now planning to go out into the garden and commune with nature again, not that he expected to derive any solace from doing so. He was still in the depths. Listlessly, he observed that the Garden Room seemed to have become the centre of a conference, but he paid its occupants but slight attention and was making for the French window, when Bill's powerful voice halted him in his tracks.

"Yesterday, Smedley was not in possession of the diary of the late Carmen Flores. To-day he is. There isn't a studio in Hollywood that won't pay through the nose for it."

Smedley corroborated this.

"I was on the phone to Colossal-Exquisite last night. They say they'll give fifty thousand."

"Fifty thousand!" gasped Adela.

"Fifty thousand," said Smedley.

Adela rose slowly to her feet.

"You mean that they . . . You mean fifty thousand *dollars?*"

"Fifty thousand dollars," said Smedley.

Joe tottered to the sofa, and collapsed on it. His head was spinning. It seemed to him that an unseen orchestra had begun to play soft music in the Garden Room.

"Have you closed with the offer?" asked Bill.

"No. I'm waiting till all the bids are in. I'm expecting big things from Medulla-Oblongata-Glutz."

"But you can't get less than fifty thousand."

"That's right," said Smedley. He took the diary from his pocket, and gazed at it reverently. "Isn't it astounding that a small book like this should be worth fifty grand!"

"It must be red-hot stuff. Have you read any of it?"

"I can't. It's in Spanish."

"Too bad."

"Quite all right," said Smedley, quick to point out the bright side. "One of the gardeners at the Lulabelle Mahaffy place down the road is a Mexican. I'm going to take it around to him and have him translate it. We're good friends. He gave me a shot of that Mexican drink once that they call—no, I've forgotten the name, but it lifts the top of your head off."

On Adela during these exchanges there had descended a curious calm. It was as if she had been thinking and had been rewarded with an idea whose effects had been to still the tumult within her. Her fingers were twitching a little, but her voice, when she spoke, was quiet and unusually amiable.

"I picked up a little Spanish when I made that personal goodwill tour in South America," she said. "I might be able to help you. May I look?"

"Sure," said Smedley cordially. Speak civilly to Smedley Cork and he would speak civilly to you. "There's an entry for the twenty-first of April that I'd like to have translated. It's got six exclamation marks against it in the margin."

He gave Adela the book. Her fingers, as she took it, were twitching more noticeably than ever. She started for the door, and Smedley, suddenly filled with a nameless fear, gave tongue.

"Hey! Where are you off to?"

Adela turned.

"A thing as valuable as this ought not to be left lying about. I will put it in the safe in the projection room."

"You will not. I want it on my person."

Adela unmasked her batteries.

"Well, you aren't going to have it on your person," she said crisply. "For five years, Smedley, you have been living on me, and it is high time you made some contribution to the household expenses. This is it."

"But—but—"

"This is it," said Adela. "Fifty thousand dollars. A very nice first instalment. And, Wilhelmina," she said, changing the subject, "will you kindly go and take off those damned dungarees. You look like a rag-picker."

8

THE SLAM of the closing door was drowned by the cry, resembling in its general features the howl of some bereaved beast of the jungle, which broke from Smedley's lips. Phipps, in his remarks to Bill on the previous day with reference to the attitude of Mrs. Adela Cork toward those whom she found exploring her bedroom, had spoken of the emotional behaviour of tigresses when robbed of their cubs. It is to be doubted whether even the most neurotic tigress could have put more naked anguish into what in motion picure circles is called a 'take' than Smedley was now doing. His eyes seemed to protrude from their sockets, and a third chin had been added to his normal two by the limp sagging of his jaw.

Bill, also, appeared a little taken aback by this unforeseen development.

"My God!"said Bill. "Hi-jacked!"

Smedley had joined Joe on the sofa.

"In broad daylight!" he moaned incredulously. His bosom swelled with righteous indignation. "I'll—I'll write to the *Los Angeles Examiner.*"

"No wonder that woman rose to impressive heights on the silent screen."

"But she can't do this," cried Joe.

"I know she can't." said Bill. "But she has."

She crossed the room with a firm step and touched the bell. She was a woman of action, not one of your weak, fluttering women who waste precious time in lamentations. It had taken her scarcely a moment to see what Napoleon would have done in a crisis like this. Put Napoleon in a tight corner, and the first thing he did was summon up his reserves and send them into battle.

This was what Bill now proposed to do. The ringing of that bell was the bugle call which would bring Phipps hurrying to the front line, and it was on Phipps that she was relying to snatch victory out of defeat. If something valuable has been wrested from you and deposited in a safe and you have at your call a butler who has taken twenty lessons in the art of opening safes and become good at it, it is mere common sense to avail yourself of his skill.

Smedley was still vibrating. He raised his hands in a passionate gesture.

"I'll write to *Variety!*"

Bill regarded him maternally.

"Pipe down, Smedley."

"I won't pipe down. I'll write to Walter Winchell."

"No need to get excited," said Bill. "Absolutely not, as Lord Topham would say. Ah, Phipps."

The butler had manifested himself silently in the doorway.

"You rang, madam?"

"Yes. Come in. Phipps," said Bill, "I'm afraid the moment has arrived when we must cease to hide your light beneath a bushel."

"Madam?"

"Smedley, have you ever served on a jury?"

As far as an English butler can quiver, Phipps quivered. He gave Bill a startled look.

"Madam, please!"

Bill ignored the interruption.

"I was on one some little time ago," she said. "The one that sent Phipps here up the river for three years."

"Madam, you promised——"

"And do you know what he had done to earn that three years sojourn in the coop? Do you know what he got his scholarship at Sing-Sing for? Safeblowing."

If she had anticipated a stunned reaction to her words, she was not disappointed. Smedley stopped blowing invisible bubbles and stared dumbly at the butler. Kay gave a sharp squeak and stared dumbly at the butler. Joe said "What?" He, too, stared dumbly at the butler. Phipps stared dumbly at Bill. Not even Julius Caesar, receiving Brutus's dagger thrust, could have packed more pain and disappointment into a glance. Those reproachful eyes made Bill feel that something in the nature of an apology was in order.

"I'm sorry, Phipps," she said, "but this is a military necessity."

Smedley found speech.

"You mean," he said, marvelling, "that Phipps—*Phipps*—was a safe-blower?"

"And a darned good one, too. He blew a beautiful safe."

"Then——"

"Exactly. That is why I brought up the subject. Phipps, we've got a job for you."

Though far from having recovered completely from one of the worst shocks of his life, the butler was sufficiently himself again to be able to speak.

"Madam?"

"We want you to open Mrs. Cork's safe. The one in the projection room."

"But, madam, I have retired."

"Then this is where you make a comeback."

Icy resolution descended upon Phipps. It was those operative words 'Mrs. Cork's safe' that steeled him to resist to the uttermost this call upon his services. As Lyly so neatly put it in his *Euphues,* the burned child dreadeth the fire, and a butler who has twice been caught by Mrs. Cork hunting for diaries in her bedroom does not lightly undertake the even more perilous task of burgling safes belonging to a woman of her intimidating personality. Call on James Phipps to make a burglarious entry into Fort Knox and it is possible that he might decide to oblige, but Mrs. Cork's safes were immune.

"No, madam," he said respectfully, but firmly.

"Ah, come on."

"No, madam."

"Think well, Phipps. Are you prepared to stand before the bar of world opinion as a man who refused to bust a safe to oblige an old friend?"

"Yes, madam."

"I should have mentioned at the outset," said Bill, "that your cut will be five thousand dollars."

Phipps started. His iron front began to waver. His eyes, which had been hard and uncompromising, softened, and there came into them the gleam which always comes into the eyes of butlers when they see an opportunity of making quick money. The vision of Adela Cork sneaking up behind him and tapping him on the shoulder as he crouched before her safe began to fade. Every man has his price, and five thousand dollars was about Phipps's.

"That is a lot of money, madam," he said, impressed.

"It's a hell of a lot of money," said Smedley, thoroughly concurring.

Bill checked this parsimonious trend of thought with an impatient gesture. How like Smedley, she felt, to haggle at a time like this.

"Customary agent's commission of ten per cent," she said. "We mustn't be tightwads. You don't want Phipps to think he's working for Gaspard the Miser. Five thousand of the best, Phipps."

"Five thousand," murmured the butler reverently.

"Are you with us?"

"Yes, madam."

A general sense of relaxation came over those present, such as occurs at a theatrical conference when the man with the money has been induced to sign on the dotted line.

"Good," said Bill. "Well, here's the story outline. Last night, Mr. Smedley found the diary."

"Oh, my Gawd!"

Bill patted his shoulder tenderly.

"I know, I know. I know just how you feel. But there it is. Mr. Smedley found the diary last night, and this morning Mrs. Cork swiped it from him and put it in the safe in the projection room. Will you reswipe it for us?"

That vision of Adela creeping up behind him flashed once more before the butler's eyes. A momentary shudder, and he was strong again.

"For five thousand dollars, yes, madam."

"Fine. Then we will meet at Philippi—or, rather, here—to-night. Say at one o'clock in the morning."

"One o'clock in the morning. Very good, madam. Will that be all, madam?"

"That will be all."

"Thank you, madam."

"Thank *you*, Phipps."

"Bill," cried Smedley, "you're a marvel. What a brain, what a brain!"

"Wonderful," said Kay. "Stupendous."

"Colossal," said Joe.

"Super-colossal," said Smedley.

"You can always trust me, boys," said Bill. "The Old Reliable."

Adela came in. She was wearing the contented look of a woman who has just locked the door of her personal safe on a diary valued at a minimum of fifty thousand dollars. Then her eyes flashed with all their old fire.

"Wilhelmina!" she cried. "Those dungarees! Are you aware that Mr. Glutz's car is coming up the drive?"

"Sorry," said Bill. "I was thinking of other things. I will rush up immediately and gown myself in some clinging material which will accentuate rather than hide my graceful outlines."

"Well, be quick."

"Forked lightning, my dear Adela, forked lightning."

9

SMEDLEY CORK, first of the little group of Phipps's admirers and supporters to arrive at the tryst, stood at the open French window of the Garden Room, staring into the night with unseeing eyes. From somewhere outside the closed door there came the *ping* of a clock striking one, and he heard it with a feeling of amazement. Only one o'clock? He could scarcely believe it. For though in actual fact not more than five minutes had elapsed since he had crept furtively down the stairs and come to the meeting place, it seemed to him that he had been waiting there for weeks. He was faintly surprised that he had not put out tendrils, like a Virginia creeper.

Strained nerves play these tricks on us, and Smedley's nerves were strained at the moment to their uttermost. Reason told him that it was improbable that his sister-in-law, a woman who was fond of her sleep, would take it into her head to roam the house at this hour, but the hideous possibility of such a disaster had not failed to present itself to his shrinking mind, and the native hue of resolution on his face was sicklied o'er with the pale cast of thought. As he stood there waiting for zero hour, his substantial frame twitched and quivered and rippled, as if he had been an Ouled Nail dancer about to go into her muscle dance.

The door opened noiselessly, and Bill came in. She was in her customary excellent spirits. Others might view with concern the shape of things to come, but not Wilhelmina Shannon. She was looking forward with bright enthusiasm to a pleasant and instructive evening.

"Hello, there, Smedley," she boomed in her breezy, genial way, and Smedley leaped like an Ouled Nail dancer who has trodden on a tin-tack.

"I wish you wouldn't bellow at a fellow suddenly like that, Bill," he said aggrievedly, having descended to terra firma. He was panting heavily and not feeling at all easy about his blood pressure. "If anyone had told me that an old friend like you would come and sneak up behind a man at a time like this and yell in his ear without the slightest preliminary warning, I wouldn't have believed it."

"Sorry, old sport."

"Too late to be sorry now," said Smedley moodily. "You made me bite my tongue off at the roots. Where's Phipps?"

"He'll be here."

"It's past one."

"Only just," said Bill. She joined him at the window and gazed out on the night. "What were you doing? Admiring the stars? A fine display. Glorious technicolor. Look how the floor of heaven is thick inlaid with patines of bright gold. In such a night as this, when the sweet wind did gently kiss the trees——"

"For God's sake, Bill!"

"Some other time, eh? Not in the mood, no? Just as you say. Still, you can't deny that yonder stars are well worth looking at. Bright, twinkling and extremely neatly arranged. A credit to Southern California. I'll tell you something about those stars, Smedley. There's not the smallest orb which thou beholdest, but in his motion like an angel sings, still quiring to the young-eyed Cherubim. Worth knowing, that. Stop fluttering like a butterfly in a storm. What's the matter with you? Nervous?"

"I'm all of a twitter."

"Too bad. Ah, Joe," said Bill, as the door opened again. "Come in and help me hold Smedley's hand. He's got the heeby-jeebies."

Joe regarded the sufferer with a sympathetic eye. He, too, was by no means free from that distressing malady. He was conscious of an unpleasant sensation of having been plunged into the middle of a B. picture of the more violent type and this was making him gulp a good deal. His had been a sheltered life, and it is disconcerting for a young man who has lived a sheltered life, to find himself involved in happenings of a melodramatic nature. To him, as to Smedley, there had come the thought that they might at any moment be joined by his formidable hostess, and it was not an agreeable reflection. Estimating Mrs. Cork's probable reactions to the discovery that her nearest and dearest were planning to burgle her safe, his imagination boggled—as Phipps would have said, perceptibly. He had conceived a wholesome awe of the ex-Empress of Stormy Emotions. Running over in his mind the women of his acquaintance who could legitimately be classed as dangerous specimens whose bite spelled death, he was inclined to place Adela Shannon Cork at the very top of the list. She had that certain something that the others had not got.

"Where's Phipps?" he asked, having swallowed a little painfully, for something—possibly his heart—seemed to be obstructing his throat.

"He's coming," said Bill. "The hour will produce the man."

Smedley whinnied like a frightened horse.

"But it hasn't produced the man, damn it. Here it is past one and not a sign of him. You keep saying he's coming, but he doesn't come. I'm going up to his room, to see if he's there. I shall probably find him curled up in bed, fast asleep. Curse the fellow. Letting us down like this. If that's the sort of butler England is turning out nowadays. I'm sorry for them."

He hurried from the room, puffing emotionally, and Bill clicked her tongue disapprovingly, like a Spartan mother who had expected better things of a favourite son.

"Smedley gets so agitated."

"I don't blame him," said Joe. "I'm agitated myself."

Bill snorted scornfully.

"You men! Just neurotic wrecks, all of you. No sang-froid."

"All right, I lack sang-froid and I'm a neurotic wreck. But I repeat that I am agitated. That's my story and I stick to it. My feet are chilly, and there's something with long hairy legs running up and down my spine. Suppose this ghastly butler doesn't show up."

"He'll show up."

"Well, suppose he can't open the safe?"

To Bill, who with eleven other good men and women true had sat for several days in a jury box while the absent man's capabilities were expatiated on by an eloquent District Attorney, who made a capital story out of it, the question was a laughable one.

"Of course he can open the safe. He's an expert. You should have read what the papers said of him at the time of the trial. He got rave notices."

Joe became calmer.

"He did?"

"He certainly did."

"He has your confidence?"

"Implicit."

Joe expelled a deep breath.

"Bill, you put heart into me."

"That's good."

"I suppose it's because one doesn't associate a butler with safeblowing that I was doubtful for a moment. I always thought butlers went about saying 'Yes, m'lord,' 'No, m'lord,' 'Pardon me, m'lady, Her Grace the Duchess is on the telephone. She desires me to ask if you can spare her a cup of sugar,' and all that sort of thing, not blowing safes. But if he carries your guarantee, that's a different matter. I feel now that prosperity is just around the corner."

"Let's sing to every citizen and for'gner prosperity is just around the corner."

"Yes, let's. Bill, you know all about women, I take it?"

"I've met a couple."

"Women like money. Right?"

"Right."

"And they like a man who does things. A man, I mean, who is what the French call an *om sayrioo*. Correct?"

"Correct."

"So if Phipps gets that diary and Smedley gives us our twenty thousand and I become a plutocratic partner in a flourishing firm of authors' representatives, it's going to make a whale of a lot of difference, don't you think? With Kay, I mean. She'll feel a new respect for me."

"She will probably throw herself on your chest and cry 'My hero!' "

"Exactly. Something more or less along those lines is what I'm budgeting for. But we need Phipps."

"We do."

"Without Phipps we can accomplish nothing constructive."

"Nothing."

"Then what it all boils down to is, Where the hell is Phipps? Ah!" said Joe, breaking off and uttering the ejaculation with satisfaction and relief. The door was opening again.

It was, however, not the missing man, but Kay who came in. She was looking charming in pyjamas, mules and a dressing-gown, and at any other time Joe's heart would have leaped up like that of the poet Wordsworth when he, the poet Wordsworth, beheld a rainbow in the sky. Now he merely stared at her bleakly, as if by failing to a be a butler with a gift for blowing safes she had disappointed him.

"You!" he said.

"Come aboard, sir," said Kay. "Where's Phipps?"

Bill's manner, too, was austere.

"Now don't you begin," she said, "I thought I told you to go to bed."

"Please, sergeant, I got up."

"Well, you're a naughty girl and will probably come to a bad end, but now you're here, you can make yourself useful. You can be cutting sandwiches."

"You can't want sandwiches after that enormous dinner."

"I always want sandwiches," said Bill. Her momentary annoyance had vanished. She scrutinized Kay critically.

"An attractive little cheesemite, isn't she, Joe? Get those eyes."

"I've got 'em."

"Thank you, Bill. I'm glad you think I have nice eyes."

Joe could not pass this. The first agony of seeing somebody who was not Phipps coming in at the door had abated, and he was able to take in those pyjamas, that dressing-gown and the mules. The wistful thought came to him that, if he and Kay had a little home, this was how she would look in it of an evening.

"Nice!" he said. "Good God! what an adjective!"

"What Joe means," explained Bill, "is that with your limited vocabulary you have failed to spike the *mot juste*. In analysing your appearance, he feels, we must not be satisfied with the first weak word that comes along. We must pull up our socks and dredge the Thesaurus. You probably consider, Joe, that those eyes of hers are more like twin stars than anything?"

"Twin stars is nearer it. You're on the right lines."

"And her brow? Alabaster?"

"I'll accept alabaster."

Kay took a seat, kicked off one of the mules and tried unsuccessfully to catch it on her toe. Like her Aunt Wilhelmina, she was in capital spirits and feeling none of the tremors which afflicted the more timorous males.

"If you two have quite finished discussing me——" she said.

"Finished?" said Bill. "Why, we've scarcely begun. We've barely scratched the surface. I like her bone structure, Joe. She has small, delicate bones."

Joe endorsed this.

"That was the first thing I noticed about her the day we met, her small, delicate bones. 'Gosh!' I said to myself. 'This girl's got small, delicate bones.' "

"And what happened then?" asked Kay.

"His heart stood still," said Bill. "I should have mentioned that when Joe was a boy, he promised his mother he would never marry a girl who didn't have small, delicate bones. Well, Smedley? Did you find him curled up in bed?"

Smedley had come puffing in, more agitated than ever. It was plain that the mystery of the missing butler was preying heavily on what may loosely be called his mind.

"Not a sign of him. He's not in his room. What on earth can have happened to the fellow?" He broke off, leaping in the old familiar way, his eyes protruding from their sockets. "What's that?"

"What's what?"

"I heard something. Outside there. Footsteps."

"Be calm, Smedley," said Bill. "It's probably Phipps. I'll bet it's Phipps. It *is* Phipps," she concluded, as a dignified figure detached itself from the darkness outside the French windows. "Good evening, Phipps."

"Good evening, madam," said the butler.

10

WITH THE arrival of the star performer, the spearhead of the movement and, if one may so describe him, the pilot on whom they were counting to weather the storm, a general feeling of relief and relaxation spread itself among the other members of the expeditionary force. Smedley grunted. So did Joe. Kay smiled a welcoming smile. And Bill, as if lost to all sense of what was fitting, went so far as to pat the man on the shoulder. Dressed in what appeared to be his Sunday best, his gaze calm and steady, he seemed so competent, so reliable, so obviously capable of conducting to a successful conclusion any task to which he set the hand holding the bowler hat without which no English butler stirs abroad.

"Well met by moonlight, proud Phipps," said Bill. "We thought you were never coming."

"I am a little late, I fear, madam. I was detained. I am sorry."

"Not at all. But I admit that we had begun to be somewhat anxious. Mr. Smedley in particular had reached a condition where he could have given Mariana at the Moated Grange six bisques and a beating. What detained you?"

"I was in conference with Mr. Glutz, madam."

Smedley's eyes, which had returned to their sockets, popped out again.

"Mr. who?"

"Glutz, sir. Of Medulla-Oblongata-Glutz. The gentleman who was with us for luncheon to-day. He sent for me to discuss details of my contract."

"Your *what?*"

The butler placed his bowler hat on the desk, carefully and a little formally, like Royalty laying a foundation stone.

"My contract, sir. If I might explain. I had withdrawn to my pantry at the conclusion of the midday meal, and Mr. Glutz presented himself there and after a few courteous preliminaries opened negotiations with a view to my playing butler roles in his organization."

"Good God."

"Yes, sir, I must confess to having experienced a slight feeling of surprise myself when I heard him formulate his proposition. Indeed, I fancied for a moment that this was a mere passing pleasantry on the gentleman's part—what is known in my native country as a bit of spoof and in the United States of Northern America as ribbing. But I soon perceived that he was in earnest. Apparently, he had been greatly impressed by my deportment at the luncheon table."

"I don't wonder," said Bill. "You were right in midseason form. It was buttling plus."

"Thank you, madam. One desires to give satisfaction. Mr. Glutz expressed much the same opinion. He appeared to feel that if talents like mine—artistry like mine, he was kind enough to say—were transferred to the silver screen, nothing but good could result. He then made me the offer to which I have referred, and I accepted it."

He ceased, walked to the bowler hat, lovingly flicked a speck of dust off it, and returned to the statuesque pose which he was wont to assume at meal times, looking as if he were about to have his portrait painted by an artist who specialized in butlers. On his audience an awed silence had descended. It is always impressive to be present at the birth of a star.

"Well, well," said Smedley.

"Fancy!" said Kay.

"So now you're in pix," said Joe.

"Yes, sir."

"Extraordinary how everybody in Hollywood wants to get into pix," said Bill.

"Yes, madam. The aspiration would appear to be universal."

Bill said it was something in the air, and Phipps said, So one would be disposed to imagine, madam, adding that oddly enough he had occasionally toyed with the idea of embarking on a motion-picture career, but had never seemed to find the time to get around to it: and the conversation might have continued in this purely professional vein, had not Smedley, recovering from his first reactions to the sensational news item, become peevish and fussy again.

"But why on earth had you got to see him at this time of night?" he demanded, not perhaps unreasonably. "One o'clock in the morning. Good God!"

A well-trained butler's eyebrows never actually rise, but Phipps's flickered as if on the verge of upward movement, and in his voice, as he replied, there was the merest hint of rebuke.

"My domestic duties would not allow me to leave the house before eleven-thirty, sir, and Mr. Glutz was insistent that the negotiations be completed without delay. I took the view that his wish was law."

"Quite right," said Bill. "Always keep in with the boss, however much he looks like a lobster. Mr. Glutz does look like a lobster, doesn't he?"

"There is perhaps a resemblance to the crustacean you mention, madam."

"Though what does that matter, provided his heart is in the right place?"

"Precisely, madam."

"People have told me I look like a German Boxer."

"A most attractive Boxer, madam."

"Nice of you to say so, Phipps. Has he given you a good contract?"

"Eminently satisfactory, thank you, madam."

"Watch those options."

"Yes, madam."

"Well, I shall follow your future career with considerable interest."

"Thank you, madam. I shall endeavour to give satisfaction."

Smedley, who had a one-track mind, struck the practical note.

"Well, now you're here, let's get to work. We've wasted half the night."

"It won't take long," Bill assured him, "if Phipps is the man he used to be. Eh, Phipps?"

The butler seemed to hesitate. He looked like a butler about to break bad news.

"I am sorry, madam," he said apologetically, "but I fear I have a slight disappointment for you."

"Eh?"

"I have come to inform you—regretfully—that I am unable to undertake the desired task."

If he had expected to make a sensation, he was not wrong. His words had the effect of a bombshell.

"What?" cried Joe.

"Oh, Phipps!" cried Kay.

"Not undertake it?" bleated Smedley. "What do you mean?"

It was plain that the spearhead of the movement was embarrassed. He departed from his official impassivity to the extent of shuffling a foot along the carpet and twiddling his fingers. Then his eyes fell on the bowler hat, and he seemed to draw strength from it.

"This unforeseen development has naturally effected a considerable alteration in my plans, sir. As an artist in the employ of Medulla-Oblongata-Glutz, I cannot run the risk of being discovered burgling safes. There is a morality clause in my contract."

"A *what?*"

"Morality clause, sir. Para Six."

Smedley exploded. His blood pressure had now reached unprecedented heights. A doctor, scanning his empurpled face, would have clicked his tongue concernedly—or perhaps would have rubbed his hands, scenting business at ten dollars a visit.

"I never heard such infernal nonsense in my life."

"I am sorry, sir. But I fear I cannot recede from my position."

"But think of the five thousand."

"A trivial sum, sir. We motion-picture actors regard five thousand dollars as the merest small change."

"Don't talk like that," cried Smedley, shocked to the core. "It—it's blasphemous."

Phipps turned to Bill, in whom he seemed to see a level-headed ally and supporter.

"I am sure *you* will understand that I cannot jeopardize my contract, madam."

"Of course not. Your art comes first."

"Precisely, madam."

"You've signed on the dotted line, and you must stay signed."

"Exactly, madam."

"But, damn it——"

"Hush, Smedley. Be calm."

"Calm!"

"What you need," said Bill, "is a drink. Could you bring us a few fluid ounces of the blushful Hippocrene, Phipps?"

"Certainly, madam. What would you desire?"

Smedley sank into a chair.

"Bring every darned bottle you can lay your hands on!"

"Very good, sir," said Phipps.

He retrieved the bowler hat from the desk, seemed for an instant about to place it on his head, recollected himself in time and left the room on his errand of mercy.

Silence reigned for some moments after his departure. Smedley in his chair was looking like a man who for two pins would have buried his face in his hands. Joe had gone to the French window and was staring up at the stars with a lack-lustre eye. Kay had crossed to where Smedley sat and was stroking his head in a rather feverish manner. Only Bill was unmoved.

"Well," said Smedley, from the depths, "this is a nice thing to happen."

"Just Hollywood," said Bill.

"If a man's a butler, why can't he *be* a butler, instead of gallivanting around getting contracts from studios? And all this nonsense about morality clauses."

"Cheer up, Smedley. All is not lost. I have the situation well in hand," said Bill. And such was the magnetism of her personality, that a faint hope stirred in Smedley's bosom. It might be, he felt, that even the present impasse would yield to treatment from one whom, though he did not want to marry her, he had always recognized as a woman of impressive gifts, well worthy of the title of The Old Reliable. He raised a haggard face.

"What are you going to do?"

"I am going to have a drink."

Joe, at the window, barked bitterly like the seal to which Kay had once compared him.

"Fine," he said. "Splendid. You're going to have a drink, are you? That has taken a great weight off my mind. I was worrying myself sick, wondering if you were going to have a drink."

"And having had it," proceeded Bill equably, "I shall press one on Phipps. When he comes back, I propose to ply him with strong liquor and—after his calm judgment has been sufficiently unbalanced—taunt him."

"Taunt him?"

"What do you mean, taunt him?" asked Smedley, puzzled but still hopeful.

"Sting his professional pride with a few well-judged sneers. Scoff and mock at him for having lost his grip. It ought to work. Phipps, you must remember, till he saw the light, was a very eminent safeblower, and you can't be an eminent safeblower without being a sensitive artist, proud of your skill and resentful of criticism. Imagine how Shakespeare would have felt if, after he had retired to Stratford, somebody had come along and congratulated him on having got out of the theatre game just in time, because it was obvious to everyone that he had been slipping."

The door opened, and Phipps came in, swaying slightly under the weight of an enormous tray filled with bottles and glasses. He placed it on the desk.

"I have made a wide selection, madam," he said.

"You certainly have," said Bill. "Start pouring, Joe."

"Right," said Joe, becoming busy. "Champagne, Bill?"

"Just a drop, perhaps. I often say that there's nothing like a little something at this time of night to pick you up. Thank you, Joe. But you haven't got yours, Phipps."

"Nothing for me, thank you, madam."

"Oh, come. We must drink success to your new venture. You are embarking on a career which is going to make you loved, worshipped, idolized by the prince in his palace, the peasant in his cot, the explorer in the jungle and the Eskimo in his frozen igloo, and your launching must be celebrated with fitting rites. Properly speaking, we ought to break a bottle over your head."

"Well, a very mild one, madam. I have always been somewhat susceptible to the effects of alcohol. It was that that led to me being on trial on the occasion when you were a member of the jury, madam."

"Really?"

"Yes, madam. The constables would never have apprehended me if I had not been under the influence."

"Of course, yes, I remember. It came out in the evidence, didn't it? Your employer heard noises in the night, tracked them down to the library, where his safe was, and there you were, lying back in a chair with your feet on the table and a bottle in your hand, singing Sweet Adeline."

"Precisely, madam. It rendered me conspicuous."

During these exchanges, Bill, her massive form interposed between the butler and the desk, had been selecting with almost loving care one bottle after another and blending their contents in a large tumbler. It was liquid dynamite that she was concocting, but her words, as she handed him the mixture, were reassuring.

"Try this for size," said Bill. "I think you'll like it. I call it the Wilhelmina Shannon Special. Mild—practically a soft drink—but refreshing."

"Thank you, madam," said Phipps, accepting the glass and raising it to his lips with a respectful "Happy days, madam." He sipped tentatively, then more deeply, finally drained the bumper with evident relish.

"How was it?" asked Bill.

"Extremely good, madam."

"Will you have another one?"

"I believe I will, madam."

Bill took the glass from him and put a second Wilhelmina Shannon Special in preparation.

"Tell me about yourself, Phipps," she said, chatting as she mixed. "Our paths parted after that trial. I, so to speak, took the high road, and you took the low road. Let us pick up the threads. What happened after you graduated from Sing-Sing?"

"I secured a position as a butler once more. Thank you, madam," said Phipps, taking the glass.

"No difficulty about getting signed up?"

"Oh, no, madam. I had a number of excellent references from employers in England, and I came to California, affecting to be a newly arrived immigrant. Ladies and gentlemen in California rarely read the New York papers, I have found. And, after all, three years had passed since my unpleasant experience. I suffered no inconvenience whatsoever."

"And how about the old life work?"

"Madam?"

"Did you continue to pass the potatoes with one hand and blow safes with the other?"

"Oh, no, madam."

"Just buttled?"

"Precisely, madam."

"So it's about four years since you did a job?"

"Yes, madam."

"Then no wonder you've lost your nerve," said Bill.

The butler started. A dull flush spread itself over his face, deepening the colour already implanted there by the Wilhelmina Shannon Specials.

"Madam?" he said.

Bill was friendly, but frank.

"Oh, you can't fool us, Phipps. That was a good story of yours about your morality clause, but we see through it." She turned to Joe. "Right?"

"Right," said Joe.

"It's perfectly plain that after your long lay-off, you realized that you were

no longer the man you had been. You had lost your grip, and you knew it."
She turned to Kay. "Right?"

"Right," said Kay.

"Listen," said Phipps.

He spoke harshly and in a manner quite lacking in his customary smooth
deference. His voice had taken on a novel roughness. His head, as he had
said, had never been strong, and there had been that in the beverage assembled by his hostess which might have roughened the voice of a seasoned
toper. It was as though the butler in him had fallen from him like a garment,
revealing the natural man beneath. That his *amour-propre* had been deeply
wounded was plainly to be seen.

"Oh, don't think we're blaming you," said Bill. "Some people might say
you were a spineless poltroon——"

"*What?*"

"—but that's all nonsense. You aren't a poltroon, you're just prudent. You
know when a thing is beyond your powers and you decline to take it on. We
respect you for it. We applaud your good sense. We admire you enormously.
Right?"

"Right," said Joe.

Phipps scowled darkly. His eyes were hard and hostile.

"You think I'm scared to bust that pete upstairs?"

"It seems the reasonable explanation. And I don't wonder. It's a tough
job."

"Tough? A lousy little country house pete? Listen, I've busted banks."

"You mean piggy banks?"

"No, I don't mean piggy banks. I'll show you," said Phipps, and started for
the door. "I'll show you," he repeated, his hand on the handle.

"But where are your tools?" bleated Smedley.

"He doesn't need tools," said Bill. "He does it all with his finger tips, like
Jimmy Valentine. He is a most gifted artist—or, rather, was."

"*Was?*" cried Phipps. He wrenched the door open. "Come on. Let's go."

"I'll come with you," said Smedley, entranced.

"So will I," said Joe. "And in case you feel faint——"

He took up the tray and added himself to the procession. Bill closed the
door behind them and came back to Kay, who was regarding her with the
light of admiration and respect in her eyes. It was a light that often came into
the eyes of those privileged to observe The Old Reliable when at her best.

"So that's that," said Bill. "Amazing what you can do with a little tact. And
now that we are alone, my girl, sit down and listen to me, because I've a bone
to pick with you. What's all this I hear about you and Joe?"

KAY LAUGHED.

"Oh, Joe!" she said.

An austere frown darkened Bill's brow. She disapproved of this spirit of levity. Ever a staunch friend, she had been much touched by Joe's story of his romance, with its modern avoidance of the happy ending. Feeling as she did about Smedley, she could understand and sympathize.

"Don't giggle in that obscene way," she said sternly. "He's a very fine young fellow, Joe Davenport, and he loves you."

"So he keeps telling me."

" 'Bill,' he said to me only the day before yesterday, and if there weren't tears in his eyes as he spoke, I don't know a tear in the eye when I see one, 'Bill, old sport, I love that girl.' And then a lot of stuff about depression and debility and night sweats and loss of appetite. And in addition to the tear in his eye, there was a choking sob in his voice, and he writhed like a dynamo. He worships you, that boy. He adores you. He would die for one little rose from your hair. And does he get one? Not so much as a blasted petal. Instead of thanking heaven, fasting, for a good man's love, you reply to his pleadings with the horse's laugh and slip him the brusheroo. Nice goings-on, I must say."

Kay stooped over and kissed the top of Bill's head. She had had a feeling that this was going to be good, and she saw that she had not been mistaken.

"You're very eloquent, Bill."

"Of course I'm eloquent. I'm speaking from a full heart on top of three glasses of champagne. Why are you pulling this hard-to-get stuff on Joe? What's wrong with the poor fish?"

"He knows. I told him exactly why I wouldn't marry him, when we had lunch together the day before I left New York."

"Aren't you going to marry him?"

"No."

"You're crazy."

"He's crazy."

"About you."

"About everything."

"Why do you say that?"

"Well, isn't he?"

"Not in the least. A man I respect and admire. Don't you like him?"

"Yes. Very much. He's fun."

"I'm glad you didn't say 'He's a good sort.' "

"Why, is that bad?"

"Fatal. It would have meant that there was no hope for him. It's what the boys used to say of me twenty years ago. 'Oh, Bill,' they'd say. 'Dear old Bill. I like Bill. She's a good sort.' And then they'd leave me flat on my keister and go off and buy candy and orchids for the other girls, blister their insides."

"Is that why you're a solitary chip drifting down the river of life?"

"That's why. Often a bridesmaid but never a bride."

"You poor old ruin."

"Don't call me a poor old ruin. Does respect for an aunt mean nothing to you? And don't try to steer me off the subject of Joe. Fourteen times you've refused him, he tells me."

"Fifteen. He proposed again in the rose garden this afternoon."

Bill snorted indignantly. She rose and walked with measured step to the desk, intending to restore her composure with more champagne, found that the tray of drinks was no longer there, snorted again, this time with disappointment, sighed heavily and returned to her seat.

"Well, I don't understand you," she said. "I simply don't understand you. The workings of your mind are a sealed book to me. If I were a girl and Joe Davenport came along and wanted to marry me, I'd grapple him to my soul with hoops of steel. Gosh, when one looks around and sees what a jerk the average young man is, the idea of a girl with any sense in her head turning down a fellow like Joe is incredible."

"He seems to have made a great impression on you."

"He has. I regard him as a son."

"Grandson."

"I said son. Yes, I regard him as a son, and you know how I've always felt about you. You're as fresh as an April breeze, you get off impertinent cracks about grandsons, you mock at my grey hairs and will probably sooner or later bring them in sorrow to the grave, but I love you."

"Mutual, Bill."

"Don't interrupt. I say I love you. And I have your best interests at heart. I consider that this J. Davenport is the right man for you, and it is my dearest wish to park myself in a ringside pew and bellow The Voice That Breathed O'er Eden while you and he go centre-aisle-ing. It beats me why you aren't thinking along the same lines. It isn't as if you had anything against the poor simp. You admit you like him."

"Of course I like him. How could anyone help liking Joe?"

"Then what's the trouble?"

Kay was silent for a moment. There had come into her face that grave, intent look which attracted Joe so much. With the toe of one of her mules, she traced an arabesque on the carpet.

"Shall I take my hair down, Bill?"

"Certainly. Tell me all."

"Well, then, I could fall in love with Joe in a minute—like *that*—if I'd let myself."

"And why don't you?"

Kay went to the French window and looked up at the stars.

"I'm—wary."

"How do you mean, wary?"

"Well . . . Bill, how do you look on marriage? I mean, is it a solemn, sacred what-d'you-call-it that's going to last the rest of your life—or a sort of comic week-end like some of these Hollywood things? I think it's pretty solemn and sacred, and that's where Joe and I seem to differ. No, don't interrupt, or I shall never be able to explain. What I'm really trying to say is that I can't bring myself to trust Joe. I can't believe he's sincere."

With a powerful effort, Bill had managed to restrain herself from breaking in on what she considered the most absurd speech to which she had ever listened, and she was a woman who had sat in on a hundred studio conferences, but she could maintain silence no longer.

"Sincere? Joe? For heaven's sake! How often do you want him to ask you to marry him before it filters through into your fat little head that he's fond of you?"

"It isn't how often he asks me, it's how he asks me. He does it as if the whole thing were a tremendous joke. And I don't regard love as a joke. I'm stuffy and sentimental and take it seriously. I want someone who takes it as seriously as I do, not someone who can't make love to a girl without making her feel as if she were the stooge in a vaudeville act. How does he expect me to feel," said Kay, becoming vehement, for the grievance was one that had long been festering within her, "when his idea of romantic wooing is to grin like a Cheshire cat and say 'Don't look now, but will you marry me?' When a girl's with the man she loves, she doesn't want to feel as if she had been wrecked on a desert island with Milton Berle."

There was silence for a moment.

"Then—just between us girls—you do love Joe?"

"Of course I do," said Kay. "I've loved him right from the start. But I don't trust him."

Silence fell again. Bill began to see that this was going to be difficult.

"I know what you mean," she said at length. "Joe *is* apt to clown. The light comedy manner. The kidding approach. But don't forget that clowning is often just a defensive armour against shyness."

"You aren't trying to tell me that Joe's shy?"

"Of course he's shy—with you. Every man's shy when he's really in love. That's why he acts like that. He's like a small boy trying to ease the embarrassment of wooing the belle of the kindergarten by standing on his head. Don't you be deceived by the surface manner, my girl. Look past it to the palpitating heart within."

"You think Joe has a palpitating heart?"

"You betcher."

"So do I. I think it palpitates for every girl he meets who isn't an absolute gargoyle. I've seen his little red book."

"His what?"

"Telephone numbers, Bill. Telephone numbers of blondes, brunettes, redheads and subsidiary blondes. Don't you understand the facts of life, my child? Joe is a butterfly, flitting from flower to flower and making love to every girl he meets."

"Is that what butterflies do?"

"You can't stop 'em. He's another Dick Mills."

"Another who?"

"A man I was once engaged to. We broke it off."

"Was he a butterfly?"

"Yes, Bill, he was."

"And you feel that Joe is like him?"

"The same type."

"You're all wrong."

"I don't think so."

Bill swelled belligerently. Her blue eyes flashed fire. Though of a more equable temperament than her sister Adela and not so ready as that formidable woman to decline on all occasions to Stand Nonsense, she could be pushed just so far. Like Mr. Churchill, there were things up with which she would not put.

"It doesn't matter what you think, my girl. Let me tell you something for your files. It is my unshakeable opinion that you and Joe were made for one another. I have studied you both with loving care, I am convinced that you would hit it off like ham and eggs, and I shall omit no word or act to promote the merger. I intend to bring you together, if it's the last thing I do. And you know me. The Old Reliable. And now go and cut those sandwiches. All this talking has made me hungry."

As Kay started for the door, it opened and Smedley came in, startling both of them. In the pressure of other matters, they had quite forgotten Smedley. Smedley was looking agitated.

"Where are you going?" he asked. "Not up to the projection room?"

"She's going to the kitchen to cut sandwiches," said Bill. "I thought we needed a little sustenance, to keep the machine from breaking down."

"I'm glad," said Smedley, relieved. "I wouldn't want you to go up there just now. Those drinks you gave Phipps, Bill, have had a curious effect on him. They seem to have—er—melted his reserve. He keeps stopping work to tell risky stories."

"Dear, dear. Off colour?"

"Very. There was one about a strip-tease dancer and a performing flea . . ." He looked at Kay, and paused. "But it wouldn't interest you."

"I've heard it," said Kay, and went off to cut sandwiches.

Smedley mopped his forehead. His morale seemed to have hit a new low. The rush and swirl of the night's events had plainly left him weak. Marcus Aurelius, who held that nothing happens to anybody which he is not fitted by nature to bear, would have had a hard time selling that idea to Smedley Cork.

"I'm worried, Bill," said Smedley.

"You're always worried."

"Well, haven't I enough to worry me? When I think of what it means to me to have Phipps open that safe! And he won't concentrate. He lets his mind wander. He's displaying a frivolous side to his nature which I wouldn't have believed existed. Do you know that just before I left he was proposing to imitate four Hawaiians? The man's blotto."

Bill nodded.

"I ought to be more careful with those Wilhelmina Shannon Specials," she said. "The trouble is, I don't know my own strength."

"And it isn't only that he refuses to get down to his job. It's the noise he's making. Loud bursts of fiendish laughter. I'm so afraid he'll wake Adela."

"Her room's on the other side of the house."

"But even so."

Blll shook her head.

"You know, looking back," she said, "where we made our big mistake was in not giving Adela a Mickey Finn. It would have—" She broke off. "Good heavens!"

"What's the matter?"

Bill was feeling in the pocket of her slacks. When she brought her hand out, there was a small white pellet in it.

"This is a Mickey Finn," she said. "It was given me from his personal stockpile by a bartender on Third Avenue, a dear old friend of mine. He said it would be bound to come in handy one of these days, and how right he was. I had intended to slip it into Adela's bedtime Ovaltine, and I forgot."

"And now too late."

"And now too late," said Bill. "Too late, too——"

Her voice trailed away. From just outside the door there had come the sound of a loud and raucous laugh. She looked at Smedley, and he looked at her, with a wild surmise.

"Good God!" said Smedley. "That's Phipps."

"Or could it have been a hyena?" said Bill.

It was Phipps. He came in, followed by Joe, laughing heartily like one of the Chorus of Villagers in an old-fashioned comic opera. Tray in hand, he selected a bottle, went to the sofa, seated himself on it and leaned back comfortably against the cushions. It was plain that for the time being, he had shelved all idea of work and was regarding this as a purely social occasion.

12

"Good evening, all," said Phipps genially, and refreshed himself from the bottle. Whatever prudent concern he might once have felt regarding his constitutional inability to absorb alcoholic stimulants in large quantities without paying the penalty had clearly vanished. Wine is a mocker and strong drink is raging, and he liked it that way. Any time wine wanted to mock him, his whole demeanor suggested, it was all right with James Phipps, and the same went for strong drink when it wished to rage. "Good evening, all," he said. "I will now imitate four Hawaiians."

His obvious eagerness to spare no effort to make the party go would have touched and delighted some such person as a fun-loving Babylonian monarch of the old school, always on the lookout for sympathetic fellow-revellers to help the Babylonian orgy along, but to Smedley his words seemed to presage doom and disaster. What it was that four Hawaiians did when performing for the public entertainment, he did not know, but instinct told him that it was probably something pretty loud, and he quivered apprehensively. Adela's room might, as Bill had said, be on the other side of the house, but, as he had said to Bill, 'even so.'

"No, no!" he squeaked, like a mouse in pain.

"Then I'll sing Sweet Adeline," said Phipps with the air of a man who only strove to please. His repertory was wide, and if the audience did not want the four Hawaiians, Sweet Adeline would do just as well.

This time it was Joe who lodged a protest. Joe was fully as agitated as Smedley. He was familiar wih Sweet Adeline. He had sung that popular song himself in clubhouse locker rooms, and none knew better than he that its melody contained certain barbershop chords which, dished out as this sozzled major-domo would dish them out, must inevitably penetrate bricks and mortar like butter, rousing a sleeping hostess from her slumbers as if the Last Trump had sounded. Once more there rose before his eyes the vision of Mrs. Adela Shannon Cork sailing in through the door in a dressing-gown, and that thing with the long hairy legs went galloping up and down his spine again.

"No, please, Phipps," he urged.

The butler stiffened. He was in genial, pleasure-seeking mood and all prepared to unbend with the boys, but even at the risk of spoiling the harmony he felt obliged to insist on the deference due to his position. Once allow the lower middle classes to become familiar, and where were you?

"Mister Phipps, if *you* please," he said coldly.

Bill, always tactful, added her weight to the rebuke.

"Yes, be careful how you speak to Mr. Phipps, Joe. You can see he's fractious. I think he's teething. But I wouldn't sing Sweet Adeline, Mr. Phipps."

"Why wouldn't I sing Sweet Adeline?"

"You'll wake sweet Adela."

"You mean Ma Cork?"

"Ma Cork is correct."

Phipps mused. He took another sip from his bottle.

"Ma Cork," he said meditatively. "Now, there's a woman I never cared for. How would it be to go and give her a jolly good punch in the nose?"

It was a suggestion which at any other time would have enchanted Smedley, for if ever there was a woman who from early childhood had been asking, nay clamouring, for a good sock on the beezer, that woman in his opinion was his sister-in-law Adela. But now he shuddered from head to foot and uttered another of his mouselike squeaks.

"No, no!"

"Not give her a punch in the nose? Just as you say," said Phipps agreeably. He could be as reasonable as the next man if you treated him with proper respect. "Then let's have a gargle. Not you, Smedley," he went on. "You've had enough. The old coot's been mopping it up like a vacuum cleaner," he explained amusedly. He surveyed the coot with an indulgent eye. "Old drunken Smedley!" he said. "Where were you last night, you old jail bird? Hey, Smedley?"

Smedley smiled a wry, preoccupied smile. Phipps, piqued, raised his voice a little.

"HEY, SMEDLEY!!"

Bill said 'Hush!' Joe said 'Hush!' Smedley leaped as if he had been unexpectedly bitten by a shark.

Phipps's sense of grievance deepened. It seemed to him that these people were deliberately going out of their way to ruffle him. When he said: 'Hey!' they said: 'Hush!', and as for the old lush Smedley, who was patently pie-eyed, he didn't so much as bother to answer when spoken to civilly. One would have to be pretty sharp, felt Phipps, on this sort of thing.

"Well, why doesn't he say Hey when I say Hey? When a gentleman says Hey to another gentleman, he expects the other gentleman to say Hey to him."

Smedley was prompt to retrieve his social lapse.

"Hey," he said hastily.

"Hey, what?"

"Hey, Mr. Phipps."

The butler frowned. His mood had now definitely darkened. Gone was that warmth of bonhomie and goodwill which had filled him when he came into the room, making him the little brother of all mankind and more like a walking sunbeam than anything. He found in Smedley's manner a formality and lack of chumminess of which he thoroughly disapproved. It was as though he had started hobnobbing with a Babylonian monarch and the Babylonian monarch had suddenly turned around and snubbed him, as Babylonian monarchs are so apt to do.

"Come, come," he said. "None of your standoffishness. Say Hey, Jimmy."

"Hey, Jimmy."

Phipps, a perfectionist, was not yet satisfied.

"Say it again, more loving like."

"Hey, Jimmy."

Phipps relaxed. Smedley's intonation had not been altogether that of a love bird passing a remark to another love bird, but it had been near enough to mollify him. Genuine feeling in it, it seemed to him.

"That's better. Can't have you sticking on dog just because you're a ruddy Society butterfly."

"Don't you like ruddy Society butterflies?" asked Bill, interested.

Phipps shook his head austerely.

"No. Don't approve of 'em. Comes the Revolution, they'll be hanging on lamp posts. The whole system's wrong. Ain't I a man? ... AIN'T I, SMEDLEY?"

Smedley leaped.

"Yes, yes, of course you are, Jimmy."

"Ain't I a gentleman?"

"Of course, Jimmy, of course."

"Then fetch me a cushion for me head, you old souse. Come on, now. Hurry. I want a little service around here."

Smedley brought the cushion and propped it behind his head.

"Comfortable—Jimmy?" he said, between his teeth.

The butler froze him with a glance.

"Who are you calling Jimmy? Address me as Mr. Phipps."

"I'm sorry, Mr. Phipps."

"And so you ought to be. I know your sort, know 'em well. Grinding the face of the poor and taking the bread out of the mouths of the widow and the orphan. Comes the Revolution, blood'll be running in streams down Park Avenue and Sutton Place'll be all cluttered up with corpses."

Smedley drew Bill aside.

"If this is going to continue," he muttered, "I cannot answer for the consequences, Bill. My blood pressure is rising."

"Comes the Revolution" Bill reminded him, "you won't have any blood. It'll be running down Park Avenue."

"I'm going up to listen at Adela's door. Make sure she's asleep. Anything to get away for a moment from that sozzled son of a . . . " He caught Phipps's eye and broke off. He smiled a difficult smile. "Hey, Mr. Phipps!"

The butler's eye was too glazed for fire to flash from it, but his manner showed that he was offended.

"How many times have I got to tell you to call me Jimmy?"

"I'm sorry, Jimmy."

"Mister Phipps, if you *don't* mind," said the butler sternly.

Smedley, plainly unequal to the intellectual pressure of the conversation, gave it up and hurried out. Bill, glad to be relieved of his disturbing presence, struck the business note.

"Well, Mr. Phipps," she said, "how's it coming? If you are feeling sufficiently rested, you might be having another go at that safe."

"Yes," agreed Joe. "We mustn't waste any more time."

He had said the wrong thing. The butler stiffened again. For some reason, possibly because of that earlier lapse into familiarity, he seemed to have taken a dislike to Joe. He gave him an unpleasant look.

"What's it got to do with *you*, may I ask?"

"Everything. You see, it's this way—Mr. Smedley—"

"You mean old drunken Smedley?"

"That's right. Old drunken Smedley is in with Miss Shannon——"

"You mean old dogfaced Bill here?"

"That's right. Old drunken Smedley is in with old dog-faced Bill here and me on a business deal. He's putting up the money."

"What money?"

"The money he'll get when he gets that diary."

"What diary?"

"The diary in the safe."

"What safe?" asked Phipps keenly, like prosecuting attorney questioning some rat of the underworld as to where he was on the night of June the fifteenth.

Joe looked at Bill. Like Smedley, he found Phipps's conversational methods a little bewildering.

"The safe you're going to open, Mr. Phipps."

"Who says I'm going to open any safes?"

"I don't," said Bill, taking charge in her competent way. "You couldn't do it."

"Do what?"

"Open that safe."

Phipps was silent for a space, digesting this.

"You say I couldn't open that safe?"

"No. It's hopeless to think of attempting it. Four years ago you would have been able to, yes, but not now. We're all agreed on that."

"On what?"

"That you were a good man once, but you've lost your nerve. We went into it all before, if you remember, and we came to the conclusion that you no longer had the stuff. You're finished."

"Ho!"

"A pity, but there it is. Not your fault, of course, but you're a back number. As a safeblower, you're washed up. You buttle like nobody's business, you have a bright future on the silver screen, but—you—can't—open—the safe."

Wine when it is red—or, as in the case of Phipps, who was drinking *crème de menthe*, green—stingeth like an adder, and so do adverse criticisms of his skill as an artist. Phipps was thus in the position of a man who is stung by two adders simultaneously, and his flushed face grew darker.

"Ho!" he said. "Can't open the safe, eh? Can't open the ruddy safe? Well, just for that I *will* open the ruddy safe."

Joe shot a quick, reverential look at Bill. Leave it to The Old Reliable, he was feeling. The Old Reliable would always see you through.

"Thank you, Phipps," he said.

"Thank *you*, sir," said the butler automatically. "I mean," he added quickly, correcting himself, "What you thanking me for?"

"I told you. You say you're going to open the safe. Well, if you open the safe, we'll get our money."

"Ho? And when you do, I suppose you think you're going to marry that young Kay? What a hope. You haven't a chance, you poor fish. *I* heard her turning you down in the rose garden this afternoon."

Joe started.

"What?"

"Like a bedspread."

Joe blushed a pretty pink. He had not supposed that he had been playing to an audience.

"You weren't there?"

"Yes, I was."

"I didn't see you."

"Nobody don't ever see me."

"They call him The Shadow," said Bill.

"And I'll tell you what struck me about the episode," proceeded Phipps, having looked once more upon the wine when it was green. "Your methods are wrong. You're too lighthearted and yumorous. You won't win the heart of a sensitive girl by cracking gags. What you want to do is to fold her in your arms and kiss her."

"He daren't," said Bill. "It isn't safe. He once kissed a girl in Paris and she shot clear up to the top of the Eiffel Tower."

"Ho?"

"Just closed her eyes with a little moan of ecstasy and floated up—and up—and up."

To illustrate, Bill twiddled her fingers, and the butler stared at them austerely.

"Don't do that!" he said sharply. "It makes me think of spiders."

"I'm sorry. You dislike spiders?"

"Yes, I do. Spiders!" said Phipps darkly. "I could tell you something about spiders. You ask me, if you want to hear all about spiders."

"Comes the Revolution, spiders will be running down Park Avenue."

"Ah," said Phipps, as if conceding this as probably correct. He yawned, and swung his feet up on the sofa. "Well, I don't know what you two are going to do," he said. "I'm going to get a little shut-eye. Good night, all. Time for Bedfordshire."

His eyes closed. He gurgled a couple of times. Then, still clutching the bottle, he slept.

13

JOE LOOKED at Bill, dismayed. In this world one should be prepared for everything, or where is one, but he had not been prepared for this. It had come on him as a complete surprise.

"Now what?" he said.

The new development appeared to have left Bill unconcerned. She regarded the horizontal butler with something of the tender affection of a mother bending over the cradle of her sleeping child, and adjusted the pillow behind his head, which looked like slipping.

"Probably all for the best," she said. "A little folding of the hands in sleep will do him good, and we have the rest of the night to operate in. Did you ever see a blotto butler before?"

"Never."

"Nor I. In which connection, would state that I'd rather see than be one. When the cold grey light of the dawn comes stealing in through yonder windows in an hour or so, you and I will be in the pink and as fresh as daisies, but one shudders to think how Jimmy Phipps will be feeling. On the morning after a binge like that, the state of man, as Shakespeare says, suffers the nature of an insurrection. There should be a big run on the bromo-seltzer ere long. But lets not wander from the point. Though brilliantly lit and not always too coherent in his remarks, the recent pickled herring said one very sensible and significant thing. About your methods of conducting your wooing. Were you listening?"

"I was."

"He was right, you know. He touched the spot. Your methods *are* wrong. I've been talking to Kay. That girl loves you, Joe."

"What?"

"She told me so in so many words. The way she actually phrased it has slipped my memory, but the gist of her remarks was that when in your presence she feels as though there was only a thin sheet of tissue paper between her and heaven. And if that isn't love, what is?"

Joe reeled.

"Bill, if you're kidding me—"

"Of course I'm not kidding you. What on earth would I want to kid you for? She loves you, I tell you. You're the cream in her coffee, you're the salt in her stew. But she's wary . . . cagey . . . She's suspicious of you."

"Suspicious? Why?"

"Because you clown all the time."

"I'm shy."

"I told her that, but she didn't believe me. She looks on you as an insubstantial butterfly, flitting from flower to flower and sipping. Are you a sipper?"

"No, I'm not a sipper."

"You don't play around with girls?"

"Certainly not."

"Then how about your little red book of telephone numbers?" said Bill.

If she had slapped a wet towel across Joe's face, the effect could not have been more pronounced. When you slap a wet towel across a man's face, he gasps and totters. The eyes widen. The colour deepens. The mouth falls open like a fish's and stays open. It was so with Joe now.

"Red book?" he stammered.

"Red book."

"Little red book?"

"Little red book."

"Little red book of telephone numbers?"

"Little red book of telephone numbers."

The sensation of having been struck with a wet towel left Joe. He became indignant, like a good man unjustly persecuted.

"Why the dickens does everybody make such a song and dance about my little red book of telephone numbers?" he demanded hotly. "Every red-blooded man has his little red book of telephone numbers. Children start keeping them in the kindergarten. And Kay knows all about my little red book. I explained carefully and fully to her the last time we lunched together that no importance whatsoever was to be attached to that little red book. I told her that the girls in that little red book were mere vestiges of a past that is dead and gone. I've forgotten half their damned names. They are nothing to me, nothing."

"Less than the dust beneath your chariot wheels?"

"Considerably less. I wouldn't call one of them up to please a dying grandmother. They're ghosts, I tell you. Spectres. Wraiths."

"Just wisps of ectoplasm?"

"Exactly. Just wisps of ectoplasm. Listen, Bill. There isn't a girl that exists for me in the world except Kay. She stands alone. Turn me loose on a street corner and have Helen of Troy, Cleopatra, Mrs. Langtry, Hedy Lamarr and La Belle Dame Sans Merci parade past me in one-piece bathing suits, and I wouldn't even bother to whistle at them."

Bill was touched by his simple eloquence.

"Well, that sounds pretty satisfactory. Summing it up, then, you are as pure as the driven snow?"

"If not purer."

"Good. Then all you have to do, as I see it, is to change the radio comic approach. You can't run a business that way. Cut the Bob Hope stuff down to a minimum. There are two methods of winning a girl's heart," said Bill. "The first is to be the dominant male—the caveman, and take her heart by storm. As an illustration of what I mean, I once wrote for *Passion Magazine* where the hero was no end of a character. He was one of the huntin', ridin' and shootin' set of Old Westbury, Long Island, and he had dark, sullen fits of rage, under the influence of which he would grab his girl by the back hair and drag her about the room with clenched teeth. His teeth were clenched, of course, not hers. Hers just rattled. I throw this out as a suggestion."

"I'm not going to drag Kay about rooms by her hair."

"It would be a delicate attention. It might just turn the scale. The girl in my story loved it. 'Oh, Gerald, Gerald,' she said, 'you do something to me.' "

"No."

"All right, then, cut business with hair. But you could seize her by the shoulders and shake her like a rat."

"No, I couldn't."

"Why not?"

"Because I couldn't."

"You're a difficult fellow to help," said Bill. "You don't meet one half-way. You seem to have forgotten the old Superba-Llewellen slogan, Service and Co-operation."

She took the Mickey Finn from her pocket and joggled it thoughtfully in the palm of her hand.

"What's that?" asked Joe.

"An aspirin. I sleep badly. Well, if you won't be a caveman, we must try the second method and melt her heart instead of storming it. We must build you up for sympathy."

"How do you mean?"

"It's quite simple . . . Thirsty work, these conferences. How about a refresher?"

"That sounds like a good idea. Champagne?"

"I think so. Stick to the old and tried."

Bill went to the tray, filled two glasses and adroitly dropped the present from her Third Avenue bartender friend into the one which she handed to Joe.

"Yes," she said. "We must build you up for sympathy."

"But how?"

"It's quite simple."

"You said that before."

"And I say it again. You know the old poem, Oh, woman, in our hours of ease . . ."

"Uncertain, coy and hard to please . . . Yes, I used to recite it as a kid."

"It must have sounded wonderful. Why do I miss these things? Well, you remember, then, that we have it straight from the horse's mouth that it requires only a little pain and anguish wringing the brow to turn a girl into a ministering angel. When pain and anguish wring the brow, a ministering angel, thou. It's all in the book of words."

"So what?"

"Well, take the case of Kay. I am convinced that if Kay, who is now down in the kitchen cutting wholesome sandwiches, were to come in here and find you lying prone and senseless on the floor, her heart would melt like a nut sundae in the Sahara desert. She would fling herself on your prostrate form and shower kisses on your upturned face. That's what Kay would do, if she came in here and found you lying prone and senseless on the floor."

"But why would I be lying prone and senseless on the floor?"

Bill nodded. She saw what he meant.

"Yes, that wants thinking out. Well, suppose Phipps in a fit of drunken fury had knocked you cold with that bottle he is nursing as a mother nurses her child?"

"But he hasn't."

"True. Then suppose I had slipped a Mickey Finn in that drink of yours."

"But you didn't."

"True, true. I'm just thinking aloud. Well, here's luck."

"Luck," said Joe.

They drained their glasses.

"Mickey Finn," said Bill pensively, "I wonder why those things are called that?"

"Wasn't there supposed to have been a bartender named Mickey Finn who invented them?"

"Mencken says not, and he probably knows. Mencken knows everything. Any idea how they work?"

"Yes, oddly enough, I have. It came up in a picture I was doing just before they fired me. Apparently you feel no ill effects at first. Then, if you shake your head—like this . . ."

Bill, quick on her feet, caught him as he started to fall. She lowered him gently to the floor, gave him a look in which commiseration and satisfaction were nicely blended, then crossed to the sofa and shook Phipps by the shoulder.

It is never easy to rouse an intoxicated butler who is in the process of sleeping off two Wilhelmina Shannon Specials and a bottle of *crème de menthe*, and for some time it seemed as though her efforts were to be unrewarded. But presently signs of animation began to appear in the rigid limbs. Phipps grunted. He stirred, he moved, he seemed to feel the rush of life along his keel. Another grunt, and he sat up, blinking.

"Hullo?" he said, speaking in a husky whisper, like a spirit at a séance. "What goes on?"

14

"I AM sorry to disturb your slumbers, Mr. Phipps," said Bill apologetically, "but I can't seem to bring him to."

"Eh?"

Bill indicated the remains on the floor.

"Perhaps you could lend a hand?" she said. "Two heads are better than one."

Phipps rose unsteadily from the sofa. It appeared to his disordered senses that there was a body on the carpet, as had so often happened in the whodunits which were his favourite reading. In those works it was almost impossible to come into a room without finding bodies on the carpet. The best you could say of this one was that there was not a dagger of Oriental design sticking in its back. He closed his eyes, hoping that this might cause the cadaver to disappear. But when he opened them, it was still there.

"What's the matter with him?" he quavered. "What's he lying there for?"
Bill raised her eyebrows.

"Surely you recall that, doubtless with the best motives, you socked him on the occiput with your bottle?"

"My—Gawd! Did I?"

"Don't tell me you've forgotten?"

"I can't remember a thing," said the butler pallidly. "What happened?"

"Well, it started with you getting into an argument about the Claims to Apostolic Succession of the Church of Abyssinia?"

"About *what?*"

"Don't you remember the Church of Abyssinia?"

"I never heard of the Church of Abyssinia."

"Well, it's a sort of church they have out Abyssinia way and you and Joe Davenport got arguing about its claims to Apostolic Succession. He took one view, you took another. You said this, he said that. Hot words ensued. Angry passions rose. You gradually bumped him with the bottle. A crash, a cry, and smiling the boy fell dead."

"He's not *dead?*"

"I was only making a good story of it."

"Well, I wish you wouldn't," said Phipps, passing a hand across his ashen forehead. He collapsed into a chair and sat puffing unhappily. He was still doing so when the door opened and Smedley came in, followed by Kay, who was carrying a large plate of sandwiches, at which Bill looked with an approving eye. She was feeling just about ready for a little snack.

"Adela must be asleep," said Smedley. "I stood outside her door for quite a time, listening, but I couldn't hear anything. Hello," he went on, Joe having caught his eye. "What's this?"

"Stretcher case," said Bill briefly. "Phipps hit him with a bottle. We were just chatting about it when you came in."

Kay's eyes widened. The blood slowly left her face. She stood for an instant, staring, and the plate of sandwiches trembled in her hand. Bill, always doing the right thing, took it gently from her. Kay seemed to come to life. With a cry she flung herself beside Joe's prostrate form.

"Oh, Joe, Joe!" she wailed.

Bill helped herself to a sandwich with a quick, gratified smile. It is always pleasant for a kind-hearted woman who wants to bring the young folks together in springtime to see that she has succeeded in doing so. She finished the sandwich and took another. Sardine, she was glad to note. She liked sardine sandwiches.

"Hit him with a bottle?" said Smedley.

"In a moment of heat," Bill explained. "The Phippses get very heated at moments."

"Good God!"

"Yes, a disagreeable thing to have happened. Spoiled the party, as you might say. But there is a bright side. It has had the effect of sobering him."

"It has? Then listen . . ."

"I believe he's dead," said Kay, raising a white face.

"Oh, I shouldn't think so," said Smedley. He dismissed this side issue and returned to the important subject. "He's sober, is he?"

"Quite. He could say truly rural."

"Then now's the time for him to get to work. No more fooling about. Phipps!"

"Sir?" said that reveller, now once more his old respectful butlerine self.

"Get busy."

"Yes, sir."

"No more nonsense."

"No, sir."

"His master's voice," said Bill, starting on her third sandwich.

Kay, she saw with approval, was now showering burning kisses on Joe's upturned face. This, it will be remembered, was the business she had arranged for her, and it was nice to see it working out so smoothly. She felt like a director whose cast is on its toes and giving of its best.

"Oh, Joe! Joe, darling!" cried Kay. She looked up. "He's alive."

"Really?"

"He just moved."

"Fine," said Bill. "This is excellent news. No electric chair for you this time, Phipps."

"I am relieved, madam."

"Later on, perhaps."

"Yes, madam."

Kay was glaring balefully. Hitherto, she had always liked Phipps, but now it seemed to her that she had never met a beastlier butler.

"You might have killed him," she said. She spoke bitterly and with clenched teeth, like Bill's huntin', ridin' and shootin' friend from Old Westbury, and would have hissed the words if there had been an 's' in them.

Phipps, still respectful, disputed this point.

"I would not go so far as to say that, miss. Just a simple slosh on the head, such as so often occurs during a religious argument. But if I might be permitted to say so, I would like to express regret and contrition for having taken such a liberty. From the bottom of me heart, miss . . ."

Smedley broke in with his usual impatience. He was in no mood for oratory.

"Now don't stand there making speeches. This isn't the Fourth of July."

"No, sir."

"Action, man, action."

"Yes, sir."

"Follow me."

"Yes, sir. Very good, sir."

The door closed behind them. Bill smiled maternally at Kay and joined her at the sick-bed. She looked down at the invalid, who was now showing definite signs of coming out of his coma.

"He'll be functioning again in a minute," she said encouragingly. "Bet you ten cents I know what he'll say when he opens his eyes. 'Where am I?' "

Joe opened his eyes.

"Where am I?" he asked.

"Gimme those ten cents," said Bill.

Joe sat up.

"Oh, gosh!" he said.

"Oh, Joe!" said Kay.

"My head!" said Joe.

"Painful, no doubt," said Bill. "What you need is air. We'll get you into the garden. Lend me a hand, Kay."

"I'll bathe your head, darling," said Kay tenderly.

Joe blinked.

"Did you say 'darling'?"

"Of course I did."

Joe blinked again.

"And just now . . . Was it just a lovely dream or did you kiss me?"

"Of course she kissed you," said Bill. "Why wouldn't she kiss you? Weren't you listening when I told you she loves you? Can you navigate?"

"I think so."

"Then we'll take you out and bathe your head in Adela's jewelled swimming pool."

Joe blinked for the third time. Even so trivial a muscular effort as blinking affected his head as if some earnest hand were driving red-hot spikes into it, but the agony, though acute, was forgotten in the thrill of ecstasy which shot through him. It seemed to him once again that soft music was playing in the Garden Room. Familiar objects had taken on a new beauty. Even Bill's rugged face, which good judges had compared to that of a German Boxer, now showed itself as something entitling her to get her telephone number into the most discriminating man's little red book.

As for Kay, the thought struck him that if you slapped a pair of wings on her, she could step straight into any gathering of Cherubim and Seraphim and no questions asked. He gazed at her in a stunned way.

"You love me?"

"Certainly she loves you," said Bill. "How many times have I to keep telling you? She worships you. She adores you. She would die for one little rose from your hair. But you'll be able to discuss all that while she's dunking your head in the swimming pool. Come along, and take it easy. I'll bet you're feeling like someone who has annoyed Errol Flynn."

Supporting the injured man between them, they passed through the French windows. And scarcely had they disappeared when the door opened and Adela came in, followed by a limp and drowsy Lord Topham. Adela was alert and bristling, her escort practically walking in his sleep. He tottered to a chair, sank into it and closed his eyes.

15

THE TROUBLE about going up to a sister-in-law's room and listening at her door to make sure she is asleep is that, if your breathing is at all inclined to be stertorous, you are apt to wake her. Although he was not aware of it, Smedley on his recent visit to the exterior of Adela's sleeping apartment had breathed very stertorously. What with the strain of being accessory before the fact to a safeblowing and the emotional disturbance occasioned by hearing Phipps address him as old drunken Smedley, he had puffed and panted like a racehorse at the conclusion of a stiff Grand National.

He had also caused boards to creak and once, overbalancing, had brought his hand sharply against the panel of the door. Indeed, practically the only thing he had not done was to make a noise like an alarm clock, and he had been operating less than a minute and a half when Adela stirred on her pillow, sat up and finally, hearing that bang on the door, got up. With the air of an Amazon donning her armor before going into battle, she put on a dressing-gown and stood listening.

The sounds outside had ceased. A cautious peep a moment later showed that nobody was there. But somebody had been there, and she proposed to look into the matter thoroughly. There was nothing of the poltroon about Adela Shannon Cork. Any one of a dozen silent picture directors could have told you that, and so could each of her three late husbands. As has previously been indicated, she was a woman who stood no nonsense, and under the head of nonsense she classed the presence of unlawful intruders in her house beween the hours of one and two in the morning.

But even the most intrepid of women likes on such an occasion as this to have an ally, so after the briefest of delays she proceeded to Lord Topham's room, and with much more difficulty than Smedley had experienced in waking her, roused him to at least a temporary activity.

He appeared now to have turned in again for the night, and she addressed him sharply.

"Lord Topham!"

Gentle breathing was her guest's only reply. Lord Topham was a man who, though resembling Napoleon Bonaparte in no other way, shared with him the ability to drop off the moment his head touched the pillow—or, as in the present case, the back of a chair.

She raised her voice.

"Lord Topham!"

The mists of sleep were not proof against that urgent cry. The visitor from across the seas opened his eyes. Napoleon in similar circumstances would probably have opened his. Adela's voice lacked the booming thunderousness of Bill's, but it was very penetrating when annoyance caused her to raise it.

"Eh?"

"Wake up."

"Was I asleep?"

"Yes, you were."

Lord Topham considered the point, remembered that a moment ago he had been dancing the rhumba in Piccadilly Circus, and nodded.

"That's right. I was. I was dreaming of Toots."

"Of *what?*"

"Girl I know in London. I dreamed that we were treading the measure in Piccadilly Circus. Of all places. Well, I mean to say," said Lord Topham, smiling a little at the quaint idea, "would one? In Piccadilly Circus, I mean to say, what?"

Adela was not a psychiatrist, ever ready to listen to people's dreams and interpret them. She made no comment other than an impatient sniff. Then she uttered a sharp exclamation. Her eye, roving about the room, had fallen on the tray of bottles.

"Look!"

Lord Topham sighed sentimentally.

"I'll tell you about Toots. I love her like billy-o, and we had a row just before I sailed for America. She's a sweet girl——"

"Look at those bottles!"

"—but touchy."

"Who put those bottles there?"

"Very touchy. A queen of her sex, but touchy. Absolutely."

"Who—put—those—bottles—there? I was right. There are burglars in the house."

Lord Topham heaved another sigh. This seemed to him about as good a time as any to unbare his soul concerning the tragedy which had been darkening it.

"Takes offence rather readily, if you know what I mean, though an angel in every possible respect. You'll scarcely believe this, but just because I told her her new hat made her look like Boris Karloff, she hauled off and biffed me on the side of the head, observing as she did so that she never wanted to see or speak to me again in this world or the next. Well, a fellow has his pride, what? I admit I drew myself up to my full height——"

"Be quiet. Listen."

Adela's gaze had shifted to the ceiling. A muffled sound had proceeded from the projection room above. This was because Smedley, becoming conscious of an imperious desire for a restorative and knowing that all the materials were downstairs, had started for the door and tripped over a footstool.

"There is someone in the projection room. Lord Topham! ... LORD TOPHAM!"

Lord Topham woke, like Abou ben Adhem, from a deep dream of peace. There crossed his mind the passing thought that he was having a rather disturbed night.

"Hullo?'"

"Go up."

"Where?"

"Upstairs."

"Why?"

"There are burglars in the projection room."

"Then I'm dashed if I'm going there," said Lord Topham. "I was about to tell you, when I dozed off, that I wrote Toots a well-expressed air mail letter the day before yesterday, saying that the fault was mine and pleading for a reconciliation. I'd look a silly ass going and getting bumped off by a bunch of bally burglars before I had time to get an answer. What? Well, I mean to say! I'm expecting a cable any moment."

Many people would have approved of his attitude. A prudent and sensible young man, they would have said, with his head screwed on the right way. But Adela could not see eye to eye with them. She uttered an indignant snort and prowled restlessly about the room like a caged lioness. It was not long before she discovered the open French window.

"Lord Topham!"

"Now what?"

"The window is open."

"The window?"

"The window."

"Open?"

"Yes."

Lord Topham, though drowsy, could grasp a simple point like this. With a brief "The window? Oh, ah, the window. You mean the window?" he looked in the direction indicated.

"Yes," he said. "Absolutley. Quite. I see exactly what you mean. Open as per esteemed memo. Did you say that there were burglars in the house?"

"Yes."

"Then mark my words, that's how they got in," said Lord Topham, and went to sleep.

"And there's someone coming along the corridor!" cried Adela, stiffening from head to foot. "Lord Topham ... LORD TOPHAM!!"

"I say, must you? What's the matter now?"

"I can hear someone coming along the corridor."

"No, really? Well, well."

Adela snatched a bottle from the table and pressed it into her companion's hand. He peered at it as if, though this was far from being the case, he were seeing a bottle for the first time.

"What's this?"

"You will need a weapon."

"Who, me?"

"Yes."

"A weapon?"

"Yes."

"Why?"

"The moment he appears, strike him with it."

"Who?"

"The man in the corridor."

"But I don't want to go striking men in corridors."

The door opened, revealing a portly form, at the sight of which Adela's pent-up emotions released themselves in an exasperated scream.

"Smedley!" she cried.

"Oof!" cried Smedley.

"Do I strike him?" inquired Lord Topham.

"What on earth," said Adela, "are you doing wandering about the house at this time of night, Smedley?"

Smedley stood in the doorway, gulping painfully and endeavouring with little success to adjust himself to the severest of all the shocks which had tried his morale in the course of this night of terror. It is not pleasant for a nervous man who comes into a room expecting a Bourbon highball to find there a sister-in-law who even under the most favourable conditions has always made him feel like a toad beneath the harrow.

He continued to gulp. Strange wordless sounds proceeded from his pallid lips. His resemblance to the sheeted dead who squeaked and gibbered in the Roman streets a little ere the mightiest Julius fell was extraordinarily close, though to Lord Topham, who was unfamiliar with the play in which this powerful image occurs, he suggested more a cat about to have a fit. In his boyhood Lord Topham had owned a large tortoiseshell which had distressed himself and family by behaving just as Smedley was behaving now.

To ease the strain, he repeated his question.

"Do I strike him?"

"No."

"Not strike him?"

"No."

"Right ho," said Lord Topham agreeably. "I merely asked."

Adela glared.

"Well, Smedley?"

Smedley at last found speech.

"I—I couldn't sleep. What—what brings you here, Adela?"

"I heard noises outside my room. Footsteps, and someone breathing. I woke Lord Topham and we came down and saw those bottles."

Smedley, still almost too shocked for utterance, contrived with an effort to keep the conversation going.

"Bottles?"

"Bottles."

"Oh, yes . . . Bottles. I—I think Phipps must have put them there," said Smedley, casting an agonized glance at the ceiling.

Adela uttered an impatient 'Tchah!' She had never had a high opinion of her brother-in-law's intelligence, but tonight he seemed to have sunk to new depths of idiocy.

"What in the name of goodness would Phipps be doing, strewing five hundred and fifty-seven bottles about the room?"

"Butlers do put bottles all over the place," urged Smedley.

Lord Topham endorsed this dictum. His had been a life into which butlers had entered rather largely, and he knew their habits.

"Absolutely. Quite. He's right. They do, I mean, what? They're noted for it. Bottles, bottles everywhere, in case you want a drink."

Adela snorted. It was a hard thing to say of anyone, but in her opinion Lord Topham's mentality was about equal to Smedley's.

"And I suppose it's Phipps making those noises in the projection room?" she said witheringly.

Smedley uttered a cry of agony. He was so used to tripping over footstools or his feet or anything that was handy that it had not occurred to him that there had been noises in the projection room. If Adela had heard such noises, it seemed to him that it would be only a matter of moments before she was up and tracing them to their source. And then what?

He stood there, squeaking and gibbering, completely at a loss as to how to deal with the appalling situation. Then relief flooded his soul. Bill was coming in through the French window, looking so solid, so dependable that, it only faintly, hope stirred in its winding cloths. It might be that matters had reached such a pass as to be beyond the power of human control, but if anyone could take arms against this sea of troubles and by opposing end them, it was good old Bill.

Adela beheld her sister with less pleasure.

"Wilhelmina!"

"Oh, hello, Adela. Hello, Smedley. Pip-pip, Lord Topham."

"Toodle-oo, Miss Shannon. Do I strike her?" he asked, for it seemed silly to him to have been issued equpiment—bottle, one, people striking for use of—and not to employ it in action.

"Oh, be quiet," snapped Adela. "What are you doing here, Wilhelmina?"

"Just strolling. I couldn't sleep. What are you?"

"I heard noises."

"Imagination."

"It was not imagination. There is someone in the projection room."

A tenseness came upon Bill. Not so good, this, she was feeling, not so good. She divined, correctly, that Smedley must have been falling over himself and raising enough uproar to wake the whole populace within miles. Phipps, that silent artist, she acquitted of blame.

"Someone in the projection room?"

"I heard the floor creaking."

"Mice."

"Mice be damned. It's a burglar."

"Have you been up there?"

"Of course I haven't. I don't want the top of my head blown off."

"Precisely how I feel," said Lord Topham. "I was explaining to our dear good hostess here that just before I left England I had a row with my girl Toots, and I've written her a well-expressed air mail letter pleading for a reconciliation and am expecting a reply at any moment, so naturally I am reluctant to get the old lemon blown into hash by nocturnal marauders before that reply arrives—a reply, I may say, which I am hoping will be favourable. True, I left the dear sweet creature foaming rather freely at the mouth and tearing my photographs up and stamping on them, but what I always say is that Time, the great healer——"

"Oh, be quiet!"

"Poor Lord Topham," said Bill. "You get about as much chance to talk in this house as a parrot living with Tallulah Bankhead. You had a row with your girl, did you?"

"A frightful row. Battle of the century. It was about her new hat, which I described—injudiciously, I see now, as making her look like——"

"Lord Topham!"

"Hullo?"

Adela spoke with a strained calm.

"I do not wish to hear about your friend Toots."

"But is she my friend? That's the moot point."

"To hell and damnation with your blasted Toots!" cried Adela, reverting, as she so often did in moments of emotion, to the breezy *argot* of the old silent film days, when a girl had to be able to express herself if she wanted to get anywhere. Her calm had exploded into fragments. She could not have regarded the young peer with more stormy distaste if she had caught him trying to steal a scene from her. "Will you kindly stop talking about this miserable creature, who has probably got platinum hair and a lisp and is the scum of the underworld. All I am interested in at the moment is the burglar in the projection room."

Bill shook her head.

"There isn't a burglar in the projection room."

"I tell you there is."

"Shall I go and investigate?"

"What good would you be? No, we'll wait for the police."

Smedley collapsed on the sofa. This was the end.

"Per-per police?"

"I telephoned them from my bedroom. Why they are not here is more than I can imagine. I suppose they're walking. It would be just like those half-

witted imbeciles they call policemen in Beverly Hills to . . . Ah!" said Adela.
"And about time."

A sergeant and a patrolman were coming through the French window.

16

THE SERGEANT was a tough, formidable sergeant, who looked as if he had been hewn from the living rock. The patrolman was a tough, formidable patrolman, who gave the same impression. They came in with the measured tread of men conscious of their ability to uphold the Law and make the hardiest criminal say Uncle.

"Good evening, ma'am," said the sergeant.

Adela was still in difficult mood. Women of her wealth grow to expect their orders to be filled with speed and promptness.

"Good evening," she said. "You've taken your time coming. What were you doing? Playing Canasta?"

The sergeant seemed wounded.

"Came as quick as we could, ma'am. You're reporting a burglary?"

Adela gave him a full whammy.

"Don't they tell you *anything* at police headquarters? Yes, as I went to the trouble of explaining carefully over the telephone, there are burglars in the house. They are up in the projection room."

"Where's that?"

"The room immediately above this one. Smedley, show the officers up to the projection room."

Smedley quivered like a Roman Emperor hearing the leader of the band of assassins which has just filed into his private apartments say "Well, here we are, Galba"—or Vitellius or Caligula or whatever the name might be. He cast an imploring glance at Bill, as if pleading with her not to fail him in this dark hour.

Bill as always, did her best.

"There aren't any burglars in the projection room. Absurd."

"Absurd, my foot. I heard strange noises."

Bill caught the sergeant's eye. Her own twinkled.

"She heard strange noises, sergeant. Ha, ha. We women! Poor, timid, fluttering creatures."

"Listen! Any time *I* flutter . . ."

"Just bundles of nerves, aren't we, sergeant?"

"Yes, ma'am. My wife's like that."

"My wife's like that," said the patrolman.

"All women are like that," said Bill. "It's something to do with the bone structure of our heads."

The sergeant said Maybe you're right, ma'am. The patrolman said Yes, she had a point there. His wife, said the patrolman, was a great believer in omens and portents and would you ever catch that woman walking under a ladder, no, ma'am: and the sergeant said his wife always said 'Rabbits, rabbits, rabbits' on the first day of the month, because she held the view that if you said 'Rabbits, rabbits, rabbits' on the first day of the month, you got a present within the next two weeks. Silly, said the sergeant, but there it was.

"Listen," said Adela, who was showing signs of becoming overwrought.

"Just a moment, Adela," said Bill. "Sit down," she said to the arms of the Law, "and tell us all about your wives."

It was a tempting offer, and for a moment the sergeant seemed to waver. But a splendid spirit animates the police force of Beverly Hills, and he was strong again.

"Not just now, ma'am," he said. "I guess we'd best take a look at this projection room the lady wants us to take a look at."

"Waste of time," said Bill judicially.

"Yes," agreed Smedley, speaking with a feverish earnestness. "And you wouldn't like the projection room. Honestly."

"Besides, there's no hurry," said Bill. "Good heavens, the night's yet young. Take a couple of chairs and have a drink."

A passer-by at this point might have supposed that an ammunition dump had exploded in the near neighbourhood. But it was only Adela.

"Sweet suffering soupspoons!" cried Adela, raising her hands to heaven in a passionate gesture. "Take a couple of chairs! Have a drink! What *is* this? A college reunion?"

The sergeant shook his head. The bottles on the tray had not escaped his notice, for the police are trained to observe, and his eye had gleamed at the suggestion that he should investigate their contents. It was a pity, he felt, that this admirable woman who looked like a German Boxer was not in charge of the proceedings. Bill, in his opinion, had nice ideas, and it would have been a pleasure to fall in with them. But apparently it was this other dame, whose face seemed oddly familiar for some reason, who was directing operations, and her views were less in keeping with the trend of modern thought.

"No, thank you, ma'am," he said virtuously. "Not while we're on duty. Come on, Bill."

"Is your name Bill?" said Bill.

The patrolman said it was, and Bill said Well, well, well.

"So is mine," said Bill. "What an amazing coincidence. Let's curl up on the sofa and have a long talk about it."

"Later on, ma'am," said the sergeant. He glanced up at the ceiling, and there came into his face that keen look which policemen wear when constabulary duty is to be done. "Seems to me I do hear something up there," he said. "A kind of creaking noise."

"All very old houses creak at night," said Bill. "This one, I believe, dates back to the early Cecil de Mille period."

"Ask me," said the patrolman, "it's more like a sort of scratching sound."

Bill cocked an ear.

"Ah, yes," she said. "I know what that is. That is my sister's poodle. He has a sensitive skin, and he is like the young lady of Natchez, who said: 'Where Ah itches, Ah scratches.' Are you fond of dogs, sergeant?"

"Yes, ma'am. I've a dog at home—"

"What sort?"

"A Scotty, ma'am."

"No nicer breed. Very intelligent animals, Scotties."

"Intelligent? You said it. Say, listen," said the sergeant.

"Say, listen," said the patrolman, who wanted to speak of his Boston terrier, Buster.

"Say, listen," said Adela, who had been fermenting rather freely during these exchanges. "Listen, you Keystone Kops, are you or are you not going up to that projection room?"

"Sure, lady, sure," said the sergeant. "Come on, Bill."

They started for the door, and Smedley uttered the soft little moan of despair of the man who feels that the doom has come upon him. Tripping over his feet, he fell against the sergeant, who fell against Adela, who asked him what he imagined he was playing at. Football? inquired Adela. Or Postman's Knock?

"Pardon, lady," said the sergeant courteously. "The gentleman bumped me." He paused, staring. "Say, aren't you Adela Shannon?"

"I am."

"Well, I'll be a son-of-a," said the sergeant. "I seen you in the old silents. You remember Adela Shannon, Bill?"

"Sure," said the patrolman. "She used to be the Empress of Stormy Emotion."

"She still is," said Bill. "So you're interested in pictures, are you sergeant?"

"Yes, ma'am. Are you connected with pix?"

"No longer. I had a job with Superba-Llewellyn, but they fired me."

"Too bad. Still, that's how it goes."

"That's how it goes."

The patrolman laughed a bitter laugh.

"Yes, that's how it goes—in Hollywood," he said. "Ha!"

Bill looked at him, interested. She turned to the sergeant.

"He doesn't seem to like Hollywood."

"No, ma'am."

Adela clenched her teeth. Her fists were already clenched. She spoke with the strained sweetness of a woman who is holding herself in with all the resolution at her disposal, knowing that if she relaxes for an instant, she will spring into the air, howling like a Banshee. No less than Smedley, who was now a mere jelly, she was finding the proceedings something of a strain. The zealous officers were affecting her like a Viennese director she remembered from the old days, a man at whose head she had once been compelled in the interests of her art to throw one of the swords used by the Roman soldiers in Hail, Caesar.

"Might I have your attention for a moment, Mr. Louis B. Mayer, and you, Mr. Zanuck," she said. "Do you intend during the next hour or so to get some action, or is this conference going on for ever? Did you come here to arrest burglars or just to chat about motion pictures? I merely wish to know how matters stand," said Adela, all charm and consideration.

Bill rebuked her gently.

"You're so impatient, Adela. We have the night before us. Why doesn't your friend like Hollywood?"

The sergeant's brow darkened.

"He tried for a job at Medulla-Oblongata-Glutz last week, and they turned him down on account he wanted to do whimsical comedy and they said he wasn't right for whimsical comedy."

"You're kidding me."

"No, ma'am, that's what they said."

"Astounding. He looks all right for whimsical comedy to *me*."

"Sure I'm all right for whimsical comedy," said the patrolman. "But it's all a closed ring. That's what it is, just a closed ring. If you're new talent, you haven't a chance."

"It's tough," said Bill.

"You're right, it's tough," said the sergeant. "Say, listen. When I tried to muscle in at Colossal-Superhuman, they had the nerve to say I lacked dramatic intensity."

"It's incredible."

A sigh like the wind blowing through the cracks in a broken heart escaped Adela. Her spirit was broken.

"God give me strength!" she moaned. "I telephone for policemen, and they send me a couple of ham actors. I shall go to bed. Lord Topham . . . LORD TOPHAM!"

Lord Topham sat up, blinking.

"Hullo? Is that Toots?"

Adela was silent for a moment. She seemed to be swallowing something.

"No," she said at length, speaking with some difficulty. "It is not Toots. Lord Topham, you have been about as much use up to now as a pain in the neck. Would it be too much to ask you to accompany me to my bedroom?"

"Accompany you to your—?"

"With burglars in every nook and cranny of the house, I don't propose to go up two flights of stairs alone."

Lord Topham seemed relieved.

"Oh, yes, yes, yes, yes, yes," he said. "I thought for a moment . . . Ha, ha, silly of me. Absolutely. Yes, yes, yes, yes, of course. I see what you mean."

"Bring that bottle."

"Eh? Oh the jolly old bottle? Quite, quite."

"And any time you get through talking about your dramatic intensity," said Adela, addressing the sergeant, "you will find the burglars in the projection room. I'll shout through the door and tell them to be sure to wait. Come, Lord Topham."

"Ladies first," said Lord Topham gallantly.

"Ladies first, my left eyeball," said Adela. "Why, they may be lurking in the corridor."

Lord Topham went out, followed by Adela. The sergeant, who appeared to have been stung by her parting words, became active.

"Come on, let's go."

"Oh, not yet," begged Smedley.

"Yes, sir. We have our duty to do."

"But I want to hear all about this gentleman's whimsical comedy," said Bill. "Do sit down and have a drink."

"Thank you, no, ma'am."

"Say when."

"When," said the sergeant.

"You?"

"Not for me, ma'am."

"Say when."

"When," said the patrolman.

"That's better," said Bill. "Now we're set. Now we're cosy. Why did Medulla-Oblongata-Glutz think you were not right for whimsical comedy?"

"Search me," said the patrolman, moodily. "What's Clark Gable got that I haven't got?"

"A moustache, ten million dollars and Lady Sylvia Ashley."

The sergeant saw that there had been a misunderstanding.

"He is alluding to talent, ma'am."

"Oh, talent?"

"Yes, talent," said the patrolman. "I got talent. I know it. I feel it *here*," said the patrolman, slapping his chest.

Bill cocked an eye at the sergeant.

"You have talent, too?"

"Sure I got talent," said the sergeant. "And who says I lack dramatic intensity? Listen. 'Drop that gun, you rat. You know me. Tough Tom Hennessy, the cop that always gets his man. Ah, would you? Bang, bang.' That's where I shoot and plug him," explained the sergeant. "It's a little thing I threw together with a view to showing myself in a dramatic role. There's more of it, but that'll give you the idea."

"It's wonderful," said Bill. "A poignant and uplifting cameo of life as it is lived to-day, purifying the emotions with pity and terror."

The sergeant simpered modestly, one massive foot drawing circles on the carpet.

"Thanks, ma'am."

"Not at all."

"Care to look in at the station house some day, I'll show you my stills."

"I can hardly wait."

"Yes, ma'am, that's the sort of thing I can do. But they turn me down."

"That's Hollywood."

"That's Hollywood."

"You're right, that's Hollywood," said the patrolman. "Lookit, ma'am. Watch. What's this?"

He smiled.

"Joy?" said Bill.

"Joy is right. And this?"

He tightened his lips.

"Grief!"

"Grief is right. And this?"

He raised his eyebrows.

"Horror?"

"You betcher, horror. And I can do hate, too. But it's whimsical comedy I'm best at. Like where the fellow meets the girl and starts kidding her. But could I drive that into their thick skulls at M-O-G? No, ma'am. They turned me down."

"That's Hollywood," said Bill.

"That's Hollywood," said the sergeant.

"You're right, that's Hollywood," said the patrolman.

"Bright city of sorrows," said Bill. "Ah, Phipps."

The butler had come shimmering through the door. If he felt any surprise or alarm at observing policemen on the premises, he gave no sign of it. He was his usual dignified self.

"I came to see if there was anything more you required, madam."

"Not a thing, thank you," said Bill.

"Say, who's this?" said the sergeant.

"My sister's butler. Sergeant—?"

"Ward, ma'am. And Patrolman Morehouse."

"Thank you. Mr. Phipps. Sergeant Ward and Patrolman Morehouse."

"How do you do?" said Phipps.

"Pleased to meet you," said the sergeant.

"Hi!" said the patrolman, also indicating pleasure.

Bill showed a womanly concern for the butler's well-being.

"You're up late, Phipps. Couldn't you sleep, either?"

"No, madam. I experienced an annoying wakefulness. Most unusual with me, madam."

"You should have tried counting sheep."

"I did, madam, but without avail. So finally, I took the liberty of proceeding to the projection room and running off Forever Amber."

The sergeant uttered an exclamation.

"What's that? Was it you in that projection room?"

"Yes, sir."

It was plain that the sergeant now saw it all. His trained mind had leaped to the significance of the butler's story.

"Then there you are. There you have the whole mystery explained and the case cleaned up. The lady thought it was burglars."

"Mrs. Cork," explained Bill. "She has just left us. She heard noises and became alarmed."

"I am sorry, madam. I endeavoured to be as silent as possible."

"I'm sure you did."

The sergeant wiped his lips, and rose.

"Well, we'll be getting along. Good night, ma'am."

"Good night. Take care of that dramatic intensity."

"I will, ma'am."

"And good luck to your artistic efforts."

"Thank you, ma'am. But one kind of loses heart. The more you submit yourself to these casting offices, the more they give you the old runaround."

"That's Hollywood."

"That's Hollywood."

"You're right, that's Hollywood," said the patrolman. "That tinsel town where tragedy lies hid behind a thousand false smiles, and—"

"Ah, come on," said the sergeant.

Bill closed the French window behind them, and Smedley breathed the first carefree breath he had breathed since the dark doings of the night had begun.

"Bill," he said, "you're a marvel."

"Thank you, Smedley. As Phipps would say, I desire to give satisfaction."

"A marvel," repeated Smedley. He turned to Phipps. "Those cops were going up to the projection room, but she kept them talking and headed them off."

"Indeed sir? The experience must have occasioned you a great deal of anxiety, madam."

"Yes, it was a close thing," said Bill. "Lucky they were interested in pictures."

Joe and Kay came in through the French window.

"Joe's feeling better," said Kay.

"Good. And you look radiant."

"Can you wonder?" said Joe. "She's going to marry me."

"Ah, you fixed it up all right. I thought you would. Kay, an aunt's blessing."

"Thank you, Bill."

"In my opinion, nice work. You probably feel the same, Smedley?"

Smedley executed a brief dance step. It might have signified joy, but more probably irritation. Smedley lacked Patrolman Morehouse's skill in registering.

"Yes, yes, yes," he said, "but I haven't time to bother about that now. You got it, Phipps?"

"Sir?"

"The diary."

"Oh, yes, sir. Without any difficulty."

"Good work, Phipps," said Joe.

"Thank you, sir."

"Splendid, Phipps," said Kay.

"Thank you, miss."

"Gimme," said Smedley.

A look of respectful regret came into the butler's face.

"I am sorry, sir, but what you suggest is not feasible, sir."

Smedley stared.

"What do you mean? You said you had got it."

"Yes, sir. And I propose to keep it."

"What?"

"Yes, sir. Would there be anything further, sir? Thank you, sir. Good night."

He shimmered out, leaving a stunned silence behind him.

"My God!" said Bill, the first to break it. "Hi-jacked *again!*" She paused, wrestling with her feelings. "Go on, Smedley," she said at length. "*You* say it. I'm a lady."

17

THERE ARE, as everybody knows, many ways of measuring time, and from the earliest ages learned men have argued earnestly in favour of their different systems, with not a little bad blood, one is sorry to say, arising between the representatives of the various schools of thought.

Hipparchus of Rhodes, for instance, who had his own ideas on the way time should be measured, once referred to Marinus of Tyre, who held different opinions, as 'Marinus the flat tire,' which, though extraordinarily witty, was pretty bitter: and when Purbach and Regiomontanus were told the views of Achmed Ibn Abdallah of Baghdad, they laughed themselves cross-eyed. Purbach, who was a hard nut, said that Achmed Ibn Abdallah knew about as much about measuring time as his grandmother's cat, a notoriously backward animal, and when kind-hearted Regiomontanus in his tolerant way urged that Achmed Ibn was just a young fellow trying to get along and one ought not to judge him too harshly, Purbach said 'Oh, yeah?' and Regiomontanus said 'Yeah,' and Purbach said Was that so, and Regiomontanus said Yes, that was so, and Purbach said Regiomontanus made him sick. It was their first quarrel.

Tycho Brahe, the eminent Dane, measured time by means of altitudes, quadrants, azimuths, cross-staves, armillary spheres and parallactic rules, and the general opinion in Denmark was that he had got the thing down cold.

And then in 1863 along came Dollen with his *Die Zeitbestimmung Vermittelst Des Tragbaren Durchgangsinstruments Im Vertical e Des Polarsterns*—a best seller in its day, subsequently made into a musical by Rodgers and Hammerstein, who called it North Atlantic, a much better marquee title—and proved that Tycho, by mistaking an azimuth for an armillary sphere one night after the annual dinner of the alumni of Copenhagen University, had got his calculations all wrong, throwing the whole thing back into the melting pot.

The truth is that time cannot be measured. To Smedley, slumped in his chair on the terrace on the following morning, it seemed to be standing still. Melancholy had marked him for her own, and each leaden moment that dragged itself by took on the semblance of an hour. To Phipps, on the other hand, chanting a gay air in his pantry, the golden minutes seemed to race. Tra-la, sang Phipps, and Tiddly-om-pom-pom. In all Beverly Hills there was, as of even date, no sunnier butler. Lord Topham had described the previous day as the maddest and merriest of all the glad new year, but it seemed to Phipps that the current one relegated it to second place. God was in His heaven and all was right with the world, he felt. A contract with Medulla-Oblongata-Glutz in one pocket and a fifty thousand dollar diary in the other—what more could a man want?

Well, the way his head was feeling after last night, perhaps a bromo-seltzer. He rose and mixed himself one. And as he drained it, singing between the sips like somebody in a drinking chorus in an opera, his eye fell on the clock. Nearly noon? Time for old Smedley's yoghurt.

Smedley had closed his eyes when the butler arrived on the terrace, and was not aware of his presence till he spoke behind him.

"Good morning, sir," said Phipps, and Smedley skipped as nearly like the high hills as is within the scope of a seated man.

"Oof!" he said. "You startled me."

"That will cure your hiccups, sir."

"I don't have hiccups."

"I am sorry, sir. I was not aware of that."

Smedley, who had been in one of his daydreams, now realized for the first time that the voice which had broken in on his reverie was that of Southern California's most prominent viper. A viper to end all vipers.

"Well, viper," he said, injecting a wealth of hate and abhorrence into the salutation and with mouth and eye-brows registering scorn, disgust and loathing in a manner which would have extorted the admiration of Patrolman Morehouse, himself no mean specialist in that direction.

"Sir?"

"I said viper."

"Very good, sir. Your yoghurt, sir."

"Take that stuff away."

Joe and Kay came on to the terrace. They had been wandering through the rose garden, discussing ways and means. Kay's view was that love was all and that so long as they had each other, what did anything else matter? It was enough for her, she said, that she was going to marry Joe, because Joe was a woolly baa-lamb. Joe, while conceding that he was a woolly baa-lamb and admitting that love was swell, had rather tended to argue that a bit of the stuff would also come in handy, and from this the conversation turned naturally to Phipps, who in such a dastardly manner had placed that bit of stuff beyond their reach. It would be gratifying, said Joe, to have a word with Phipps. So, coming on to the terrace and seeing him there, he had it.

"Ha!" he said. "Well, you sneaking, chiselling, two-timing, horn-swoggling highbinder!"

"Good morning, sir."

Kay, too, was severe.

"I wonder you can look us in the face, Phipps."

The butler sighed regretfully. His innate chivalry made the thought of having given offence to Youth and Beauty an unpleasant one.

"I am sorry to have been compelled to occasion you inconvenience, miss, but as Miss Shannon so well put it, it was military necessity. One cannot make an omelette without breaking eggs."

He winced a little. Those overnight potations had left him in a condition where he would have preferred not to think of eggs. His breakfast that morning had consisted of a slice of Melba toast and three pots of black coffee, and even the Melba toast had seemed at the time excessive.

Joe had thought of another one.

"You wolf in butler's clothing!"

"Yes, sir. Precisely, sir," said Phipps deferentially. He turned to Smedley. "If you persist in refusing to drink your yoghurt, sir, I shall have no option but to inform Mrs. Cork."

Smedley endeavoured, as usual unsuccessfully, to snap his fingers.

"That for Mrs. Cork!"

"Very good, sir."

"You can go to Mrs. Cork and tell her, with my compliments, to boil her head."

"Very good, sir. I will bear your instructions in mind."

The butler withdrew, to all appearances oblivious of the fact that six eyes were boring holes in his back, and the emotions of the three on the terrace found expression in words.

"The snake!" said Smedley.

"The hound!" said Joe.

"The reptile!" said Kay.

This made them all feel a little better, but only a little, for it was apparent to the dullest mind that what the crisis which had been precipitated called for was not words, but action. It was Smedley who clothed this thought in speech.

"We've got to do something," said Smedley.

"But what?" said Joe.

"Yes, what?" said Kay.

There, Smedley admitted, they had him.

"Well, I'll tell you one thing," he said. "It's no good trying to formulate a plan of action without Bill. Where is Bill?"

"In the Garden Room," said Kay. "I saw her as we passed. I think she's working on Aunt Adela's *Memoirs.*"

"Then come on," said Smedley.

Left to himself, he would rather not have revisited the Garden Room, with all its sad memories, but if Bill was there, to the Garden Room he must go. It was imperative that the conduct of affairs be handed over to The Old Reliable without delay. The thought crossed his mind that if Bill was capable of concentrating on Adela's *Memoirs* on the morning after a night like last night, she must be a woman of iron, and it encouraged him. There are certain difficult situations in life where a woman of iron at one's side is just what one most needs.

Bill, as fresh, so far as the eye could discern, as an infant newly risen from its afternoon nap, was seated at the desk, prattling away into the dictaphone as if without a care in the world.

"Ah, Hollywood, Hollywood," said Bill. "Bright city of sorrows, where fame deceives and temptation lurks, where souls are shrivelled in the furnace of desire and beauty is broken on sin's cruel wheel."And if that was not the stuff to give them, she felt, she was vastly mistaken. There was a flat dullness about the story of Adela's life which made the injection of some such purple patch from time to time a necessity. Absolutely, as Lord Topham would have said.

Observing the procession filing in at the French window, she suspended her activities.

"Hello, boys and girls. Heavens, Smedley, you look like something left over from the Ark," she said, and marvelled at the mysteries of a woman's heart, which can preserve its love for a man intact even when his appearance is that of flotsam and jetsam. For in describing Smedley as something left over from the Ark, she was really giving him the breaks. Actually, he resembled more closely one of those mildewed pieces of refuse found in dustbins, which are passed over with a disdainful jerk of the head by the discriminating alley cat.

Smedley exhibited pique. None knew better than he that he was not his usual spruce self and, like Regiomontanus, he felt that allowances ought to be made.

"How do you expect me to look?" he protested. "I haven't been to bed for two nights. Bill, what are we going to do?"

"About Phipps?"

"Of course about Phipps. What else did you think we'd got on our minds?"

Bill nodded sympathetically.

"It's a problem," she agreed. "I ought to have reflected, before enlisting Phipps's services, that he is a man of infinite guile."

"I'll sue him," cried Smedley. "I'll fight the case to the Supreme Court."

"M'm."

"Yes," said Smedley, deflated, "I suppose you're right. Then is there nothing we can do?"

"Can't you force him to give it up?" said Kay.

This pleased Smedley. The right spirit, he considered.

"Good idea. Intimidate the fellow. Stick lighted matches between his toes."

Bill was obliged to discourage this Utopian dream.

"My dear Smedley, you can't stick lighted matches between the toes of an English butler. He would raise his eyebrows and freeze you with a glance. You'd feel as if he had caught you using the wrong fork. No, the only thing is to try an appeal to his better nature." She rose, and pressed the bell. "I guarantee no results. For all we know, Phipps hasn't a better nature." She regarded Joe solicitously. "You're looking very gloomy, Joe. Feeling a little low?"

"I could walk under a cockroach."

"Cheer up. There is still joy in the world, still the happy laughter of children and the singing of bluebirds."

"That's all right about bluebirds. I want to get married, and I'm down to my last ten dollars."

Bill stared.

"Last ten dollars? What's become of that thousand you had?"

Joe's manner betrayed a certain embarrassment.

"Well, I'll tell you, Bill. You remember that gambling joint, Perelli's, we were talking about a couple of days ago? After the party broke up last night, I thought I'd go down there and try to make a fast buck."

"Did you make a fast buck?"

"Unfortunately, no. But there's always a bright side. Perelli did."

"He cleaned you out?"

"Except for ten dollars."

"You unbalanced young boll weevil! Kay's right. You're not an *homme sérieux.*"

Kay flared up.

"He is not an unbalanced boll weevil. And what do you mean, saying he's not an *homme sérieux?* I think it was very sensible of him to go to Perelli's. It wasn't his fault he didn't win."

Bill let it go. This, she felt, was love.

"And anyway, darling," said Kay, "I don't know what you are worrying about. Two can live as cheap as one."

Bill regarded her admiringly.

"You do say some bright things, child. If that's your normal form, Joe won't have a dull moment in your little home."

"In our little gutter, you mean," corrected Joe.

"Joe says we shall have to starve in the gutter."

"You can't," said Bill. "There aren't any gutters in Hollywood. Ah, come in, Phipps."

The butler had manifested himself.

"You rang, madam?"

"Yes. Good morning, Phipps."

"Good morning, madam."

"Quite a night last night."

"Yes, madam."

"No ill effects, I trust?"

"I have a slight headache, madam."

"Well earned. You should keep off the sauce, Phipps."

"Yes, madam."

"And now what about things?"

"On what particular point do you desire information, madam?"

Bill did not find his manner promising. Anything less resembling a butler likely to be talked with honeyed words into giving up a diary worth fifty thousand dollars she had never beheld. She persevered, however.

"About the diary. You remember it? It hasn't slipped your mind?"

"No, madam."

"Having slept on the matter, you still propose to keep it?"

"Yes, madam."

"And sell it and convert the proceeds to your own use?"

"Yes, madam."

"Well, I don't want to hurt your feelings," said Bill, "but you must have a soul like a stevedore's undervest."

The butler seemed rather pleased than otherwise. A faint twitch of the upper lip showed that if he had not been an English butler, he might have smiled.

"A very striking image, madam."

"Has it occurred to you that you will have some exceedingly nasty questions to answer about this on Judgment Day?"

"No doubt, madam."

"But you don't quail?"

"No, madam."

Bill gave it up.

"All right, Phipps. You may withdraw."

"Very good, madam."

"What do you like at Santa Anita to-day?"

"Betty Hutton, madam, in the fourth race."

"Thank you, Phipps."

"Thank *you*, madam."

18

THE DOOR closed. Bill lit a cigarette.

"Well," she said, "I did my best. Nobody can do more. When you come up against Battling Phipps, you certainly know you've been in a fight."

The door reopened.

"Excuse me, madam," said Phipps. "I inadvertently omitted to deliver a message entrusted to me by Mrs. Cork. Mrs. Cork presents her compliments and would be glad if Mr. Smedley would join her in the projection room at his earliest convenience."

Smedley did one of his quick dance steps.

"What? What does she want?"

"Mrs. Cork did not honour me with her confidence, sir. But when I left her, she was standing scrutinizing the safe——"

Oh, gosh!"

"—and heaving gently, sir, like a welsh rabbit about to come to the height of its fever. Thank you, sir."

The door closed again.

"Phipps has a very happy gift of phrase," said Bill.

Smedley was plucking at his collar.

"Bill, she's found out."

"She was bound to sooner or later."

"She suspects me. What'll I do."

"Stick to stout denial."

"Stout denial?"

"Stout denial. You can't beat it. Get tough. Say 'Oh, yeah?' and 'Jussa minute, jussa minute,' and when speaking, speak out of the side of the mouth."

"Like Perelli," said Joe.

"Does Mr. Perelli speak out of the side of his mouth?"

"All the time."

"Then there's your model, Smedley. Imagine that you're the proprietor of a prosperous gambling hell and that Adela is a disappointed client who is trying to sell you the idea that the wheel is crooked."

Smedley went out, gulping unhappily. Bill wandered to the French window and looked out on the sunlit garden. Kay came to Joe, who after his brief observation about Mr. Perelli had returned to the depths.

"Cheer up, darling," she said. "You still have me."

"And ten dollars."

"I call ten dollars quite a lot."

"Yes, but when I leave here, I shall have to tip Phipps with it. Is that a bitter thought? If not," said Joe, "how would you describe it?" He looked at Bill, who was waving a friendly hand at someone in the garden. "What are you waving at?"

Bill turned.

"Come here, Joe." She pointed. "What do you see?"

Joe followed her finger with a dull eye.

"Clouds," he said. "Black, inky clouds. And murky shadows threatening doom, disaster and despair. Oh, you mean the figure in the foreground?"

"Right. My Lord Topham. He is coming this way, you observe. How have you been getting along with Lord Topham since your arrival?"

"Pretty well. He was telling me about the trouble he has been having with a girl in England called Toots. Apparently she gave him the brusheroo, and he's a bit down about it."

"You were sympathetic, I hope?"

"Oh, yes."

"Good. Then he probably looks on you as a bosom friend. A very rich young man, Lord Topham, I understand," said Bill meditatively. "One of England's richest, Adela tells me. Something to do with chain stores or provision markets, if I am not mistaken. Anyway, however he gets the stuff, he's got it."

Joe started. This opened up a new line of thought.

"Good Lord, Bill, you weren't thinking of touching Topham?"

"It is always a sound business principle, when you need twenty thousand dollars, to go to the man who's got twenty thousand dollars."

"Bill, you're a genius."

"That's what I kept telling those people at Superba-Llewellyn, but they wouldn't listen to me."

"Pitch it strong, old friend."

"I will, Joe, I will."

The Lord Topham who a moment later dragged his long legs across the threshold of the French window and added his presence to the little group of thinkers in the Garden Room differed substantially from the exuberant young athlete who had made a similar entrance almost exactly twenty-four hours earlier. Then, it will be remembered, he had had a song on his lips and a gleam in his eye as the result of having broken a hundred on the golf links. For even an anxious lover, awaiting a reply to his well-expressed air mail letter from the girl with whom he has had a falling-out, will temporarily forget the sex angle after doing eighteen holes in ninety-seven strokes for the first time in his life. The Lord Topham of twenty-four hours ago, though the vultures of anxiety had presumably been gnawing at his vitals, had stood before the world as a definitely chirpy man.

Vastly different was the sombre figure that now loomed up behind its eleven-inch cigarette holder. The face was drawn, the eyes haggard, the general appearance that of one who has searched for the leak in life's gaspipe with a lighted candle. Even such a man, so faint, so spiritless, so dead, so dull in look, so woebegone, drew Priam's curtain in the dead of night and would have told him half his Troy was burned. One might have supposed, looking at him, that Lord Topham had been out on the links again and had not been able to do better than a hundred and fifty-seven, taking fourteen at the long dog-leg hole and losing six balls in the lake at the second.

Actually, what was causing his despondency was the fact that shortly after breakfast he had received the cable he had been expecting, and it had been a red-hot one. Miss Gladys ('Toots') Fauntleroy was one of those girls who do not object to letting the sun go down on their wrath, and it is to be doubted whether a more vitriolic ten-bobsworth had crossed the Atlantic Ocean since the days of the late Florenz Ziegfeld. It had caused hope to die and despair to take possession of Lord Topham's soul, and had engendered in him a comprehensive dislike for the whole human race. It was, in short, the worst possible moment anyone could have selected to approach him with the idea of getting into his ribs for twenty thousand dollars.

The newcomer's gloom did not impress itself on those present, so self-centred do we all tend to be in this world. Obsessed with their own personal problems, they merely saw a fabulously rich young man coming in through a French window. They did not pause to ask themselves if his heart was intact or broken, but cluttered joyously about him, giving him a great reception.

"Lord Topham!" cried Kay. "Do come in, Lord Topham."

"Yes, do," cried Joe. "Just the man we wanted to see."

"The very person," said Bill. "Lord Topham, old boy, could we have a word with you, Lord Topham, old boy?"

She patted his shoulder lovingly and another man in his position might have been pleased and touched by the warmth of her affection. He merely glowered down at her hand as if it had been one of those spiders for which Phipps had so strong a distaste.

"What the dickens are you doing?"

"Just patting your shoulder, Lord Topham, old boy, old boy."

"Well, bally well don't," said the old boy morosely.

A chill crept into the hearts of the reception committee. They looked at one another with a growing feeling of uneasiness. Something was wrong, they felt, something was seriously wrong. This was not the effervescent young man they had hoped to see. More like some sort of a changeling. It was with a feeling that little of a constructive nature was likely to result that Joe approached the main item on the agenda paper.

"Listen, Lord Topham. It is within your power to bring joy and happiness into quite a number of human lives."

"Then I'm dashed if I'm going to do it," said Lord Topham. "Would it interest you to know how I feel about the human species? I hope it jolly well chokes. I don't mind telling you that I got a cable from my girl Toots this morning which has definitely turned me into a mis-what's-the-word. I mean one of those blokes who get fed up with their fellow men and go and live in caves and grow beards and subsist on berries from the bush and water from the spring. Don't talk to me about bringing joy into human lives. I have to do without joy, so why shouldn't the ruddy human lives? To blazes with them. Let 'em eat cake."

"But if you don't help me, I'm ruined."

"Well, that's fine," said Lord Topham, brightening a little.

Phipps came softly in, and Bill regarded him with an unfriendly eye.

"You again?" she said. "The way you keep shimmering in and out, one would think you were the family spectre."

The butler preserved his equanimity.

"I came to inform his lordship that he was wanted on the telephone, madam. A transatlantic call, m'lord."

Lord Topham quivered. The cigarette holder, which he had replaced between his lips at the conclusion of his powerful speech, fell to the ground, dashing its cigarette to fragments.

"Eh? What? A transatlantic call? Who is it?"

"A Miss Fauntleroy, m'lord."

"What! Good God! Good Lord! Good heavens! Well, I'm dashed. Well, I'm blowed. Well, I'll be jiggered. Gangway, gangway, gangway!" cried Lord Topham, and was out of the room before one could have said 'What ho.' It seemed incredible that that elongated form, a moment ago so limp, could be capable of such speed on the flat.

Phipps, about to follow, was stopped by Bill.

"Oh, Phipps," said Bill.

"Madam?"

"One moment, if I may delay your progress. Could you bring us some strengthening cocktails?"

"Certainly, madam."

"Thank you, but don't go. When we were chatting just now, there was a point I omitted to touch on."

"Yes, madam?"

"It is this. Had you a mother, Phipps?"

"Yes, madam."

"Had she a knee?"

"Yes, madam."

"Then did you not learn at that knee to do the square thing by all and sundry and not to go about steeping yourself in crime?"

"No, madam."

"H'm. Negligence somewhere. All right, Phipps. Push off. Don't forget those cocktails."

"I will put them in preparation immediately, madam."

The door closed.

"Now what would Phipps's mother be like?" mused Bill. "Something on the lines of Queen Victoria, I imagine." She turned to Joe. "Did you say 'Oh, hell!'?"

"Yes."

"I thought you did, and it wrung my heart. You take a dim view of the situation?"

"I do."

"I don't. I have high hopes of Lord Topham."

"What, after the way he was talking just now?"

"Forget the way he was talking just now. Since then his girl has called him on the transatlantic telephone. Girls don't dig down into their jeans for the price of a transatlantic telephone call unless love has re-awakened in their hearts, dispelling like the morning sun the mists of doubt and misunderstanding. I shall be greatly surprised if this does not mean that the second phase has set in—where the female love bird weeps on the male love bird's chest and says can he ever forgive her for speaking those cruel words."

"Oh, Bill!" cried Kay.

"If such is the case, I don't think I am wrong in assuming that the milk of human kindness will have come surging back into the Topham bosom like a tidal wave, sweetening his outlook and rendering him a good and easy prospect."

Joe nodded.

"Gosh, I believe you're right."

"I feel sure of it. We shall see a very different Lord Topham in a moment or two."

"And then you'll talk to him?"

"And then I'll talk to him."

Footsteps sounded in the corridor, gay, galloping footsteps. The door was dashed open, and something that might have been a ray of sunshine in form-fitting grey flannel came curvetting over the threshold.

"I say," cried this new and improved edition of Lord Topham. "Everything's fine. Everything's all right. Everything's splendid."

Bill patted his shoulder, this time without provoking a protest.

"Precisely what I was hoping when I heard that your heart throb was on the telephone. Get them calling up on the telephone, and it's in the bag. She loves you still?"

"Absolutely. She cried buckets, and I said: 'There, there!' "

"You could hardly have put it more neatly."

"She said she had toothache when she sent that cable."

"That soured her outlook?"

"Oh, definitely."

"You mean absolutely, don't you?"

"That's right. Absolutely."

"Well, well, well, I couldn't be more pleased. I'm delighted. We're all delighted. And now, Lord Topham, could you spare me a moment?"

"Oh, rather."

"Fine."

Bill led the young man to the sofa, deposited him there and took a seat at his side.

"Tell me, Lord Topham—or may I call you Topham?"

"Do. Or Toppy. Most of my pals call me Toppy."

"What is your first name?"

"Lancelot. But I prefer to hush it up."

"Then shall we settle for Toppy?"

"Absolutely."

"Right. You notice I am patting your shoulder again, Toppy. Would you like to know why?"

"Very much. I was just wondering."

"I do it in a congratulatory spirit. Because I am going, Toppy, old boy, to let you in on a big thing."

"Really?"

"Absolutely. Tell me, my dear Toppy, have you ever seen a man in a fur coat, with three chins, riding in a Rolls-Royce with a blonde on each knee and smoking a five-dollar cigar? Because, if so, you can be pretty sure he was a literary agent."

"A what?"

"A literary agent."

"What's that?"

"A literary agent—or authors' representative—is a man who sits in an arm-chair with his feet on a desk, full of caviare and champagne, and gives a couple of minutes to the authors who come crawling in on all fours, begging him to handle their output. Should he consent to do so, he takes ten per cent of the kitty."

"What kitty would that be?"

"I refer to all emoluments received from these authors' works, which amount to very large sums indeed. Thus, we will suppose that this authors' representative sells a story by some client of his to a prominent editor for—well, taking a figure at random, forty thousand dollars. His cut would be four thousand."

"It sounds like a jolly good show."

"It is a jolly good show. Four thousand bucks for telling his secretary to shove a wad of typescript into an envelope and address, stamp and mail it is unquestionably nice sugar. And it's going on all the time."

"All the time?"

"Practically without cessation. You would be astounded if you knew the amount of money that pours into the coffers of an authors' representative. New clients every hour of the day coming in and pleading to be allowed to give him ten per cent. Well, take an instance. He is sitting in his office one day after a lunch of nightingales' tongues washed down with Imperial Tokay, and in comes someone whom for want of a better name we will call Erle Stanley Gardner. He says: 'Good afternoon, my dear authors' representative, would you as a favour to me agree to accept a tenth of my annual earnings? I should mention that I write sixteen books a year, and if only I can get out of the habit of eating, I think I could work it up to twenty. In short, counting in everything, serial, motion picture, radio, television and other rights, I should imagine that your take-home pay on me alone would be at least fifty or sixty thousand dollars per annum. Will you accept me as a client, my dear authors' representative?' And the authors' representative yawns and says he will try to fit him in. 'Thank you, thank you,' says Erle Stanley Gardner, and goes out. And scarcely has he left than in come Frank Yerby and Somerset Maugham. They say: 'Good afternoon . . .' and—well, you get the idea. It's a bonanza."

"A what?"

"A gold mine."

"Oh, absolutely."

"I knew you would see it, my dear Toppy. I knew I could rely on your swift intelligence. You have a mind like a razor. Now then, the point is that Joe here and I have the opportunity of buying an old established business of this nature."

"An authors' representative business?"

"Just that."

"You'll make a fortune."

"Exactly. The same thought occurred to me. We shall have to spend the rest of our lives thinking up ways of doing down the income tax authorities. And all we need, to begin operations——"

"You'll have more money than you know what to do with."

"We shall sprain our wrists, clipping coupons. And all we need——"

"So what I would suggest," said Lord Topham, "is that you slip me a hundred dollars as a temporary loan."

Bill swayed a little.

"Eh?"

"You see," said Lord Topham, "owing to circumstances over which I have no control and which give me a headache whenever I try to understand them, I can't get a penny of my money out of England, not a solitary dashed penny. My pals tell me it's got something to do with there being a Labor Government, composed, as you doubtless know, of the most frightful cads and bounders. Well, this leaves me considerably strapped for the ready, so if you want to earn the undying gratitude of a bloke who is down to a cigarette case and a little small change, now's your chance."

Bill looked up.

"Joe."

"Yes?"

"Did you hear what I heard?"

"I did."

"Then it wasn't just a ghastly dream."

Lord Topham was going on to explain further.

"What put it into my mind to ask you was what you were saying about your extraordinary wealth. Here, on the one hand, I said to myself, is this dear, sweet creature rolling in the stuff, and here, on the other hand, am I, unable to raise a bean on account of the sinister goings-on of this bally Labor Government who go about seeking whom they may devour. So pretty naturally the thought floated into my mind 'Well, dash it!' I mean, a hundred dollars means nothing to you . . ."

A weary look came into Bill's rugged face.

"Have you a hundred dollars, Joe? No, I remember you haven't. Then I suppose . . . Here you are, Toppy."

"Thanks," said Lord Topham. "Thanks most awfully. Yo ho! You know what this means? It means that I can now go to Santa Anita this afternoon with a light heart, ready for any fate. Phipps tells me Betty Hutton is a snip for the fourth and . . . Well, in a nutshell, my dear good preserver, thanks awfully. May heaven bless you, my jolly old multimillionairess. Yo ho!" said Lord Topham. "Yo frightfully absolutely ho!"

He passed through the French window on winged feet.

19

BILL DREW a deep breath. Her face was careworn, as if hers was the head upon which all the sorrows of the world had come, and when at length she found speech, she spoke dully.

"So that's that," she said. "A disappointment, Joe."

"Quite."

"Upsetting."

"Most."

"Yes, distinctly upsetting. Until that last awful moment everything seemed to be going so well. It makes me feel as if I had been chasing rainbows and one of them had turned and bitten me in the leg. If only I had remembered to give a thought to existing financial conditions in the British Isles, I would have been spared a painful experience. My last hundred dollars—gone—just like that. And for what? To enable a goofy English peer to back his fancy on the Santa Anita racecourse. Oh, well, I suppose it all comes under the head of the Marshall Plan. Ah, Smedley," she said, as the door opened. "What news from the throbbing centre of things?"

Smedley was looking warm and glassy-eyed, like a sensitive director of a shaky limited liability company emerging from a stormy meeting of shareholders. It was plain that whatever had passed between him and his sister-in-law in the projection room had not been in the nature of a love feast.

"She's as mad as a wet hen," he said.

"Too bad," said Bill. "One hates to cause Adela distress. What happened?"

"She swears we've got the thing."

"She little knows. Did you try stout denial?"

"Yes, but it didn't do any good. You can't drive an idea out of Adela's head, once it's in it. You know what she's like."

"I do, indeed."

Smedley mopped his forehead. There was a suggestion in his deportment of Shadrach, Meshach and Abednego coming out of the burning fiery furnace.

"Gosh, I'm a nervous wreck. I wish I had a drink."

"Phipps will be bringing cocktails in a moment. Ah," said Bill. "Here, if I mistake not, is our client now."

Phipps entered, bearing a loaded tray that tinkled musically. He laid it on the desk with his usual air of being a plenipotentiary to some great court delivering important documents.

"So what was the upshot?" said Bill.

"Eh?" said Smedley, who had been eyeing the cocktails.

"How did it all come out in the end?"

"Adela? Oh, she stuck to it that we had opened the safe, and she seemed to think you were the one who had got the diary. She put on a big act, and finished by saying she had phoned for the police."

"What?"

A sudden light came into Bill's eye. Her despondency had left her. She was once more The Old Reliable in full command of the situation.

"The police are coming here? Then I think I see daylight. It's better than the arrival of the United States Marines. Phipps!"

"Madam?"

"I greatly fear, Phipps, that you are in a spot. Did you hear what Mr. Smedley said?"

"No, madam. My attention was occupied with depositing the cocktails, madam."

Bill gave him a sympathetic look.

"Stick close to those cocktails, Brother Phipps. You'll be needing one in just a moment. Mr. Smedley said that Mrs. Cork has sent for the cops."

"Indeed, madam?"

"I admire your icy coolness. In your place I would be trembling like a leaf."

"I do not follow your drift, madam."

"I will continue snowing. The officers of the Law are on their way here, and what will they do when they get here, these officers of the Law? They will spread a dragnet. They will case the joint. They will go through the place with a fine-tooth comb."

"So I imagine, madam."

"They will find your hiding place, the secret nook where you have cached that diary. And then what?"

The butler remained politely puzzled.

"Are you hinting that they might suspect me of the robbery, madam?"

Bill laughed raspingly.

"Well, considering that you have an established place in the hall of fame as an expert safeblower, whom else would they suspect? It begins to look like a sticky week-end for you, Phipps."

"I disagree with you, madam. It is true that the constables will probably discover the object under advisement, but I have merely to explain that in abstracting it I was operating on Mr. Smedley's behalf. My position was that of an agent acting for a principal."

Bill raised her eyebrows.

"I don't understand you. Are you suggesting that you were *asked* to open the safe? You don't know anything about this, do you, Smedley?"

"Not a thing."

"You never asked Phipps to open the safe?"

"Certainly not."

"Did you, Joe?"

"No."

"Kay?"

"No."

"Nor did I. The trouble with you, Phipps, is that you will insist on trying to hide your light beneath a bushel. Quite independently and on your own you conceive this brilliant idea of busting the safe and pinching its contents, and you try to give the credit to others. It shows a generous spirit which one cannot help but admire, and in recognition of our admiration we should like to do something for you. Hand the thing over to Mr. Smedley, and he will take charge of it. Then you won't have anything to worry about. You follow my reasoning?"

"Yes, madam."

"I thought you would. Go and get it."

"I have it on my person, madam."

Without any visible emotion the butler drew the book from his pocket, placed it on a salver and brought it to Smedley, who took it like a trout jumping at a fly.

"Would there be anything further, madam?"

"No, thank you, Phipps. You will receive your agent's commission, of course."

Smedley started.

"What, after this?"

"Certainly. We must keep the books straight. And we agents stick together. You will receive your cut in due course, Phipps."

"Thank you, madam."

"Sorry you have been troubled."

"Not at all, madam."

"After all, you have your Art."

"Precisely, madam," said Phipps, and made a decorous withdrawal.

Joe was eyeing Bill devoutly, like a man gazing at some great public monument. His feelings were for a moment too deep for utterance, but eventually he managed to tell Bill she was a marvel.

"She certainly is," said Kay.

"She ought to have that brian of hers pickled and presented to some national museum," said Smedley, equally enthusiastic.

"When she's done with it."

"When she's done with it, of course," assented Smedley. "Well, I'm off to see that gardener at the Lulabelle Mahaffys to get him to translate this thing for me. I shall be in a stronger position to bargain with those fellows at Colossal-Exquisite if I know what's in it."

"You are going to close with Colossal-Exquisite's offer?" said Bill.

"If it's still firm. Fifty thousand dollars is a nice round sum."

Bill agreed.

"Very nice. Very round. Yes, I'd take it. Get their check, lay aside five thousand for Phipps, slip Joe and me our twenty thousand, and you'll be set."

Smedley, who had been making for the French window, briskly like a man to whom time is money, paused. He seemed perplexed.

"Joe and you? Twenty thousand? I don't get this. What are you talking about?"

"For the literary agency."

"What literary agency?"

"You told me you would put up the money for it," said Joe.

Smedley stared.

"I said I would put up money for a literary agency? When?"

"The night before last. When we were at Mocambo."

"This is the first I have heard of this."

"What! But we were talking about it for hours. Don't you remember?"

Bill was looking grave.

"I was afraid this might happen, Joe. Smedley has a memory like a sieve."

Smedley bridled.

"I have an excellent memory," he said stiffly. "But I certainly have not the slightest recollection of ever having heard a literary agency mentioned. What is this literary agency?"

"The one Bill and I want to buy."

"And you construed some passing remark of mine into a promise that I would lend you the money?"

"Passing remark be damned. We discussed it for about an hour and a half. You kept patting me on the back and telling me over and over again——"

Smedley shook his head.

"Some mistake. The thing's absurd on the face of it. I wouldn't put up money for a literary agency. Much too risky. I'm going to go back to New York and get into the producing game again. I shall take an office and let it be known that I am prepared to consider scripts. Bless my soul, it will be quite like old times. Well, I can't stand here talking," said Smedley. "See you all later."

He went out, and Joe and Kay, after an instant's stunned silence, came to life and bounded after him. Their voices died away across the garden, and Bill sat down at the dictaphone.

"Ah, Hollywood, Hollywood," said Bill. "Home of mean glories and spangled wretchedness, where the deathless fire burns for the outspread wings of the guileless moth, whose streets are bathed in the shamed tears of betrayed maidens."

She looked up as the door opened.

"Ah, Adela," she said welcomingly. "I thought you might be looking in. Yo ho! Yo frightfully absolutely ho!"

20

ADELA WAS looking even more formidable than usual, and her voice when, after fixing Bill for some moments with a baleful stare, she finally spoke, vibrated with stormy emotion.

"So there you are, Wilhelmina."

It took more than a vibrating voice to lower Bill's morale. She nodded with what seemed to her sister insufferable heartiness.

"Yes, here I am, working away as always. I was just recording your views on Hollywood at the time when Bioscope wouldn't give you a job."

Adela continued to stare balefully.

"Never mind my views on Hollywood. Wilhelmina, I would like a word with you."

"A thousand."

"Five will do. Wilhelmina, where is that diary?"

Bill wrinkled her forehead.

"Diary? Diary?" Her face cleared. "Oh, you mean the one you were taking care of for Smedley? Isn't it in your safe?"

"You know very well it is not in my safe."

"I thought you put it there."

"I did, and it is there no longer. I will give you two minutes to produce it."

"Me?"

"After that I wash my hands of the matter and the Law can take its course."

Bill held up a hand.

"Wait. It's coming back. Yes, I thought that line was familiar. It was a sub-title in your Gilded Sinners. Do you remember? Where you came in and found your sister burgling the safe?"

"As happened last night."

"I don't understand you."

Her pent-up feelings were too much for Adela. She picked up a cocktail glass and flung it emotionally against the opposite wall.

"Sweet artichokes of Jerusalem!" she cried. "Do you want it in words of one syllable? Then you shall have it. You—stole—that—diary."

"Diary is three syllables."

There was a pause. Bill, too, picked up a cocktail glass, but with the intention of making a better use of it than her sister had done. She rattled the shaker with pleasurable anticipation. No other sound broke the silence. Adela was clenching and unclenching her fists, and her eyes were stony. Her late husband, Alfred Cork, encountering her in this mood one morning after he had been out all night playing poker, had taken one look at her and left for

Mexico City without stopping to pack. On Bill her demeanour seemed to have made a less pronounced impression. She filled her glass, and drank its amber contents with a satisfied sigh.

"Well?" said Adela. "Are you going to have the effrontery to deny it?"

Bill seemed amused. She refilled her glass, paying a silent tribute to the absent Phipps. Jimmy Phipps might be about as slippery a customer as ever breathed the pure air of Beverly Hills, with a moral code which would have caused comment in Alcatraz, but he knew how to mix cocktails.

"But, my dear Adela, I can't open safes."

"You have friends who can. Your friends are well known to be the scum of the earth, thugs who would stick at nothing."

"The only friend of mine on the premises last night was Joe Davenport, and you can hardly suspect Joe of being a safeblower. Why, you might just as well suspect Phipps. No," said Bill, sipping the butler's masterpiece reverently. "An outside job, if you ask me."

"An outside job!"

"That's right. Probably the work of an international gang. Damn' clever, these international gangs. Have a cocktail?"

"I will not have a cocktail."

"You're missing something good. Unlike the international gang."

Bill's respect for Phipps deepened. The man seemed to have everything. Not only could he mix the perfect martini, but as a word-painter he stood second to none. He had described Adela as looking like a welsh rabbit about to come to the height of its fever, and it was such a welsh rabbit at the critical stage of its preparation that she now resembled. In times of crisis, Smedley was a great shaker in every limb, but he would have had to yield first place to Adela Shannon Cork.

"So you wish me to believe," said Adela, having struggled with her feelings, "that it was just a coincidence that my safe was burgled on the one night when it contained that diary?"

"A pure coincidence."

"A pretty coincidence."

"And I'm afraid, a most unfortunate coincidence—for you."

Adela stared.

"What do you mean?"

Bill shrugged her shoulders.

"Surely it's obvious?"

"Not to me."

Bill's manner became grave. There was concern in it, and sympathy. She hesitated a moment, as if reluctant to break the bad news. One could see she was sorry for Adela.

"Well, consider your position," she said. "Smedley had a firm offer of fifty thousand dollars for that diary. He wanted to keep it on his person, but you officiously insisted on taking it from him and putting it in your safe. In other words, you voluntarily assumed full responsibility for it."

"Nonsense."

"You won't find it nonsense when Smedley brings a suit against you for fifty thousand dollars."

"What?"

"Don't forget that he has three witnesses to testify that you took the thing against his expressed wishes. There isn't a jury in America that won't give him your head on a charger."

"Nonsense."

"Keep on saying 'Nonsense,' if it comforts you. I'm merely stating the cold facts. Fifty thousand dollars is what that intelligent jury will award to Smedley, without so much as leaving the jury box. Fortunately you're a millionairess, so it doesn't matter to you. Unless you're one of those women who don't like having to pay out fifty thousand dollars. Some women don't."

Adela groped her way to the sofa and collapsed on it.

"But—but——"

"I told you you ought to have a cocktail."

"But this is absurd."

"Not absurd. Disastrous. I can't see how the cleverest lawyer could make out any case for you. Smedley will win hands down."

Adela had taken out her handkerchief and was twisting it agitatedly. Much, if not all, of her stormy emotion had been drained from her. When she spoke, there was quite a fluttering note in her voice.

"But, Wilhelmina——"

"Yes, Adela?"

"But, Wilhelmina, can't you reason with Smedley?"

Bill finished her cocktail and sighed contentedly.

"Now we're getting down to it," she said with satisfaction. "Now we're arriving somewhere. I *have* reasoned with Smedley."

"You have?"

"Yes, he was in here just now, breathing fire and fury. I never saw a man so worked up. Adamant, he was. Insisted on the full amount and not a cent less. You should have seen him striding about the room like a tiger. I doubted at first if I would be able to do anything with him. But I kept after him. I pointed out what a nuisance these lawsuits were and urged him to agree to a settlement. And in the end, you'll be glad to hear, I beat him down to thirty thousand."

"Thirty thousand!"

"I knew you'd be pleased," said Bill. She looked at her sister incredulously. "Do you mean you *aren't* pleased?"

Adela choked.

"It's highway robbery."

Bill could not follow her.

"I would call it a perfectly ordinary business transaction. Owing to you, Smedley is down fifty thousand dollars. He very decently agrees to accept thirty. Pretty square of him, I should have said. Still, have it your own way. Let him bring his suit, if that's the way you want it. If you would rather pay fifty thousand than thirty thousand, that's your affair. Eccentric, though, it seems to me."

"But, Wilhelmina——"

Bill pointed out another aspect of the matter.

"Of course, it will mean a lot of unpleasant publicity, I'm afraid. You won't show up well at the trial, you know. The impression the public will get from the evidence is that you're the sort of woman who is not to be trusted alone with anything that isn't nailed down. When your friends see you coming, they will hurriedly store their little valuables in a stout chest and sit on the lid till you are out of sight. Louella Parsons is hardly likely to refrain from comment on the affair, nor is Hedda Hopper. And I should imagine that the *Hollywood Reporter* would consider you front-page stuff. But as I say," said Bill, "have it your own way."

The picture she had conjured up decided Adela. She rose.

"Oh, very well." She paused for a moment, to overcome a sudden urge to scream and break the remaining cocktail glasses. "It's an outrage, but . . . Oh, very well."

Bill nodded approvingly. One likes to see one's flesh and blood reasonable.

"Good," she said. "I'm glad you're taking the sensible view. Trot along to your boudoir and write the check. Make it out to me. Smedley has appointed me his agent, to handle the affair." She accompanied Adela to the door. "Gosh, how relieved you must be feeling," she said. "You would probably like to go into a buck and wing dance."

Phipps appeared.

"The constables are here, madam."

"Oh, damn the constables," said Adela, and sailed past him.

Bill gave the butler a grave look.

"You must excuse Mrs. Cork, Phipps, if she is a little brusque. She has just had a bereavement."

"I am sorry, madam."

"I, too. Still, these things are sent to us for a purpose. Maybe to make us more spiritual."

"Quite possibly, madam."

"You're looking a bit spiritual yourself, Phipps."

"Thank you, madam."

"Not at all. Show the officers in."

"Very good, madam."

Joe and Kay came through the French window. They were looking dejected.

"Well?" said Bill.

"No luck," said Joe.

"He wouldn't listen," said Kay.

This caused Bill no surprise.

"Smedley is a bad listener. He reminds me of the deaf adder with whom the charmers had so much trouble. But cheer up, Joe. All is well."

Joe stared.

"All is *what?*"

"Everything's fine."

"Who says so?"

"I say so."

"The constables, madam," announced Phipps.

Sergeant Ward entered, followed by Patrolman Morehouse. Bill greeted them effusively.

"Well, well, well," she said. "How delightful seeing you again."

"Good morning, ma'am."

"I was thinking only just now how nice it would be if you were to drop in once more. Too often in this world we meet a strange face and say to ourselves: 'Have I found a friend? I believe I have found a friend. Yes, by golly, I'm *sure* I've found a friend,' and then—*bing*—the face pops off and you never see it again." She peered at them. "But you're looking extraordinarily cheerful," she said. "Has some good fortune come your way?"

The sergeant beamed. The patrolman beamed.

"I'll say it has," said the patrolman. "Tell her, sarge."

"Well, ma'am. Got a call this morning from the Medulla-Oblongata-Glutz casting office. We start tomorrow."

"Well, well. Joy cometh in the morning."

"Yes, ma'am. Of course, it's only extra work."

"Only extra work right now," said Patrolman Morehouse.

"Sure," said Sergeant Ward. "Just for the moment. We expect to rise in our profession."

"Of course you'll rise," said Bill. "Like rockets. First, extra work, then bit parts, then big parts, then bigger parts, and finally stardom."

"Ah!" said the sergeant. "Hot dog!"

"Hot dog," said the patrolman.

"You'll be bigger than Gary Cooper."

"Hell, yes," said the sergeant. "What's Gary Cooper ever done?"

Adela came in. She had a slip of paper in her hand, but there was nothing in her demeanor to indicate that she enjoyed carrying it. She came to Bill and gave it to her, reluctantly like a woman parting with life blood.

"There," she said.

"Thank you, Adela."

"And may I remark that I wish you had been strangled at birth."

The sergeant saluted.

"You sent for us, ma'am?"

"Yes," said Bill, "but it was a mistake. My sister thought her safe had been robbed last night. It wasn't."

"Ah? Well, that's how it goes," said the sergeant.

"That's how it goes," said the patrolman.

"Good morning," said Adela.

"Good morning, ma'am," said the sergeant.

"Hey!" said the patrolman. "Excuse me, lady, but may I have your autograph, ma'am?"

Adela paused at the door. She swallowed once or twice before speaking.

"You may not," she said. "And one more word out of you on the subject of autographs—or any other subject—and I'll pull your fat head off and make you swallow it. Good MORNING."

The door slammed. The sergeant looked at the patrolman. The patrolman looked at the sergeant.

"Women!" said the sergeant.

"Women!" said the patrolman.

"Can you beat them!" said the sergeant.

"Why, yes," said Bill. "Sometimes. But you need to be a woman yourself and very, very clever—like me. Here, Joe," she said, and handed him the check.

He looked at it listlessly, then staggered.

"Bill! Good heavens, Bill!"

Bill patted her chest.

"The Old Reliable!" she said. "Which way did Smedley go? I want a word with him."

21

THE HOME of the Lulabelle Mahaffys, whose gardens were tended by the Mexican gentleman with whom Smedley had gone to confer, stood some two hundred yards down the road from the Carmen Flores place, and it did not take Bill long to cover the distance. She had just arrived in sight of the gate, when she saw Smedley come out and start walking toward her. He was whistling, and there was a jauntiness in his step which bespoke the soul at rest.

"Well?" she said. "Did you see him?"

"Oh, hello, Bill," said Smedley. "No, he wasn't there. It's his day off. But it doesn't matter. I was just coming back to ask you to lend me that jalopy of yours. I want to go down and see those people at Colossal-Exquisite. Bless my soul," said Smedley, casting an approving glance at the blue sky, "what a glorious day."

"For you."

Smedley was not a man of quick perceptions, but even he could appreciate that this morning, which had brought such happiness to him, had been more sparing with the ecstasy as regarded others. He recalled now, what he had neglected to observe at the time of their meeting, that both his niece Kay and that young fellow Davenport had exhibited not a few signs of distress of mind when chatting with him.

"What was all that nonsense young Davenport was talking about a literary agency?" he asked. "He seemed very excited about it, but I was too busy to listen."

"Joe and I were thinking of buying one."

"You? Are you in it too?"

"That's right. As was carefully explained to you. You're like a Wednesday matinée audience, Smedley. You miss the finer points."

Smedley puffed—remorsefully, it seemed.

"Well, I'm sorry, Bill."

"Don't give it a thought."

"But you can understand how I'm placed, a sensible woman like you. I can't afford to go putting up money for literary agencies."

"You prefer something safer and more conservative, like backing shows on Broadway?"

"That's where the big money is," said Smedley defensively. "How much do you think someone would have made if they'd bought in on *Oklahoma?*"

"Or *South Pacific.*"

"Or *Arsenic And Old Lace.*"

"Or *Ladies, I Beg You,*" said Bill, mentioning the little stinker adapted from the French which had cost the other the last thousands of his waning capital.

Smedley blushed. He did not like to be reminded of *Ladies, I Beg You.*

"That was just an unfortunate accident."

"So that's what you call it?"

"It can't happen again. I shall be bringing to the business now a wealth of experience and a ripened judgment."

"Ripened judgment, did you say?"

"Ripened judgment."

"I see. Ripened judgment. God bless you, Smedley," said Bill, giving him the tender look a mother gives her idiot child. She was feeling, not for the first time, that it was criminal to allow her old friend to run around loose, without a woman's hand to guide him. Somewhere in America, she told herself, there might be a more pronounced fathead than this man she had loved so long, but it would be a weary search, trying to find him.

A klaxon tooted in their rear. If it is possible for a tooter to toot respectfully and deferentially, this tooter did. They turned, and saw approaching a natty little roadster, at whose wheel sat Phipps. It is a very impoverished butler in Beverly Hills who does not own his natty little roadster.

He drew up beside them, and Bill noted suitcases on the seat. It seemed that Phipps was flitting.

"Hello, my bright and bounding Phipps," she said. "You off?"

"Yes, madam."

"Leaving us for good?"

"Yes, madam."

"Rather sudden?"

"Yes, madam. Strictly speaking my tenure of office should not have expired until the day after tomorrow, but I chanced to encounter Mrs. Cork not long since, and she expressed a wish that I should curtail my stay."

"She told you to get the hell out?"

"That was substantially the purport of her words, madam. Mrs. Cork seemed somewhat stirred."

"I told you she had had a bereavement."

"Yes, madam."

"So this—is good-bye?"

"Yes, madam."

Bill dabbed at her eyes.

"Well, it's been nice seeing you."

"Thank you, madam."

"I'll say this for you, Brother Phipps, that when you're around, there's never a dull moment. We part with no hard feelings, I trust?"

"Madam?"

"About the diary."

"Oh, no, madam. None whatever."

"I'm glad you can take the big, broad view."

"I find it easier to do so, madam, because the brochure which I handed to Mr. Smedley at the conclusion of our recent conversation was not the diary of the late Miss Flores."

Smedley, who had been gazing stiffly into the middle distance, as if resolved not to show himself aware of the presence of one whom he considered, and always would consider, a viper of the first water, suddenly ceased to be aloof and detached. He transferred his gaze to the butler, and his eyes popped, as was their custom when he was deeply moved.

"What?"

"No, sir."

"What are you talking about?"

"It was a little thing I borrowed from the cook, sir."

"But it's in Spanish."

"I think you will find that it is not, sir, if you will examine it, sir."

Smedley whipped the volume from his pocket, gave it a quick glance and registered triumph.

"Spanish!"

"You are mistaken, sir."

"Damn it, man, look for yourself."

Phipps took the book in his deferential way.

"Yes, sir, I was wrong." He put the book in his pocket. "You are quite right, sir. Spanish. Good day, sir. Good day, madam."

He placed a shapely foot on the accelerator.

"Hey!" cried Smedley.

But there was no answer. Phipps had said his say. The car gathered speed. It turned the corner, beyond which lay the broad road leading to Beverly Hills. Like some lovely dream that vanishes at daybreak, James Phipps had gone out of their lives.

That Smedley was reluctant to see him go was manifest in his whole bearing. He did not actually say 'Oh, for the touch of the vanished hand!' but the words were implicit in his actions. Breaking into a clumsy gallop, he started in pursuit. But these natty roadsters are hard to catch, particularly if you are a man of elderly middle age and sedentary habits. If Smedley had been capable of doing the quarter-mile in forty-nine seconds, he might have accomplished something to his advantage, but his distance was the ten-yard dash, and he was not very good even at that.

Presently he came back to Bill, panting and passing a handkerchief over a streaming brow, and Bill stared at him with honest amazement.

"If I hadn't seen it with my own eyes," said Bill, "I wouldn't have believed it. You *gave* it to him. You handed it to him. If you had served it up to him on an individual skewer smothered in onions, you couldn't have done more."

Smedley writhed beneath her scorn.

"Well, how could I know he was going to——"

"Of course you couldn't," said Bill, "After having exactly the same thing happen yesterday with Adela, how could the thought have entered your mind? And what possible reason could you have to suspect a man like Phipps of anything in the least resembling raw work? All your dealings with him must have established him in your mind as a stainless soul and a paragon of spotless rectitude. Honestly, Smedley, you ought to be in some sort of home."

"Well, I——"

"Or married," said Bill.

Smedley quivered as if the two simple words had been a couple of harpoons plunged into his shrinking flesh. He shot an apprehensive look at Bill, and did not like the determined expression on her rugged face.

"Yes," she said, "that's what you need—marriage. You want someone to look after you and shield you from the world, and by the greatest good luck I know the very woman to do it. Smedley, I have been potty about you for twenty years—heaven knows why——"

"Bill, please!"

"And, if you didn't suspect it, what probably misled you was the fact that I never told my love, but let concealment like a worm i' the bud feed on my damask cheek. I pined in thought, and with a green and yellow melancholy——"

"No, Bill, really!"

"—sat like Patience on a monument, smiling at grief. But now I have changed my act, and, like Adela, I intend to stand no nonsense. I cannot offer you luxury, Smedley. All I have to lay at your feet is a literary agency which Adela is backing to the tune of thirty thousand dollars."

Smedley had not supposed that anything would have had the power to divert his mind from the hideous vision of matrimony which her words had brought before his eyes, but this did.

"Adela?" he gasped. "She's given you thirty thousand dollars?"

"With a merry smile and a jolly pat on the back. And to-morrow Joe and I start for New York and get our noses down to the grindstone. It will be hard work, of course, and it would be nice to have you at our side, doing your bit. For I am convinced that in a literary agency you would find your niche, Smedley. You have the presence which would impress authors. I can just see you giving them five minutes. Editors, too. That Roman Emperor deportment of yours would lay editors out cold. But I can see why you hesitate. You are reluctant to give up your life of luxury under Adela's roof, with yoghurt flowing like water and Adela always on hand for a stimulating chat . . . By the way, I wonder how you stand with Adela just now. She may be the least bit sore with you after all that has occurred, and when Adela is sore with anyone, she shows it in her manner."

Smedley paled.

"Oh, gosh!"

"Yes, you may not find those chats with her so stimulating, after all. You'd better marry me, Smedley."

"But, Bill——"

"I am only speaking for your own good."

"But, Bill . . . Marriage . . ."

"What's wrong with marriage? It's fine. Why, look at the men who liked it so much that, once started, they couldn't stop, and just went on marrying everything in sight. Look at Brigham Young. Look at Henry the Eighth. Look at King Solomon. Those boys knew when they were on a good thing."

Out of the night that covered him, black as the pit from pole to pole, there shone on Smedley a faint glimmer of light. Something like hope dawned in him. He weighed what she had just said.

Brigham Young—Henry the Eighth—King Solomon—knowledgeable fellows, all of them, men whose judgment you could trust. And they had liked being married, so much so that, as Bill had indicated, they made a regular hobby of it. Might it not quite easily prove, mused Smedley, that marriage was not, as it was generally called, the fate that is worse than death, but something that has its points?

Bill saw his drawn face light up. She linked her arm in his and gave it a squeeze.

"Wilt thou, Smedley," she said, "take this Wilhelmina?"

"I will," said Smedley in a low but firm voice.

Bill kissed him tenderly.

"That's my little man," she said. "This afternoon we'll go out in my jalopy and start pricing ministers."